Wilt on High

Wilt on High

Tom Sharpe

Random House   New York

Library of Congress Cataloging in Publication Data
Sharpe, Tom.
Wilt on high.
I. Title
PR6069.H345W54 1985   823'.914   84-45756
ISBN 0-394-54480-3

Manufactured in the United States of America

First American Edition
24689753

1

'Days of wine and roses,' said Wilt to himself. It was an inconsequential remark but sitting on the Finance and General Purposes Committee at the Tech needed some relief and for the fifth year running Dr Mayfield had risen to his feet and announced, 'We must put the Fenland College of Arts and Technology on the map.'

'I should have thought it was there already,' said Dr Board, resorting as usual to the literal to preserve his sanity. 'In fact to the best of my knowledge it's been there since 1895 when –'

'You know perfectly well what I mean,' interrupted Dr Mayfield. 'The fact of the matter is that the College has reached the point of no return.'

'From what?' asked Dr Board.

Dr Mayfield turned to the Principal. 'The point I am trying to make –' he began, but Dr Board hadn't finished. 'Is apparently that we are either an aircraft halfway to its destination or a cartographical feature. Or possibly both.'

The Principal sighed and thought about early retirement. 'Dr Board,' he said, 'we are here to discuss ways and means of maintaining our present course structure and staffing levels in the face of the Local Education Authority and Central Government pressure to reduce the College to an adjunct of the Department of Unemployment.'

Dr Board raised an eyebrow. 'Really? I thought we were here to teach. Of course, I may be mistaken but when I first entered the profession, that's what I was led to believe. Now I learn that we're here to maintain course structures, whatever they may be, and staffing levels. In plain English, jobs for the boys.'

'And girls,' said the Head of Catering, who hadn't been listening too carefully. Dr Board eyed her critically.

'And doubtless one or two creatures of indeterminate gender,' he murmured. 'Now, if Dr Mayfield –'

1

'Is allowed to continue,' interrupted the Principal, 'we may arrive at a decision by lunchtime.'

Dr Mayfield continued. Wilt stared out of the window at the new Electronics Building and wondered for the umpteenth time what it was about committees that turned educated and relatively intelligent men and women, all of them graduates of universities, into bitter and boring and argumentative people whose sole purpose seemed to be to hear themselves speak and prove everyone else wrong. And committees had come to dominate the Tech. In the old days, he had been able to come to work and spend his mornings and afternoons trying to teach or at least to awaken some intellectual curiosity in classes of Turners and Fitters or even Plasterers and Printers, and if they hadn't learnt much from him, he had been able to go home in the evening with the knowledge that he had gained something from them.

Now everything was different. Even his title, Head of Liberal Studies, had been changed to that of Communication Skills and Expressive Attainment, and he spent his time on committees or drawing up memoranda and so-called consultative documents or reading similarly meaningless documents from other departments. It was the same throughout the Tech. The Head of Building, whose literacy had always been in some doubt, had been forced to justify classes in Bricklaying and Plastering in a 45-page discussion paper on 'Modular Construction and Internal Surface Application', a work of such monumental boredom and bad grammar, that Dr Board had suggested forwarding it to the RIBA with the recommendation that he be given a Fellowship in Architectural Semanticism – or alternatively Cementicism. There had been a similar row over the monograph submitted by the Head of Catering on 'Dietetic Advances In Multi-Phased Institutional Provisioning', to which Dr Mayfield had taken exception on the grounds that the emphasis on faggots and Queen's Pudding might lead to a misunderstanding in certain quarters. Dr Cox, Head of Science, had demanded to know what a Multi-Phased Institution was, and what the hell was wrong with faggots, he'd been brought up on them. Dr Mayfield had explained he was referring to gays and the Head of Catering had confused the issue still further by denying she was a feminist. Wilt had sat

2

through the controversy in silent wondering, as he did now, at the curious modern assumption that you could alter acts by using words in a different way. A cook was a cook no matter that you call him a Culinary Scientist. And calling a gasfitter a Gaseous and Liquefaction Engineer didn't alter the fact that he had taken a course in Gasfitting.

He was just considering how long it would be before they called him an Educational Scientist or even a Mental Processing Officer, when he was drawn from this reverie by a question of 'contact hours'.

'If I could have a breakdown of departmental timetabling on a real-time contact hour basis,' said Dr Mayfield, 'we could computerize those areas of overlap which under present circumstances render our staffing levels unviable on a cost-effective analysis.'

There was a silence while the Heads of Departments tried to figure this out. Dr Board snorted and the Principal rose to the bait. 'Well, Board?' he asked.

'Not particularly,' said the Head of Modern Languages, 'but thank you for enquiring all the same.'

'You know very well what Dr Mayfield wants.'

'Only on the basis of past experience and linguistic guess-work,' said Dr Board. 'What puzzles me in the present instance is his use of the phrase "real-time contact hours". Now according to my vocabulary ...'

'Dr Board,' said the Principal, wishing to God he could sack the man, 'what we want to know is quite simply the number of contact hours the members of your department do per week.'

Dr Board made a show of consulting a small notebook. 'None,' he said finally.

'None?'

'That's what I said.'

'Are you trying to say your staff do no teaching at all? That's a downright lie. If it isn't ...'

'I didn't say anything about teaching and no one asked me to. Dr Mayfield quite specifically asked for "real time" –'

'I don't give a damn about real-time. He means actual.'

'So do I,' said Dr Board, 'and if any of my lecturers have

3

been touching their students even for a minute, let alone an hour, I'd –'

'Board,' snarled the Principal, 'you're trying my patience too far. Answer the question.'

'I have. Contact means touching, and a contact hour must therefore mean a touching hour. Nothing more and nothing less. Consult any dictionary you choose, and you'll find it derives directly from the Latin, *contactus*. The infinitive is *contigere* and the past participle *contactum*, and whichever way you look at it, it still means touch. It cannot mean to teach.'

'Dear God,' said the Principal, through clenched teeth, but Dr Board hadn't finished.

'Now I don't know what Dr Mayfield encourages in Sociology and for all I know he may go in for touch teaching, or, what I believe is called in the vernacular "group groping", but in my department ...'

'Shut up,' shouted the Principal, now well beyond the end of his tether. 'You will all submit in writing the number of teaching hours, the actual teaching hours, each member of your department does ...'

As the meeting broke up, Dr Board walked down the corridor with Wilt. 'It's not often one can strike a blow for linguistic accuracy,' he said, 'but at least I've thrown a spanner in Mayfield's clockwork mind. The man's mad.'

It was a theme Wilt took up with Peter Braintree in the public bar of The Pig In A Poke half an hour later.

'The whole system is loony,' he said over a second pint, 'Mayfield's given up empire-building with degree courses and he's on a cost-effectiveness kick now.'

'Don't tell me,' said Braintree. 'We've already lost half our textbook allocation this year, and Foster and Carston have been bullied into early retirement. At this rate I'll end up teaching *King Lear* to a class of sixty with eight copies of the play to go round.'

'At least you're teaching something. You want to try Expressive Attainment with Motor Mechanics Three. Expressive Attainment! The sods know all there is to be known about cars in the first place, and I haven't a clue what Expressive

Attainment means. Talk about wasting the taxpayers' money. And anyway, I spend more of my time on committees than I do supposedly teaching. That's what galls me.'

'How's Eva?' asked Braintree, recognizing Wilt's mood and trying to change the subject.

'*Plus ça change, plus c'est la même chose.* Mind you, that's not entirely true. At least she's off Suffrage for Little Children and Votes at Eleven Plus. After those two blokes from PIE came round soliciting and went away with thick ears.'

'Pie?'

'Pedophile Information Exchange. Used to be called child molesters. These two sods made the mistake of trying to get Eva's support for lowering the age of consent to four. I could have told them four was an unlucky number round our way, considering what the quads get up to. By the time Eva had finished with them, they must have thought 45 Oakhurst Avenue was part of some bloody zoo, and they'd broached the topic with a tigress in cub.'

'Serve the swine right.'

'Didn't serve Mr Birkenshaw right though. Samantha promptly organized the other three into CAR, otherwise known as Children Against Rape, and set up a target in the garden. Luckily the neighbours put their communal feet down before one of the little boys in the street got himself castrated. The quads were just warming up with penknives. Well, actually, they were Sabatier knives from the kitchen, and they'd got quite good with them. Emmeline could hit the damned thing's scrotum at eighteen feet, and Penelope punctured it at ten.'

'It?' said Braintree faintly.

'Mind you, it was a bit oversize. They made it out of an old football bladder and two tennis balls. But it was the penis that got the neighbours up in arms. And Mr Birkenshaw. I didn't know he had a foreskin like that. Come to think of it, I doubt if anyone else in the street did either. Not until Emmeline wrote his name on the damned French letter and fixed wrapping paper from the Christmas cake round the end and the wind carried it ten gardens at peak viewing time on Saturday afternoon. It ended up hanging from the cherry tree in Mrs Lorrimer's on the corner. That way you could see BIRKENSHAW down all four streets quite clearly.'

'Good Lord,' said Braintree. 'What on earth did Mr Birkenshaw have to say about it?'

'Not much yet,' said Wilt, 'he's still in shock. Spent most of Saturday night at the cop shop trying to convince them he isn't the Phantom Flasher. They've been trying to catch that lunatic for years and this time they thought they'd got him.'

'What? Birkenshaw? They're out of their tinies, the man's a Town Councillor.

'Was,' said Wilt. 'I doubt if he'll stand again. Not after what Emmeline told the policewoman. Said she knew his prick looked like that because he'd lured her into his back garden and waggled the thing at her.'

'Lured her?' said Braintree dubiously. 'With all due respect to your daughters, Henry, I wouldn't have said they were exactly lurable. Ingenious, perhaps, and ...'

'Diabolical,' said Wilt. 'Don't think I mind what you say about them. I have to live with the hell-cats. Of course she wasn't lured. She's had a vendetta with his little pussy for months because it comes and knocks the stuffing out of ours. She was probably trying to poison the brute. Anyway, she was in his garden and according to her he waggled it. Not his version of course. Claimed he always pees on the compost heap and if little girls choose to lurk ... Anyway, that didn't go down with the policewoman very well either. Said it was unhygienic.'

'Where was Eva while this was going on.'

'Oh, here and there,' said Wilt airily. 'Apart from practically accusing Mr Birkenshaw of being related to the Yorkshire Ripper ... I managed to stop that one going down in the police report by saying she was hysterical. Talk about drawing fire. At least I had the policewoman there to protect me and as far as I know the law of slander doesn't apply to ten-year-olds. If it does, we'll have to emigrate. As it is, I'm having to work nights to keep them at that blasted school for so-called gifted children. The cost is astronomic.'

'I thought Eva was getting something off by helping out there.'

'Helped out is more accurate. In fact, ordered off the

premises,' said Wilt and asked for two more pints.

'What on earth for? I'd have thought they'd have been only too glad to have someone as energetic as Eva as an unpaid ancillary cleaning up and doing the cooking.'

'Not when the said ancillary takes it into her head to brighten up their micro-computers with metal polish. Anyway, she screwed the lot and it was a miracle we didn't have to replace them. Mind you, I wouldn't have minded handing over the ones we've got in the house. The place is a deathtrap of I triple E cables and floppy discs, and I can never get near the TV. And when I do, something called a dot matrix printer goes off somewhere and sounds like a hornets' nest in a hurry. And all for what? So that four girls of average if fiendish intelligence can steal a march on snotty-nosed small boys in the scholastic rat-race.'

'We're just old-fashioned,' said Braintree with a sigh. 'The fact is the computer's here to stay and children know how to use them and we don't. Even the language.'

'Don't talk to me about that gobbledygook. I used to think a poke was a crude form of sex. Instead it's something numerical in a programme and a programme's not what it was. Nothing is. Even bugs and bytes. And to pay for this electronic extravaganza, I spend Tuesday night at the prison teaching a bloody gangster what I don't know about E. M. Forster and Fridays at Baconheath Airbase giving lectures on British Culture and Institutions to a load of Yanks with time on their hands till Armageddon.'

'I shouldn't let the news of that leak out to Mavis Mottram,' said Braintree as they finished their beer and left the pub. 'She's taken up Banning the Bomb with a vengeance. She's been on to Betty about it and I'm surprised she hasn't roped Eva in.'

'She tried but it didn't work, for a change. Eva's too busy worrying about the quads to get involved in demonstrations.'

'All the same, I'd keep quiet about the airbase job. You don't want Mavis picketing your house.'

But Wilt wasn't sure. 'Oh, I don't know. It might make us slightly more popular with the neighbours. At the moment they've got it into their thick heads that I'm either a potential mass-murderer or a left-wing revolutionary because I teach at the Tech. Being picketed by Mavis on the wholly false grounds that I'm in favour of the Bomb might improve my image.' They walked back to the Tech by way of the cemetery.

At 45 Oakhurst Avenue, it was one of Eva Wilt's better days. There were days, better days and one of those days. Days were just days when nothing went wrong and she drove the quads to school without too much quarrelling, and came home to do the housework and went shopping and had a tuna-fish salad for lunch and did some mending afterwards and planted something in the garden and picked the children up from school and nothing particularly nasty happened. On one of those days everything went wrong. The quads quarrelled before, during and after breakfast, Henry lost his temper with them and she found herself having to defend them when she knew all the time he was right, the toast got stuck in the toaster and she was late getting the girls to school and something went wrong with the Hoover or the loo wouldn't flush and nothing seemed to be right with the world, so that she was tempted to have a glass of sherry before lunch and that was no good because then she'd want a nap afterwards and the rest of the day would be spent trying to catch up with what she had to do. But on one of her better days she did all the things she did on days and was somehow uplifted by the thought that the quads were doing wonderfully well at The School for The Mentally Gifted and would definitely get scholarships and go on to become doctors or scientists or something really creative, and that it was lovely to be alive in an age when all this was possible and not like it had been when she was a girl and had to do what she was told. It was on such days that she even considered having her mother to live with them instead of being in the old people's home in Luton and wasting all that money. Only considered it, of course, because Henry couldn't stand the old lady and had threatened to walk out and find himself digs if she ever stayed more than three days in the house.

'I'm not having that old bag polluting the atmosphere with her fags and her filthy habits,' he had shouted so loudly that even Mrs Hoggart, who had been in the bathroom at the time, didn't need her hearing aid to get the gist of the message.

'And another thing. The next time I come down to breakfast and find she's been lacing the teapot with brandy, and my brandy at that, I'll strangle the old bitch.'

'You've got no right to talk like that. After all, she is family –'

'Family?' yelled Wilt, 'I'll say she's family. Your fucking family, not mine. I don't foist my father on you –'

'Your father smells like an old badger,' Eva had retaliated, 'he's unhygienic. At least Mother washes.'

'And doesn't she need to, considering all the muck she smears on her beastly mug. Webster wasn't the only one to see the skull beneath the skin. I was trying to shave the other morning ...'

'Who's Webster?' demanded Eva before Wilt could repeat the disgusting account of Mrs Hoggart's emergence from behind the shower curtain in the altogether.

'Nobody. It's from a poem, and talking about uncorseted breasts the old hag ...'

'Don't you dare call her that. She's my mother and one day you'll be old and helpless and need –'

'Yes, well maybe, but I'm not helpless now and the last thing I need is that old Dracula in drag haunting the house and smoking in bed. It's a wonder she didn't burn the place down with that flaming duvet.'

It was the memory of that terrible outburst and the smouldering duvet that had prevented Eva from giving in to her better-day intentions. Besides, there had been truth in what Henry had said, even if he had put it quite horribly. Eva's feelings for her mother had always been ambiguous and part of her wish to have her in the house sprang from the desire for revenge. She'd show her what a really good mother was. And so on one of her better days, she telephoned her and told the old lady how wonderfully the quads were getting on and what a happy atmosphere there was in the home and how even Henry related to the children – Mrs Hoggart invariably broke into a hacking cough at this point – and on the best of days, invited her over for the weekend only to regret it almost as soon as she'd put the phone down. By then it had become one of those days.

But today she resisted the temptation and went round to

Mavis Mottram's to have a heart-to-heart with her before lunch. She just hoped Mavis wouldn't try recruiting her for the Ban the Bomb demo.

Mavis did. 'It's no use your saying you have your hands full with the quads, Eva,' she said, when Eva had pointed out that she couldn't possibly leave the children with Henry, and what would happen if she were sent to prison. 'If there's a nuclear war you won't have any children. They'll all be dead in the first second. I mean Baconheath puts us in a first-strike situation. The Russians would be forced to take it out to protect themselves and we'd all go with it.'

Eva tried to puzzle this out. 'I don't see why we'd be a first-strike target if the Russians were being attacked,' she said finally, 'wouldn't it be a second strike?'

Mavis sighed. It was always so difficult to get things across to Eva. It always had been, and with the barrier of the quads behind which to retreat, it was practically impossible nowadays. 'Wars don't start like that. They start over trivial little things like the Archduke Ferdinand being assassinated at Sarajevo in 1914,' she said, putting it as simply as her work with the Open University allowed. But Eva was not impressed.

'I don't call assassinating people trivial,' she said. 'It's wicked and stupid.'

Mavis cursed herself. She ought to have remembered that Eva's experience with terrorists had prejudiced her against political murders. 'Of course it is. I'm not saying it isn't. What I'm –'

'It must have been terrible for his wife,' said Eva, pursuing her line of domestic consequences.

'Since she happened to be killed with him, I don't suppose she cared all that much,' said Mavis bitterly. There was something quite horribly anti-social about the whole Wilt family but she ploughed on. 'The whole point I'm trying to make is that the most terrible war in the history of mankind, up till then, happened because of an accident. A man and his wife were shot by a fanatic, and the result was that millions of ordinary people died. That sort of accident could happen again, and this time there'd be no one left. The human race would be extinct. You don't want that to happen, do you?'

Eva looked unhappily at a china figurine on the mantelshelf.

She knew it had been a mistake to come anywhere near Mavis on one of her better days. 'It's just that I don't see what I can do to stop it,' she said and threw Wilt into the fray. 'And anyway, Henry says the Russians won't stop making the bomb and they've got nerve gas too, and Hitler had as well, and he'd have used it if he'd known we hadn't during the war.' Mavis took the bait.

'That's because he's got a vested interest in things staying the way they are,' she said. 'All men have. That's why they're against the women's peace movement. They feel threatened because we're taking the initiative and in a sense the bomb is symbolic of the male orgasm. It's potency on a mass destruction level.'

'I hadn't thought of it like that,' said Eva, who wasn't quite sure how a thing that killed everyone could be a symbol of an orgasm. 'And after all, he used to be a member of CND.'

'"Used to",' sniffed Mavis, 'but not any longer. Men just want us to be passive and stay in a subordinate sex role.'

'I'm sure Henry doesn't. I mean he's not very active sexually,' said Eva, still preoccupied with exploding bombs and orgasms.

'That's because you're a normal person,' said Mavis. 'If you hated sex he'd be pawing you all the time. Instead, he maintains his power by refusing you your rights.'

'I wouldn't say that.'

'Well, I would, and it's no use your claiming anything different.'

It was Eva's turn to look sceptical. Mavis had complained too often in the past about her husband's numerous affairs. 'But you're always saying Patrick's too sex-oriented.'

'Was,' said Mavis with rather sinister emphasis. 'His days of gadding about are over. He's learning what the male menopause is like. Prematurely.'

'Prematurely? I should think it must be. He's only forty-one, isn't he?'

'Forty,' said Mavis, 'but he's aged lately, thanks to Dr Kores.'

'Dr Kores? You don't mean to say Patrick went to her after that dreadful article she wrote in the *News*? Henry burnt the paper before the girls could read it.'

'Henry would. That's typical. He's anti freedom of information.'

'Well, it wasn't a very nice article, was it? I mean it's all very well to say that men are ... well ... only biological sperm banks but I don't think it's right to want them all neutered after they've had two children. Our cat sleeps all day and he's –'

'Honestly, Eva, you're so naïve. She didn't say anything about neutering them. She was simply pointing out that women have to suffer all the agonies of childbirth, not to mention the curse, and with the population explosion the world will face mass starvation unless something's done.'

'I can't see Henry being done. Not that way,' said Eva. 'He won't even let anyone talk about vasectomy. Says it has unwanted side-effects.'

Mavis snorted. 'As if the Pill didn't too, and far more dangerous ones. But the multi-national pharmaceutical corporations couldn't care less. All they are interested in is profits and they're controlled by men too.'

'I suppose so,' said Eva, who'd got used to hearing about multi-national companies though she still didn't know exactly what they were, and was completely at a loss with 'pharmaceutical'. 'All the same, I'm surprised Patrick agreed.'

'Agreed?'

'To have a vasectomy.'

'Who said anything about him having a vasectomy?'

'But you said he went to Dr Kores.'

'*I* went,' said Mavis grimly. 'I thought to myself, "I've had just about enough of you gallivanting about with other women, my boy, and Dr Kores may be able to help." And I was right. She gave me something to reduce his sex drive.'

'And he took it?' said Eva, genuinely astounded now.

'Oh, he takes it all right. He's always been keen on vitamins, especially Vitamin E. So I just swapped the capsules in the bottle. They're some sort of hormone or steroid and he takes one in the morning and two at night. Of course, they're still in the experimental stage but she told me they'd worked very well with pigs and they can't do any harm. I mean he's put on some weight and he's complained about his teats being a bit swollen, but he's certainly quietened down a lot. He never goes out in the evening. Just sits in front of the telly and dozes off. It's made quite a change.'

'I should think it has,' said Eva, remembering how randy Patrick Mottram had always been. 'But are you really sure it's safe?'

'Absolutely. Dr Kores assured me they're going to use it on gays and transvestites who are frightened of a sex-change operation. It shrinks the testicles or something.'

'That doesn't sound very nice. I wouldn't want Henry's shrinking.'

'I daresay not,' said Mavis, who had once made a pass at Wilt at a party, and still resented the fact that he hadn't responded. 'In his case she could probably give you something to stimulate him.'

'Do you really think so?'

'You can always try,' said Mavis. 'Dr Kores does understand women's problems and that's more than you can say for most doctors.'

'But I didn't think she was a proper doctor like Dr Buchman. Isn't she something in the University?'

Mavis Mottram stifled an impulse to say that, yes, she was a consultant in animal husbandry at that, which should suit Henry Wilt's needs even better than Patrick's.

'The two aren't mutually incompatible, Eva. I mean there is a medical school at the University, you know. Anyway, the point is, she's set up a clinic for women with problems, and I do think you'd find her very sympathetic and helpful.'

By the time Eva left and returned to 45 Oakhurst Avenue and a lunch of celery soup with bran magi-mixed into it, she was convinced. She would phone Dr Kores and go and see her about Henry. She was also rather pleased with herself. She had managed to divert Mavis from the depressing topic of the Bomb and on to alternative medicine and the need for women to determine the future because men had made such a mess of the past. Eva was all for that, and when she drove down to fetch the quads it was definitely one of her better days. New possibilities were burgeoning all over the place.

2

They were burgeoning all over the place for Wilt as well, but he wouldn't have put the day into the category of one of his better ones. He had returned to his office smelling of The Pig In A Poke's best bitter and hoping he could do some work on his lecture at the airbase without being disturbed, only to find the County Advisor on Communication Skills waiting for him with another man in a dark suit. 'This is Mr Scudd from the Ministry of Education,' said the Advisor. 'He's making a series of random visits to Colleges of Further Education on behalf of the Minister, to ascertain the degree of relevance of certain curricula.'

'How do you do,' said Wilt, and retreated behind his desk. He didn't like the County Advisor very much, but it was as nothing to his terror of men in dark grey suits, and three-piece ones at that, who acted on behalf of the Minister of Education. 'Do take a seat.'

Mr Scudd stood his ground. 'I don't think there's anything to be gained from sitting in your office discussing theoretical assumptions,' he said. 'My particular mandate is to report my observations, my personal observations, of what is actually taking place on the classroom floor.'

'Quite,' said Wilt, hoping to hell nothing was actually taking place on any of his classroom floors. There had been a singularly nasty incident some years before when he'd had to stop what had the makings of a multiple rape of a rather too attractive student teacher by Tyres Two, who'd been inflamed by a passage in *By Love Possessed* which had been recommended by the Head of English.

'Then if you'll lead the way,' said Mr Scudd and opened the door. Behind him, even the County Advisor had assumed a hangdog look. Wilt led the way into the corridor.

'I wonder if you'd mind commenting on the ideological bias of your staff,' said Mr Scudd, promptly disrupting Wilt's

14

desperate attempt to decide which class it would be safest to take the man into. 'I noticed you had a number of books on Marxism–Leninism in your office.'

'As a matter of fact, I do,' said Wilt and bided his time. If the sod had come on some sort of political witch-hunt, the emollient response seemed best. That way the bastard would land with his bum in the butter, but fast.

'And you consider them suitable reading matter for the working-class apprentices?'

'I can think of worse,' said Wilt.

'Really? So you admit to a left-wing tendency in your teaching.'

'Admit? I didn't admit to anything. You said I had books on Marxism–Leninism in my office. I don't see what that's got to do with what I teach.'

'But you also said you could think of worse reading material for your students,' said Mr Scudd.

'Yes,' said Wilt, 'that's exactly what I said.' The bloke was really getting on his wick now.

'Would you mind amplifying that statement?'

'Glad to. How about *Naked Lunch* for starters?'

'*Naked Lunch*?'

'Or *Last Exit From Brooklyn*. Nice healthy reading stuff for young minds, don't you think?'

'Dear God,' muttered the County Advisor, who had gone quite ashen.

Mr Scudd didn't look any too good either, though he inclined to puce rather than grey. 'Are you seriously telling me that you regard those two revolting books ... that you encourage the reading of books like that?'

Wilt stopped outside a lecture room in which Mr Ridgeway was fighting a losing battle with a class of first-year A-level students who didn't want to hear what he thought about Bismark. 'Who said anything about encouraging students to read any particular books?' he asked above the din.

Mr Scudd's eyes narrowed. 'I don't think you quite understand the tenor of my questions,' he said, 'I am here ...' He stopped. The noise coming from Ridgeway's class made conversation inaudible.

'So I've noticed,' shouted Wilt.

The County Advisor staggered to intervene. 'I really think, Mr Wilt,' he began, but Mr Scudd was staring maniacally through the glass pane at the class. At the back, a youth had just passed what looked suspiciously like a joint to a girl with yellow hair in Mohawk style who could have done with a bra.

'Would you say this was a typical class?' he demanded and turned back to Wilt to make himself heard.

'Typical of what?' said Wilt, who was beginning to enjoy the situation. Ridgeway's inability to interest or control supposedly high motivated A-level students would prepare Scudd nicely for the docility of Cake Two and Major Millfield.

'Typical of the way your students are allowed to behave.'

'My students? Nothing to do with me. That's History, not Communication Skills.' And before Mr Scudd could ask what the hell they were doing standing outside a classroom with bedlam going on inside, Wilt had walked on down the corridor.

'You still haven't answered my question,' said Mr Scudd when he had caught up.

'Which one?'

Mr Scudd tried to remember. The sight of that bloody girl had thrown his concentration. 'The one about the pornographic and revoltingly violent reading matter,' he said finally.

'Interesting,' said Wilt. 'Very interesting.'

'What's interesting?'

'That you read that sort of stuff. I certainly don't.'

They went up a staircase and Mr Scudd made use of the handkerchief he kept folded for decoration in his breast pocket. 'I don't read that filth,' he said breathlessly when they reached the top landing.

'Glad to hear it,' said Wilt.

'And I'd be glad to hear why you raised the issue.' Mr Scudd's patience was on a short leash.

'I didn't,' said Wilt, who, having reached the classroom in which Major Millfield was taking Cake Two, had reassured himself that the class was as orderly as he'd hoped. 'You raised it in connection with some historical literature you found in my office.'

'You call Lenin's *State and Revolution* historical literature? I most certainly don't. It's communist propaganda of a particularly virulent kind, and I find the notion that it's being fed to young minds in your department extremely sinister.'

Wilt permitted himself a smile. 'Do go on,' he said. 'There's nothing I enjoy more than listening to a highly trained intelligence leapfrogging common sense and coming to the wrong conclusions. It gives me renewed faith in parliamentary democracy.'

Mr Scudd took a deep breath. In a career spanning some thirty years of uninterrupted authority and bolstered by an inflation-linked pension in the near future, he had come to have a high regard for his own intelligence and he had no intention of having it disparaged now. 'Mr Wilt,' he said, 'I would be grateful to know what conclusions I am supposed to draw from the observation that the Head of Communication Skills at this College has a shelf full of works of Lenin in his office.'

'Personally, I'd be inclined not to draw any,' said Wilt, 'but if you press me ...'

'I most certainly do,' said Mr Scudd.

'Well, one thing's for certain. I wouldn't suppose that the bloke was a raving Marxist.'

'Not a very positive answer.'

'Not a very positive question, come to that,' said Wilt. 'You asked me what conclusions I'd arrive at and when I tell you I wouldn't arrive at any, you're still not satisfied. I don't see what more I can do.'

But before Mr Scudd could reply, the County Advisor forced himself to intervene. 'I think Mr Scudd simply wants to know if there's any political bias in the teaching in your department.'

'Masses,' said Wilt.

'Masses?' said Mr Scudd.

'Masses?' echoed the County Advisor.

'Absolutely stuffed with it. In fact, if you were to ask me ...'

'I am,' said Mr Scudd. 'That's precisely what I'm doing.'

'What?' said Wilt.

'Asking you how much political bias there is,' said Mr Scudd, having recourse to his handkerchief again.

'In the first place, I've told you, and in the second, I thought you said you didn't think there was anything to be gained from discussing theoretical assumptions and you'd come to see for yourself what went on on the classroom floor. Right?' Mr Scudd swallowed and looked desperately at the County Advisor, but Wilt went on. 'Right. Well you just take a shuftie in there where Major Millfield is having a class with Fulltime Caterers brackets Confectionery and Bakery close brackets Year Two, affectionately known as Cake Two, and then come and tell me how much political bias you've managed to squeeze out of the visit.' And without waiting for any further questions, Wilt went back down the stairs to his office.

'Squeeze out?' said the Principal two hours later. 'You have to ask the Minister of Education's Personal Private Secretary how much political bias he can squeeze out of Cake Two?'

'Oh, is that who he was, the Minister of Education's own Personal Private Secretary?' said Wilt. 'Well, what do you know about that? Now if he'd been an HMI ...'

'Wilt,' said the Principal with some difficulty, 'if you think that bastard isn't going to lumber us with one of Her Majesty's Inspectors – in fact I shouldn't be surprised if the entire Inspectorate doesn't descend upon us – and all thanks to you, you'd better think again.'

Wilt looked round at the ad hoc committee that had been set up to deal with the crisis. It consisted of the Principal, the V-P, the County Advisor and, for no apparent reason, the Bursar. 'It's no skin off my nose how many Inspectors he rustles up. Only too glad to have them.'

'You may be but I rather doubt ...' The Principal hesitated. The County Advisor's presence didn't make for a free flow of opinion on the deficiencies of other departments. 'I take it that any remarks I make will be treated as off the record and entirely confidential,' he said finally.

'Absolutely,' said the County Advisor, 'I'm only interested in Liberal Studies and ...'

'How nice to hear that term used again. That's the second time this afternoon,' said Wilt.

'And you might have added the bloody studies,' snarled the Advisor, 'instead of leaving the wretched man with the impression that that other idiot lecturer was a fee-paying member of the Young Liberals and a personal friend of Peter Tatchell.'

'Mr Tatchell isn't a Young Liberal,' said Wilt. 'To the best of my knowledge he's a member of the Labour Party, left of centre of course, but ...'

'And a fucking homosexual.'

'I've no idea. Anyway, I thought the compassionate word was "gay".'

'Shit,' muttered the Principal.

'Or that if you prefer,' said Wilt, 'though I'd hardly describe the term as compassionate. Anyway, as I was saying ...'

'I am not interested in what you are saying. It's what you said in front of Mr Scudd that matters. You deliberately led him to believe that this College, instead of being devoted to Further Education ...'

'I like that "devoted". I really do,' interrupted Wilt.

'Yes, devoted to Further Education, Wilt, and you led him to think we employ nobody but paid-up members of the Communist Party and at the other extreme a bunch of lunatics from the National Front.'

'Major Millfield isn't a member of any party to the best of my knowledge,' said Wilt. 'The fact that he was discussing the social implications of immigration policies –'

'Immigration policies!' exploded the County Advisor. 'He was doing no such thing. He was talking about cannibalism among wogs in Africa and some swine who keeps heads in his fridge.'

'Idi Amin,' said Wilt.

'Never mind who. The fact remains that he was demonstrating a degree of racial bias that could get him prosecuted by the Race Relations Board and you had to tell Mr Scudd to go in and listen.'

'How the hell was I to know what the Major was on about? The class was quiet and I had to warn the other lecturers that the sod was on his way. I mean if you choose to pitch up out of the blue with a bloke who's got no official status ...'

'Official status?' said the Principal. 'I've already told you Mr Scudd just happens to be –'

'Oh, I know all that and it still doesn't add up. The point is he walks into my office with Mr Reading here, noses his way through the books on the shelf, and promptly accuses me of being an agent of the bleeding Comintern.'

'And that's another thing,' said the Principal. 'You deliberately left him with the impression that you use Lenin's whatever it was called ...'

'*The State and Revolution*,' said Wilt.

'As teaching material with day-release apprentices. Am I right, Mr Reading?'

The County Advisor nodded weakly. He still hadn't recovered from those heads in the fridge or the subsequent visit to Nursery Nurses who had been deep in a discussion on the impossible and utterly horrifying topic of post-natal abortion for the physically handicapped. The bloody woman had been in favour of it.

'And that's just the beginning,' continued the Principal, but Wilt had had enough.

'The end,' he said. 'If he'd bothered to be polite, it might have been different but he wasn't. And he wasn't even observant enough to see that those Lenin books belong to the History Department, were stamped to that effect, and were covered with dust. To the best of my knowledge, they've been on that shelf ever since my office was changed and they used to use them for the A-level special subject on the Russian Revolution.'

'Then why didn't you tell him that?'

'Because he didn't ask. I don't see why I should volunteer information to total strangers.'

'What about *Naked Lunch*? You volunteered that all right,' said the County Advisor.

'Only because he asked for worse reading material and I couldn't think of anything more foul.'

'Thank the Lord for small mercies,' murmured the Principal.

'But you definitely stated that the teaching in your department is stuffed – yes, you definitely used the word "stuffed" – with political bias. I heard you myself,' continued the County Advisor.

'Quite right too,' said Wilt. 'Considering I'm lumbered with forty-nine members of staff, including part-timers, and all the teaching they ever do is to natter away to classes and keep them quiet for an hour, I should think their political opinions must cover the entire spectrum, wouldn't you?'

'That isn't the impression you gave him.'

'I'm not here to give impressions,' said Wilt, 'I'm a teacher as a matter of unquestionable fact, not a damned public-relations expert. All right, now I've got to take a class of Electronics Engineers for Mr Stott who's away ill.'

'What's the matter with him?' asked the Principal inadvertently.

'Having another nervous breakdown. Understandably,' said Wilt and left the room.

Behind him the members of the Committee looked wanly at the door. 'Do you really imagine this man Scudd will get the Minister to call for an enquiry?' asked the Vice-Principal.

'That's what he told me,' said the Advisor. 'There are certain to be questions in the House after what he saw and heard. It wasn't simply the sex that got his goat, though that was bad enough in all conscience. The man's a Catholic and the emphasis on contraception –'

'Don't,' whispered the Principal.

'No, the thing that really upset him was being told to go and fuck himself by a drunken lout in Motor Mechanics Three. And Wilt, of course.'

'Isn't there something we can do about Wilt?' the Principal asked despairingly as he and the Vice-Principal returned to their offices.

'I don't see what,' said the V–P. 'He inherited half his staff and since he can't get rid of them, he has to do what he can.'

'What Wilt can do is land us with questions in Parliament, the total mobilization of Her Majesty's Inspectorate and a public enquiry into the way this place is run.'

'I shouldn't have thought they'd go to the lengths of a public enquiry. This man Scudd may have influence but I very much doubt ...'

'I wouldn't. I saw the swine before he left and he was practically demented. What in God's name is post-natal abortion anyway?'

'Sounds rather like murder ...' the Vice-Principal began, but the Principal was way ahead of him on a thought process that would lead to his forced retirement. 'Infanticide. That's it. Wanted to know if I was aware that we were running a course on Infanticide for future Nannies and asked if we had an evening class for Senior Citizens on Euthanasia or Do-It-Yourself Suicide. We haven't, have we?'

'Not to my knowledge.'

'If we had I'd ask Wilt to run it. That bloody man will be the end of me.'

At the Ipford Police Station, Inspector Flint shared his feelings. Wilt had already screwed his chances of becoming a Superintendent and Flint's misery had been compounded by the career of one of his sons, Ian, who had left school and home before taking his A-levels, and after graduating on marijuana and a suspended prison sentence had gone on to be seized by Customs and Excise loaded with cocaine at Dover. 'Bang goes any hope of promotion,' Flint had said morosely when his son was sent down for five years, and had brought down on his own head the wrath of Mrs Flint who blamed him for her son's delinquency. 'If you hadn't been so interested in your own blooming work and getting on and all, and had taken a proper father's interest in him, he wouldn't be where he is now,' she had shouted at him, 'but no, it had to be Yes Sir, No Sir, Oh certainly Sir, and any rotten night work you could get. And week-ends. And what did Ian ever see of his own father? Nothing. And when he did it was always this crime or that villain and how blooming clever you'd been to nick him. That's what your career's done for your family. B. all.'

And for once in his life, Flint wasn't sure she wasn't right. He couldn't bring himself to put it more positively than that. He'd always been right. Or in the right. You had to be to be a good copper, and he certainly hadn't been a bent one. And his career had had to come first.

'You can talk,' he'd said somewhat gratuitously, since it was about the only thing he'd ever allowed her to do apart from the shopping and washing up and cleaning the house and whining on about Ian, feeding the cat and the dog and generally skivvying for him. 'If I hadn't worked my backside off, we wouldn't have the house or the car and you wouldn't have been able to take the little bastard to the Costa ...'

'Don't you dare call him that!' Mrs Flint had shouted, putting the hot iron on his shirt and scorching it in her anger.

'I'll call him what I bloody well like. He's a rotten villain like all the rest of them.'

'And you're a rotten father. About the only thing you ever did as a father was screw me, and I mean screw, because it wasn't anything else as far as I was concerned.' Flint had taken himself out of the house and back to the police station thinking dark thoughts about women and how their place was in the home, or ought to be, and he was going to be the laughing-stock of the Fenland Constabulary with cracks about him visiting the nick over in Bedford to see his own home-grown convict and a drug pusher at that, and what he'd do to the first sod who called him Snowy and harrying ... And all the time there was, on the very edge of his mind, a sense of grievance against Henry fucking Wilt. It had always been there, but now it came back stronger than ever: Wilt had buggered his career with that doll of his and then the siege. Oh, yes, he'd almost admired Wilt at one stage but that was a long time ago, a very long time indeed. The little sod was sitting pretty in his house at Oakhurst Avenue and a good salary at the ruddy Tech, and one day he'd probably be the Principal of the stinking place. Whereas any hope Flint had ever had of rising to Super, and being posted to some place Wilt wasn't, had gone up in smoke. He was stuck with being Inspector Flint for the rest of his natural, and stuck with Ipford. As if to emphasize his lack of any hope, they'd brought Inspector Hodge in as Head of the Drug Squad and a right smart-arse he was too. Oh, they'd tried to butter over the crack, but the Super had called Flint in to tell him personally, and that had to mean something. That he was a dead-beat and they couldn't trust him in the drugs game, because his son was inside. Which had brought on another of his headaches which he'd always thought were migraines, only this time the police doctor had diagnosed hypertension and put him on pills.

'Of course I'm hypertense,' Flint had told the quack. 'With the number of brainy bastards round here who ought to be behind bars, any decent police officer's got to be tense. He wouldn't be any good at nailing the shits if he weren't. It's an occupational hazard.'

'It's whatever you like to call it, but I'm telling you you've got high blood pressure and ...'

'That's not what you said a moment ago,' Flint had flashed

back. 'You stated I had tension. Now then, which is it, hypertension or high blood pressure?'

'Inspector,' the doctor had said, 'you're not interrogating a suspect now.' (Flint had his reservations about that.) 'And I'm telling you as simply as I can that hypertension and high blood pressure are one and the same thing. I'm putting you on one diuretic a day –'

'One what?'

'It helps you pass water.'

'As if I needed anything to make me do that. I'm up twice in the blasted night as it is.'

'Then you'd better cut down on your drinking. That'll help your blood pressure, too.'

'How? You tell me not to be tense and the one thing that helps is a beer or two in the local.'

'Or eight,' said the doctor, who'd seen Flint in the pub. 'Anyway, it'll bring your weight down.'

'And make me piss less. So you give me a pill to make me piss more and tell me to drink less. Doesn't make sense.'

By the time Inspector Flint left the surgery, he still didn't know what the pills he had to take did for him. Even the doctor hadn't been able to explain how beta-blockers worked. Just said they did and Flint would have to stay on them until he died.

A month later the Inspector could tell the doctor how they worked. 'Can't even type any more,' he said, displaying a pair of large hands with white fingers. 'Look at them. Like bloody celery sticks that have been blanched.'

'Bound to have some side-effects. I'll give you something to relieve those symptoms.'

'I don't want any more of the piss pills,' said Flint. 'Those bleeding things are dehydrating me. I'm on the bloody trot all the time and it's obvious there's not enough blood left in me to get to my fingers. And that's not all. You want to try working some villain over and being taken short just when he's coming up with a confession. I tell you, it's affecting my work.'

The doctor looked at him suspiciously and thought wistfully of the days when his patients didn't answer back and police officers were of a different calibre to Flint. Besides, he didn't

24

like the expression 'working some villain over'. 'We'll just have to try you out on some other medications,' he said, and was startled by the Inspector's reaction.

'Try me out on some other medicines?' he said belligerently. 'Who are you supposed to be treating, me or the bloody medicines? I'm the one with blood pressure, not them. And I don't like being experimented with. I'm not some bleeding dog, you know.'

'I suppose not,' said the doctor, and had doubled the Inspector's dose of beta-blockers but under a different trade name, added some pills to counter the effect on his fingers, and changed the name of the diuretics. Flint had gone back to his office from the chemist feeling like a walking medicine cabinet.

A week later, he was hard put to it to say what he felt like. 'Fucking awful is all I know,' he told Sergeant Yates who'd been unwise enough to enquire. 'I must have passed more bleeding water in the last six weeks than the Aswan Dam. And I've learnt one thing, this bloody town doesn't have enough public lavatories.'

'I should have thought there were enough to be going on with,' said Yates, who'd once had the unhappy experience of being arrested by a uniformed constable while loitering in the public toilets near the cinema in plain clothes trying to apprehend a genuine loo-lounger.

'Well, you can think again,' snapped Flint. 'I was caught short in Canton Street yesterday, and do you think I could find one? Not on your nelly. Had to use a lane between two houses and nearly got nabbed by a woman hanging her washing on the line. One of these days I'll be done for flashing.'

'Talking about flashing, we've had another report of a case down by the river. Tried it out on a woman of fifty this time.'

'Makes a change from those Wilt bitches and Councillor Birkenshaw. Get a good look at the brute?'

'She said she couldn't see it very well because he was on the other side but she had the impression it wasn't very big.'

'It? It?' shouted Flint. 'I'm not interested in it. I'm talking about the bugger's mug. How the hell do you think we're going to identify the maniac. Have a prick parade and ask

25

the victims to go along studying cocks? The next thing you'll be doing is issuing identikits of penises.'

'She couldn't see his face. He was looking down.'

'And peeing, I daresay. Probably on the same fucking tablets I'm doomed to. Anyway, I wouldn't take the evidence of a fifty-year-old blasted woman. They're all sex-mad at that age. I should know. My old woman's practically off her rocker about it and I keep telling her that the ruddy quack's lowered my blood pressure so much I couldn't get the fucking thing up even if I wanted to. Know what she said?'

'No,' said Sergeant Yates, who found the subject rather distasteful, and anyway it was obvious he didn't know what Mrs Flint had said and he didn't want to hear. The whole notion of anyone wanting the Inspector was beyond him. 'She had the gall to tell me to do it the other way.'

'The other way?' said Yates in spite of himself.

'The old soixante-neuf. Disgusting. And probably illegal. And if anyone thinks I'm going to go down at my age, and on my ruddy missus at that, they're clean off their fucking rockers.'

'I should think they'd have to be,' said the Sergeant almost pitifully. He'd always been relatively fond of old Flint, but there were limits. In a frantic attempt to change the topic to something less revolting, he mentioned the Head of the Drug Squad. He was just in time. The Inspector had just begun a repulsive description of Mrs Flint's attempts to stimulate him. 'Hodge? What's that bloody cock-sucker want now?' Flint bawled, still managing to combine the two subjects.

'Phone-tapping facilities,' said Yates. 'Reckons he's on to a heroin syndicate. And a big one.'

'Where?'

'Won't say, not to me any road.'

'What's he want my permission for? Got to ask the Super or the Chief Constable and I don't come into it. Or do I?' It had dawned on Flint that this might be a subtle dig at him about his son. 'If that bastard thinks he's going to take the piss out of me ...' he muttered and stopped.

'I shouldn't think he could,' said Yates, getting his own back, 'not with those tablets you're on.'

But Flint hadn't heard. His mind had veered off along lines

determined more than he knew by beta-blockers, vaso-dilators and all the other drugs he was on, but which combined with his natural hatred for Hodge and the accumulated worries of his job and his family to turn him into an exceedingly nasty man. If the Head of the Drug Squad thought he was going to put one over on him he'd got another think coming. 'There are more ways of stuffing a cat than filling it with cream,' he said with a gruesome smile.

Sergeant Yates looked at him doubtfully. 'Shouldn't it be the other way round?' he asked, and immediately regretted any reference to other way round. He'd had enough of Mrs Flint's thwarted sex life, and stuffing cats was definitely out. The old man must be off his rocker.

'Quite right,' said the Inspector. 'We'll fill the bugger with cream all right. Got any idea who he wants to tap?'

'He's not telling me that sort of thing. He reckons the uniform branch aren't to be trusted and he doesn't want any leaks.' The word was too much for Inspector Flint. He shot out of his chair and was presently finding temporary relief in the toilet.

By the time he returned to his office, his mood had changed to the almost dementedly cheerful. 'Tell him we'll give him all the co-operation he needs,' he told the Sergeant, 'only too pleased to help.'

'Are you sure?'

'Of course I'm sure. He's only got to come and see me. Tell him that.'

'If you say so,' said Yates and left the room a puzzled man. Flint sat on in a state of drug-induced bemusement. There was only one bright spot on his limited horizon. If that bastard Hodge wanted to foul up his career by making unauthorized phone taps, Flint would do all he could to encourage him. Fortified by this sudden surge of optimism, he absent-mindedly helped himself to another beta-blocker.

3

But already things were moving in a direction the Inspector would have found even more encouraging. Wilt had emerged from the meeting of the crisis committee rather too pleased with his performance. If Mr Scudd really had the influence with the Minister of Education he had claimed to, there might well be a full-scale inspection by the HMIs. Wilt welcomed the prospect. He had frequently thought about the advantages of such a confrontation. For one thing, he'd be able to demand an explicit statement on what the Ministry really thought Liberal Studies were about. Communication Skills and Expressive Attainment they weren't. Since the day some twenty years before when he'd joined the Tech staff, he'd never had a clear knowledge and nobody had been able to tell him. He'd started off with the peculiar dictum enunciated by Mr Morris, the then Head of Department, that what he was supposed to be doing was 'Exposing Day Release Apprentices to Culture', which had meant getting the poor devils to read *Lord Of The Flies* and *Candide*, and then discuss what they thought the books were about, and countering their opinions with his own. As far as Wilt could see, the whole thing had been counter-productive and as he had expressed it, if anyone was being exposed to anything, the lecturers were being exposed to the collective barbarism of the apprentices which accounted for the number who had nervous breakdowns or became milkmen with degrees. And his own attempt to change the curriculum to more practical matters, like how to fill in Income Tax forms, claim Unemployment Benefit, and generally move with some confidence through the maze of bureaucratic complications that had turned the Welfare State into a piggy-bank for the middle classes and literate skivers, and an incomprehensible and humiliating nightmare of forms and jargon for the provident poor, had been thwarted by the lunatic theories of so-called educa-

28

tionalists of the sixties like Dr Mayfield, and the equally irrational spending policies of the seventies. Wilt had persisted in his protestations that Liberal Studies didn't need video cameras and audio-visual aids galore, but could do with a clear statement from somebody about the purpose of Liberal Studies.

It had been an unwise request. Dr Mayfield and the County Advisor had both produced memoranda nobody could understand, there had been a dozen committee meetings at which nothing had been decided, except that since all the video cameras were available they might as well be used, and that Communication Skills and Expressive Attainment were more suited to the spirit of the times than Liberal Studies. In the event the education cuts had stymied the audio-visual aids and the fact that useless lecturers in more academic departments couldn't be sacked had meant that Wilt had been lumbered with even more deadbeats. If Her Majesty's Inspectors did descend, they might be able to clear the log jam and make some sense, Wilt would be only too pleased. Besides, he rather prided himself on his ability to hold his own in confrontations.

His optimism was premature. Having spent fifty minutes listening to Electronic Engineers explaining the meaning of cable television to him, he returned to his office to find his secretary, Mrs Bristol, in a flap. 'Oh, Mr Wilt,' she said as he came down the corridor. 'You've got to come quickly. She's there again and it's not the first time.'

'What isn't?' asked Wilt from behind a pile of *Shane* he had never used.

'That I've seen her there.'

'Seen whom where?'

'Her. In the loo.'

'Her in the loo?' said Wilt, hoping to hell Mrs Bristol wasn't having another of her 'turns'. She'd once gone all funny-peculiar when one of the girls in Cake Three had announced in all innocence, that she had five buns in the oven. 'I don't know what you're talking about.'

Nor, it appeared, did Mrs Bristol. 'She's got this needle thing and . . .' she petered out.

'Needle thing?'

'Syringe,' said Mrs Bristol, 'and it's in her arm and full of blood and ...'

'Oh my God,' said Wilt, and headed past her to the door. 'Which loo?'

'The Ladies' staff one.'

Wilt halted in his tracks. 'Are you telling me one of the members of staff is shooting herself full of heroin in the Ladies' staff lavatory?'

Mrs Bristol *had* gone all funny now. 'I'd have recognized her if she'd been staff. It was a girl. Oh, do something Mr Wilt. She may do herself an injury.'

'You can say that again,' said Wilt, and bolted down the corridor and the flight of stairs to the toilet on the landing and went in. He was confronted by six cubicles, a row of washbasins, a long mirror and a paper-towel dispenser. There was no sign of any girl. On the other hand, the door of the third cubicle was shut and someone was making unpleasant sounds inside. Wilt hesitated. In less desperate circumstances, he might have supposed Mr Rusker, whose wife was a fibre freak, was having one of his problem days again. But Mr Rusker didn't use the Ladies' lavatory. Perhaps if he knelt down he might get a glimpse. Wilt decided against it. (*A*) He didn't want glimpses and (*B*) it had begun to dawn on him that he was, to put it mildly, in a delicate situation and bending down and peeping under doors in ladies' lavatories was open to misinterpretation. Better to wait outside. The girl, if there was a girl and not some peculiar figment of Mrs Bristol's imagination, would have to come out some time.

With one last glance in the trash can for a hypodermic, Wilt tiptoed towards the door. He didn't reach it. Behind him a cubicle door opened. 'I thought so,' a voice shouted, 'a filthy Peeping Tom!' Wilt knew that voice. It belonged to Miss Hare, a senior lecturer in Physical Education, whom he had once likened rather too audibly in the staff-room to Myra Hindley in drag. A moment later, his arm had been wrenched up to the back of his neck and his face was in contact with the tiled wall.

'You little pervert,' Miss Hare continued, jumping to the nastiest, and, from Wilt's point of view, the least desirable conclusion. The last person he'd want to peep at was Miss

Hare. Only a pervert would. It didn't seem the time to say so.

'I was just looking –' he began, but Miss Hare quite evidently had not forgotten the crack about Myra Hindley.

'You can keep your explanation for the police,' she screamed, and reinforced the remark by banging his face against the tiles. She was still enjoying the process, and Wilt wasn't, when the door opened and Mrs Stoley from Geography came in.

'Caught the voyeur in the act,' said Miss Hare. 'Call the police.' Against the wall, Wilt tried to offer his point of view and failed. Having Miss Hare's ample knee in the small of his back didn't help and his false tooth had come out.

'But that's Mr Wilt,' said Mrs Stoley uncertainly.

'Of course it's Wilt. It's just the sort of thing you'd expect from him.'

'Well . . .' began Mrs Stoley, who evidently hadn't.

'Oh for goodness sake get a move on. I don't want the little runt to escape.'

'Am I trying to?' Wilt mumbled and had his nose rammed against the wall for his pains.

'If you say so,' said Mrs Stoley and left the room only to return five minutes later with the Principal and the V-P. By then, Miss Hare had transferred Wilt to the floor and was kneeling on him.

'What on earth's going on?' demanded the Principal. Miss Hare got up.

'Caught in the act of peeping at my private parts,' she said. 'He was trying to escape when I grabbed him.'

'Wasn't,' said Wilt groping for his false tooth and inadvisedly putting it back in his mouth. It tasted of some extremely strong disinfectant which hadn't been formulated as a mouthwash, and was doing things to his tongue. As he scrambled to his feet, and made a dash for the washbasins, Miss Hare applied a half-nelson.

'For God's sake let go,' yelled Wilt, by now convinced he was about to die of carbolic poisoning. 'This is all a terrible mistake.'

'Yours,' said Miss Hare and cut off his air supply.

The Principal looked dubiously at them. While he might have enjoyed Wilt's discomfiture in other circumstances, the sight of him being strangled by an athletically built woman like Miss Hare whose skirt had come down was more than he could stomach.

'I think it would be best if you let him go,' he said as Wilt's face darkened and his tongue stuck out. 'He seems to be bleeding rather badly.'

'Serves him right,' said Miss Hare, reluctantly letting Wilt breathe again. He stumbled to a basin and turned the tap on.

'Wilt,' said the Principal, 'what is the meaning of this?' But Wilt had his false tooth out again and was trying desperately to wash his mouth out under the tap.

'Hadn't we better wait for the police before he makes a statement?' asked Miss Hare.

'The police?' squawked the Principal and the V-P simultaneously. 'You're not seriously suggesting the police should be called in to deal with this ... er ... affair.'

'I am,' Wilt mumbled from the basin. Even Miss Hare looked startled.

'You are?' she said. 'You have the nerve to come in here and peer at ...'

'Balls,' said Wilt, whose tongue seemed to be resuming its normal size, though it still tasted like a recently sterilized toilet bend.

'How dare you,' shouted Miss Hare, and was on the point of getting to grips with him again when the V-P intervened. 'I think we should hear Wilt's version before we do anything hasty, don't you?' Miss Hare obviously didn't, but she stopped in her tracks. 'I've already told you precisely what he was doing,' she said.

'Yes, well let me tell you what ...'

'He was bending over and looking under the door,' continued Miss Hare remorselessly.

'Wasn't,' said Wilt.

'Don't you dare lie. I always knew you were a pervert. Remember that revolting incident with the doll?' she said, appealing to the Principal. The Principal didn't need reminding but it was Wilt who answered.

'Mrs Bristol,' he mumbled, dabbing his nose with a paper towel, 'Mrs Bristol's the one who started this.'

'Mrs Bristol?'

'Wilt's secretary,' explained the V-P.

'Are you suggesting you were looking for your secretary in here?' asked the Principal. 'Is that what you're saying?'

'No, I'm not. I'm saying Mrs Bristol will tell you why I was here and I want you to hear it from her before that damned bulldozer on anabolic steroids starts knocking hell out of me again.'

'I'm not standing here being insulted by a ...'

'Then you'd better pull your skirt up,' said the V-P, whose sympathies were entirely with Wilt.

The little group made their way up the stairs, past a class of English A-level students who'd just ended an hour with Mr Gallen on The Pastoral Element in Wordsworth's *Prelude*, and were consequently unprepared for the urban element of Wilt's bleeding nose. Nor was Mrs Bristol. 'Oh dear, Mr Wilt, what have you done to yourself?' she asked. 'She didn't attack you?'

'Tell them,' said Wilt. 'You tell them.'

'Tell them what?'

'What you told me,' snapped Wilt, but Mrs Bristol was too concerned about his condition and the Principal and the V-P's presence had unnerved her. 'You mean about –'

'I mean ... Never mind what I mean,' said Wilt lividly, 'just tell them what I was doing in the Ladies' lavatory, that's all.'

Mrs Bristol's face registered even more confusion. 'But I don't know,' she said, 'I wasn't there.'

'I know you weren't there, dammit. What they want to know is why I was.'

'Well ...' Mrs Bristol began, and lost her nerve again, 'Haven't you told them?'

'Caesar's ghost,' said Wilt, 'can't you just spit it out. Here I am accused of being a peeping Tom by Miss Burke and Hare over there ...'

'You call me that again and your own mother wouldn't recognize you,' said Miss Hare.

'Since she's been dead for ten years, I don't suppose she would now,' said Wilt, retreating behind his desk. By the time the PE teacher had been restrained, the Principal was trying

33

to make some sense out of an increasingly confused situation. 'Can someone please shed some light on this sordid business?' he asked.

'If anyone can, she can,' said Wilt, indicating his secretary. 'After all, she set me up.'

'Set you up, Mr Wilt? I never did anything of the sort. All I said was there was a girl in the staff toilet with a hypodermic and I didn't know who she was and ...' Intimidated by the look of horror on the Principal's face, she ground to a halt. 'Have I said something wrong?'

'You saw a girl with a hypodermic in the staff toilet? And told Mr Wilt about it?'

Mrs Bristol nodded dumbly.

'When you say "girl" I presume you don't mean a member of the staff?'

'I'm sure it wasn't. I didn't see her face but I'd have known surely. And she had this awful syringe filled with blood and ...' She looked at Wilt for assistance.

'You said she was taking drugs.'

'There was no one in that toilet while I was there,' said Miss Hare, 'I'd have heard them.'

'I suppose it could have been someone with diabetes,' said the V-P, 'some adult student who wouldn't want to use the students' toilet for obvious reasons.'

'Oh quite,' said Wilt, 'I mean we all know diabetics go round with hypodermics full of blood. She was obviously flushing back to get the maximum dose.'

'Flushing back?' said the Principal weakly.

'That's what the junkies do,' said the V-P. 'They inject themselves and then –'

'I don't want to know,' said the Principal.

'Well, if she was taking heroin –'

'Heroin! That's all we need,' said the Principal, and sat down miserably.

'If you ask me,' said Miss Hare, 'the whole thing's a fabrication. I was in there ten minutes ...'

'Doing what?' asked Wilt. 'Apart from attacking me.'

'Something feminine, if you must know.'

'Like taking steroids. Well, let me tell you that when I went down there and I wasn't there more than ...'

34

It was Mrs Bristol's turn to intervene. 'Down, did you say down?'

'Of course I said down. What did you expect me to say? Up?'

'But the toilet's on the fourth floor, not the second. That's where she was.'

'Now you tell us. And where the hell do you think I went?'

'But I always go upstairs,' said Mrs Bristol. 'It keeps me in trim. You know that. I mean one's got to get some exercise and ...'

'Oh, belt up,' said Wilt, and dabbed his nose with a blood-stained handkerchief.

'Right, let's get this straight,' said the Principal, deciding it was time to exercise some authority. 'Mrs Bristol tells Wilt here there is a girl upstairs injecting herself with something or other and instead of going upstairs, Wilt goes down to the toilet on the second floor and ...'

'Gets beaten to a pulp by Ms Blackbelt Burke here,' said Wilt who was beginning to regain the initiative. 'And I don't suppose it's occurred to anyone to go up and see if that junkie's still there.'

But the Vice-Principal had already left.

'If that little turd calls me Burke again ...' said Miss Hare menacingly. 'Anyway, I still think we should call the police. I mean, why did Wilt go downstairs instead of up? I find that peculiar.'

'Because I don't use the Ladies' or, in your case, the Bisexual Toilets, that's why.'

'Oh for God's sake,' said the Principal, 'there's obviously been some mistake and if we all keep calm ...'

The Vice-Principal returned. 'No sign of her,' he said.

The Principal got to his feet. 'Well, that's that. Evidently there's been some mistake. Mrs Bristol may have imagined ...'

But any aspersions on Mrs Bristol's imagination he was about to make were stopped by the V-P's next words.

'But I did find this in the trash can,' he said, and produced a blood-stained lump of paper towel, which looked like Wilt's handkerchief.

The Principal regarded it with disgust. 'That hardly proves anything. Women do bleed occasionally.'

'Call it a jamrag and be done with it,' said Wilt viciously.

He was getting fed up with bleeding himself. Miss Hare turned on him.

'That's typical, you foulmouthed sexist,' she snapped.

'I was merely interpreting what the Principal was ...'

'And more conclusively, this,' interrupted the V-P, this time producing a hypodermic needle.

It was Mrs Bristol's turn to bridle. 'There, what did I tell you. I wasn't imagining anything. There was a girl up there injecting herself and I did see her. Now what are you going to do?'

'Now we mustn't jump to conclusions just because ...' the Principal began.

'Call the police. I demand that you call the police,' said Miss Hare, determined to take this opportunity for airing her opinions about Wilt and Peeping Toms as widely as possible.

'Miss Burke,' said the Principal, flustered into sharing Wilt's feelings about the PE lecturer, 'this is a matter that needs cool heads.'

'Miss Hare's my name and if you haven't the decency ... And where do you think you're going?'

Wilt had taken the opportunity to sidle to the door. 'To the men's toilet to assess the damage you did, then the Blood Transfusion Unit for a refill and after that, if I can make it, to my doctor and the most litigious lawyer I can find to sue you for assault and battery.' And before Miss Hare could reach him, Wilt was off down the corridor and had closeted himself in the Men's toilet.

Behind him Miss Hare vented her fury on the Principal. 'Right, that does it,' she shouted. 'If you don't call the police, I will. I want the facts of this case spelt out loud and clear so that if that little sex-maniac goes anywhere near a lawyer, the public are going to learn the sort of people who teach here. I want this whole disgusting matter dealt with openly.'

It was the last thing the Principal wanted. 'I really don't think that's wise,' he said. 'After all, Wilt could have made a natural mistake.'

Miss Hare wasn't to be mollified. 'The mistake Wilt made wasn't natural. And besides, Mrs Bristol did see a girl taking heroin.'

36

'We don't know that. There could be some quite ordinary explanation.'

'The police will find out soon enough once they've got that syringe,' said Miss Hare adamantly. 'Now then, are you going to phone them or am I?'

'If you put it like that, I suppose we'll have to,' said the Principal, eyeing her with loathing. He picked up the phone.

4

In the Men's toilet, Wilt surveyed his face in the mirror. It looked as unpleasant as it felt. His nose was swollen, there were streaks of blood on his chin and Miss Hare had managed to open an old cut above his right eye. Wilt washed his face in a basin and thought dismally about tetanus. Then he took his false tooth out and studied his tongue. It was not, as he had expected, twice its normal size, but it still tasted of disinfectant. He rinsed his mouth out under the tap with the slightly cheering thought that if his taste buds were anything to go by a tetanus germ wouldn't stand an earthly of surviving. After that, he put his tooth back and wondered yet again what it was about him that invited misunderstanding and catastrophe.

The face in the mirror told him nothing. It was a very ordinary face and Wilt had no illusions about it being handsome. And yet for all its ordinariness, it had to be the façade behind which lurked an extraordinary mind. In the past he had liked to think it was an original mind or, at the very least, an individual one. Not that that helped much. Every mind had to be individual and that didn't make everyone accident-prone, to put it mildly. No, the fact of the matter was that he lacked a sense of his own authority.

'You just let things happen to you,' he told the face in the mirror. 'It's about time you made them happen for you.' But as he said it, he knew it would never be like that. He would never be a dominating person, a man of power whose orders were obeyed without question. It wasn't his nature. To be more accurate, he lacked the stamina and drive to deal in details, to quibble over procedure and win allies and out-manoeuvre opponents, in short, to concentrate his attention on the means of gaining power. Worse still, he despised the people who had that drive. Invariably, they limited themselves to a view of the world in which they alone were important

38

and to hell with what other people wanted. And they were everywhere, these committee Hitlers, especially at the Tech. It was about time they were challenged. Perhaps one day he would ...

He was interrupted in this daydream by the entrance of the Vice-Principal. 'Ah, there you are, Henry,' he said, 'I thought I'd better let you know that we've had to call in the police.'

'About what?' asked Wilt, suddenly alarmed at the thought of Eva's reaction if Miss Hare accused him of being a voyeur.

'Drugs in the college.'

'Oh, that. A bit late in the day, isn't it? Been going on ever since I can remember.'

'You mean you knew about it?'

'I thought everyone did. It's common knowledge. Anyway, it's obvious we're bound to have a few junkies with all the students we've got,' said Wilt, and made good his escape while the Vice-Principal was still busy at the urinal. Five minutes later, he had left the Tech and was immersed once more in those speculative thoughts that seemed to occupy so much of his time when he was alone. Why was it, for instance, that he was so concerned with power when he wasn't really prepared to do anything about it? After all, he was earning a comfortable salary – it would have been a really good one if Eva hadn't spent so much of it on the quads' education – and objectively he had nothing to complain about. Objectively. And a fat lot that meant. What mattered was how one felt. On that score, Wilt came bottom even on days when he hadn't had his face mashed by Ms Hare.

Take Peter Braintree for example. He didn't have any sense of futility or lack of power. He had even refused promotion because it would have meant giving up teaching and taking on administrative duties. Instead, he was content to give his lectures on English literature and go home to Betty and the children and spend his evenings playing trains or making model aeroplanes when he'd finished marking essays. And at the weekends, he'd go off to watch a football match or play cricket. It was the same during the holidays. The Braintrees always went off camping and walking and came back cheerful, with none of the rows and catastrophes that seemed an inevitable part of the Wilt family excursions. In his own way, Wilt envied him, while having to admit that his envy was muted by a contempt he knew to be wholly unjustified. In the modern world, in any world, it wasn't enough just to be content and hope that everything would turn out for the best in the end. In Wilt's experience, they turned out for the worst, e.g. Miss Hare. On the other hand, when he did try to do something the result was catastrophic. There didn't seem to be any middle way.

He was still puzzling over the problem when he crossed Bilton Street and walked up Hillbrow Avenue. Here too, the signs told him that almost everyone was content with his lot. The cherry trees were in bloom, and pink and white petals littered the pavement like confetti. Wilt noted each front garden, most of them neat and bright with wallflowers, but some, where academics from the University lived, unkempt and overgrown with weeds. On the corner of Pritchard Street, Mr Sands was busy among his heathers and azaleas, proving to an uninterested world that it was possible for a retired bank manager to find satisfaction by growing acid-loving plants on an alkaline soil. Mr Sands had explained the difficulties to Wilt one day, and the need to replace all the topsoil with peat to lower the pH. Since Wilt had no idea what pH stood for, he hadn't a clue what Mr Sands had been talking out, and in any case, he had been more interested in Mr Sands' character and the enigma of his contentment. The man had spent forty years presumably fascinated by the movement of money from one account to the other, fluctuations in the interest rate and the granting of loans and overdrafts, and now all he seemed prepared to talk about were the needs of his camellias and miniature conifers. It didn't make sense and was just as unfathomable as the character of Mrs Cranley who had once figured so spectacularly in a trial to do with a brothel in Mayfair, but who now sang in the choir at St Stephens and wrote children's stories filled with remorseless whimsy and an appalling innocence. It was all beyond him. He could only deduce one fact from his observations. People could and did change their lives from one moment to the next, and quite fundamentally at that. And if they could, there was no reason why he shouldn't. Fortified with the knowledge, he strode on more confidently and with the determination not to put up with any nonsense from the quads tonight.

As usual he was proved wrong. He had no sooner opened the front door, than he was under siege. 'Ooh, Daddy, what have you done to your face?' demanded Josephine.

'Nothing,' said Wilt, and tried to escape upstairs before the real inquisition could begin. He needed a bath and his clothes stank of disinfectant. He was stopped by Emmeline who was playing with her hamster halfway up.

'Don't step on Percival,' she said, 'she's pregnant.'

'Pregnant?' said Wilt, momentarily nonplussed. 'He can't be. It's impossible.'

'Percival's a she, so it is.'

'A she? But the man at the petshop guaranteed the thing was a male. I asked him specifically.'

'And she's not a thing,' said Emmeline. 'She's an expectant mummy.'

'Better not be,' said Wilt. 'I'm not having the house overrun by an exploding population of hamsters. Anyway, how do you know?'

'Because we put her in with Julian's to see if they'd fight to the death like the book said, and Percival went into a trance and didn't do anything.'

'Sensible fellow,' said Wilt, immediately identifying with Percival in such horrid circumstances.

'She's not a fellow. Mummy hamsters always go into a trance when they want to be done.'

'Done?' said Wilt inadvisedly.

'What you do to Mummy on Sunday mornings and Mummy goes all funny afterwards.'

'Christ,' said Wilt, cursing Eva for not shutting the bedroom door. Besides, the mixture of accuracy and baby-talk was getting to him. 'Anyway, never mind what we do. I want to . . .'

'Does Mummy go into a trance, too?' asked Penelope, who was coming down the stairs with a doll in a pram.

'It's not something I'm prepared to discuss,' said Wilt. 'I need a bath and I'm going to have one. And now.'

'Can't,' said Josephine. 'Sammy's having her hair washed. She's got nits. You smell funny too. What's that on your collar?'

'And all down the front of your shirt.' This from Penelope.

'Blood,' said Wilt, endowing the word with as much threat as he could. He pushed past the pram and went into the bedroom, wondering what it was about the quads that gave them some awful sort of collective authority. Four separate daughters wouldn't have had the same degree of assertiveness and the quads had definitely inherited Eva's capacity for making the worst of things. As he undressed, he could hear Penelope bearing the glad tidings of his misfortune to Eva through the bathroom door.

'Daddy's come home smelling of disinfectant and he's cut his face.'

'He's taking off his trousers and there's blood all down his shirt,' Josephine chimed in.

'Oh, great,' said Wilt. 'That ought to bring her out like a scalded cat.'

But it was Emmeline's announcement that Daddy had said Mummy went into a trance when she wanted a fuck that caused the trouble.

'Don't use that word,' yelled Wilt. 'If I've told you once I've told you a thousand times and I never said anything about your bleeding mother going into a trance. I said –'

'What did you call me?' Eva shouted, storming out of the bathroom. Wilt pulled up his Y-fronts again and sighed. On the landing, Emmeline was describing with clinical accuracy the mating habits of female hamsters, and attributing the description to Wilt.

'I didn't call you a bloody hamster. That's a downright lie. I don't know the first thing about the fucking things and I certainly never wanted them in –'

'There you go,' shouted Eva. 'One moment you're telling the children not to use filthy language and the next you're using it yourself. You can't expect them to –'

'I don't expect them to lie. That's far worse than the sort of language they use and anyway Penelope used it first. I –'

'And you've absolutely no right to discuss our sex life with them.'

'I don't and I wasn't,' said Wilt. 'All I said was I didn't want the house overrun by blasted hamsters. The man in the shop sold me that mentally deficient rat as a male, not a bloody breeding machine.'

'Now you're being disgustingly sexist as well,' yelled Eva.

Wilt stared wildly round the bedroom. 'I am not being sexist,' he said finally. 'It just happens to be a well-known fact that hamsters –'

But Eva had seized on his inconsistency. 'Oh yes you are. The way you talk anyone would think women were the only ones who wanted you-know-what.'

'You-know-what my foot. Those four little bints out there know what without you-know-whating –'

'How dare you call your own daughters bints? That's a disgusting word.'

'Fits,' said Wilt, 'and as for their being my own daughters, I can tell you it's –'

'I shouldn't,' said Eva.

Wilt didn't. Push Eva too far and there was no knowing what would happen. Besides, he'd had enough of women's power in action for one day. 'All right, I apologize,' he said. 'It was a stupid thing to say.'

'I should think it was,' said Eva, coming off the boil and picking his shirt off the floor. 'How on earth did you get all this blood on your new shirt?'

'Slipped and fell in the gents,' said Wilt, deciding the time was hardly appropriate for a more accurate account. 'That's why it smells like that.'

'In the gents?' said Eva suspiciously. 'You fell over in the gents?'

Wilt gritted his teeth. He could see any number of awful consequences developing if the truth leaked out but he'd already committed himself.

'On a bar of soap,' he said. 'Some idiot had left it on the floor.'

'And another idiot stepped on it,' said Eva, scooping up Wilt's jacket and trousers and depositing them in a plastic basket. 'You can take these to the dry-cleaners on the way to work tomorrow.'

'Right,' said Wilt, and headed for the bathroom.

'You can't go in there yet. I'm still washing Samantha's

hair and I'm not having you prancing around in the altogether ...'

'Then I'll wear my pants in the shower,' said Wilt and was presently hidden behind the shower curtain listening to Penelope telling the world that female hamsters frequently bit the male's testicles after copulating.

'I wonder they bother to wait. Talk about having your cake and eating it,' muttered Wilt, and absentmindedly soaped his Y-fronts.

'I heard that,' said Eva and promptly turned the hot tap on in the bath. Behind the shower curtain Wilt juddered under a stream of cold water. With a grunt of despair, he wrenched at the cold tap and stepped from the shower.

'Daddy's foaming at his panties,' squealed the quads delightedly.

Wilt lurched at them rabidly. 'Not the only fucking place he'll be foaming if you don't get the hell out of here,' he shouted.

Eva turned the hot tap in the bath off. 'That's no way to set an example,' she said, 'talking like that. You should be ashamed of yourself.'

'Like hell I should. I've had a bloody awful day at the Tech and I've got to go out to the prison to teach that ghastly creature McCullum, and I no sooner step into the bosom of my menagerie than I –'

The front doorbell rang loudly downstairs. 'That's bound to be Mr Leach nextdoor come to complain again,' said Eva.

'Sod Mr Leach,' said Wilt and stepped back under the shower.

This time he learnt what it felt like to be scalded.

5

Things were hotting up for other people in Ipford as well. The Principal for one. He had just arrived home and was opening the drinks cabinet in the hope of dulling his memory of a disastrous day, when the phone rang. It was the Vice-Principal. 'I'm afraid I've got some rather disturbing news,' he said with a lugubrious satisfaction the Principal recognized. He connected it with funerals. 'It's about that girl we were looking for ...' The Principal reached for the gin bottle and missed the rest of the sentence. He got back in time to hear something about the boiler-room. 'Say that again,' he said, holding the bottle between his knees and trying to open it with one hand.

'I said the caretaker found her in the boiler-room.'

'In the boiler-room? What on earth was she doing there?'

'Dying,' said the Vice-Principal, affecting an even more sombre tone.

'Dying?' The Principal had the bottle open now and poured himself a large gin. This was even more awful than he expected.

'I'm afraid so.'

'Where is she now?' asked the Principal, trying to stave off the worst.

'Still in the boiler-room.'

'Still in the ... But good God man, if she's in that condition, why the devil haven't you got her to hospital?'

'She isn't in that condition,' said the Vice-Principal and paused. He too had had a hard day. 'What I said was that she was dying. The fact of the matter is that she's dead.'

'Oh, my God,' said the Principal and swigged neat gin. It was better than nothing. 'You mean she died of an overdose?'

'Presumably. I suppose the police will find out.'

The Principal finished the rest of the gin. 'When did this happen?'

'About an hour ago.'

'An hour ago? I was still in my office an hour ago. Why the hell wasn't I told?'

'The caretaker thought she was drunk first of all and fetched Mrs Ruckner. She was taking an ethnic needlework class with Home Economics in the Morris block and –'

'Never mind about that now,' snapped the Principal. 'A girl's dead on the premises and you have to go on about Mrs Ruckner and ethnic needlework.'

'I'm not going on about Mrs Ruckner,' said the Vice-Principal, driven to some defiance, 'I'm merely trying to explain.'

'Oh, all right, I've heard you. So what have you done with her?'

'Who? Mrs Ruckner?'

'No, the damned girl, for God's sake. There's no need to be flippant.'

'If you're going to adopt that tone of voice, you'd better come here and see for yourself,' said the Vice-Principal and put the phone down.

'You bloody shit,' said the Principal, unintentionally addressing his wife who had just entered the room.

At Ipford Police Station the atmosphere was fairly acrimonious too. 'Don't give me that,' said Flint who had returned from a fruitless visit to the Mental Hospital to interview a patient who had confessed (quite falsely) to being the Phantom Flasher. 'Give it to Hodge. He's drugs and I've had my fill of the bloody Tech.'

'Inspector Hodge is out,' said the Sergeant, 'and they specially asked for you. Personally.'

'Pull the other one,' said Flint. 'Someone's hoaxing you. The last person they want to see is me. And it's mutual.'

'No hoax, sir. It was the Vice-Principal himself. Name of Avon. My lad goes there so I know.'

Flint stared at him incredulously. 'Your son goes to that hell-hole? And you let him? You must be out of your mind. I wouldn't let a son of mine within a mile of the place.'

'Possibly not,' said the Sergeant, tactfully avoiding the observation that since Flint's son was doing a five-year stretch, he wasn't likely to be going any place. 'All the same, he's an

46

apprentice plumber. Got day-release classes and he can't opt out of them. There's a law about it.'

'You want my opinion, there ought to be a law stopping youngsters having anything to do with the sods who teach there. When I think of Wilt ...' He shook his head in despair.

'Mr Avon said something about your discreet approach being needed,' the Sergeant went on, 'and anyway, they don't know how she died. I mean, it doesn't have to be an overdose.'

Flint perked up. 'Discreet approach my arse,' he muttered. 'Still, a genuine murder there makes a change.' He lumbered to his feet and went down to the car pool and drove down to Nott Road and the Tech. A patrol car was parked outside the gates. Flint swept past it and parked deliberately in the space reserved for the Bursar. Then with the diminished confidence he always felt when returning to the Tech, he entered the building. The Vice-Principal was waiting for him by the Enquiries Desk. 'Ah, Inspector, I'm so glad you could come.'

Flint regarded him suspiciously. His previous visits hadn't been welcomed. 'All right, where's the body?' he said abruptly and was pleased to see the Vice-Principal wince.

'Er ... in the boiler-room,' he said. 'But first there's the question of discretion. If we can avoid a great deal of publicity it would really be most helpful.'

Inspector Flint cheered up. When the sods started squealing about publicity and the need for discretion, things had got to be bad. On the other hand, he'd had enough lousy publicity from the Tech himself. 'If it's anything to do with Wilt ...' he began, but the Vice-Principal shook his head.

'Nothing like that, I assure you,' he said. 'At least, not directly.'

'What's that mean, not directly?' said Flint warily. With Wilt, nothing was ever direct.

'Well, he was the first to be told that Miss Lynchknowle had taken an overdose but he went to the wrong loo.'

'Went to the wrong loo?' said Flint and bared his teeth in a mock smile. A second later the smile had gone. He'd smelt trouble. 'Miss who?'

'Lynchknowle. That's what I meant about ... well, the need for discretion. I mean ...'

'You don't have to tell me. I know, don't I just,' said Flint
rather more coarsely than the Vice-Principal liked. 'The Lord
Lieutenant's daughter gets knocked off here and you don't
want him to ...' He stopped and looked hard at the V-P.
'How come she was here in the first place? Don't tell me she
was shacked up with one of your so-called students.'

'She was one of our students,' said the Vice-Principal, trying
to maintain some dignity in the face of Flint's patent scepti-
cism. 'She was Senior Secs Three and ...'

'Senior Sex Three? What sort of course is that, for hell's
sake? Meat One was sick enough considering they were a load
of butcher's boys, but if your telling me you've been running
a class for prostitutes and one of them's Lord Lynchknowle's
ruddy daughter ...'

'Senior Secretaries,' spluttered the Vice-Principal, 'a very
respectable course. We've always had excellent results.'

'Like deaths,' said Flint. 'All right, let's have a look at your
latest victim.'

With the certainty now that he'd done the wrong thing
in asking for Flint, the Vice-Principal led the way across the
quad.

But the Inspector hadn't finished. 'I hear you've been
putting it out as a self-administered OD. Right?'

'OD?'

'Overdose.'

'Of course. You're not seriously suggesting it could have
been anything else?'

Inspector Flint fingered his moustache. 'I'm not in a position
to suggest anything. Yet. I'm asking why you say she died of
drugs.'

'Well, Mrs Bristol saw a girl injecting herself in the staff
toilet and went to fetch Wilt ...'

'Why Wilt of all people? Last person I'd fetch.'

'Mrs Bristol is Wilt's secretary,' said the V-P and went on
to explain the confused course of events. Flint listened grimly.
The only part he enjoyed was hearing how Wilt had been
dealt with by Miss Hare. She sounded like a woman after his
own heart. The rest fitted in with his preconceptions of the
Tech.

'One thing's certain,' he said when the Vice-Principal had

48

finished, 'I'm not drawing any conclusions until I've made a thorough examination. And I do mean thorough. The way you've told it doesn't make sense. One unidentified girl takes a fix in a toilet and the next thing you know Miss Lynchknowle is found dead in the boiler-room. How come you assume it's the same girl?'

The Vice-Principal said it just seemed logical. 'Not to me it doesn't,' said Flint. 'And what was she doing in the boiler-room?'

The Vice-Principal looked miserably down the steps at the door and resisted the temptation to say she'd been dying. That might work with the Principal but Inspector Flint's manner didn't suggest he'd respond kindly to statements of the obvious. 'I've no idea. Perhaps she just felt like going somewhere dark and warm.'

'And perhaps she didn't,' said Flint. 'Anyway, I'll soon find out.'

'I just hope you will be discreet,' said the V-P, 'I mean it's a very sensitive ...'

'Bugger discretion,' said Flint, 'all I'm interested in is the truth.'

Twenty minutes later, when the Principal arrived, it was all too obvious that the Inspector's search for the truth had assumed quite alarming dimensions. The fact was that Mrs Ruckner, more accustomed to the niceties of ethnic needlework than resuscitation, had allowed the body to slip behind the boiler: that the boiler hadn't been turned off added a macabre element to the scene. Flint had refused to allow it to be moved until it had been photographed from every possible angle, and he had summoned fingerprint and forensic experts from the Murder Squad along with the police surgeon. The Tech car park was lined with squad cars and an ambulance and the buildings themselves seemed to be infested with policemen. And all this in full view of students arriving for evening classes. To the Principal, it appeared as if the Inspector was intent on attracting the maximum adverse publicity.

'Is the man mad?' he demanded of the Vice-Principal, stepping over a white tape that had been laid on the ground outside the steps to the boiler-room.

'He says he's treating it as a murder case until he's proved it isn't,' said the Vice-Principal weakly, 'and I wouldn't go down there if I were you.'

'Why the hell not?'

'Well, for one thing there's a dead body and ...'

'Of course there's a dead body,' said the Principal, who had been in the War and frequently mentioned the fact. 'Nothing to be squeamish about.'

'If you say so. All the same ...'

But the Principal had already gone down the steps into the boiler-room. He was escorted out a moment later looking decidedly unwell. 'Jesus wept! You could have told me they were holding an autopsy on the spot,' he muttered. 'How the hell did she get in that state?'

'I rather think Mrs Ruckner ...'

'Mrs Ruckner? Mrs Ruckner?' gurgled the Principal, trying to equate what he had just seen in some way with the tenuous figure of the part-time lecturer in ethnic needlework and finding it impossible. 'What the hell has Mrs Ruckner got to do with that ... that ...'

But before he could express himself at all clearly, they were joined by Inspector Flint. 'Well, at least we've got a real dead corpse this time,' he said, timing his cheerfulness nicely. 'Makes a change for the Tech, doesn't it?'

The Principal eyed him with loathing. Whatever Flint might feel about the desirability of real dead corpses littering the Tech he didn't share Flint's opinions. 'Now look here, Inspector ...' he began in an attempt to assert some authority.

But Flint had opened a cardboard box. 'I think you had better look in here first,' he said. 'Is this the sort of printed matter you encourage your students to read?'

The Principal stared down into the box with a horrid fascination. If the cover of the top magazine was anything to go by – it depicted two women, a rack and a revoltingly androgynous man clad in chains and a ... the Principal preferred not to think what it looked like – the entire box was filled with printed matter he wouldn't have wanted his students to know about, let alone read.

'Certainly not,' he said, 'that's downright pornography.'

'Hard core,' said Flint, 'and there's more where this little

lot came from. Puts a new complexion on things, doesn't it?'
'Dear God,' muttered the Principal, as Flint trotted off across the quad, 'are we to be spared nothing? That bloody man seems to find the whole horrible business positively enjoyable.'
'It's probably because of that terrible incident with Wilt some years back,' said the V-P. 'I don't think he's ever forgotten it.'
'Nor have I,' said the Principal, looking gloomily round at the buildings in which he had once hoped to make a name for himself. And in a sense it seemed he had. Thanks to so many things that were connected, in his mind, with Wilt. It was the one topic on which he would have agreed with the Inspector. The little bastard ought to be locked up.

And in a sense Wilt was. To prevent Eva from learning that he spent Friday evenings at Baconheath Airbase he devoted himself on Mondays to tutoring a Mr McCullum at Ipford Prison and then led her to suppose he had another tutorial with him four evenings later. He felt rather guilty about this subterfuge but excused himself with the thought that if Eva wanted to buy an expensive education plus computers for four daughters, she couldn't seriously expect his salary, however augmented by HM Prison Service, to pay for it. The airbase lectures did that and anyway Mr McCullum's company constituted a form of penance. It also had the effect of assuaging Wilt's sense of guilt. Not that his pupil didn't do his damnedest to instil one. A sociology lecturer from the Open University had given him a solid grounding in that subject and Wilt's attempts to further Mr McCullum's interest in E. M. Forster and *Howards End* were constantly interrupted by the convict's comments on the socio-economically disadvantaged environment which had led him to end up where and what he was. He was also fairly fluent on the class war, the need for a preferably bloody revolution and the total redistribution of wealth. Since he had spent his entire life pursuing riches by highly illegal and unpleasant means, ones which involved the deaths of four people and the use of a blowtorch as a persuader on several gentlemen in his debt, thus earning himself the soubriquet 'Fireworks Harry' and 25 years from a socially

51

prejudiced judge, Wilt found the argument somewhat suspect. He didn't much like Mr McCullum's changes of mood either. They varied from whining self-pity, and the claim that he was deliberately being turned into a cabbage, through bouts of religious fervour during which the name Longford came up rather too often, and finally to a bloody-minded belligerence when he threatened to roast the fucking narks who'd shopped him. On the whole, Wilt preferred McCullum the cabbage and was glad that the tutorials were conducted through a grill of substantial wire mesh and in the presence of an even more substantial warder. After Miss Hare and the verbal battering he'd had from Eva, he could do with some protection and this evening Mr McCullum's mood had nothing to do with vegetables. 'Listen,' he told Wilt thickly, 'you don't have a clue, do you? Think you know everything but you haven't done time. Same with this E. M. Forster. He was a middle-class scrubber too.'

'Possibly,' said Wilt, recognizing that this was not one of the nights on which to press Mr McCullum too frankly on the need to stick to the subject. 'He was certainly middle-class. On the other hand, this may have endowed him with the sensitivity needed to –'

'Fuck sensitivity. Lived with a pig, that's how sensitive he was, dirty sod.'

Wilt considered this estimation of the private life of the great author dubious. So, evidently, did the warder. 'Pig?' said Wilt, 'I don't think he did you know. Are you sure?'

'Course I'm sure. Fucking pig by the name of Buckingham.'

'Oh, him,' said Wilt, cursing himself for having encouraged the beastly man to read Forster's biography as background material to the novels. He should have realized that any mention of policemen was calculated to put 'Fireworks Harry' in a foul mood. 'Anyway, if we look at his work as a writer, as an observer of the social scene and ...'

McCullum wasn't having any of that. 'The social scene my eye and Betty Martin. Spent more time looking up his own arsehole.'

'Well, metaphorically I suppose you could ...'

'Literally,' snarled McCullum, and turned the pages of the book. 'How about this? January second "... have the illusion

I am charming and beautiful ... blah, blah ... but would powder my nose if I wasn't found out ... blah, blah ... The anus is clotted with hairs ..." And that's in your blooming Forster's diary. A self-confessed narcissistic fairy.'

'Must have used a mirror, I suppose,' said Wilt, temporarily thrown by this revelation. 'All the same his novels reflect ...'

'I know what you're going to say,' interrupted McCullum. 'They have social relevance for their time. Balls. He could have got nicked for what he did, slumming it with one of the State's sodding hatchet men. His books have got about as much social relevance as Barbara bloody Cartland's. And we all know what they are, don't we? Literary asparagus.'

'Literary asparagus?'

'Chambermaid's delight,' said Mr McCullum with peculiar relish.

'It's an interesting theory,' said Wilt, who had no idea what the beastly man was talking about, 'though personally I'd have thought Barbara Cartland's work was pure escapism whereas ...'

'That's enough of that,' interrupted the warder, 'I don't want to hear that word again. You're supposed to be talking about books.'

'Listen to Wilberforce,' said McCullum, still looking fixedly at Wilt, 'bloody marvellous vocabulary he's got, hasn't he?'

Behind him the warder bridled. 'My name's not Wilberforce and you know it,' he snapped.

'Well then, I wasn't talking about you, was I?' said McCullum. 'I mean everyone knows you're Mr Gerard, not some fucking idiot who has to get someone literate to read the racing results for him. Now as Mr Wilt here was saying ...'

Wilt tried to remember. 'About Barbara Cartland being moron fodder,' prompted McCullum.

'Oh yes, well according to your theories, reading romantic novels is even more detrimental to working-class consciousness than ... What's the matter?'

Mr McCullum was smiling horribly at him through the mesh. 'Screw's pissed off,' he hissed. 'Knew he would. Got him on my payroll and his wife reads Barbara Cartland so he couldn't stand to listen. Here, take this.'

53

Wilt looked at the rolled-up piece of paper McCullum was thrusting through the wire. 'What is it?'

'My weekly essay.'

'But you write that in your notebook.'

'Think of it like that,' said McCullum, 'and stash it fast.'

'I'll do no ...'

Mr McCullum's ferocious expression had returned. 'You will,' he said.

Wilt put the roll in his pocket and 'Fireworks' relaxed. 'Don't make much of a living, do you?' he asked. 'Live in a semi and drive an Escort. No big house with a Jag on the forecourt, eh?'

'Not exactly,' said Wilt, whose taste had never been drawn to Jaguars. Eva was dangerous enough in a small car.

'Right. Well now's your chance to earn 50K.'

'50K?'

'Grand. Cash,' said McCullum and glanced at the door behind him. So did Wilt, hopefully, but there was no sign of the warder. 'Cash?'

'Old notes. Small denominations and no traceability. Right?'

'Wrong,' said Wilt firmly. 'If you think you can bribe me into ...'

'Gob it,' said McCullum with a nasty grunt. 'You've got a wife and four daughters and you live in a brick and mortar, address 45 Oakhurst Avenue. You drive an Escort, pale dog-turd, number-plate HPR 791 N. Bank at Lloyds, account number 0737 ... want me to go on?' Wilt didn't. He got to his feet but Mr McCullum hadn't finished. 'Sit down while you've still got knees,' he hissed. 'And daughters.'

Wilt sat down. He was suddenly feeling rather weak. 'What do you want?' he asked.

Mr McCullum smiled. 'Nothing. Nothing at all. You just go off home and check that piece of paper and everything's going to be just jake.'

'And if I don't?' asked Wilt feeling weaker still.

'Sudden bereavement is a sad affair,' said McCullum, 'very sad. Specially for cripples.'

Wilt gazed through the wire mesh and wondered, not for the first time in his life, though by the sound of things it might be the last, what it was about him that attracted the horrible.

And McCullum was horrible, horrible and evilly efficient. And why should the evil be so efficient? 'I still want to know what's on that paper,' he said.

'Nothing,' said McCullum, 'it's just a sign. Now as I see it Forster was the typical product of a middle-class background. Lots of lolly and lived with his old Ma ...'

'Bugger E. M. Forster's mother,' said Wilt. 'What I want to know is why you think I'm going to ...'

But any hope he had of discussing his future was ended by the return of the warder. 'You can cut the lecture, we're shutting up shop.'

'See you next week, Mr Wilt,' said McCullum with a leer as he was led back to his cell. Wilt doubted it. If there was one thing on which he was determined, it was that he would never see the swine again. Twenty-five years was far too short a sentence for a murdering gangster. Life should mean life and nothing less. He wandered miserably down the passage towards the main gates, conscious of the paper in his pocket and the awful alternatives before him. The obvious thing to do was to report McCullum's threats to the warder on the gate. But the bastard had said he had one warder on his payroll and if one, why not more? In fact, looking back over the months, Wilt could remember several occasions when McCullum had indicated that he had a great deal of influence in the prison. And outside too, because he'd even known the number of Wilt's bank account. No, he'd have to report to someone in authority, not an ordinary screw.

'Had a nice little session with "Fireworks"?' enquired the warder at the end of the corridor with what Wilt considered to be sinister emphasis. Yes, definitely he'd have to speak to someone in authority.

At the main gate it was even worse. 'Anything to declare, Mr Wilt?' said the warder there with a grin, 'I mean we can't tempt you to stay inside, can we?'

'Certainly not,' said Wilt hurriedly.

'You could do worse than join us, you know. All mod cons and telly and the grub's not at all bad nowadays. A nice little cell with a couple of friendly mates. And they do say it's a healthy life. None of the stress you get outside ...'

But Wilt didn't wait to hear any more. He stepped out into

what he had previously regarded as freedom. It didn't seem so free now. Even the houses across the road, bathed in the evening sunshine, had lost their moderate attraction; instead, their windows were empty and menacing. He got into his car and drove a mile along Gill Road before pulling into a side street and stopping. Then making sure no one was watching him, he took the piece of paper out of his pocket and unrolled it. The paper was blank. Blank? That didn't make sense. He held it up to the light and stared at it but the paper was unlined and as far as he could see, had absolutely nothing written on it. Even when he held it horizontally and squinted along it he could make out no indentations on the surface to suggest that a message had been written on it with a matchstick or the blunt end of a pencil. A man was coming towards him along the pavement. With a sense of guilt, Wilt put the paper on the floor and took a road map from the dashboard and pretended to be looking at it until the man had passed. Even then he checked in the rear-view mirror before picking up the paper again. It remained what it had been before, a blank piece of notepaper with a ragged edge as though it had been torn very roughly from a pad. Perhaps the swine had used invisible ink. Invisible ink? How the hell would he get invisible ink in prison? He couldn't unless ... Something in Wilt's literary memories stirred. Hadn't Graham Greene or Muggeridge mentioned using bird-shit as ink when he was a spy in the Second World War? Or was it lemon juice? Not that it mattered much. Invisible ink was meant to be invisible and if that bastard had intended him to read it, he'd have told him how. Unless, of course, the swine was clear round the bend and in Wilt's opinion, anyone who'd murdered four people and tortured others with a blowtorch as part of the process of earning a living had to be bloody well demented. Not that that let McCullum off the hook in the least. The bugger was a murderer whether he was sane or not, and the sooner he fulfilled his own predictions and became a cabbage the better. Pity he hadn't been born one.

With a fresh sense of desperation, Wilt drove on to The Glassblowers' Arms to think things out over a drink.

6

'All right, call it off,' said Inspector Flint, helping himself to a plastic cup of coffee from the dispenser and stumping into his office.

'Call it off?' said Sergeant Yates, following him in.

'That's what I said. I knew it was an OD from the start. Obvious. Gave those old windbags a nasty turn all the same, and they could do with a bit of reality. Live in a bloody dream world where everything's nice and hygienic because it's been put into words. That way they don't happen, do they?'

'I hadn't thought of it like that,' said Yates.

The Inspector took a magazine out of the cardboard box and studied a photograph of a threesome grotesquely inter-twined. 'Bloody disgusting,' he said.

Sergeant Yates peered over his shoulder. 'You wouldn't think anyone would have the nerve to be shot doing that, would you?'

'Anyone who does that ought to be shot, if you ask me,' said Flint. 'Though mind you they're not really doing it. Can't be. You'd get ruptured or something. Found this little lot in that boiler-room and it didn't do that murky Principal a bit of good. Turned a very queer colour, he did.'

'Not his, are they?' asked Yates.

Flint shut the magazine and dumped it back in the box. 'You never know, my son, you never know. Not with so-called educated people you don't. It's all hidden behind words with them. They look all right from the outside, but it's what goes on in here that's really weird.' Flint tapped his forehead significantly. 'And that's something else again.'

'I suppose it must be,' said Yates. 'Specially when it's hygienic into the bargain.'

Flint looked at him suspiciously. He never knew if Sergeant

Yates was as stupid as he made out. 'You trying to be funny or something?'

'Of course not. Only first you said they lived in a hygienic dream world of words; and then you say they're kinky in the head. I was just putting the two together.'

'Well, don't,' said Flint. 'Don't even try. Just get me Hodge. The Drug Squad can take this mess over, and good luck to them.' The Sergeant went out, leaving Flint studying his pale fingers and thinking weird thoughts of his own about Hodge, the Tech and the possibilities that might result from bringing the Head of the Drug Squad and that infernal institution together. And Wilt. It was an interesting prospect, particularly when he remembered Hodge's request for phone-tapping facilities and his generally conspiratorial air. Kept his cards close to his chest, did Inspector Hodge, and a fat lot of good it had done him so far. Well, two could play at that game, and if ever there was a quicksand of misinformation and inconsequentiality, it had to be the Tech and Wilt. Flint reversed the order. Wilt and the Tech. And Wilt had been vaguely connected with the dead girl, if only by going to the wrong toilet. The word alerted Flint to his own immediate needs. Those bloody pills had struck again.

He hurried down the passage for a pee and as he stood there, standing and staring at the tiled wall and a notice which said, 'Don't drop your cigarette ends in the urinal. It makes them soggy and difficult to light,' his disgust changed to inspiration. There was a lesson to be learned from that notice if he could only see it. It had to do with the connection between a reasonable request and an utterly revolting supposition. The word 'inconsequential' came to mind again. Sticking Inspector Bloody Hodge onto Wilt would be like tying two cats together by their tails and seeing which one came out on top. And if Wilt didn't, Flint had sorely misjudged the little shit. And behind Wilt there was Eva and those foul quads and if that frightful combination didn't foul Hodge's career up as effectively as it had wrecked Flint's, the Inspector deserved promotion. With the delightful thought that he'd be getting his own back on Wilt too, he returned to his office and was presently doodling figures of infinite confusion which was exactly what he hoped to initiate.

58

He was still happily immersed in this daydream of revenge when Yates returned. 'Hodge is out,' he reported. 'Left a message he'd be back shortly.'

'Typical,' said Flint. 'The sod's probably lurking in some coffee bar trying to make up his mind which dolly bird he's going to nail.'

Yates sighed. Ever since Flint had been on those ruddy penis-blockers or whatever they were called, he'd had girls on his mind. 'Why shouldn't he be doing that?' he asked.

'Because that's the way the sod works. A right shoddy copper. Pulls some babe in arms in for smoking pot and then tries to turn her into a supergrass. Been watching too much TV.'

He was interrupted by the preliminary report from the Lab. 'Massive heroin dose,' the technician told him, 'that's for starters. She'd used something else we haven't identified yet. Could be a new product. It's certainly not the usual. Might be "Embalming Fluid" though.'

'Embalming Fluid? What the hell would she be doing with that?' said Flint with a genuine and justified revulsion.

'It's a name for another of these hallucinogens like LSD only worse. Anyway, we'll let you know.'

'Don't,' said Flint. 'Deal direct with Hodge. It's his pigeon now.'

He put the phone down and shook his head sorrowfully. 'Says she fixed herself with heroin and some filth called Embalming Fluid,' he told Yates. 'You wouldn't credit it, would you? Embalming Fluid! I don't know what the world's coming to.'

Fifty miles away, Lord Lynchknowle's dinner had been interrupted by the arrival of a police car and the news of his daughter's death. The fact that it had come between the mackerel pâté and the game pie, and on the wine side, an excellent Montrachet and a Chateau Lafite 1962, several bottles of which he'd opened to impress the Home Secretary and two old friends from the Foreign Office, particularly annoyed him. Not that he intended to let the news spoil his meal by announcing it before he'd finished, but he could foresee an ugly episode with his wife afterwards for no better reason than that he had come back to the table with the rather unfortunate remark that it was nothing important. Of course, he could always excuse himself on the grounds that hospitality came first, and old Freddie was the Home Secretary after all, and he wasn't going to let that Lafite '62 go to waste, but somehow he knew Hilary was going to kick up the devil of a fuss about it afterwards. He sat on over the Stilton in a pensive mood wishing to God he'd never married her. Looking back over the years, he could see that his mother had been right when she'd warned him that there was bad blood in 'that family', the Puckertons.

'You can't breed bad blood out, you know,' she'd said, and as a breeder of bull terriers, she'd known what she was talking about. 'It'll come out in the end, mark my words.'

And it had, in that damned girl Penny. Silly bitch should have stuck to showjumping instead of getting it into her head she was going to be some sort of intellectual and skiving off to that rotten Tech in Ipford and mixing with the scum there. All Hilary's fault, too, for encouraging the girl. Not that she'd see it that way. All the blame would be on his side. Oh well, he'd have to do something to pacify her. Phone the Chief Constable perhaps and get Charles to put the boot in. His eyes wandered round the table and rested moodily on the Home Secretary. That was it, have a word with Freddie before he left and see that the police got their marching orders from the top.

By the time he was able to get the Home Secretary alone, a process that required him to lurk in the darkness outside the cloakroom and listen to some frank observations about himself by the hired waitresses in the kitchen, Lord Lynchknowle had worked himself up into a state of indignation that was positively public-spirited. 'It's not simply a personal matter, Freddie,' he told the Home Secretary, when the latter was finally convinced Lynchknowle's daughter was dead and that he wasn't indulging that curious taste for which he'd been renowned at school. 'There she was at this bloody awful Tech at the mercy of all these drug pedlars. You've got to put a stop to it.'

'Of course, of course,' said the Home Secretary, backing

into a hatstand and a collection of shooting sticks and umbrellas. 'I'm deeply sorry –'

'It's no use you damned politicians being sorry,' continued Lynchknowle, forcing him back against a clutter of raincoats, 'I begin to understand the man-in-the-street's disenchantment with the parliamentary process.' (The Home Secretary doubted it) 'What's more, words'll mend no fences' (the Home Secretary didn't doubt that) 'and I want action.'

'And you'll have it, Percy,' the Home Secretary assured him, 'I guarantee that. I'll get the top men at Scotland Yard onto it tomorrow first thing and no mistake.' He reached for the little notebook he used to appease influential supporters. 'What did you say the name of the place was?'

'Ipford,' said Lord Lynchknowle, still glowering at him.

'And she was at the University there?'

'At the Tech.'

'Really?' said the Home Secretary, with just enough inflexion in his voice to lower Lord Lynchknowle's resolve.

'All her mother's fault,' he said defensively.

'Quite. All the same, if you will allow your daughters to go to Technical Colleges, not that I'm against them you understand, but a man in your position can't be too careful ...'

In the hall, Lady Lynchknowle caught the phrase.

'What are you two men doing down there?' she asked shrilly.

'Nothing, dear, nothing,' said Lord Lynchknowle. It was a remark he was to regret an hour later when the guests had gone.

'Nothing?' shrieked Lady Lynchknowle, who had by then recovered from the condolences the Home Secretary had offered so unexpectedly. 'You dare to stand there and call Penny's death nothing?'

'I am not actually standing, my dear,' said Lynchknowle from the depths of an armchair. But his wife was not to be deflected so easily.

'And you sat through dinner knowing she was lying there on a marble slab? I knew you were a callous swine but ...'

'What the hell else was I supposed to do?' yelled Lynchknowle, before she could get into her stride. 'Come back to the table and announce that your daughter was a damned junkie? You'd have loved that, wouldn't you? I can just hear you now ...'

'You can't,' shrieked his wife, making her fury heard in the servants' quarters. Lynchknowle lumbered to his feet and slammed the door. 'And don't think you're going to –'

'Shut up,' he bawled, 'I've spoken to Freddie and he's putting Scotland Yard onto the case and now I'm going to call Charles. As Chief Constable he can –'

'And what good is that going to do? He can't bring her back to me!'

'Nobody can, dammit. And if you hadn't put the idea into her empty head that she was capable of earning her own living when it was as clear as daylight she was as thick as two short planks, none of this would have happened.' Lord Lychknowle picked up the phone and dialled the Chief Constable.

At The Glassblowers' Arms, Wilt was on the phone too. He had spent the time trying to think of some way to circumvent whatever ghastly plans McCullum had in mind for him without revealing his own identity to the prison authorities. It wasn't easy.

After two large whiskies, Wilt had plucked up enough courage to phone the prison, had refused to give his name and had asked for the Governor's home number. It wasn't in the phone book. 'It's ex-directory.' said the warder in the office.

'Quite,' said Wilt. 'That's why I'm asking.'

'And that's why I can't give it to you. If the Governor wanted every criminal in the district to know where he could be subjected to threats, he'd put it there wouldn't he?'

'Yes,' said Wilt. 'On the other hand, when a member of the public is being threatened by some of your inmates, how on earth is he supposed to inform the Governor that there's going to be a mass breakout?'

'Mass breakout? What do you know about plans for a mass breakout?'

'Enough to want to speak to the Governor.' There was a pause while the warder considered this and Wilt fed the phone with another coin.

'Why can't you tell me?' the warder asked finally.

Wilt ignored the question. 'Listen,' he said with a desperate earnestness that sprang from the knowledge that having come so far he couldn't back down, and that if he didn't convince the man that this was a genuine crisis, McCullum's accomplices would shortly be doing something ghastly to his knees, 'I assure you that this is a deeply serious matter. I wish to speak to the Governor privately. I will call back in ten minutes. All right?'

'It may not be possible to reach him in that time, sir,' said the warder, recognizing the voice of genuine desperation. 'If you can give me your number, I'll get him to call you.'

'It's Ipford 23194,' he said, 'and I'm not joking.'

'No, sir,' said the warder. 'I'll be back to you as soon as I can.'

Wilt put the phone down and wandered back to his whisky at the bar uncomfortably aware that he was now committed to a course of action that could have horrendous consequences. He finished his whisky and ordered another to dull the thought that he'd given the warder the phone number of the pub where he was well-known. 'At least it proved to him that I was being serious,' he thought and wondered what it was about the bureaucratic mentality that made communication so difficult. The main thing was to get in touch with the Governor as soon as possible and explain the situation to him. Once McCullum had been transferred to another prison, he'd be off the hook.

At HM Prison Ipford, the information that a mass escape was imminent was already causing repercussions. The Chief Warder, summoned from his bed, had tried to telephone the Governor. 'The blasted man must be out to dinner somewhere,' he said when the phone had rung for several minutes without being answered. 'Are you certain it wasn't a hoax call?'

The warder on duty shook his head. 'Sounded genuine to me,' he said. 'Educated voice and obviously frightened. In fact, I have an idea I recognized it.'

'Recognized it?'

'Couldn't put a name to it but he sounded familiar somehow. Anyway, if it wasn't genuine, why did he give me his phone number so quick?' The Chief Warder looked at the number and dialled it. The line was engaged. A girl at The Glass-blowers' Arms was talking to her boyfriend. 'Why didn't he give his name?'

'Sounded frightened to death like I told you. Said something about being threatened. And with some of the swine we've got in here ...'

The Chief Warder didn't need telling. 'Right. We're not taking any chances. Put the emergency plan into action pronto. And keep trying to contact the bloody Governor.'

Half an hour later, the Governor returned home to find the phone in his study ringing. 'Yes, what is it?'

'Mass breakout threatened,' the warder told him, 'a man ...' But the Governor wasn't waiting. He'd been living in terror for years that something of this sort was going to happen. 'I'll be right over,' he shouted and dashed for his car. By the time he reached the prison his fears had been turned to panic by the wail of police sirens and the presence on the road of several fire engines travelling at high speed in front of him. As he ran towards the gate, he was stopped by three policemen.

'Where do you think you're going?' a sergeant demanded. The Governor looked at him lividly.

'Since I happen to be the Governor,' he said, 'the Governor of this prison, you understand, I'm going inside. Now if you'll kindly stand aside.'

'Any means of identification, sir?' asked the Sergeant. 'My orders require me to prevent anyone leaving or entering.'

The Governor rummaged through the pockets of his suit and produced a five-pound note and a comb. 'Now look here, officer ...' he began, but the Sergeant was already looking. At the five-pound note. He ignored the comb.

'I shouldn't try that one if I were you,' he said.

'Try what one? I don't seem to have anything else on me.'

'You heard that one, Constable,' said the sergeant, 'Attempting to offer a bribe to –'

'A bribe ... offer a bribe? Who said anything about offering a bribe?' exploded the Governor. 'You ask me for means of identification and when I try to produce some, you start talking about bribes. Ask the warder on the gate to identify me, dammit.' It took another five minutes of protest to get inside the prison and by then his nerves were in no state to deal at all adequately with the situation. 'You've done what?' he screamed at the Chief Warder.

'Moved all the men from the top floors to the cells below, sir. Thought it better in case they got onto the roof. Of course, they're a bit cramped but ...'

'Cramped? They were four to a one-man cell already. You mean to say they're eight now? It's a wonder they haven't started rioting already.' He was interrupted by the sound of screams from C Block. As Prison Officer Blaggs hurried away, the Governor tried to find out what was happening. It was almost as difficult as getting into the prison had been. A battle was apparently raging on the third floor of A Wing. 'That'll be due to putting Fidley and Gosling in with Stanforth and Haydow,' the warder in the office said.

'Fidley and ... Put two child murderers in with a couple of decent honest-to-God armed bank robbers? Blaggs must be mad. How long did it take them to die?'

'I don't think they're dead yet,' said the warder with rather more disappointment in his voice than the Governor approved. 'Last I heard, they'd managed to stop Haydow from castrating Fidley. That was when Mr Blaggs decided to intervene.'

'You mean the lunatic waited?' asked the Governor.

'Not exactly, sir. You see, there was this fire in D Block –'

'Fire in D Block? What fire in D Block?'

'Moore set fire to his mattress, sir, and by the time –' But the Governor was no longer listening. He knew now that his career was at stake. All it needed to finish him was for that lunatic Blaggs to have acted as an accessory to murder by packing all the swine in the Top Security Block into one cell. He was just on his way to make quite certain when Chief Warder Blaggs returned. 'Everything's under control, sir,' he said cheerfully.

'Under control?' spluttered the Governor. 'Under control? If you think the Home Secretary's going to think "under control" means having child killers castrated by other prisoners, I can assure you you're not up-to-date with contemporary regulations. Now then, about Top Security.'

'Nothing to worry about there, sir. They're all sleeping like babes.'

'Odd,' said the Governor. 'If there was going to be an

attempted breakout you'd think they were bound to be involved. You're sure they're not shamming?'

'Positive, sir,' said Blaggs proudly. 'The first thing I did, sir, by way of a precaution, was to lace their cocoa with that double-strength sleeping stuff.'

'Sweet Jesus,' moaned the Governor, trying to imagine the consequences of the Chief Warder's experiment in preventive sedation if news leaked out to the Howard League for Penal Reform. 'Did you say "double strength"?'

The Chief Warder nodded. 'Same stuff we had to use on Fidley that time he saw the Shirley Temple film and went bananas. Mind you, he's not going to get a hard-on after tonight, not if he's wise.'

'But that was double-strength phenobarb,' squawked the Governor.

'That's right, sir. So I gave them double strength like it said. Went out like lights they did.'

The Governor could well believe it. 'You've gone and given four times the proper dose to those men,' he moaned, 'probably killed the brutes. That stuff's lethal. I never told you to do that.'

Chief Warder Blaggs looked crestfallen. 'I was only doing what I thought best, sir. I mean those swine are a menace to society. Half of them are psychopathic killers.'

'Not the only psychopaths round here,' muttered the Governor. He was about to order a medical team into the prison to stomach-pump the villains Blaggs had sedated, when the warder by the phone intervened. 'We could always say Wilson poisoned them,' he said, 'I mean, that's what they're terrified of. Remember that time they went on dirty strike and Mr Blaggs here let Wilson do some washing up in the kitchen?'

The Governor did, and would have preferred to forget it. Putting a mass poisoner anywhere near a kitchen had always struck him as insane.

'Did the trick, sir. They come off dirtying their cells double quick.'

'And went on hunger strike instead,' said the Governor.

'And Wilson didn't like it much either, come to that,' said the warder, for whom the incident evidently had pleasant

66

memories. 'Said we'd no right making him wash up in boxing gloves. Proper peeved he was –'

'Shut up,' yelled the Governor, trying to get back to a world of comparative sanity, but he was interrupted by the phone.

'It's for you, sir,' said the Chief Warder significantly.

The Governor grabbed it. 'I understand you have some information to give me about an escape plan,' he said, and realized he was talking to the buzz of a pay phone. But before he could ask the Chief Warder how he knew it was for him, the coin dropped. The Governor repeated his statement.

'That's what I'm phoning about,' said the caller. 'Is there any truth in the rumour?'

'Any truth in the ...' said the Governor. 'How the devil would I know? You were the one to bring the matter up.'

'News to me,' said the man. 'That is Ipford Prison, isn't it?'

'Of course it's Ipford Prison and what's more, I'm the Governor. Who the hell did you think I was?'

'Nobody,' said the man, now sounding decidedly perplexed, 'nobody at all. Well, not nobody exactly but ... well ... you don't sound like a Prison Governor. Anyway, all I'm trying to find out is if there's been an escape or not.'

'Listen,' said the Governor, beginning to share the caller's doubts about his own identity, 'you phoned earlier in the evening with information about an escape plot and –'

'I did? You off your rocker or something? I've been out covering a burst bloody bulkloader on Bliston Road for the last three bloody hours and if you think I've had time to call you, you're bleeding barmy.'

The Governor struggled with the alliteration before realizing something else was wrong. 'And who am I speaking to?' he asked, mustering what little patience he still retained.

'The name's Nailtes,' said the man, 'and I'm from the *Ipford Evening News* and –'

The Governor slammed the phone down and turned on Blaggs. 'A bloody fine mess you've landed us in,' he shouted. 'That was the *Evening News* wanting to know if there's been an escape.'

Chief Warder Blaggs looked dutifully abashed. 'I'm sorry if there's been some mistake ...' he began and brought a fresh torrent of abuse on his head.

'Mistake? Mistake?' yelled the Governor. 'Some maniac rings up with some fucking cock-and-bull story about an escape and you have to poison . . .' But further discussion was interrupted by news of a fresh crisis. Three safebreakers, who had been transferred from a cell designed to hold one Victorian convict to another occupied by four Grievous Bodily Harm merchants from Glasgow, known as the Gay Gorbals, had begun to fulfil Wilt's prophesy by escaping and demanding to be closeted with some heterosexual murderers for protection.

The Governor found them arguing their case with warders in B Block. 'We're not going in with a load of arse-bandits and that's a fact,' said the spokesman.

'It's only a temporary move,' said the Governor, himself temporizing. 'In the morning –'

'We'll be suffering from AIDS,' said the safebreaker.

'Aids?'

'Auto-Immune Deficiency Syndrome. We want some good, clean murderer, not those filthy swine with anal herpes. A stretch is one thing and so's a bang to rights but not the sort of stretch those Scotch sods would give us and we're fucked if we're going to be banged to wrong. This is supposed to be a prison, not Dotheboys Hall.'

By the time the Governor had pacified them and sent them back to their own cell, he was beginning to have his doubts about the place himself. In his opinion, the prison felt more like a mad-house. His next visit, this time to Top Security, made an even worse impression. A sepulchral silence hung over the floodlit building and, as the Governor passed from cell to cell, he had the illusion of being in a charnel-house. Wherever he looked, men who in other circumstances he would happily have seen dead, looked as though they were. Only the occasional ghastly snore suggested otherwise. For the rest, the inmates hung over the sides of their beds or lay grotesquely supine on the floor in attitudes that seemed to indicate that rigor mortis had already set in.

'Just let me find the swine who started this little lot,' he muttered. 'I'll . . . I'll . . . I'll . . .' He gave up. There was nothing in the book of legal punishments that would fit the crime.

7

By the time Wilt left The Glassblowers' Arms, his desperation
had been alleviated by beer and his inability to get anywhere
near the phone. He'd moved onto beer after three whiskies,
and the change had made it difficult for him to be in two
places at the same time, a prerequisite, it seemed, for finding
the phone unoccupied. For the first half hour, a girl had been
engaged in an intense conversation on reversed charges, and
when Wilt had returned from the toilet, her place had been
taken by an aggressive youth who had told him to bugger off.
After that, there seemed to be some conspiracy to keep him
away from the phone. A succession of people had used it and
Wilt had ended up sitting at the bar and drinking, and generally
arriving at the conclusion that things weren't so bad after all,
even if he did have to walk home instead of driving.

'The bastard's in prison,' he told himself as he left the pub.
'And what's more, he's not coming out for twenty years, so
what have I got to worry about? Can't hurt me, can
he?'

All the same, as he made his way along the narrow streets
towards the river, he kept glancing over his shoulder and
wondering if he was being followed. But apart from a man
with a small dog and a couple who passed him on bicycles,
he was alone and could find no evidence of menace. Doubtless
that would come later. Wilt tried to figure out a scenario.
Presumably, McCullum had given him the piece of paper as
a token message, an indication that he was to be some sort
of link-man. Well, there was an easy way out of that one; he
wouldn't go near the bloody prison again. Might make things
awkward as far as Eva was concerned though. He'd just have
to make himself scarce on Monday nights and pretend he
was still teaching the loathsome McCullum. Shouldn't be too
difficult and anyway, Eva was so engrossed in the quads and
their so-called development, she hardly noticed what he was

doing. The main thing was that he still had the airbase job and that brought the real money in.

But in the meantime, he had more immediate problems to deal with. Like what to tell Eva when he got home. He looked at his watch and saw that it was midnight. After midnight and without the car. Eva would certainly demand an explanation. What a bloody world it was, where he spent his days dealing with idiotic bureaucrats who interfered at the Tech, and was threatened by maniacs in prison, and after all that, came home to be bullied into lying by a wife who didn't believe he'd done a stroke of work all day. And in a bloody world, only the bloody-minded made any mark. The bloody-minded and the cunning. People with drive and determination. Wilt stopped under a street light and looked at the heathers and azaleas in Mr Sands' garden for the second time that day, but this time with a resurgence of those dangerous drives and determinations which beer and the world's irrationality induced in him. He would assert himself. He would do something to distinguish himself from the mass of dull, stupid people who accepted what life handed out to them and then passed on probably into oblivion (Wilt was never sure about that) without leaving more than the fallacious memories of their children and the fading snapshots in the family album. Wilt would be ... well, anyway, Wilt would be Wilt, whatever that was. He'd have to give the matter some thought in the morning.

In the meantime, he'd deal with Eva. He wasn't going to stand any nonsense about where have you been? or what have you been up to this time? He'd tell her to mind her own ... No, that wouldn't do. It was the sort of challenge the damned woman was waiting for and would only provoke her into keeping him awake half the night discussing what was wrong with their marriage. Wilt knew what was wrong with their marriage; it had been going on for twenty years and Eva had had quads instead of having one at a time. Which was typical of her. Talk about never doing things by halves. But that was beside the point. Or was it? Perhaps she'd had quads to compensate in some ghastly deterministic and genetical way for marrying only half a man. Wilt's mind shot off on a tangent once again as he considered the fact, if it was one, that after wars the birthrate of males shot up as if nature with

70

a capital N was automatically compensating for their shortage. If Nature was that intelligent, it ought to have known better than to make him attractive to Eva, and vice versa. He was driven from this line of thought by another attribute of Nature. This time its call. Well, he wasn't peeing in a rose bush again. Once was enough.

He hurried up the street and was presently letting himself surreptitiously into 45 Oakhurst Avenue with the resolve that if Eva was awake he would say the car had broken down and he'd taken it to a garage. It was better to be cunning than bloody-minded after all. In the event, there was no need to be anything more than quiet. Eva, who had spent the evening mending the quads' clothes and who had discovered that they had cut imitation flies in their knickers as a blow for sexual equality, was fast asleep. Wilt climbed carefully into bed beside her and lay in the darkness thinking about drive and determination.

Drive and determination were very much in the air at the police station. Lord Lynchknowle's phone call to the Chief Constable, and the news that the Home Secretary had promised Scotland Yard's assistance, had put the skids under the Superintendent and had jerked him from his chair in front of the telly and back to the station for an urgent conference.

'I want results and I don't care how you get them,' he told the meeting of senior officers inadvisedly. 'I'm not having us known as the Fenland equivalent of Soho or Piccadilly Circus or wherever they push this muck. Is that clear? I want action.'

Flint smirked. For once he was glad of Inspector Hodge's presence. Besides, he could honestly claim that he had gone straight to the Tech and had made a very thorough investigation of the cause of death. 'I think you'll find all the preliminary details in my report, sir,' he said. 'Death was due to a massive overdose of heroin and something called Embalming Fluid. Hodge might know.'

'It's Phencyclidine or PCP,' he said. 'Comes under a whole series of names like Super Grass, Hog, Angel Dust and Killer Weed.'

The Superintendent didn't want a catalogue of names. 'What's the filth do, apart from kill kids, of course?'

71

'It's like LSD only a hell of a sight worse,' said Hodge. 'Puts them into psychosis if they smoke the stuff too much and generally blows their minds. It's bloody murder.'

'So we've gathered,' said the Superintendent. 'Where'd she get it is what I want to know. Me and the Chief Constable *and* the Home Secretary.'

'Hard to say,' said Hodge. 'It's a Yankee habit. Haven't seen it over here before.'

'So she went to the States and bought it there on holiday? Is that what you're saying?'

'She wouldn't have fixed herself with the stuff if she had,' said Hodge, 'she'd have known better. Could have got it from someone in the University, I suppose.'

'Well, wherever she got it,' said the Superintendent grimly, 'I want that source traced, and fast. In fact, I want this town clean of heroin and every other drug before we have Scotland Yard descending on us like a ton of bricks and proving we're nothing but a bunch of country hicks. Those aren't my words, they're the Chief Constable's. Now then, we're quite certain she took this stuff herself? She couldn't have been ... well, given it against her will?'

'Not according to my information,' said Flint, recognizing the attempt to shift the investigation in his direction and clear Lord Lynchknowle's name from any connection with the drug scene. 'She was seen shooting herself with it in one of the Staff toilets at the Tech. If shooting's the right word,' said Flint, and looked across at Hodge, hoping to shift onto him the burden of keeping Scotland Yard at bay while screening the Lynchknowles.

The Superintendent wasn't interested. 'Whatever,' he said. 'So there's no question of foul play?'

Flint shook his head. The whole beastly business of drugs was foul play but now didn't seem the time to discuss the question. What was important from Flint's point of view was to land Hodge with the problem up to his eyebrows. Let him foul this case up and his head really would be on the chopping-block. 'Mind you,' he said, 'I did find it suspicious she was using the Staff toilet. Could be that's the connection.'

'What is?' demanded the Superintendent.

'Well, I'm not saying they are and I'm not saying they're

not,' said Flint, with what he liked to think was subtle equivocation. 'All I'm saying is some of the staff could be.'

'Could be what, for Christ's sake?'

'Involved in pushing,' said Flint. 'I mean, that's why it's been so difficult to get a lead on where the stuff's coming from. Nobody'd suspect lecturers to be pushing the muck, would they?' He paused before putting the boot in. 'Take Wilt for example, Mr Henry Wilt. Now there's a bloke I wouldn't trust further than I could throw him and even then I wouldn't turn my back. This isn't the first time we've had trouble over there, you know. I've got a file on that sod as thick as a telephone directory and then some. And he's Head of the Liberal Studies Department at that. You should see some of the drop-outs he's got working for him. Beats me why Lord Lynchknowle let his daughter go to the Tech in the first place.' He paused again. Out of the corner of his eye he could see Inspector Hodge making notes. The bastard was taking the bait. So was the Superintendent.

'You may have something there, Inspector,' he said. 'A lot of teachers are hangovers from the sixties and seventies and that rotten scene. And the fact that she was spotted in the Staff toilet . . .' It was this that did it. By the time the meeting broke up, Hodge was committed to a thorough investigation of the Tech and had been given permission to send in undercover agents.

'Let me have a list of the names and I'll forward it to the Chief Constable,' said the Superintendent. 'With the Home Secretary involved, there shouldn't be any difficulty, but for God's sake, get some results.'

'Yes, sir,' said Inspector Hodge, and went off to his office a happy man.

So did Flint. Before leaving the station, he called in on the Head of the Drug Squad with Wilt's file. 'If this is any use . . .' he said and dropped it on the desk with apparent reluctance. 'And any other help I can give you, you've only to ask.'

'I will,' said Inspector Hodge, with the opposite intention. If one thing was certain, it was that Flint would get no credit for breaking the case. And so, while Flint drove home and unwisely helped himself to a brown ale before going to bed,

Hodge sat on in his office planning the campaign that would lead to his promotion.

He was still there two hours later. Outside, the street lamps had gone off and Ipford slept, but Hodge sat on, his mind already infected with the virus of ambition and hope. He had gone carefully through Flint's report on the discovery of the body and for once he could find no fault with the Inspector's conclusions. They were confirmed by the preliminary report from Forensic. The victim had died from an overdose of heroin mixed with Emblaming Fluid. It was this last which interested Hodge.

'American,' he muttered yet again, and checked with the Police National Computer on the incidence of its use. Negligible, as he had thought. All the same, the drug was extremely dangerous and its spread in the States had been so rapid that it had been described as the syphilis of drug abuse. Crack this case and Hodge's name would be known, not simply in Ipford, but through the Lord Lieutenant to the Home Secretary and ... Hodge's dreams pursued his name before returning to the present. He picked up Wilt's file doubtfully. He hadn't been in Ipford at the time of the Great Doll Case and its ghastly effects on Flint's career, but he'd heard about it in the canteen, where it was generally acknowledged that Mr Henry Wilt had outfoxed Inspector Flint. Made him look a damned fool was the usual verdict, but it had never been clear what Wilt had really been up to. No one in his right mind went round burying inflatable dolls dressed in his wife's clothes at the bottom of piling-holes with twenty tons of concrete on top of them. And Wilt had. It followed that either Wilt hadn't been in his right mind, or that he'd been covering some other crime. Diverting suspicion. Anyway, the sod had got away with whatever he'd been up to and had screwed Flint into the bargain. So Flint had a grudge against the bastard. That was generally acknowledged too.

It was therefore with justified suspicion that Hodge turned to Wilt's file and began to read in detail the transcript of his interrogation. And as he read, a certain grim respect for Wilt grew in his mind. The sod hadn't budged from his story, in spite of being kept awake and deluged with questions. And he had made Flint look the idiot he was. Hodge could see that, just as he could see why Flint had a grudge against him. But above all his own intuition told him that Wilt had to have been guilty of something. Just had to be. And he'd been too clever for the old bugger. Which explained why Flint had been prepared to hand the file over to him. He wanted this Wilt nailed. Only natural. All the same, knowing Flint's attitude to him, Hodge was amazed he had given him the file. Not with all that stuff showing what a moron he was. Must be something else there. Like the old man knew when he was beaten? And certainly he looked it lately. Sounded it too, so maybe giving him the file was tacitly acknowledging the fact. Hodge smiled to himself. He'd always known he was the better man and that his chance to prove it would come. Well, now it bloody well had.

He turned back to Flint's report on Miss Lynchknowle again and read it through carefully. There was nothing wrong with Flint's methods and it was only when he came to the bit about Wilt having gone to the wrong toilet that Inspector Hodge saw where the old man had made a mistake. He read through it again.

'Principal reported Wilt went to toilet on the second floor when he should have gone to the one on fourth floor.' And later 'Wilt's secretary, Mrs Bristol, said she told Wilt to go to Ladies' staff toilet on the fourth floor. Claimed she'd seen girl there before.' It fitted. Another of clever Mr Wilt's little moves, to go to the wrong toilet. But Flint hadn't spotted that or he'd have interviewed the sod. Hodge made a mental note to check Mr Wilt's movements. But surreptitiously. There was no point in putting him on his guard. Hodge made more notes. 'Tech laboratory facilities provide means of making Embalming Fluid. Check,' was one. 'Source heroin,' another. And all the time while he concentrated, part of his mind ran on different lines, involving romantic-sounding places like the 'Golden Triangle' and the 'Golden Crescent', those jungle areas of Thailand and Burma and Laos, or in the case of the 'Golden Crescent', the laboratories of Pakistan from which heroin came into Europe. In Hodge's mind, small dark men, Pakis, Turks, Iranians and Arabs, converged on Britain by donkey or container truck or the occasional ship: always at night, a black and sinister movement of the deadly opiates financed by men who lived in large houses and belonged to country clubs and had yachts. And then there was the Sicilian Connexion with Mafia murders almost daily on the streets of Palermo. And finally the 'pushers' in England, little runts like Flint's son doing his time in Bedford. That again could be an explanation for Flint's change of attitude, his ruddy son. But the romantic picture of distant lands and evil men was the dominant one, and Hodge himself the dominant figure in it, a lone ranger in the war against the most insidious of all crimes.

Reality was different of course, and converged with Hodge's mental geography only in the fact that heroin did come from Asia and Sicily and that an epidemic of terrible addiction had come to Europe, and only the most determined and intelligent police action and international co-operation would bring it to a halt. Which, since the Inspector in spite of his rank was neither intelligent nor possessed of more than a vivid imagination, was where he came unstuck. In place of intelligence, there was only determination, the determination of a man without a family and with few friends, but with a mission. And so Inspector Hodge worked on through the night planning the action he intended to take. It was four in the morning when he finally left the station and walked round the corner to his flat for a few hours' sleep. Even then, he lay in the darkness gloating over Flint's discomfiture. 'The sod's getting his comeuppance,' he thought before falling asleep.

On the other side of Ipford, in a small house with a neat garden distinguished by a nicely symmetrical goldfish pond with a stone cherub in the middle, Inspector Flint would have agreed, though the cause of his problem had rather more to do with brown ale and those bloody piss pills than with Hodge's future. On the latter score, he was quietly confident. He went back to bed wondering if it wouldn't be a wise move to take some leave. He had a fortnight due to him, and anyway he could justifiably claim his doctor had told him to take it easy. A trip to the Costa Brava, or maybe Malta? The only trouble there was that Mrs Flint tended to get randy in the heat. It was about the only time she did these days, thank God. Perhaps Cornwall would be a better bet. On the other

hand, it would be a pity to miss watching Hodge come unstuck
and if Wilt didn't run rings round the shit, Flint wasn't the
man he thought he was. Talk about tying two cats together
by their tails!

And so the night wore on. At the Prison, the activities Wilt
had initiated went on. At two, another prisoner in D Block
set fire to his mattress, only to have it extinguished by an
enterprising burglar using the slop bucket. But it was in Top
Security that matters were more serious. The Governor had
been disconcerted to find two prisoners wide awake in
McCullum's cell, and because it was McCullum's cell, he had
been wary of entering without at least six warders to ensure
his safety, and six warders were hard to find, partly because
they shared the Governor's apprehension and partly because
they were busy elsewhere. Lacking their support, the Governor
was forced to conduct a dialogue with McCullum's companions through the cell door. Known as the Bull and the
Bear, they acted as McCullum's bodyguards.

'Why aren't you men asleep?' demanded the Governor.

'Might be if you hadn't turned the ruddy light on,' said the
Bull, who had once made the mistake of falling madly in love
with a bank manager's wife, only to be betrayed when he had
fulfilled her hopes by murdering her husband and robbing the
bank of fifty thousand pounds. She had gone on to marry a
stockbroker.

'That's no way to speak to me,' said the Governor, peering
suspiciously through the peep-hole. Unlike the other two
prisoners, McCullum appeared to be fast asleep. One hand
hung limply over the side of his bunk, and his face was
unnaturally pallid. Considering that the swine was usually
a nasty ruddy colour, the Governor was perturbed. If anyone was likely to be involved in an escape plot, he'd have
sworn McCullum was. In which case, he'd have been
... The Governor wasn't sure what he'd have been, but he
certainly wouldn't have been fast asleep, with his face that
ghastly grey colour, while the Bull and the Bear were wide
awake. There was something distinctly fishy about his being
asleep.

'McCullum,' shouted the Governor, 'McCullum, wake up.'

McCullum didn't move. 'Blimey,' said the Bear, sitting up. 'What the fuck's going on?'

'McCullum,' yelled the Governor, 'I am ordering you to wake up.'

'What the fuck's up with you?' yelled the Bull. 'Middle of the bleeding night and some screw has to go off his nut and go round fucking waking people up. We got fucking rights, you know, even if we are in nick and Mac isn't going to like this.'

The Governor clenched his teeth and counted to ten. Being called a screw wasn't what he liked either. 'I am simply trying to ascertain that Mr McCullum is all right,' he said. 'Now will you kindly wake him up.'

'All right? All right? Why shouldn't he be all right?' asked the Bear.

The Governor didn't say. 'It's merely a precautionary measure,' he answered. McCullum's refusal to show any sign of life – and in fact from his attitude and complexion to show just the opposite – was getting to him. If it had been anyone else, he'd have opened the cell door and gone in. But the swine could well be shamming, and with the Bull and the Bear to help him, might be planning to overpower a warder going in to see what was wrong. With a silent curse on the Chief Warder for making his life so difficult, the Governor hurried off to get assistance. Behind him, the Bull and the Bear expressed their feelings about fucking screws who left the fucking light on all fucking night, when it occurred to them that there might be something to be said for checking McCullum after all. The next moment, Top Security was made hellish by their shouts.

'He's fucking dead,' screamed the Bear, while the Bull made a rudimentary attempt to resuscitate McCullum by applying what he thought was artificial respiration, and which in fact meant hurling himself on the body and expelling what remained of breath from his victim's lungs.

'Give him the fucking kiss of life,' ordered the Bear, but the Bull had reservations. If McCullum wasn't dead, he had no intention of bringing him back to consciousness to find he was being kissed, and if he had coughed it, he didn't fancy kissing a corpse.

'Squeamish sod,' yelled the Bear, when the Bull stated his

views on the question. 'Here, let me get at him.' But even then he was put off by McCullum's coldness. 'You bloody murderers,' he shouted through the cell door.

'You've done it this time,' said the Governor. He had found the Chief Warder in the office enjoying a cup of coffee. 'You and your infernal sedatives.'

'Me?' said the Chief Warder.

The Governor took a deep breath. 'Either McCullum's dead or he's shamming very convincingly. Get me ten warders and the doctor. If we hurry, we may be in time to save him.'

They rushed down the passage, but the Chief Warder had yet to be convinced. 'I gave him the same dose as everyone else. He's having you on.'

Even when they had secured the ten warders and were outside the cell door, he delayed matters. 'I suggest you leave this to us, sir,' he said. 'If they take hostages, you ought to be on the outside to conduct negotiations. We're dealing with three extremely dangerous men, you know.' The Governor doubted it. Two seemed more probable.

Chief Warder Blaggs peered into the cell. 'Could have painted his face with chalk or something,' he said. 'He's a right crafty devil.'

'And pissed himself into the bargain?'

'Never does things by halves, does our Mac,' said the Chief Warder. 'All right, stand clear of the door in there. We're coming in.' A moment later the cell was filled with prison officers and in the mêlée that followed, the late McCullum received some post mortem injuries which did nothing to improve his appearance. But there was no doubt he was dead. It hardly needed the prison doctor to diagnose death as due to acute barbiturate poisoning.

'Well, how was I to know that the Bull and the Bear were going to give him their cups of cocoa?' said the Chief Warder plaintively, at a meeting held in the Governor's office to discuss the crisis.

'That's something you're going to have to explain to the Home Office enquiry,' said the Governor.

They were interrupted by a prison officer who announced that a cache of drugs had been found in McCullum's sodden mattress. The Governor looked out at the dawn sky and groaned.

'Oh, and one other thing, sir,' said the warder. 'Mr Coven in the office has remembered where he heard that voice on the telephone. He thought he recognized it at the time. Says it was Mr Wilt.'

'Mr Wilt?' said the Governor. 'Who the hell's Mr Wilt?'

'A lecturer from the Tech or somewhere who's been teaching McCullum English. Comes every Monday.'

'McCullum? Teaching McCullum English? And Coven's certain he was the one who phoned?' In spite of his fatigue, the Governor was wide awake now.

'Definitely, sir. Says he thought it was familiar and naturally when he heard "Fireworks" Harry'd snuffed it, he made the connection.'

So had the Governor. With his career in jeopardy he was prepared to act decisively. 'Right,' he said, casting discretion to the draught that blew under the door. 'McCullum died of food poisoning. That's the official line. Next...'

'What do you mean, "food poisoning"?' asked the prison doctor. 'Death was due to an overdose of phenobarbitone and I'm not going on record as saying –'

'And where was the poison? In his cocoa, of course,' snapped the Governor. 'And if cocoa isn't food, I don't know what is. So we put it out as food poisoning.' He paused and looked at the doctor. 'Unless you want to go down as the doctor who nearly poisoned thirty-six prisoners.'

'Me? I didn't have anything to do with it. That goon went and dosed the sods.' He pointed at Chief Warder Blaggs, but the Chief Warder had spotted the out.

'On your instructions,' he said with a meaningful glance at the Governor. 'I mean I couldn't have laid my hands on that stuff if you hadn't authorized it, could I now? You always keep the drugs cupboard in the dispensary locked, don't you? Be irresponsible not to, I'd have thought.'

'But I never did...' the doctor began, but the Governor stopped him.

'I'm afraid Mr Blaggs has a point there,' he said. 'Of course if you want to dispute the facts with the Board of Enquiry, that is your privilege. And doubtless the Press would make some-

80

thing of it. PRISON DOCTOR INVOLVED IN POISONING CONVICT would look well in the *Sun*, don't you think?'

'If he had drugs in his cell, I suppose we could say he died of an overdose,' said the doctor.

8

'There's no use in saying you didn't come home late last night because you did,' said Eva. It was breakfast, and, as usual, Wilt was being cross-examined by his nearest and dearest. On her other days, Eva left it to the quads to make the meal a misery for him by asking questions about computers or bio-chemistry about which he knew absolutely nothing. But this morning the absence of the car had given her the opportunity to get her own questions in.

'I didn't say I didn't come in late,' said Wilt through a mouthful of muesli. Eva was still into organic foods and her home-made muesli, designed to guarantee an adequate supply of roughage, did just that and more.

'That's a double negative,' said Emmeline.

Wilt looked at her balefully. 'I know it is,' he said, and spat out the husk of a sunflower seed.

'Then you weren't telling the truth,' Emmeline continued. 'Two negatives make a positive and you didn't say you had come in late.'

'And I didn't say I hadn't,' said Wilt, struggling with his daughter's logic and trying to use his tongue to get the bran off the top of his dentures. The damned stuff seemed to get everywhere.

'There's no need to mumble,' said Eva. 'What I want to know is where the car is.'

'I've already told you. I left it in a car park. I'll get a mechanic to go round and see what's wrong with the thing.'

'You could have done that last night. How do you expect me to take the girls to school?'

'I suppose they could always walk,' said Wilt, extracting a raisin from his mouth with his fingers and examining it offensively. 'It's an organic form of transportation, you know. Unlike this junior prune which would appear to have led a sedentary life and a sedimentary death. I wonder why it is that health foods so frequently contain objects calculated to kill. Now take this –'

'I am not interested in your comments,' said Eva. 'You're just trying to wriggle out of it and if you expect me to...'

'Walk?' interrupted Wilt. 'God forbid. The adipose tissue with which you –'

'Don't you adipose me, Henry Wilt,' Eva began, only to be interrupted by Penelope.

'What's adipose?'

'Mummy is,' said Wilt. 'As to the meaning, it means fat, fatty deposits and appertaining to fat.'

'I am not fat,' said Eva firmly, 'and if you think I'm spending my precious time walking three miles there and three miles back twice a day you're wrong.'

'As usual,' said Wilt. 'Of course. I was forgetting that the gender arrangements of this household leave me in a minority of one.'

'What are gender arrangements?' demanded Samantha.

'Sex,' said Wilt bitterly and got up from the table.

Behind him Eva snorted. She was never prepared to discuss sex in front of the quads. 'It's all very well for you,' she said, reverting to the question of the car which provided a genuine grievance. 'All you have to do is –'

'Catch a bus,' said Wilt, and hurried out of the house before Eva could think of a suitable reply. In fact there was no need. He caught a lift with Chesterton from the Electronics Department and listened to his gripes about financial cuts and why they didn't make them in Communication Skills and get rid of some of those Liberal Studies deadbeats.

'Oh well, you know how it is,' said Wilt as he got out of the car at the Tech. 'We have to make good the inexactitudes of science.'

'I didn't know there were any,' said Chesterton.

'The human element,' said Wilt enigmatically, and went through the library to the lift and his office. The human element was waiting for him.

'You're late, Henry,' said the Vice-Principal.

Wilt looked at him closely. He usually got on rather well with the V-P. 'You're looking pretty late yourself,' he said. 'In fact, if I hadn't heard you speak, I'd say you were a standing corpse. Been whooping it up with the wife?'

The Vice-Principal shuddered. He still hadn't got over the horror of seeing his first dead body in the flesh, rather than on the box, and trying to drown the memory in brandy hadn't helped. 'Where the hell did you get to last night?'

'Oh, here and there, don't you know,' said Wilt. He had no intention of telling the V-P he did extra-mural teaching.

'No, I don't,' said the V-P. 'I tried calling your house and all I got was some infernal answering service.'

'That'd be one of the computers,' said Wilt. 'The quads have this programme. It runs on tape, I think. Quite useful really. Did it tell you to fuck off?'

'Several times,' said the Vice-Principal.

'The wonders of science. I've just been listening to Chesterton praising –'

'And I've just been listening to the Police Inspector,' cut in the V-P, 'on the subject of Miss Lynchknowle. He wants to see you.'

Wilt swallowed. Miss Lynchknowle hadn't anything to do with the prison. It didn't make sense. In any case, they couldn't have got on to him so quickly. Or could they? 'Miss Lynchknowle? What about her?'

'You mean you haven't heard?'

'Heard what?' said Wilt.

'She's the girl who was in the toilet,' said the V-P. 'She was found dead in the boiler-room last night.'

'Oh God,' said Wilt. 'How awful.'

'Quite. Anyway, we had the police swarming all over the place last night and this morning there's a new man here. He wants a word with you.'

They walked down the corridor to the Principal's office. Inspector Hodge was waiting there with another policeman. 'Just a matter of routine, Mr Wilt,' he said when the Vice-Principal had shut the door. 'We've already interviewed Mrs Bristol and several other members of the staff. Now I understand you taught the late Miss Lynchknowle?'

Wilt nodded. His previous experience with the police didn't dispose him to say more than he had to. The sods always chose the most damning interpretation.

'You taught her English?' continued the Inspector.

84

'I teach Senior Secretaries Three English, yes,' said Wilt.

'On Thursday afternoons at 2.15 p.m?'

Wilt nodded again.

'And did you notice anything odd about her?'

'Odd?'

'Anything to suggest that she might be an addict, sir.'

Wilt tried to think. Senior Secretaries were all odd as far as he was concerned. Certainly in the context of the Tech. For one thing, they came from 'better families' than most of his other students and seemed to have stepped out of the fifties with their perms and their talk about Mummies and Daddies who were all wealthy farmers or something in the Army. 'I suppose she was a bit different from the other girls in the class,' he said finally. 'There was this duck, for instance.'

'Duck?' said Hodge.

'Yes, she used to bring a duck she called Humphrey with her to class. Bloody nuisance having a duck in a lesson but I suppose it was a comfort to her having a furry thing like that.'

'Furry?' said Hodge. 'Ducks aren't furry. They have feathers.'

'Not this one,' said Wilt. 'Like a teddy bear. You know, stuffed. You don't think I'd have a live duck shitting all over the place in my class, do you?'

Inspector Hodge said nothing. He was beginning to dislike Wilt.

'Apart from that particular addiction, I can't think of anything else remarkable about her. I mean, she didn't twitch or seem unduly pale or even go in for those sudden changes of mood you tend to find with junkies.'

'I see,' said Hodge, holding back the comment that Mr Wilt seemed exceedingly well-informed on the matter of symptoms. 'And would you say there was much drug-taking at the College?'

'Not to my knowledge,' said Wilt. 'Though, come to think of it, I suppose there must be some with the numbers we've got. I wouldn't know. Not my scene.'

'Quite, sir,' said the Inspector, simulating respect.

'And now, if you don't mind,' said Wilt, 'I have work to do.' The Inspector didn't mind.

'Not much there,' said the Sergeant when he'd left.

'Never is with the really clever sods,' said Hodge.

'I still don't understand why you didn't ask him about going to the wrong toilet and what the secretary said.'

Hodge smiled. 'If you really want to know, it's because I don't intend to raise his suspicions one little iota. That's why. I've been checking on Mr Wilt and he's a canny fellow, he is. Scuppered old Flint, didn't he? And why? I'll tell you. Because Flint was fool enough to do what Wilt wanted. He pulled him in and put him through the wringer and Mr Wilt got away with bloody murder. I'm not getting caught the same way.'

'But he never did commit any murder. It was only a fucking inflatable doll he'd buried,' said the Sergeant.

'Oh, come off it. You don't think the bugger did that without he had a reason? That's a load of bull. No, he was pulling some other job and he wanted a cover, him and his missus, so they fly a kite and Flint falls for it. That old fart wouldn't know a decoy if it was shoved under his bloody snout. He was so busy grilling Wilt about that doll he couldn't see the wood for the trees.'

Sergeant Runk fought his way through the mixed metaphors and came out none the wiser. 'All the same,' he said finally, 'I can't see a lecturer here being into drugs, not pushing anyway. Where's the lifestyle? No big house and car. No country-club set. He doesn't fit the bill.'

'And no big salary here either,' said Hodge. 'So maybe he's saving up for his old age. Anyway, we'll check him out and he won't ever know.'

'I should have thought there were more likely prospects round about,' said the Sergeant. 'What about that Greek restaurant bloke Macropolis or something you've been bugging? We know he's been into heroin. And there's that fly boy down the Siltown Road with the garage we had for GBH. He was on the needle himself.'

'Yea, well he's inside, isn't he? And Mr Macropolis is out of the country right now. Anyway, I'm not saying it is Wilt. She could have been down in London getting it for all we know. In which case, it's off our patch. All I'm saying is, I'm keeping an open mind and Mr Wilt interests me, that's all.'

And Wilt was to interest him still further when they returned to the police station an hour later. 'Super wants to see you,' said the Duty Sergeant. 'He's got the Prison Governor with him.'

'Prison Governor?' said Hodge. 'What's he want?'

'You,' said the Sergeant, 'hopefully.'

Inspector Hodge ignored the crack and went down the passage to the Superintendent's office. When he came out half an hour later, his mind was alive with circumstantial evidence, all of which pointed most peculiarly to Wilt. Wilt had been teaching one of the most notorious gangsters in Britain, now thankfully dead of an overdose of one of his own drugs. (The prison authorities had decided to use the presence of so much heroin in McCullum's mattress as the cause of death, rather than the phenobarb one, much to Chief Warder Blaggs' relief.) Wilt had been closeted with McCullum at the very time Miss Lynchknowle's body had been discovered. And, most significantly of all, Wilt, within an hour of leaving the prison and presumably on learning that the police were busy at the Tech, had rung the prison anonymously with a phoney message about a mass break-out and McCullum had promptly taken an overdose.

If that little lot didn't add up to something approaching a certainty that Wilt was involved, Hodge didn't know one. Anyway, add it to what he already knew of Wilt's past and it was certain. On the other hand, there was still the awkward little matter of proof. It was one of the disadvantages of the English legal system, and one Hodge would happily have dispensed with in his crusade against the underworld, that you had first to persuade the Director of Public Prosecutions that there was a case to be answered, and then go on to present evidence that would convince a senile judge and a jury of do-gooders, half of whom had already been nobbled, that an obvious villain was guilty. And Wilt wasn't an obvious villain. The bastard was as subtle as hell and to send the sod down would require evidence that was as hard as ferro-concrete.

'Listen,' Hodge said to Sergeant Runk and the small team of plain-clothes policemen who constituted his private crime squad, 'I don't want any balls-ups so this has got to be strictly covert and I mean covert. No one, not even the Super, is to know it's going on, so we'll code-name it Flint. That way, no one will suspect. Anyone can say Flint round this station and it doesn't register. That's one. Two is, I want Mr Wilt tailed twenty-four hours continuous. And another tail on his missus. No messing. I want to know what those people do every moment of the day and night from now on in.'

'Isn't that going to be a bit difficult?' asked Sergeant Runk. 'Day *and* night. There's no way we can put a tail in the house and ...'

'Bug it is what we'll do,' said Hodge. 'Later. First off we're going to patternize their lives on a time-schedule basis. Right?'

'Right,' echoed the team. In their time, they had patternized the lives of a fish-and-chip merchant and his family who Hodge had suspected were into hard-core porn; a retired choirmaster – this time for boys; and a Mr and Mrs Pateli for nothing better than their name. In each case the patternizing had failed to confirm the Inspector's suspicions, which were in fact wholly groundless, but had established as incontrovertible facts that the fish-and-chip merchant opened his shop at 6 p.m. except Sundays, that the choirmaster was having a happy and vigorous love affair with a wrestler's wife, and in any case had an aversion amounting almost to an allergy for small boys, and that the Patelis went to the Public Library every Tuesday, that Mr Pateli did full-time unpaid work with the Mentally Handicapped, while Mrs Pateli did Meals on Wheels. Hodge had justified the time and expense by arguing that these were training sessions in preparation for the real thing.

'And this is it,' continued Hodge. 'If we can nail this one down before Scotland Yard takes over we'll be quids in. We're also going into a surveillance mode at the Tech. I'm going over to see the Principal about it now. In the meantime, Pete and Reg can move into the canteen and the Student's Common Room and make out they're mature students chucked out for dope at Essex or some other University.'

Within an hour, Operation Flint was underway. Pete and Reg, suitably dressed in leather garments that would have alarmed the most hardened Hell's Angels, had already emptied the Students' Common Room at the Tech by their language and their ready assumption that everyone there was on heroin. In the Principal's office, Inspector Hodge was having more or less the same effect on the Principal and the V-P, who found the notion that the Tech was the centre for drug distribution in Fenland particularly horrifying. They didn't much like the idea of being lumbered with fifteen educationally sub-normal coppers as mature students.

'At this time of year?' said the Principal. 'Dammit, it's April. We don't enrol mature students this term. We don't enrol any, come to that. They come in September. And anyway, where the hell would we put them?'

'I suppose we could always call them "Student Teachers",' said the V-P. 'That way they could sit in on any classes they wanted to without having to say very much.'

'Still going to look bloody peculiar,' said the Principal. 'And frankly, I don't like it at all.'

But it was the Inspector's assertion that the Lord Lieutenant, the Chief Constable and, worst of all, the Home Secretary didn't like what had been going on at the Tech that turned the scales.

'God, what a ghastly man,' said the Principal, when Hodge had left. 'I thought Flint was foul enough, but this one's even bloodier. What is it about policemen that is so unpleasant? When I was a boy, they were quite different.'

'I suppose the criminals were, too,' said the V-P. 'I mean, it can't be much fun with sawn-off shotguns and hooligans hurling Molotov cocktails at you. Enough to turn any man bloody.'

'Odd,' said the Principal, and left it at that.

Meanwhile Hodge had put the Wilts under surveillance. 'What's been happening?' he asked Sergeant Runk.

'Wilt's still at the Tech so we haven't been able to pick him up yet, and his missus hasn't done anything much except the shopping.'

But even as he spoke, Eva was already acting in a manner calculated to heighten suspicion. She had been inspired to phone Dr Kores for an appointment. Where the inspiration came from she couldn't have said, but it had partly to do with an article she had read in her supermarket magazine on sex and the menopause entitled 'No Pause In The Pause, The Importance of Foreplay In The Forties', and partly with the glimpse she'd had of Patrick Mottram at the check-out counter where he usually chatted up the prettiest girl. On this occasion, he had ogled the chocolate bars instead and had ambled off with the glazed eyes of a man for whom the secret consumption of half a pound of Cadbury's Fruit and Nut was the height of sensual experience. If Dr Kores could reduce the randiest man in Ipford to such an awful condition, there was every possibility she could produce the opposite effect in Henry.

Over lunch, Eva had read the article again and, as always on the subject of sex, she was puzzled. All her friends seemed to have so much of it, either with their husbands or with someone, and obviously it was important, otherwise people wouldn't write and talk so much about it. All the same, Eva still had difficulty reconciling it with the way she'd been brought up. Mind you, her mother had been quite wrong going on about remaining a virgin until she was married. Eva could see that now. She certainly wasn't going to do the same with the quads. Not that she'd have them turn into little tarts like the Hatten girls, wearing make-up at fourteen and going around with rough boys on motorbikes. But later on, when they were eighteen and at university, then it would be all right. They'd need experience before they got married instead of getting married to get ... Eva stopped herself. That wasn't true, she hadn't married Henry just for sex. They'd been genuinely in love. Of course, Henry had groped and fiddled but never nastily like some of the boys she'd gone out with. If anything, he'd been rather shy and embarrassed and she'd had to encourage him. Mavis was right to call her a full-blooded woman. She did like sex but only with Henry. She wasn't going to have affairs, especially not with the quads in the house. You had to set an example and broken homes were bad. On the other hand, so were homes where both parents were always quarrelling and hated one another. So divorce was a good thing too. Not that anything like that threatened her marriage. It was just that she had a right to a more fulfilling love life and if Henry was too shy to ask for help, and he certainly was, she'd have to do it for him. So she had phoned Dr Kores and had been surprised to learn that she could come at half past two.

Eva had set off with an unnoticed escort of two cars and four policemen and had caught the bus at the bottom of Perry Road to Silton and Dr Kores' shambolic herb farm. 'I don't suppose she has time to keep it tidy,' Eva thought as she made her way past a number of old frames and a rusty cultivator to the house. All the same, she was slightly dismayed by the lack of organization. If it had been her garden, it wouldn't have looked like that. But then anything organic tended to go its own way, and Dr Kores did have a reputation as an eccentric. In fact, she had prepared herself to be confronted by some wizened old creature with a plaid shawl when the door opened and a severe woman in a white coat stood looking at her through strangely tinted dark glasses.

'Ms Wilt?' she said. Was there just the hint of a V for the W? But before Eva could consider this question, she was being ushered down the hallway and into a consulting-room. Eva looked round apprehensively as the doctor took a seat behind the desk. 'You are having problems?' she asked.

Eva sat down. 'Yes,' she said, fiddling with the clasp of her handbag and wishing she hadn't made the appointment.

'With your husband I think you said, yes?'

'Well, not with him exactly,' said Eva, coming to Henry's defence. After all, it wasn't his fault he wasn't as energetic as some other men. 'It's just that he's ... well ... not as active as he might be.'

'Sexually active?' Eva nodded.

'How old?' continued Dr Kores.

'You mean Henry? Forty-three. He'll be forty-four next March. He's a –'

But Dr Kores was clearly uninterested in Wilt's astrological sign. 'And the sexual gradient has been steep?'

'I suppose so,' said Eva, wondering what a sexual gradient was.

'Maximum weekly activity please.'

Eva looked anxiously at an Anglepoise lamp and tried to think. 'Well, when we were first married...' she paused.

'Go on,' Dr Kores ordered.

'Well, Henry did it three times one night I remember,' said Eva, blurting the statement out. 'He only did it once of course.'

The doctor's ballpen stopped. 'Please explain,' she said. 'First you said he was sexually active three times in one night. And second you said he was only once. Are you saying there was seminal ejaculation only on the first occasion?'

'I don't really know,' said Eva. 'It's not easy to tell, is it?'

Dr Kores eyed her doubtfully. 'Let me put it another way. Was there a penile spasm at the climax of each episode?'

'I suppose so,' said Eva. 'It's so long ago now and all I remember is that he was ever so tired next day.'

'In which year did this take place?' asked the doctor, having written down 'Penile spasm uncertain.'

'1963. In July,' said Eva. 'I remember that because we were on a walking holiday in the Peak District and Henry said he'd peaked out.'

'Very amusing,' said Dr Kores dryly. 'And that is his maximum sexual attainment?'

'He did it twice in 1970 on his birthday...'

'And the plateau was how many times a week?' asked Dr Kores, evidently determined to prevent Eva from intruding anything remotely human into the discussion.

'The plateau? Oh, well it used to be once or twice but now I'm lucky if it's once a month and sometimes we go even longer.'

Dr Kores licked her thin lips and put the pen down. 'Mrs Wilt,' she said, leaning on the desk and forming a triangle with her fingertips and thumbs. 'I deal exclusively with the problems of the female in a male-dominated social context, and to speak frankly, I find your attitude to your relationship with your husband unduly submissive.'

'Do you really?' said Eva, beginning to perk up. 'Henry always says I'm too bossy.'

'Please,' said the doctor with something approaching a shudder, 'I'm not in the least interested in your husband's opinions or in his person. If you choose to be, that is your business. Mine is to help you as an entirely independent being and, to be truthful, I find your self-objectivization highly distasteful.'

'I'm sorry,' said Eva, wondering what on earth self-objectivization was.

'For instance, you have repeatedly stated that and I quote "He did it three times" and again "He did it twice..."'

'But he did,' Eva protested.

'And who was the "It"? You?' said the doctor vehemently.

'I didn't mean it that way...' Eva began but Dr Kores was

not to be stopped. 'And the very word "did" or "done" is a tacit acceptance of marital rape. What would your husband say if you were to do him?'

'Oh, I don't think Henry'd like that,' said Eva, 'I mean, he's not very big and . . .'

'If you don't mind,' said the doctor, 'size does not come into it. The question of attitude is predominant. I am only prepared to help you if you make a determined effort to see yourself as the leader in the relationship.' Behind the blue tinted spectacles her eyes narrowed.

'I'll certainly try,' said Eva.

'You will succeed,' said the doctor sibilantly. 'It is of the essence. Repeat after me "I will succeed."'

'I will succeed,' said Eva.

'I am superior,' said Dr Kores.

'Yes,' said Eva.

'Not "Yes",' hissed the doctor, gazing even more peculiarly into Eva's eyes, 'but "I am superior".'

'I am superior,' said Eva obediently.

'Now both.'

'Both,' said Eva.

'Not that. I want you to repeat both remarks. First . . .'

'I will succeed,' said Eva, finally getting the message, 'I am superior.'

'Again.'

'I will succeed. I am superior.'

'Good,' said the doctor. 'It is vital that you establish the correct psychic attitude if I am to help you. You will repeat those auto-instructs three hundred times a day. Do you understand?'

'Yes,' said Eva. 'I am superior. I will succeed.'

'Again,' said the doctor.

For the next five minutes Eva sat fixed in her chair and repeated the assertions while Dr Kores stared unblinking into her eyes. 'Enough,' she said finally. 'You understand what this means, of course?'

'Sort of,' said Eva. 'It's to do with what Mavis Mottram says about women taking the leading role in the world, isn't it?'

Dr Kores sat back in her chair with a thin smile. 'Ms Wilt,' she said, 'for thirty-five years I have made a continuous study of the sexual superiority of the feminine in the mammalian world. Even as a child, I was inspired by the mating habits of arachnida – my mother was something of an expert in the field before so unfortunately marrying my father, you understand.'

Eva nodded. Fortunately for her she had missed the reference to spiders but she was too fascinated not to understand that whatever Dr Kores was saying was somehow important. She had the future of the quads in mind.

'But,' continued the doctor, 'my own work has been concentrated upon the higher forms of life and, in particular, the infinitely superior talents of the feminine in the sphere of survival. At every level of development, the role of the male is subordinate and the female demonstrates an adaptability which preserves the species. Only in the human world, and then solely in the social context rather than the purely biological, has this process been reversed. This reversal has been achieved by the competitive and militaristic nature of society in which the brute force of the masculine has found justification for the suppression of the feminine. Would you agree?'

'Yes, I suppose so,' said Eva, who had found the argument difficult to follow but could see that it made some sort of sense.

'Good,' said Dr Kores. 'And now we have arrived at a world crisis in which the extermination of life on earth has been made probable by the masculine distortion of scientific development for military purposes. Only we women can save the future.' She paused and let Eva savour the prospect. 'Fortunately, science has also put into our hands the means of so doing. The purely physical strength of the male has lost its advantage in the automated society of the present. Man is redundant and with the age of the computer, it is women who will have power. You have, of course, read of the work done at St Andrew's. It is proven that women have the larger corpus collossum than men.'

'Corpus collossum?' said Eva.

'One hundred million brain cells, neural fibre connecting the hemispheres of the brain and essential in the transfer of information. In working with the computer, this interchange has the highest significance. It could well be to the electronic age what the muscle was to the age of the physical...'

94

For another twenty minutes, Dr Kores talked on, swinging between an almost demented fervour for the feminine, rational argument and the statement of fact. To Eva, ever prone to accept enthusiasm uncritically, the doctor seemed to embody all that was most admirable about the intellectual world to which she had never belonged. It was only when the doctor seemed to sag in her chair that Eva remembered the reason she had come. 'About Henry...' she said hesitantly.

For a moment, Dr Kores continued to focus on a future in which there were probably no men, before dragging herself back to the present. 'Oh yes, your husband,' she said almost absently. 'You wish for something to stimulate him sexually, yes?'

'If it's possible,' said Eva. 'He's never been...'

But Dr Kores interrupted her with a harsh laugh.

'Ms Wilt,' she said, 'have you considered the possibility that your husband's lack of sexual activity may be only apparent?'

'I don't quite understand.'

'Another woman perhaps?'

'Oh, no,' said Eva. 'Henry isn't like that. He really isn't.'

'Or latent homosexuality?'

'He wouldn't have married me if he'd been like that, would he?' said Eva, now genuinely shocked.

Dr Kores looked at her critically. It was at moments like this that her faith in the innate superiority of the feminine was put to the test. 'It has been known,' she said through clenched teeth and was about to enter into a discussion of the family life of Oscar Wilde when the bell rang in the hall.

'Excuse me a moment,' she said and hurried out. When she returned it was through another door. 'My dispensary,' she explained. 'I have there a tincture which may prove beneficial. The dose is, however, critical. Like many medications, it contains elements that taken in excess will produce definite contra-indication. I must warn you not to exceed the stated dose by as much as five millilitres. I have supplied a syringe for the utmost accuracy in measurement. Within those limits, the tincture will produce the desired result. Beyond them, I cannot be held responsible. You will naturally treat the matter with the utmost confidentiality. As a scientist, I cannot be held responsible for the misapplication of proven formulae.'

Eva put the plastic bottle in her bag and went down the hall. As she passed the rusty cultivator and the broken frames, her mind was in a maelstrom of contradictory impressions. There had been something weird about Dr Kores. It wasn't what she said that was wrong, Eva could see her words made good sense. It was rather in the way she said them and how she behaved. She'd have to discuss it with Mavis. All the same, as she stood at the bus stop she found herself repeating 'I am superior. I will succeed' almost involuntarily.

A hundred yards away, two of Inspector Hodge's plain-clothes men watched her and made notes of the time and place. The patternizing of the Wilts' lives had begun in earnest.

9

And it continued. For two days, teams of detectives kept watch on the Wilts and reported back to Inspector Hodge who found the signals unambiguous. Eva's visit to Dr Kores was particularly damning.

'Herb farm? She went to a herb farm in Silton?' said the Inspector incredulously. After forty-eight almost sleepless hours and as many cups of black coffee, he could have done with some alternative medicine himself. 'And she came out with a large plastic bottle?'

'Apparently,' said the detective. Trying to keep up with Eva had taken its toll. So had the quads. 'For all I know, she went in with one. All we saw was her taking the bottle out of her bag when she was waiting for the bus.'

Hodge ignored the logic. As far as he was concerned, suspects who visited herb farms, and had bottles in their bags afterwards, were definitely guilty.

But it was Mavis Mottram's arrival at 45 Oakhurst Avenue later that afternoon that interested him most. 'Subject collects children from school at 3.30,' he read from the written report 'gets home and a woman drives up in a mini.'

'Correct.'

'What's she look like?'

'Forty, if she's a day. Dark hair. Five foot four. Blue anorak and khaki trousers with leg-warmers. Goes in at 3.55, leaving at 4.20.'

'So she could have collected the bottle?'

'Could have, I suppose, but she hadn't got a bag and there was no sign of it.'

'Then what?'

'Nothing till the nextdoor neighbour comes home at 5.30. Look, it's all there in my report.'

'I know it is,' said Hodge, 'I'm just trying to get the picture. How did you know his name was Gamer?'

'Blimey, I'd have to be stone deaf not to, the way she gave it to him, not to mention his wife carrying on something chronic.'

'So what happened?'

'This bloke Gamer goes in the door of 43,' said the detective, 'and five minutes later he's out again like a scalded cat with his wife trying to stop him. Dashes round to the Wilts' and tries to go in the side gate round the back of the house. Grabs the latch on the gate and the next moment he's flat on his back in the flower bed, twitching like he's got St Vitus' dance and his missus is yelling like they've killed him.'

'So what you're saying is the back gate was electrified?' said Hodge.

'I'm not saying it. He did. As soon as he could speak, that is, and had stopped twitching. Mrs Wilt comes out and wants to know what he's doing in her wallflowers. By the time he's got to his feet, just, and is yelling that her fucking hellcats – his words, not mine – have tried to murder him by stealing some statuette he's got in his back garden, and they've put in theirs, and wiring up the back gate to the fucking mains. And Mrs Wilt tells him not to be so silly and kindly not to use filthy language in front of her daughters. After that, things got a bit confusing with him wanting his statue and her saying she hadn't got it, and wouldn't have it if he gave it to her because it's dirty.'

'Dirty?' muttered Hodge. 'What's dirty about it?'

'It's one of those ones of a small boy peeing. Got it on his pond. She practically called him a pervert. And all the time his wife is pleading with him to come on home and never mind the ruddy statue, they can always get another one when they've sold the house. That got to him. "Sell the house?" he yells, "Who to? Even a raving lunatic wouldn't buy a house next to the bloody Wilts." Probably right at that.'

'And what happened in the end?' asked Hodge, making a mental note that he'd have an ally in Mr Gamer.

'She insists he come through the house and see if his statue's there, because she's not going to have her girls called thieves.'

'And he went?' said Hodge incredulously.

'Hesitantly,' said the detective. 'Came out shaken and swearing he'd definitely seen it there and if she didn't believe those kids had tried to kill him, why were all the lights in the house on the blink. That had her, and he pointed out there was a piece of wire still tied to the bootscraper outside the back gate.'

'Interesting,' said Hodge. 'And was there?'

'Must have been, because she got all flustered then, especially when he said it was evidence to show the police.'

'Naturally, with that bottle of dope still in the house,' said Hodge. 'No wonder they'd fixed the back door.' A new theory had been formulated in his mind. 'I tell you we're on to something, this time.'

Even the Superintendent, who shared Flint's view that Inspector Hodge was a greater menace to the public than half the petty crooks he arrested and would gladly have put the sod on traffic duty, had to admit that for once the Inspector seemed to be on the right track. 'This fellow Wilt's got to be guilty of something,' he muttered as he studied the report of Wilt's extraordinary movements during his lunch break.

In fact, Wilt had been on the look-out for McCullum's associates and had almost immediately spotted the two detectives in an unmarked car when he'd walked out of the Tech to pick up the Escort at the back of The Glassblowers' Arms, and had promptly taken evasive action with an expertise he'd learnt from watching old thrillers on TV. As a result, he'd doubled back down side roads, had disappeared up alleyways, had bought a number of wholly unnecessary items in crowded shops and had even bolted in the front doors of Boots and out the back before heading for the pub.

'Returned to the Tech car park at 2.15,' said the Superintendent. 'Where'd he been?'

'I'm afraid we lost him,' said Hodge. 'The man's an expert. All we know is he came back driving fast and practically ran for the building.'

Nor had Wilt's behaviour on leaving the Tech that evening been calculated to inspire confidence in his innocence. Anyone who walked out of the front gate wearing dark glasses, a coat with the collar turned up and a wig (Wilt had borrowed one from the Drama Department) and spent half an hour sitting on a bench by the bowling green on Midway Park, scrutinizing the passing traffic before sneaking back to the Tech car park, had definitely put himself into the category of a prime suspect.

'Think he was waiting for someone?' the Superintendent asked.

'More likely trying to warn them off,' said Hodge. 'They've probably got a system of signalling. His accomplices drive past and see him sitting there and get the message.'

'I suppose so,' said the Superintendent, who couldn't think of anything else that made sense. 'So we can expect an early arrest. I'll tell the Chief Constable.'

'I wouldn't say that, sir,' said Hodge, 'just that we've got a definite lead. If I'm right, this is obviously a highly organized syndicate. I don't want to rush into an early arrest when this man could lead us to the main source.'

'There is that,' said the Superintendent gloomily. He had been hoping that Hodge's handling of the case would prove so inept that he could call in the Regional Crime Squad. Instead the confounded man seemed to be making a success of it. And after that he'd doubtless apply for promotion and get it. Hopefully somewhere else. If not, the Superintendent would apply for a transfer himself. And there was still a chance Hodge would foul things up.

At the Tech, Hodge had. His insistence on putting plain-clothes detectives in, masquerading as apprentices or even more unsatisfactorily as Trainee Teachers, was playing havoc with staff morale.

'I can't stand it,' Dr Cox, Head of Science, told the Principal. 'It's bad enough trying to teach some of the students we get, without having a man poking about who doesn't know the difference between a Bunsen burner and a flamethrower. He practically burnt down the lab. on the third floor. And as for being any sort of teacher...'

'He doesn't have to say anything. After all, they're only here to observe.'

'In theory,' said Dr Cox. 'In practice, he keeps taking my students into corners and asking them if they can get him some Embalming Fluid. Anyone would think I was running a funeral home.'

The Principal explained the term. 'God Almighty, no wonder the wretched fellow asked to stay behind last night to check the chemical inventory.'

It was the same in botany. 'How was I to know she was a policewoman?' Miss Ryfield complained. 'And anyway I had no idea students were growing marijuana as pot plants in the greenhouses. She seems to hold me responsible.' Only Dr Board viewed the situation at all philosophically. Thanks to the fact that none of the policemen spoke French, his department had been spared intrusion.

'After all, it is 1984,' he announced to an ad hoc committee in the staff room, 'and as far as I can tell, discipline has improved enormously.'

'Not in my department,' said Mr Spirey of Building. 'I've had five punch-ups in Plasterers and Bricklayers and Mr Gilders is in hospital with bicycle-chain wounds.'

'Bicycle-chain wounds?'

'Someone called the young thug from the police station a fucking pig and Mr Gilders tried to intervene.'

'And I suppose the apprentices were arrested for carrying offensive weapons?' said Dr Mayfield.

The Head of Building shook his head. 'No, it was the policeman who had the bicycle chain. Mind you, they made a right mess of him afterwards,' he added with some satisfaction.

But it was among Senior Secretaries that Hodge's investigations had been carried out most vigorously. 'If this goes on much longer, our exam results will be appalling,' said Miss Dill. 'You have no idea the effect of having girls taken out of class and interrogated is having on their typing performance. The impression seems to be that the College is a hotbed of vice.'

'Would that it were,' said Dr Board. 'But, as usual, the papers have got it all wrong. Still, page 3 is something.' And he produced a copy of the *Sun* and a photograph of Miss Lynchknowle in the nude, taken in Barbados the previous summer. The caption read DRUG HEIRESS DEAD AT TECH.

'Of course I've seen the papers and the publicity is disgraceful,' said the Principal to the members of the Education Committee. Originally called to discuss the impending visitation of HMIs, it was now more concerned with the new crisis. 'The point I am trying to make is that this is an isolated incident and . . .'

'It isn't,' said Councillor Blighte-Smythe. 'I have here a list of catastrophes which have bedevilled the College since your appointment. First there was that awful business with the Liberal Studies lecturer who ...'

Mrs Chatterway, whose views were indefatigably progressive, intervened. 'I hardly think there's anything to be gained by dwelling on the past,' she said.

'Why not?' demanded Mr Squidley. 'It's time someone was held accountable for what goes on there. As tax- and rate-payers, we have a right to a decent practical education for our children and ...'

'How many children do you have at the Tech?' snapped Mrs Chatterway.

Mr Squidley looked at her in disgust. 'None, thank God,' he said. 'I wouldn't let one of my kids anywhere near the place.'

'If we could just keep to the point,' said the Chief Education Officer.

'I am,' said Mr Squidley, 'very much to the point, and the point is that as an employer, I'm not paying good money to have apprentices turned into junkies by a lot of fifth-rate academic drop-outs.'

'I resent that,' said the Principal. 'In the first place, Miss Lynchknowle wasn't an apprentice, and in the second we have some extremely dedicated –'

'Dangerous nutters,' said Councillor Blighte-Smythe.

'I was going to say "dedicated teachers".'

'Which doubtless accounts for the fact that the Minister of Education's secretary is pushing for the appointment of a board of enquiry to investigate the teaching of Marxism-Leninism in the Liberal Studies Department. If that isn't a clear indication something's wrong, I don't know what is.'

'I object. I object most strongly,' said Mrs Chatterway. 'The real cause of the problem lies in spending cuts. If we are to give our young people a proper sense of social responsibility and care and concern –'

'Oh God, not that again,' muttered Mr Squidley. 'If half the louts I have to employ could even read and bloody write ...'

The Principal glanced significantly at the Chief Education

Officer and felt more comfortable. The Education Committee would come to no sensible conclusions. It never did.

At 45 Oakhurst Avenue, Wilt glanced nervously out of the window. Ever since his lunch break and the discovery that he was being followed, he'd been on edge. In fact, he had driven home with his eyes so firmly fixed on the rear-view mirror that he had failed to notice the traffic lights on Nott Road and had banged into the back of the police car which had taken the precaution of tailing him from the front. The resulting exchange with the two plain-clothes men who were fortunately unarmed had done a lot to confirm his view that his life was in danger.

And Eva had hardly been sympathetic. 'You never do look where you're going,' she said, when he explained why the car had a crumpled bumper and radiator. 'You're just hopeless.'

'You'd feel fairly hopeless if you'd had the sort of day I've had,' said Wilt and helped himself to a bottle of home-brew. He took a swig of the stuff and looked at his glass dubiously.

'Must have left the bloody sugar out, or something,' he muttered, but Eva quickly switched the conversation to the incident with Mr Gamer. Wilt listened half-heartedly. His beer didn't usually taste like that and anyway it wasn't always quite so flat.

'As if girls their age could lift a horrid statue like that over the fence,' said Eva, concluding a singularly biased account of the incident.

Wilt dragged his attention away from his beer. 'Oh, I don't know. That probably explains what they were doing with Mr Boykins' block and tackle the other day. I wondered why they'd become so interested in physics.'

'But to say they'd tried to electrocute him,' said Eva indignantly.

'You tell me why the whole damned house was out,' said Wilt. 'The main fuse was blown, that's why. Don't tell me a mouse got into the toaster again either, because I checked. Anyway, that mouse didn't blow all the fuses and if I hadn't objected to having putrefying mouse savoury for breakfast instead of toast and marmalade, you'd never have noticed.'

'That was quite different,' said Eva. 'The poor thing got in there looking for crumbs. That's why it died.'

'And Mr Gamer damn near died because he was looking for his ruddy garden ornament,' said Wilt. 'And I can tell you who gave your brood that idea, the blooming mouse, that's who. One of these days they'll get the hang of the electric chair and I'll come home and find the Radleys' boy with a saucepan on his head and a damned great cable running to the cooker plug, as dead as a dodo.'

'They'd never do anything like that,' said Eva. 'They know better. You always look on the worst side of things.'

'Reality,' said Wilt, 'that's what I look at and what I see is four lethal girls who make Myra Hindley seem like a suitable candidate for a kindergarten teacher.'

'You're just being horrid,' said Eva.

'So's this bloody beer,' said Wilt as he opened another bottle. He took a mouthful and swore, but his words were drowned by the Magimix which Eva had switched on, in part to make an apple and carrot slaw because it was so good for the quads, but also to express her irritation. Henry could never admit the girls were bright and intelligent and good. They were always bad to him.

So was the beer. Eva's addition of five millilitres of Dr Kores' sexual stimulant to each bottle of Wilt's Best Bitter had given the stuff a new edge to it and, besides, it was flat. 'Must have left the screw top loose on this batch,' Wilt muttered as the Magimix came to a halt.

'What did you say?' Eva asked unpleasantly. She always suspected Wilt of using the cover of the Magimix, or the coffee-grinder to express his true thoughts.

'Nothing at all,' said Wilt, preferring to keep off the topic of beer. Eva was always going on about what it did to his liver and for once he believed her. On the other hand, if McCullum's thugs were going to duff him up, he intended to be drunk when they started, even if the muck did taste peculiar. It was better than nothing.

On the other side of Ipford, Inspector Flint sat in front of the telly and gazed abstractedly at a film on the life-cycle of the giant turtle. He didn't give a damn about turtles or their sex life. About the only thing he found in their favour was that they had the sense not to worry about their offspring and left the little buggers to hatch out on a distant beach or, better still, to get eaten by predators. Anyway, the sods lived two hundred years and presumably didn't have high blood pressure.

Instead, his thoughts reverted to Hodge and the Lynchknowle girl. Having pointed the Head of the Drug Squad towards the morass of inconsequentiality that was Wilt's particular forte, it had begun to dawn on him that he might gain some kudos by solving the case himself. For one thing, Wilt wasn't into drugs. Flint was certain of that. He knew Wilt was up to something – stood to reason – but his copper's instinct told him that drugs didn't fit.

So someone else had supplied the girl with the muck that had killed her. With all the slow persistence of a giant turtle swimming in the depths of the Pacific, Flint went over the facts. The girl dead on heroin and PCP: a definite fact. Wilt teaching that bastard McCullum (also dead from drugs): another fact. Wilt making a phone call to the prison: not a fact, merely a probability. An interesting probability for all that, and if you subtracted Wilt from the case there was absolutely nothing to go on. Flint picked up the paper and looked at the dead girl's photo. Taken in Barbados. Smart set and half of them on drugs. If she'd got the stuff in that circle Hodge hadn't got a hope in hell. They kept their secrets. Anyway, it might be worth checking up on his findings so far. Flint switched off the TV and went into the hall. 'I'm just going out to stretch my legs,' he called out to his wife and was answered by a grim silence. Mrs Flint didn't give a damn what he did with his legs.

Twenty minutes later, he was in his office with the report on the interview with Lord and Lady Lynchknowle in front of him. Naturally, it had never dawned on them that Linda was on drugs. Flint recognized the symptoms and the desire to clear themselves of all blame. 'About as much parental care as those bloody turtles,' he muttered and turned to the interview with the girl who'd shared a flat with Miss Lynchknowle.

This time there was something more positive. No, Penny hadn't been to London for ages. Never went anywhere, in fact, not even home at weekends. Discos occasionally, but generally a loner and had given up her boyfriend at the university before Christmas etcetera. No recent visitors either. Occasionally, she'd go out of an evening to a coffee bar or just wander along by the river. She'd seen her down there twice on her way back from the cinema. Whereabouts exactly? Near the marina. Flint made a note of that, and also of the fact that the Sergeant who'd visited her had asked the right questions. Flint noted the names of some of the coffee bars. There was no point in visiting them, they'd be covered by Hodge and, besides, Flint had no intention of being seen to be interested in the case. Above all, though, he knew he was acting on intuition, the 'smell' of the case which came from his long experience and his knowledge that whatever else Wilt was – and the Inspector had his own views on the matter – he wasn't pushing drugs. All the same, it would be interesting to know if he had made that phone call to the prison on the night McCullum took an overdose. There was something strangely coincidental about that incident, too. It was easy enough to hear the story from Mr Blaggs. Flint had known the Chief Warder for years and had frequently had the pleasure of consigning prisoners to his dubious care.

And so presently he was standing in the pub near the prison discussing Wilt with the Chief Warder with a frankness Wilt would have found only partly reassuring. 'If you want my opinion,' said Mr Blaggs, 'educating villains is anti-social. Only gives them more brains than they need. Makes your job more difficult when they come out, doesn't it?'

Flint had to agree that it didn't make it any easier. 'But you don't reckon Wilt had anything to do with Mac's having a cache of junk in his cell?' he asked.

'Wilt? Never. A bloody do-gooder, that's what he is. Mind you, I'm not saying they're not daft enough, because I know for a fact they are. What I'm saying is, a nick ought to be a prison, not a fucking finishing-school for turning half-witted petty thieves into first-rate bank robbers with degrees in law.'

'That's not what Mac was studying for, is it?' asked Flint.

Mr Blaggs laughed. 'Didn't need to,' he said. 'He had enough cash on the outside, he had a fistful of legal beavers on his payroll.'

'So how come Wilt's supposed to have made this phone call?' asked Flint.

'Just what Bill Coven thought, he took the call,' said Blaggs, and looked significantly at his glass. Flint ordered two more pints. 'He just thought he recognized Wilt's voice,' Blaggs continued, satisfied that he was getting his money's worth for information. 'Could have been anyone.'

Flint paid for the beer and tried to think what to ask next. 'And you've got no idea how Mac got his dope then?' he asked finally.

'Know exactly,' said Blaggs proudly. 'Another bloody do-gooder only this time a fucking prison visitor. If you ask me, they should ban all vi –'

'A prison visitor?' interrupted Flint, before the Chief Warder could express his views on a proper prison regime, which involved perpetual solitary confinement for all convicts and mandatory hanging for murderers, rapists and anyone insulting a prison officer. 'You mean a visitor to the prison?'

'I don't. I mean an authorized prison visitor, a bloody licensed busybody. They come in and treat us officers like we've committed the ruddy crimes and the villains are all bloody orphans who didn't get enough teat when they were toddlers. Right, well, this bitch of a PV, name of Jardin, was the one McCullum got to bring his stuff in.'

'Christ,' said Flint. 'What did she do that for?'

'Scared,' said Blaggs. 'Some of Mac's nastier mates on the outside paid her a visit with razors and a bottle of nitric acid and threatened to leave her looking like a cross between a dog's dinner and a leper with acne unless ... You get the message?'

'Yes,' said Flint, who'd begun to sympathize with the prison visitor, though for the life of him he couldn't visualize what a leper with acne looked like. 'And you mean she walked in and announced the fact?'

'Oh dear me, no,' said Blaggs. 'Starts off we've done for Mr – I ask you, *Mister*? – fucking McCullum ourselves. Practically said I'd hanged the sod myself, not that I'd have minded. So we took her down the morgue – of course it just happened the prison quack was doing an autopsy at the time and didn't much like the look of things by the sound of it, using a saw he was, too – and he wasn't having any crap about anyone doing anything to the bugger. Right, well when she'd come to, like, and he's saying the swine died of drug overdose and anyone who said different'd end up in court for slander, she cracked. Tears all over the place and practically down on her knees in front of the Governor. And it all comes out how she's been running heroin into the prison for months. Ever so bleeding sorry and all.'

'I should bloody well think so,' said Flint. 'When's she going to be charged?'

Mr Blaggs drank his beer mournfully. 'Never,' he grunted.

'Never? But smuggling anything, let alone drugs, into a prison is an indictable offence.'

'Don't tell me,' said Blaggs. 'On the other hand, the Governor don't want no scandal, can't afford one with his job up for grabs and anyway, she'd done a social service in a way by shoving the bugger where he belongs.'

'There is that,' said Flint. 'Does Hodge know this?'

The Chief Warder shook his head. 'Like I said, the Governor don't want no publicity. Anyway, she claimed she thought the stuff was talcum powder. Like hell, but you know what a Rumpole would do with a defence like that. Prison authorities entirely to blame, and so on. Negligence, the lot.'

'Did she say where she got the heroin?' asked Flint.

'Picked it up back of a telephone box on the London Road at night. Never saw the blokes who delivered it.'

'And it won't have been any of the lot who'd threatened her either.'

By the time the Inspector left the pub, he was a happy man. Hodge was way off line, and Flint had a conscience-stricken prison visitor to question. He wasn't even worried about the effect of four pints of the best bitter being flushed through his system by those bloody piss-pills. He'd already charted his route home by way of three relatively clean public lavatories.

10

But if Flint's mood had changed for the better, Inspector Hodge's hadn't. His interpretation of Wilt's behaviour had been coloured by the accident at the end of Nott Road. 'The bastard's got to know we're onto him, ramming a police car like that,' he told Sergeant Runk, 'so what's he do?'

'Buggered if I know,' said the Sergeant, who preferred early nights and couldn't think at all clearly at one in the morning.

'He goes for an early arrest, knowing we've got no hard evidence and will have to let him go.'

'What's he want us to do that for?'

'Because if we pull him in again he can start squealing about harassment and civil bloody liberties,' said Hodge.

'Seems an odd way of going about things,' said Runk.

'And what about sending your wife out to a herb farm to pick up a load of drugs on the very day after a girl dies of the filth? Isn't that a bit odd too?' Hodge demanded.

'Definitely,' said Runk. 'In fact, I can't think of anything odder. Any normal criminal would lie bloody low.'

Inspector Hodge smiled unpleasantly. 'Exactly. But we're not dealing with any ordinary criminal. That's the point I'm trying to make. We've got one of the cleverest monkeys I've ever had to catch on our hands.'

Sergeant Runk couldn't see it. 'Not if he sends his missus out to get a bottle of the stuff when we're watching her, he's not clever. Downright stupid.'

Hodge shook his head sadly. It was always difficult to get the Sergeant to understand the complexities of the criminal mind. 'Suppose there was nothing remotely like drugs in that bottle she was seen carrying?' he asked.

Sergeant Runk dragged his thoughts back from beds and tried to concentrate. 'Seems a bit of a wasted journey,' was all he could find to say.

'It's also intended to lead us up the garden path,' said Hodge.

'And that's his tactics. You've only to look at Wilt's record to see that. Take that doll caper for instance. He had old Flint by the short and curlies there, and why? Because the stupid fool pulled him in for questioning when all the evidence he had to go on was a blown-up doll of Mrs Wilt down a piling-hole with twenty tons of concrete on top of her. And where was the real Mrs Wilt all that week? Out on a boat with a couple of hippie Yanks who were into drugs up to their eyeballs and Flint lets them flee the country without grilling them about what they'd really been doing down the coast. Sticks out a mile they were smuggling and Wilt had set himself up for a decoy and kept Flint busy digging up a plastic doll. That's how cunning Wilt is.'

'I suppose when you put it like that it makes sense,' said Runk. 'And you reckon he's using the same tactics now.'

'Leopards,' said Hodge.

'Leopards?'

'Don't change their bleeding spots.'

'Oh, them,' said the Sergeant, who could have done without ellipses at that time of night.

'Only this time he's not dealing with some old-fashioned dead-beat copper like Flint,' said Hodge, now thoroughly convinced by the persuasiveness of his argument. 'He's dealing with me.'

'Makes a change. And talking about changes, I'd like to go ...'

'To 45 Oakhurst Avenue,' said Hodge decisively, 'that's where you're going. I want Mr Smart-Arse Wilt's car wired for sound and we're calling off the physical observation. This time it's going to be electronic all the way.'

'Not if I have anything to do with it,' said Runk defiantly, 'I've enough sense to know better than start tinkering with a sod like Wilt's car. Besides, I've got a wife and three kids to –'

'What the hell's your family got to do with it?' said Hodge. 'All I'm saying is, we'll go round there while they're asleep –'

'Asleep? A bloke who electrifies his back gate, you think he takes chances with his bloody car? You can do what you like, but I'm buggered if I'm going to meet my Maker charred to a fucking cinder by a maniac who's linked his car to the national grid. Not for you or anyone else.'

But Hodge was not to be stopped. 'We can check it's safe,' he insisted.

'How?' asked Runk, who was wide awake now. 'Let a police dog pee against the thing and see if he gets 32,000 volts up his prick? You've got to be joking.'

'I'm not,' said Hodge. 'I'm telling. Go and get the equipment.' Half an hour later, a desperately nervous Sergeant wearing gum boots and electrically safe rubber gloves eased the door of Wilt's car open. He'd already been round it four times to check there were no wires running from the house and had earthed it with a copper rod. Even so, he was taking no chances and was a trifle surprised that the thing didn't explode.

'All right, now where do you want the tape recorder?' he asked when the Inspector finally joined him.

'Somewhere where we can get at the tape easily,' Hodge whispered.

Runk groped under the dash and tried to find a space. 'Too bloody obvious,' said Hodge. 'Stick it under his seat.'

'Anything you say,' said Runk and stuffed the recorder into the springs. The sooner he was out of the damned car, the better. 'And what about the transmitter?'

'One in the boot and the other...'

'Other?' said Runk. 'You're going to get him picked up by the TV licence-detector vans at this rate. One of these sets has a radius of five miles.'

'I'm not taking chances,' said Hodge. 'If he finds one, he won't look for the other.'

'Not unless he has his car serviced.'

'Put it where no one looks.'

In the end, and then only after a lot of disagreement, the Sergeant attached one radio magnetically in a corner of the boot and was lying under the car searching for a hiding-place for the second when the lights came on in the Wilts' bedroom. 'I told you the swine wouldn't take any chances,' he whispered frantically as the Inspector fought his way in beside him. 'Now we're for it.'

Hodge said nothing. With his face pressed against an oily patch of tarmac and something that smelt disgustingly of cats, he was incapable of speech.

*

111

So was Wilt. The effect of Dr Kores' sexual stimulant added to his homebrew – Wilt had surreptitiously finished six bottles in an effort to find one that didn't taste peculiar – had been to leave him mentally befuddled and with the distinct impression that something like a battalion of army ants had taken possession of his penis and were busily digging in. Either that, or one of the quads had dementedly shoved the electric toothbrush up it while he was asleep. It didn't seem likely. But then again the sensation he was experiencing didn't seem in the least likely either. As he switched on the bedside lamp and hurled the sheet back to see what on earth was wrong, he glimpsed an expanse of red panties beside him. Eva in red panties? Or was she on fire too?

Wilt stumbled out of bed and fought a losing battle with his pyjama cord before dragging the damned things down without bothering to undo them and pointed the Anglepoise at the offending organ in an effort to identify the cause of his agony. The beastly creature (Wilt had always granted his penis a certain degree of autonomy or, more accurately, had never wholly associated himself with its activities) looked normal enough but it certainly didn't feel normal, not by a long chalk. Perhaps if he put some cold cream on it...

He hobbled across to Eva's dressing-table and searched among the jars. Where the hell did she keep the cold cream? In the end, he chose one that called itself a moisturizer. That'd do. It didn't. By the time he'd smeared half the jar on himself and a good deal on the pillow, the burning sensation seemed to have got worse. And whatever was going on was taking place *inside*. The army ants weren't digging in, the sods were digging out. For one insane moment he considered using an aerosol of Flykil to flush them out, but decided against it. God alone knew what a load of pressurized insecticide would do to his bladder and anyway the bloody thing was full enough already. Perhaps if he had a pee ... Still clutching the moisturizer, he hobbled through to the bathroom. 'Must have been a fucking lunatic who first called it relieving oneself,' he thought when he'd finished. About the only relief he'd found was that he hadn't peed blood and there didn't appear to be any ants in the pan afterwards. And peeing hadn't helped. If anything, it had made things even worse. 'The bloody thing'll ignite in a minute,' Wilt muttered, and was considering using the shower hose as a fire extinguisher when a better idea occurred to him. There was no point in smearing moisturizer on the outside. The stuff was needed internally. But how the hell to get it there? A tube of toothpaste caught his eye. That was what he needed. Oh no, it wasn't. Not with toothpaste. With moisturizer. Why didn't they pack the muck in tubes?

Wilt opened the medicine cupboard and groped among the old razors, the bottles of aspirin and cough mixture for a tube of something vaguely suitable for squeezing up his penis but apart from Eva's hair remover ... 'Sod that for a lark,' said Wilt, who had once accidentally brushed his teeth with the stuff, 'I'm not shoving that defoliant up any place.' It would have to be the moisturizing cream or nothing. And it wasn't going to be nothing. With a fresh and frenzied sense of desperation, he lurched from the bathroom clutching the jar and stumbled downstairs to the kitchen and was presently scrabbling in the drawer by the sink. A moment later he had found what he was looking for.

Upstairs, Eva turned over. For some time she had been vaguely aware that her back was cold but too vaguely to do anything about it. Now she was also aware that the light was on and that the bed beside her was empty and the bedclothes had been flung back. Which explained why she'd been freezing. Henry had evidently gone to the lavatory. Eva pulled the blankets back and lay awake waiting for him to return. Perhaps he'd be in the mood to make love. After all, he'd had two bottles of his beer and Dr Kores' aphrodisiac and she'd put on her red panties and it was much nicer to make love in the middle of the night when the quads were fast asleep than on Sunday mornings when they weren't, and she had to get up and shut the door in case they came in. Even that wasn't guaranteed to work. Eva would always remember one awful occasion when Henry had almost made it and she had suddenly smelt smoke and there'd been a series of screams from the quads. 'Fire! Fire!' they'd yelled, and she and Henry had hurled themselves from the bed and onto the landing in the altogether only to find the quads there with her jam-making pan filled with burning newspaper. It had been one of those rare occasions when she'd had to agree with Henry about the need for a thorough thrashing. Not that the quads had had one. They'd been down the stairs and out of the front door before Wilt could catch them and he'd been unable to pursue them down the street without a stitch of clothing on. No, it was much nicer at night and she was just wondering if she ought to take her panties off now and not wait, when a crash from downstairs put the thought out of her mind.

Eva climbed out of bed and putting a dressing-gown on, went down to investigate. The next moment all thoughts of making love had gone. Wilt was standing in the middle of the kitchen with her cake-icing syringe in one hand and his penis in the other. In fact, the two seemed to be joined together.

Eva groped for words. 'And what do you think you're doing?' she demanded when she could speak.

Wilt turned a crimson face towards her. 'Doing?' he asked, conscious that the situation was one that was open to any number of interpretations and none of them nice.

'That's what I said, doing,' said Eva.

Wilt looked down at the syringe. 'As a matter of fact...' he began, but Eva was ahead of him.

'That's my icing syringe.'

'I know it is. And this is my John Thomas,' said Wilt. Eva regarded the two objects with equal disgust. She would never be able to ice a cake with the syringe again and how she could ever have found anything faintly attractive about Wilt's John Thomas was beyond her. 'And for your information,' he continued, 'that is your moisturizing cream on the floor.'

Eva stared down at the jar. Even by the peculiar standards of 45 Oakhurst Avenue there was something disorientating about the conjunction – and conjunction was the right word – of Wilt's thingamajig and the icing syringe and the presence on the kitchen floor of a jar of her moisturizing cream. She sat down on a stool.

'And for your further information,' Wilt went on, but Eva stopped him. 'I don't want to hear,' she said.

Wilt glared at her lividly. 'And I don't want to feel,' he snarled. 'If you think I find any satisfaction in squirting whatever's in that emulsifier you use for your face up my whatsit at three o'clock in the morning, I can assure you I don't.'

114

'I don't see why you're doing it then,' said Eva, beginning to have an awful feeling herself.

'Because, if I didn't know better, I'd think some bloody sadist had larded my waterworks with pepper, that's why.'

'With pepper?'

'Or ground glass and curry powder,' said Wilt. 'Add a soupçon of mustard gas and you'll have the general picture. Or sensation. Something ghastly anyway. And now if you don't mind...'

But before he could get to work with the icing syringe again Eva had stopped him. 'There must be an antidote,' she said. 'I'll phone Dr Kores.'

Wilt's eyes bulged in his head. 'You'll do what?' he demanded.

'I said I'll –'

'I heard you,' shouted Wilt. 'You said you'd ring that bloody herbal homothrope Dr Kores and I want to know why.'

Eva looked desperately round the kitchen but there was no comfort now to be found in the Magimix or the le Creuset saucepans hanging by the stove and certainly none in the herb chart on the wall. That beastly woman had poisoned Henry and it was all her own fault for having listened to Mavis. But Wilt was staring at her dangerously and she had to do something immediately. 'I just think you ought to see a doctor,' she said. 'I mean, it could be serious.'

'Could be?' yelled Wilt, now thoroughly alarmed. 'It fucking well is and you still haven't told me –'

'Well, if you must know,' interrupted Eva, fighting back, 'you shouldn't have had so much beer.'

'Beer? My God, you bitch, I knew there was something wrong with the muck,' shouted Wilt and hurled himself at her across the kitchen.

'I only meant –' Eva began, and then dodged round the pine table to avoid the syringe. She was saved by the quads.

'What's Daddy doing with cream all over his genitals?' asked Emmeline. Wilt stopped in his tracks and stared at the four faces in the doorway. As usual, the quads were employing tactics that always nonplussed him. To combine the whimsy of 'Daddy', particularly with the inflection Emmeline gave the word, with the anatomically exact was calculated to dis-

115

concert him. And why not ask him instead of referring to him so objectively? For a moment he hesitated and Eva seized her opportunity.

'That's nothing to do with you,' she said and ostentatiously shielded them from the sight. 'It's just that your father isn't very well and –'

'That's right,' shouted Wilt, who could see what was coming, 'slap all the blame on me.'

'I'm not blaming you,' said Eva over her shoulder. 'It's –'

'That you lace my beer with some infernal irritant and bloody well poison me, and then you have the gall to tell them I'm not very well. I'll say I'm not well. I'm –'

A hammering sound from the Gamers' wall diverted his attention. As Wilt hurled the syringe at the Laughing Cavalier his mother-in-law had given them when she'd sold her house and which Eva claimed reminded her of her happy childhood there, Eva hustled the quads upstairs. When she came down again, Wilt had resorted to ice-cubes.

'I do think you ought to see a doctor,' she said.

'I should have seen one before I married you,' said Wilt. 'I suppose you realize I might be dead by now. What the hell did you put in my beer?'

Eva looked miserable. 'I only wanted to help our marriage,' she said, 'and Mavis Mottram said –'

'I'll strangle the bitch!'

'She said Dr Kores had helped Patrick and –'

'Helped Patrick?' said Wilt, momentarily distracted from his ice-packed penis. 'The last time I saw him he looked as if he could do with a bra. Said something about not having to shave so much either.'

'That's what I mean. Dr Kores gave Mavis something to cool his sexual ardour and I thought...' She paused. Wilt was looking at her dangerously again.

'Go on, though I'd question the use of "thought".'

'Well, that she might have something that would pep...'

'Pep?' said Wilt. 'Why not say ginger and have done with it? And why the hell should I need pepping up anyway? I'm a working man ... or was, with four damned daughters, not some demented sex pistol of seventeen.'

'I just thought ... I mean it occurred to me if she could do

116

so much for Patrick...' (here Wilt snorted) '... she might be able to help us to have a ... well, a more fulfilling sex life.'

'By poisoning me with Spanish Fly? Some fulfilment that is,' said Wilt. 'Well, let me tell you something now. For your information, I am not some fucking sex processor like that Magimix, and if you want the sort of sex life those idiotic women's magazines you read seem to suggest is your due, like fifteen times a week, you'd better find another husband because I'm buggered if I'm up to it. And the way I feel now, you'll be lucky if I'm ever up to it again.'

'Oh Henry!'

'Sod off,' said Wilt, and hobbled through to the downstairs loo with his mixing bowl of ice cubes. At least they seemed to help and the pain was easing off now.

As the sound of discord inside the house died down, Inspector Hodge and the Sergeant made their way back down Oakhurst Avenue to their car. They hadn't been able to hear what was being said, but the fact that there had been some sort of terrible row had heightened Hodge's opinion that the Wilts were no ordinary criminals. 'The pressure's beginning to tell,' he told Sergeant Runk. 'If we don't find him calling on his friends within a day or two, I'm not the man I think I am.'

'If I don't get some sleep, I won't be either,' said Runk, 'and I'm not surprised that bloke next door wants to sell his house. Must be hell living next to people like that.'

'Won't have to much longer,' said Hodge, but the mention of Mr Gamer had put a new idea in his mind. With a bit of collaboration from the Gamers, he'd be in a position to hear everything that went on in the Wilts' house. On the other hand, with their car transformed into a mobile radio station, he was expecting an early arrest.

11

All the following day, while Wilt lay in bed with a hot-water bottle he'd converted into an ice-pack by putting it into the freezer compartment of the fridge and Inspector Hodge monitored Eva's movements about Ipford, Flint followed his own line of investigation. He checked with Forensic and learnt that the high-grade heroin found in McCullum's cell corresponded in every way to that discovered in Miss Lynchknowle's flat and almost certainly came from the same source. He spent an hour with Mrs Jardin, the prison visitor, wondering at the remarkable capacity for self-deception that had already allowed her to put the blame on everyone else for McCullum's death. Society was to blame for creating the villain, the education authorities for his wholly inadequate schooling, commerce and industry for failing to provide him with a responsible job, the judge for sentencing him . . .

'He was a victim of circumstances,' said Mrs Jardin.

'You might say that about everybody,' said Flint, looking at a corner cupboard containing pieces of silver that suggested Mrs Jardin's circumstances allowed her the wherewithal to be the victim of her own sentimentality. 'For instance, the three men who threatened to carve you up with –'

'Don't,' said Mrs Jardin, shuddering at the memory.

'Well, they were victims too, weren't they? So's a rabid dog, but that's no great comfort when you're bitten by one, and I put drug pushers in that category.' Mrs Jardin had to agree. 'So you wouldn't recognize them again?' asked Flint, 'not if they were wearing stockings over their heads like you said.'

'They were. And gloves.'

'And they took you down the London Road and showed you where the drop was going to be made.'

'Behind the telephone box opposite the turn-off to Brindlay. I was to stop and go into the phone box and pretend to make a call, and then, if no one was about, I had to come out and pick up the package and go straight home. They said they'd be watching me.'

'And I don't suppose it ever occurred to you to go straight to the police and report the matter?' asked Flint.

'Naturally it did. That was my first thought, but they said they had more than one officer on their payroll.'

Flint sighed. It was an old tactic, and for all he knew the sods had been telling the truth. There were bent coppers, a lot more than when he'd joined the force, but then there hadn't been the big gangs and the money to bribe, and if bribery failed, to pay for a contract killing. The good old days when someone was always hanged if a policeman was murdered, even if it was the wrong man. Now, thanks to the do-gooders like Mrs Jardin, and Christie lying in the witness box and getting that mentally subnormal Evans topped for murders Christie himself had committed, the deterrent was no longer there. The world Flint had known had gone by the board, so he couldn't really blame her for giving in to threats. All the same, he was going to remain what he had always been, an honest and hardworking policeman.

'Even so we could have given you protection,' he said, 'and they wouldn't have been bothered with you once you'd stopped visiting McCullum.'

'I know that now,' said Mrs Jardin, 'but at the time I was too frightened to think clearly.'

Or at all, thought Flint, but he didn't say it. Instead, he concentrated on the method of delivery. No one dropped a consignment of heroin behind a telephone kiosk without ensuring it was going to be picked up. Then again, they didn't hang around after the drop. So there had to be some way of communicating. 'What would have happened if you'd been ill?' he asked. 'Just supposing you couldn't have collected the package, what then?'

Mrs Jardin looked at him with a mixture of contempt and bewilderment she evidently felt when faced with someone who concentrated so insistently on practical matters and neglected moral issues. Besides, he was a policeman and ill-educated. Policemen didn't find absolution as victims. 'I don't know,' she said.

But Flint was getting angry. 'Come off the high horse,' he said, 'you can squeal you were forced into being a runner, but we can still charge you with pushing drugs and into a prison at that. Who did you have to phone?'

Mrs Jardin crumbled. 'I don't know his name. I had to call a number and...'

'What number?'

'Just a number. I can't –'

'Get it,' said Flint. Mrs Jardin went out of the room and Flint sat looking at the titles in the bookshelves. They meant very little to him and told him only that she'd read or at least bought a great many books on sociology, economics, the Third World and penal reform. It didn't impress Flint. If the woman had really wanted to do something about the conditions of prisoners, she'd have got a job as a wardress and lived on low wages, instead of dabbling in prison visits and talking about the poor calibre of the staff who had to do society's dirty work. Stick up her taxes to build better prisons and she'd soon start squealing. Talk about hypocrisy.

Mrs Jardin came back with a piece of paper. 'That's the number,' she said, handing it to him. Flint looked at it. A London phone box.

'When did you have to call?'

'They said between 9.30 and 9.40 at night the day before I had to collect the packet.'

Flint changed direction. 'How many times did you collect?'

'Only three.'

He got to his feet. It was no use. They'd know Mac was dead, even if it hadn't been announced in the papers, so there was no point in supposing they'd make another drop, but at least they were operating out of London. Hodge was on the wrong track. On the other hand, Flint himself couldn't be said to be on the right one. The trail stopped at Mrs Jardin and a public telephone in London. If McCullum had still been alive...

Flint left the house and drove over to the prison. 'I'd like to take a look at Mac's list of visitors,' he told Chief Warder Blaggs, and spent half an hour writing names in his notebook, together with addresses.

'Someone in that little lot had to be running messages,' he

said when he finished. 'Not that I expect to get anywhere, but it's worth trying.'

Afterwards, back at the Station, he had checked them on the Central Records Computer and cross-referenced for drug dealing, but the one link he was looking for, some petty criminal living in Ipford or nearby, was missing. And he wasn't going to waste his time trying to tackle London. In fact, if he were truthful, he had to admit he was wasting his time even in Ipford except . . . except that something told him he wasn't. It nagged at his mind. Sitting in his office, he followed that instinct. The girl had been seen by her flat-mate down by the marina. Several times. But the marina was just another place like the telephone kiosk on the London Road. It had to be something more definite, something he could check out.

Flint picked up the phone and called the Drug Addiction Study Unit at the Ipford Hospital.

By lunchtime, Wilt was up and about. To be exact, he'd been up and about several times during the morning, in part to get another hot-water bottle from the freezer, but more often in a determined effort not to masturbate himself to death. It was all very well Eva supposing she'd benefit from the effects of whatever diabolical irritant she'd added to his homebrew, but to Wilt's way of thinking, a wife who'd damned near poisoned her husband didn't deserve what few sexual benefits he had to offer. Give her an inkling of satisfaction from this experiment and next time he'd land up in hospital with internal bleeding and a permanent erection. As it was, he had a hard time with his penis.

'I'll freeze the damn thing down,' had been Wilt's first thought and for a while it had worked, though painfully. But after a time he had drifted off to sleep and had woken an hour later with the awful impression that he'd taken it into his head to have an affair with a freshly caught Dover Sole. Wilt hurled himself off the thing and had then taken the bottle downstairs to put it back in the fridge before realizing that this wouldn't be particularly hygienic. He was in the process of washing it when the front doorbell rang. Wilt dropped the bottle on the draining-board, retrieved it from the sink when it slithered off and finally tried wedging it between the upturned teapot and a casserole dish in the drying rack, before going to answer the call.

It was not the postman as he expected, but Mavis Mottram. 'What are you doing at home?' she asked.

Wilt sheltered behind the door and pulled his dressing-gown tightly round him. 'Well, as a matter of fact ...' he began.

Mavis pushed past him and went through to the kitchen. 'I just came round to see if Eva could organize the food side of things.'

'What things?' asked Wilt, looking at her with loathing. It was thanks to this woman that Eva had consulted Dr Kores. Mavis ignored the question. In her dual rôle as militant feminist and secretary of Mothers Against The Bomb, she evidently considered Wilt to be part of the male sub-species. 'Is she going to be back soon?' she went on.

Wilt smiled unpleasantly and shut the kitchen door behind him. If Mavis Mottram was going to treat him like a moron, he felt inclined to behave like one. 'How do you know she's not here?' he asked, testing the blade of a rather blunt bread-knife against his thumb.

'The car's not outside and I thought ... well, you usually take it ...' She stopped.

Wilt put the breadknife on the magnetic holder next to the Sabatier ones. It looked out of place. 'Phallic,' he said. 'Interesting.'

'What is?'

'Lawrentian,' said Wilt, and retrieved the icing syringe from a plastic bucket where Eva had been soaking it in Dettol in an attempt to persuade herself she would be able to use the thing again.

'Lawrentian?' said Mavis, beginning to sound genuinely alarmed.

Wilt put the syringe on the counter and wiped his hands. Eva's washing-up gloves caught his eye. 'I agree,' he said and began putting the gloves on.

'What on earth are you talking about?' asked Mavis, suddenly remembering Wilt and the inflated doll. She moved round the kitchen table towards the door and then thought better of it. Wilt in a dressing-gown and no pyjama trousers, and now wearing a pair of rubber gloves and holding a cake-icing syringe, was an extremely disturbing sight. 'Anyway, if you'll ask her to call me, I'll explain about the food side of ...' Her voice trailed off.

Wilt was smiling again. He was also squirting a yellowish liquid into the air from the syringe. Images of some demented doctor in an early horror movie flickered in her mind. 'You were saying something about her not being here,' said Wilt and stepped back in front of the door. 'Do go on.'

'Go on about what?' said Mavis with a distinct quaver.

'About her not being here. I find your interest curious, don't you?'

'Curious?' mumbled Mavis, desperately trying to find some thread of sanity in his inconsequential remarks. 'What's curious about it? She's obviously out shopping and –'

'Obviously?' asked Wilt, and gazed vacantly past her out of the window and down the garden. 'I wouldn't have said anything was obvious.'

Mavis involuntarily followed his gaze and found the back garden almost as sinister as Wilt with washing-up gloves and that bloody syringe. With a fresh effort, she forced herself to turn back and speak normally. 'I'll be off now,' she said and moved forward.

Wilt's fixed smile crumbled. 'Oh, not so soon,' he said. 'Why not put the kettle on and have some coffee? After all, that's what you'd do if Eva was here. You'd sit down and have a nice talk. And you and Eva had so much in common.'

'Had?' said Mavis and wished to God she'd kept her mouth shut. Wilt's awful smile was back again. 'Well, if you'd like a cup yourself, I suppose I've got time.' She crossed to the electric kettle and took it to the sink. The hot-water bottle was lying on the bottom. Mavis lifted it out and experienced another ghastly frisson. The hot-water bottle wasn't simply not hot, it was icy cold. And behind her Wilt had begun to grunt alarmingly. For a moment Mavis hesitated before swinging round. This time there was no mistaking the threat she was facing. It was staring at her from between the folds of Wilt's dressing-gown. With a squeal, she hurled herself at the back door, dragged it open, shot out and with a clatter of dustbin lids, was through the gate and heading for the car.

Behind her Wilt dropped the syringe back into the bucket and tried to get his hands out of the washing-up gloves by pulling on the fingers. It wasn't the best method and it was some time before he'd rid himself of the wretched things and had grabbed the second bottle from the freezer. 'Bugger the woman,' he muttered as he clutched the bottle to his penis and tried to think of what to do next. If she went to the police ... No, she wasn't likely to do that but all the same, it would be as well to take precautions. Regardless of hygiene, he flung the bottle from the sink into the freezer and hobbled upstairs. 'At least we've seen the last of Mavis M,' he thought as he got back into bed. That was some consolation for the reputation he was already doubtless acquiring. As usual, he was entirely wrong.

Twenty minutes later, Eva, who had been intercepted by Mavis on her way home, drove up to the house.

'Henry,' she shouted as soon as she was inside the front door. 'You come straight down here and explain what you were doing with Mavis.'

'Sod off,' said Wilt.

'What did you say?'

'Nothing. I was just groaning.'

'No, you weren't. I distinctly heard you say something,' said Eva on her way upstairs.

Wilt got out of bed and girded his loins with the water bottle. 'Now you just listen to me,' he said before Eva could get a word in, 'I've had all I can stand from everybody, you, Mavis-moron-Mottram, that poisoner Kores, the quads and the bloody thugs who've been following me. In fact the whole fucking modern world with its emphasis on me being nice and docile and passive and everyone else doing their own thing and to hell with the consequences. (*A*) I am not a thing, and (*B*) I'm not going to be done any more. Not by you, or Mavis, or, for that matter, the damned quads. And I don't give a tuppenny stuff what received opinions you suck up like some dehydrated sponge from the hacks who write articles on progressive education and sex for geriatrics and health through fucking hemlock –'

'Hemlock's a poison. No one . . .' Eva began, trying to divert his fury.

'And so's the ideological codswallop you fill your head with,' shouted Wilt. 'Permissive cyanide, page three nudes for the so-called intelligentsia or video nasties for the unemployed, all fucking placebos for them that can't think or feel. And if you don't know what a placebo is, try looking it up in a dictionary.'

He paused for breath and Eva grabbed her opportunity. 'You know very well what I think about video nasties,' she said, 'I wouldn't dream of letting the girls see anything like that.'

'Right,' yelled Wilt, 'so how about letting me and Mr bleeding Gamer off the hook. Has it ever occurred to you that you've got genuine non-video actual nasties, pre-pubescent horrors, in those four daughters? Oh no, not them. They're special, they're unique, they're flipping geniuses. We mustn't do anything to retard their intellectual development, like teaching them some manners or how to behave in a civilized fashion. Oh no, we're your modern model parents holding the ring while those four ignoble little savages turn themselves into computer-addicted technocrats with about as much moral sense as Ilse Koch on a bad day.'

'Who's Ilse Koch?' asked Eva.

'Just a mass murderess in a concentration camp,' said Wilt, 'and don't get the idea I'm on a right-wing, flog 'em and hang 'em reactionary high because I'm not, and those idiots don't think either. I'm just mister stick-in-the-middle who doesn't know which way to jump. But my God I do think! Or try to. Now leave me in peace and discomfort and go and tell your mate Mavis that the next time she doesn't want to see an involuntary erection, not to advise you to go anywhere near Castrator Kores.'

Eva went downstairs feeling strangely invigorated. It was a long time since she'd heard Henry state his feelings so strongly and, while she didn't understand everything he'd said, and she certainly didn't think he'd been fair about the quads, it was somehow reassuring to have him assert his authority in the house. It made her feel better about having been to that awful Dr Kores with all her silly talk about . . . what was it? ... 'the sexual superiority of the female in the mammalian world'. Eva didn't want to be superior in everything and anyway, she wasn't just a mammal. She was a human being. That wasn't the same thing at all.

12

By the following evening, it would have been difficult to say what Inspector Hodge was. Since Wilt hadn't emerged from the house, the Inspector had spent the best part of two days tracing Eva's progress to and from the school and round Ipford in the bugged Escort.

'It's good practice,' he told Sergeant Runk, as they followed her in a van Hodge had converted to a listening-post.

'For what?' asked the Sergeant, pinning a mark on the town map to indicate that Eva now parked behind Sainsbury's. She'd already been to Tesco's and Fine Fare. 'So we learn where to get the best discount on washing powder?'

'For when he decides to move.'

'When,' said Runk. 'So far he hasn't been out of the house all day.'

'He's sent her out to check she hasn't got a tail on her,' said Hodge. 'In the meantime, he's lying low.'

'Which you said was just the thing he wasn't doing,' said Runk. 'I said he was and you said ...'

'I know what I said. But that was when he knew he was being followed. It's different now.'

'I'll say,' said Runk. 'So the sod sends us on a tour of shopping centres and we haven't got a clue what's going on.'

They had that night. Runk, who had insisted on having the afternoon off for some shut-eye if he was to work at night, retrieved the tape from under the seat and replaced it with a new one. It was one o'clock in the morning. Half an hour later, Hodge, whose childhood had been spent in a house where sex was never mentioned, was listening to the quads discussing Wilt's condition with a frankness that appalled him. If anything was needed to convince him that Mr and Mrs Wilt were died-in-the-wool criminals, it was Emmeline's repeated demand to know why Daddy had been up in the night putting cake icing on his penis. Eva's explanation didn't

127

help either. 'He wasn't feeling very well, dear. He'd had too much beer and he couldn't sleep, so he went down to the kitchen to see if he could ice cake and...'

'I wouldn't like the sort of cake he was icing,' interrupted Samantha. 'And anyway, it was face-cream.'

'I know, dear, but he was practising and he spilt it.'

'Up his cock?' demanded Penelope, which gave Eva the opportunity to tell her never to use that word. 'It's not nice,' she said, 'it's not nice to say things like that and you're not going to tell anyone at school.'

'It wasn't very nice of Daddy to use the icing syringe to pump face-cream up his penis,' said Emmeline.

By the time the discussion was over, and Eva had dropped the quads off at the school, Hodge was ashen. Sergeant Runk wasn't feeling very well either.

'I don't believe it, I don't believe a bloody word of it,' muttered the Inspector.

'I wish to God I didn't,' said Runk. 'I've heard some revolting things in my time but that lot takes the cake.'

'Don't mention that word,' Hodge said. 'I still don't believe it. No man in his right mind would do a thing like that. They're having us on.'

'Oh, I don't know. I knew a bloke once who used to butter his wick with strawberry jam and have his missus –'

'Shut up,' shouted Hodge, 'if there's one thing I can't stand it's filth and I've had my fill of that for one night.'

'So's Wilt, by the sound of it,' said Runk, 'walking about with his prick in a jug of ice cubes like that. Can't have been just face-cream or icing-sugar he had in that syringe.'

'Dear God,' said Hodge. 'You're not suggesting he was fixing himself with a cake-icing syringe, are you? He'd be bloody dead by now, and anyhow the fucking thing would leak.'

'Not if he mixed the junk with cold cream. That'd explain it, wouldn't it?'

'It might do,' Hodge admitted. 'I suppose if people can sniff the filthy muck, there's no knowing what they can do with it. Not that it helps us much what he does.'

'Of course it does,' said the Sergeant, who had suddenly seen a way of ending the tedium of sitting through the night

128

in the van. 'It means he's got the stuff in the house.'

'Or up his pipe,' said Hodge.

'Wherever. Anyway, there's bound to be enough around to haul him in and give him a good going over.'

But the Inspector had his sights set on more ambitious targets. 'A fat lot of good that's going to do us,' he said, 'even if he did crack, and if you'd read what he did to old Flint you'd know better –'

'But this'd be different,' Runk interrupted. 'First off, he'd be cold turkey. Don't have to question him. Leave him in a cell for three days without a fix and he'd be bleating like a fucking baa-lamb.'

'Yes, and I know who for,' said the Inspector. 'His ruddy mouthpiece.'

'Yes, but we'd have his missus too, remember. And anyway this time we'd have hard evidence and it would just be a matter of charging him. He wouldn't get bail on a heroin charge.'

'True,' said Hodge grudgingly, 'if we had hard evidence. "If."'

'Well, there's bound to be with him getting the stuff all over his pyjamas like those kids said. Forensic would have an easy time. Take that cake-icing syringe for a starter. And then there are towels and drying-up cloths. Blimey, the place must be alive with the stuff. Even the fleas on the cat must be addicts the way he's been splashing it round.'

'That's what worries me,' said Hodge. 'Whoever heard of a pusher splashing it round? No way. They're too bloody careful. Especially when the heat's on like it is now. You know what I think?' Sergeant Runk shook his head. In his opinion the Inspector was incapable of thought. 'I think the bastard's trying the old come-on. Wants us to arrest him. He's trying to trap us into it. That explains the whole thing.'

'Doesn't explain anything to me,' said Runk despairingly.

'Listen,' said Hodge, 'what we've heard on that tape just now is too bizarre to be credible, right? Right. You've never heard of a junkie fixing his cock and I haven't either. But apparently, this Wilt does. Not only that, but he makes a fucking mess, does it in the middle of the night and with a cake-icing syringe and makes sure his kids find him in the kitchen doing it. For why? Because he wants the little bitches to shoot their mouths off about it in public and for us to hear about it. That's why. Well, I'm not falling for it. I'm going to take my time and wait for Mr Clever Wilt to lead me to his source. I'm not interested in single pushers, this time I'm going to pull in the whole ruddy network.'

And having satisfied himself with this interpretation of Wilt's extraordinary behaviour, the Inspector sat on, savouring his eventual triumph. In his mind's eye, he could see Wilt in the dock with a dozen big-time criminals, none of whom the likes of Flint had ever suspected. They'd be moneyed men with large houses who played golf and belonged to the best clubs, and after sentencing them, the Judge would compliment Inspector Hodge on his brilliant handling of the case. No one would ever call him inefficient again. He'd be famous and his photograph would be in all the papers.

Wilt's thoughts followed rather similar lines, though with a different emphasis. The effects of Eva's enthusiasm for aphrodisiacs were still making themselves felt and, more disastrously, had given him what appeared to be a permanent erection. 'Of course I'm confined to the bloody house,' he said when Eva complained that she didn't want him wandering about in his dressing-gown on her weekly coffee morning. 'You don't expect me to go back to the Tech with the thing sticking out like a ramrod.'

'Well, I don't want you making an exhibition of yourself in front of Betty and the others like you did with Mavis.'

'Mavis got what she deserved,' said Wilt. 'I didn't ask the woman into the house, she just marched in, and anyway if she hadn't put you on to poisoner Kores I wouldn't be wandering around with a coat-hanger strapped to my waist, would I?'

'What's the coat-hanger for?'

'To keep the flipping dressing-gown off the inflamed thing,' said Wilt. 'If you knew what it felt like to have stuff like a heavy blanket rubbing against the end of a pressurized and highly sensitive –'

'I don't want to hear,' said Eva.

'And I don't want to feel,' Wilt retorted. 'Hence the coat-hanger. And what's more, you want to try bending your knees and leaning forward at the same time every time you have to pee. It's bloody agony. As it is I've banged my head on the wall twice and I haven't had a crap in two days. I can't even sit down to read. It's either flat on my back in bed with the wastepaper basket for protection or up and about with the coat-hanger. And up and about it is. At this rate, they'll have to build a special coffin with a periscope when I cough it.'

Eva looked at him doubtfully. 'Perhaps you ought to go and see a doctor if it's that serious.'

'How?' snapped Wilt. 'If you think I'm going to walk down the road looking like a pregnant sex-change artist, forget it. I'd be arrested before I was half-way there and the local rag would have a field day. TECH TEACHER ON PERMANENT HIGH. And you'd really love it if I got called Pumpkin Penis Percy. So you have your Tupperware Party and I'll stick around upstairs.'

Wilt went carefully up to the bedroom and took refuge under the wastepaper basket. Presently, he heard voices from below. Eva's Community Care Committee had begun to arrive. Wilt wondered how many of them had already heard Mavis' version of the episode in the kitchen and were secretly delighted that Eva was married to a homicidal flasher. Not that they would ever admit as much. No, it would be 'Did you hear about poor Eva's awful husband?' or 'I can't think how she can bring herself to stay in the same house with that frightful Henry,' but in fact the target for their malice would be Eva herself. Which was just as it should be, considering that she'd doctored his beer with whatever poison Dr Kores had given her. Wilt lay back and wondered about the doctor and presently fell into a daydream in which he sued her for some enormous sum on the grounds of ... What sort of grounds were there? Invasion of Penisy? Or Deprivation of Scrotal Rights? Or just plain Poisoning. That wouldn't work because Eva had administered the stuff and presumably if you took it in the correct doses it wouldn't have such awful effects. And, of course, the Kores bitch wasn't to know that Eva never did things by halves. In her book, if a little of something was good for you, twice as much was better. Even Charlie, the cat, knew that, and had developed an uncanny knack of disappearing for several days the moment Eva put down a saucer of cream laced with worm powder. But then Charlie was no fool and evidently still remembered the experience of having his innards scoured out by twice the recommended dosage. The poor brute had come limping back into the house after a week in the bushes at the bottom of the garden looking like a tapeworm with fur and had promptly been put on a high-pilchard diet to build him up.

Well, if a cat could learn from experience, there was no excuse for Wilt. On the other hand, Charlie didn't exactly have to live with Eva, but could shove off at the first sign of trouble. 'Lucky blighter,' Wilt muttered and wondered what would happen if he rang up one night and said he wasn't coming home for a week. He could just imagine the explosion on the other end of the line, and if he put the phone down without coming up with a really plausible explanation, he'd never hear the end of it when he did come home. And why? Because the truth was always too insane or incredible. Just about as incredible as the events of the week which had started with that idiot from the Ministry of Education and had gone on through Miss Hare's use of karate in the Ladies' lavatory to McCullum's threats and the men in the car who'd followed him. Add that little lot together with an overdose of Spanish Fly, and you had a truth no one would believe. Anyway, there was no point in lying there speculating about things he couldn't alter.

'Emulate the cat,' said Wilt to himself and went through to the bathroom to check in the mirror how his penis was getting on. It certainly felt better, and when he removed the wastepaper basket, he was delighted to find it had begun to droop. He had a shower and shaved and by the time Eva's little group had broken up, he was able to go downstairs wearing his trousers. 'How did the hen party go?' he asked.

Eva rose to the provocation. 'I see you're back to your normal sexist self. Anyway, it wasn't any sort of party. We're having that next Friday. Here.'

'Here?'

'That's right. It's going to be a fancy-dress party with prizes for the best costume and a raffle to raise money for the Harmony Community Play-Group.'

'Yes, and I'm sending a bill to all the people you're inviting to pay for the insurance in advance. Remember what happened to the Vurkells when Polly Merton sued them for falling downstairs blind drunk.'

'That was quite different,' said Eva. 'It was all Mary's fault for having a loose stair carpet. She never did look after the house properly. It was always a mess.'

'So was Polly Merton when she hit the hall floor. It was a wonder she wasn't killed,' said Wilt. 'Anyway, that's not the point. The Vurkells' house was wrecked and the insurance company wouldn't pay up because he'd been breaking the by-laws by running an illegal casino with that roulette wheel of his.'

'There you are,' said Eva. 'We're not breaking the law by holding a raffle for charity.'

'I'd check it out if I were you, and you can check me out too,' said Wilt. 'I've had enough trouble with my private parts these last two days without wearing that Francis Drake outfit you rigged me out in last Christmas.'

'You looked very nice in it. Even Mr Persner said you deserved a prize.'

'For wearing your grandmother's camiknickers stuffed with straw, I daresay I did, but I certainly didn't feel nice. In any case, I've got my prisoner to teach that night.'

'You could cancel that for once,' said Eva.

'What, just before the exams? Certainly not,' said Wilt. 'You invite a mob of costumed fools to invade the house for the good of charity without consulting me, you mustn't expect me to stop my charitable work.'

'In that case, you'll be going out tonight then?' said Eva. 'Today's Friday and you've got to keep up the good work, haven't you?'

'Good Lord,' said Wilt, who'd lost track of the days. It *was* Friday and he had forgotten to prepare anything for the lecture to his class at Baconheath. Spurred on by Eva's sarcasm and the knowledge that he'd end up the following Friday in straw-filled camiknickers or even as Puss in Boots in a black leotard which fitted far too tightly, Wilt spent the afternoon working over some old notes on British Culture and Institutions. They were entitled 'The Need For Deference, Paternalism and The Class Structure' and were designed to be provocative.

By six o'clock he had finished his supper, and half an hour later was driving out along the fen roads towards the airbase rather faster then usual. His penis was playing up again and it had only been by strapping it to his lower stomach with a long bandage and a cricket box that he'd been able to make himself comfortable and not provocatively indecent.

Behind him, the two monitoring vans followed his progress and Inspector Hodge was jubilant. 'I knew it. I knew he'd have to move,' he told Sergeant Runk as they listened to the signals coming from the Escort. 'Now we're getting somewhere.'

'If he's as smart as you say he is, it could be up the garden path,' said Runk.

But Hodge was consulting the map. The coast lay ahead. Apart from that, there were only a few villages, the bleak flatness of the fens and ... 'Any moment he'll switch west,' he predicted. His hopes had turned to certainty. Wilt was heading for the US Airbase at Baconheath and the American connection was complete.

In Ipford prison, Inspector Flint stared into the Bull's face. 'How many years have you still to do?' he asked. 'Twelve?'

'Not with remission,' said the Bull. 'Only eight. I've got good behaviour.'

'Had,' said Flint. 'You lost that when you knocked Mac off.'

'Knocked Mac off? I never did. That's a bloody lie. I never touched him. He –'

'That's not what the Bear says,' interrupted Flint, and opened a file. 'He says you'd been saving up those sleeping pills so you could murder Mac and take over from him. Want to read his statement? It's all down in black and white and nicely signed. Here, take a dekko.'

He pushed the paper across the table but the Bull was on his feet. 'You can't pull that fucking one on me,' he shouted and was promptly pushed back into his chair by the Chief Warder.

'Can,' said Flint, leaning forward and staring into the Bull's frightened eyes. 'You wanted to take over from McCullum, didn't you? Jealous of him, weren't you? Got greedy. Thought you'd grab a nice little operation run from inside and you'd come out in eight years with a pension as long as your arm all safely stashed away by your widow.'

'Widow?' The Bull's face was ashen now. 'What you mean, widow?'

Flint smiled. 'Just as I say. Widow. Because you aren't ever going to get out now. Eight years back to twelve and a life stretch for murdering Mac adds up to twenty-seven by my reckoning, and for all those twenty-seven years, you're going to be doing solitary for your own protection. I can't see you making it, can you?'

The Bull stared at him pathetically. 'You're setting me up.'

'I don't want to hear your defence,' said Flint, and got to his feet. 'Save the blarney for the court. Maybe you'll get some nice judge to believe you. Especially with your record. Oh, and I shouldn't count on the missus to help. She's been shacked up with Joe Slavey for six months, or didn't you know?'

He moved towards the door, but the Bull had broken. 'I didn't do it, I swear to God I didn't, Mr Flint. Mac was like a brother to me. I'd never...'

Flint put the boot in again. 'Plead insanity is my advice,' he said. 'You'll be better off in Broadmoor. Buggered if I'd want Brady or the Ripper as a neighbour for the rest of my natural.' For a moment he paused by the door. 'Let me know if he wants to make a statement,' he said to the Chief Warder. 'I mean, I suppose he could help...'

There was no need to go on. Even the Bull had got the message. 'What do you want to know?'

It was Flint's turn to think. Take the pressure off too quickly and all he'd get would be garbage. On the other hand, strike while the iron was hot. 'The lot,' he said. 'How the operations work. Who does what. What the links are. You name it, I want it. Every fucking thing!'

The Bull swallowed. 'I don't know everything,' he said, looking unhappily at the Chief Warder.

'Don't mind me,' said Mr Blaggs. 'I'm not here. Just part of the furniture.'

'Start with how Mac got himself junk,' said Flint. It was best to begin with something he already knew. The Bull told him and Flint wrote it all down with a growing sense of satisfaction. He hadn't known about Prison Officer Lane being bent.

'You'll get me slit for this,' said the Bull when he'd finished with Mrs Jardin, the Prison Visitor.

'I don't know why,' said Flint. 'Mr Blaggs here isn't going to say who told him and it doesn't necessarily have to come out at your trial.'

'Christ,' said the Bull. 'You're not still going on with that, are you?'

'You tell me,' said Flint, maintaining the pressure. By the time he left the prison three hours later, Inspector Flint was almost a happy man. True, the Bull hadn't told him everything, but then he hadn't expected him too. In all likelihood, the fool didn't know much more, but he'd given Flint enough names to be going on with. Best of all, he'd grassed too far to back out, even if the threat of a murder charge lost its effect. The Bull would indeed get himself sliced by some other prisoner if the news ever got out. And the Bear was going to be Flint's next target.

'Being a copper's a dirty business sometimes,' he thought as he drove back to the police station. But drugs and violence were dirtier still. Flint went up to his office and began to check out some names.

Ted Lingon's name rang a bell – two bells, when he put his lists together. And Lingon ran a garage. Promising. But who was Annie Mosgrave?

'Who?' said Major Glaushof.

'Some guy who teaches English or something evenings. Name of Wilt,' said the Duty Lieutenant. 'H. Wilt.'

'I'll be right over,' said Glaushof. He put the phone down and went through to his wife.

'Don't wait up, honey,' he said, 'I've got a problem.'

'Me too,' said Mrs Glaushof, and settled back to watch Dallas on BBC. It was kind of reassuring to know Texas was still there and it wasn't damp and raining all the time and goddam cold like Baconheath, and people still thought big and did big things. So she shouldn't have married an Airbase Security Officer with a thing going for German Shepherds. And to think he'd seemed so romantic when she'd met him back from Iran. Some security there. She should have known.

Outside, Glaushof climbed into his jeep with the three dogs and drove off between the houses towards the gates to Civilian Quarters. A group of men were standing well back from Wilt's Escort in the parking lot. Glaushof deliberately skidded the jeep to a stop and got out.

'What is it?' he asked. 'A bomb?'

'Jesus, I don't know,' said the Lieutenant, who was listening to a receiver. 'Could be anything.'

'Like he's left his CB on,' a Corporal explained, 'only there's two of them and they're bleeping.'

'Know any Brit who has two CBs running continuously the same time?' asked the Lieutenant. 'No way, and the frequency's wrong. Way too high.'

'So it could be a bomb,' said Glaushof. 'Why the fuck did you let it in?'

In the darkness and under threat of being blown to bits by whatever diabolical device the car concealed, Glaushof edged away. The little group followed him.

'Guy comes every Friday, gives his lecture, has coffee and goes on home no problem,' said the Lieutenant.

'So you let him drive right through with that lot buzzing and you don't stop him,' said Glaushof. 'We could have a Beirut bomb blast on our hands.'

'We didn't pick up the bleep till later.'

'Too later,' said Glaushof, 'I'm not taking any chances. I want the sand trucks brought up but fast. We're going to seal that car. Move.'

'It ain't no bomb,' said the Corporal, 'not sending like that. With a bomb the signals would be coming in.'

'Whatever,' said Glaushof, 'it's a breach of security and it's going to be sealed.'

'If you say so, Major,' said the Corporal and disappeared across the parking lot. For a moment, Glaushof hesitated and considered what other action he should take. At least he'd acted promptly to protect the base and his own career. As Base Security Officer, he'd always been against these foreign lecturers coming in with their subversive talks. He'd already discovered a geographer who'd sneaked a whole lot of shit about the dangers to bird-life from noise pollution and kerosene into his lectures on the development of the English landscape. Glaushof had had him busted as a member of Greenpeace. A car with radios transmitting continuously suggested something much more serious. And something much more serious could be just what he needed.

Glaushof ran through a mental checklist of enemies of the Free World: terrorists, Russian spies, subversives, women from Greenham Common ... whatever. It didn't matter. The key thing was that Base Intelligence had fouled things up and it was up to him to rub their faces in the shit. Glaushof smiled to himself at the prospect. If there was one man he detested, it was the Intelligence Officer. Nobody heard of Glaushof, but Colonel Urwin with his line to the Pentagon and his wife in with the Base Commander's so they were invited to play Bridge Saturday nights, oh sure, he was a big noise. And a Yale man. Screw him. Glaushof intended to. 'This guy ... what did you say his name is?' he asked the Lieutenant.

'Wilt,' said the Lieutenant.

'Where are you holding him?'

'Not holding him anyplace,' said the Lieutenant. 'Called you first thing we picked up the signals.'

'So where is he?'

'I guess he's over lecturing someplace,' said the Lieutenant. 'His details are in the guardhouse. Schedule and all.'

They hurried across the parking lot to the gates to the civilian quarters and Glaushof studied the entry in Wilt's file. It was brief and uninformative. 'Lecture Hall 9,' said the Lieutenant. 'You want me to have him picked up?'

'No,' said Glaushof, 'not yet. Just see no one gets out, is all.'

'No way he can except over the new fence,' said the Lieutenant, 'and I don't see him getting far. I've switched the current on.'

'Fine,' said Glaushof. 'So he comes out you stop him.'

'Yes, sir,' said the Lieutenant, and went out to check the guards, while Glaushof picked up the phone and called the Security Patrol. 'I want Lecture Hall 9 surrounded,' he said, 'but nobody to move till I come.'

He sat on staring distractedly at the centrepage of *Playgirl* featuring a male nude which had been pinned to the wall. If this bastard Wilt could be persuaded to talk, Glaushof's career would be made. So how to get him in the right frame of mind? First of all, he had to know what was in that car. He was still puzzling over tactics when the Lieutenant coughed discreetly behind him. Glaushof reacted violently. He didn't like the implications of that cough. 'Did you pin this up?' he shouted at the Lieutenant.

'Negative,' said the Lieutenant, who disliked the question almost as much as Glaushof had hated the cough. 'No, sir, I did not. That's Captain Clodiak.'

'That's Captain Clodiak?' said Glaushof, turning back to examine the picture again. 'I knew she ... he ... You've got to be kidding, Lieutenant. That's not the Captain Clodiak I know.'

'She put it there, sir. She likes that sort of thing.'

'Yes, well I guess she's a pretty feisty woman,' said Glaushof to avoid the accusation that he was discriminatory. In career prospect terms, it was almost as dangerous as being called a faggot. Not almost; it was worse.

'I happen to be Church of God,' said the Lieutenant, 'and that is irreligious according to my denomination.'

But Glaushof wasn't to be drawn into a discussion. 'Could be,' he said. 'Some other time, huh?' He went out and back to the parking lot where the Corporal, now accompanied by a Major and several men from the Demolition and Excavation section, had surrounded Wilt's car with four gigantic dumpers filled with sand, sweeping aside a dozen other vehicles in the process. As he approached, Glaushof was blinded by two searchlights which had suddenly been switched on. 'Douse those mothers,' he shouted, stumbling about in the glare. 'You want them to know in Moscow what we're doing?' In the darkness that followed this pronouncement, Glaushof banged into the wheelhub of one of the dumptrucks.

'Okay, so I go in without lights,' said the Corporal. 'No problem. You think it's a bomb, I don't. Bombs don't transmit CB.' And before Glaushof could remind him to call him 'Sir' in future, the Corporal had walked across to the car.

'Mr Wilt,' said Mrs Ofrey, 'would you like to elucidate on the question of the rôle of women in British society with particular regard to the part played in professional life by the Right Honorable Prime Minister Mrs Thatcher and...'

Wilt stared at her and wondered why Mrs Ofrey always read her questions from a card and why they seldom had anything to do with what he had been talking about. She must spend the rest of the week thinking them up. And the questions always had to do with the Queen and Mrs Thatcher, presumably because Mrs Ofrey had once dined at Woburn Abbey with the Duke and Duchess of Bedford and their hospitality had affected her deeply. But at least this evening he was giving her his undivided attention.

From the moment he'd entered the lecture room, he'd been having problems. The bandage he had wound round his loins had come undone on the drive over, and before he could do anything about it one end had begun to worm its way down his right trouser leg. To make matters worse, Captain Clodiak had come late and had seated herself in front of him with her legs crossed, and had promptly forced Wilt to press himself

140

against the lectern to quell yet another erection or, at least, hide the event from his audience. And by concentrating on Mrs Ofrey, he had so far managed to avoid a second glance at Captain Clodiak.

But there were disadvantages in concentrating so intently on Mrs Ofrey too. Even though she wore enough curiously patterned knitwear to have subsidized several crofters in Western Scotland, and her few charms were sufficiently muted by wool to make some sort of antidote to the terrifying chic of Captain Clodiak – Wilt had already noted the Captain's blouse and what he took to be a combat skirt in shantung silk – Mrs Ofrey was still a woman. In any case, she evidently liked to be socially exclusive and sat by herself to the left of the rest of the class, and by the time he'd got halfway through his lecture, he'd become positively wry-necked in his regard for her. Wilt had switched his attention to an acned clerk from the PX stores whose other courses were karate and aerobics and whose interest in British Culture was limited to unravelling the mysteries of cricket. That hadn't worked too well either, and after ten minutes of almost constant eye-contact and Wilt's deprecating observations on the effect of women's suffrage on the voting patterns in elections since 1928, the man had begun to shift awkwardly in his chair and Wilt had suddenly realized the fellow thought he was being propositioned. Not wanting to be beaten to pulp by a karate expert, he had tried alternating between Mrs Ofrey and the wall behind the rest of the class, but each time it seemed that Captain Clodiak was smiling more significantly. Wilt had clung to the lectern in the hope that he'd manage to get through the hour without ejaculating into his trousers. He was so worried about this that he hardly noticed that Mrs Ofrey had finished her question. 'Would you say that view was correct?' she said by way of a prompt.

'Well ... er ... yes,' said Wilt, who couldn't recall what the question was anyway. Something to do with the Monarchy being a matriarchy. 'Yes, I suppose in a general way I'd go along with you,' he said, wedging himself more firmly against the lectern. 'On the other hand, just because a country has a female ruler, I don't think we can assume it's not male-dominated. After all, we had Queen Boadicea in Pre-Roman

Britain and I wouldn't have thought there was an awful lot of Women's Lib about then, would you?'

'I wasn't asking about the feminist movement,' said Mrs Ofrey, with a nasty inflection that suggested she was a pre-Eisenhower American, 'my question was directed to the matriarchal nature of the Monarchy.'

'Quite,' said Wilt, fighting for time. Something desperate seemed to have happened to the cricket box. He'd lost touch with the thing. 'Though just because we've have a number of Queens ... well, I suppose we've had almost as many as we've had kings ... must have had more, come to think of it? Is that right? I mean, each king had to have a queen...'

'Henry VIII had a whole heap of them,' said an astronavigational expert, whose reading tastes seemed to suggest she would have preferred life in some sort of airconditioned and deodorized Middle Ages. 'He must have been some man.'

'Definitely,' said Wilt, grateful for her intervention. At this rate, the discussion might spread and leave him free to find that damned box again. 'In fact he had five. There was Katherine of...'

'Excuse me asking, Mr Wilt,' interrupted an engineer, 'but do old Queens count as Queens? Like they're widows. Is a King's widow still a Queen?'

'She's a Queen Mother,' said Wilt, who by this time had his hand in his pocket and was searching for the box. 'It's purely titular of course. She –'

'Did you say "titular"?' asked Captain Clodiak, endowing the word with qualities Wilt had never intended and certainly didn't need now. And her voice suited her face. Captain Clodiak came from the South. 'Would you care to amplify what titular means?'

'Amplify?' said Wilt weakly. But before he could answer, the engineer had interrupted again.

'Pardon me breaking in, Mr Wilt,' he said, 'but you've got kind of something hanging out of your leg.'

'I have?' said Wilt, clutching the lectern even more closely. The attention of the entire class was now focused on his right leg. Wilt tried to hide it behind his left.

'And by the look of it I'd say it was something important to you.'

142

Wilt knew damned well what it was. With a lurch, he let go of the lectern and grabbed his trouser leg in a vain attempt to stop the box but the beastly thing had already evaded him. It hung for a moment almost coyly half out of the trouser cuff and then slid onto his shoe. Wilt's hand shot out and smothered the brute and the next moment he was trying to get it into his pocket. The box didn't budge. Still attached to the bandage by the plaster he had used, it refused to come without the bandage. As Wilt tried to drag it away it became obvious he was in danger of splitting the seam of his trousers. It was also fairly obvious that the other end of the bandage was still round his waist and had no intention of coming off. At this rate, he'd end up half-naked in front of the class and suffering from a strangulated hernia into the bargain. On the other hand, he could hardly stay half-crouching there and any attempt to drag the bloody thing up the inside of his trousers from the top was bound to be misinterpreted. In fact, by the sound of things, his predicament already had been. Even from his peculiar position, Wilt was aware that Captain Clodiak had got to her feet, a bleeper was sounding and the astro-navigator was saying something about codpieces.

Only the engineer was being at all constructive. 'Is that a medical problem you got there?' he asked and missed Wilt's contorted reply that it wasn't. 'I mean, we've got the best facilities for the treatment of infections of the urino-genital tract this side of Frankfurt and I can call up a medic ...'

Wilt relinquished his hold on the box and stood up. It might be embarrassing to have a cricket box hanging out of his trousers but it was infinitely preferable to being examined in his present state by an airbase doctor. God knows what the man would make of a runaway erection. 'I don't need any doctor,' he squawked. 'It's just ... well, I was playing cricket before I came here and in a hurry not to be late I forgot ... Well, I'm sure you understand.'

Mrs Ofrey clearly didn't. With some remark about the niceties of life being wanting, she marched out of the hall in the wake of Captain Clodiak. Before Wilt could say that all he needed was to get to the toilet, the acned clerk had intervened. 'Say, Mr Wilt,' he said, 'I didn't know you were a cricket player. Why, only three weeks ago you were saying you couldn't tell me what you English call a curve ball.'

'Some other time,' said Wilt, 'right now I need to get to ... er ... a washroom.'

'You sure you don't want –'

'Definitely,' said Wilt, 'I am perfectly all right. It's just a ... never mind.'

He hobbled out of the hall and was presently ensconced in a cubicle fighting a battle with the box, the bandage and his trousers. Behind him, the class were discussing this latest manifestation of British Culture with a greater degree of interest than they had shown for Wilt's views on voting patterns. 'I still say he don't know anything about cricket,' said the PX clerk, only to be countered by the navigator and the engineer who were more interested in Wilt's medical condition. 'I had an uncle in Idaho had to wear a support. It's nothing unusual. Fell off a ladder when he was painting the house one spring,' said the engineer. 'Those things can be real serious.'

'I told you, Major,' said the Corporal, 'two radio transmitters, one tape recorder, no bomb.'

'Definitely?' asked Glaushof, trying to keep the disappointment out of his voice.

'Definite,' said the Corporal and was supported in this by the Major from the Demolition and Excavation Section who wanted to know whether he could order his men to move the dumpers back. As they rolled away leaving Wilt's Escort isolated in the middle of the parking lot, Glaushof tried to salvage some opportunity from the situation. After all, Colonel Urwin, the Intelligence Officer, was away for the weekend and in his absence Glaushof could have done with a crisis.

'He had to come in here with that equipment for some reason,' he said, 'transmitting like that. Any ideas on the matter, Major?'

'Could be it's a dummy run to check if they can bring a bomb in and explode it by remote control,' said the Major, whose expertise tended to make him one-track-minded.

'Except he was transmitting, not receiving,' said the Corporal. 'They'd need signals in, not out, for a bomb. And what's with the recorder?'

144

'Not my department,' said the Major. 'Explosively, it's clean. I'll go file my report.'

Glaushof took the plunge. 'With me,' he said. 'You file it with me and no one else. We've got to shroud this.'

'We've done that once already with the safety trucks and quite unnecessarily.'

'Sure,' said Glaushof, 'but we still gotta find out what this is all about. I'm in charge of security and I don't like it, some Limey bastard coming in with all this equipment. Either it's a dummy run like you said, or it's something else.'

'It's got to be something else,' said the Corporal, 'obviously. With the equipment he's using, you could tape lice fucking twenty miles away it's that sensitive.'

'So his wife's getting evidence for a divorce,' said the Major.

'Must be goddam desperate for it,' said the Corporal, 'using two transmitters and a recorder. And that stuff's not general issue. I never seen a civilian using homers that sophisticated.'

'Homers?' said Glaushof, who had been preoccupied by the concept of lice fucking. 'How do you mean, homers?'

'Like they're direction indicators. Signals go out and two guys pick it up on their sets and they've got where he is precise.'

'Jesus!' said Glaushof. 'You mean the Russkies could have sent this guy Wilt in as an agent so they can pin-point right where we are?'

'They're doing that already infra-red by satellite. They don't need some guy coming in waving a radio flag,' said the Corporal. 'Not unless they want to lose him.'

'Lose him? What would they want to do that for?'

'I don't know,' continued the Corporal. 'You're Security, I'm just Technical and why anybody wants to do things isn't my province. All I do know is I wouldn't send any agent of mine any place I didn't want him caught with those signals spelling out he was coming. Like putting a fucking mouse in a room with a cat and it can't stop fucking squeaking.'

But Glaushof was not to be deterred. 'The fact of the matter is this Wilt came in with unauthorized spy equipment and he isn't going out.'

'So they're going to know he's here from those signals,' said the Corporal.

Glaushof glared at him. The man's common sense had become intensely irritating. Here was his opportunity to hit back. 'You don't mean to tell me those radios are still operational?' he shouted.

'Sure,' said the Colonel. 'You tell me and the Major here to check the car for bombs. You didn't say nothing about screwing his transmission equipment. Bombs, you said.'

'Correct,' said the Major. 'That's what you did say. Bombs.'

'I know I said bombs,' yelled Glaushof, 'you think I need telling?' He stopped and turned his attention lividly on the car. If the radios were still working, presumably the enemy already knew they'd been discovered, in which case ... His mind raced on, following lines which led to catastrophe. He had to make a momentous decision, and now. Glaushof did. 'Right, we're going in,' he said, 'and you're going out.'

Five minutes later, in spite of his protests that he wasn't driving any fucking car thirty miles with fucking spooks following his fucking progress, not unless he had a fucking escort, the Corporal drove out of the base. The tape in the recorder had been removed and replaced with a new one, but in all other respects there was nothing to indicate that the car had been tampered with. Glaushof's instructions had been quite explicit. 'You drive right back and dump it outside his house,' he had told the Corporal. 'You've got the Major here with you to bring you back and if there's any problems, he'll take care of them. Those bastards want to know where their boy is they can start looking at home. They're going to have trouble finding him here.'

'Ain't going to have no trouble finding me,' said the Corporal, who knew never to argue with a senior officer. He should have stuck to dumb insolence.

For a moment, Glaushof watched as the two vehicles disappeared across the bleak night landscape. He had never liked it but now it had taken on an even more sinister aspect. It was across those flatlands that the wind blew from Russia non-stop from the Urals. In Glaushof's mind, it was an infected wind which, having blown around the domes and turrets of the Kremlin, threatened the very future of the world. And now somewhere out there someone was listening. Glaushof turned away. He was going to find out who those sinister listeners were.

14

'I got the whole place wrapped up, sir, and he's still inside,' said Lieutenant Harah when Glaushof finally reached Lecture Hall 9. Glaushof didn't need telling. He had had enough trouble himself getting through the cordon the Lieutenant had thrown up around the hall and in other circumstances would have expressed himself irritably on the Lieutenant's thoroughness. But the situation was too serious for recrimination, and besides he respected his second-in-command's expertise. As head of the APPS, the Anti Perimeter Penetration Squad, Lieutenant Harah had been through training at Fort Knox, in Panama and had seen action at Greenham Common disguised as a British bobby where he had qualified for a Purple Heart after being bitten in the leg by a mother of four, an experience which had left him with a useful bias against women. Glaushof appreciated his misogyny. At least one man in Baconheath could be relied on not to lay Mona Glaushof and Harah wasn't going to play footsy with any CND women if and when they tried breaking into Baconheath.

On the other hand, he seemed to have gone too far this time. Quite apart from the six hit-squad men in gas masks by the glass fronted door to the lecture hall and a number of others crouching under the windows round the side a small group of women were standing with their heads up against the wall of the next building.

'What are those?' Glaushof asked. He had a nasty suspicion he recognized Mrs Ofrey's Scottish knitwear.

'Suspected women,' said Lieutenant Harah.

'What do you mean "suspected women"?' demanded Glaushof. 'Either they're women or they aren't.'

'They came out dressed as women, sir,' said the Lieutenant, 'doesn't mean to say they are. Could be the terrorist dressed as one. You want me to check them out?'

'No,' said Glaushof, wishing to hell he had given the order

147

to storm the building before he had put in an appearance himself. It wasn't going to look too good spread-eagling the wife of the Chief Administrative Officer against a wall with a gun at her head, and to have her checked out sexually by Lieutenant Harah would really foul things up. On the other hand even Mrs Ofrey could hardly complain about being rescued from a possible hostage situation.

'You sure there's no way he could have got out?'

'Absolute,' said the Lieutenant. 'I got marksmen on the next block in case he makes the roof and the utilities tunnels are sealed. All we got to do is toss a canister of Agent Incapacitating in there and there's going to be no trouble.'

Glaushof glanced nervously at the row of women and doubted it. There was going to be trouble and maybe it would be better if that trouble could be seen to be serious. 'I'll get those women under cover and then you go in,' he said. 'And no shooting unless he fires first. I want this guy taken for interrogation. You got that?'

'Absolute, sir,' said the Lieutenant. 'He gets a whiff of AI he wouldn't find a trigger to pull if he wanted to.'

'Okay. Give me five minutes and then go,' said Glaushof and crossed to Mrs Ofrey.

'If you ladies will just step this way,' he said, and dismissing the men who were holding them hurried the little group round the corner and into the lobby of another lecture hall. Mrs Ofrey was clearly annoyed.

'What do you mean –' she began but Glaushof raised a hand. 'If you'll just let me explain,' he said, 'I realize you have been inconvenienced but we have an infiltration situation on our hands and we couldn't afford the possibility of you being held hostage.' He paused and was glad to see that even Mrs Ofrey had taken the message. 'How absolutely dreadful,' she murmured.

It was Captain Clodiak's reaction that surprised him. 'Infiltration situation? We just had the usual class no problem,' she said, 'I didn't see anybody new. Are you saying there's somebody in there we don't know about?'

Glaushof hesitated. He had hoped to keep the question of Wilt's identity as a secret agent to himself and not have news of it spreading round the base like wildfire. He certainly didn't want it getting out until he had completed his interrogation and had all the information he needed to prove that the Intelligence Section, and in particular that bland bastard Colonel Urwin, hadn't screened a foreign employee properly. That way the Colonel would take a fall and they could hardly avoid promoting Glaushof. Let Intelligence get wind of what was going on and the plan might backfire. Glaushof fell back on the 'Eyes off' routine.

'I don't think it advisable at this moment in time to elucidate the matter further. This is a top-security matter. Any leak could severely prejudice the defensive capabilities of Strategic Air Command in Europe. I must insist on a total information blackout.'

For a moment the pronouncement had the effect he had wanted. Even Mrs Ofrey looked satisfactorily stunned. Then Captain Clodiak broke the silence. 'I don't get it,' she said. 'There's us and this Wilt guy in there, nobody else. Right?' Glaushof said nothing. 'So you bring up the stormtroopers and have us pinned against the wall as soon as we walk out and now you tell us it's an infiltration situation. I don't believe you, Major, I just don't believe you. The only infiltration I know of is what that bastard sexist lieutenant did up my ass and I intend to formalize a complaint against Lieutenant Harah and you can pull as many phoney agents out of your pinhead imagination as you like, you still aren't going to stop me.'

Glaushof gulped. He could see he'd been right to describe the Captain as a feisty woman and entirely wrong to have allowed Lieutenant Harah to act on his own. He'd also been fairly wrong in his estimation of the Lieutenant's antipathy for women though even Glaushof had to admit that Captain Clodiak was a remarkably attractive woman. In an attempt to save the situation he tried a sympathetic smile. It came out lopsided. 'I'm sure Lieutenant Harah had no intention of –' he began.

'So what's with the hand?' snapped the Captain. 'You think I don't know intentions when I feel them? Is that what you think?'

'Perhaps he was doing a weapon check,' said Glaushof, who knew now he would have to do something really astonishing to regain control of the situation. He was saved by the sound of breaking glass. Lieutenant Harah had waited exactly five minutes before taking action.

It had taken Wilt rather more than five minutes to unravel the bandage and slide it down his trouser leg and reassemble the box in a position where it would afford him some measure of protection from the spasmodic antics of his penis. In the end he had succeeded and had just tied the entire contraption together rather uncomfortably when there was a knock on the door.

'You okay, Mr Wilt?' asked the engineer.

'Yes, thank you,' said Wilt as politely as his irritation allowed. It was always the same with nice idiots. The sods offered to help in precisely the wrong way. All Wilt wanted now was to get the hell out of the base without any further embarrassment. But the engineer didn't understand the situation. 'I was just telling Pete how I had an uncle in Idaho had the same support problem,' said the engineer through the door.

'Really?' said Wilt, feigning interest while actually struggling to pull his zip up. A thread of bandage had evidently got caught in the thing. Wilt tried pulling it down.

'Yea. He went around for years with this bulky thing on until my Auntie Annie heard of this surgeon in Kansas City and she took my Uncle Rolf down there and of course he didn't want to go but he never did regret it. I can give you his name if you like.'

'Fuck,' said Wilt. A stitch on the bottom of his zip sounded as though it had torn.

'Did you say something, Mr Wilt?' asked the engineer.

'No,' said Wilt.

There was a moment's silence while the engineer evidently considered his next move and Wilt tried holding the bottom of the zip to his trousers while wrenching the tag at the same time. 'As I see it, and you've got to understand I'm not a medical man myself I'm an engineer so I know about structural failure, there's muscle deterioration in the lower –'

'Listen,' said Wilt. 'Right now where I've got a structural failure is in the zip on my trousers. Something's got caught in it and it's stuck.'

150

'Which side?' asked the engineer.

'Which side is what?' demanded Wilt.

'The ... er ... thing that's stuck in it?'

Wilt peered down at the zip. In the confines of the toilet it was difficult to see which side anything was. 'How the hell would I know?'

'You pulling it up or down?' continued the engineer.

'Up,' said Wilt.

'Sometimes helps to pull it down first.'

'It's already bloody down,' said Wilt allowing his irritation to get the better of him. 'I wouldn't be trying to pull the fucking thing up if it wasn't down, would I?'

'I guess not,' said the engineer with a degree of bland patience that was even more irritating than his desire to be helpful. 'Just the same if it isn't right down it could be the thing ...' He paused. 'Mr Wilt, just what is it you've got in the zip?'

Inside the toilet Wilt stared dementedly at a notice which not only instructed him to wash his hands but seemed to suppose he needed telling how to. 'Count to ten,' he muttered to himself and was surprised to find that the zip had freed itself. He'd also been freed from the unwanted helpfulness of the engineer. A crash of breaking glass had evidently disturbed the man's blandness. 'Jesus, what's going on?' he yelled.

It was not a question Wilt could answer. And by the sound of things outside he didn't want to. Somewhere a door burst open and running feet in the corridor were interspersed with muffled orders to freeze. Inside the toilet Wilt froze. Accustomed as he had recently become to the hazards seemingly inherent in going to the lavatory anywhere outside his own house, the experience of being locked in a cubicle with a hit squad of Anti Perimeter Penetration men bursting into the building was new to him.

It was fairly new to the engineer. As the canisters of Agent Incapacitating hit the floor and masked men armed with automatic weapons broke through the door he lost all interest in the problems of Wilt's zip and headed back into the lecture hall only to collide with the navigator and the PX clerk who were dashing the other way. In the confusion that followed Agent Incapacitating lived up to its name. The PX clerk tried

151

to disentangle himself from the engineer who was doing his best to avoid him and the navigator embraced them both under the illusion he was moving in the other direction.

As they fell to the ground Lieutenant Harah loomed over them large and quite extraordinarily sinister in his gas mask. 'Which of you is Wilt?' he yelled. His voice, distorted both by the mask and by the effects of the gas on their nervous systems, reached them slowly. Not even the voluble engineer was able to help him. 'Take them all out,' he ordered and the three men were dragged from the building gurgling sentences that sounded as if a portable recorder with faulty batteries was being played under water.

In his cubicle Wilt listened to the awful noises with growing apprehension. Breaking glass, strangely muffled shouts and the clump of boots had played no part in his previous visits to the airbase and he couldn't for the life of him imagine what they portended. Whatever it was he'd had enough trouble for one evening without wishing to invite any more. It seemed safest to stay where he was and wait until whatever was happening had stopped. Wilt switched off the light and sat down on the seat.

Outside, Lieutenant Harah's men reported thickly that the hall was clear. In spite of the eddies of gas the Lieutenant could see that. Peering through the eyepiece of his gas mask he surveyed the empty seats with a sense of anti-climax. He had rather hoped the infiltrator would put up a show of resistance, and the ease with which the bastard had been taken had disappointed him. On the other hand he could also see that it had been a mistake to bring in the assault dogs without equipping them with gas masks. Agent Incapacitating evidently affected them too. One of them was slithering about the floor snarling in slow motion while another, in an attempt to scratch its right ear, was waving a hindfoot about in a most disturbing manner.

'Okay, that's it,' he said and marched out to question his three prisoners. Like the assault dogs they had been totally incapacitated and he had no idea which was the foreign agent he was supposed to be detaining. They were all dressed in civilian clothes and in no state to say who or what they were. Lieutenant Harah reported to Glaushof. 'I think you better check them out, sir. I don't know which son of a bitch is which.'

'Wilt,' said Glaushof, glaring at the gas mask, 'his name is Wilt. He's a foreign employee. Shouldn't be any difficulty recognizing the bastard.'

'All Limeys look the same to me,' said the Lieutenant, and was promptly rewarded with a chop across his throat and a knee in his groin by Captain Clodiak who had just recognized her sexist assailant through his gas mask. As the Lieutenant doubled up she grabbed his arm and Glaushof was surprised to see how easily his second-in-command was swept off his feet by a woman.

'Remarkable,' he said. 'It's a genuine privilege to witness –'

'Cut the crap,' said Captain Clodiak, dusting her hands and looking as though she would like to demonstrate her expertise in karate on another man. 'That creep said a sexist remark and you said Wilt. Am I right?' Glaushof looked puzzled. He hadn't recognized 'son of a bitch' as being sexist and he didn't want to discuss Wilt in front of the other women. On the other hand he didn't have any idea what Wilt looked like and someone had to identify him. 'Maybe we'd better step outside to discuss this, Captain,' he said and went out the door.

Captain Clodiak followed him warily. 'What do we have to discuss?' she asked.

'Like Wilt,' said Glaushof.

'You're crazy. I heard you just now. Wilt an agent?'

'Incontrovertible,' said Glaushof, pulling brevity.

'How so?' said Clodiak, responding in kind.

'Infiltrated the perimeter with enough radio transmitting equipment hidden in his car to signal our position to Moscow or the moon. I mean it, Captain. What's more it's not civilian equipment you can buy in a store. It's official.' said Glaushof and was relieved to notice the disbelief fade from her face. 'And right now, I'm going to need help identifying him.'

They went round the corner and were confronted by the sight of three men lying face down on the ground in front

153

of Lecture Hall 9 guarded by two incapacitated assault dogs and the APP team.

'Okay, men, the Captain here is going to identify him,' said Glaushof and prodded the PX clerk with his foot. 'Turn over, you.' The clerk tried to turn over but succeeded only in crawling sideways on top of the engineer, who promptly went into convulsions. Glaushof looked at the two contorted figures with disgust before having his attention distracted even more disturbingly by an assault dog that had urinated on his shoe without lifting its leg.

'Get that filthy beast off me,' he shouted and was joined in his protests by the engineer who objected just as strongly though less comprehensibly to the apparent attempts the PX clerk was making to bugger him. By the time the dog had been removed, a process that required the efforts of three men on the end of its chain, and some sort of order was restored on the ground Captain Clodiak's expression had changed again. 'I thought you said you wanted Wilt identified,' she said, 'Well, he's not here.'

'Not here? You mean ...' Glaushof looked suspiciously at the broken door of the lecture hall.

'They're the men the Lieutenant told us to grab,' said one of the hit-squad. 'There wasn't anyone else in the hall I saw.'

'There's gotta be,' yelled Glaushof. 'Where's Harah?'

'In there where you –'

'I know where he is. Just get him and fast.'

'Yessir,' said the man and disappeared.

'You seem to have got yourself a problem,' said Captain Clodiak.

Glaushof tried to shrug it off. 'He can't have broken through the cordon and even if he has he's going to burn on the fence or get himself arrested at the gate.' he said. 'I'm not worried.'

All the same he found himself glancing round at the familiar dull buildings and the roadways between them with a new sense of suspicion as though somehow they had changed character and had become accomplices to the absent Wilt. With an insight that was alarmingly strange to him he realized how much Baconheath meant to him; it was home, his own little fortress in a foreign land with its comfortable jet noises linking him to his own hometown, Eiderburg, Michigan, and the abattoir down the road where the hogs were killed. As a boy he had woken to the sound of their squeals and an F111 screaming for take-off had the same comforting effect on him. But more than anything else Baconheath with its perimeter fence and guarded gates had been America for him, his own country, powerful, independent and freed from danger by his constant vigilance and the sheer enormity of its arsenal. Squatting there behind the wire and isolated by the flat reaches of the Fens from the old crumbling villages and market towns with their idle, inefficient shopkeepers and their dirty pubs where strange people drank warm, unhygienic beer, Baconheath had been an oasis of brisk efficiency and modernity, and proof that the great US of A was still the New World and would remain so.

But now Glaushof's vision had shifted and for a moment he felt somehow disassociated from the place. These buildings were hiding this Wilt from him and until he found the bastard Baconheath would be infected. Glaushof forced himself out of this nightmare and was confronted by another. Lieutenant Harah came round the corner. He was clearly still paying for his sexist attitude to Captain Clodiak and had to be supported by two APPS men. Glaushof had almost been prepared for that. The garbled noises the Lieutenant was making were something else again and could hardly be explained by a kick in the groin.

'It's the AI, sir,' one of the men explained, 'I guess he must have loosed off a canister in the lobby.'

'Loosed off a canister? In the lobby?' Glaushof squawked, appalled at the terrible consequences to his career such a lunatic action seemed certain to provoke. 'Not with those women –'

'Affirmative,' ejaculated Lieutenant Harah without warning. Glaushof turned on him.

'What do you mean, affirmative?'

'Absolute,' Harah's voice hit a new high. And stuck there. 'Absolute absolute absolute absolute ...'

'Gag that bastard,' shouted Glaushof and shot round the corner of the building to see what he could do to rescue the situation. It was beyond hope. For whatever insane reason Lieutenant Harah, perhaps in an attempt to defend himself against a second strike from Captain Clodiak, had wrenched

155

the pin from a gas grenade before realizing that his gas mask had come off in his fall. Gazing through the glass doors at the bizarre scenes in the lobby, Glaushof was no longer worried about Mrs Ofrey's interference. Draped over the back of a chair with her hair touching the floor and happily obscuring her face, the wife of the Chief Administrative Executive resembled nothing so much as a large and incontinent highland ewe which had been put rather prematurely through a Fair Isle knitting machine. The rest of the class were in no better shape. The astro-navigation officer lay on her back, evidently re-enacting a peculiarly passive sexual experience, while several other students of British Culture and Institutions looked as though they were extras in some film depicting the end of the world. Once again Glaushof experienced the ghastly sensation of being at odds with his environment and it was only by calling up reserves of approximate sanity that he took control of himself.

'Get them out of there,' he shouted, 'and call the medics. We got a maniac on the loose.'

'Got something,' said Captain Clodiak. 'That Lieutenant Harah's going to have a lot to answer for. I can't see General Ofrey being too pleased with a dead wife. He'll just have to play three-handed bridge with the Commander.'

But Glaushof had had enough of the Captain's objective standpoint. 'You're responsible for this,' he said with a new menace in his voice. 'You talk about questions you're going to have to answer some yourself. Like you deliberately assaulted Lieutenant Harah in the execution of his duty and –'

'Like the execution of his duty includes getting his hand up my ...' interrupted the Captain furiously and then stopped and stared. 'Oh my God,' she said and Glaushof, who had been preparing for another demonstration of karate, followed her gaze.

In the broken doorway of Lecture Hall 9 a hapless figure was trying to stand up. As they watched, it failed.

15

Fifteen miles away Wilt's Escort beeped its erratic way towards Ipford. Since no one had thought to provide the Corporal with adequate directions and he had distrusted Glaushof's assurances that he would be well protected by the Major and the men in the truck behind him, he had taken his own precautions before and after leaving the base. He had provided himself with a heavy automatic and had computed a route which would cause maximum confusion to anyone trying to cross-reference his position on their receivers. He had achieved his object. In short, he had travelled twenty quite extraordinarily complicated miles in no time at all. Half an hour after leaving Baconheath he was still only five miles from the base. After that he had shot off towards Ipford and had spent twenty minutes pretending to change a tyre in a tunnel under the motorway before emerging on a minor road which ran for several miles very conveniently next to a line of high-tension electricity pylons. Two more tunnels and fifteen miles on a road that wound along below the bank of a dyked river, and Inspector Hodge and the men in the other listening van were desperately transmitting messages to one another in an attempt to make out where the hell he had got to. More awkwardly still, they couldn't be entirely sure where they were either.

The Major shared their dilemma. He hadn't expected the Corporal to take evasive action or to drive – when he wasn't lurking in tunnels – at excessive speed along winding roads that had presumably been designed for single-file horse traffic and had been dangerous even then. But the Major didn't care. If the Corporal wanted to take off like a scalded cat that was his problem. 'He wants an armed escort he better stay with us,' he told his driver as they skidded round a muddy ninety-degree bend and nearly landed in a deep water-filled drain. 'I'm not ending my life in a ditch so slow down for Chrissake.'

'So how do we keep up with him?' asked the driver, who had been thoroughly enjoying himself.

'We don't. If he's going any place outside hell it's Ipford. I've got the address here. Take the motorway first chance you get and we'll wait for him where he's supposed to be going.'

'Yes sir,' said the driver reluctantly and switched back to the main road at the next turn-off.

Sergeant Runk would have done the same had he been given the chance but the Corporal's tactics had confirmed all Inspector Hodge's wildest dreams. 'He's trying to lose us,' he shouted shortly after the Corporal left the airbase and began to dice with death. 'That must mean he's carrying dope.'

'That or he's practising for the Monte Carlo Rally,' said Runk.

Hodge wasn't amused. 'Rubbish. The little bastard goes into Baconheath, spends an hour and a half and comes out doing eighty along mud roads no one in their right minds would do forty on in daylight and backtracks five times the way he's done – he must have something he values in that car.'

'Can't be his life, and that's for certain,' said Runk who was struggling to keep his seat. 'Why don't we just call up a patrol car and pull him for speeding? That way we can have him searched for whatever he's carrying.'

'Good idea,' said Hodge and had been about to send out instructions when the Corporal had taken radio refuge in the motorway tunnel and they'd lost him for twenty minutes. Hodge had spent the time blaming Runk for failing to have an accurate fix on his last position and calling for help from the second van. The Corporal's subsequent route near the power lines and below the river bank had made matters still more awkward. By then the Inspector had no idea what to do, but his conviction that he was dealing with a mastercriminal had been confirmed beyond doubt.

'He's obviously passed the stuff on to a third party and if we go for a search he'll plead innocence,' he muttered.

Even Runk had to agree that all the evidence pointed that way. 'He also happens to know his car's been wired for sound,' he said. 'The route he's following he's got to know. So where do we go from here?'

Hodge hesitated. For a moment he considered applying for a warrant and conducting so thorough a search of the Wilts' house that even the minutest trace of heroin or Embalming Fluid would come to light. But if it didn't ... 'There's always the tape recorder,' he said finally. 'He may have missed that in which case we'll get the conversations he had with the pick-up artist.'

Sergeant Runk doubted it. 'If you ask me,' he said, 'the only way you're going to get solid evidence on this bugger is by sending Forensic in to do a search with vacuum-cleaners that'd suck an elephant through a drain pipe. He may be as canny as they come but those lab blokes know their onions. I reckon that's the sane way of going about it.'

But Hodge wasn't to be persuaded. He had no intention of handing the case over to someone else when it was patently obvious he was on the right track. 'We'll see what's on that tape first,' he said as they headed back towards Ipford. 'We'll give him an hour to get to sleep and then you can move in and get it.'

'And have the rest of the bloody day off,' said Runk. 'You may be one of Nature's insomniacs but if I don't get my eight hours I won't be fit for –'

'I am not an insomniac,' snapped the Inspector. They drove on in silence broken only by the bleeps coming from Wilt's car. They were louder now. Ten minutes later the van was parked at the bottom of Perry Road and Wilt's car was announcing its presence from Oakhurst Avenue.

'You've got to hand it to the little sod,' said Hodge. 'I mean you'd never dream to look at him he could drive like that. Just shows you can never tell.'

An hour later Sergeant Runk stumbled out of his van and walked up Perry Road. 'It's not there,' he said when he got back.

'Not there? It's bloody well got to be,' said the Inspector, 'it's still coming over loud and clear.'

'That's as may be,' said Runk. 'For all I care the little shit's tucked up in bed with the fucking transmitters but what I do know is that it's not outside his house.'

'What about the garage?' Runk snorted.

159

'The garage? Have you ever had a dekko in that garage? It's a ruddy furniture depository, that garage is. Stuffed to the roof with junk when I saw it and if you're telling me he's spent the last two days shifting it all out into the back garden so as he could get his car in there ...'

'We'll soon see about that,' said Hodge and presently the van was driving slowly past 45 Oakhurst Avenue and the Sergeant had been proved right.

'What did I tell you?' he said. 'I said he hadn't put it in the garage.'

'What you didn't say was he'd parked the thing there,' said Hodge, pointing through the windscreen at the mud-stained Escort which the Corporal, who hadn't been prepared to waste time checking house numbers in the middle of the night, had left outside Number 65.

'Well I'm buggered,' said Runk. 'Why'd he want to do a thing like that?'

'We'll see if that tape has anything to tell us,' said the Inspector. 'You hop out here and we'll go on round the corner.'

But for once Sergeant Runk wasn t to be budged. 'If you want that bloody tape you go and get it,' he said. 'A bloke like this Wilt doesn't leave his car down the road without a good reason and I'm not learning too bleeding late what that reason is, and that's final.'

In the end it was Hodge who approached the car warily and had just started to grope under the front seat when Mrs Willoughby's Great Dane gave tongue inside the house.

'What did I tell you?' said Runk as the Inspector clambered in beside him puffing frantically. 'I knew there was a trap there somewhere but you wouldn't listen.'

Inspector Hodge was too preoccupied to listen to him even now. In his mind's ear he could still hear the baying of that dreadful dog and the sound of its terrible paws on the front door of the Willoughbys' house.

He was still shaken by the experience when they arrived back at the station. 'I'll get him, I'll get him,' he muttered as he made his way wearily up the steps. But the threat lacked substance. He had been outwitted yet again and for the first time he appreciated Sergeant Runk's need for sleep. Perhaps after a few hours his mind would come up with a new plan.

In Wilt's case the need for sleep was paramount too. The effects of Agent Incapacitating on a body already weakened by the administration of Dr Kores' sexual cordial had reduced him to a state in which he hardly knew who he was and was quite incapable of answering questions. He vaguely remembered escaping from a cubicle, or rather of being locked in one, but for the rest his mind was a jumble of images, the sum total of which made no sense at all. Men with masks, guns, being dragged, thrown into a jeep, driven, more dragging, lights in a bare room and a man shouting dementedly at him, all formed kaleidoscopic patterns which constantly rearranged themselves in his mind and made no sense at all. They just happened or were happening or even, because the man shouting at him still seemed somehow remote, had happened to him in some previous existence and one he would prefer not to relive. And even when Wilt tried to explain that things, whatever they were, were not what they seemed, the shouting man wasn't prepared to listen.

It was hardly surprising. The strange noises Wilt was in fact making hardly came into the category of utterances and certainly weren't explanations.

'Scrambled,' said the doctor Glaushof had summoned to try and inject some sense into Wilt's communications system. 'That's what you get with AI Two. You'll be lucky if he ever talks sense again.'

'AI Two? We used standard issue Agent Incapaciting,' said Glaushof. 'Nobody's been throwing AI Two around. That's reserved for Soviet suicide squads.'

'Sure,' said the doctor, 'I'm just telling you what I diagnose. You'd better check the canisters out.'

'I'll check that lunatic Harah out too,' said Glaushof and hurried from the room. When he returned Wilt had assumed a foetal position and was fast asleep.

'AI Two,' Glaushof admitted lugubriously. 'What do we do now?'

'I've done what I can,' said the doctor, 'dispensing with two hypodermics. 'Loaded him with enough Antidote AI to keep him out of the official brain-death category ...'

161

'Brain-death category? But I've got to interrogate the bastard. I can't have him cabbaging on me. He's some sort of infiltrating fucking agent and I got to find out where he's from.'

'Major Glaushof,' said the doctor wearily, 'it is now like zero three hundred hours and there's eight women, three men, one lieutenant and this ...' he pointed at Wilt 'and all of them suffering from nerve-gas toxicity and you think I can save any of them from chemically induced psychosis I'll do it but I'm not putting a suspected terrorist wearing a scrotal guard at the head of my list of priorities. If you want to interrogate him you'll have to wait. And pray. Oh yes, and if he doesn't come out of coma in eight hours let me know, maybe we can use him for spare-part surgery.'

'Hold it there, doctor,' he said. 'One word out of any of these people about there being –'

'Gassed?' said the doctor incredulously. 'I don't think you realize what you've done, Major. They're not going to remember a thing.'

'There being an agent here,' shouted Glaushof. 'Of course they've been gassed. Lieutenant Harah did that.'

'If you say so,' said the doctor. 'My business is physical welfare not base security and I guess you'll be able to explain Mrs Ofrey's condition to the General. Just don't call on me to say she and seven other women are naturally psychotic.'

Glaushof considered the implications of this request and found them decidedly awkward. On the other hand there was always Lieutenant Harah ... 'Tell me, doc,' he said, 'just how sick is Harah?'

'About as sick as a man who's been kicked in the groin and inhaled AI Two can be,' said the doctor. 'And that's not taking his mental condition beforehand into account either. He should have been wearing one of these.' He held up the box.

Glaushof looked at it speculatively and then glanced at Wilt. 'What would a terrorist want with one of those things?' he asked.

'Could be he expected what Lieutenant Harah got,' said the doctor, and left the room.

Glaushof followed him into the next office and sent for

162

Captain Clodiak. 'Take a seat, Captain,' he said. 'Now I want a breakdown of exactly what happened in there tonight.'

'What happened in there? You think I know? There's this maniac Harah ...'

Glaushof held up a hand. 'I think you should know that Lieutenant Harah is an extremely sick man right now.'

'What's with the now?' said Clodiak. 'He always was. Sick in the head.'

'It's not his head I'm thinking about.'

Captain Clodiak chewed gum. 'So he's got balls where his brain should be. Do I care?'

'I'd advise you to,' said Glaushof. 'Assaulting a junior officer carries a very heavy penalty.'

'Yea, well the same goes for sexually assaulting a senior one.'

'Could be,' said Glaushof, 'but I think you're going to have a hard time proving it.'

'Are you telling me I'm a liar?' demanded the Captain.

'No. Definitely not. I believe you but what I'm asking is, will anyone else?'

'I've got witnesses.'

'Had,' said Glaushof. 'From what the doctors tell me they're not going to be very reliable. In fact I'd go so far as to say they don't even come into the category of witnesses any longer. Agent Incapacitating does things to the memory. I think you ought to know that. And Lieutenant Harah's injuries have been medically documented. I don't think you're going to be in a position to dispute them. Doesn't mean you have to, but I'd advise you to co-operate with this department.'

Captain Clodiak studied his face. It wasn't a pleasant face but there was no disputing the fact that her situation wasn't one which allowed her too many options. 'What do you want me to do?' she asked.

'I want to hear what this Wilt said and all. In his lectures. Did he give any indications he was a communist?'

'Not that I knew,' said the Captain. 'I'd have reported it if he had.'

'So what did he say?'

'Mostly talked about things like parliament and voting patterns and how people in England see things.'

163

'See things?' said Glaushof, trying to think why an attractive woman like Ms Clodiak would want to go to lectures he'd have paid money to avoid. 'What sort of things?'

'Religion and marriage and ... just things.'

At the end of an hour, Glaushof had learnt nothing.

16

Eva sat in the kitchen and looked at the clock again. It was five o'clock in the morning and she had been up since two indulging herself in the luxury of a great many emotions. Her first reaction when going to bed had been one of annoyance. 'He's been to the pub again and got drunk,' she had thought. 'Well, he won't get any sympathy from me if he has a hangover.' Then she had lain awake getting angrier by the minute until one o'clock when worry had taken over. It wasn't like Henry to stay out that late. Perhaps something had happened to him. She went over various possibilities, ranging from car crashes to his getting arrested for being drunk and disorderly, and finally worked herself up to the point where she knew that something terrible had been done to him at the prison. After all he was teaching that dreadful murderer McCullum and when he'd come home on Monday night he'd been looking very peculiar. Of course he'd been drinking but all the same she remembered saying ... No, that hadn't been Monday night because she'd been asleep when he got back. It must have been Tuesday morning. Yes, that was it. She'd said he looked peculiar and come to think of it what she really thought was that he had looked scared. And he'd said he'd left the car in a car park and when he'd come home in the evening he'd kept looking out the front window in the strangest way. He'd had an accident with the car too and while at the time she had just put that down to his usual absent-mindedness now that she came to think about it ... At that point Eva had turned the light on and got out of bed. Something terrible had been going on and she hadn't even known it.

Which brought her round to anger again. Henry should have told her but he never did tell her really important things. He thought she was too stupid and perhaps she wasn't very clever when it came to arguing about books and saying the right things at parties but at least she was practical and nobody

165

could say that the quads weren't getting a good education.

So the night passed. Eva sat in the kitchen and made cups of tea and worried and was angry and then blamed herself and wondered who to telephone and then decided it was best not to call anyone because they'd only be cross at being woken in the middle of the night and anyway there might be a perfectly natural explanation like the car had broken down or he'd gone to the Braintrees for a drink and had had to stay there because of the police and the breathalyser which would have been the sensible thing to do and so perhaps she ought to go back to bed and get some sleep ... And always beside this bustle of conflicting thoughts and feelings there was the sense of guilt and the knowledge that she had been stupid to have listened to Mavis or to have gone anywhere near Dr Kores. Anyway, what did Mavis know about sex? She'd never really said what went on between her and Patrick in bed – it wasn't one of those things Eva would have dreamt of asking and even if she had Mavis wouldn't have told her – and all she'd ever heard was that Patrick was having affairs with other women. There might be good reasons for that too. Perhaps Mavis was frigid or wanted to be too dominant or masculine or wasn't very clean or something. Whatever the reason it was quite wrong of her to give Patrick those horrid steroid things or hormones and turn him into a sleepy fat person – well, you could hardly call him a man any longer could you? – who sat in front of the telly every night and couldn't get on with his work properly. Besides, Henry wasn't a bad husband. It was just that he was absent-minded and was always thinking about something or other that had no connection at all with what he was supposed to be doing. Like the time he'd been peeling the potatoes for Sunday lunch and he'd suddenly said the Vicar made Polonius sound like a bloody genius and there's been no reason to say that because they hadn't been to church for two Sundays running and she'd wanted to know who Polonius was and he wasn't anyone at all, just some character in a play.

No, you couldn't expect Henry to be practical and she didn't. And of course they'd had their tiffs and disagreements, particularly about the quads. Why couldn't he see they were special? Well, he did, but not in the right way, and calling them 'clones' wasn't helpful. Eva could think of other things he'd said that weren't nice either. And then there was that dreadful business the other night with the cake icer. Goodness only knew what effect that had had on the girls' ideas about men. And that really was the trouble with Henry, he didn't know what romantic meant. Eva got up from the kitchen table and was presently calming her nerves by cleaning out the pantry. She was interrupted at six-thirty by Emmeline in her pyjamas.

'What are you doing?' she asked so unnecessarily that Eva rose to the bait.

'It's perfectly obvious,' she snapped. 'There's no need to ask stupid questions.'

'It wasn't obvious to Einstein,' said Emmeline, using the well-tried technique of luring Eva into a topic about which she knew nothing but which she had to approve.

'What wasn't?'

'That the shortest distance between two points is a straight line.'

'Well it is, isn't it?' said Eva, moving a tin of Epicure marmalade from the shelf with pilchards and tuna fish on it to the jam section where it looked out of place.

'Of course it isn't. Everyone knows that. It's a curve. Where's Daddy?'

'I don't see how . . . What do you mean "Where's Daddy?"' said Eva, completely thrown by this leap from the inconceivable to the immediate.

'I was asking where he is,' said Emmeline. 'He's not in, is he?'

'No, he isn't,' said Eva, torn now between an inclination to give vent to her irritation and the need to keep calm. 'He's out.'

'Where's he gone?' asked Emmeline.

'He hasn't gone anywhere,' said Eva and moved the marmalade back to the pilchard shelf. Tins didn't look right among the jam-jars. 'He spent the night at the Braintrees.'

'I suppose he got drunk again,' said Emmeline. 'Do you think he's an alcoholic?'

Eva clutched a coffee jar dangerously. 'Don't you dare talk about your father like that!' she snapped. 'Of course he has a drink when he comes home at night. Nearly everyone does.

167

It's quite normal and I won't have you saying things about your father.'

'You say things about him,' said Emmeline, 'I heard you call him –'

'Never mind what I say,' said Eva. 'That's quite different.'

'It isn't different,' Emmeline persisted, 'not when you say he's an alcoholic and anyway I was only asking a question and you're always telling us to –'

'Go up to your room at once,' said Eva. 'You're not speaking to me in that fashion. I won't have it.'

Emmeline retreated and Eva slumped down at the kitchen table again. It was really too trying of Henry not to have instilled some sense of respect in the quads. It was always left to her to be the disciplinarian. He should have more authority. She went back into the larder and saw to it that the packets and jars and tins did exactly what she wanted. By the time she had finished she felt a little better. Finally she chased the quads into dressing quickly.

'We'll have to catch the bus this morning,' she announced when they came in to breakfast. 'Daddy has the car and –'

'He hasn't,' said Penelope, 'Mrs Willoughby has.'

Eva, who had been pouring tea, spilt it. 'What did you say?' Penelope looked smug. 'Mrs Willoughby has the car.'

'Mrs Willoughby? Yes, I know I've spilt some tea, Samantha. What do you mean, Penny? She can't have.'

'She has,' said Penelope looking smugger still. 'The milkman told me.'

'The milkman? He must have been mistaken,' said Eva.

'He isn't. He's scared stiff of the Hound of Oakhurst Avenue and he only delivers at the gate and that's where our car is. I went and saw it.'

'And was your father there?'

'No, it was empty.'

Eva put the teapot down unsteadily and tried to think what this meant. If Henry wasn't in the car . . .

'Perhaps Daddy's been eaten by the Hound,' suggested Josephine.

'The Hound doesn't eat people. It just tears their throats out and leaves their bodies on the waste ground at the bottom of the garden,' said Emmeline.

'It doesn't. It only barks. It's quite nice if you give it lamb chops and things,' said Samantha, unintentionally dragging Eva's attention away from the frightful possibility that Henry might in his drunken state have mistaken the house and ended up mauled to death by a Great Dane. And then again with Dr Kores' potion still coursing through his veins ...

Penelope put the idea into words. 'He's more likely to have been eaten by Mrs Willoughby,' she said. 'Mr Gamer says she's sex-mad. I heard him tell Mrs Gamer that when she said she wanted it.'

'Wanted what?' demanded Eva, too stunned by this latest revelation to be concerned about the chops missing from the deep-freeze. She could deal with that matter later.

'The usual thing,' said Penelope with a look of distaste. 'She's always going on about it and Mr Gamer said she was getting just like Mrs Willoughby after Mr Willoughby died on the job and he wasn't going the same way.'

'That's not true,' said Eva in spite of herself.

'It is too,' said Penelope. 'Sammy heard him, didn't you?' Samantha nodded.

'He was in the garage playing with himself like Paul in 3B does and we could hear ever so easily,' she said. 'And he's got lots of *Playboys* in there and books and she came in and said ...'

'I don't want to hear,' said Eva, finally dragging her attention away from this fascinating topic. 'It's time to get your things on. I'll go and fetch the car ...' She stopped. It was clearly one thing to say she was going to fetch the car from a neighbour's front garden, but just as clearly there were snags. If Henry was in Mrs Willoughby's house she'd never be able to live the scandal down. All the same something had to be done and it was a scandal enough already for the neighbours to see the Escort there. With the same determination with which Eva always dealt with embarrassing situations she put on her coat and marched out of the front door. Presently she was sitting in the Escort trying to start it. As usual when she was in a hurry the starter motor churned over and nothing happened. To be exact, something did but not what she had hoped. The front door opened and the Great Dane loped out followed by Mrs Willoughby in a dressing-gown. It was, in Eva's opinion, just the sort of dressing-gown a sex-mad widow would wear. Eva wound down the window to explain that she was just collecting the car and promptly wound it up again. Whatever Samantha's finer feelings might persuade her about the dog, Eva mistrusted it.

'I'm just going to take the girls to school,' she said by way of rather inadequate explanation.

Outside the Great Dane barked and Mrs Willoughby mouthed something that Eva couldn't hear. She wound the window down two inches. 'I said I'm just going to . . .' she began.

Ten minutes later, after an exceedingly acrimonious exchange in which Mrs Willoughby had challenged Eva's right to park in other people's drives and Eva had only been prevented by the presence of the Hound from demanding the right to search the house for her Henry and had been forced to confine herself to a moral critique of the dressing-gown, she drove the quads furiously to school. Only when they had left was Eva thrown back on her own worries. If Henry hadn't left the car at that awful woman's – and she really couldn't see him braving the Great Dane unless he'd been blind drunk and then he wouldn't have held much interest for Mrs Willoughby – someone else must have. Eva drove to the Braintrees and came away even more worried. Betty was sure Peter had said he hadn't seen Henry nearly all week. It was the same at the Tech. Wilt's office was empty and Mrs Bristol was adamant that he hadn't been in since Wednesday. Which left only the prison.

With a terrible sense of foreboding Eva used the phone in Wilt's office. By the time she put it down again panic had set in. Henry not at the prison since Monday? But he taught that murderer every Friday . . . He didn't. He never had. And he wasn't going to teach him on Mondays either now because Mac wasn't a burden on the state, as you might say. But he had given McCullum lessons on Friday. Oh no, he hadn't. Prisoners in that category couldn't have cosy little chats every night of the week, now could they? Yes, he was quite sure. Mr Wilt never came to the prison on Fridays.

Sitting alone in the office, Eva's reactions swung from panic to anger and back again. Henry had been deceiving her. He'd lied. Mavis was right, he had had another woman all the time.

170

But he couldn't have. She'd have known. He couldn't keep a thing like that to himself. He wasn't practical or cunning enough. There'd have been something to tell her like hairs on his coat or lipstick or powder or something. And why? But before she could consider that question Mrs Bristol had poked her head round the door to ask if she'd like a cup of coffee. Eva braced herself to face reality. No one was going to have the satisfaction of seeing her break down.

'No thank you,' she said, 'it's very kind of you but I must be off.' And without allowing Mrs Bristol the opportunity to ask anything more Eva marched out and walked down the stairs with an air of deliberate fortitude. It had almost cracked by the time she had reached the car but she hung on until she had driven back to Oakhurst Avenue. Even then, with all the evidence of treachery around her in the shape of Henry's raincoat and the shoes he'd put out to polish and hadn't and his briefcase in the hall, she refused to give way to self-pity. Something was wrong. Something that proved Henry hadn't walked out on her. If only she could think.

It had something to do with the car. Henry would never have left it in Mrs Willoughby's drive. No, that wasn't it. It was ... She dropped the car keys on the kitchen table and recognized their importance. They'd been in the car when she'd gone to fetch it and among them on the ring was the key to 45 Oakhurst Avenue. Henry had left her without any warning and without leaving a message but he had left the key to the house? Eva didn't believe it. Not for one moment. In that case her instinct had been right and something dreadful had happened to him. Eva put the kettle on and tried to think what to do.

'Listen, Ted,' said Flint. 'You play it the way you want. If you scratch my back I'll scratch yours. No problems. All I'm saying is –'

'If I scratch your back,' said Lingon, 'I won't have a fucking back to be scratched. Not one you'd want to scratch anyway, even if you could find it under some bloody motorway. Now would you mind just getting out of here?'

Inspector Flint settled himself in a chair and looked round the tiny office in the corner of the scruffy garage. Apart from a filing cabinet, the usual nudey calendar, a telephone and the desk, the only thing it contained of any interest to him was Mr Lingon. And in Flint's view Mr Lingon was a thing, a rather nasty thing, a squat, seedy and corrupt thing. 'Business good?' he asked with as little interest as possible. Outside the glass cubicle a mechanic was hosing down a Lingon Coach which claimed to be de luxe.

Mr Lingon grunted and lit a cigarette from the stub of his last one. 'It was till you turned up,' he said. 'Now do me a favour and leave me alone. I don't know what you're on about.'

'Smack,' said Flint.

'Smack? What's that supposed to mean?'

Flint ignored the question. 'How many years did you do last time?' he enquired.

'Oh Jesus,' said Lingon. 'I've been inside. Years ago. But you sods never let up, do you? Not you. A little bit of breaking and entering, someone gets done over two miles away. You name it, who do you come and see? Who's on record? Ted Lingon. Go and put the pressure on him. That's all you buggers can ever think of. No imagination.'

Flint shifted his attention from the mechanic and looked at Mr Lingon. 'Who needs imagination?' he said. 'A nice signed statement, witnessed and everything clean and above-board and no trade. Much better than imagination. Stands up in court.'

'Statement? What statement?' Mr Lingon was looking uneasy now.

'Don't you want to know who from first?'

'All right. Who?'

'Clive Swannell.'

'That old poove? You've got to be joking. He wouldn't –' He stopped suddenly. 'You're trying it on.'

Flint smiled confidently. 'How about the Rocker then?'

Lingon stubbed his cigarette out and said nothing.

'I've got it down in black and white. From the Rocker too. Adds up, doesn't it? Want me to go on?'

'I don't know what you're talking about, Inspector,' said Lingon. 'And now if you don't mind ...'

'Next on the list,' said Flint, savouring the pressure, 'there's

172

a nice little piece down Chingford called Annie Mosgrave. Fond of Pakis, she is. And Chinese threesomes. Sort of cosmopolitan, isn't she? But she writes a nice clean hand and she doesn't want some bloke with a meat cleaver coming round one night.'

'You're fucking lying. That's what you're doing,' said Lingon, shifting in his seat and fumbling with the cigarette packet.

Flint shrugged. 'Of course I am. I mean I would be. Stupid old copper like me's bound to lie. Specially when he's got signed statements locked away. And don't think I'm going to do you the favour of locking you away too, Teddie boy. No, I don't like drug buggers. Not one little bit.' He leant forward and smiled. 'No, I'm just going to attend the inquest. Your inquest, Teddie dear. I might even try to identify you. Difficult of course. It will be, won't it? No feet, no hands, teeth all wrenched out ... that is if there is a head and they haven't burnt it after they've done the rest of what was you over. And they do take their time over it. Nasty really. Remember Chris down in Thurrock. Must have been a terrible way to die, bleeding like that. Tore his –'

'Shut up,' shouted Lingon, now ashen and shaking.

Flint got up. 'For now,' he said. 'But only for now. You don't want to do business: that's fine with me. I'll walk out of here and you won't be seeing me again. No, it'll be some bloke you don't even know comes in. Wants to hire a coach to take a party to Buxton. Money on the table, no hassle and the next fucking thing you know is you'll be wishing it had been me instead of one of Mac's mates with a pair of secateurs.'

'Mac's dead,' said Lingon almost in a whisper.

'So they tell me,' said Flint. 'But Roddie Eaton's still out and about and running things. Funny bloke, Roddie. Likes hurting people, according to my sources, specially when they've got enough knowledge to put him away for life and he can't be certain they won't talk.'

'That's not me,' said Lingon. 'I'm no squealer.'

'Want to bet on it? You'll be screaming your rotten little heart out before they've even begun,' said Flint and opened the door.

But Lingon signalled him back. 'I need guarantees,' he said. 'I got to have them.'

Flint shook his head. 'I told you. I'm a stupid old copper. I'm not selling the Queen's pardon. If you want to come and see me and tell me all about it, I'll be there. Till one o'clock.' He looked at his watch. 'You've got exactly one hour twelve minutes. After that you'd better shut up shop and buy yourself a shotgun. And it won't do you any good picking up that phone because I'll know. And the same if you leave here to use a call-box. And by five past one Roddie will know too.'

Flint walked out past the coach. The rotten little bastard would come. He was sure of that and everything was fitting nicely, or nastily, into place. And Hodge was screwed too. It was all very satisfactory and only went to prove what he had always said, that there was nothing like years of experience. It helped to have a son in prison for drug smuggling too, but Inspector Flint had no intention of mentioning his sources of information to the Superintendent when he made his report.

17

'An infiltrating agent?' boomed the Airforce General commanding Baconheath. 'Why wasn't I informed immediately?'

'Yes sir, that's a good question, sir,' said Glaushof.

'It is not, Major, it's a lousy question. It isn't even a question I should have to ask. I shouldn't have to ask any questions. In fact I'm not here to ask questions. I run a tight ship and I expect my men to answer their own questions.'

'And that's the way I took it, sir,' said Glaushof.

'Took what?'

'Took the situation, sir, faced with an infiltrating agent. I said to myself –'

'I am not interested in what you said to yourself, Major. I am only interested in results,' shouted the General. 'And I want to know what results you've achieved. By my count the results you've achieved amount to the gassing of ten Airforce personnel or their dependants.'

'Eleven, sir,' said Glaushof.

'Eleven? That's even worse.'

'Twelve with the agent Wilt, sir.'

'Then how come you just told me eleven?' demanded the General, toying with the model of a B52.

'Lieutenant Harah, sir, was gassed in the course of the action, sir, and I am proud to report that without his courage in the face of determined resistance by the enemy we could have encountered heavy casualties and possibly a hostage situation. Sir.'

General Belmonte put the B52 down and reached for a bottle of Scotch before remembering he was supposed to be in command of the situation. 'Nobody told me about a resistance situation,' he said rather more amicably.

'No, sir. It didn't seem advisable to issue a press release in the light of current opinion, sir,' said Glaushof. Having managed to avoid the General's questions he was prepared to apply more direct pressure. If there was one thing the Commander hated it was any mention of publicity. Glaushof mentioned it. 'As I see it, sir, the publicity –'

'Jesus, Glaushof,' shouted the General, 'how many times have I got to remind you there is to be no publicity? That is Directive Number One and comes from the highest authority. No publicity, dammit. You think we can defend the Free World against the enemy if we have publicity? I want that clearly understood. No publicity for Chrissake.'

'Understood, General,' said Glaushof. 'Which is why I've ordered a security blackout, a total no-traffic command to all information services. I mean if it got out we'd had an infiltration problem ...'

He paused to allow the General to get his strength back for a further assault on publicity. It came in waves. When the bombardment had finished Glaushof produced his real target. 'If you'll permit me to say so, sir, I think we're going to be faced with an informational problem on the Intelligence side.'

'You do, do you? Well, let me tell you something, Major, and this is an order, a top priority directive order, that there is to be a security blackout, a total no-traffic command to all information services. That is my order, you understand.'

'Yes, sir,' said Glaushof, 'I'll institute it immediately to the Intelligence Command. I mean if we had a leak to the press there ...'

'Major Glaushof, that is an order I have given you. I want it instituted pre-immediate to all services.'

'Including Intelligence, sir?'

'Of course including Intelligence ,' bawled the General. 'Our Intelligence services are the best in the world and I'm not jeopardizing standards of excellence by exposing them to media harassment. Is that clear?'

'Yessir,' said Glaushof and promptly left the office to order an armed guard to be placed on Intelligence HQ and to instruct all personnel to initiate a total no-traffic command. Since no one knew at all precisely what a no-traffic command was the various interpretations put on it ranged from a ban on all vehicles entering or leaving civilian quarters to a full alert on the airfield, the latter having been intermittently in force throughout the night thanks to wafts of Agent Incapacitating Two sounding off the toxic-weapon-detection sensors. By mid-morning the diverse rumours circulating were so manifestly at odds with one another that Glaushof felt safe enough to bawl his wife out over Lieutenant Harah's sexual insubordination before catching up on his sleep. He wanted to be in good shape to interrogate Wilt.

But when, two hours later, he arrived at the guarded room in the hospital Wilt was evidently in no mood to answer questions. 'Why don't you just go away and let me get some sleep?' he said blearily and turned on his side.

Glaushof glared at his back.

'Give him another shot,' he told the doctor.

'Give him another shot of what?'

'Whatever you gave him last night.'

'I wasn't on duty last night,' said the doctor. 'And anyhow who are you to tell me what to give him?'

Glaushof turned his attention away from Wilt's back and glared instead at the doctor. 'I'm Glaushof. Major Glaushof, doctor, just in case you haven't heard of me. And I'm ordering you to give this commie bastard something that'll jerk him out of that bed so I can question him.'

The doctor shrugged. 'If you say so, Major,' he said and studied Wilt's chart. 'What would you recommend?'

'Me?' said Glaushof. 'How the hell would I know? I'm not a goddam doctor.'

'So happens I am,' said the doctor, 'and I'm telling you I am not administering any further medication to this patient right now. The guy's been exposed to a toxic agent –'

He got no further. With a nasty grunt Glaushof shoved him through the doorway into the corridor. 'Now you just listen to me,' he snarled, 'I don't want to hear no crap about medical ethics. What we've got in there is a dangerous enemy agent and he doesn't even come into the category of a patient. Do you read me?'

'Sure,' said the doctor nervously. 'Sure, I read you. Loud and clear. So now will you take your hands off me?'

Glaushof let go of his coat. 'You just get something'll make the bastard talk and fast,' he said. 'We've got a security problem on our hands.'

'I'll say we have,' said the doctor and hurried away from it. Twenty minutes later a thoroughly confused Wilt was bundled out of the hospital building under a blanket and driven at high speed to Glaushof's office where he was placed on a chair. Glaushof had switched on the tape recorder. 'Okay, now you're going to tell us,' he said.

'Tell you what?' asked Wilt.

'Who sent you?' said Glaushof.

Wilt considered the question. As far as he could tell it didn't have much bearing on what was happening to him except that it had nothing whatsoever to do with reality. 'Sent me?' he said. 'Is that what you said?'

'That's what I said.'

'I thought it was,' said Wilt and relapsed into a meditative silence.

'So?' said Glaushof.

'So what?' asked Wilt, in an attempt to restore his morale slightly by combining insult with enquiry.

'So who sent you?'

Wilt sought inspiration in a portrait of President Eisenhower behind Glaushof's head and found a void. 'Sent me?' he said, and regretted it. Glaushof's expression contrasted unpleasantly with that of the late President. 'Nobody sent me.'

'Listen,' said Glaushof, 'this far you've had it easy. Doesn't mean it's going to stay that way. It could get very nasty. Now, are you going to talk or not?'

'I'm perfectly prepared to talk,' said Wilt, 'though I must say your definition of easy isn't mine. I mean being gassed and –'

'You want to hear my definition of nasty?' asked Glaushof.

'No,' said Wilt hastily, 'Certainly not.'

'So talk.'

Wilt swallowed. 'Any particular subject you're interested in?' he enquired.

'Like who your contacts are,' said Glaushof.

'Contacts?' said Wilt.

'Who you're working for. And I don't want to hear any

crap about teaching at the Fenland College Of Arts and Technology. I want to know who set this operation up.'

'Yes,' said Wilt, once more entering a mental maze and losing himself. 'Now when you say "this operation" I wonder if you'd mind ...' He stopped. Glaushof was staring at him even more awfully than before. 'I mean I don't know what you're talking about.'

'You don't, huh?'

'I'm afraid not. I mean if I did –'

Glaushof shook a finger under Wilt's nose. 'A guy could die in here and nobody would know,' he said. 'If you want to go that way you've only to say so.'

'I don't,' said Wilt, trying to focus on the finger as a means of avoiding the prospect of his going any way. 'If you'd just ask me some questions I could answer ...'

Glaushof backed off. 'Let's start with where you got the transmitters,' he said.

'Transmitters?' said Wilt. 'Did you say transmitters? What transmitters?'

'The ones in your car.'

'The ones in my car?' said Wilt. 'Are you sure?'

Glaushof gripped the edge of the desk behind him and thought wistfully about killing people. 'You think you can come in here, into United States territory and –'

'England,' said Wilt stolidly. 'To be precise the United Kingdom of England, Scotland –'

'Jesus,' said Glaushof, 'You little commie bastard, you have the nerve to talk about the Royal Family ...'

'My own country,' said Wilt, finding strength in the assuredness that he was British. It was something he had never really thought much about before. 'And for your information, I am not a communist. Possibly a bastard, though I like to think otherwise. You'd have to ask my mother about that and she's been dead ten years. But definitely not a communist.'

'So what's with the radio transmitters in your car?'

'You said that before and I've no idea what you're talking about. Are you sure you're not mistaking me for someone else.'

'You're named Wilt, aren't you?' shouted Glaushof.

'Yes.'

'And you drive a beat-up Ford, registration plates HPR 791 N, right?'

Wilt nodded. 'I suppose you could put it like that,' he said. 'Though frankly my wife –'

'You saying your wife put those transmitters in your car?'

'Good Lord no. She hasn't a clue about things like that. Anyway, what on earth would she want to do that for?'

'That's what you're here to tell me, boy,' said Glaushof. 'You ain't leaving till you do, you better believe it.'

Wilt looked at him and shook his head. 'I must say I find that difficult,' he muttered. 'I come here to give a lecture on British Culture, such as it is, and the next thing I know I'm in the middle of some sort of raid and there's gas all over the place and I wake up in a bed with doctors sticking needles into me and ...'

He stopped. Glaushof had taken a revolver out of the desk drawer and was loading it. Wilt watched him apprehensively. 'Excuse me,' he said, 'but I'd be grateful if you'd put that ... er ... thing away. I don't know what you've got in mind but I can assure you I am not the person you should be talking to.'

'No? So who should that be, your controller?'

'Controller?' said Wilt.

'Controller,' said Glaushof.

'That's what I thought you said, though to be perfectly honest I still don't see that it helps very much. I don't even know what a controller is.'

'Then you better start inventing one. Like the guy in Moscow who tells you what to do.'

'Look,' said Wilt, desperately trying to get back to some sort of reality which didn't include controllers in Moscow who told him what to do, 'there's obviously been some terrible mistake.'

'Yea, and you made it coming in here with that equipment. I'm going to give you one last chance,' said Glaushof, looking along the barrel of the gun with a significance Wilt found deeply alarming. 'Either you spell it out like it is or ...'

'Quite,' said Wilt. 'Point taken, to use a ghastly expression. What do you want me to tell you?'

180

'The whole deal. How you were recruited, who you contact and where, what information you've given ...'

Wilt stared miserably out the window as the list rolled on. He had never supposed the world to be a particularly sensible place and airbases were particularly nonsensical, but to be taken for a Soviet spy by a lunatic American who played with revolvers was to enter a new realm of insanity. Perhaps that's what had happened. He'd gone clean out of his tiny. No, he hadn't. The gun was proof of some kind of reality, one that was taken for granted by millions of people all over the world but which had somehow never come anywhere near Oakhurst Avenue or the Tech or Ipford. In a sense his own little world with its fundamental beliefs in education and books and, for want of a better word, sensibility, was the unreal one, a dream which no one could ever hope to live in for long. Or at all, if this madman with his cliché talk of guys dying in here and nobody knowing had his way. Wilt turned back and made one last attempt to regain the world he knew.

'All right,' he said, 'if you want the facts I'll give them to you but only with men from MI5 present. As a British subject I demand that right.'

Glaushof snorted. 'Your rights ended the moment you passed that guardhouse,' he said. 'You're telling me what you know. I'm not playing footsy with a lot of suspect faggots from British Intelligence. No way. Now talk.'

'If it's all the same to you I think it would be better written down,' said Wilt, playing for time and trying frantically to think what he could possibly confess. 'I mean, all I need is a pen and some sheets of paper.'

For a moment Glaushof hesitated before deciding that there was something to be said for a confession written out in Wilt's own hand. That way no one could say he'd beaten it out of the little bastard. 'Okay,' he said. 'You can use that table.'

Three hours later Wilt had finished and six pages were covered with his neat and practically illegible handwriting. Glaushof took them and tried to read. 'What you trying to do? Didn't anybody ever teach you to write properly?'

Wilt shook his head wearily. 'If you can't read, take it to someone who can. I've had it,' he said and put his head on his arms on the table. Glaushof looked at his white face and had to agree. He wasn't feeling too good himself. But at least Colonel Urwin and the idiots in Intelligence were going to feel worse. With a fresh surge of energy he went into the office next door, made photocopies of the pages and was presently marching past the guards outside Communications. 'I want transcripts made of these,' he told the head of the typists' pool. 'And absolute security.' Then he sat down and waited.

18

'A warrant? A search warrant for 45 Oakhurst Avenue? You want to apply for a search warrant?' said the Superintendent.

'Yes, sir,' said Inspector Hodge, wondering why it was that what seemed like a perfectly reasonable request to him should need querying quite so repetitively. 'All the evidence indicates the Wilts to be carriers.'

'I'm not sure the magistrate is going to agree,' said the Superintendent. 'Circumstantial evidence is all it amounts to.'

'Nothing circumstantial about Wilt going out to that airbase and giving us the run-around, and I wouldn't say her going to that herb farm was circumstantial either. It's all there in my report.'

'Yes,' said the Superintendent, managing to imbue the word with doubt. 'What's not there is one shred of hard evidence.'

'That's why we need the search, sir,' said Hodge. 'There've got to be traces of the stuff in the house. Stands to reason.'

'If he's what you say he is,' said the Superintendent.

'Look,' said Hodge, 'he knew he was being tailed when he went out to Baconheath. He had to know. Drives around in circles for half an hour when he comes out and gives us the slip –'

'And that's another thing,' interrupted the Superintendent, 'your bugging the blighter's car without authorization. I consider that highly reprehensible. I want that understood clearly right now. Anyway, he may have been drunk.'

'Drunk?' said Hodge, finding it difficult to make the transition between unauthorized bugging being reprehensible, which in his opinion it wasn't, and Wilt being drunk.

'When he came out of Baconheath. Didn't know whether he was coming or going and went round in circles. Those Yanks drink rye. Sickly muck but it goes down so easily you don't notice.'

Inspector Hodge considered the suggestion and rejected it.

'I don't see how a drunk could drive that fast, not on those roads without killing himself. And choosing a route that'd take him out of radio contact.'

The Superintendent studied the report again. It didn't make comfortable reading. On the other hand there was something in what Hodge had said. 'If he wasn't pissed why leave the car outside someone else's house?' he asked but Hodge had already concocted an answer to that one.

'Shows how clever the little bastard is,' he said. 'Not giving anything away, that bloke. He knows we're onto him and he needs an explanation for all that run-around he's given us so he plays pissed.'

'If he's that bloody clever you're not going to find anything in his house and that's for sure,' said the Superintendent and shook his head. 'No, he'd never have the stuff on his own doorstep. He'd have it stored somewhere miles away.'

'He's still got to move it,' said Hodge, 'and that means the car. Look, sir, Wilt's the one who goes to the airbase, he collects the stuff there and on the way home he hands it over to a third party who distributes it. That explains why he took such pains to lose us. There was a whole twenty minutes when we weren't picking up any signals. That could have been when he was offloading.'

'Could have been,' said the Superintendent, impressed in spite of himself. 'Still, that only goes to prove my point. You go for a search warrant for his house you're going to end up with egg all over your face. More important, so am I. So that's out. You'll have to think of some other way.'

Hodge returned to his office and took it out on Sergeant Runk. 'The way they carry on it's a bloody wonder we ever nick any bugger. And you had to go and sign for those fucking transmitters ...'

'You don't think they give them out without being signed for,' said Runk.

'You didn't have to land me in the shit by putting "Authorized by Superintendent Wilkinson for covert surveillance." He loved that.'

'Well, wasn't it? I mean I thought you'd got permission ...'

'Oh no, you didn't. We pulled that stroke in the middle

184

of the night and he'd been home since five. And now we've got to retrieve the bloody things. That's something you can do tonight.'

And having, as he hoped, ensured that the Sergeant would spend the day regretting his indiscretion, the Inspector got up and stared out of the window for inspiration. If he couldn't get a search warrant ... He was still pondering the question when his attention was distracted by a car parked down below. It looked hideously familiar.

The Wilts' Escort. What the hell was it doing outside the police station?

Eva sat in Flint's office and held back the tears. 'I didn't know who else to come to,' she said. 'I've been to the Tech and phoned the prison and Mrs Braintree hasn't seen him and he usually goes there if he's ... well, if he wants a change. But he hasn't been there or the hospital or anywhere else I can think of and I know you don't like him or anything but you are a policeman and you have been ... helpful in the past. And you do know Henry.' She stopped and looked appealingly at the Inspector.

It wasn't a look that held much appeal for Flint and he certainly didn't like the notion that he knew Wilt. He'd tried to understand the blighter, but even at his most optimistic he'd never supposed for one moment that he'd got anywhere near fathoming the horrible depths of Wilt's extraordinary character. The sod came into the category of an enigma made all the more impossible to understand by his choice of Eva as a wife. It was a relationship Flint had always preferred not to think about, but here she was sitting foursquare on a chair in his office telling him, evidently without the slightest regard for his feelings, even as though it were some sort of compliment, that he knew her Henry. 'Has he ever gone off like this before?' he asked, with the private thought that in Wilt's shoes he'd have been off like a flash – before the wedding.

'No, never,' said Eva, 'that's what's so worrying. I know you think he's ... peculiar, but he's really been a good husband.'

'I'm sure he has,' said Flint for want of anything more reassuring to say. 'You don't think he's suffering from amnesia.'

'Amnesia?'

'Loss of memory,' said Flint. 'It hits people who've been under strain. Has anything been happening lately that might have caused him to flip ... to have a nervous breakdown?'

'I can't think of anything in particular,' said Eva, determined to keep any mention of Dr Kores and that dreadful tonic out of the conversation. 'Of course the children get on his nerves sometimes and there was that horrible business at the Tech the other day with that girl dying. Henry was ever so upset. And he's been teaching at the prison ...' She stopped again as she remembered what had been really worrying her. 'He's been teaching a dreadful man called McCullum on Monday evenings and Fridays. That's what he told me anyway, only when I phoned the prison they said he never had.'

'Had what?' asked Flint.

'Never been there on Fridays,' said Eva, tears welling up in her eyes at this proof that Henry, her Henry, had lied to her.

'But he went out every Friday and that's where he told you he was going?'

Eva nodded dumbly and for a moment Flint almost felt sorry for her. A fat middle-aged woman with four bloody tear-away kids who turned the house into a blooming bearpit and she hadn't known what Wilt was up to? Talk about being as thick as two short planks. Well, it was about time she learnt. 'Look, Mrs Wilt, I know this isn't easy to ...' he began but to his amazement Eva was there before him.

'I know what you're going to say,' she interrupted, 'but it isn't true. If it had been another woman why did he leave the car in Mrs Willoughby's?'

'Leave the car in Mrs Willoughby's? Who's Mrs Willoughby?'

'She lives at Number 65, and that's where the car was this morning. I had to go and get it. Why would he want to do that?'

It was on the tip of Flint's tongue to say that's what he'd have done in Wilt's place, dump the car down the road and run like hell, when something else occurred to him.

'You wait here,' he said and left the room. In the corridor he hesitated for a moment and tried to think who to ask. He certainly wasn't approaching Hodge but there was always Sergeant Runk. And Yates could find out for him. He turned into the open-plan office where the Sergeant was sitting at a typewriter.

'Got an enquiry for you, Yates,' he said. 'Have a word with your mate Runk and find out where they tailed Wilt last night. I've got his missus in my office. And don't let him know I'm interested, understand? Just a casual enquiry on your part.' He sat on the edge of the desk while Yates was gone five minutes.

'Right balls-up,' said the Sergeant when he returned. 'They followed the little bugger out to Baconheath airbase with a radio tail. He's in there an hour and a half and comes out driving like a maniac. Runkie reckons Wilt knew they were on to him, the way he drove. Anyway they lost him, and when they did find the car it was outside some house down the road from the Wilts' with a fucking big dog trying to tear the front door down to get at Hodge. That's about the strength of it.'

Flint nodded, and kept his excitement to himself. He'd already done enough to make Hodge look the fucking idiot he was; he'd broken the Bull and Clive Swannell and that little shit Lingon, signed statements and all; and all the time Hodge had been harrying Wilt. So why drop him in it any further?

Why not? The deeper the bugger sank the less he'd be likely to surface. And not only Hodge but Wilt too. The bastard had been the original cause of all Flint's misfortunes and to be able to drag him through the mire together with Hodge was justice at its most perfect. Besides, Flint still had to make the catch with Lingon, so a diversion was just what he needed. And if ever there was a diversion ready to hand it was sitting in his office in the shape of Mrs Eva Wilt. The only problem was how to point her in Hodge's direction without anyone learning what he had done. It was a risk he had to take. He'd better check first, though. Flint went to a phone and looked up the Baconheath number.

'Inspector Hodge speaking,' he said, slurring the name so that it might well have been Squash or Hedge, 'I'm calling from Ipford Police Station in connection with a Mr Wilt ... A Mr Henry Wilt of 45 Oakhurst Avenue, Ipford. I understand he visited you last night.' He waited while someone said he'd check.

It took a long time and another American came on the line. 'You enquiring about someone called Wilt?' he asked.

'That's correct,' said Flint.

'And you say you're police?'

'Yes,' said Flint, noting the hesitancy in the questioner with intense interest.

'If you'll give me your name and the number to call I'll get back to you,' said the American. Flint put the phone down quietly. He'd learnt what he needed and he wasn't having any Yank check his credentials.

He went back to his office and sat down with a calculated sigh. 'I'm afraid you're not going to like what I'm going to tell you, Mrs Wilt,' he said.

Eva didn't. She left the police station white-faced with fury. Not only had Henry lied to her but he'd been cheating her for months and she hadn't had an inkling.

Behind her Flint sat on in his office staring almost ecstatically at a wall-map of Ipford. Henry Wilt, Henry Bloody Wilt, was going to get his comeuppance this time. And he was out there somewhere, somewhere in one of those little streets, holed up with a dolly bird who must have money or he would be back at his job at the Tech.

No, he wouldn't. Not with Eva in pursuit. No wonder the bugger had left the car down the road. If he'd any sense he'd have left town by now. The bloody woman would murder him. Flint smiled at the thought. Now that *would* be poetic justice, no mistake.

'It's more than my life's worth. I mean I'd do it, I'd happily do it but what if it gets out?' said Mr Gamer.

'It won't,' said Hodge, 'I can give you a solemn assurance on that. You won't even know they're there.'

Mr Gamer looked mournfully round the restaurant. He usually had sandwiches and a cup of coffee for lunch and he wasn't sure how well Boneless Chicken Curry washed down with a bottle of Blue Nun was going to agree with him. Still, the Inspector was paying and he could always get some Solvol on the way back to the shop. 'It's not just me either, it's the wife. If you knew what that woman has been through these last twelve months you wouldn't believe me. You really wouldn't.'

'I would,' said Hodge. If it was anything like what he'd been through in the last four days, Mrs Gamer must be a woman with an iron constitution.

'It's even worse in the school holidays,' Mr Gamer continued. 'Those fucking girls . . . I don't usually swear but there's a point where you've got to . . . I mean you can't begin to know how awful they are.' He stopped and looked closely into Hodge's face. 'One of these days they're going to kill someone,' he whispered. 'They bloody near did for me on Tuesday. I'd have been as dead as a dodo if I hadn't been wearing rubber-soled shoes. Stole my statue from the garden and when I went round to get it . . .'

Hodge listened sympathetically. 'Criminal,' he said. 'You should have reported it to us straight away. Even now if you made a formal complaint . . .'

'You think I'd dare? Never. If it meant having them all carted off to prison straightaway I might but it doesn't work like that. They'd come home from court and . . . it doesn't bear thinking about. Take that poor sod down the road, Councillor Birkenshaw. He had his name up in lights on a french letter with a foreskin on it. Floated right down the street it did and then they went and accused him of showing his privates to them. He had a horrible time trying to prove he hadn't. And look where he is. In hospital. No, it's not worth the risk.'

'I can see what you mean,' said Hodge. 'But this way they wouldn't ever find out. All we need is your permission to –'

'I blame the bloody mother,' Mr Gamer went on, encouraged by the Blue Nun and the Inspector's apparent sympathy. 'If she didn't encourage the little bitches to be like boys and take an interest in mechanical things it'd help. But no, they've got to be inventors and geniuses. Mind you, it takes some sort of genius to do what they did to Dickens' lawnmower. Brand new, it was, and God knows what exactly they did to it. Supercharged it with a camping-gas cylinder and altered the gear ratio too so it went like the clappers. And it's not as though he's a well man. Anyway, he started the bloody thing up and before he could stop it was off down the lawn at about eighty and mowing their new carpet in the lounge. Smashed the piano too, come to think of it. They had to call the fire brigade to put it out.'

'Why didn't he sue the parents?' asked Hodge, fascinated in spite of himself.

Mr Gamer sighed. 'You don't understand,' he said. 'You have to live through it to understand. You don't think they admit what they've done? Of course they don't. And who's going to believe old Duckens when he says four ruddy girls that age could change the sprocket on the driveshaft and superglue the clutch? No one. Mind if I help myself.'

Hodge poured another glass. Clearly Mr Gamer was a broken man. 'All right,' he said. 'Now supposing you know nothing about it. Just suppose a man from the Gas Board comes to check the meter –'

'And that's another thing,' said Mr Gamer almost dementedly, 'gas. The bill! Four hundred and fifty fucking pounds for a summer quarter! You don't believe me, do you? I didn't believe it either. Had that meter changed and checked and it still came to the same. I still don't know how they did it. Must have been while we were on holiday. If only I could find out!'

'Look,' said Hodge, 'you let my man install the equipment and you've a very good chance of getting rid of the Wilts for ever. And I mean that. For ever.'

Mr Gamer gazed into his glass and considered this glorious prospect. 'For ever?'

'For ever.'

'Done,' said Mr Gamer.

Later that afternoon Sergeant Runk, feeling distinctly uncomfortable in a Gas Board uniform, and with Mrs Gamer asking pitifully what could possibly be wrong with the chimney because they'd had it lined when the central heating was put in, was up in the roof space. By the time he left he had managed to feed microphones through a gap in the bricks so that they lay hidden among the insulating chips above the Wilts' bedrooms. 45 Oakhurst Avenue had been wired for sound.

19

'I think we've got one hell of a problem, sir,' said the Corporal. 'Major Glaushof ordered me to ditch the car back at the Wilt guy's house and I did. All I can say is those transmitters weren't civilian. I had a good look at them and they were hi-tech British.'

Colonel Urwin, Senior Intelligence Officer USAF Baconheath, pondered the problem by looking coolly at a sporting print on the wall. It wasn't a very good one but its depiction of a fox in the far distance, being chased by a motley crowd of thin, fat, pale, or red-faced Englishmen on horseback, always served to remind him that it was as well not to underestimate the British. Better still, it paid to seem to be one of them. To that end he played golf with an ancient set of clubs and spent his idler moments tracing his family tree in the archives of various universities and the graveyards of Lincolnshire churches. In short, he kept an almost subterranean profile and was proud of the fact that he had on several occasions been taken for a master from one of the better public schools. It was a rôle that suited him exactly and fitted in with his professional creed that discretion was the better part of valour.

'British?' he said thoughtfully. 'That could mean anything or nothing. And you say Major Glaushof has put down a security clamp?'

'General Belmonte's orders, sir.'

The Colonel said nothing. In his opinion the Base Commander's IQ was only slightly higher than that of the egregious Glaushof. Anyone who could call four no trumps without a diamond in his hand had to be a cretin. 'So the situation is that Glaushof has this man Wilt in custody and is presumably torturing him and no one is supposed to know he's here. The operative word being "supposed". Obviously whoever sent him knows he never returned to Ipford.'

'Yes, sir,' said the Corporal. 'And the Major's been trying to get a message on line to Washington.'

'See it's coded garbage,' said the Colonel, 'and get a copy to me.'

'Yes, sir,' said the Corporal and disappeared.

Colonel Urwin looked across at his deputy. 'Seems we could have a hornet's nest,' he said. 'What do you make of it?'

Captain Fortune shrugged. 'Could be any number of options,' he said. 'I don't like the sound of that hardware.'

'Kamikaze,' said the Colonel. 'No one would come in transmitting.'

'Libyans or Khomeini might.'

Colonel Urwin shook his head. 'No way. When they hit they don't signal their punches. They'd come in loaded with explosives first time. So who's scoring?'

'The Brits?'

'That's my line of thinking,' said the Colonel, and wandered across to take a closer look at the sporting print. 'The only question is who are they hunting, Mr Henry Wilt or us?'

'I've checked our records and there's nothing on Wilt. CND in the sixties, otherwise non-political.'

'University?'

'Yes,' said the Captain.

'Which one?'

The Captain consulted the computer file. 'Cambridge. Majored in English.'

'Otherwise, nothing?'

'Nothing we know of. British Intelligence would know.'

'And we're not asking,' said the Colonel, coming to a decision. 'If Glaushof wants to play Lone Ranger with the General's consent he's welcome to the fan-shit. We stay clear and come up with the real answer when it's needed.'

'I still don't like that hardware in the car,' said the Captain.

'And I don't like Glaushof,' said the Colonel. 'I have an idea the Ofreys don't either. Let him dig his own grave.' He paused. 'Is there anyone with any intelligence who knows what really happened, apart from that Corporal?'

'Captain Clodiak filed a complaint against Harah for sexual

harassment. And she's on the list of students attending Wilt's lectures.'

'Right, we'll start digging back into this fiasco there,' said the Colonel.

'Let's get back to this Radek,' said Glaushof, 'I want to know who he is.'

'I've told you, a Czech writer and he's been dead since God knows when so there is no way I could have met him,' said Wilt.

'If you're lying you will. Shortly,' said Glaushof. Having read the transcripts of Wilt's confession that he had been re-cruited by a KGB agent called Yuri Orlov and had a contact man called Karl Radek, Glaushof was now determined to find out exactly what information Wilt had passed to the Russians. Understandably it was proving decidedly harder than getting Wilt to admit he was an agent. Twice Glaushof had used the threat of instant death, but without any useful result. Wilt had asked for time to think and had then come up with H-bombs. 'H-bombs? You've been telling this bastard Radek we've got H-bombs stashed here?'

'Yes,' said Wilt.

'They know that already.'

'That's what Radek said. He said they wanted more than that.'

'So what did you give him, the BBs?'

'BBs?' said Wilt 'You mean airguns?'

'Binary bombs.'

'Never heard of them.'

'Safest nerve-gas bombs in the world,' said Glaushof proudly, 'We could kill every living fucking thing from Moscow to Peking with BBs and they wouldn't even know a thing.'

'Really?' said Wilt. 'I must say I find your definition of safe peculiar. What are the dangerous ones capable of?'

'Shit,' said Glaushof, wishing he was somewhere under-developed like El Salvador and could use more forceful methods. 'You don't talk you're going to regret you ever met me.'

Wilt studied the Major critically. With each unfulfilled threat he was gaining more confidence but it still seemed inadvisable to point out that he already regretted meeting the bloody man. Best to keep things cool. 'I'm only telling you what you want to know,' he said.

'And you didn't give them any other information?'

'I don't know any. Ask the students in my class. They'll tell you I wouldn't know a bomb from a banana.'

'So you say,' muttered Glaushof. He'd already questioned the students and, in the case of Mrs Ofrey, had learnt more about her opinion of him than about Wilt. And Captain Clodiak hadn't been helpful either. The only evidence she'd been able to produce that Wilt was a communist had been his insistence that the National Health Service was a good thing. And so by degrees of inconsequentiality they had come full circle back to this KGB man Radek whom Wilt had claimed was his contact and now said was a Czech writer and dead at that. And with each hour Glaushof's chances of promoting himself were slipping away. There had to be some way of getting the information he needed. He was just wondering if there wasn't some truth drug he could use when he caught sight of the scrotal guard on his desk. 'How come you were wearing this?' he asked.

Wilt looked at the cricket box bitterly. The events of the previous evening seemed strangely distant in these new and more frightening circumstances but there had been a moment when he had supposed the box to be in some way responsible for his predicament. If it hadn't come undone, he wouldn't have been in the loo and ...

'I was having trouble with a hernia,' he said. It seemed a safe explanation.

It wasn't. Glaushof's mind had turned grossly to sex.

Eva's was already there. Ever since she had left Flint she had been obsessed with it. Henry, her Henry, had left her for another woman and an American airbase slut at that. And there could be no doubt about it. Inspector Flint hadn't told her in any nasty way. He'd simply said that Henry had been out to Bacon-heath. He didn't have to say any more. Henry had been going out every Friday night telling her he was going to the prison and all the time ... No, she wasn't going to give way. With

194

a sense of terrible purpose Eva drove to Canton Street. Mavis had been right after all and Mavis had known how to deal with Patrick's infidelities. Best of all, as secretary of Mothers Against The Bomb she hated the Americans at Baconheath. Mavis would know what to do.

Mavis did. But first she had to have her gloat. 'You wouldn't listen to me, Eva,' she said. 'I've always said there was something seedy and deceitful about Henry but you would have it that he was a good, faithful husband. Though after what he tried to do to me the other morning I don't see how ...'

'I'm sorry,' said Eva, 'but I thought that was my fault for going to Dr Kores and giving him that ... Oh dear, you don't think that's what's made him do this?'

'No, I don't,' said Mavis, 'not for one moment. If he's been deceiving you for six months with this woman, Dr Kores' herbal mixture had nothing to do with it. Of course he'll try to use that as an excuse when it comes to the divorce.'

'But I don't want a divorce,' said Eva, 'I just want to lay my hands on that woman.'

'In that case, if you're going to be a sexual helot –'

'A what?' said Eva, appalled at the word.

'Slave, dear,' said Mavis, recognizing her mistake, 'a serf, a skivvy who's just there to do the cooking and cleaning.'

Eva subsided. All she wanted to be was a good wife and mother and bring the girls up to take their rightful place in the technological world. At the top. 'But I don't even know the beastly woman's name,' she said, getting back to practicalities.

Mavis applied her mind to the problem. 'Bill Paisley might know,' she said finally. 'He's been teaching out there and he's at the Open University with Patrick. I'll give him a ring.'

Eva sat on in the kitchen, sunk in apparent lethargy. But underneath she was tensing herself for the confrontation. No matter what Mavis said no one was going to take Henry away from her. The quads were going to have a father and a proper home and the best education Wilt's salary could provide, never mind what people said or how much her own pride was hurt. Pride was a sin and anyway Henry would pay for it.

She was going over in her mind what she would say to him when Mavis returned triumphantly. 'Bill Paisley knows all about it,' she said. 'Apparently Henry has been teaching a class of women British Culture and it doesn't take much imagination to see what's happened.' She looked at a scrap of paper. 'The Development of British Culture and Institutions, Lecture Hall 9. And the person to contact is the Education Officer. He's given me the number to call. If you want me to, I'll do it for you.'

Eva nodded gratefully. 'I'd only lose my temper and get agitated,' she said, 'and you're so good at organizing things.'

Mavis went back to the hall. For the next ten minutes Eva could hear her talking with increasing vehemence. Then the phone was slammed down.

'The nerve of the man,' Mavis said, storming back into the kitchen pale-faced with anger. 'First they wouldn't put me through to him and it was only when I said I was from the Library Service and wanted to speak to the Education Officer about the free supply of books that I got to him. And then it was "No comment, ma'am. I'm sorry but no comment."'

'But you did ask about Henry?' said Eva who couldn't see what the Library Service or the free supply of books could possibly have to do with her problem.

'Of course I did,' snapped Mavis. 'I said Mr Wilt had suggested I contact him about the Library Service supplying books on English Culture and that's when he clammed up.' She paused thoughtfully. 'You know I could almost swear he sounded scared.'

'Scared? Why should he be scared?'

'I don't know. It was when I mentioned the name "Wilt,"' said Mavis. 'But we're going to drive out there now and find out.'

Captain Clodiak sat in Colonel Urwin's office. Unlike the other buildings at Baconheath which had been inherited from the RAF or which resembled prefabricated and sub-economic housing estates, Intelligence Headquarters was strangely at odds with the military nature of the base. It was in fact a large red-brick mansion built at the turn of the century by a retired mining engineer with a taste for theatrical Tudor, an eye to the value of black fen soil and a dislike for the icy

winds that blew from Siberia. As a consequence the house
had a mock baronial hall, oak-panelled walls and a highly
efficient central-heating system and accorded perfectly with
Colonel Urwin's sense of irony. It also set him apart from
the rest of the base and lent weight to his conviction that
military men were dangerous idiots and incapable of speaking
E. B. White's English. What was needed was intelligence, brains
as well as brawn. Captain Clodiak seemed endowed with both.
Colonel Urwin listened to her account of Wilt's capture with
very close interest. It was forcing him to reassess the situation.
'So you're saying that he definitely seemed uneasy right through
the lexture?' he said.

'No question,' said Clodiak. 'He kept squirming behind the
lecturn like he was in pain. And his lecture was all over the
place. Incoherent. Usually he takes off on tangents but he
comes back to the main theme. This time he rambled and
then this bandage came down his leg and he went to pieces.'

The Colonel looked across at Captain Fortune. 'Do we
know anything about the need for bandages?'

'I've checked with the medics and they don't know. The
guy came in gassed and no other sign of injuries.'

'Let's go back from there to previous behaviour. Anything
unusual?' Captain Clodiak shook her head.

'Nothing I noticed. He's hetero, got nice manners, doesn't
make passes, he's probably got some hang-ups, like he's a
depressive. Nothing I'd class as unusual in an Englishman.'

'And yet he was definitely uneasy? And there's no question
about the bandage?'

'None,' said Clodiak.

'Thank you for your help,' said the Colonel. 'If anything
else comes to mind come back to us.' And having seen her
out into the passage he turned to look at the sporting print
for inspiration. 'It begins to sound as though someone's been
leaning on him,' he said finally.

'You can bet your life Glaushof has,' said Fortune. 'A guy
who confesses that easy has to have had some treatment.'

'What's he confessed to? Nothing. Absolute zero.'

'He's admitted being recruited by this Orlov and having a
contact man in a Karl Radek. I wouldn't say that was nothing.'

'The one being a dissident who's doing time in Siberia,' said

197

Urwin, 'and Karl Radek was a Czech writer who died in a Gulag in 1940. Not the easiest man to contact.'

'They could be cover names.'

'Could be. Just. I'd choose something less obviously phoney myself. And why Russians? If they're from the Embassy ... yes, I suppose so. Except that he met quote Orlov unquote in the bus station in Ipford which is outside Soviet embassy staff permitted radius. And where does he meet friend Radek? Every Wednesday afternoon by the bowling green on Midway Park. Every Wednesday same place same time? Out of the question. Our friends from the KGB may play dumb occasionally but not that dumb. Glaushof's been dealt the hand he asked for and that doesn't happen by accident.'

'Leaves Glaushof up shit creek,' said Fortune.

But Colonel Urwin wasn't satisfied. 'Leaves us all there if we don't take care,' he said. 'Let's go through the options again. Wilt's a genuine Russian probe? Out for the reasons given. Someone running a check on our security? Could be some goon in Washington came up with the idea. They've got Shi'ite suicide squads on the brain. Why use an Englishman? They don't tell him his car's being used to make the test more effective. If so why's he panicking during the lecture? That's what I get back to, his behaviour in that lecture hall. That's where I really begin to pick up the scent. Go from there to this "confession" which only an illiterate like Glaushof would believe and the state of Denmark really is beginning to stink to high heaven. And Glaushof's handling it? Not any more, Ed. I'm pulling rank.'

'How? He's got a security blanket from the General.'

'That's where I'm pulling rank,' said the Colonel. 'Old B52 may think he commands this base but I'm going to have to disillusion the old warrior. About a great many things.' He pressed a button on the phone. 'Get me Central Intelligence,' he said.

20

'Orders are no one in,' said the guard on the gate, 'I'm sorry but that's how it is.'

'Look,' said Mavis, 'all we've come to do is speak to the officer in charge of Education. His name is Bluejohn and –'

'Still applies, no one in.'

Mavis took a deep breath and tried to keep calm. 'In that case I'd like to speak to him here,' she said. 'If we can't come in, perhaps he'd be good enough to come out.'

'I can check,' said the guard and went into the gatehouse.

'It's no use,' said Eva, looking at the barrier and the high barbed-wire fence. Behind the barrier a series of drums filled with concrete had been laid out on the roadway to form a zigzag through which vehicles could only wind their way very slowly. 'They're not going to tell us anything.'

'And I want to know why,' said Mavis.

'It might help if you weren't wearing that Mothers Against The Bomb badge,' said Eva.

Mavis took it off reluctantly. 'It's utterly disgusting,' she said. 'This is supposed to be a free country and –'

She was interrupted by the appearance of a lieutenant. He stood in the doorway of the gatehouse and looked at them for a moment before walking over. 'I'm sorry ladies,' he said, 'but we're running a security exercise. It's only temporary so if you come back tomorrow maybe ...'

'Tomorrow is no good,' said Mavis. 'We want to see Mr Bluejohn today. Now if you'll be good enough to telephone him or give him a message, we'd be most obliged.'

'Sure, I can do that,' said the Lieutenant. 'What do you want me to say?'

'Just that Mrs Wilt is here and would like to make some enquiries about her husband, Mr Henry Wilt. He's been teaching a class here on British Culture.'

'Oh him, Mr Wilt? I've heard of him from Captain Clodiak,'

said the Lieutenant, expansively. 'She's been attending his course and she says he's real good. No problem, I'll check with the EO.'

'What did I tell you?' said Mavis as he went back into the guardhouse. '*She* says he's real good. I wonder what your Henry's being so good at now.'

Eva hardly heard. Any lingering doubt that Henry had been deceiving her had gone and she was staring through the wire at the drab houses and prefabricated buildings with the feeling that she was looking ahead into the drabness and barren years of her future life. Henry had run off with some woman, perhaps this same Captain Clodiak, and she was going to be left to bring up the quads on her own and be poor and known as a ... A one-parent family? But there was no family without a father and where was she going to get the money to keep the girls at school? She'd have to go on Social Security and queue up with all those other women ... She wouldn't. She'd go out to work. She'd do anything to make up for ... The images in her mind, images of emptiness and of her own fortitude, were interrupted by the return of the Lieutenant.

His manner had changed. 'I'm sorry,' he said abruptly, 'there's been a mistake. I've got to tell you that. Now if you'll move off. We've got this security exercise on.'

'Mistake? What mistake?' said Mavis, reacting to his brusqueness with all her own pent-up hatred. 'You said Mrs Wilt's husband ...'

'I didn't say anything,' said the Lieutenant and, turning on his heel, ordered the barrier to be lifted to allow a truck to come through.

'Well!' said Mavis furiously. 'Of all the nerve! I've never heard such a bare-faced lie in my life. You heard what he said just a moment ago and now –'

But Eva was moving forward with a new determination. Henry was in the camp. She knew that now. She'd seen the look on the Lieutenant's face, the changed look, the blankness that had been in such contrast to his previous manner, and she'd known. Without thinking she moved into the drabness of life without Henry, into that desert beyond the barrier. She was going to find him and have it out with him. A figure got in her way and tried to stop her. There was a flurry of arms and he fell. Three more men, only figures in her mind, and she was being held and dragged back. From somewhere seemingly distant she heard Mavis shout, 'Go limp. Go limp.' Eva went limp and the next moment she was lying on the ground with two men beside her and a third dragging on an arm.

Three minutes later, covered with dust and with the heels of her shoes scuffed and her tights torn, she was dragged beneath the barrier and dumped on the road. And during that time she had uttered no sound other than to pant with exertion. She sat there for a moment and then got to her knees and looked back into the camp with an intensity that was more dangerous in its implications than her brief battle with the guards.

'Lady, you got no right to come in here. You're just asking for trouble,' said the Lieutenant. Eva said nothing. She helped herself up from the kneeling position and walked back to the car.

'Eva dear, are you all right?' asked Mavis.

Eva nodded. 'Just take me home,' she said. For once Mavis had nothing to say. Eva's strength of purpose needed no words.

Wilt's did. With time running out on him, Glaushof had resorted to a new form of interrogation. Unable to use more forceful methods he had decided on what he considered to be the subtle approach. Since it involved the collaboration of Mrs Glaushof clad in garments Glaushof and possibly even Lieutenant Harah had found so alluring – jackboots, suspender belts and teatless bras figured high in Glaushof's compendium of erotica – Wilt, who had been hustled yet again into a car and driven to the Glaushof's house, found himself suddenly lying on a heart-shaped bed clad in the hospital gown and confronted by an apparition in black, red and several shades of pink. The boots were black, the suspender belt and panties were red and the bra was black fringed with pink. The rest of Mrs Glaushof was, thanks to her frequent use of a sun lamp, mostly brown and definitely drunk. Ever since Glausie, as she had once called him, had bawled her out for sharing her mixed charms with those of Lieutenant Harah she had been hitting the Scotch. She had also hit a bottle of Chanel

No 5 or had lathered herself with the stuff. Wilt couldn't
decide which. And didn't want to. It was enough to be
cloistered (the word seemed singularly inappropriate in the
circumstances) in a room with an alcoholic prostitute who
told him to call her Mona.

'What?' said Wilt.

'Mona, baby,' said Mrs Glaushof, breathing whisky into
his face and fondling his cheek.

'I am not your baby,' said Wilt.

'Oh, but you are, honey. You're just what momma needed.'

'And you're not my mother,' said Wilt, wishing the hell the
woman was. She'd have been dead ten years. Mrs Glaushof's
hand strayed down his body. 'Shit,' said Wilt. That damned
poison was beginning to work again.

'That's better, baby,' Mrs Glaushof whispered as Wilt
stiffened. 'You and me's going to have the best of times.'

'You and I,' said Wilt, frantically trying to find some relief
in correct syntax, 'and you may consider – Ouch!'

'Is baby going to be good to momma now?' asked Mrs
Glaushof, sliding her tongue between his lips. Wilt tried to
focus on her eyes and found it impossible. He also found it
impossible to reply without unclenching his teeth and Mrs
Glaushof's reptilian tongue, tasting as it did of alcohol and
tobacco, was so busily exploring his gums that any move that
might allow it to go any further seemed inadvisable. For one
insane moment it crossed his mind to bite the filthy thing but
considering what she had in her hand the consequences didn't
bear thinking about. Instead he tried to concentrate on less
tangible things. What the hell was he doing lying on a quilted
bed with a sex-mad woman clutching his balls when only half
an hour ago a homicidal maniac had been threatening to
plaster his brains on the ceiling with a .38 unless he talked
about binary bombs? It didn't make even the vaguest sense
but before he could arrive at any sane conclusion Mrs
Glaushof had relinquished her probe.

'Baby's steaming me up,' she moaned and promptly bit his
neck.

'That's as maybe,' said Wilt, making a mental note to brush
his teeth as soon as possible. 'The fact of the matter is that
I . . .'

202

Mrs Glaushof pinched his cheeks. 'Rosebud,' she whimpered.

'Wosebud?' said Wilt with difficulty.

'Your mouth's like a wosebud,' said Mrs Glaushof, digging her nails still further into his cheeks, 'a lovely wosebud.'

'It doethn't tathte like one,' said Wilt and instantly regretted it. Mrs Glaushof had hoisted herself up him and he was facing a nipple fringed with pink lace.

'Suck momma,' said Mrs Glaushof.

'Thod off,' said Wilt. Further comment was stifled by the nipple and Mrs Glaushof's breast which was worming around on his face. As Mrs Glaushof pressed down on him Wilt fought for breath.

In the bathroom next door Glaushof was having the same problem. Staring through the two-way mirror he'd installed to watch Mrs Glaushof putting on the regalia of his fantasies while he bathed, he had begun to regret his new tactics. Subtle they weren't. The bloody woman had clearly gone clean over the top. Glaushof's own patriotism had led him to suppose that his wife would do her duty by cosying up to a Russian spy, but he hadn't expected her to screw the bastard. What was even worse was that she was so obviously enjoying the process.

Glaushof wasn't. Gritting his teeth he stared lividly through the mirror and tried not to think about Lieutenant Harah. It didn't help. In the end, driven by the thought that the Lieutenant had lain on that same bed while Mona gave him the works he was now witnessing, Glaushof charged out of the bathroom. 'For Chrissake,' he yelled from the landing, 'I told you to soften the son of a bitch up, not turn him on.'

'So what's wrong?' said Mrs Glaushof, in the process of changing nipples. 'You think I don't know what I'm doing?'

'I'm buggered if I do,' squawked Wilt, taking the opportunity to get some air. Mrs Glaushof scrambled off him and headed for the door.

'No, I don't,' said Glaushof, 'I think you're –'

'Screw off,' screamed Mrs Glaushof. 'This guy's got a hard-on for me.'

'I can see that,' said Glaushof morosely, 'and if you think that's softening him up you're fucking crazy.'

Mrs Glaushof divested herself of a boot. 'Crazy, am I?' she
bawled and hurled the boot at his head with surprising
accuracy. 'So what's an old man like you know about crazy?
You couldn't get it up if I didn't wear fucking Nazi jackboots.'
The second boot hurtled through the door. 'I got to dress up
like I'm fucking Hitler in drag before you're anywhere near
a man and that ain't saying much. Like this guy's got a prick
like the Washington Monument compared to yours.'

'Listen,' shouted Glaushof, 'lay off my prick. That's a
commie agent you got in there. He's dangerous!'

'I'll say,' said Mrs Glaushof now liberating herself from the
bra. 'Is he ever.'

'No, I'm not,' said Wilt, lurching away from the bed. Mrs
Glaushof staggered out of the suspender belt.

'I'm telling you you could get yourself deep in trouble,'
Glaushof called. He'd taken refuge from any further missiles
round the corner.

'Deep in it is,' Mrs Glaushof shouted back and slammed
the door and locked it. Before Wilt could move she had tossed
the key out of the window and was heading for him. 'Red
Square here I come.'

'I'm not Red Square. I don't know why everyone keeps
thinking –' Wilt began, but Mrs Glaushof wasn't into thought.
With an agility that took him by complete surprise she threw
him back on to the bed and knelt over him.

'Choo choo, baby,' she moaned and this time there was no
mistaking her meaning. Faced with this horrible prospect Wilt
lived up to Glaushof's warning that he was a dangerous man
and sank his teeth into her thigh. In the bathroom Glaushof
almost cheered.

'Countermand my orders? Countermand my orders? You're
telling me to countermand my orders?' said General Belmonte
dropping several decibels in his disbelief. 'We have an enemy
agent infiltration situation with possible bombing implications
and you're telling me to countermand my orders?'

'Asking, General,' said the Colonel gently. 'I am simply
saying that the political consequences could be disastrous.'

'Having my base blown apart by a fucking fanatic is
disastrous too and I'm not standing for it,' said the General.

'No, sir, I am not having a body count of thousands of innocent American service personnel and their dependants on my conscience. Major Glaushof's handling of the situation has been absolutely correct. No one knows we've got this bastard and he can beat the shit out of him for all I care. I am not –'

'Correction, sir,' interrupted the Colonel, 'a number of people know we're holding this man. The British police called in enquiring about him. And a woman claiming to be his wife has already had to be ejected at the main gate. Now if you want the media to get hold –'

'The media?' bellowed the General. 'Don't mention that fucking word in my presence. I have given Glaushof a Directive Number One, Toppest Priority, there's to be no media intervention and I am not countermanding that order.'

'I am not suggesting you do. What I am saying is that the way Glaushof is handling the situation we could find ourselves in the middle of a media onslaught that would get world coverage.'

'Shit,' said the General, cringing at the prospect. In his mind's eye he could already see the television cameras mounted on trucks outside the base. There might even be women. He pulled his mind back from this vision of hell. 'What's wrong with the way Glaushof's handling it?'

'Too heavy,' said the Colonel. 'The security clamp-down's drawing attention to the fact that we do have a problem. That's one. We should cool it all off by acting normal. Two is we are presently holding a British subject and if you've given the Major permission to beat the shit out of him I imagine that's just what –'

'I didn't give him permission to do anything like that, I gave him . . . well, I guess I said he could interrogate him and . . .' He paused and tried the comradely approach. 'Hell, Joe, Glaushof may be a shitass but he has got him to confess he's a commie agent. You've got to hand it to him.'

'That confession's a dummy. I've checked it out and had negative affirmation,' said the Colonel, lapsing into the General's jargon to soften the blow.

'Negative affirmation,' said the General, evidently impressed. 'That's serious. I had no idea.'

'Exactly, sir. That's why I'm asking for an immediate de-escalation of the security directive intelligencewise. I also want this man Wilt handed over to my authority for proper questioning.'

General Belmonte considered the request almost rationally. 'If he isn't Moscow-based, what is he?'

'That's what Central Intelligence intend to find out,' said the Colonel.

Ten minutes later Colonel Urwin left the Airbase Control Centre well satisfied. The General had ordered a security stand-down and Glaushof had been relieved of his custody right to the prisoner.

Theoretically.

In practice getting Wilt out of the Glaushof's house proved rather more awkward. Having visited the Security building and learnt that Wilt had been taken off, still apparently unharmed, to be interrogated at Glaushof's house, the Colonel had driven there with two Sergeants only to realize that 'unharmed' no longer applied. Ghastly noises were emanating from upstairs.

'Sounds like someone's having themselves a whole heap of fun,' said one of the Sergeants as Mrs Glaushof threatened to castrate some horny bastard just as soon as she stopped bleeding to death and why didn't some other cocksucker open the fucking door so she could get out. In the background Glaushof could be heard telling her plaintively to keep her cool, he'd get the door undone, she didn't have to shoot the lock off and would she stop loading that fucking revolver.

Mrs Glaushof replied she didn't intend shooting the fucking lock off, she had other fucking objects in fucking mind, like him and that fucking commie agent who'd bit her and they weren't going to live to tell the tale, not once she'd got that magazine fucking loaded and why didn't shells go in the way they were fucking supposed to? For an instant Wilt's face appeared at the window, only to vanish as a bedside lamp complete with a huge lampshade smashed through the glass and hung upside-down from its cord.

Colonel Urwin studied the thing with horror. Mrs Glaushof's language was foul enough but the shade, covered with a collage of sado-masochistic images cut from magazines, pictures of kittens in baskets and puppy dogs, not to mention several crimson hearts and flowers, was aesthetically so disgusting that it almost unnerved him. The action had the opposite effect on Glaushof. Less concerned about the likelihood of his drunken wife murdering a Russian spy with a .38 she had been trying to load with what he hoped was 9 mm. ammunition than with the prospect of having his entire house torn apart and its peculiar contents revealed to the neighbours he left the comparative safety of the bathroom and charged the bedroom door. His timing was bad. Having foiled any hope Wilt might have held of escaping by the window Mrs Glaushof had finally loaded the revolver and pulled the trigger. The shot passed through the door, Glaushof's shoulder, and one of the tubes in the hamster's complicated plastic burrow on the staircase wall before embedding in the tufted carpet.

'Jesus Christ,' screamed Glaushof, 'you meant it! You really meant it.'

'What's that?' said Mrs Glaushof, almost as surprised by the consequences of simply pulling the trigger, though definitely less concerned. 'What you say?'

'Oh God,' moaned Glaushof, now slumped to the floor.

'You think I can't shoot the fucking lock off?' Mrs Glaushof enquired. 'You think that? You think I can't?'

'No,' yelled Glaushof. 'No, I don't think that. Jesus, I'm dying.'

'Hypochondriac,' Mrs Glaushof shouted back, evidently paying off an old domestic score. 'Stand back, I'm coming out.'

'For fuck's sake,' squealed Glaushof, eyeing the hole she'd already made in the door near one of the hinges, 'don't aim at the lock.'

'Why not?' Mrs Glaushof demanded.

It wasn't a question Glaushof was prepared to answer. In one final attempt to escape the consequences of her next fusillade he rolled sideways and hit the stairs. By the time he'd crashed to the bottom even Mrs Glaushof was concerned.

'Are you OK, Glausie?' she asked and simultaneously pulled the trigger. As the second shot punched a hole in a Liberace-style bean bag, Wilt acted. In the knowledge that her next shot might possibly do to him what it had already done to

207

Glaushof and the bag, he picked up a pink furbelowed stool and slammed it down on her head.

'Macho man,' grunted Mrs Glaushof, inappropriate to the end, and slid to the floor. For a moment Wilt hesitated. If Glaushof were still alive, and by the sound of breaking glass downstairs it seemed as though he was, there was no point in trying to break the door down. Wilt crossed to the window.

'Freeze!' shouted a man down below. Wilt froze. He was staring down at five uniformed men crouched behind handguns. And this time there was no question what they were aiming at.

21

'Logic dictates,' said Mr Gosdyke, 'that we should look at this problem rationally. Now I know that's difficult but until we have definite proof that your husband is being held at Bacon-heath against his will there really isn't any legal action we can take. You do see that?'

Eva gazed into the solicitor's face and saw only that she was wasting time. It had been Mavis' idea that she should consult Mr Gosdyke before she did anything hasty. Eva knew what 'hasty' meant. It meant being afraid of taking real risks and doing something effective.

'After all,' Mavis had said, as they drove back, 'you may be able to apply for a court order or habeas corpus or something. It's best to find out.'

But she didn't need to find out. She'd known all along that Mr Gosdyke wouldn't believe her and would talk about proof and logic. As if life was logical. Eva didn't even know what the word meant, except that it always produced in her mind the image of a railway line with a train running along it with no way of getting off it and going across fields and open countryside like a horse. And anyway when you did reach a station you still had to walk to wherever you really wanted to go. That wasn't the way life worked or people behaved when things were really desperate. It wasn't even the way the Law worked with people being sent to prison when they were old and absent-minded like Mrs Reeman who had walked out of the supermarket without paying for a jar of pickled onions and she never ate pickles. Eva knew that because she'd helped with Meals on Wheels and the old lady had said she never touched vinegar. No, the real reason had been that she'd had a pekinese called Pickles and he'd died a month before. But the Law hadn't seen that, any more than Mr Gosdyke could understand that she already had the proof that Henry was in the airbase because he hadn't been there when the officer's manner had changed so suddenly.

'So there's nothing you can do?' she said and got up.

'Not unless we can obtain proof that your husband really is being held against ...' But Eva was already through the door and had cut out the sounds of those ineffectual words. She went down the stairs and out into the street and found Mavis waiting for her in the Mombasa Coffee House.

'Well, did he have any advice?' asked Mavis.

'No,' said Eva, 'he just said there was nothing he could do without proof.'

'Perhaps Henry'll telephone you tonight. Now that he knows you've been out there and they must have told him ...'

Eva shook her head. 'Why should they have told him?'

'Look, Eva, I've been thinking,' said Mavis, 'Henry's been deceiving you for six months. Now I know what you're going to say but you can't get away from it.'

'He hasn't been deceiving me the way you mean,' said Eva. 'I know that.'

Mavis sighed. It was so difficult to make Eva understand that men were all the same, even a sexually subnormal one like Wilt. 'He's been going out to Baconheath every Friday evening and all that time he's been telling you he's got this prison job. You've got to admit that, haven't you?'

'I suppose so,' said Eva, and ordered tea. She wasn't in the mood for anything foreign like coffee. Americans drank coffee.

'The question you have to ask yourself is why didn't he tell you where he was going?'

'Because he didn't want me to know,' said Eva.

'And why didn't he want you to know?'

Eva said nothing.

'Because he was doing something you wouldn't like. And we all know what men don't think their wives would like to know, don't we?'

'I know Henry,' said Eva.

'Of course you do but we none of us know what even those closest to us are really like.'

'You knew all about Patrick's chasing other women,' said Eva, fighting back. 'You were always going on about his being

210

unfaithful. That's why you got those steroid pills from that beastly Dr Kores and now all he does is sit in front of the telly.'

'Yes,' said Mavis, cursing herself for ever mentioning the fact. 'All right, but you said Henry was undersexed. Anyway that only goes to prove my point. I don't know what Dr Kores put in the mixture she gave you ...'

'Flies,' said Eva.

'Flies?'

'Spanish flies. That's what Henry called them. He said they could have killed him.'

'But they didn't,' said Mavis. 'What I'm trying to get across is that the reason he wasn't performing adequately may have been –'

'He's not a dog, you know,' said Eva.

'What's that got to do with it?'

'Performing. You talk as though he were something in a circus.'

'You know perfectly well what I meant.'

They were interrupted by the arrival of the tea. 'All I'm saying,' Mavis continued when the waitress had left, 'is that what you took for Henry's being undersexed –'

'I said he wasn't very active. That's what I said,' said Eva.

Mavis stirred her coffee and tried to keep calm. 'He may not have wanted you, dear,' she said finally, 'because for the last six months he has been spending every Friday night in bed with some American servicewoman at that airbase. That's what I've been trying to tell you.'

'If that had been the case,' said Eva, bridling, 'I don't see how he could have come home at ten thirty, not if he was teaching as well. He never left the house until nearly seven and it takes at least three-quarters of an hour to drive out there. Two three-quarters make ...'

'One and a half hours,' snapped Mavis. 'That doesn't prove anything. He could have had a class of one.'

'Of one?'

'One person, Eva dear.'

'They're not allowed to have only one person in a class,' said Eva. 'Not at the Tech. If they don't have ten ...'

'Well, Baconheath may be different,' said Mavis, 'and

anyway they fiddle these things. My bet is that Henry's teaching consisted of taking off his clothes and –'

'Which just shows how much you know about him,' interrupted Eva. 'Henry taking his clothes off in front of another woman! That'll be the day. He's too shy.'

'Shy?' said Mavis, and was about to say that he hadn't been so shy with her the other morning. But the dangerous look had come back on to Eva's face and she thought better of it. It was still there ten minutes later when they went out to car park to fetch the quads from school.

'Okay, let's take it from there,' said Colonel Urwin. 'You say you didn't shoot Major Glaushof.'

'Of course I didn't,' said Wilt. 'What would I do a thing like that for? She was trying to blow the lock off the door.'

'That's not the version I've got here,' said the Colonel, referring to a file on the desk in front of him, 'according to which you attempted to rape Mrs Glaushof orally and when she refused to co-operate you bit her leg. Major Glaushof tried to intervene by breaking the door down and you shot him through it.'

'Rape her orally?' said Wilt, 'what the hell does that mean?'

'I prefer not to think,' said the Colonel with a shudder.

'Listen,' said Wilt, 'if anyone was being raped orally I was. I don't know if you've ever been in close proximity to that woman's muff but I have and I can tell you the only way out was to bite the bitch.'

Colonel Urwin tried to erase this awful image. His security classification rated him 'highly heterosexual' but there were limits and Mrs Glaushof's muff was unquestionably off them. 'That doesn't exactly gel with your statement that she was attempting to escape from the room by blowing the lock off with a .38, does it? Would you mind explaining what she was doing that for?'

'I told you she was trying ... well, I've told you what she was trying to do and as a way out I bit her. That's when she got mad and went for the gun.'

'It still doesn't explain why the door was locked and she

212

had to blow the lock. Are you saying Major Glaushof had locked you in?'

'She'd thrown the fucking key out of the window,' said Wilt wearily, 'and if you don't believe me go and look for the thing outside.'

'Because she found you so sexually desirable she wanted to rape you ... orally?' said the Colonel.

'Because she was drunk.'

Colonel Urwin got up and consulted the sporting print for inspiration. It wasn't easy to find. About the only thing that rang true was that Glaushof's ghastly wife had been drunk. 'What I still don't understand is why you were there in the first place.'

'You think I do?' said Wilt. 'I came out here on Friday night to give a lecture and the next thing I know I've been gassed, injected, dressed up like something that's going to be operated on, driven all over the place with a fucking blanket over my head and asked insane questions about radio transformers in my car –'

'Transmitters,' said the Colonel.

'Whatever,' said Wilt. 'And told if I don't confess to being a Russian spy or a fanatical raving Shi'ite Muslim I'm going to have my brains plastered all over the ceiling. And that's just for starters. After that I'm in a horrible bedroom with a woman dressed up like a prostitute who hurls keys out of the window and shoves her dugs in my mouth and then threatens to suffocate me with her cunt. And you're asking me for an explanation?' He sank back in his chair and sighed hopelessly.

'That still doesn't –'

'Oh, for God's sake,' said Wilt. 'If you want insanity explained go and ask that homicidal maniac Major. I've had a bellyful.'

The Colonel got up and went out the door. 'What do you make of him?' he asked Captain Fortune who had been sitting with a technician recording the interview.

'I've got to say he convinces me,' said Fortune. 'That Mona Glaushof would screw a fucking skunk if there weren't nothing better to hand.'

'I'll say,' said the technician. 'She's been humping Lieutenant

Harah like he's a human vibrator. The guy's been taking mega-vitamins to keep up.'

'Dear God,' said the Colonel, 'and Glaushof's in charge of security. What's he doing letting Mona Messalina loose on this one for?'

'Got a two-way mirror in the bathroom,' said the Captain. 'Could be he gets his thrills through it.'

'A two-way mirror in the bathroom? The bastard's got to be sick watching his wife screwing a guy he thinks is a Russian agent.'

'Maybe he thought the Russkies have got a different technique. Something he could learn,' said the technician.

'I want a check run on that key outside the house,' said the Colonel and went out into the passage.

'Well?' he asked.

'Nothing fits,' said the Captain. 'That corporal in Electronics is no fool. He's certain the equipment he saw in the car was British classified. Definitely non-Russian. No record of it ever being used by anyone else.'

'Are you suggesting he was under surveillance by British Security?'

'It's a possibility.'

'It would be if he hadn't demanded MI5 attendance the moment Glaushof started putting the heat on,' said Urwin. 'Have you ever heard of a Moscow agent calling for British Intelligence when he's been blown? I haven't.'

'So we go back to your theory that the Brits were running an exercise on base security systems. About the only thing that adds up.'

'Nothing adds up for me. If it had been a routine check they'd have come to his rescue by now. And why has he clammed? No point in sweating it out. Against that we've got those transmitters and the fact that Clodiak says he was nervous and agitated all through the lecture. That indicates he's no expert and I don't believe he ever knew his car was tagged. Where's the sense?'

'You want me to question him?' asked the Captain.

'No, I'll go on. Just keep the tape running. We're going to need some help in this.'

He went back into his office and found Wilt lying on the

couch fast asleep. 'Just a few more questions, Mr Wilt,' he said. Wilt stared blearily up at him and sat up.

'What questions?'

The Colonel took a bottle from a cupboard. 'Care for a Scotch?'

'I'd care to go home,' said Wilt.

22

In Ipford Police Station Inspector Flint was savouring his triumph. 'It's all there, sir,' he told the Superintendent, indicating a pile of folders on the desk. 'And it's local. Swannell made the contact on a skiing trip to Switzerland. Nice clean place, Switzerland, and of course he says he was the one who was approached by this Italian. Threatened him, he says, and of course our Clive's a nervous bloke as you know.'

'Could have fooled me,' said the Superintendent. 'We nearly did the bugger for attempted murder three years ago. Got away because the bloke he scarred wouldn't press charges.'

'I was being ironical, sir,' said Flint. 'Just saying his story for him.'

'Go on. How did it work?'

'Simple really,' continued Flint, 'nothing too complicated. First they had to have a courier who didn't know what he was doing. So they put the frighteners on Ted Lingon. Threaten him with a nitric acid facial if he doesn't co-operate with his coach tours to the continent. Or so he claims. Anyway he's got a regular run to the Black Forest with overnight stops. The stuff's loaded aboard at Heidelberg without the driver knowing, comes through to Ostend and the night ferry to Dover and halfway across one of the crew dumps the muck over the side. Always on the night run so no one sees. Picked up by a friend of Annie Mosgrave's who happens to be in his floating gin palace nearby and ...'

'Hang on a minute,' said the Superintendent. 'How the hell would anyone find a package of heroin in mid-Channel at night?'

'The same way Hodge has been keeping tabs on Wilt. The muck's in a bloody great suitcase with buoyancy and a radio signal that comes on the moment it hits the water. Bloke beams in on it, hauls it aboard and brings it round to a marker buoy in the Estuary and leaves it there for a frogman to pick up when the gin palace is back in the marina.'

'Seems a risky way of going about things,' said the Superintendent, 'I wouldn't trust tides and currents with that amount of money involved.'

'Oh, they did enough practice runs to feel safe and tying it to the chain of the marker buoy made that part easy,' said Flint. 'And after that it was split three ways with the Hong Kong Charlies handling the London end and Roddie Eaton fixing this area and Edinburgh.'

The Superintendent studied his fingernails and considered the implications of Flint's discoveries. On the whole they seemed entirely satisfactory, but he had a nasty feeling that the Inspector's methods might not look too good in court. In fact it was best not to dwell on them. Defending counsel could be relied on to spell them out in detail to the jury. Threats to prisoners in gaol, murder charges that were never brought ... On the other hand if Flint had succeeded, that idiot Hodge would be scuppered. That was worth a great many risks.

'Are you quite certain Swannell and the rest haven't been spinning you a yarn?' he asked. 'I mean I'm not doubting you or anything but if we go ahead now and they retract those statements in court, which they will do –'

'I'm not relying on their statements,' said Flint. 'There's hard evidence. I think when the search warrants are issued we'll find enough heroin and Embalming Fluid on their premises and clothing to satisfy Forensic. They've got to have spilt some when they were splitting the packages, haven't they?'

The Superintendent didn't answer. There were some things he preferred not to know and Flint's actions were too dubious for comfort. Still if the Inspector had broken a drug ring the Chief Constable and the Home Secretary would be well satisfied, and with crime organized the way it was nowadays there was no point in being too scrupulous. 'All right,' he said finally, 'I'll apply for the warrants.'

'Thank you, sir,' said Flint and turned to go. But the Superintendent stopped him.

'About Inspector Hodge,' he said. 'I take it he's been following a different line of investigation.'

'American airbases,' said Flint. 'He's got it into his head that's where the stuff's been coming in.'

'In that case we'd better call him off.'

But Flint had other plans in mind. 'If I might make a suggestion, sir,' he said, 'the fact that the Drug Squad is pointing in the wrong direction has its advantages. I mean Hodge has drawn attention away from our investigations and it would be a pity to put up a warning signal until we've made our arrests. In fact it might help to encourage him a bit.'

The Superintendent looked at him doubtfully. The last thing the Head of the Drug Squad needed was encouraging. He was demented enough already. On the other hand ...

'And how exactly is he to be encouraged?' he asked.

'I suppose you could say the Chief Constable was looking for an early arrest,' said Flint. 'It's the truth after all.'

'I suppose there's that to it,' said the Superintendent wearily. 'All right, but you'd better be right with your own cases.'

'I will be, sir,' said Flint and left the room. He went down to the car pool where Sergeant Yates was waiting.

'The warrants are all settled,' he said. 'Have you got the stuff?'

Sergeant Yates nodded and indicated a plastic packet on the back seat. 'Couldn't get a lot,' he said, 'Runkie reckoned we'd no right to it. I had to tell him it was needed for a lab check.'

'Which it will be,' said Flint. 'And it's all the same batch?'

'It's that all right.'

'No problem then,' said Flint as they drove out, 'we'll look at Lingon's coach first and then Swannell's boat and the back garden and leave enough for Forensic to pick up.'

'What about Roddie Eaton?'

Flint took a pair of cotton gloves from his pocket. 'I thought we'd leave these in his dustbin,' he said. 'We'll use them on the coach first. No need to bother going to Annie's. There will be something there anyway, and besides, the rest of them will try to get lighter sentences by pointing the finger at her. All we need is three of them as guilty as sin and facing twenty years and they'll drop everyone else in the shit with them.'

'Bloody awful way of going about police work,' said Yates after a pause. 'Planting evidence and all.'

'Oh, I don't know,' said Flint. 'We know they're traffickers, they know it, and all we're doing is giving them a bit of their own medicine. Homeopathic, I call it.'

That wasn't the way Inspector Hodge would have described his work. His obsessive interest in the Wilts' extraordinary domestic activities had been alarmingly aggravated by the noises coming from the listening devices installed in the roof space. The quads were to blame. Driven up to their rooms by Eva who wanted them out of the way so that she could think what to do about Henry, they had taken revenge by playing long-playing records of Heavy Metal at one hundred watts per channel. From where Hodge and Runk sat in the van it sounded as though 45 Oakhurst Avenue was being blown apart by an endless series of rythmic explosions.

'What the fuck's wrong with those bugs?' Hodge squealed, dragging the earphones from his head.

'Nothing,' shouted the operator. 'They're highly sensitive ...'

'So am I,' yelled Hodge, stubbing his little finger into his ear in an attempt to get his hearing back, 'and something's definitely wrong.'

'They're just picking up one hell of a lot of interference. Could be any number of things produce that effect.'

'Like a fifty-megaton rock concert,' said Runk. 'Bloody woman must be stone deaf.'

'Like hell,' said Hodge. 'This is deliberate. They must have scanned the place and spotted they were being bugged. And turn that damned thing off. I can't hear myself think.'

'Never known anyone who could,' said Runk. 'Thinking doesn't make a sound. It's an –'

'Shut up,' yelled Hodge, who didn't need a lecture on the workings of the brain. For the next twenty minutes he sat in comparative silence trying to figure out his next move. At every stage of his campaign he had been outmanoeuvred and all because he hadn't been given the authority and back-up he needed. And now the Superintendent had sent a message demanding an immediate arrest. Hodge had countered with a request for a search warrant and had been answered with a vague remark that the matter would be considered. Which meant, of course, that he'd never get that warrant. He was on the point of returning to the station and demanding the right to raid the house when Sergeant Runk interrupted his train of thought.

'That jam session's stopped,' he said. 'Coming through nice and quiet.'

Hodge grabbed the earphones and listened. Apart from a rattling sound he couldn't identify (but which came in fact from Emmeline's hamster Percival getting some exercise in her wheel) the house in Oakhurst Avenue was silent. Odd. The place hadn't ever been silent before when the Wilts were at home. 'The car still outside?' he asked the technician.

The man turned to the car monitor. 'Nothing coming through,' he muttered and swung the aerial. 'They must have been using that din to dismantle the transmitters.'

Behind him Inspector Hodge verged on apoplexy. 'Jesus, you moron,' he yelled, 'you mean you haven't been checking that fucking car all this time?'

'What do you think I am? A bleeding octopus with ears?' the radio man shouted back. 'First I have to cope with all those stupid bugs you laced the house with and at the same time I've got two direction indicators to listen in to. And what's more I'm not a moron.'

But before Hodge could get into a real fight Sergeant Runk had intervened. 'I'm getting a faint signal from the car,' he said. 'Must be ten miles away.'

'Where?' yelled Hodge.

'East, as before,' said Runk. 'They're heading back to Baconheath.'

'Then get after them,' Hodge shouted, 'this time the shit isn't going to get back home before I've nabbed him. I'll seal that fucking base off if it's the last thing I do.'

Oblivious of the ill-feeling building up behind her Eva drove steadily towards the airbase. She had no conscious plan, only the determination to force the truth, and Wilt, out of somebody even if that meant setting fire to the car or lying naked in the roadway outside the gates. Anything to gain publicity.

220

And for once Mavis had agreed with her and been helpful too. She had organized a group of Mothers Against The Bomb, some of whom were in fact grandmothers, had hired a coach and had telephoned all the London papers and BBC and Fenland Television to ensure maximum coverage for the demonstration.

'It gives us an opportunity to focus the world's attention on the seductive nature of capitalist military-industrial world domination,' she had said, leaving Eva with only the vaguest idea what she meant but with the distinct feeling that Wilt was the 'It' at the beginning of the sentence. Not that Eva cared what anyone said; it was what they did that counted. And Mavis's demonstration would help divert attention away from her own efforts to get into the camp. Or, if she failed to do that, she would see to it that the name Henry Wilt reached the millions of viewers who watched the news that night.

'Now I want you all to behave nicely,' she told the quads as they drove up to the camp gates. 'Just do what Mummy tells you and everything is going to be all right.'

'It isn't going to be all right if Daddy's been staying with an American lady,' said Josephine.

'Fucking,' said Penelope, 'not staying with.'

Eva braked sharply. 'Who said that?' she demanded, turning a livid face on the quads in the back seat.

'Mavis Motty did,' said Penelope. 'She's always going on about fucking.'

Eva took a deep breath. There were times when the quads' language, so carefully nurtured towards mature self-expression at the School for the Mentally Gifted, seemed appallingly inappropriate. And this was one of those times. 'I don't care what Mavis said,' she declared, 'and anyway it isn't like that. Your father has simply been stupid again. We don't know what's happened to him. That's why we've come here. Now you behave yourselves and –'

'If we don't know what's happened to him how do you know he's been stupid?' asked Samantha, who had always been hot on logic.

'Shut up,' said Eva and started the car again.

Behind her the quads silently assumed the guise of four nice

221

little girls. It was misleading. As usual they had prepared themselves for the expedition with alarming ingenuity. Emmeline had armed herself with several hatpins that had once belonged to Grandma Wilt; Penelope had filled two bicycle pumps with ammonia and sealed the ends with chewing-gum; Samantha had broken into all their piggy banks and had then bought every tin of pepper she could from a perplexed greengrocer; while Josephine had taken several of Eva's largest and most pointed Sabatier knives from the magnet board in the kitchen. In short, the quads were happily looking forward to disabling as many airbase guards as they could and were only afraid that the affair would pass off peacefully. In the event their fears were almost realized.

As they stopped at the gatehouse and were approached by a sentry there were none of those signs of preparedness that had been so obvious the day before. In an effort to maintain that everything was normal and in a 'No Panic Situation' Colonel Urwin had ordered the removal of the concrete blocks in the roadway and had instilled a fresh sense of politeness in the officer in charge of entry to civilian quarters. A large Englishwoman with permed hair and a carload of small girls didn't seem to pose any threat to USAAF security.

'If you'll just pull over there I'll call up the Education Office for you,' he told Eva who had decided not to mention Captain Clodiak this time. Eva drove past the barrier and parked. This was proving much easier than she had expected. In fact for a moment she doubted her judgement. Perhaps Henry wasn't there after all and she had made some terrible mistake. The notion didn't last long. Once again the Wilts' Escort had signalled its presence and Eva was just telling the quads that everything was going to be all right when the Lieutenant appeared from the guardhouse with two armed sentries. 'Pardon me, ma'am,' he said, 'but I'd be glad if you'd step over to the office.'

'What for?' asked Eva.

'Just a routine matter.'

For a moment Eva gazed blankly up at his face and tried to think. She had steeled herself for a confrontation and words like 'stepping over to the office' and 'a routine matter' were somehow threateningly bland. All the same she opened the door and got out.

'And the children too,' said the Lieutenant. 'Everybody out of there.'

'Don't you touch my daughters,' said Eva, now thoroughly alarmed. It was obvious she had been tricked into the base. But this was the opportunity the quads had been waiting for. As the Lieutenant reached for the door handle Penelope poked the end of the bicycle pump through the window and Josephine pointed a carving knife. It was Eva's action that saved him from the knife. She wrenched at his arm and at the same time the ammonia hit him. As the stuff wafted up from his soaked jacket and the two sentries hurled themselves on Eva, the Lieutenant gasped for air and dashed for the guardhouse vaguely aware of the sound of girlish laughter behind him. It sounded demonic to him. Half suffocated he stumbled into the office and pressed the Alert button.

'It rather sounds as if we have another problem,' said Colonel Urwin as sirens wailed over the base.

'Don't include me,' said Wilt. 'I've got problems of my own like trying to explain to my wife what the hell's been happening to me the last God knows how many days.'

But the Colonel was on the phone to the guardhouse. For a moment he listened and then turned to Wilt. 'Your wife a fat woman with four daughters?'

'You could put it like that, I suppose,' said Wilt, 'though frankly I'd leave the "fat" bit out if you meet her. Why?'

'Because that's what just hit the main gate,' said the Colonel and went back to the phone. 'Hold everything ... What do you mean you can't? She's not ... Jesus ... Okay, okay. And cut those fucking sirens.' There was a pause and the Colonel held the phone away from his ear and stared at Wilt. Eva's shouted demands were clearly audible now that the sirens had stopped.

'Give me back my husband,' she yelled, 'and take your filthy paws off me ... If you go anywhere near those children ...' The Colonel put the phone down.

'Very determined woman, is Eva,' said Wilt by way of explanation.

'So I've gathered,' said the Colonel, 'and what I want to know is what she's doing here.'

'By the sounds of things, looking for me.'

'Only you told us she didn't know you were here. So how come she's out there fighting mad and ...' He stopped. Captain Fortune had entered the room.

'I think you ought to know the General's on the line,' he announced. 'Wants to know what's going on.'

'And he thinks *I* know?' said the Colonel.

'Well, someone has to.'

'Like him,' said the Colonel, indicating Wilt, 'and he's not saying.'

'Only because I haven't a clue,' said Wilt with increasing confidence, 'and without wishing to be unnecessarily didactic I'd say no one in the whole wide world knows what the hell's going on anywhere. Half the world's population is starving and the overfed half have a fucking death-wish, and –'

'Oh for Chrissake,' said the Colonel, and came to a sudden decision. 'We're taking this bastard out. Now.'

But Wilt was on his feet. He had watched too many American movies not to have ambivalent feelings about being 'taken out'. 'Oh, no you're not,' he said backing up against the wall. 'And you can cut the bastard abuse too. I didn't do anything to start this fucking madhouse and I've got my family to think about.'

Colonel Urwin looked at the sporting print hopelessly. He'd been right to suspect the British of having hidden depths he would never understand. No wonder the French spoke of 'perfidious Albion'. The bastards would always behave in ways one least expected. In the meantime he had to produce some explanation that would satisfy the General. 'Just say we've got a purely domestic problem on our hands,' he told the Captain, 'and rout Glaushof out. Base security is his baby.'

But before the Captain could leave the room Wilt had reacted again. 'You let that maniac anywhere near my kids and someone's going to get hurt,' he shouted, 'I'm not having them gassed like I was.'

'In that case you better exercise some parental control yourself,' said the Colonel grimly, and headed for the door.

23

By the time they reached the parking lot by the gates it was clear that the situation had deteriorated. In an entirely unnecessary effort to rescue their mother from the sentries – Eva had already felled one of the men with a knee-jerk to the groin she had learnt at a Rape Resistance Evening Class – the quads had abandoned the Wilts' car and, by dusting the second sentry with pepper, had put him out of action. After that they had occupied the gatehouse itself and were now holding the Lieutenant hostage inside. Since he had torn off his uniform to escape the ammonia fumes and the quads had armed themselves with his revolver and that of the sentry writhing on the ground outside, they had been able to isolate the guardhouse even more effectively by threatening the driver of an oil tanker which had made the mistake of arriving at the barrier and forcing him to offload several hundred gallons of fuel oil on to the roadway before driving tentatively into the base.

Even Eva had been appalled at the result. As the stuff swilled across the tarmac Lieutenant Harah had driven up rather too hurriedly in a jeep and had tried to brake. The jeep was now enmeshed in the perimeter fence and Lieutenant Harah, having crawled from it, was calling for reinforcements. 'We have a real penetration situation here,' he bawled into his walkie-talkie. 'A bunch of leftist terrorists have taken over the guardhouse.'

'They're not terrorists, they're just little girls,' Eva shouted from inside, only to have her words drowned by the Alert siren which Samantha had activated.

Outside in the roadway Mavis Mottram's busload of Mothers Against The Bomb had gathered in a line and had handcuffed themselves together before padlocking the ends of the line to the fence on either side of the gateway and were dancing something approximate to the can-can and chanting 'End the arms race, save the human' in full view of three TV

225

cameras and a dozen photographers. Above their heads an enormous and remarkable balloon, shaped and veined like an erect penis, swung slowly in the breeze exposing the rather confusing messages, 'Wombs Not Tombs' and 'Screw Cruise Not Us' painted on opposite sides. As Wilt and Colonel Urwin watched, the balloon, evidently force-fed by a hydrogen cylinder, shed its few human pretensions in the shape of an enormous plastic foreskin and turned itself into a gigantic rocket.

'This is going to kill old B52,' muttered the Colonel who had until then been enjoying the spectacle of Lieutenant Harah covered in oil and trying to get to his feet. 'And I can't see the President liking it too much either. That fucking phallus has got to hit prime time with all those cameras.'

A fire truck shot round the corner past them and in a jeep behind it came Major Glaushof, his right arm in a sling and his face the colour of putty.

'Jesus,' said Captain Fortune, 'if that fire truck hits the oil were going to have a body count of thirty of the Mothers.'

But the truck had stopped and men were deploying hoses. Behind them and the human chain Inspector Hodge and Sergeant Runk had driven up and were staring wildly about them. In front the women still kicked up their legs and chanted, the firemen had begun to spray foam on to the oil and Lieutenant Harah, and Glaushof was gesticulating with one hand to a troop of Anti Perimeter Penetration Squad men who had formed up as near the Mothers Against The Bomb as they could get and were preparing to discharge canisters of Agent Incapacitating at them.

'For fuck's sake hold it,' yelled Glaushof but his words were drowned out by the Alert Siren. As the canisters dropped into the roadway at the feet of the human chain Colonel Urwin shut his eyes. He knew now that Glaushof was a doomed man, but his own career was in jeopardy. 'We've got to get those fucking kids out of there before the cameras start playing on them,' he bawled at Captain Fortune. 'Go in and get them.'

The Captain looked at the foam, the oil and the drifting gas. Already a number of MABs had dropped to the ground and Samantha had added to the hazards of approaching the guardhouse by accidentally-on-purpose firing a revolver through one of the windows, an action which had drawn answering fire from Glaushof's APP Squad.

'You think I'm risking my life ...' the Captain began but it was Wilt who took the initiative. Wading through the oil and foam he made it to the guardhouse and presently four small girls and a large woman came out with him. Hodge didn't see them. Like the cameramen his attention was elsewhere, but unlike them he was no longer interested in the disaster taking place at the gates. A canister of AI had persuaded him to leave the scene as quickly as possible. It had also made it difficult to drive. As the police van backed into the bus and then shot forward and ricocheted off a cameraman's car before sliding off the road and onto its side, he had a moment of understanding. Inspector Flint hadn't been such an old fool after all. Anyone who tangled with the Wilt family had to come off worst.

Colonel Urwin shared his feelings. 'We're going to get you out of here in a chopper,' he told Wilt as more women slumped across the gateway.

'And what about my car?' said Wilt. 'If you think I'm leaving ...'

But his protest was shouted down by the quads. And Eva.

'We want to go up in a helicopter,' they squealed in unison.

'Just take me away from all this,' said Eva.

Ten minutes later Wilt looked down from a thousand feet at the pattern of runways and roads, buildings and bunkers and at the tiny group of women being carried from the gate to waiting ambulances. For the first time he felt some sympathy for Mavis Mottram. For all her faults she had been right to pit herself against the banal enormity of the airbase. The place had all the characteristics of a potential extermination camp. True, nobody was being herded into gas chambers and there was no smoke rising from crematoria. But the blind obedience to orders was there, instilled in Glaushof and even in Colonel Urwin. Everyone in fact, except Mavis Mottram and the human chain of women at the gate. The others would all obey orders if the time came and the real holocaust would begin. And this time there would be no liberators, no successive generations to erect memorials to the dead or learn lessons from past horrors. There would be only silence. The wind and the sea the only voices left. And it was the same in Russia and the occupied countries of the Eastern Europe. Worse. There Mavis Mottram was already silenced, confined to a prison or a psychiatric ward because she was idiosyncratically sane. No TV cameras or photographers depicted the new death camps. And twenty million Russians had died to make their country safe from genocide, only to have Stalin's successors too afraid of their own people to allow them to discuss the alternatives to building more machines to wipe life off the face of the earth.

It was all insane, childish and bestial. But above all it was banal. As banal as the Tech and Dr Mayfield's empire-building and the Principal's concern to keep his own job and avoid unfavourable publicity, never mind what the staff thought or the students would have preferred to learn. Which was what he was going back to. In fact nothing had changed. Eva would go on with her wild enthusiasms; the quads might even grow up to be civilized human beings. Wilt rather doubted it. Civilized human beings were a myth, legendary creatures who existed only in writers' imaginations, their foibles and faults expurgated and their occasional self-sacrifices magnified. With the quads that was impossible. The best that could be hoped was that they would remain as independent and uncomfortably non-conforming as they were now. And at least they were enjoying the flight.

Five miles outside the base the helicopter set down beside an empty road.

'You can drop off here,' said the Colonel, 'I'll try and get a car out to you.'

'But we want to go all the way home by helicopter,' shouted Samantha above the roar of the rotors, and was joined by Penelope who insisted she wanted to parachute on to Oakhurst Avenue. It was too much for Eva. Grabbing the quads in turn she bundled them out on to the beaten grass and jumped down beside them. Wilt followed. For a moment the air around him was thick with the downblast and then the helicopter had lifted off and was swinging away. By the time it had disappeared Eva had found her voice.

'Now look what you've been and done,' she said. Wilt stared

round at the empty landscape. After the interrogation he had been through he was in no mood for Eva's whingeing.

'Let's start walking,' he said. 'Nobody's coming out to pick us up and we'd better find a bus stop.'

He climbed the bank onto the road and set off along it. In the distance there was a sudden flash and a small ball of flame. Major Glaushof had fired a tracer round into Mavis Mottram's inflated penis. The fireball and the little mushroom cloud of smoke above it would be on the evening TV news in full colour. Perhaps something had been achieved after all.

24

It was the end of term at the Tech and the staff were seated in the auditorium, as evidently bored as the students they themselves had previously lectured there. Now it was the Principal's turn. He had spent ten excruciating minutes doing his best to disguise his true feelings for Mr Spirey of the Building Department who was finally retiring, and another twenty trying to explain why financial cuts had ended any hope of rebuilding the engineering block at the very time when the College had been granted the staggering sum of a quarter of a million pounds by an anonymous donor for the purchase of textbooks. In the front row Wilt sat poker-faced among the other Heads of Departments and feigned indifference. Only he and the Principal knew the source of the donation and neither of them could ever tell. The Official Secrets Act had seen to that. The money was the price of Wilt's silence. The deal had been negotiated by two nervous officials from the United States Embassy and in the presence of two rather more menacing individuals ostensibly from the legal division of the Home Office. Not that Wilt had been worried by their attitude. Throughout the discussion he had basked in the sense of his own innocence and even Eva had been overawed and then impressed by the offer of a new car. But Wilt had turned that down. It was enough to know that the Principal, while never understanding why, would always be unhappily aware that the Fenland College of Arts and Technology was once again indebted to a man he would have liked to fire. Now he was lumbered with Wilt until he retired himself.

Only the quads had been difficult to silence. They had enjoyed pumping ammonia over the Lieutenant and disabling sentries with pepper too much not to want to make their exploits known.

'We were only rescuing Daddy from that sexy woman,' said

Samantha when Eva rather unwisely asked them to promise never to talk about what had happened.

'And you'll have to rescue your Mother and me from Dartmoor if you don't keep your damned traps shut,' Wilt had snapped. 'And you know what that means.'

'What?' asked Emmeline, who seemed to be looking forward to the prospect of a prison break.

'It means you'll be taken into care by horrible foster parents and not as a bloody group either. You'll be split up and you won't be allowed to visit one another and . . .' Wilt had launched into a positively Dickensian description of foster homes and the horrors of child abuse. By the time he'd finished the quads were cowed and Eva had been in tears. Which was the first time that had happened and was another minor triumph. It wouldn't last, of course, but by the time they spilled the beans the immediate dangers would be over and nobody would believe them anyway.

But the argument had aroused Eva's suspicions again. 'I still want to know why you lied to me all those months about teaching at the prison,' she said as they undressed that night.

Wilt had an answer for that one too. 'You heard what those men from MI5 said about the Official Secrets Act.'

'MI5?' said Eva. 'They were from the Home Office. What's MI5 got to do with it?'

'Home Office, my foot, Military Intelligence,' said Wilt. 'And if you choose to send the quads to the most expensive school for pseudo-prodigies and expect us not to starve . . .'

The argument had rumbled on into the night but Eva hadn't needed much convincing. The officials from the Embassy had impressed her too much with their apologies and there had been no talk of women. Besides, she had her Henry home again and it was obviously best to forget that anything had happened at Baconheath.

And so Wilt sat on beside Dr Board with a slight sense of accomplishment. If he was fated to fall foul of other people's stupidity and misunderstanding he had the satisfaction of knowing that he was no one's victim. Or only temporarily. In the end he beat them and circumstances. It was better than being a successful bore like Dr Mayfield – or worse still, a resentful failure.

'Wonders never cease,' said Dr Board when the Principal finally sat down and they began to file out of the auditorium, 'A quarter of a million in actual textbooks? It must be a unique event in British education. Millionaires who give donations usually provide better buildings for worse students. This one seems to be a genius.'

Wilt said nothing. Perhaps having some commonsense was a form of genius.

At Ipford Police Station ex-Inspector Hodge, now merely Sergeant Hodge, sat at a computer terminal in Traffic Control and tried to confine his thoughts to problems connected with flow-patterns and off-peak parking systems. It wasn't easy. He still hadn't recovered from the effects of Agent Incapacitating or, worse still, from the enquiry into his actions the Superintendent had started and the Chief Constable had headed.

And Sergeant Runk hadn't been exactly helpful. 'Inspector Hodge gave me to understand the Superintendent had authorized the bugging of Mr Wilt's car,' he said in evidence. 'I was acting on his orders. It was the same with their house.'

'Their house? You mean to say their house was bugged too?'

'Yes, sir. It still is for all I know,' said Runk, 'we had the collaboration of the neighbours, Mr Gamer and his wife.'

'Dear God,' muttered the Chief Constable, 'if this ever gets to the gutter press ...'

'I don't think it will, sir,' said Runk, 'Mr Gamer has moved out and his missus has put the house up for sale.'

'Then get those bloody devices out of there before someone has the place surveyed,' snarled the Chief Constable before dealing with Hodge. By the time he had finished the Inspector was on the verge of a breakdown himself and had been demoted to Sergeant in the Traffic Section with the threat of being transferred to the police dog training school as a target if he put his foot wrong just once again.

To add insult to injury he had seen Flint promoted to Head of the Drug Squad.

'The chap seems to have a natural talent for that kind of work,' said the Chief Constable. 'He's done a remarkable job.'

232

The Superintendent had his reservations but he kept them to himself. 'I think it runs in the family,' he said judiciously. And for a fortnight during the trial Flint's name had appeared almost daily in the *Ipford Chronicle* and even in some of the national dailies. The police canteen too had buzzed with his praises. Flint the Drug Buster. Almost Flint the Terror of the Courtroom. In spite of all the efforts the defence counsel had made, with every justification, to question the legality of his methods, Flint had countered with facts and figures, times, dates, places and with exhibits, all of which were authentic. He had stepped down from the witness box still retaining the image of the old-fashioned copper with his integrity actually enhanced by the innuendoes. It was enough for the public to look from him to the row of sleazy defendants in the dock to see where the interests of justice lay. Certainly the Judge and jury had been convinced. The accused had gone down with sentences that ranged from nine years to twelve and Flint had gone up to Superintendent.

But Flint's achievement led beyond the courtroom to areas where discretion still prevailed.

'She brought the stuff back from her cousins in California?' spluttered Lord Lynchknowle when the Chief Constable visited him. 'I don't believe a word of it. Downright lie.'

'Afraid not, old chap. Absolutely definite. Smuggled the muck back in a bottle of duty-free whisky.'

'Good God. I thought she'd got it at that rotten Tech. Never did agree with her going there. All her mother's fault.' He paused and stared vacuously out across the rolling meadows. 'What did you say the stuff was called?'

'Embalming Fluid,' said the Chief Constable. 'Or Angel Dust. They usually smoke it.'

'Don't see how you can smoke embalming fluid,' said Lord Lynchknowle. 'Mind you, there's no understanding women, is there?'

'None at all,' said the Chief Constable and with the assurance that the coroner's verdict would be one of accidental death he left to deal with other women whose behaviour was beyond his comprehension.

In fact it was at Baconheath that the results of Hodge's

obsession with the Wilt family were being felt most keenly. Outside the airbase Mavis Mottram's group of Mothers Against The Bomb had been joined by women from all over the country and had turned into a much bigger demonstration. A camp of makeshift huts and tents was strung out along the perimeter fence, and relations between the Americans and the Fenland Constabulary had not been improved by scenes on TV of middle-aged and largely respectable British women being gassed and dragged in handcuffs to camouflaged ambulances.

To make matters even more awkward Mavis' tactics of blockading the civilian quarters had led to several violent incidents between US women who wanted to escape the boredom of the base to go souvenir-hunting in Ipford or Norwich and MABs who refused to let them out or, more infuriatingly, allowed them to leave only to stop them going back. These fracas were seen on TV with a regularity that had brought the Home Secretary and the Secretary of State for Defence into conflict, each insisting that the other was responsible for maintaining law and order.

Only Patrick Mottram had benefited. In Mavis' absence he had come off Dr Kores' hormones and had resumed his normal habits with Open University students.

Inside the airbase, too, everything had changed. General Belmonte, still suffering from the effect of seeing a giant penis circumcise itself and then turn into a rocket and explode, had been retired to a home for demented veterans in Arizona where he was kept comfortably sedated and could sit in the sun dreaming of happy days when his B52 had blasted the empty jungle in Vietnam. Colonel Urwin had returned to Washington and a cat-run garden in which he grew scented narcissi to perfection and employed his considerable intelligence to the problem of improving Anglo-American relations.

It was Glaushof who had suffered the most. He had been flown to the most isolated and radioactive testing ground in Nevada and consigned to duties in which his own personal security was in constant danger and his sole responsibility. And sole was the word. Mona Glaushof with Lieutenant Harah in tow had hit Reno for a divorce and was living comfortably

234

in Texas on the alimony. It was a change from the dank Fenlands and the sun never ceased to shine.

It shone too on Eva and 45 Oakhurst Avenue as she bustled about the house and wondered what to have for supper. It was nice to have Henry home and somehow more assertive than he had been before. 'Perhaps,' she thought as she Hoovered the stairs, 'we ought to get away by ourselves for a week or two this summer.' And her thoughts turned to the Costa Brava.

But it was a problem Wilt had already solved. Sitting in The Pig In A Poke with Peter Braintree he ordered two more pints.

'After all I've been through this term I'm not having my summer made hellish in some foul camp site by the quads,' he said cheerfully. 'I've made other arrangements. There's an adventure school in Wales where they do rock-climbing and pony-trekking. They can work their energy off on that and the instructors. I've rented a cottage in Dorset and I'm going down there to read *Jude The Obscure* again.'

'Seems a bit of a gloomy book to take on holiday,' said Braintree.

'Salutary,' said Wilt, 'a nice reminder that the world's always been a crazy place and that we don't have such a bad time of it teaching at the Tech. Besides, it's an antidote to the notion that intellectual aspirations get you anywhere.'

'Talking about aspirations,' said Braintree, 'what on earth are you going to do with the thirty thousand quid this lunatic philanthropist has allotted your department for textbooks?'

Wilt smiled into his pint of best bitter. 'Lunatic philanthropists' was just about right for the Americans with their airbases and nuclear weapons, and the educated idiots in the State Department who assumed that even the most ineffectual liberal do-gooder must be a homicidal Stalinist and a member of the KGB – and who then shelled out billions of dollars trying to undo the damage they'd done.

'Well, for one thing I'm going to donate two hundred copies of *Lord of the Flies* to Inspector Flint,' he said finally.

235

'To Flint? Why him of all people? What's he want with the damned things?'

'He's the one who told Eva I was out at ...' Wilt stopped. There was no point in breaking the Official Secrets Act. 'It's a prize,' he went on, 'for the first copper to arrest the Phantom Flasher. It seems an appropriate title.'

'I daresay it does,' said Braintree. 'Still, two hundred copies is a bit disproportionate. I can't imagine even the most literate policeman wanting to read two hundred copies of the same book.'

'He can always hand them out to the poor sods at the airbase. Must be hell trying to cope with Mavis Mottram. Not that I disagree with her views but the bloody woman is definitely demented.'

'Still leaves you with a hell of a lot of new books to buy,' said Braintree. 'I mean, it's all right for me because the English Department needs books but I shouldn't have thought Communication and –'

'Don't use those words. I'm going back to Liberal Studies and to hell with all that bloody jargon. And if Mayfield and the rest of the social-economic structure merchants don't like it, they can lump it. I'm having it my way from now on.'

'You sound very confident,' said Braintree.

'Yes,' said Wilt with a smile.

And he was.

MORTAL
WORDS

Kathryn Lasky Knight

SUMMIT BOOKS
NEW YORK · LONDON · TORONTO
SYDNEY · TOKYO · SINGAPORE

SUMMIT BOOKS
Simon & Schuster Building
Rockefeller Center
1230 Avenue of the Americas
New York, New York 10020

Copyright © 1990 by Kathryn Lasky Knight
All rights reserved
including the right of reproduction
in whole or in part in any form.
SUMMIT BOOKS and colophon are
trademarks of Simon & Schuster Inc.
Manufactured in the United States of America

10 9 8 7 6 5 4 3 2 1

Library of Congress Cataloging in Publication Data

Knight, Kathryn Lasky.
    Mortal words / Kathryn Lasky Knight.
        p.   cm.
    I. Title.
PS3561.N485M6   1990
813'.54—dc20   90–35919
ISBN 0–671–68446–9   CIP

FOR ERIC SWENSON

1   "So how are the dragon-fanged
      tulips?" Calista asked the small
elderly woman sitting next to her in the car as they swung out
onto Mount Auburn Street. They were headed toward the Larz
Anderson Bridge, which crossed the Charles River to Boston
from Cambridge.

"Blagghh!!" The sound gurgled up like scalding phlegm,
and Margaret McGowan made a face to match it. She kept her
eyes fastened on the wings of the light-up fairy that was the
hood ornament on Calista's Volkswagen. "You've got to treat
them like annuals, Calista. Even the dragons. Very wimpy."
Although she had lived in the States for over three decades,
Margaret still had a trace of Scottish brogue that was a wonderful condiment to her speech when she spoke like this.

Calista laughed. She liked Margaret a lot. Margaret was an
author of children's books. Calista was an illustrator. They were
both on their way to a children's literature conference in downtown Boston where they were to speak on their art. Margaret did
not illustrate at all but was an eloquent spinner of high-fantasy
novels for young children, high fantasy being that genre of
fiction that pulled heavily on Arthurian legend and the general
arsenal of Celtic and Nordic mythic elements. Thus, her well-
crafted stories were laced with quests, magical forests, and
wizards. Calista was the more well known of the two. She was in
fact renowned in the field of children's literature. She illustrated
fairy tales, folktales, and small stories of her own. Her reputation had been built over the last twenty years, and her books
were consistently best-sellers. She had twice won the Caldecott
Medal for Best Children's Picture Book of the Year. The second

11

medal had been announced just months before for her version of *Puss in Boots*. She would be the drawing card at today's event.

"Don't tell me you have to treat tulips as annuals, I just planted hundreds last fall. I got some of those dragon-fanged ones, too, because they looked so good in your garden."

"Not dragon-fanged, my dear. Dragon Flames. That's how they are listed in the catalog."

"Well, whatever, they look great."

"Not this year. Although I can't really tell yet. It's still too early. I mean, my grape hyacinths are just starting."

"You get more sun than I do on your side of Cambridge." They lived on opposites sides of Harvard Square, Calista in a very old neighborhood with the largest trees in Cambridge and where such luminaries as William James and George Santayana once lived and where it had been said that when those two old lugubrious souls got together, "even the dogs howled." Margaret lived on a small street off Brattle where the sidewalks were still brick but the trees were not as big and the flowers could be flashier because of more sun.

"Stop moaning about my tulips. Tell me who else is on this panel with us," Margaret said.

"Norman Petrakis. You know, the nonfiction writer for children."

"Oh, yes, of course. I met him at an American Library Association meeting a couple of years ago. Charming, handsome."

"I know," Calista said.

"So?" A delicately curved eyebrow shot up and hovered in the suspension of fine wrinkles of her brow. "He's closer to your age than mine, my dear."

"Well," Calista said noncommittally, and shrugged her shoulders.

They were driving east on Storrow Drive, now hugging the Charles River. Some of the crew teams were out on the river.

"Well, what? Is he married?"

"No."

"Is he gay?"

"No. Nothing's wrong at all."

The only thing that was wrong was that Calista hated these conversations. Norman was enormously attractive both physically and intellectually. She should be so lucky. But that was the problem. Luck had not been in the cards since she had been widowed over three years ago. Colossal bad luck with men— well, just two, really. Her husband, who had been murdered, and then a man whose name fought to remain unspoken even in silence. Gun-shy, was she? You bet. But there was no denying it: Norman Petrakis was attractive. And she could do worse, and her luck could be better.

The auditorium was packed to capacity. It was a typical mixture for a children's literature conference—ninety percent librarians, the rest students of children's literature and library science, teachers, and parents. It was a panel discussion on directions in children's literature. It was being held at the Hynes Auditorium in downtown Boston.

Calista had made few appearances since her husband's murder three years before. After cracking that peculiar case with the help of her son, Charley, she had become a full-fledged celebrity. Her books, which had always sold well, now sold extraordinarily well. She had called her most recent Caldecott Medal her *Butterfield 8* award, likening it to the time Liz Taylor won an Oscar for a less-than-great performance simply because she had nearly died of pneumonia. When one's husband gets murdered and son nearly killed in trying to solve the crime, it seemed to provide more than adequate grounds for universal sympathy. The world had felt sorry for her; hence, the award. That was how she interpreted it, although everyone else had told her it wasn't so.

She peeked out now from behind the curtain. Norman Petrakis had already taken his seat and was chatting, while the mikes were off, with David Cummings, the moderator of the panel and an editor of children's books himself. In the audience she spotted her editor, Janet Weiss, who had flown up from New York and just made it in time, as her plane was late. She'd dashed backstage to give Calista a quick kiss before finding a seat. Calista wished that Janet could be right there next to her

13

on the panel. She was so comforting. But where the hell was Margaret? Calista was having a bad case of butterflies and didn't want to have to walk out there alone.

"Ready?" She spun around. Margaret looked more frail here in the wings of the stage than she had in the tight confines of Calista's VW. Frail but still spirited. She had a gnomelike quality and could have stepped out from one of her own books. Her thin gray hair seemed to hover rather than actually grow from her head. She had been wearing a knit hat in the car, and now that she was without it Calista noticed that Margaret's hair was much thinner than she had remembered. She could see some of her scalp. It seemed rather like a patchy fog blowing off a headland.

"Oh, Margaret! I'm feeling very jittery. I don't want to have to walk out there alone."

"Me too!" She grasped Calista's hand and grimaced, her pale blue eyes flickering softly. "Let's go." Calista felt a gentle tug, and they walked onstage holding hands like two little kinder-garteners on the first day of school. A ripple of applause began and then rolled into a crushing sound like a breaking wave.

"That's for you, my dear!" Margaret whispered.

"But it's not for my work."

"Don't be silly!"

They took their seats as the moderator introduced them and briefly explained the format and procedure of the panel. Each of the three participants would give a brief talk, ten minutes, on their work, and then the session would be thrown open for questions. First Margaret, then Norman, and then Calista. Calista was in the hot spot. Margaret was an easy one to follow. Unlike her books, she was not particularly organized as a speaker. Her talk tended to ramble. She interrupted herself repeatedly. Norman, on the other hand, was brief, witty, and to the point. He had wonderful anecdotes about his previous career as a high school science teacher. He was very attractive in a donnish sort of way. His black hair was flecked with some gray. He had a slightly beaked nose and deep green eyes that peered out from behind black-wire-rimmed glasses. And there was a dimple in his left cheek that was not really flirtatious but very engaging. Most attractive, Calista thought as she observed him

14

speaking. There might be other places she would prefer to be following him to than the speaker's podium.

"And now my time is up," Norman was saying. "And I think that we all want to hear from our third speaker."

How gallant! Calista thought. She wished that all these other writers wouldn't be so self-effacing just because she had won the damn medal. She was not going to talk about *Puss in Boots* anyhow. She had to save that for her acceptance speech in Dallas. She would talk about her animal characters Owl and Hedge and "the buddy theme" in literature, or something like that.

She finished her talk in under ten minutes, and now the floor was open for questions. There were several for Calista, and then the audience began to ask Norman about the differences between writing for children and his twice monthly science column for *The New York Times*. The questions were fairly predictable. A hand went up in the back of the room, and a rather wan-looking man in his early thirties stood up. "My question," he began, "is really for all of you because, although all of your work appears quite different . . ."

It was the word *appears* that made something deep within Calista flinch. "It seems to be part of an increasing trend . . ." With the word *trend* Calista knew they were heading for trouble. "A trend toward secular humanism." An audible groan rolled through the auditorium.

"Oh, shit!" Norman muttered.

"Mr. Petrakis," the man continued. Something turned in Calista's stomach. She could feel Norman tense beside her at the table. "In a book of yours in which you write about human evolution for children, are you not supporting a particular religious belief?" There was a stunned silence, and then a single hiss scrawled across the still air of the auditorium.

"Sir, are you finished with your question?" David Cummings spoke in an icy voice.

"No, not yet. I would really ask the same question of Miss McGowan. In her portrayal of medieval kings and the like, is she not really portraying and suggesting our Lord Jesus Christ as a mythic figure?" There was a roar of boos now.

Margaret McGowan looked absolutely white. From the

15

corner of her eye Calista could see her rather thin hand with its bulging veins begin to tremble.

"Get him out of here!" someone yelled.

Norman coughed, hunched forward a bit, and picked up his mike. "No. I'll take this," he said emphatically. "My views on human evolution have absolutely nothing to do with my own private religious beliefs." He emphasized the word *private*.

"But for a Christian nation . . ." the man continued.

That always pissed Calista off royally. She started to speak, but by the time she realized that her mike was not turned on the man was full steam into his diatribe. "We find that it is intolerable to foist on our children a so-called evolutionary theory that is inimical to religion and morality."

"I do not understand first of all why you refer to this as a so-called theory and then—"

Calista opened her eyes wide and looked at Norman. He was actually going to try to address this buffoon and continue a dialogue. The man interrupted him, however. "It is a philosophy that, along with books like Miss McGowan's, fosters godlessness, promiscuity."

"Well, I never!" gasped Margaret. The audience was beginning to hiss loudly.

"Now hold it right there, sir," Petrakis barked. "It is not a philosophy. It is a testable theory, a theory that says species do not remain fixed and immutable. It has been proven in countless lab experiments using thousands of millions of fruit flies, not to mention the evidence of the fossil record. Recent biochemical evidence establishes a molecular time clock that indicates precisely when the apes separated from early humans. I would ask you now what proof you have that this theory causes godlessness and promiscuity?"

"It is well known, Mr. Petrakis, that it has crept into all forms of modern thought—Marx, Freud, Nitzi . . ."

"Nitzi?" Calista wondered aloud. Nietzsche, she guessed. But the pitch of the man's voice was becoming higher. The air seemed shrill with the rasp of a blind paranoia, demagoguery. It was as if a poison gas had begun to fill the room.

"This is frightening," whispered Margaret. It was then that

16

Calista became furious. What right had this man to disrupt and frighten, to come in here wielding his ignorance like an M-16?

"Order! Order." David switched off his mike and looked at Norman weakly. "Jeez, I didn't think to bring a gavel."

Calista switched on her mike and leaned forward. "What about me!" Her voice was just a scratch in the angry tumult. There was a slight quieting as people realized she was trying to say something. "What about me?" she repeated. "I feel left out." People began to laugh.

"Well, you, Mrs. Jacobs." There was a hush now as the man began to speak. "Your Owl and Hedge books, which you call a celebration of friendship, and also in your book *Nick in the Night,* where you have portrayed a small boy in the nude, are supporting homosexuality, and as a known heterosexual fornicator . . ."

The crowd went crazy. Some people collared the fellow and began moving him out. David Cummings was down off the podium yelling for security.

Calista's head swam. She felt Norman's hand on her arm and Margaret's birdlike grasp of her wrist. "Don't worry! Don't worry!" she felt compelled to reassure them.

David Cummings was now leaning across the table toward her. "He's just one of the nuts planted by those fundamentalist groups. They've been going around doing this lately. They broke up an International Reading Association meeting and a New York Library Conference. Just incredibly offensive, into book burning, the whole works."

"Don't worry about me. This is nothing." Calista felt compulsive about reassuring these people. How could they ever realize that after having your husband murdered, then to be seduced by a CIA agent while trying to solve the crime, and nearly losing your child, all of which subsequently became front-page news, to be called a "fornicator" at a children's literature conference was hardly grounds for a mental crack-up. "I'm fine," she kept saying. What she meant was, "I'm tough."

Janet Weiss came bustling up. "Are you all right, Cal?"

"I'm fine, what about you?" Calista replied.

Janet, usually as neat as a bandbox, looked totally disheveled.

A hairpin was hanging absurdly over one ear, her blouse was untucked, and one leg of her panty hose was torn from her knee to her ankle. She was also missing one shoe.

"What happened to you?" Calista gasped as she took in the full impact of her editor's physical state.

"I tackled the bastard."

"You?!" Calista was stunned.

"Yeah, me and these two rather wimpy-looking, but very effective, graduate students who 'escorted' him out. Come on," Janet said, "I'm taking this whole crew for dinner and a good stiff drink first." She nodded at Margaret and Norman and Calista.

"With one shoe?" Calista asked.

"No, it's back there somewhere where I was sitting."

The crowd had cleared out, and Janet had found her shoe, minus one heel.

"Did you hit him with it and with luck left it spiked in his groin?" Calista said as Janet limped into the Genji, a Japanese restaurant on Newbury Street.

"I can't really remember." She then turned to Norman. "This was an inspired notion of yours, Norman, coming to a Japanese restaurant. I suppose I could even check my shoes with my coat." But she took them off and carried them to the table.

"Perfect atmosphere after that fracas," Margaret said, patting her forehead with the warm damp cloth that the kimono-clad waitress had just given her. They passed up the hot tea and the sake for vodka martinis. All except for Norman, who asked for bourbon on the rocks.

"Bourbon!" said Margaret dreamily. "How charming. I haven't heard of anyone ordering bourbon in years. Are you from the South, Norman, originally?"

"Originally? No, from Athens originally."

"Oh, of course, dear."

Margaret McGowan, Calista thought, in a certain sense was just the way children's book authors were supposed to be—full of wonder and bewilderment, ready to walk through looking glasses into magical realms. But then she might say something totally off-the-wall, as she was about to do right now. Calista

18

felt it coming. Raising her glass, Margaret smiled sweetly. "To Calista, one of the nicest fornicators I know!" She blushed furiously. "I mean, of course, not that I actually know." But the table was already laughing.

"We know what you mean, Margaret," Norman said, giving her a clap on the back.

"Well," Margaret said, furrowing her brow, "this attack was no laughing matter."

"Hardly." Janet Weiss shook her head. "I don't know. I think we're really sliding backwards."

"How do you mean?" Calista asked.

"We get more letters now. It's scarier in a way. The letters aren't so specific. It's not just like the ones we got over *Nick in the Night,* where people were upset about the nudity, or complaints of miscegenation when we have a book illustrating a white rabbit and a black rabbit playing together."

"Rabbit miscegenation?" Norman asked.

"Oh, yes, my dear. When I worked at Harper and Row—this was years ago—we did a book called *The Rabbits' Wedding,* and boy, did we take flak. And then there was *Sylvester and the Magic Pebble.*"

"Who could object to that book?" Margaret asked. "The one about the donkey, right?"

"Yes. It was fine that Sylvester was a donkey, but not so fine that the policeman was a pig."

"Oh, God!" Norman sipped his bourbon. Calista noticed his dimple again as he looked across the rim of his glass at her. It was definitely not a flirtatious dimple. It was simply a part of the grammar of his face. She liked the face and the intelligence behind the eyes.

"Oh, yes. William Steig, that sweet man, was accused of ridiculing law and order," Janet continued.

"So what's worse now?" Calista asked.

"It tends to be more general, which is scarier as far as I'm concerned. We get complaints from groups about books that are 'overly imaginative.' Paranoia about books that lead children into 'imaginative forays' that will encourage everything from defying authority to masturbation. It used to be that people who were into censorship simply took paragraphs or words out

19

of context. They didn't read. Well, they still don't read, but now they don't take even a word out of context. They just have their minds made up: imagination's no good. Everything must be fact. And some facts are ungodly, as we heard today. It's scary."

"It sure is." Norman nodded. "The Arkansas creationist law was challenged and overridden . . . what? five or six years ago? But those creationist groups just formed up again and seem to have come back stronger."

"And I am loath to say"—Janet picked up her drink and swirled it—"that our publishing brethren in the textbook divisions of certain companies listen to these groups."

"They do." Calista nodded. "You should see Charley's science textbook. It devotes all of two pages to evolution and two sentences to Charles Darwin. Of course, the teachers in Charley's school don't rely all that much on the textbooks anyway and bring in other stuff to supplement. Thank God. But that textbook is a joke when it comes to evolution."

"That's for Texas," Norman said.

"Why Texas?" asked Margaret.

"Because Texas buys more textbooks than any other state. And if it is adopted, as they say, by the Texas Board of Education for use in the school system, it means millions of dollars for the company. I've got an article coming out about all this in the *Times* next month."

"After the one on designer genes?" Calista asked. "I just love that title."

"What?" exclaimed Margaret. "I take it it's not about Calvin what's-his-name."

"No." Norman laughed. "It's all sorts of things—cloning, cancer research, a lot with twins research and that whole project up at the University of Minnesota, and then the human gene project."

"What's that?" Margaret asked.

"It's a plan to decipher all the human genes, the entire set."

"And then there's all that stuff, isn't there, with DNA profiling and its use in solving crimes," Janet said.

"Oh, yes. That's become the most important breakthrough

since fingerprinting, and there is the molecular time clock stuff which gets back to evolution again."

"Molecular what?" asked Janet.

"Molecular time clock. It's a particular kind of genetic research where they look very closely at the blood proteins. You can compare them between species. The more closely related two species are, the more similar their blood proteins are expected to be. The greater the difference between the blood proteins, the longer ago these two species forked apart, or diverged. The DNA tells the tale within the blood proteins. Zebras from horses, for example, diverged relatively recently."

"And more to the point, remembering our friend in the audience . . ." Calista paused. "What about apes and humans?"

"Aha!" Norman's eyes sparkled warmly across his drink at Calista in a way that caused a little flutter within her. Her question was obviously appreciated. That excited her. He was attractive, and he was smart.

"You mean the Texas school board isn't going to like the answer," she said, laughing.

"Not at all! Humans and apes diverged within the last five or six million years."

"No kidding!" Janet gasped. "I didn't realize it was that recent."

"Truly kissing cousins, then," Margaret added.

"More than that, my dear," Norman said. "If you look at the DNA, you will find that there is less than a fraction of one percent difference between our chromosomes and those of a chimpanzee. Chimps and humans diverged within a very narrow range of time. Say within the last four million years, we shared an ancestor with chimps. In fact, there is more genetic similarity between humans and chimpanzees than between chimps and gorillas."

"Amazing!" Janet said. "So that's what they do in these high-tech gene labs."

"No, just a very little of that, actually. Most of the genetic work is related to cancer research. That's how they get into all this cloning business and the transgenic mice, which is basically transplanting human genes into mice so they can study growth of tumors. They do a lot of that right here in Boston, or rather Cambridge, at the Martin Institute."

"Charley is supposed to have some sort of student internship there through his school," Calista added.

"Do you think there could ever possibly be a nonfiction book in that for children?" Margaret asked.

"I don't know. It's technically very complicated. DNA, RNA, and now all this new stuff with the mitochondrial DNA."

"What about cloning? If you just limited the book to a very simplified explanation of what cloning is, what they've done so far. Kids, you know, are fascinated by that. They all know about cloning in a vague sort of way."

"Yes, Charley knows about it," Calista offered.

"Well, Charley!" Janet exclaimed. "We can hardly go by Charley as a measure for the average kid."

Calista blushed slightly. She had walked right into that one. She did have a very bright thirteen-year-old. He was, in the parlance, "gifted." The gift, in Calista's mind, came from his late father, Tom Jacobs, one of the world's foremost astrophysicists. But gifts had funny ways of turning into terrible burdens. Calista had assiduously avoided sending him to fancy private schools. She had done her homework in this area and found the programs not to be that special, but dreadfully elitist. He could get the so-called enrichment by virtue of living in Cambridge and through their own Harvard connections. But by going to a normal public school, she felt, he received the gift of learning how to get along in a world that was made of diverse people with diverse IQs. She and Tom had both agreed on this. A good public school had more to offer than the most high-powered prep school.

The conversation shifted now to trout fishing. Norman was quite interested, and he knew that Calista was an experienced trout fisherman.

"Fisherman, fisherwoman?" He laughed. "What does one say?"

"Fisherman is fine," Calista said.

"For God's sake, don't neuter it!" Margaret exclaimed.

"Calista, did you see the sign in the window of that little restaurant on Brattle Street advertising for a 'waitron'?"

"Oh, God!"

"Where do you go fishing?" Norman asked.

"Vermont, mostly. I have a vacation home there. When I get a chance I like to go out to Montana. It's the best. The Yellowstone, the Madison, the Gallatin rivers. You can't beat them."

They talked streams and flies, and Calista promised that if there were time after tomorrow morning's session at the conference, she would personally escort Norman to her favorite rod and tackle shop.

"You are all, of course, welcome any time to come to my summer place in Scotland. You know I'm in the Mecca for trout fishermen and women," Margaret said.

"Oh, I've always wanted to go to Scotland." Janet sighed.

"Well, you and that lovely husband of yours should come."

There was an uncomfortable pause. "I'm afraid, Margaret, that Jack and I have separated."

"Oh, dear, I'm so sorry."

"Well, it was a long time coming, but it's a good thing to be on the other side of now."

"Yes, yes. I know how it feels. You know I was divorced years ago. It was awful when we were going through it, but gradually I began to reclaim a part of my life that I had nearly forgotten about. At first, however, before I really sorted things out, I had this inexorable urge toward chintz."

"Chintz?" they all said at once.

"Yes, chintz. You know, men don't like chintz that much, and so women always have to keep it under control in home decor. I just chintzed everything up. . . . And then there is the other urge, of course." She paused briefly. "I slept around a bit. But everybody does that after a divorce."

"Margaret, you are something else!" Norman said.

After dinner they put Margaret in a cab to go home. Norman was staying at the Sheraton only a few blocks away. The evening was mild for early April, so Calista and Janet had decided to walk all the way down to the Ritz where Janet was staying.

Now, however, as they walked with Norman, Calista felt it to be slightly awkward. One of them should be with this attractive man, not both of them, and it should be Janet. She needed it more than Calista after that rotten drunk of a husband who only sobered up long enough to have an affair with Janet's old boss! She wished now she had just driven Margaret home.

"It's so clear tonight," Norman said. He paused and looked up. "I don't believe it!"

"Believe what?" Calista and Janet both said at once.

"Look, ladies! Over the Hancock Building. You can see part of Auriga, my favorite constellation—the Charioteer!" The soft wonder of his voice melted into the darkness. "Look, even the tracers," he said, pointing with his finger toward some trailing stars.

Oh, dear, Calista thought. One of us should be alone with this lovely man.

2

She had just finished taking a shower after sending Charley off to school the next morning. When she turned off the water she heard the phone ringing furiously. She grabbed a towel, raced out of her bathroom, and did a dive across the bed to reach the phone on the other side.

"Yes!" she nearly barked. "Or rather, yes," she said in a gentler, less rasping voice.

"Calista!" Janet's voice seemed breathy and trembling on the other end.

"What is it!" A black fear began to fill her.

"Norman. He's dead."

"What!" Calista gasped.

"Murdered."

"No!"

A limo was sent from the Boston office of J. T. Thayer and Sons, Calista's publisher, to pick up Calista, and soon she arrived. Ethan Thayer, the patriarch of the firm, walked through the door, having flown up from their main office in New York.

"I know this is terrible for you, Calista. Too much violence in a young lifetime." He patted her hair and took her by the arm.

They went to a conference room down the corridor, where Margaret McGowan sat with two Boston policemen. Ethan seemed to know more about the procedures and what to expect than Calista.

"They just want to ask you and Janet and Margaret a few questions since you were the last ones to see him. David Cummings is coming over with Norman's editor from Sundial. He's meeting him at the airport now, I think."

He looked up as two men arrived. Calista recognized them. They were lawyers for the publishing house. But she couldn't remember their names.

"Calista, you met our counsels here in Boston, Fred Begelman and John Kieffer."

"Yes, of course."

Margaret was practically a basket case until Ethan got the bright idea of getting her a little shot of good rye whiskey that was kept in a cabinet in his office. Calista declined. They had tried to answer as best they could all of the lieutenant's and the other man's questions. But it was hard for Calista to concentrate, and she had so many questions of her own. She felt vague and distracted, but Janet seemed equally so.

"So you can't think of any enemies Mr. Petrakis might have had?"

"Enemies?" Calista whispered.

"We told you about the obnoxious man at the conference," Janet said.

"He hated us all!" Calista said, and saw Margaret's pale blue eyes widen in the horror at this sudden realization.

"Yes, we'll run an MCIC on all the fundamentalist groups, and we're checking through Sundial to see if Mr. Petrakis had received any kind of threatening mail recently over the publication of his book on human evolution. The conference people are checking all of their registrations." Lieutenant McCafferty paused. "Mrs. Jacobs, have you ever received any threatening mail or calls?"

25

"Why, certainly," Calista said crisply. "You know, of course, of my little run-in with the CIA a few years ago." Her voice was drenched in sarcasm. "That was very threatening, to say the least. It nearly resulted in the—"

Ethan Thayer grimaced. "Calista, they're talking about offensive mail in regard to your books."

"Oh, well, yes," she continued. "All the time, from all sorts of groups. The born agains, the Moral Majority."

Ethan Thayer coughed and began to speak. "Calista's talking about a picture book of hers called *Nick in the Night*. It's about a little four- or five-year-old boy who dreams he can fly and takes a magical flight through the night. Very innocent, but sometimes his nightshirt gets caught in a gust of wind and you can see his . . . er . . . er, anatomy."

"Here!" Calista jumped up. There were shelves full of books published by J. T. Thayer and Sons just behind where the cops were sitting. Jeez, she thought, sometimes Ethan's genteel ways were cumbersome. She plucked a book off the shelf. Flipping through it quickly, she found the pictures in question and showed them to the two policemen. "See, there's a penis. They don't like them." She felt Ethan wince.

"It was the first time that there had ever been that sort of nudity in a children's book," Ethan began to explain. "It was all very tastefully done, mind you. But some people objected."

"Huh." The lieutenant was impassive. It was clear to Calista that Ethan's overweening delicacy was ridiculous.

"And then, of course, there were those radical feminist groups, and remember SCUM?"

"SCUM," said the plainclothesman, the one without a name tag.

"Society for Cutting Up Men," Calista said. "Remember them? One of them shot Andy Warhol."

"Yeah," said the plainclothesman. "They don't like you, either?"

"They don't like my princesses."

"Your princesses?" McCafferty looked up and tapped a gold-edged front tooth with his pen.

"Oh, yes!" Ethan's face brightened. He clearly preferred keeping his authors away from discussions of anatomy in favor of the more nuts and bolts aspects of fairy tales. "Calista does the most extraordinary princesses. You should see."

Oh, God! Calista thought. She dearly loved Ethan. He was the most devoted, supportive man in the world, but he could be wearisome, she thought. These guys did not want to hear how beautiful her princesses were. They wanted to know about how SCUM had written her those scummy letters.

"Yeah." She broke in to Ethan's eulogy for her princesses. "You know. I do stuff like *Sleeping Beauty, The Twelve Dancing Princesses.* You know, your basic fairy-tale princess stuff, and I like drawing boobs, and I like drawing hair, and these radical feminists can never get beyond that; you know, they're so doctrinaire. They see that and they immediately think wimpy female. My princesses are distinctly unmagical. They rely on brains more than potions. They are wily, you know, more in the mold of a Ulysses."

"Yes." Janet nodded, although she was uncertain as to how much Boston's finest was really absorbing of this brief foray into the genre of children's literature.

"And what about you, Miss McGowan?"

"Yes?" Margaret looked up from her glass of rye.

"Do you ever receive any offensive mail about your work?"

"Well, now." She spoke slowly. "It depends on what you call offensive. Just last week I received a letter from a little boy. It was one of twenty letters from a class out in Elgin, Illinois. The teacher, if you can believe this, made the entire class write me a letter after they had read one of my books, *The Twilight of Kyre.* It's the first in the Knights of Kyre chronicles. It's bad enough thinking of a roomful of children being forced to read one of my books, let alone having to write me. So this little boy writes, 'You are a complete bore. I hated your book. I'm being forced to write this and I hope you drop dead so I won't ever have to read another one of your darn books.' Now that is offensive. But I can hardly say I blame him."

Both cops nodded.

"But," she continued, "if you're talking penises . . ."

27

Ethan Thayer visibly blanched. He had not been expecting this from Margaret's quarter. He reached inside his pocket for his nitroglycerin tablets. For Ethan Thayer, scion of one of the oldest publishing families and chairman of the board of one of the few remaining houses that had not been swallowed and conglomeratized, this had obviously become an angina-producing situation.

"Well," Margaret continued, "I don't have them in my books because, you know, there's so much armor and all. It would be very awkward. There are not that many illustrations in my novels anyhow, and, well, somehow I can't imagine showing a troll in the buff. There are lots of trolls in my books. It could get a little revolting. But as we were saying, that goon at the conference seems to think I've done something to his Lord Jesus Christ. I really loathe this proprietary manner in which people speak of God. The possessive pronoun, when used with God, is rather like lemon in milk—it curdles."

Calista wanted to get back to the murder. "You say it was a very professional job." No one so far had asked many details of the death. "What do you mean?"

"It was quick and quiet," the plainclothesman said.

"As opposed to noisy and messy?" Margaret asked.

The cops exchanged uneasy looks. Janet and Calista looked at one another.

"What aren't you telling us?" Calista demanded suddenly.

"Uh . . ." David Cummings, who had just arrived with the editor from Sundial, shifted on his chair and began to speak for the first time. "Calista, there were some very . . ." He paused and compressed his lips into a bloodless line. "Some messy details that I think you'd rather not know about."

Calista looked straight at him. She was a beautiful woman in her early forties with a luxuriant tumble of prematurely silver-gray hair. It was her trademark, but suddenly she looked older than Margaret McGowan. Her dark hooded eyes, normally warm, twinkling, and slightly mysterious, had turned lifeless and opaque. "David," she said in a low, dusty voice, "death is a mess." And she didn't need to tell him that she knew that better than most. She turned sharply toward the two cops. "Now what happened?"

Janet Weiss was thinking that if these two dudes didn't know about Calista's princesses before, they did now.

"Well, ma'am," McCafferty began, "there was a lot of blood, considering the MO."

"MO?" Calista's mind was going in slow motion. These guys always talked in letters, initials. What was the MO? The method? Hadn't they said something before about strangulation?

"Garroting."

"Isn't that something the Mafia does?" Janet asked.

The plainclothesman shifted on his seat. "Yes, they've been known to. They don't have an exclusive, though."

"There wouldn't be much blood from that," Calista said. "Where did it all come from?"

"That's what we'd like to know. Some from him."

"Some?" Calista was bewildered. "What do you mean, some?" McCafferty fiddled with his ballpoint pen and looked over toward his partner.

"Not enough," the plainclothesman said almost abruptly.

"Not enough?" Calista asked. "Enough for what?"

"For the writing on the wall."

"Who wrote on the wall?" Margaret McGowan's voice sounded like sandpaper in the still room.

"The murderer, presumably," McCafferty replied.

"What did he write?" Calista leaned forward. Neither man answered. "Tell us, what did the murderer write?" She clenched her fist and hammered it on the table.

"Monkey's Uncle." The plainclothes detective said the words in a low voice.

Calista settled back in her chair and primly folded her hands in her lap. She felt her eyes fill up, but she knew she would not cry. She was the most disciplined person on earth. It was both her blessing and her curse. She had needed to know these loathsome details so she could get beyond them. But now she knew precisely what her duty was. She must remember Norman Petrakis, this gentle man, as she had last seen him. The man who had found the Charioteer over the Hancock Building in the black velvet of a Boston night. She would look for the Charioteer every night through its ascendant spring, as it made its

29

transit across the skies until it slid out of sight in midsummer. Then she would wait for it again in the cool nights of autumn.

3

There was never any hiding of anything from Charley. Luckily Charley would not be coming home directly after school, so she would not have to tell him immediately. It was the night of the big performance of his school at the Loeb Drama Center, and he would be participating in it. It was called *City Step* and was a collaborative program between Harvard undergraduates and Cambridge Public School kids. It was a dance program that was somewhere in tempo and energy between aerobics and jazz. Each spring they gave a performance at the Loeb, home of the American Repertory Theater on Brattle Street. Charley would be upset about Petrakis. Although he did not know him personally, he had a shelf full of Petrakis's books, especially those that were devoted to model airplanes, flight, and aeronautical engineering.

There was no way Calista would miss Charley's performance or spoil it with this news. There was time for a drink, another shower, and a bite to eat before the performance. She put on a nice sedate pair of trousers and an elegantly cut Armani jacket. It was a man's jacket, and she had found it in Filene's basement. Out of habit she still went to the men's section even though she didn't have a man to buy for anymore. The deals she had picked up for Tom! Every once in a while she found something in what she called their Napoleonic Division that would fit her. This jacket was one. She liked to look nice for Charley especially when a lot of his buddies were around. Although he wore the most repulsive and outlandish clothes, and on occasion she had to censor his T-shirts for their suggestive inscriptions, he had very rigid and conservative sartorial guidelines for his mother. He wanted her to look "normal." Sometimes she apparently looked abnormal, like the time she had worn a Celtics jersey—

number 33 no less, Larry Bird's number—with a pair of white silk trousers to some event. Charley was mortified. "I know you like Larry Bird. I like Larry Bird, but you shouldn't wear that in public. It's not like a normal mother."

She managed to get to the theater in ample time and send a message backstage to Charley that she was there. It was a wonderful performance. The kids were so high, so beautiful, so pleased and proud of their marvelous dancing and of their marvelous bodies. It had actually been easy for Calista to forget the horror of the last few hours. Nothing could attest more to life than the one hundred kids from the public schools in all shades and sizes, plus the twenty from Harvard who had worked so lovingly with them, as they lit up the stage with their energy, their rhythm, and their faith in themselves. The energy was absolutely contagious. The audience had gone wild and demanded encore after encore. The *Harvard Crimson* and the *Boston Globe* and the *Cambridge Chronicle* all hailed it as one of Harvard's finest hours—those hours when the kids of Cambridge came together to dance. Yes, it had been easy for those two hours to forget what had happened, to drive out the images, that were somehow etched on her brain—images of strangulations and of words scrawled in blood on hotel room walls.

After the performance Calista and Charley and his friend Matthew McPhail and his mother and father had gone to the Border Cafe on Church Street, a favorite Mexican restaurant of the kids. Charley and Matthew were still high on the performance and high on the fact that the teachers had suspended any real homework for this week due to the performance.

"Too bad we can't do this all year long. Just think, no homework, no book reports."

"Oh, book reports!" Charley exclaimed. "I hate book reports. They are so stupid. Why do we have to do book reports? There is absolutely no good reason."

"If you want to be a book review critic," offered Joan McPhail.

"Never!" Charley said. "Critics are a dirty word in our house."

"Charley!" Calista blushed furiously. "That's not true."

31

"You hate 'em. You said so."

"Why?" Fred McPhail asked. "They always give your mother wonderful reviews."

"Most always," Calista said. "So it's only the ones who don't. that I hate. And I don't really hate them. I just think they're stupid. I never said that I hated them, Charley."

"Well, you said that one was stupid."

"Yes, but it's not the same thing. And anyhow I don't think book reports are a bad thing."

"Yeah," said Charley, "but it's so much more fun doing stuff like *City Step*."

"Or Project Look Ahead," Matthew said.

"Oh, yes. When does that start?" Joan asked.

"Next week," Charley said, referring to another program in the Cambridge Public Schools which teamed junior high and high school students with professionals in the area.

"And you're both going to be at the Martin Institute, right?" Fred asked.

"Yes," Matthew said. "We just don't know which labs yet."

"Yeah," said Charley. "If we could only dance in *City Step* and then do this real-life stuff—that should be what school is. You should never have to sit down and write book reports or take spelling or math tests. You should just do it in real-life situations."

Calista smiled at her son. "You mean no practice, no drills, no skill stuff?"

"I mean nothing boring, is what I mean. Working in labs isn't boring, building stuff isn't boring, but being tested is boring and being programmed is, too. Hands-on, like Dad used to say—real experience!" Charley smiled a sweet-sad look to his mom.

That look of Charley's always got her. But she wouldn't trade it for the world. He would remember his dad even though he had shared barely a decade with him. She had shared nearly two decades. A sliver of time, it seemed. But when she looked at Charley's face and that expression, she knew it had added up to much more.

Calista took a sip of her beer now. The din of the restaurant

32

had become like a white noise to her. It was easy to fall into private silences and remember. Calista had met Tom in her junior year in college. After graduation and when she was starting her career as a children's book illustrator, she divided her week between New York and Princeton, where Tom was still working. Gradually she moved most of her stuff down to Princeton. Easier for an illustrator to move a drawing board to Princeton than for a particle physicist to move an accelerator to New York. Tom called Calista's New York place her "morality apartment." Although by the end of three years when they got married Calista was fairly certain her parents knew that she was virtually and unvirtuously living in Princeton. They got married and then went to Cal Tech and then to Harvard.

Joan McPhail was looking out of the corner of her eye at Calista. Calista sensed that she was worried that this talk of Tom was disturbing her. It wasn't the talk of Tom, really. It was the creeping red-tinged shadows of the violence, of the bizarre bloody images of Norman Petrakis's murder, that were stealing back into her now. The wild energy and joy of the children's dancing was beginning to dissolve.

They stepped out onto the curb of Church Street. A wet chill air smacked them in the face.

"This doesn't feel like April weather," Joan said.

"And what does April weather in New England feel like?" Fred asked.

"Probably this," Joan said. "I can't seem to remember that Boston doesn't have a spring. Lived here ten years and can't remember. Virginia had such lovely springs."

"Indiana, too," Calista added.

"I keep forgetting that you come originally from Indiana, Calista," Fred said.

"The springs were very nice," she replied almost tersely, as if to suggest that there were few other charms. She was watching the boys. They were running ahead with their skateboards under their arms. Charley and Matthew and their friends rarely went anyplace without their skateboards. The gates on the far side of Harvard Yard would be closed at this hour. The boys had crossed Mass. Ave. As soon as they reached the other side and the sidewalk that led around the west side of the yard, they put down their boards and took off skimming by Harvard and Hollis halls and Holden Chapel. Calista smiled to herself as she watched the lithe youngsters whiz by those plain homely brick buildings behind the iron gates of the yard. Built in the Colonial period, they were among the oldest buildings of the college. Charley sliced through a cone of light from a street lamp that illuminated for a brief instant his fierce red hair. He wore it long, and now it flared in the apparent wind of his movement, flared in an aureole of flames, a ring of fire, actually, more than a halo. Siva, the cosmic dancer! The Hindu god! Siva, the Creator and the Destroyer, the deity who moved in a ring of fire while balancing the forces of creation and destruction. Charley wheeled on through the night, rounding the corner by Philip Brooks House onto one of the paths that crisscrossed the space between the Science Center and the north side of Harvard Yard.

"The springs—that's it for Indiana?" Fred said.

Calista had not meant to get so lost in her thoughts and visions of Charley.

"Oh!" She laughed. "Well, the dogwoods are beautiful, and the redbud. There are just miles and miles of redbud. You go down into southern Indiana in May and you've never seen such stretches of pink and red. And there are cornfields."

"And that's about it," Joan said. Calista was not sure if it was a statement or a question.

"Well, that used to be it. But in Indianapolis, where I come from, the cornfields have been eaten up."

"By what?" Fred asked.

"Shopping malls." Calista sighed, thinking of her last trip to the Midwest. "Indiana has been malled—malled to death." She paused. They turned the corner, following their boys. She supposed that the space that the boys were now whizzing through could be considered a kind of shopless mall. A long wide rectangle crisscrossed by paths culminating in Memorial Hall. Some had described Memorial Hall as a cathedral mated with a railroad terminal. Calista, however, thought of the Victorian edifice as the Matterhorn of Harvard in its somber, inescapable thereness.

34

On the left side of the shopless mall was the Science Center. Built from poured concrete and steel, it was by reputation exemplary of the New Brutalism in architecture, but to Calista the building seemed more funky than brutal with its clear expression of mechanical and structural elements. Generators, air-conditioning, and heat stacks erupted through the roof— the building's guts encased in massive concrete cubes. Suspension trusses rose over the roof, forming low-slung triangles from which the two major auditorium ceilings were hung. The effect on this night of gathering mist was that of a cubistic jumble of concrete blocks hovering just above the ground.

The boys were having a great time. Pedestrian traffic was light. A few students walked from the Science Library toward the Holworthy Gate, which apparently was still open into the yard, and Charley and Matthew, showing no fatigue from their nighttime dance performance, were beginning yet another performance.

"Is that what you call an Ollie?" Joan asked as she saw first her own son and then Charley go airborne on a stretch of path.

"I think so," said Calista. "What I don't understand is what is a power slide?"

"Me neither," said Fred. "Hey, Charley," he called. "Demonstrate a power slide for us."

Charley crouched down on the board and grabbed the edge. One side of the board lifted, and it was now traveling on only its outer wheels. He shaved the edge of the path leaning backward and, picking up speed, headed toward a grouping of rocks from the base of which rose a very fine spray of water.

"Why would they have that fountain on now?" Fred asked. "On a night like this? There's enough humidity around already."

"Who knows. But Charley's going to get wet. Charley!" she called, but it was useless. He was already slaloming through the maze of rocks.

"What did you call those, Calista—meadow muffins?"

"Yeah. The fountain's a nice idea, but the rocks look like piles of cow manure. I've never seen uglier rocks. They're so rounded and even, and the way they've got them lined up, so rigid and predictable."

"I see what you mean," Joan said. "The rocks you have in that Japanese garden of yours are much more interesting."

"I mean it's a nice idea, the spray and everything. But round turdlike rocks set in asphalt would give a Japanese gardener pause, if not cardiac arrest, I would think," Calista said thoughtfully.

Charley emerged from the spray of the rock fountain beaded with a fine dew.

At the corner of Oxford and Kirkland the two families parted ways. The McPhails headed up Oxford to the house they had recently purchased on Gorham, less than a half mile from their old house, and Calista and Charley headed straight up Kirkland to their house on James Place tucked behind the Harvard museums and the law and the divinity schools of the university. They had lived there for almost fifteen years—Calista as an almost new bride, then young mother, and almost now, well, yes, middle-aged mother and widow.

4
The sky appeared marbled with clouds, and the trees with just a stain of green in their bare dark branches seemed more frail than ever. Calista resisted making a comment about the weather, however. She had just told Charley about the murder of Norman Petrakis. Weather talk was after all the conversational counterpart to hamburger filler, and she had been tempted in order to break the tension, or perhaps simply to try to move the conversation, the mood, into more neutral territory. But she knew this was not right or good. Charley needed to digest this piece of news. Even though Charley did not personally know Petrakis, and he was not a friend, still a reader had lost a favorite author. And this carried with it its own kind of sadness. He was particularly fond of the series Petrakis had done on the making of model airplanes.

Charley now dragged his fork in a light tracery over the

surface of the yolk of his fried egg. Then he jabbed at it in one swift motion. "Did he have children?" he asked.

"No," Calista replied.

"Well, I guess that's someone less to miss him."

For a dreadful and seemingly unending minute they were drawn back to that awful time three years before when Tom Jacobs had died. At the time, of course, they did not realize he had been murdered. And when they had found out a year later, it had been like experiencing those awful days all over again. Tom Jacobs had been an outspoken opponent to nuclear arms. Three years before, he had died a peculiar death in the desert that at first had appeared to be natural—as natural as a rattlesnake bite could ever appear, Calista thought bitterly. It had been Charley and Calista who had ultimately proved that indeed it had not been a snake with malice aforethought, but a human, and that although the CIA had not been directly implicated, they were not precisely heartbroken to see Tom Jacobs out of this administration's hair. Tom Jacobs, when not contemplating the mysteries of the origins of the universe and building theoretical models, liked to build little machines. One of these little machines was called the Time Slicer. It could not only do very refined dating based on magnetic variations in certain rocks and minerals, but it could also detect underground nuclear testing.

Jacobs had been in the desert with the Time Slicer at the specific request of Archie Baldwin, a Smithsonian archaeologist. Baldwin had suspected that a Paleo-Indian site was being seeded, that the artifacts were phonies and had been brought in from other locations. At that time he had no way of knowing that Peter Gardiner, the archaeologist, was crossing over into a deep paranoia, and that in fact the mission he was sending Jacobs on would end in tragedy. It was because of the information that this machine could yield that Tom Jacobs had died, that a child had become orphaned and a woman widowed. Right after Tom's death Calista had been plenty upset with Baldwin, although she had never met him. But a year later Charley himself had very nearly gotten killed in the process of trying to solve the murder. And this time it had been Baldwin who had saved Charley's life. Calista was eternally grateful.

Although Norman Petrakis's death had none of the same intensity for Calista and Charley, the fact that it was a murder brought with it a chilling resonance. Charley ate silently for a while. Calista looked out the window and watched clouds build. They were high and thin, and they stretched like snaggly fingers clawing the sky. She had drawn witches with fingers like that—in *Hansel and Gretel* and the ogress in *Rapunzel*—those dreadful fingers clutching the scissors in one hand and wrenching the girl's head back with the other.

"Why?" Charley finally said. "Why would anybody do that? A children's book author?" Calista winced quietly to herself. "Why? How did it happen?"

Calista told the story, starting with the obnoxious man in the audience and finishing with the peculiar words scrawled in blood. Charley bit his lip as he concentrated on the story. It was a habit that he shared with his mother. Calista marveled that either one of them had a lip left to bite.

"It doesn't fit," he said at last.

"What doesn't fit?"

"I'm not sure," Charley said vaguely. "But it's something about the blood on the wall, the words *Monkey's Uncle,* and this dude at the conference."

"Well, I told you what the police said—that it was too much blood to have come from a person murdered that way."

"Yeah, yeah. I know you said that. But it's more than that that doesn't fit."

"What?"

"I'm not sure." His expression was blank. The dull eyes and the nearly motionless face would signal to most people that something less than scintillating was occurring in the cranium, but Calista knew it was just the opposite. She had seen that same expression on Tom's face and was convinced that it had been encoded in the DNA as precisely as the red hair and the pale gray eyes and all the other hereditary baggage. It was the expression that went with contemplating uncertainty, with the endless fascination and astonishment at the unpredictable nature of things. Tom and now Charley were particularly agile at dealing with uncertainty on an intellectual level. They found an odd kind of comfort in pondering the breaks in patterns. Tom had

38

been the world's foremost theoretician of black holes, those quirks in the cosmos where all the known rules of gravity and physics break down. And something had now broken down in the pattern of the story of Norman Petrakis's murder that intrigued Charley, that made his face grow stony in its contemplation and his pale gray eyes become as opaque as the cloud-marbled sky.

The news story of Norman Petrakis's murder was buried on a back page of the *Boston Globe*. Calista showed it to Charley, and he read it quickly while he zipped his parka. The news account did not even mention the scrawl of blood on the hotel wall.

"It doesn't fit, that's for sure," Charley said, clamping his lips into a firm line. He slung his backpack over his shoulders and, grabbing his skateboard, went out the door to catch the school bus at the end of the block.

Calista had aimed to kiss his cheek but wound up with his earlobe instead. "Take care," she called.

Her drawing board was set up. The text for *Marian's Tale* was finally edited, the dummy approved, and now the galleys of the text had come back from the typesetter, all the drawings pencil-sketched in, and she was ready to begin finished artwork; to blow up the dummy into the dazzling experience—a children's picture book. There were two times that were most exciting in the process of creating a picture book. The first point occurred after the story had been written and it was time to plan the layout and make the dummy. The dummy was a miniature of the book. And Calista's dummies were even more miniature than most, often measuring only two and one-half inches by three for a book that in its final form would have a trim size of eleven by fourteen. But these tiny dummies in their intensity and exquisite detail possessed a shimmering brilliance. In a retrospective of Calista's work the previous year at the Morgan Library in New York, one critic had likened them to Fabergé Easter eggs. "Looks like you laid an egg," Charley had commented when he heard of the critics' praise.

The second exciting moment in creating a picture book came when it was time to blow up the dummy into the finished art. She was at that point now. She had spent two and a half months working on small pencil sketches, and now she was ready to start with pen and ink and paint. She should have been tremendously excited. Her drawing board was ready, the galleys chopped up into the proper blocks of text, and on her Plexiglas cookbook holder to the left of the drawing board in her study was a two-hundred-dollar book of the *Très Riches Heures du Duc de Berry*—the most exquisite reproduction to date of the *Book of Hours* that was in the Musée Condé in Chantilly.

It was the medieval pictorial conventions of the books of hours that would play a dominant role in the graphic style of *Marian's Tale.* Calista liked the gilt of these books of hours, but she liked the skies even more. The Limburg brothers, the early illustrators of the duke's first books, had an extraordinary feeling for both the countryside and the luxury of the court. Together the brothers were probably the most brilliant illustrators of architecture in history. Between that book and her frequent trips to Harvard's Houghton Library, where there was a treasure trove of other books of hours, she was set to work on a splendid tale—Robin Hood as told from Maid Marian's point of view. But now she balked. It was hard to get into the gilt and the splendor of the books of hours or the lush verdancy of Sherwood Forest with those other images, the ones of the bloody scrawl, so fresh in her mind. She would procrastinate just a bit.

She went out her back door. It was time for a turn through her garden. She was a great and eager monitor of the earliest vernal stirrings. By this third week in April the crocuses were past history. But she nearly shrieked as she spied the sudden start of red in the bed by her brick terrace. Spurting from the earth like blood, the small tulips grew low and scarlet near the ground. She had forgotten about the new exotic mixture of early blooming tulips that she had put in last fall, and she certainly had not remembered that these were such a violent shade of red. She believed that they were called Little Red Riding Hoods. The catalog had not done them justice. But then again, since the murder of Norman Petrakis her imagination had been working overtime.

Calista held a spectrum of color in her brain that was constantly shimmering even in the dark. She hardly had need of waves of light striking her retina to get excited about a color. It was as if her optic nerve could do it alone without retinal stimulus. Now it was getting a little out of hand, particularly in terms of the hues of red. She tried to convince herself that the gush of red tulips from the black wet earth did not look like a major artery bursting open. They had delicate little cup-shaped blossoms that the catalog had promised would look just like Little Red Riding Hood's hood. That had done it for her. She had ordered thirty-six bulbs. Calista had been a Red Riding Hood freak as a child. Always wore a red cape and hood. Even had one now that she had made up for herself from bright red wool.

She continued walking around the garden. Under a mountain laurel that she had pruned back violently last year, the earth was stippled with a jeweled potpourri of miniature bulbs just springing forth. There were dwarf irises, snowdrops, something called Dasystemon that exploded from the earth like yellow shooting stars. She must come out and sketch them before they went by. They reminded her of some of the borders in the books of hours, particularly the plates of the biblical passages. She squinted at the ground, and the blues and golds merged. The *Fall of the Rebel Angels?* One of the Limburgs' best with the extraordinary cascade of angels from the sky. Yes, the snowdrops still dewy could be the silver helmets at the heavenly host's feet. And the blue dwarf irises would be the tunics of the falling rebel angels. Those dashes of color were enough to send her back into the house and her studio.

5

I shall make you love books more than your mother.—from *The Instruction of Dua Khety,* Egyptian text of the Middle Kingdom.

The inscription had been beautifully transcribed with a calligraphic pen onto handcrafted marbled paper. It hung just to the right of the heavy walnut sliding door to Calista's studio on a paneled wall, directly above a cast-iron grill. Another calligraphic inscription below it read, *"Hey, there's ladies here!"* The second one was attributable to Mel Brooks, a quote from the 2,000-year-old man alluding to the discovery of women on the planet.

In the studio there were, of course, the tools of an artist. The ink pots, the sable brushes in gradations of size purchased dearly in Chinatown, a stack of Wattnum board, one of her favorite surfaces for drawing, paints, acrylics, oils, watercolors. All of the walls except for one were dark walnut and shelved with books, mostly reference books—bestiaries, costume design books, hundreds of horticulture books. For her work she needed to know not just how a plant or an animal or a dress looked then as well as now, but also how people's imaginations worked then. She had a deep and passionate interest in the evolutionary pressures that had been exerted not merely on the human form that turned hominid to human in terms of opposable thumbs and upright posture, but most particularly in those transformations of the brain. Calista was interested in what throughout the ages had frightened people. What made them laugh? What did they find intolerable? How did they perceive children, and how did children perceive them?

No one perceived children more peculiarly in Calista's mind than the Victorians. She had a valuable collection of nineteenth-century first-edition children's books and drawings that included Beatrix Potter, Randolph Caldecott, Arthur Rackham, and others. There were also in this collection numerous arcane cookbooks. One was a book of Elizabethan cookery, and she periodically threatened Charley with hedgehog *en dorée.* Charley was a dedicated McDonald's fan and the only child in Cambridge who still ate white bread as far as Calista could ascertain.

So the room seemed more of a study than a studio, a Victorian study at that, with its love seat upholstered in red-and-white velvet candy cane stripes flanked on either end by small Tiffany lamps. Tasseled ivory curtains hung in the three windows of the bay. The floor had been painted a lacquer green and was mostly covered by a worn but still elegant ancient Oriental rug that sparkled like old rubies in the evening light of the room.

On her drawing table were numerous small toys. Calista liked to fiddle when she got stuck. Her favorite "toys," though, were her trout flies that she tied herself. She even had clamped to the table an Anderson Model C flytier's vise. On a small stand now rested her most recent efforts. She had retied the entire life cycle of the mayfly from nymph to dun and on through to its maturity and spent stages.

Opposite her desk was an eighteenth-century wing chair. Elegant and quiet, it contrasted nicely with the striped love seat. Charley often sat on it talking with his mom as she worked. Now, however, it was occupied by one of Calista's stuffed animals, one of the good buddies of the Hedge and Owl series. The two characters had been made into stuffed animals and sold at F.A.O. Schwarz and department stores. They had become hot items. All those yuppies were starting to reproduce, and Hedge and Owl dolls were as indispensable to them as the cappuccino machines.

She sighed, opened a bottle of ink, and reached for her favorite thin-nibbed pen and what she called her eyelash brush. The trim size of this book was ten and one-half by eight and one-half inches. This was her world now. It must be for the next seven hours. She could not allow anything intrusive to disturb her. There could be no thoughts of bloody scrawls, only very deliberate strokes of this number three pen. It was safe, it was confined, and she controlled everything that happened here on this small field of white.

The frontispiece of the book faced her. The design spilled over onto the title page. It looked simple. It looked spare. But it was not. The blank space that occupied nearly 75 percent of the page was important. In spite of the borders, which were a fairly direct borrowing from the elaborate ones of the *Book of Hours of the Duc de Berry,* the illustrations on these two pages had to have a movement and tension. They had to leap beyond the decorative frame and lead into the story. Illustration was an interpretive art: it added to the text. It illuminated meaning, shed light, and even sometimes created mystery simultaneously, but it never translated directly. If it did, the magic of the book stopped. The pictures became oddly opaque. The text must flow ceaselessly, and the images of the pictures should intertwine subtly. It must all appear seamless, effortless—a knock-off. This was what picture book illustration was about.

Calista was a person who lived inside of books, particularly picture books. And although there were values embedded in her stories, she never preached. She was a storyteller first and last, which meant that her imagination was important, but her reader's imagination was more important. It felt good now to be entering this forum with its eight-by-ten dimensions, to be inside her books where she could control the characters, where the world was predictable. Nottingham, after all, was a simple place. You knew who the bad guys were, and the crimes were not high crimes of murder. And most of the time only the bad guys died for good.

The illustration sketched in pencil showed an arrow being shot from a narrow slot in a stone wall and sailing over a cultivated garden into the blankness of the facing page. From the extreme edge of the facing page, as if growing from the paper's edge, were the inky greens of the forest's foliage with a sliver of a tree trunk showing. The gulf of white separated the lush verdant forest from the stone convent. And always through the book there would be this tantalizing juxtaposition of the world of stone and built form against that of the wildness and green freedom of the forest. This was the torsion of the book. *Marian's Tale* began in a convent. For that was where in Calista's retelling Maid Marian had fled to escape the amorous attentions of the foul-breathed, pockmarked greedy Prince John. Research had shown that Marian had not entered the cycle of the Robin Hood tales until well into the sixteenth century. She did so as Matilda Fitzwalter, the historical wife of Robin Hood. She had been toyed with ever since in retellings.

Three years before, Ethan Thayer had bought the rights to the novel-length Paul Creswick version, and Calista had done the first paintings since N. C. Wyeth's for the book. She had had to stick to the text, but this other idea of a tale told from Marian's point of view began to simmer on some back burner of her brain. Now it was her turn, Calista's version of the tale. It was to be Marian's tale, and everything would be different. No more matinee idols for Robin, and Marian would be different, too.

She had found an almost suitable face on the subway one day. There was a guy who had gotten on at Kenmore Square and off at Charles Street. Luckily, when the train comes between those two stops it rides into daylight for a short stretch on the Longfellow Bridge over the Charles River. The man's face was not really a handsome one at all in the classical sense. It was too rough. Great bone structure, but hacked, or perhaps rough-hewn, rather than chiseled. This had resulted in startling collisions of the facial planes. It was a face, she had suspected, that was slightly too old in its structure for the person. He would have to grow into it. And as the train rushed into the light of day, he looked up directly at Calista. The incongruity of the rather puerile mud brown eyes confirmed her suspicions. Some faces could sustain such oxymoronic quirks. Others could not. The latter was the case with this face. She would have to think about the eyes, but she'd take the bone structure.

For Marian she had the eyes worked out. They would be slightly vampy, a touch of Louise Brooks and Anita Loos. As she worked on the frontispiece she began to softly whistle "Diamonds Are a Girl's Best Friend." She loved that song. She had loved the movie. There was a baby in one of her early books that had Marilyn Monroe eyes. She was listening to Morning Pro Musica, but Robert J Lurtsenia was sighing deeply over the news at that moment as she sketched out the stones of the tower. She caught herself subconsciously waiting for Robert J to mention something on the news about Petrakis. But there was no reference. She forced herself back to the business at hand— crosshatching the stonework.

By eleven forty-five she had the tower inked in and had begun the dense crosshatching that would give volume and shadow to the stones. A Hanson Romantic concerto was swirling through the air. She felt a twinge of hunger but decided on a coffee break instead. She walked to the kitchen and poured herself a cup of coffee from the electric pot she kept going. Back at her desk she reached into a tin box that was the shape of the Albert Hall in London for a *biscotti*. She was thinking about that

45

color of green, the one of the books of hours and the one of Sherwood Forest, and how she would make it flow from one page to the other in the border motifs and then into the forest.

She tapped her feet lightly as she bit into the cookie. Robert J was sighing again. She couldn't bear any more grim reports about a devastating earthquake in Peru. She resumed tapping her feet gently on the floor. Gads! She just remembered her tap-dancing class was tonight. She never missed her tap class. Charley was mortally embarrassed to have a mother who took tap dancing. Why couldn't she take aerobics like other mothers? He had sworn her to secrecy about this vice of hers and made her promise she would never perform anywhere at all ever in his lifetime in this galaxy.

"Do lobsters ever get rabies?" he had asked once when he had caught her practicing.

"I don't think so. Why?" she had answered.

"Well, if they did and walked upright, they would look like you tap-dancing."

This did not deter her. She enjoyed the exercise and looked forward to her class that evening.

She worked through the afternoon. By four o'clock she had finished the pen-and-ink work on the frontispiece and title page. She would have to think seriously about color now. She knew it was time to quit. She had to think about that transition of green in the borders, and at the end of a long day she was not up for it. But she wasn't up for thoughts of murder, either. And it seemed as soon as she stopped working that was what she thought of—Norman Petrakis. Why hadn't the police ever called her back? They had said that they would keep in touch and tell her if they had any leads. But she had heard nothing, and it had barely been mentioned in the newspaper. She supposed there would be no harm in calling up the Boston Police Department. She could ask to talk to one of the detectives. She ransacked her brain for the cops' names. McCafferty, she was almost positive that was one. She dialed the number and asked for Lieutenant McCafferty. He wasn't in. How about his partner? What partner? The one that had been on the Petrakis murder case? Petrakis murder? Oh, yeah, it seemed to ring a distant bell, but she had better call back in the morning when

46

someone who knew more about it would be on duty. "Doesn't anybody know anything about this?" Calista asked with a slight desperation in her voice.

"Don't worry," the officer on duty said.

"Don't worry?!" she screamed.

"Honey . . . ,"

Oh, yuck, Calista thought. How far could you get with a cop who calls you honey? He was going on now about a series of drug-related murders in the Mattapan section of Boston. Innocent people getting cut down by stray bullets and how this was using most of the homicide detectives. In short, the death of Norman Petrakis had failed to become a top priority. It did not fit into a pattern of violence that was threatening the city; therefore Norman had become just a statistic to be swallowed up in the morass of other forgotten souls whose demises failed to pique the interest of the department because of the circumstances. If Norman had been ensnared somehow into the web of drugs, either as an operative or an innocent bystander and died within that ring of fire, then someone would have been working on it. But dying alone in a hotel room with a bloody scrawl on the wall, well, that fit into no patterns and was so bizarre as to not be considered a threat in at least an endemic sense. There was something ineffably sad about it all.

6

Charley had soccer practice after school. Calista left a message with the school secretary that he should take the Mount Auburn Street bus out to Watertown Square and meet her at Stellina's, their favorite Italian restaurant, for dinner after her tap class. She went upstairs and grabbed her tap-dancing gear along with her swimming suit. She always stopped in at the Mount Auburn Club to swim off the tap sweat and take a sauna and steam after class. People at the Mount Auburn Club were not into tap dancing. They were into aerobics with a vengeance, squash, tennis, networking parties where business cards were traded while eating sushi and sipping burgundy, a combination of food that appalled Calista almost as much as the meadow muffin rocks set in asphalt. But indeed there had been a notice on the club board for a sushi-and-burgundy-tasting party.

Mindy Berkhauer was over sixty years old and the tap teacher. She had briefly been a Rockette, and she talked just like Dr. Ruth while she tap-danced. She didn't talk about sex, though. She talked about listening for the correct sounds of the taps. She talked about "feathering" a brush stroke and digging in on the cramp roll. And she was loaded with anecdotal material—about Flo Ziegfeld, Ann Miller, Fred Astaire. It was a lot more interesting than Dr. Ruth and "Vhat form of birth control are you using?" Much more "Vell, you know who Cab Callovay really vas mad for? . . . Ach! Calista, no, no, dahlink. You're not breaking vith the knees."

At six-thirty Calista was sitting naked in the steam room of the Mount Auburn Club. Through the miasma of the humid clouds came the disembodied voices of two other women. One was special counsel to the governor of Massachusetts, and the other one was a vice-president of the Boston Stock Exchange. They were discussing something about the Governor's Commission on Affirmative Action. Heavy-duty group. The women's locker room was laced with talk like this. There was a preponderance of attorneys, computer software people, and therapists. They spent a lot of time helping other women achieve power and serving on governor's and mayor's commissions and panels. Calista had once served on a panel for the arts. But nothing got done, and she got a fancy certificate to commemorate the experience of serving on a panel that had accomplished absolutely nothing. Calista didn't listen that much when she went to the club. She looked at the naked bodies. There was an incredible range of form and size and coloring. She studied these bodies surreptitiously. It was part of her job. For beneath every clothed body that she drew was a moving, naked one. All plump bodies in children's books tended to look like jugs, roly-poly vessels with no movement or animation. But Calista had had a plump grandmother. She had died when Calista was very young, but she still had a vivid image of her whirling about a kitchen, lightly, full of grace and rhythm. She had of course never seen that grandmother undressed, never had the opportunity to study the anatomy of a plump, active woman. Here she did. Women trotted all over the huge locker room naked as jaybirds, their bodies pink and glistening from the steam room or the sauna. They lotioned themselves, sprayed themselves. The pleasant *thwack*ing sound of after-bath splash being slapped onto different kinds of flesh punctuated the air. There were all sorts of buttocks. It might surprise many people, Calista thought, to discover that fat women did not necessarily have fat fannies. Often their posteriors were surprisingly flat, and their cheeks drooped into flaccid little creases. And there were ways that breasts that had nursed infants sagged that Calista found beautiful, and there were stomachs that had folds across them that were as attractive as the trampoline-taut tummies that had been winched in by merciless numbers of sit-ups every day.

She found the peculiar, the irregular, as charming and sensual as the honed-to-perfection aerobicised body. This locker room was the best drawing class available. She even had a preview of her own body thirty, forty years hence. She had picked out her seventy-year-old counterpart. The tummy was flat but wrinkled as crepe paper. The skin gathered around the sunken navel like a drooping eyelid. The deflated breasts were slung like little pouches on either side of the sternum, which appeared almost concave with its bones exposed like the ribs in the hull of a finely built dory. The buttocks too had grown bonier, hollowing out on the sides, and the cleft was now just a shadow more than a neat little pleat between two rounded mounds. Where there was enough flesh, it had simply collapsed into very fine wrinkles and thin little folds. Where there was not enough flesh, it had drawn back tightly to reveal the scaffolding, the hinges, the levers, and the ropy musculature of the body. Such was the fate of thin women. It was not really a bad fate at all. The body looked used, worked in the best sense of the word. One could read those ridges, those valleys and hollows, like a geologist reading the stratigraphy of an outcrop. Erosion was beautiful. Erosion meant something had happened. Erosion

49

meant history and, in that wonderful phrase of John McPhee, deep time. Calista found great beauty and mystery in this.

Calista herself was more circumspect in her naked peregrinations around the locker room. She always requested a locker near a vanity with a hairdryer so she would not have to walk too far. And she usually put on her underwear and often her stockings or tights before beginning to dry her hair and moisturize her face. Drying and moisturizing were the A to Z of Calista's beauty routine. However, if she were going to something fancy and felt she looked exceedingly pale, she would then put on rouge and some eye makeup.

At seven-fifteen she was sitting in one of the booths at Stellina's inhaling garlic and wondering where Charley was. Just at that moment he came through the door. She could tell by his slicked-back hair that he had actually showered before coming to dinner. Bravo, she thought. One small step for hygiene, one big step for mankind and maturity.

"Hi, sweetie. I ordered you that melted cheese thing on bread with tomatoes. Thought you'd like it."

"I'm famished. I'd eat it melted on a shoe." Charley slid onto the seat opposite her.

Stellina's was one step up from a diner in terms of its decor. The food was one step ahead of Lutèce, as far as Calista was concerned, and at a fraction of the price, needless to say. Most important, it represented a common ground, foodwise, upon which she and Charley could meet. Charley, to say the least, was rather pedestrian in his tastes, aside from his undying fondness and loyalty to squishy white nonnutritious bread, air bread. The waitress came with the appetizers—crostados. The chopped tomatoes on top were sprinkled liberally with basil, olive oil, and garlic, and the smell was heaven. Calista believed firmly that if there was a God, heaven would smell like garlic, basil, and tomatoes.

"Umm, this is good," Charley said, taking his first bite. "What kind of cheese did you say this was?"

"Goat's milk. But don't let it prejudice you," she added quickly.

"No, no, not at all. Who'd ever think a goat could do anything as nice as this. No, this is almost as good as Velveeta."

"Charley!"

He laughed. He loved teasing his mom.

For their main course Charley had spaghetti with the plainest sauce they served, and Calista had òsso buco and risotto Milanese.

"What are you doing?" Charley asked as he watched her take her knife and poke at a bone.

"I'm poking out the marrow."

"You're what?" He looked aghast.

"Poking out the marrow," she repeated. "That's what you do. These are veal shanks. The marrow's in the holes. It's the best part."

Charley lowered his eyes and reached for his water glass. "I've got a marrow-eating mother," he muttered.

"Yes, and she tap-dances, too! What trials!"

He took several swallows of water and put down his glass. "You know I got a French test tomorrow, and I got to pass it or else."

"I don't understand why you're not doing better in French."

"Why! That's easy. Because Madame Morganstern yaps in French constantly. She never says a word in English. How does she expect us to learn anything? It was much better with Mr. O'Flaherty."

"Mr. O'Flaherty was the biggest oaf I ever met."

"He talked slow."

"He thought slow. You can't take a football coach and make him the French teacher."

"I disagree entirely. He said the words so we could understand them."

"He had the thickest Charlestown accent I ever heard."

"He wasn't from Charlestown. He's from Somerville."

"Well, it doesn't matter. You'll never hear a French r coming out of O'Flaherty's mouth."

"Nobody in the greater Boston area says r anyhow."

"But you're learning French, not Boston."

"It doesn't matter. And it's not the pronunciation that's

51

going to flunk us. It's the grammar. O'Flaherty could explain the grammar real good."

"Really well, Charley, as long as we're speaking about grammar."

"Well, you know what I mean."

"Yeah, but I even had grave doubts on that score with O'Flaherty. On that one test last year it was quite apparent that he did not understand the subjunctive tense in the way he structured those questions."

"Subjunctive?" Charley said vaguely. "That's the would-be one, right?"

"The conditional tense, that's right."

"Well, you see, that explains it. O'Flaherty is a man of action, a coach. He operates in the here and now." Charley's eyes were twinkling. He loved arguing with his mother this way.

"Oh." Calista nodded. "Yes, that would explain why he should be on the football field rather than in the French class."

"No," Charley said emphatically. "Except for the subjunctive the guy was great. He explained all that stuff perfectly, in English. This lady, Morganstern, she's not even French and we've got to call her Madame. We never had to call him, you know . . ." He paused. "You know," he repeated. "The word for 'Mister.'"

Calista rolled her eyes. "'Monsieur,' Charley. Good heavens, you don't even know that word!"

"Just slipped my mind. Anyhow, we never had to call him 'Monsieur O'Flaherty.' She's just showing off, this Morganstern lady. That's why she talks French all the time. She loves the sound of her own voice saying it. And she talks. God, does she talk! Mom, you never heard someone talk as much."

"So what about this test tomorrow? You going to pull it off or not?"

"I think I can actually do the irregular verbs part and the translation. The translation isn't going to be long. *Ne pas* long. But it's the dictation that's going to kill me. She says it so fast, and all of her words just mush together. And sometimes she spits. You should never sit in the front row in that class. Once Spider wore a raincoat."

"The Spider would. Anyway, what am I supposed to to do to help you, aside from sending foul-weather gear?"

"Pray. Say a little prayer for me around ten thirty-five."

They left the restaurant with Calista humming "Say a Little Prayer for Me," one of her favorite Dionne Warwick songs.

"Mother!" Charley said, turning to her, his face as red as his hair. She resisted grabbing him in a headlock and kissing his head. He looked so dear when he blushed, but then again she didn't want to deal with a resuscitation on the premises due to embarrassment. On the pubescent angst meter this would make the bell ring.

7

There were no little prayers to be said for shaky French students in any of the books of hours Calista had thus encountered. Nor was there a liturgical hour of the day that addressed any such concerns. But Calista at ten-thirty looked up from her table in the reading room of the library toward a high round window and muttered a *broche,* or Hebrew benediction. Her Hebrew wasn't worth beans, but she figured that there was more chance of there being a *broche* for someone in Charley's situation than finding something in the books of hours. She had remembered her very ancient grandfather when she was a little girl coming to visit and whispering *broches* all day long. She had thought he was talking to himself because their housekeeper had explained to her that that was what very old people often did. But she couldn't believe that he would talk to himself in such a strange language. So she asked him. He wasn't talking to himself at all. He was praying to God.

"When I talk to myself I talk Yiddish," he had said. "When I pray to God I speak Hebrew." He had then told her that there were *broches,* or blessings, for all kinds of events. There were *broches* for the expected ones—for getting up in the morning and for going to bed at night. But then there were other wonderful ones that he told her about for unexpected and lovely things that might happen and mark a day. There were *broches* for seeing a new moon, *broches* for spotting a beautiful animal, *broches* uttered upon smelling a delightful fragrance. Her parents still had hanging in their living room a very early drawing of Calista's that showed an old man, his back bent but his head lifted as he watched an owl flying overhead. It was her grandfather, and he was saying a *broche* for seeing an owl. For Calista and he had seen an owl together one summer twilight when they had taken a walk before dinner.

So if any religion was going to have a blessing for a fragile French student who didn't quite believe in the subjunctive tense, it had to be Judaism. There was only one rule in saying a *broche,* really. It must include the words *Shem U' Malchus,* the name of God affirmed as king. So Calista muttered, *"Shem U' Malchus,* make Charley think, think clearly." That was it. She didn't feel it was cricket to pray for right answers to drop straight out of heaven. She just prayed that he would think and use his God-given gifts. It was possibly the first *broche* to be uttered in Houghton Library of Harvard University.

Houghton was the rare-books library of Harvard and possessed one of the greatest collections in the world of old manuscripts. Calista had come that morning early and had now spent more than an hour just going through the slide catalog of books of hours to figure out which manuscripts would serve her best in her search for the illusive color green that she needed to see. The color distortion on the slides, of course, was monumental. There were skies that appeared green and grass that appeared blue. But she had it narrowed down now and decided that her best bets lay in a 1471 Dutch *Book of Hours* called the *Getydebok,* and another one from northern Italy of the same period, nearly the same year.

She had been allowed to bring only her magnifying glass and a pencil into the reading room. She had checked her "guns" on the other side of the red leather door. Those were the rules. No pens, no pocket books or satchels of any kind. After saying the *broche* for Charley, she walked up to the desk and filled out a form requesting to see the two books incarnate rather than in Kodachrome.

As she waited for the books she looked about her. There was a man down at the other end of the table who was doing something on e. e. cummings. He had a folder that looked like original correspondence. Calista's house was a stone's throw from the old cummings's house. Calista wondered if she should walk over and tell the cummings scholar this. The man was sort of attractive. Or maybe she should just walk up and say, "Hi, I'm one of those Cambridge ladies with the furnished souls. You know, the ones e. e. writes about who believe in Christ and Longfellow. Well, actually not exactly Christ. See, I'm Jewish, and I just said a *broche* for my son, but still you get the picture. . . ."

The librarian interrupted this reverie. She brought two rather small books. One was in a lovely flat box containing the fragments that had been left from the Italian book. The other was a very small, very fat book measuring four by five inches and was a good three inches thick. When she opened it it took Calista's breath away. She forgot about cute cummings scholars and Charley's French test. She forgot about everything except the color green. It was as if she had seen the color for the first time ever. Maybe it was like a baby seeing snow for the first time. Her mind was surprised, her eyes seemed fresh and young, and the world new and full of charms.

In the manuscript there was a large S in gilt, and within the open curves of the S a man, a crusader, perhaps, knelt in prayer on the most beautiful green grass Calista had ever seen. His sword and his shield were cast aside. It was a luminous, pellucid green. Green was the hardest color of all. Green so often turned murky or worse yet bilious and phlegmy, and she felt her own green envy at the artist's ability.

She did not know how long she looked at the page and feasted on the color green. She had never in her life had such a visceral reaction to a color. It was sensual. She could almost smell it. Somewhere deep in her brain there was a part that responded to color the way perhaps gourmands responded to food and enologists to wine. Three-quarters of an hour had passed before she even turned to the other book, the one from Italy. The color couldn't compare. The characterization, however, was quite interesting. Especially when one considered how tiny the faces were. She took out her magnifying glass to study the faces more carefully. Leave it to the Italians to make St. Andrew a sexy devil rather than one of those somber, militant types the French and the north countries seemed to favor. There was a head floating in the border, a lady's head with a face just like Mrs. Fitchborne's, Calista's old piano teacher from her girlhood. The cherubs in the corners of the border were quite arresting, too. Babies with beer bellies. These bellies were not at all the poochy tummies of babies, but real beer guts hanging out there. Their wings were exquisitely rendered. Calista sketched quickly in pencil on some small index cards she had brought with her. She went back to the Dutch book and sketched the sword and the shield of the man in the gilt S. That weaponry would be roughly of the same period as *Marian's Tale*. The sheriff's thugs would be carrying swords and shields. Marian and the boys of Sherwood would just have bows. She was after details. There was no way, however, that she could sketch that color green. She looked at the green once more. This would be hard. Calista painted in acrylics—plastics. She had started painting in them when Charley was little because they were indestructible and there was no way a toddler or rambunctious kid could mess them up. The trade-off, however, for the indestructibility of the medium was that you had to work harder to make it subtle. This green that she wanted did not come from any bottle or tube. She knew what these old illuminators had done. She had read about it extensively. This particular green she would bet dollars to doughnuts came from the same stuff that the Limburgs' *vert de flambé* came from—wild irises and massicot, a yellow crystalline mineral form of lead monoxide. All she had was Aquatex number 63. That would not do at all. She would have to build the green up carefully layer by layer starting with yellows and blues and maybe a little of her Vermont red.

8

There was a note on the mail desk. *No calls. You need more floor wax. See you Thursday, Vicki.* She had been at the library longer than she had thought if she had entirely missed Vicki, her garrulous cleaning lady, whose cleaning days Calista looked forward to. The house indeed was immaculate. She had also missed lunch and was starving, so she went directly to the kitchen.

There wasn't much inspiring in the refrigerator. A jar of Vienna sausages in brine, the kind that looked like babies' fingers, another tribute to Charley's appalling palate. He loved them. There was also a can of opened pineapple rings. God forbid someone would offer Charley a genuine fresh pineapple. Oh, this was going to be disgusting! There must be something else. She peered deeper into the fridge, hoping. There were some ominous little packages wrapped in tinfoil and something in plastic wrap that had lurked there for too long. Just throw them out, Calista! she ordered herself. Don't look at them. They'll probably have fur. Just throw them out before they walk out on their own! And to think people were worried when they had begun to set up all those recombinant DNA labs in Cambridge. For heaven's sake, she probably had a host of mutant killers right in her own refrigerator. She reached in and grabbed a fistful of little packages and marched them to the trash can. These would not rate the garbage disposal because then she would have to unwrap them. Yuck. She really must become more organized about groceries and meal planning, but it was so hard when the only other person to cook for was Charley of the leaden palate. She went back to the refrigerator. The only decent candidate in the lunch department was one tiny chunk of Jarlsberg. She supposed she could stab it with a toothpick and then put a Vienna sausage on it and then stick part of a canned pineapple ring on that. *Zut alors!* Oh, well. There was no other choice.

East meets West, she thought as she washed down the

dubious luncheon materials with a Kirin beer. God! This stuff did for bad food what ivy did for bad architecture. If she had a beer during the day, however, she needed coffee to keep her alert and full of nerve for her afternoon's work and the continuing onslaught to crack the code of green, the Rosetta stone of the painter's palette. The color green from the *Book of Hours* was still fresh in her head. She might as well try mixing it up out here while she waited for her coffee water to boil. She opened the fridge again and this time took out a small jar half-full with a dark rusty goo. Vermont red. It was actually some oxide she had skimmed off a Vermont stream where she sometimes fished. She got an egg, too. Then went to the basement for some linseed oil.

Five minutes later she took a sip of her coffee and looked at the mixture in her bowl. "You old wizard, you!" she exclaimed happily. Indeed the very color she had been searching for was beginning to come through. Give this five, ten more minutes to warm up, and the sharpness would leave it and she would have her *Book of Hours* green, or something pretty close.

She did. Ten minutes later she carried the precious color into her study.

There was something wrong. The minute she walked into the room she knew it. She felt it. The bowl began to quiver in her hands. Somebody had been there in her absence, and it was not Vicki. Vicki never came into her study, not even to clean. Something was different, not just different—wrong, out of order. There was a book on her drawing table. Right on it, leaning against her work. Nobody ever touched her work. Her work was covered. So it probably was not harmed, but if any messages were to be left, any packages, they were left either on the mail desk or perhaps the flat part of her desk, but never the drawing board. This was tantamount to touching the eggs of a bird's nest that a mother had left unguarded. It was unnatural. It was a terrible invasion. Calista stood there and stared at the book. It was one of hers, *Nick in the Night*. She began to tremble more fiercely. Her mouth felt suddenly dry. She was frightened to touch it. Frightened of her own book. But she sensed then that somehow, some way, this would no longer be her book. It had become an alien thing to her. She willed herself to pick it up.

She grasped the pages between her thumb and other fingers and flipped them. The print and pictures blurred. No note dropped out. But one of the pages . . . what was that? There was a mark on a page, on many pages. She turned back. Nothing on the first five pages, but on the sixth . . . Calista felt a wave of nausea pass over her, and the rank taste of the Vienna sausage welled up in the back of her throat. There on the sixth page was little Nick flying through the night. But instead of that swift little nude body skimming across the clouds, he now wore diapers! Her eyes widened. She turned the page. On each of the succeeding pages until the very end of the book diapers had been drawn on the little boy's figure. Tears sprang to her eyes, more for the child, Nick, than herself, for he had been invaded as well. She sat down slowly on her stool and looked about.

There was something else wrong. There was something missing. "Where's Owl?" She whispered staring at the wing chair. The stuffed animal from the Hedge and Owl series always sat there except when Charley sat there. Then he put it on the floor by the chair, but it was not there now. Hedge still resided on a high shelf that held the *Encyclopedia Britannica,* shoulder to shoulder with the last volume X-Z. "Where's Owl?" She whispered in a low trembling voice. Then she ran up to Charley's room. Owl was not there. She went to the alcove on the third floor where she kept her sewing machine and where a second Hedge resided experiencing life as a pin cushion. But Owl was not there either. She went through every room in the house searching for the stuffed animal. Owl was gone and Hedge was without a buddy!

Calista was stunned by this defacement of the book and haunted by the loss of Owl. She went back through the book again. There was something indefinably grotesque about the way the diapers had been drawn, or was it simply the effect that was grotesque? In any case she felt her character had vanished. The original Nick was lost, abducted, and in some way his memory shamed.

She wanted to cry. She had created a lovely innocent child, a little boy of three or four years old, and they had destroyed him. The whole book leered at her now. Who could have done such a thing? And how? Vicki had been here. She must call Vicki.

She tried to keep the tremor out of her voice as she spoke to one of Vicki's daughters. No, Vicki wasn't home yet. She worked afternoons, after Calista's, at the Clarks. Calista thanked Vicki's daughter for the number.

"No, Cal. No, dear. Nobody delivered anything. No, nobody came. . . . Weird. I can't imagine. . . . No, I was there all morning. I had a cigarette on your front porch, but you know I was right there by the door and the back door was locked. No, I don't understand how anyone could have gotten in."

Neither did Calista. Just as she hung up the phone rang. She nearly jumped. The kettle was now whistling, too, as she had put on more coffee water. It was as if the whole world had begun to shriek at her. She raced from her study to the kitchen to turn off the water. She wanted to run out the door, run out the door of her own house! She almost did not want to pick up the telephone. But she did.

"Calista!" The voice was raspy and tight.

"What?"

"Calista, it's me, Margaret. I just got the most awful thing."

"No!" Calista almost shouted the word.

"Yes." Margaret paused. "Yes, why did you say it that way?" It was suddenly dawning on Margaret McGowan that there was something odd about the alacrity and intensity of that "no" that had exploded out of the phone.

"Me too." Calista's voice dropped to a hoarse whisper.

"What?"

"What did you get?"

She heard Margaret suck in her breath sharply. "This horrible . . . horrible copy of my book *The Dark Knight of Kyre,* they've put a crown of thorns on Rothgar. You know the book only has a few illustrations. But in each one with Rothgar they've drawn in this crown of thorns, and—" Her voice broke. "Calista . . ."

"What?"

"It didn't come through the mail. I found it on my front hall

60

carpet. Whoever it was just dropped it right through my mail slot."

Calista would refrain from telling Margaret that she herself did not even have a mail slot. That the person had come right through a door, or a window, that the person himself had entered into her own house. His foot had actually trod on her carpeting. He had breathed the same air. She realized Margaret seemed quite bad off and appeared to be hyperventilating.

"Margaret, are you okay? Margaret!"

"Yes, dear." She breathed deeply as one might to summon up courage. "But you know, it is the last illustration that is the worst."

"Yes?" Calista asked in a small voice, not really wanting to hear.

"There are these wounds?"

"Wounds?" Calista whispered.

"Yes, wounds. Those horrible kinds of wounds. You know, like those twisted northern European painters used to paint, I don't know, in the early Renaissance. Very precise little slits spurting blood."

"Oh, God!"

"Yes, 'Oh, God,'" Margaret said weakly. "It's absolutely revolting." She paused. "But worse than revolting, Calista, it's scary." Her voice was tremulous again.

"Yes." There was silence. They were both thinking of the loathsome little man at the conference and the murder of Norman Petrakis. Was this related? Could it be? "I think I better come right over and look at this. Maybe we should talk."

"Yes, yes. I'd feel better if you'd come over."

"Okay, give me a few minutes."

She dashed around the house not looking for Owl now but checking every window and door. Nothing seemed disturbed in any other part of the house. She returned to the kitchen and screwed the top on the Vermont red and put it back in the refrigerator. Damn! Damn! she thought as she placed the jar with its deep red contents on a shelf. I don't want to think about red! I want to think about green, green! But all she could think

61

about was the scrawl on the wall in the Sheraton Hotel and now these gruesome little slits spurting blood. She sought refuge in Tom's study, where he had worked inventing the formulas that might pin down the hidden parts of the universe, where he had explored the nature of time, space-time in the cosmos, and that most alluring billionth of a second when the universe and time began.

It always calmed Calista to come into Tom's study. The desk was now covered with papers of Charley's for some report that was due soon. She sank down on the chair and absently, as if in a trance, began stacking index cards, putting some photocopied newspaper articles in the folder. The desktop didn't look all that different from when Tom had been alive and working at it. The clutter had a sameness, although the marks on the papers were different. There was still the sign—GRAVITY QUANTICIZED HERE—and the small box holding some of Tom's favorite flies, which she still used on occasion. This was her kind of sentimentality. She liked fishing with his old flies, ones that she had tied especially for him—old Marabou Streamers and Royal Wulffs and Humpies.

She opened the box now and picked up one of the flies, twirling it between her fingers. She wanted to calm herself down before going to Margaret's. She wanted to think clearly about these odd events. She did not want to be overwhelmed by their luridness. She had to think. But it was difficult. She stared out the window between the photos of Cygnus X-1 and the Crab Nebulae at the garden. The shoots of daffodils were poking up, the blossoms still sheathed in their tight green jackets. She had called this perennial garden, this view of it, Tom's black hole break, the pause that refreshed from thinking about singularities, infinite gravitational densities and imploding stars, and the inexorable events that would follow from such starry disasters. The Charioteer himself had now crashed.

And were the vile defacements of the books, were these the ripples spreading out from the event, from that starry crash, that implosion of life that splattered the night with blood?

"Hi, Mom."

This time there was no hiding it. She had not even heard the front door slam. He had probably gone upstairs first to check his E-mail, electronic mail, on the Mac in his bedroom, and now she had been caught in flagrante terrified!

"What in the world is wrong with you?" He had just bitten into an apple and was setting down his skateboard. He looked up with his luminous gray eyes into his mother's. "Mom, you look like you've seen a ghost or something."

"Charley, I received the most horrible little . . ." She paused searching for a word. "Surprise today."

Three minutes later Charley closed the book of *Nick in the Night* and gave a shudder. "Yuck."

"Yuck is right," Calista said. "And also . . ."

"What else?" Charley said looking up from the book.

"Owl has disappeared, the one that sits in the wing chair. You didn't take it anywhere, did you?"

"Me? No." Charley resumed looking at the book. "At least this isn't one of the books where the kid looks like me. That would really be creepy."

"Oh, Charley, don't say such a thing!" Oh, God, she thought, she simply could not endure another close call like the one she had had with Charley almost two years before.

"And you say Margaret McGowan got a book of hers messed up like this, too?"

"Yes, well, not exactly in the same way." She thought of the blood Margaret had described spurting from the precise little slit.

"So maybe we should go over and see Margaret's book?"

"Oh, you don't have to come, Charley."

He looked stunned. The luminosity of his eyes hardened into the same slate gray as the sky. There was no light, no hint of spring. It could have been a winter day outside and in. "Why shouldn't I come?" The voice was taut with a combination of disbelief and frustration. "If it has to do with Petrakis's murder, it . . ." But he let it go. He did not need to say any more. If it had to do with Petrakis, it could have to do with his mother. And especially if it had to do with books, it meant Mother to him, his mother, his only parent. She might be the world's most

63

famous children's book illustrator, but she had failed utterly with her own son in terms of the proscription of the Dua Khety text from the Middle Kingdom.

9

There was a particular street in Cambridge, Foster Street, that was known for its especially small houses. Built in the early 1800s for the servants of the larger houses, and sometimes mansions, on Brattle Street a block north, these houses had come to be called the Cambridge dollhouses. Clapboard structures, they stood erect and unadorned, many even shutterless, but they possessed an elegance based entirely on proportion and minimal detail. Margaret McGowan's house was one of these, and it stood as prim and starched as a Quaker lady in its fresh coat of dove gray paint and cream-colored trim. Except today there was one thing out of place, totally wrong, and Calista noticed it immediately. A raw unpainted board had been crudely nailed over the mail slot, a terrible testimony to the offense that this particular household had just suffered. The effect of the board was not a particularly remedial one, not the natural scar of a wound that had healed with time or a neat bandage for a deep cut. It seemed like another wound itself on the immaculate exterior of the house.

Margaret's house at one time had been the home of a butler and his wife. The wife had been a cook for the Longfellow household at 105 Brattle Street, and the butler had worked next door at number 101, the Oliver Hastings house, a rather grand English Regency villa. Their son had been in the employ of Professor Eben Horsford, the noted chemist who lived round the corner on Craigie Street. All quite convenient.

"These houses are so small," Charley said as they rode up on their bikes. "How does anyone fit in?"

"Margaret is very small, and she lives alone."

They had opened the front gate. "I better chain my bike,"

64

Charley said. Charley had a bike lock that cost nearly as much as the bike but did guarantee the replacement of the bike if it were stolen. Calista had a junk bike. She had had the same junk bike for fifteen years and could leave it anywhere. Nobody ever dreamed of stealing it. She occasionally treated it to a new pair of tires.

They walked up the brick path and Calista heard the latch of the front door turn. She looked up and saw it open a crack. Margaret's tiny head peeped around. Calista felt a resurgence of the same anger she had experienced during the panel at the children's book conference. The anger caused by an old woman being frightened. It made no sense that this frail, elderly person should be afraid to open wide her door; that she must peer around its edge like a frightened, hunted animal. This was not just ridiculous. It was obscene. She grew madder and madder.

"Oh, Calista, I'm so glad your're here. Oh . . ." She looked startled. "You brought Charley."

Calista had a sinking feeling that Margaret thought it was somehow grossly inappropriate that she had brought along Charley. Well, it was too late, and there was very little she could do about it. When you lived alone with a child, when you were a single parent, there were very few buffers or blinds one could put up. Sooner or later, things, be they feelings or facts, spilled out.

They went into the little house. It might be a prim Quaker lady from the outside, but inside was a different story, more like a velvet-lined jewel box sparkling with old Oriental rugs the color of garnets and walls covered with a marble-green paper. The house swirled with a secret life of its own. A Tiffany lamp, or a darn good copy of one, glowed in shades of celadon and amber in a corner. Windows were lavishly swagged in chintz draperies that were tasseled and had dragon-head tie-back fixtures on the walls. There were stuffed dragons all over the place sent by Margaret's devoted fans of the Knights of Kyre chronicles, which featured dragons prominently throughout all ten volumes. The dragons sprawled across tables covered with fringed tapestries and crawled up the delicately curved legs of a Queen Anne walnut chair. One spread its wings over the top of her fold-out writing desk. Margaret was actually one of those writers who worked at a desk that looked like what an author should be writing on. The desk had the straight lines of a Sheraton piece, and the top that folded out was inset with leather. The back of the desk rose up into a nest of cubbyholes. A small herd of miniature dragons along with some papers peered out of these. There was no word processor in sight. She was the last of a breed of writers.

In addition to the dragons there were cats, real ones stalking about, two or three at least. Calista spotted a Manx and a long-haired something or other curled up on what looked to be a gigantic velvet mushroom with fringe. It was a settee, and Margaret now shooed off the cat so Charley would have a place to sit. "Off! Off, Clicquot." The cat opened one eye and gave her the how-dare-you look that seemed to Calista common to felines and certain maître d's. Margaret hustled over and plucked it off the couch. "We'll have none of that, Clicquot," she admonished in her best Scottish nanny voice.

"Clicquot, that's a funny name," Charley said.

"She's named for Veuve Clicquot because of her beautiful coat. That's a champagne, Charley—Veuve Clicquot, in case you didn't know. Named for a Frenchwoman who was called the widow Clicquot."

"I think I've heard of it. Don't you have some of that, Mom?"

"Yes, it's my favorite champagne," Calista said.

Margaret now raised the cat high up for display and made gurgling noises at it. "Yes, you have what they call a cham-pagne coat." She turned to Charley. "It's a common color to many of this breed. And you have a bubbly personality to match except when you're being sulky like now."

"Is she a widow, too?" It just slipped out. Calista hadn't meant to say it at all.

"Well, if she is, it hasn't slowed her down! Had to have her fixed. I couldn't face another litter."

Thankfully Margaret did not connect the widow reference to La Veuve Jacobs. How self-centered can you be? Calista thought. Why should people always think of her as some archetypal widow? In any case Clicquot the cat was doing better than Calista the human as a widow. One disastrous affair over a ten-day period in last three and one-half years of widowhood was

66

hardly grounds for getting herself fixed. There was little fear of
more litters.

Charley's eyes seemed to be watering up, and it wasn't over
her widowhood. Oh, Lord, she thought, he did have allergies,
and long-haired cats could trigger them. He began to sneeze.
"Oh, dear! Charley, I bet you're allergic to Clicquot. Many
are. Don't worry. Look, Calista, I'm going to take Clicquot into
the back. In that pot over there is some Benadryl." She pointed
to a chinoiserie cache pot on an urn stand. "I keep them handy
for allergic friends. Let me get you a glass of water, and Calista,
how 'bout something stronger for us."

"Yes. I think we need it."

When Margaret returned she was carrying a tray with a glass
of water and two rather ornately cut crystal decanters. It
suddenly struck Calista that with her potions and dragons, her
tasseled velvet settees and luxurious cats, her old Orientals and
chinoiserie, Margaret's home was not a house so much as a lair of
some sort, a lair for a meeting, or would it be a mating . . . between who? Colette and Merlin seemed like the
obvious pair. And yet here was Margaret as plain as a bun, so
fragile and now so frightened. What a multifaceted person she
really was—just like her books. At first glance, or just from the
jacket copy, her books might appear to be simple adventures in
the land of high fantasy where good is always pitted against evil.
And at first glance this house seemed so constrained and correct
and positively eighteenth-century New England, giving lie all
the time to its interior. But here was Margaret now with her
many facets all singularly transfixed into one aspect of fear. She
walked stiffly toward Calista, holding out the book, open in her
hands to the page. There was something oddly ceremonial about
the way she held the book and even in the way she moved. Her
lips seemed to tremble with unspoken words, and her eyes, pale
blue eyes, faded with age, were wide and fearful. Again Calista
felt the surge of anger. Charley got up from the velvet mushroom.

"Weird," he said as he and Calista looked down at the page.
It was a full-color plate, and Rothgar was shown engulfed in the
mist from the Lake of the Deathless. It was a beautiful painting

done by Leo Krell, a marvelous artist who had been illustrating children's books for over forty years. He worked exclusively in oils, and Calista had nothing but admiration for his art. But now with a very fine-nibbed pen a crown of thorns had been drawn in on the head of Rothgar.

"Now look at this." Margaret's voice was low and dusty. She turned several pages to the next color plate. It was a picture of Rothgar on the Plain of Crystal Doom. He was not wearing his armor, but it lay in shards along with his sword, for that indeed was the fate of one who traversed the Plain of Crystal Doom. Things shattered, except for Rothgar. All his worldly possessions had shattered, but if he could repeat the incantation of the Good Wizard of Mor, there was a chance for his body. No chances here. The seven wounds of Christ had been meticulously drawn in. No ragged wounds, just neat little slits from which blood spurted, precise little teardrop-shaped spurts.

"Oh, how awful," whispered Calista. And then she looked to the immediate foreground of the picture. One of the crevices of the plain that Leo had so meticulously rendered had been painted in red so that it absolutely gushed with blood. Calista looked up at Margaret and tapped the crevice with her index finger. "Too much blood. Too much for those wounds."

"Like Norman!"

"Yes, like Norman!" Calista repeated.

10

"Yoo-hoo!" The cheerful greeting split the air and seemed to reverberate through the room with its warmth.

"Oh, goodness, it's Mammy. How comforting!" Margaret sighed.

"Mammy?" Charley wondered aloud.

"Oh, Calista, dear, do explain to Charley about Mammy, and now that she's here please both of you stay for dinner. She cooks so much better than I do." Margaret turned to go to the kitchen and then turned back. "Let me have the book a minute. I want to show Mammy this gruesome business. She might have some insights." She then scurried out to the kitchen.

What there was to explain about Mammy was that in liberal Cambridge Margaret McGowan had been blessed with a black housekeeper who had the unfortunate name of Mammy. It was not a name given to her by the descendants of some antebellum family from Peach Tree Street in Atlanta, Georgia. It was given to her by her own parents when she was born in Antigua and was a truncation of Mamita. Mammy was pushing eighty and had worked for over sixty years in Cambridge homes. Each family had tried unsuccessfully to change her name. But she was adamant. She preferred Mammy to Mamita. Some people nearly gagged saying Mammy. But she insisted. "Do I look like Aunt Jemima? Am I fat? Do I wear a kerchief and have those big shiny teeth? As Shakespeare said, what's in a name? I like Mammy. I hate Mamita. It sounds like some kind of fruit, and I don't mean one of your pansy boys. I mean a big, juicy, sweet fruit that grows on a tree, hanging there all ripe till it drops and rots. Nobody's going to call me Mamita!" She had to say all this to one old liberal, a retired editor of *The New Republic*. He stood there clenching his pipe between his teeth and rubbing the suede patches on his houndstooth jacket as he observed the stocky but trim figure that stood in front of him in the Pierre Cardin warm-up suit and New Balance running shoes. This was Mammy's work uniform. Now she worked exclusively for Margaret as a housekeeper–copy editor. She was Margaret's first reader. She told Margaret if it sounded right and when she had gone too far, and she got rid of the excess commas. Margaret was promiscuous in her use of commas. Mammy was also a better speller than Margaret. She couldn't type, though. She therefore kept the commas down to a minimum and kept the plush velvet cushions plumped up and the Jensen silver polished, or, as she put it, she "fussed with all that clutter" that Margaret kept around. When the dragons got dirty she washed them in Woolite or sent them to the cleaners. She mixed up her own potions of vinegar and baking soda to keep the Tiffany lamp sparkling and the woodwork gleaming. She even functioned as

69

something of a secretary for Margaret, organizing her fan mail, although Margaret was careful to answer each one herself.

"Well, that beats all!" Mammy said, bustling into the living room. "Howdy, Calista. This your fine son?" She was wearing little golf socks and had apparently left her shoes in the kitchen.

"Yes, Mammy. Charley, this is Mammy. Mammy, this is Charley."

"You folks stay for dinner. I fixed a nice pot roast for Margy. There's plenty. You hit a good night to come. I'm cooking. None of that awful English food she likes to cook."

"Well, Mammy, I'm afraid there is a pudding, a milk custard, in the refrigerator for dessert." She looked at Charley rather dolefully. "It's hard being British."

"Well, we'll put some rum on it and jazz it up a little," Mammy said, and then paused. "Calista, you like rum, don't you? What are you doing drinking that Scotch for?"

"Oh, I'm sorry, Calista. I didn't even know we had any rum in the house," Margaret apologized.

"You don't know what you've got in this house, lady. Let me go fetch that gal some rum. You take it with soda, don't you, Calista?" Calista nodded.

The pot roast was good, and Mammy had joined them.

"Well, what do you think we should do about this?" Margaret said, gesturing at both books that rested on a nearby Welsh sideboard. "We should report it, don't you think?"

"Who to?" Charley asked.

"The Boston Police Department, those detectives we met. I guess," Calista said. "And I suppose we should tell Janet and the folks at Thayer."

"Yes. I suppose so." Margaret nodded.

"Charley," Calista said, looking at him. "You look doubtful of this strategy."

"I'm not doubtful, exactly. I'm just not that convinced about the Boston Police Department. I mean, you tried to call that cop, or detective, the other day, didn't you, Mom? To find out how the investigation was going, and he never called you back. You called a couple of times."

"Yes, but they were probably just really busy."

"Well," said Margaret. "They didn't appear, either one of those fellows, to be mental giants to me."

"The New York Police Department must be plenty smart. They tracked that Son of Sam killer through parking tickets and their computer," Mammy offered. "They must be plenty smart."

"They did?" Charley asked with sudden interest. "That's how they did it? Tracked him down through a computer?"

"They sure did, honey," Mammy answered.

"They were probably just working within their Unix if it was parking tickets. Probably didn't even have to download from a mainframe for that," Charley reflected.

The three women looked bewildered.

"What's he talking about?" Margaret asked.

"Uh . . ." Calista hesitated. Damn, why did Mammy have to mention the Son of Sam and the computer thing? That awful feeling was coming back to her, the same that had clutched at her gut two years before when she and Charley had first begun to have suspicions that Tom's death had not been an accident, but something more. They were those same feelings, instincts, really, that at that time had warned her this was not for children. That she should put a damper on it right away. But there was no way of dampening Charley in these instances. She had learned that. "Oh," she said, turning to Margaret and Mammy and trying to sound light. "Computer jargon, you know."

"Oh, well, then count me out," Margaret said. "I know nothing about the beasts."

"Me neither," Mammy added.

But not Charley, Calista thought. Count him in. She could tell by that strangely opaque look in his eyes—he was off and running, every brain cell and neuron firing. If things hadn't seemed to fit for Charley, they still might not, but now he saw a way of possibly making them fit or getting the missing pieces. And after all, computers could talk to one another when people didn't or refused to do so. If the Boston Police Department refused to return their calls, Charley had at his disposal other means of contacting them. The chips were never down! There

71

was a whole world of electronic communication that could bypass such inconveniences as not having calls answered.

11

"How're you doing with the Benadryl?" Calista said as they wheeled their bikes down Margaret's path. "You think you can operate the heavy machinery of this bike?"

"No problem," Charley answered.

It had gotten cold, and a wet wind blew in from the northeast. "I don't believe this!" Calista called out as they were cutting across the Common on their bikes. A large wet snowflake had landed on her nose. "I mean, this really is awful, you know it!" The flakes were falling lazily through the Cambridge night.

By the time they got back to James Place it was snowing hard. They put their bikes in the garage and came up onto their front entry porch. Calista looked around nervously, half anticipating another book or little surprise. She felt a chill run down her spine that was not from the weather. She shook it off. Damn these people! They went in the house. She peered into her study cautiously.

"Is it all okay?" Charley's voice made her jump.

"Yeah, it's fine." God, she hated this. Why should he have to see her scared? This was all so wrong. She suddenly felt unbearably sorry for them both. They had been through so much, she and Charley. Why this now? Why did fear spread itself through their house, their little world, like some poison gas? She felt her anger welling up again.

Ten minutes later she climbed up the ladder of Charley's bunk bed to kiss him good night.

"Do me a favor, sweet pea!"

"What's that?" he said, turning over on his side to face her and propping himself up on one elbow.

"Cool it on this business."

72

"Yeah, well, okay. But will you try to reach those cops again?"

"Sure."

She wasn't even sure what either of them meant by "cooling it." She looked at him again. The eyes were clear. He knew that she knew that he was hot. But she still wasn't exactly sure what she meant by "cooling it." Such was the state of being a parent. Uncertainty grew as knowledge grew. Rather like surface-to-volume ratios of one to three. The volume of what you didn't know was the cube of what you did know. Or what you didn't know expanded three times faster than what you did know. Differential scaling. She studied Charley's face. That gentle curve of his cheek was gone now, vanished into the new emerging face. It still had that sweet vulnerability, but there was something else there now, something a little less innocent. She had drawn that face so many times. It had crept into so much of her work when there were young children to portray. It didn't matter whether the characters were boys or girls. They could sometimes even be animals, but there was so often a Charley-ness about them, something so quintessentially Charley. The essence now had not changed, but the contours and the light in the eyes had changed in some infinitely subtle and elusive way. She couldn't use it for young children anymore. Will Scarlet, perhaps?

The telephone rang just as she was walking out of Charley's room. It was Vicki. "Cal, I figured out how that book got in your study."

"How?"

"Well, you know, it's been bothering me all day. I just couldn't make sense out of it." Calista wished that Vicki would get to the point, but this was Vicki. She always had to give you in addition to the facts a certain emotional content. She could make a narrative out of anything. Calista was patient as Vicki continued. "So I said to myself . . . something funny did happen today, but I'd been wrestling with that rotten discolored tile in the corner of the kitchen, and you know I think sometimes the fumes get to me."

"I told you, Vicki, forget that stain. I don't want you passing out over a bucket of Clorox."

73

"Well, in any case, the doorbell rang, and it was the man to read the gas meter. So I just let him in and pointed him toward the basement. And you know how that is, they just kind of waltz in and waltz out. I heard the door slam a couple of minutes later."

"So you think it was the gas man?"

"Well, this is it . . . I say to myself, Gee, that's funny—wasn't that gas man here just last week? Or was that over at the Benchleys? You know, you work all these houses, you get a little mixed up about these things, and I got the Mr. Clean fumes and the Clorox. But he had a uniform and all that."

"It's got to be the gas man."

"Actually, now that I think about it, he had some sort of parka on and then a billed cap that said Gas Company or whatever on it—just the cap, you know."

"That ought to be easy to get," Calista said.

"But I don't understand, Calista, why would anybody, a gas man or not, want to do this?"

"I don't know."

"Well, I just thought I should call and let you know."

"Oh, I'm glad you did. At least it wasn't a break-in exactly."

"No, you won't have to go and get all the locks changed."

"Right. Well, thanks for calling."

"Try and have a good night's sleep, dear. And I'll see you the day after tomorrow."

"Yes."

It was not a break-in, yet she had never felt so violated, and the fact that she didn't have to get the locks changed was of little solace to her. The person, whoever he was, had penetrated into the heart of her home and taken a swift, precise stab into the center of her imagination through this wanton attack on her work. It was totally unnerving. She was exhausted from it all, and now she was more than ready for bed and for sleep.

The night was not really black but seemed slightly bleached by the swirling snow. And she sensed that sleep, the nice, dark, comforting numbness of sleep, was going to escape her. Lethe and Nepenthe, those muses of the night, were not on call. She

74

tried hot milk and then resorted to half of a Halcion tablet. It would not be the smooth black silk sleep that came without the pills. No, that sleep was only delivered unaided by those Greek muses that Calista fully believed resided somewhere in the brain, not perhaps the most primitive part, the limbic region up front, but still somewhere within a relatively old and venerable region. Calista tended to think of those early regions of the brain, the ones associated with primitive behavior, as venerable. Of course they were not as complex or beefed up as the other parts that dealt with rapid manipulations of great megabytes of information. Still, they did have their charms. One of these charms was the little miniature Greek muses she imagined floating about through the cortical chambers and convolutions of her midbrain. Forget that these so-called primitive brains didn't know Greeks from crocodiles. Forget the fact that this part of the brain structure evolved long before there were Greeks. There was the capacity somewhere midbrain, in the neocortex—which, when it was functioning up to snuff, did not need to be jogged by chemicals and would release the little muses quietly, no fuss, no muss—to spread the balm of sleep.

Not tonight. Calista's chemically induced sleep was fractured by fragments of dreams and images. She, indeed, felt as if she were stretched across the Plain of Crystal Doom. Nothing seemed quite whole but lay like shards of glass, ragged and sharp, in a penumbra of restless sleep, sleep that was not quite dark enough. She saw Rothgar with his crown of thorns slipped jauntily over one eye and the awful wounds spurting *vert de flambé!* The Limburgs' old color. But too much blood! Too much blood! The fissures of the plain roiled with the blood, and Charley was picking his way through the debris and wading through the bloody streams. She woke herself up. This was ridiculous. Wrestling with colors all day and all night long. She got up and washed her face.

She would fall back to sleep, she knew it. She always did after she had taken a Halcion. What a dumb name for a drug that did this to you. It was still snowing. Oh, Lord, it would probably be a snow day and school would be canceled. Only in Massachusetts did they cancel school in April. She didn't understand it. What the hell did they do in Alaska, for Christ's sake? There had to be something between mushing huskies and the anti-quated snow removal systems they had in Boston and Cambridge. Last year they had gone over the snow removal budget. Run out of money for salt or some dumb thing. They never canceled school when she was a kid out in Indiana. There was no such thing as a snow emergency. Pshaw! Snow, that's nothing. The major emergency that they anticipated back in those days was a nuclear attack! You got under your desk and covered your ears. It was the era of bomb shelter parties. People went off gaily popping corks into the face of destruction. Spit in its eye! It was the last ragged mile of an old frontier and just before the beginning of Jack Kennedy's New Frontier. Not only were there no snow emergencies, for Christ's sake, there were not even wind chill factors. People were just plain cold, and the temperature figures were given straight. It was that time long ago when spaghetti was not yet pasta and who knew, or cared, how cold it was with the wind blowing. You just went out and froze your ass. Charley had refused to go skating one evening in January at the Cambridge Skating Club when he heard that the wind chill brought the temperature down to minus 35. What had happened? Strong midwestern-Russian-Jewish stock diluted! Chicken soup and Wheaties, the occasional Heath bar, that's all it used to take. None of this pasta crap and talking wind chill factors.

Her mind was in the full lather of internal dialogue. Getting back to sleep might not be so easy. The branches on the dogwood tree outside her bedroom window were laden with snow. The thing was supposed to bloom in another three weeks. It always bloomed the first week in May. All through April you could watch the buds swell up, like engorged nipples, the same color, too, a deep, dusky red. And then they opened. For the first eight days the blossoms were the color of new potatoes. They lightened each day until they were the most delicate shade of pink. People came and took pictures of the tree during the spring. It fanned out in all of its russet-and-pink glory and covered the entire front of the house. The house appeared like a pointillist's painting through the dogwood, for the blossoms hung like a screen of pink lace. Behind this screen the mass of the dark-brown-shingled house broke up into shadowy fragments. She knew those blossoms up close, too, from her bedroom window. She knew their shape, their complicated interiors, striated with even subtler colors. She was an intimate of the swift, tough beauty of their unfolding petals. But what would happen to them now in the middle of this northeaster, what would happen to dogwood time with the heavy wet snow? Branches might break. Calista yawned. The chemical Lethe and Nepenthe were beginning to ensnare her again. This was what was wrong, of course. She felt listless and heavy-limbed herself in the face of the snow-laden limbs of her dear tree. She tried to visualize the splay of the four petals of the blossom. They could be quite perfect in their symmetry and even demonstrate what physicists called spin, a property in which a subatomic particle either maintains or does not maintain its same appearance through a complete revolution. Calista remembered hearing how the blossoms were used in Easter services as metaphors for the crucifixion with their four nail holes, one at each tip. Oh, dear! She thought of those terrible wounds again, so meticulously drawn onto the color plates of Margaret's book. And who could those horrible people be, or person, to do such a thing, to wreck books and disfigure characters in such a way? She drifted off again.

She awoke with a start. It wasn't a bad dream, at least not one she could remember. And yet there was the same kind of feeling as after a nightmare. Then she remembered. It was not a dream at all. It was something about those tulips. Of course, the Little Red Riding Hood ones. They must be frozen stiff! How could she lie there and think about tulips expiring under the icy glaze of this storm? A rescue mission was called for.

But did she really want to go out into her backyard at two o'clock in the morning? What if? She stopped the thought. But it wouldn't stop, of course. Here she had been planning, before Vicki had called about the gas man coming to read the meter, to call the locksmith tomorrow to change all her locks and now she was contemplating walking out alone into her own backyard at two in the morning. Forget the fact that there was an icy northeaster blowing. It wasn't weather that was bothering her. Then she got mad and sat bolt upright. Shit! She would not let her life be ruled by fear. This was what she resented the most. She would not become a prisoner in her own house. She would not be scared to go into her own backyard. Anger was the best palliative for fear. She got up, pulled on her long underwear under her flannel nightgown. She headed downstairs and put on her heavy wool Red Riding Hood cape. It was the easiest thing to wear over a nightgown. She then pulled on the old Muk Luks that Tom had brought her from Alaska, grabbed a pair of scissors and a basket, and stomped out the back door.

It had stopped snowing and there was an unearthly stillness. Everything was sheathed in heavy snow. The very air seemed not so much bleached now as suffused with an almost spectral light. It was weird. Was she stupid or what coming out here in the middle of the night of the same day she had received that defaced book?

But suppose the sick person who had delivered these books had wanted to enjoy Calista's shock and terror? Suppose he was out here in the bushes waiting for her to come out on this sleep-fractured night? She peered out from around the edge of her hood and began to tremble. Now hold it right there! she ordered herself. No person, no matter how sick or insane, would expect insomnia to drive someone out for a turn in his own backyard on a night like this. Her anger returned and like a vengeful catharsis swept every particle of fear from her. She was pissed! So pissed. Pissed for her sake and for Margaret's. That a decent law-abiding citizen like herself had to be scared out of her own yard! She stomped off in the direction of the tulips. The new bags of peat moss and mulch that she had just had delivered wore blankets of snow; the wheelbarrow lay turned on its side, under its wheels a glaze of ice, and Charley had not put the trash cans in the shed after taking out the garbage. She must get some of these yews pruned back, not to mention the hemlock hedge. She was making this mental list of yard chores as she rounded the bend and gasped.

Something was bleeding! That was her first thought. Like immense globules of blood the tulips swayed in the wind against the snow. The image exploded in front of her eyes. For one dreadful moment the engorged blossoms seemed to be spurting into the white night. She was breathing hard. This was crazy. She had to get these images of blood out of her head. She took out her scissors and began to cut. She could not help remembering the bloody scrawl on the hotel wall. She tried with every atom of her being to will herself to be calm, to concentrate. You cannot have your life hamstrung like this. You cannot allow these devastating inroads to cut into your psyche. You cannot! You cannot! The words puffed in her mind in a total inversion of the message of the little engine that could.

As she was bending over, intent on her work, she felt something. There in the garden, a presence. Within the shadow of her hood she turned her head slowly to the left, toward a large rock that marked the beginning of the steppingstone path—the rock that looked like the sleeping cat—and now she covered her mouth in horror. The scream froze in her throat. Perched atop the sleeping rock cat was Owl, grinning luridly at her, his mouth a bright red gash. The scream wouldn't come. But something drew her toward him. She felt this inexorable pull. The horrible face frozen in a peculiar grimace beckoned her. Clutching the tulips she slowly walked across the small patch of icy grass, in a daze, mesmerized by the stuffed animal's disfigured face, drawn into its hideousness. The owl's terror hung like a shriek in the frozen night and the little button eyes gleamed so blackly, watching her so carefully.

She could smell a familiar smell. It was the smell of paint. For some reason this comforted her. She must touch it. There was no way she could not. But fear lay coiled in her stomach as she put the tulips in the basket on her arm and picked up the stuffed animal. His head had been slashed and some stuffing exploded from one side. Her hood fell back as she stared at it, transfixed by the little owl's suddenly ghoulish face.

Close up the face did not look so ghoulish as much as pathetically disfigured. She examined it with a mixture of horror and sympathy that one might experience when seeing a facially deformed or scarred child. She could feel the wet cold on her face. Who could have done this?

As the rest of the neighborhood slept through its own frozen, untroubled night, Calista stood in her backyard at two thirty in the morning with the mauled, stuffed animal in the crook of her left arm. There was something out here. It had already come into her house once. It had defaced her book, and now it had disfigured the little owl. It moved closer and closer, becoming less and less abstract with each advance. It was striking at her imaginary children now, but would it . . . . She could not complete the thought. She raced into the house, up the stairs, and climbed the ladder to Charley's top bunk. He slept peacefully. She brushed the hair off his forehead and kissed him. He stirred slightly.

By the time she returned to her own bedroom the weird light of the night was beginning to dissolve into the thin, pale light of the dawn. The sky, which for days had looked like the marbled endpapers of a book, broke clear and fragile. She loved the frailty of this early dawn light. It washed into the bedroom.

Calista sat down now in a rocking chair near her bedroom window. The last stars still hung dimly in the dawn sky, which was now the color of eggshells. It was as if these last stars were shining through the eggshells from the far side. She watched them now wink out, one by one. She tried hard not to think about the mutilated stuffed animal. She was wondering how she would tell Charley about this latest development. There would certainly be no cooling it for him now. She should at least try to get in touch with the police before he woke up. She should give a semblance of being in control, being the director of things. After all, she was the parent in this twosome.

Toward six o'clock she called the snow link number for the Cambridge Public Schools. Sure enough, school was canceled. She went in to run a bath and turned on the switch so she could hear the start-up of Morning Pro Musica. The first five minutes of air time of the program were devoted to the sounds of birds tweeting. As Calista sank into the deep claw-footed tub, the tweets swirled around her. She poured in some bath salts and then rested her head on the bath pillow that was hooked onto the rim of the tub. She lolled in the tub, thinking with a washcloth draped over her face. She would have to call the cops this morning—while Charley was there. It did not thrill her to have to make the call with her son hanging right over her shoulder. But she had little choice. Damn the Cambridge Public Schools and their snow emergencies. And if she couldn't reach the cops? What then? How long would he cool it? What could he really do, though? He had a modem. She supposed he could use it to get into crime files or parking ticket files. The birds had finished, and the music of Francis Poulenc's piano concerto filled the steamy bathroom. Oh, God, if she could just spend all day in this warm tub listening to music. She sprinkled some more Vitiver in the tub, resoaked the washcloth, draped it over her face again, and tried to figure out how worried she should be about Charley. Was he vulnerable? Would he make himself more vulnerable by starting to poke around electronically?

There had been a time just after Tom had been murdered when Calista was really worried that Charley showed all the indications of becoming a classic nerd in the true MIT sense of the word. For what better way was there for a young kid who had just lost his father and who had trouble dealing with emotional issues than to lose himself in that strange, weird world of the computer? That world at its worst became an isolationist one conducive to setting up walls and erecting barriers between an individual, a hacker, and the rest of the real world. All the confrontations were controllable. There was logic and there was certainty and there was the pleasure of manipulating a powerful machine. Calista could see Charley being sucked deeper and deeper into the quicksand of this isolation in those months after Tom's death. It was terribly frightening to her. And although she had very little faith in psychiatrists, she had sought out one to figure out how to deal with it. The woman was helpful and gave Calista some good suggestions. Charley seemed to have gotten over the hump. His interest and prowess in skateboarding had perhaps helped as much as anything. He was not particularly good at team sports, but he had an undeniable skill and grace with the skateboard. And that was also why she was so pleased that he had enjoyed *City Step*. Not liking one's body, feeling physically inferior, was unfortunately part of the nerd syndrome. Only at MIT would they have something called the Ugliest Man on Campus Contest. But she was fairly sure that in Charley's case of incipient nerdhood, his low self-esteem in terms of body image had been a passing phase, a kind of window of vulnerability during a very stressful and vulnerable time in his life. Besides, he was, if nothing else, just too good-looking these days. He had grown rangy, and

81

there was a hint of real muscle. His hair, once an impossibly curly, bordering on kinky, mop of red, had calmed down. He now used the blow dryer regularly and went through a can of mousse every two months. Any kid who used that much mousse was a pretty poor candidate for nerddom. Of this Calista was convinced.

For now, Charley mostly used his modem for sending E-mail through the network to his various user friends, or whatever they called these network pen pals. They gossiped. They played games. They bragged. Charley said that bragging was the downfall of crackers. Crackers were evil hackers. Charley was careful to make this distinction. Hacking was something you just did for fun. It wasn't illegal and didn't make the kind of trouble that caused big-buck problems like viruses that got into defense-system mainframes. But they all bragged—hackers and crackers alike. They bragged about writing programs that could solve the Towers of Hanoi puzzle, or they bragged about getting into the TRW computer that controls all credit references. Charley mostly logged in to the recreation groups that had to do with games and skateboarding. If you had questions, you could post them and receive answers through your E-mail mailing list program.

Just a few short years after Calista and Tom had had the birds-and-the-bees talk with Charley, they had to have the hacker or cracker talk. Charley had, when he was nine, engaged in his first, and as far as Calista knew last, computer criminal act. He had managed to put himself on the subscription list for a *Dungeons and Dragons* magazine, a magazine that his parents had thought was too expensive to buy. It was the electronic equivalent of the kind of shoplifting young children sometimes do when they just want to see what it feels like to steal. Tom and Calista had made him send back a note of apology and confess to having hacked into the subscription files. He was grounded, his allowance suspended for two months, and he was made to do extra chores around the house. But it wasn't anything as bloodless as computer crime that was now occupying her thoughts, and if Charley started poking around, how long would it be before that computer started spurting blood? No, he just had to cool it. This was for her to handle through the proper channels. She flipped up the drain and felt the water sucking out around her toes.

She got dressed in her favorite cold-weather outfit, a Cal Tech sweat suit, and went downstairs to make breakfast. Charley slept like a log, and that would be her salvation. He never woke up on his own before nine. She always had to get him up on school mornings. If the Boston Police Department woke up before Charley, it would be nice. She called them at seven, but Lieutenant McCafferty was not in yet. She left her name and number. She called at seven forty-five. He'd been in but was out again. "Thanks for returning my call," she muttered. She didn't exactly know how to proceed. The thing with the stuffed animal and the book's defacement had happened in Cambridge, so theoretically she could call up the Cambridge cops. But what would they say to someone calling up and reporting a stuffed animal smeared with paint and diapers drawn on a boy in a book? And it wasn't the Cambridge Police Department's business. It was the Boston Cops' bailiwick because it was all related to the murder of Petrakis. Someone was trying to scare her and scare her good. But why? Why scare her and Margaret?

She turned on the *Today* show and made herself another cup of coffee. There was a most attractive man being interviewed by Jane Pauley. Gads, he was attractive! But what in the hell was he talking about—the Vatican as a dysfunctional family? Oh, dear! Jane was addressing him as "Father." Of course. Calista had seen his book in the window of the Harvard Coop. What was his name? Father something or other, a Dominican or Jesuit who had been silenced by the Vatican. Oh, maybe he'd get defrocked! One could always hope.

The next person on after Father Whoever was Betty Furness. Calista switched the channel. Oh, no! She knew what this was already. Somehow she just sensed it. It was a local show, and this morning they were calling in about sex. They seemed to do that topic at least once a week. What was the angle today? Sex fantasy. Great. The visiting expert was quoting something from Masters and Johnson about men wanting more, more sex, more than one woman at a time—that was one of their big fantasies. He quoted some statistic. They then took a commercial break. Was this planned or what? A voice came on singing, "You've got to give more! 'Cause you're a mom!" It showed a mom beaming as she served her child a sandwich. "You got to give one hundred percent 'cause you're a mom. So buy Twain's Bread."

"Oh, for heaven's sake!" muttered Calista. "A little guilt in the morning for Mommy, Mommy who hasn't made enough love for Daddy, that insatiable satyr! What kind of number are you doing on us?" Calista often talked to machines. Televisions, washing machines that didn't behave, hairdryers that over-heated. She had once stood in a gas station and yelled at a talking Coke machine. Charley had said it was the most embarrassing moment of his life. "Dear me! Dear me!" she now muttered as the sex experts came back on. And to think that she had the simple fantasy of one man and she'd long ago given up on Charley eating whole-wheat bread. By God, she wasn't going to feel guilty about that! She picked up the phone to try the police department again.

"Lieutenant McCafferty, please. . . . He's not in? That's what you tell me every time I call. Look, I would really like to talk to him. It's in regard to the Petrakis murder case. This is Calista Jacobs. Lieutenant McCafferty and the other man, yes, Detective Stevens, that was his name, interviewed me exten-sively after the murder. Now I have left numerous messages for them to call, and no one returns my calls, and . . ." She hesitated. She didn't want to tell all about the books and the stuffed animal on the phone to this secretary. "Well, there's been some new and unsettling, uh . . ." She searched for a word—"developments," that was it. That might excite them into thinking something was breaking. "Developments," she continued, "and I would really like to talk to them about it. . . . No . . . no, I don't want to talk to you about it. No offense, but really I think it's most appropriate that I speak directly with Lieutenant McCafferty or Detective Stevens. . . . Yes . . . yes. . . . Okay. Good-bye."

"No dice, huh?"

Calista wheeled around. It was Charley, barefoot and yawn-ing in his striped pajamas.

"Charley, how long have you been up?"

"Not long. I heard you when I was coming through the pantry. So you're not getting anyplace with the police department?"

"No, I guess you can say that." Calista sank down in her chair. She would have to tell him. "Charley . . ." She inhaled sharply.

"What?" The sleepiness had vanished instantly from his eyes.

"Something happened last night," she said. She tried to keep her voice steady.

"What?" He leaned forward across the table where he had just sat down. Calista got up and walked to a broom closet where she had put the plastic bag with the stuffed owl.

"I found Owl"—she paused—"on the cat rock in the garden," she said, taking out the stuffed figure. The paint smell rose from the bag. Owl didn't look quite as lurid in the morning light. The markings on his face seemed more like the scribbling of a child. But a shocked gray look crept across Charley's face.

"Owl was out there in the backyard."

"Yep."

Charley swallowed hard.

"I don't want you to get too frightened, Charley. I've thought about it, and I think people who do stuff like this, well, it's kind of like obscene telephone calls. This is the extent of their kicks. They don't act out any further. It's just sort of a perverse pleasure in scaring."

"But they have acted out further. They've murdered Petrakis."

"I bet it's not the same person." She said this so firmly that it surprised even her. But she felt an acute edge of truth in this statement. She would bet that it was not the same person. Different strokes for this different folks. It might all be related, but one was a compulsive graffitist and the other was a murderer, both perhaps sides of the same coin, part of a currency she did not understand as yet.

"But what's really bugging me is that I can't get hold of the cops, those two detectives who interviewed Margaret and me downtown. It's hard to just call up and say, Hey, someone marked up my book and wrecked my stuffed animal. I got to get hold of those two guys. I just don't think they're paying much

85

attention to this murder. You read about so many of these murders. They're on the front page for one day, and then what happens? Just another statistic."

"Petrakis didn't even make it to the front page."

"I know, and I just hate to think of him becoming another statistic, another unsolved crime on the roster." She sipped some of her coffee, which by now was lukewarm.

"You really feel that way, Mom?"

"Well, of course I do . . . but wait, Charley . . ." She started to hold up her hand in a cautionary gesture.

"Don't worry, Mom. Let me just try one thing, right here."

"What?" she asked cautiously.

"The police department must have a public relations office, right?"

"I suppose so. Public information or something like that."

"Okay, what's the number you've been calling?"

"Here." She pushed a piece of paper toward him. "What are you going to do?"

"It's nothing bad. It's nothing illegal."

"I should hope not."

"I just want to find out what kind of hardware they use."

"What do you mean, hardware? They use guns and night-sticks."

"Not that kind of hardware, Mom. What kind of computers. And what their operating system is."

"Well, okay. Let me get you a robe, though. You make me feel cold just to look at you, and what do you want for breakfast?"

"Uh . . . I don't know. You decide." He was already dialing. When she came downstairs again, he was just hanging up. "They gave me another number to call."

By the time Calista had sliced an orange for him, toasted him a bagel, and scrambled two eggs, he had called two more numbers and was in the middle of another call. "Well, I'm just a junior high student in Boston, and I'm supposed to do a report on computers in law enforcement, and all I want to know is the name of your computer and the operating system. Yeah, but if I write a letter and by the time that office gives clearance, it'll be beyond the deadline for my assignment, and couldn't you just please tell me . . ." He waited expectantly. "Okay," he said, and hung up the phone.

"No dice?" Calista asked.

"No dice." He did not seem all that disturbed. "You see how awful it is, Mom? I mean, here we are, two law-abiding citizens, just trying to get some information on a violent crime, the victim was our friend. Well, not exactly our friend, but certainly your friend, and they won't return your calls, and they won't tell me anything. And you and Margaret get these weird books, and they aren't even there to report it to."

He was working up to something. She could tell. "I think that's just the way it goes, Charley."

"What are you going to do about it?" He had a way of absolutely skewing her with the luminous gray light from his eyes when he was asking her one of his "no exit" questions. And this was definitely one of them.

"Well," she began cautiously, stalling like an ill-prepared student in a recitation. "I think we take this one step at a time." It even sounded like bullshit to her.

"What do you mean by that?"

"I suppose I should next call Janet Weiss or, better, Ethan Thayer, and see if he's had any feedback from the detectives, and I guess also tell him about this"—she hesitated—"latest development." At that moment the phone rang. Calista jumped for it. "Oh, hi, Matthew. . . . Yes, isn't this nice, a snow day in April. . . . Yes, just what every mother wants. Okay, here's Charley." She handed the phone to Charley. "Why don't you guys plan something for this morning, and then I'll take you both to lunch at Elsie's."

Charley took the phone. "Mom's bribing us. She said she'll take us both to lunch at Elsie's if we plan some wonderful educational activity for this morning that will make us better citizens of the world."

"I said no such thing, Charley!" Calista protested.

"She said no such thing. She just wants us out of her hair until lunch. . . . Okay. Yeah, bring that program. See you." He hung up.

"He's coming here?"

"Yep."

87

"What's he bringing with him?"

"Oh, this cool modeling program."

"Modeling?"

"Yeah, didn't I tell you about our ideas for doing this thing for the Martin Institute?"

"Oh, my God, Charley!" Calista slapped her forehead. "I forgot that yesterday was your first day over there. I never even asked you about it with all the commotion over the books and going to Margaret's. Damn! This is what makes me so mad about all this! It's so disruptive to the real stuff, the good stuff of life and the things we should be focused on and attending to."

Charley didn't answer. He just looked at her calmly with the no-exit light in his gray eyes. "So is it neat over there?"

"You mean at the Martin Institute?"

"Yes. What did you do? Are you in a lab or what? I hope you're not in the AIDS lab."

"No, don't be silly, Mom. They're not going to put kids in the AIDS lab."

"Well, where are you? What are you doing?"

"I'm in a guy's lab named Leventhal."

"Leventhal, I've heard of him. He's a big honcho in cancer research."

"Yeah, I know. I think he's the biggest according to Matthew's dad. He might even get a Nobel Prize for his work with the oncogene—see, I learned a new word on my first day."

"It's the cancer gene, right?"

"Tumor-producing genes, altered genes. When they're normal they do things like make scabs."

"Oh, Charley, that's so good. Look how much you've learned already. I think this program is wonderful. What do you have to do?"

"Not much." He made a face. "Basically Matthew and I and this other kid, Louise, she's from another school, we just have to look at all these protein bases that make up the chains of amino acids."

"You mean you look at them through a microscope?"

"No. No, I don't even know how to look through one of those electron microscopes anyway. No, you look at them through computers."

"Through computers?" She was definitely confused, but she also felt something of a letdown. She had hoped that maybe Charley would get away just a little bit from computers at the Martin Institute. She had had visions of him bending over test tubes and Bunsen burners. "How in the hell do they look at DNA or whatever through computers?"

"They have these X-ray photographs of genetic materials called autoradiographs, and they can use nuclear trace stuff and do experiments so they can figure out what the protein bases are. And they get thousands, maybe millions of sequences, and they make up into one of twenty amino acids. I don't quite understand it all."

"Just *quite?*" Calista opened her eyes wide. "I couldn't understand any of it."

"Well, I understand the fact that there are these four very fundamental bases in DNA and RNA called uracil, cytosine, and two others I can't remember, and when they link up into three they are called codons. And that these make up the twenty amino acids, which are the bases of proteins."

"What do you have to actually do?"

"I told you. I just look at the data from the autoradiographs and the other ways that they've tried to blow apart these proteins, and I look at these long chains of amino acids called peptides and I try to find stuff that might make a pattern, you know, correlations. They got the data for fifty or sixty of what they are calling the solved proteins. So we're supposed to look at those and become familiar with their sequences and then go and look at this other stuff. It's kind of boring, but I guess I'm learning a lot about DNA and all that stuff."

"I'll say. I mean, you're way ahead of me in one day, and I had two semesters of biology in college."

"You did?" Charley looked surprised.

"Yes. Don't rub it in."

"Ah, don't worry. They probably hadn't discovered any of this stuff back then."

"Ah, yes, back then at the dawn of the Pleistocene."

"You're very sensitive about your age, ever since you turned forty, which you have been for over a year now. I thought you'd get used to it."

89

"Funny about that. I'll probably be fifty before I'm used to being forty."

"I'm used to thirteen. I'm ready for fourteen, even fifteen. Definitely sixteen!"

"Don't rush it. So what is the program that Matthew is bringing over?"

"It's a modeling program that his dad got hold of. It's for molecular modeling. See, Matthew and I think we can relieve the boredom of this job if we can talk them into letting us build some models on the computer of these protein base arrangements. And then we're going to figure out how to do some really sensational graphics of all the patterns we do find or the known ones. You know, three-D stuff in color. It is so boring looking at all these gray, white, and black pictures. The Martin Institute is not into splashy graphics at all."

"Well, that sounds terribly educational and will certainly make you better citizens of the world." Calista winked.

And Charley smiled. He resisted the strong urge to wink himself.

12

"Well, it's not really illegal in the same way that the subscription to *Dungeons and Dragons* magazine was. I mean, you're not really stealing in this case."

Charley winced as he remembered that rather shameful incident. "I mean, you're not ripping anyone off," Matthew continued.

"Of course I'm not ripping anybody off. I'm not stealing, I wouldn't be hurting anything or anybody. I'd just be eavesdropping. I wouldn't disturb the files at all. It's nothing like Murray Kaploff."

"Who's Murray Kaploff?"

"A son of some friends of my mom's and dad's, and he wrote a

90

virus and it got into the NASA mainframe and cost the taxpayers ten million dollars."

"Well, this is nothing. At worst it could be considered a violation of confidentiality."

"These guys aren't doctors. They're the Boston Police Department, and if anybody's their patient, it's Mom and her old-lady friend Margaret McGowan, and they have a right to know if this book thing is connected with Petrakis's murder."

"That is so gross. I can't believe someone would murder that guy. I have every book he ever did on the planets and space. And then that stuff to your mom's books and Owl."

"Yeah, I have all the Petrakis books on making model airplanes," Charley said.

Matthew was silent for a moment and then looked up. "Well, Charley, I think they're treating you like crap—the police department."

"You do?" Charley said. There was a plangent, hopeful tone in his voice.

"Yeah."

"Does that mean you'll help me do it?"

Matthew scratched his head. He and Charley had been friends, best friends, since they were three years old and had met in nursery school. Matthew had been peripherally involved when Charley and Calista had discovered that Tom Jacobs had been murdered. Charley had turned to Matthew at that time, when he had discovered that the files, locked files in his dad's computer, had been tampered with. Charley had suspected von Sackler, the undercover CIA agent, but knew that his mother was becoming kind of romantically involved. There was no one to turn to except Matthew. They had trailed von Sackler on that night. It had been Halloween, and somehow they'd gotten into some stupid fight and Matthew had stomped off, let down his friend, and then Charley had . . . Matthew couldn't bear even now to think of it. Charley had nearly been killed. He definitely owed Charley one. They didn't have those stupid fights anymore. They had matured, and what they were doing wasn't dangerous, really, and it wasn't illegal. Well, at least no one would be hurt by it. But it would be going against a promise Matthew had made to his own parents: not to get involved with cracker bulletin boards. But they wouldn't really have to be that involved. They weren't going to do anything wrong, nothing that would hurt anybody or vandalize any systems. No viruses. He told himself that for the fiftieth time.

"Okay," Matthew said tersely, and pressed his lips together tightly as if he had just taken some particularly foul tasting medicine. "But we got to do it from your house on your machine."

"Of course. I'll take all the responsibility."

"Did your mom make you promise not to use cracker boards?"

"My mom doesn't even know they exist."

Cracker bulletin boards were like other electronic bulletin boards except that they specialized in purveying stolen information. They were electronic hock shops in that sense, and in addition to this they provided, like all bulletin boards, a way for the crackers to communicate, except they often used stolen AT&T credit cards or MCI numbers to pay for the calls. All one needed was a personal computer and a modem. It was through these boards that crackers then reported a wealth of information that they had in their possession concerning other computer systems—phone numbers, passwords, user names as well as credit card information.

"So where do we start?"

"I don't know. What are the names of some of those boards— Captain Kidd's? Isn't that one?"

"A lot of pirate names."

"Stands to reason."

"So how do we find them? From the straight bulletin boards?" Matthew asked.

"Yeah, if you watch those, you'll see listings, phone numbers that just stay on for a few minutes before the systems operator chases them off."

"Sam's—that's one. Sam's Equipment Exchange. I was over at Jerry Kline's the other day and we were in his brother's room. His brother goes to MIT, and he was looking for something on Sam's board and a couple of numbers disappeared, like, you know, within fifteen or twenty minutes. He said the systems operator was deleting them."

"You got the number for Sam's?"

"No. But it's in almost every issue of the *Computer Digest*. I think it even came in a handout they gave us when we bought our modem—you know, some sort of listing of services and bulletin boards."

Charley got up and went over to a shelf where he kept a precariously high stack of magazines. He got a few. They found the number for Sam's Equipment Exchange in the ad section of the first magazine they opened.

"Okay," said Charley. "Let me shut this down." There was a picture on the screen of nucleotides that looked like bubbles arranged in a three-dimensional pattern around a ring of nitrogen and carbon atoms. They faded from the screen. "So much for us finding the cure for cancer." Charley sighed and remembered his mother's high hopes.

They watched the board and studied the listings and messages.

"I know that sci-fi outfit. I got Software Wars from it," Matthew said, spotting one listing.

"Okay, look . . . There it is, Captain Kidd's!" Charley scribbled down a number.

"Look, Digital Pirate!"

They continued paging through the messages, pressing SPACE each time to scan the board to see how many choices there were. They then went back to write down the numbers of possible candidates. The fourth time they hit SPACE for an outfit just after Digital Pirate, the computer indicated that that particular number had been deleted.

"Wow!" they both exclaimed.

"Let's go back and see if Digital Pirate's still there," Charley said. They did. Again a message came up that the listing had been deleted. They had been printing out as they went along. They tried printing now, but the number was just not there. They tried once more to print. A message came up: "No pirates permitted to leave messages on this board."

"We got some numbers, didn't we?" Charley said, picking up the printout.

93

"Yeah, I think enough to get started."

"The sys op must really be riding the range," Charley said as he checked the printout. "Sys op" was the abbreviated form of systems operator, and the one at Sam's Equipment Exchange was obviously on line cleansing his board of the pirate influence, running a tight ship and making the crackers walk the electronic plank. But the boys had gotten enough numbers to begin, and less than a quarter of an hour after they had shut down their cancer research project, they entered the subterranean labyrinth of the world of electronic bandits. There was no one on-line at the first three of the cracker bulletin boards that they tried. They could not leave E-mail in this situation. That was rule number one. They had to be able to have someone on-line to "talk" with.

13

Calista was pleased with the green. The egg and linseed oil had worked, and she was able to thin it out to that first barely green that stained the trees in earliest spring, which was when the story opened. It had gone fast, faster than she had thought. She had used for the most part a sponge to apply the green— actually a fragment of a sponge that she had bought in Chinatown and then attached to a small stick. It worked beautifully for dabbing on the vernal stain of early spring. She was now ready to begin work on the arm of Marian. She looked at her watch. It was getting on toward lunch, but there had been no growls of hunger from above. The boys must be totally absorbed in their modeling of cancer genes, or whatever it was. It would be exciting if Charley really got hooked on this project—my son the doctor, my son the Nobel laureate! It had a more comforting ring to it than "my son the computer wizard." Lots of young computer wizards, at least in Cambridge these days, tended to go into AI—artificial intelligence, not steak sauce, as she had thought at first when she had come across the initials in a magazine article. The Tech Square-Kendall Square area was apparently the artificial intelligence center of the world. She had read a little bit more about it after that first encounter with the term. Tom had explained some of it to her. She found it weirder than any of the physics he had ever tried to explain to her, more confounding in its own way than general relativity. Hard-core AI people believed that they could build not just robots, but minds. She found the whole area very strange. Some critics thought of it as a kind of mumbo-jumbo alchemy that had nothing to do with "real intelligence"; but the devotees, the hard-core, looked upon it as the next step in human evolution. It could conceivably come up with formulas or algorithms for intuition!

At the moment her algorithms were down. She couldn't visualize what this arm of Marian's should look like. It had to look like a woman's arm, a young woman's arm, but be able to shoot like a man's! She had to convey that tensile strength of the musculature yet delicacy of bone structure. She could actually see the arm but not visualize the strength, the coiled energy, in it. Of course, that was the problem! She was coiling the energy, putting it into a potential state, whereas it had already been spent, the arrow had been shot, the energy transferred from muscle to the arrow's shaft. She needed to show a relaxed muscle. She went over to her bookshelf and got down a very worn copy of Gray's *Anatomy of the Human Body,* as well as a book of Leonardo da Vinci's drawings. For body work they were an unbeatable combination. She opened the books and imme-diately found the drawings that would help her. So much for intuition and artistic impulse. Sometimes you just simply had to know the sources to go to and look at things really hard. She felt her stomach growl. She'd stop now. It was always good to stop when you were on top, when you knew where to come back to and what precisely you had to do. No waiting around for inspiration. It wasted too much time.

Elsie's was on the corner of Mount Auburn and Holyoke streets in the heart of Harvard Square. One did not go to Elsie's for ambience. Elsie's was before ambience, definitely before pasta, before anybody had ever heard the word *upscale,* and there was no other term for a downscale eatery than greasy spoon. Elsie's made McDonald's look like Lutèce. It was Calista's theory that it was started by somebody who had gone bust in the wood veneer business, for there were at least ten different kinds of plastic wood in the place and the walls were covered with the three most rejected wallpapers in the Western Hemisphere. You didn't eat at tables but at high countertops, sitting on stools. You placed your order upon entering. There were a few quaint things about Elsie's—just a few, but present nonetheless. The windows were very nice, mullioned into lots of smaller frames in much the same style as the rest of Harvard's window architecture. The other quaint thing about Elsie's was that they eschewed the French fry. There was not a French fry on the premises. Instead they had knishes. And it was "instead." Ask for French fries and they said, "No, but we got knishes." A tad strange, but there was something rather charming about the presence of a knish on such a menu. Their hamburgers were wonderful. You could go around the corner to Bartley's Burger Cottage and get all sorts of fancy hamburgers with bacon and saga cheese and pineapple put on top, but nobody put on the grease like Elsie's. And that's what Calista liked. It wasn't simply that they were excessively greasy. It was rather the way they let the grease seep into the bun that made it all soggy and wonderfully juicy through and through. The boys liked the hamburgers, or Elsie Burgers, as the double-decker ones were called, and the video games. There was a room off the one where you gave your order devoted to video games. It was hell to go to Elsie's during reading period because all the Harvard students hogged the games. But reading period was still a few weeks away, and there would be plenty of space in the game room, as Calista pointed out to the boys. They had seemed somewhat reluctant to leave their molecular modeling project. They played the games while they waited for their orders, and then Calista came in and got them. They found a counter near the Holyoke Street window.

"So what's new in the world of oncogenes? You guys going to turn the Martin Institute on its ear?"

"Sure," said Charley. He hoped his mother wouldn't dwell

on this. He probably should never have told her so much about it.

"What's Leventhal like?"

"How should we know?" Matthew asked. "We never saw him when we were there. I saw his picture, though. He looks kind of like a Buddha, his shape, at least."

"Mom, I think you're getting your hopes up too much. Do you really think Leventhal's going to sit down with two eighth-graders and say, 'Now tell me, fellows, where do you think I should look next for the cure for cancer'?"

"They don't even talk about cancer there. They just talk about cells. They just want to find out how cells work. If they stumble across the cure for cancer, so much the better," Matthew said.

"You're right. That guy, the one who's sort of our adviser there, he's this graduate student or something. When he was showing us what he did and talking about all the stuff that he is looking at, stuff about membranes and biochemical pathways of cells, he's just talking really about how cells work, not necessarily cancer. They're hacking cells is what they're doing over there."

"Yeah," said Matthew. "It's a hack."

"A hack?" Calista was bewildered. "You mean as in computer hacking?"

"Sort of. They're just trying to tunnel into a system."

"Oh," said Calista. She took a bite of her hamburger. Was she a romantic or what?

14

Charley had been adamant about not leaving any E-mail on a cracker board. So when they returned from lunch they tried two more calls to find an on-line sys op. Their second call was to a board called Pieces of Eight, and someone was home tending the shop. Charley had logged on using his user name CHAZ. He then typed CHAT, indicating his wish to "talk" directly to the sys op. The sys op then responded:

WHAT DO YOU NEED?

Charley typed: BOSTON POLICE DEPARTMENT.

Sys op: YOU NUTZ?

Chaz: NO, VERY IMPORTANT. NEED TO GET IN.

Sys op: NO WAY JOSE. YOU'LL GET CAUGHT. NOT A GENERAL ACCESS MODEM. ALL HARD WIRE RUNNING TO EACH PRECINCT. THEY GOT TAPS ON EVERYTHING. YOU'D HAVE TO ROUTE THE CALL THROUGH EUROPE. COME ON, I CAN FIX YOU UP WITH MCI NUMBERS. YOU WANT TO GET INTO THE TRW COMPUTER? YOU NAME IT WE CAN DO IT. REPEAT NUTZ TO TRY BPD.

Chaz: GOT TO. NO CHOICE. WHAT'S THEIR HARDWARE?

Sys op: IT'S YOUR ASS. FINEST. WHY WON'T NCIC DO?

Charley and Matthew looked at each other. "What's that?" Charley asked. Matthew shrugged.

Chaz: WHAT'S NCIC?

Sys op: NATIONAL CRIME INFORMATION CENTER.

"That's not going to help me," Charley said, shaking his head. He typed again: NO. NEED BPD. LOCAL THING. PLEEZE!

Sys op: OKAY. LET ME TRY SOMETHING. I'LL CALL BACK ONE HOUR. WHAT'S YOUR NUMBER?

Chaz: NO, I'LL CALL YOU BACK ONE HOUR.

Sys Op: OKAY.

Nothing is a pain to a cracker, only a challenge. Nobody'd ever asked this before. So why not? It wasn't his ass if the kid got caught. Although he had a notion that if he could find who he wanted to find, it wouldn't be that dangerous.

Charley called back in an hour, but the sys op didn't have the stuff. He told him to call back in three hours or leave his number. But Charley wouldn't. Shortly before dinner Charley got what he wanted. Hobbit. Hobbit had just quit his job writing programs for the Boston Police Department's computer FINEST. He didn't have a general access number. He had something that was better than a general access number—a private one. He had installed it just for himself, so he didn't have to go all the way into town to fix things. He had quit three months before, but he still had his modem, and a "back door" into the system was still available. At midnight of that evening while Calista slept, CHAZ talked with HOBBIT and convinced him that he meant to do no damage, that he only wanted to get into the homicide files because his mom's friend had been murdered. It took very little convincing. Hobbit had a big fat grudge against the BPD. He probably wouldn't have cared if CHAZ trashed the whole system. So he gave CHAZ the telephone number of a modem connected to FINEST. Charley dialed and was immediately prompted to log on:

Chaz: HELLO.

Finest: RESTART.

So Charley immediately was cued by the word RESTART that this was not the proper way to log on to the computer system. They must have changed a few things since HOBBIT had left. This left only one option for Charley's next step:

Chaz: HELP.

Finest: RESTART.

Chaz: RESTART.

Finest: FMKLOG092F USER ID MISSING OR INVALID.

The next step for Chaz was to determine a valid user name and password combination. But this was easy once he was logged on, for HOBBIT had given him a few that he felt would still work. So within twenty minutes Charley was neatly logged on to the police department's computer and into the homicide files. He had never used a system like FINEST before, but the HELP command continued to be helpful and explained the nitty-gritties of moving through this electronic precinct.

There had been two people named Petrakis involved in violent crimes in the greater Boston area in the past year. Only one was male and named Norman, however, and unfortunately that file was the shortest. "Zilch," muttered Charley to himself. "Friggin' zero." The report listed Norman Petrakis's address and Social Security number, a three-line description of the crime and the detectives who were investigating the crime. There were no suspects, no leads. There wasn't even anything about fingerprints. How could there be a crime and no mention of fingerprints; even absence of fingerprints—wouldn't they at

99

least mention it? Charley wondered. There was a number by the coroner's report, but there was no coroner's report. He must have to go into another file for that. Why not try it? The former sys op had given Charley a user name and a password for FINEST. The same user name, HICKS, appeared to be valid for the coroner's file, but a different password was required. The old password didn't work. This was a flaw in the system, a stupid one that benefited Charley, for it had told him the difference between a valid user name and an invalid password pair. For the invalid password it had responded with NOT IN DIRECTORY: REINITIATE LOGON PROCEDURE. So now all Charley had to do, knowing that his user name was okay but that the password was not, was to try passwords until he found one that worked for the coroner's file with the pathologist's report. He tried to call up the old sys op for the password to the coroner's file, but the guy wasn't on-line. Charley then had to make a decision. He could try his own thirty-thousand-word dictionary of most common English words and have his computer try each one as a password. It would take about five seconds a word. Although it would be under fifteen hours, it was still too long. It could result in revealing his presence in the system and alert the current sys op. Alternatively, he could just play with inversions of the password he had already used. But he didn't see much choice. He might as well try ransacking his dictionary at least for a little while until the old sys op came back on-line.

It only took a few hundred tries. Within the hour Chaz was back in business. But for all it was worth, the coroner's report didn't yield much. Norman Petrakis in this report had become *Decedent # 70-10879. Death by asphyxiation, contusions around the throat.* There was something that referred to *blood anomalies,* followed by some numbers and letter sequences that must have referred to blood types. Charley copied it all down, including the blood anomalies H1, H2, H1-H2, K3, K4, K5. For his sixteen hours of efforts he had very little to show. He was dead tired, and there was no way his mom would let him stay home from school the next day. So much for Boston's FINEST!

15

A reasonable facsimile of spring actually did arrive. And on schedule, undeterred and unimpaired by the snowstorm, the dogwood outside Calista's window blossomed. It was still in its deep russet stage as Calista opened her eyes this early May morning. She was thinking not of the glories of spring, however, but of Norman Petrakis. The detectives had never called her back. She had informed Ethan Thayer and Janet Weiss of the defaced books and the mutilated stuffed animal. Ethan had reported this to the authorities, but nothing had happened. They were carefully screening all the mail that arrived at the publishers for both Calista and Margaret. Margaret had gone off to England to visit relatives. Calista envied her. The only places that she had relatives were Long Island, New York, and Indiana, neither of which appealed to her at the moment. Besides, would she really want to have missed the dogwood?

What she wished she could have avoided was the whole month of April. She and Charley would go to Dallas in June for the American Library Association meeting, where she would pick up her Caldecott Medal. Dallas in June could hardly be considered idyllic. Other than that, there were no big plans for travel. They had traveled quite a bit anyway in the past year—to Japan and to Italy, where Calista's work had been honored at conferences and exhibits. She had looked forward to spending most of the summer in Vermont, where they had a summer house and where Charley could help out at a nearby commercial apple orchard and make some money. She had told him that he could bring a friend, too, for the whole summer. But now those plans seemed in jeopardy, as Charley was finding his work at the Martin Institute more interesting and had been making noises about working there for the summer with Matthew and this girl Louise who apparently was very nice. It seemed that although the project of scanning the protein base sequences was very boring, figuring out snazzy graphics and presentations for molecular models on the computer was really fun. The computers they worked on were very powerful and some of the programs very exotic. So this part of the job for Charley was like being in the proverbial candy shop.

The kids had unlimited time and license to fuss with this stuff. Charley and Louise had even prepared a graphic model for the great Leventhal himself that he had used in a European conference. The people at the lab were quite pleased with the young "mentees" that they were supposed to be mentoring. She had credited Charley's growing interest with the Martin Institute in helping him to, if not forget, at least ease up on the still unsolved Petrakis case.

But she would not think of that on such a spectacular morning. She didn't have to start rousing Charley for another hour. She should hop outside quickly and see what was growing in her garden, especially since this was the day that she would start the garden illustration, a double-page spread, in *Marian's Tale*. She was planning a spectacular walled garden for the convent where Marian was holed up.

After her walk in the garden Calista went back inside and turned on the *Today* show. Jane had changed her hairstyle yet again! Wonderful to have such flexible hair. Calista had worn her hair the same way for over twenty years. The masses of chestnut brown were shot through with silvery gray and was always madly unkempt. She kept it pinned to the top of her head with a monster barrette. This morning as she had come in from the garden and caught a glimpse of herself in a mirror, her hair had looked like a satellite picture of a weather front, she thought.

Such was not the stuff TV hairdos were made of! But then again she could keep pencils in her hair. By noon she usually had at least two sticking out of her head. She had remembered that Archie Baldwin had laughed at that when he saw her do it. She wondered how he was doing. They had talked a few times on the phone, but they always seemed to miss each other when he came to Cambridge for whatever it was he did with Harvard and the Peabody Museum. Thank God they hadn't missed at the important time when he had saved Charley's life.

Therefore, it was with some surprise, having just been

thinking about Archie, that she heard the name Baldwin emanating from the television set. She turned abruptly from the stove to the set. What an odd coincidence. But it was not Archie Baldwin the man was talking about. It was that wimpy Neddy Baldwin, former governor of Massachusetts. Must be the same family, Calista thought. There were Baldwins all over. But how different they were. Ned Baldwin had been the governor years ago, before Calista and Tom had ever moved to Cambridge. After the governorship and an unsuccessful attempt to gain the Republican presidential nomination, he had gone on to a series of high, and in many cases rather ceremonial, posts—ambassadorships, special envoy positions, numerous boards and commissions. Averill Harriman he was not. He was, rather, a very wealthy, weak-brained Brahmin. And "Holy shit!" Calista muttered, and set down her coffee. There he was at a prayer breakfast with that bizarre television preacher Lorne Thurston. Good Lord, he was more weak-brained than she thought. What could he possibly be doing with that guy?

"Hi, Mom."

"Ssshhh!" Calista held out her hand to hush him.

Charley crept into the kitchen and sat down at the table, where there was a glass of orange juice waiting for him.

"I think we have to look at this whole issue of what we have been told is human evolution."

Calista's jaw dropped. She walked toward the television spellbound. This was not Lorne Thurston talking. This was Ned Baldwin, scion of one of the oldest families of the commonwealth, son of Harvard—albeit it was only genealogy, a wing and a prayer that got him through his undergraduate years— haute Episcopalian (probably a little Unitarian thrown in there, too, as was the case with many of these Yankee families), but there he was saying—let's hear that again. Oh, no! Now he was just being so folksy, and all those hick-brained fundamentalists were looking positively gleeful as he told them: "I just don't think the final word is in on all this evolution stuff, and if that's the case and there does appear to be evidence for some scientific basis for creationism, and then Genesis is—" Cheers drowned him out. The audience went wild.

"What is this?" Charley asked, staring at the television.

"This is the bully pulpit, Charley, and you'll never guess who that is up there, the one on the left."

"Who?"

"Ned Baldwin, a relative of Archie Baldwin."

"Archie Baldwin—the guy who saved my life?"

"The one and only."

"How can he have an idiot like that for a relative?"

"I'm not sure. The blood must have really thinned out at a certain point." Calista sighed. "He was, however, once governor of this state, and he's held a lot of important posts. I don't think anyone ever did think of him as a mental giant, but they didn't think of him as this, either." She gestured at the television screen. The news clip was over, and the commentator was discussing the growing popularity of Lorne Thurston, the television minister, and the rumors of his seeking political office.

"Why would this Baldwin creep be there with him?" Charley asked.

"I don't know. It's perplexing. Baldwin isn't seeking any political office. I think he's beyond that now. He just gets very fancy ambassadorships and serves on lots of important boards and commissions. There's no need for him to do this kind of thing. Why would he stick his neck out on this evolution thing? It must be so embarrassing to his family."

"If they're anything like Archie, it would be." Charley had taken an immediate liking to Archie Baldwin that seemed based on something more than the fact that the man had saved his life. There was just something about the guy that Charley liked, felt good about being around him, and yet he had only been around him for a very brief time. Somehow he couldn't match Archie up with the turkey he had just seen on television.

"Mom, are you sure they're related?"

"They've got to be. All these old Boston families are intertwined."

"And who's the other guy? What'd you say his name was?"

"Lorne Thurston. You know, you've heard of him. He's one of these TV ministers with his 'heavenly megaphone' and WATS line to God. Gets all those old folks to send in their

104

Social Security money. Got his own network, and he's even got some sort of Bible college he runs."

"You're kidding—a college, too? Where?"

"Down in Texas somewhere."

"Oh, great! Maybe I'll apply when we go to get your award in Dallas."

"You'd last about one second, Charley Jacobs."

And then out of the blue Charley turned to her. His gray eyes seemed especially limpid as Calista later recalled. "I bet," he said softly. "He must have hated Norman Petrakis."

Something cold stole through Calista. "Charley, I can't believe that he would do anything like that. I mean, these guys I should think for all their fundamentalist ways would at least begin with the fundamentals of all fundamentals, the Ten Commandments."

"Yeah, I guess you're right." He paused. "But you said that guy at the conference was really obnoxious."

"Obnoxious, but not murderous. I mean, it's really not worth murdering over—human evolution." Her words struck her as very odd, oxymoronic, to say the least.

"But it's not exactly evolution," Charley said.

"What do you mean?" Calista asked. She looked up.

"It's politics." Then he suddenly looked confused by his own words. "I think that's what I mean. I mean, it sure doesn't look like religion to me, not that I'm an expert."

Calista rolled her eyes and smiled in agreement. She and Tom had never been heavily into organized religion. They had occasionally gone to services at Sanders Theater, where Harvard held them during the Jewish holidays, and Charley had had a brief whirl with Hebrew school at Harvard Hillel. They did have a seder every year with friends, and they lit candles for Hannukah. Charley had a definite Jewish identity. They ate Jewish, they celebrated Jewish holidays, and if they believed in God, it was only one, and that was about it. Charley was right. He was no expert. But then again, to use a favorite expression of her father's, he sure could "tell shit from shinola," and when he said "politics" he was right. This wasn't religion. Nobody needed a cable network, radio stations, and a college to have a little word with God or pray. It could become very cumbersome to try to cram an entire broadcasting empire though the eye of a needle. Yes, indeed, the camels had much more of a straight shot at the pearly gates than Lorne Thurston with BBN, his Bible Broadcasting Network. It was politics. But could it be murder? No, no way, she told herself. They wouldn't risk it. It was stupid. But who says they're smart?

"No . . . no . . ." She shook her head. "I just can't believe they'd do something like this. I mean, if he were found out, it would be curtains for him, and he wouldn't be crying over his lost souls, Charley, or his flock no longer having their shepherd. He'd be crying over his private jet and his estates and, gee whiz, the guy lives like a billionaire because he is one. He just wouldn't risk all that. It's out of the question. I think that Petrakis's death was the result of one crazy person working alone." She could tell, though, that Charley did not entirely buy that. He was still hung up on the notion of Lorne Thurston and his Bible-belting vigilantes.

"But you called it a bully pulpit just a minute ago."

"Bullies, not murderers, Charley. I think there's a difference."

"Hmm." It was not the sigh of satisfaction or resolution. And as if to confirm this, Charley's eyes took on that opaque look that signaled one thing—thinking, heavy-duty thinking. Oh, shit, had she opened this whole thing up again? Just three weeks before she had been worried about him getting overanxious with the police department. Luckily he seemed to have cooled on that. But now this jerky Baldwin and God's mouthpiece had reared their ugly heads, and . . . Oh, God, she didn't even want to think about it. She began biting her lip again as she watched Charley's still face.

16

Archie Baldwin slipped the key into the front door of his Georgetown town house. He was back home after two months in the field in Mexico supervising a Mayan excavation. He had not planned to be gone for two months, but the unexpected had happened in the best sense, the most positive and serendipitous of events that can befall an archaeologist: an entire lost city had been found. What had started out as a very ordinary dig a year before, which promised to reveal some rather classic textbooky-type pre-Columbian stuff, had indeed turned into much more as the first walls of the city began to poke through the rubble. Archie's role, originally that of visiting Smithsonian scientist, a drop-in appearance by the grand old man of the field, had changed dramatically. Not that it was simply perfunctory or ceremonial before. He was after all the one who decided on funding and approved the budget for an undertaking like this, but his role in the field was peripheral. After all, he had five other digs that he was overseeing and an international traveling exhibit he was putting together for the Smithsonian. But when the "sub-Tecla" had been discovered under the Tecla in the Yucatán peninsula, everything else was put on hold.

It wasn't simply a matter of it being appropriate and fitting that the man, the dean of American archaeology, be on the premises so that an adequate interpretation could be made during excavation. He was needed in a different way in this situation. Young Willburton, the principal investigator on this site, was as smart as they came and had a very promising career in the making. It would have been most inappropriate for Archie to simply swoop down and take over. But the fact was that no one else knew how to properly excavate around the corbeled arches without them all crashing in on the rooms, thought to be temple rooms, below. They didn't teach these kids enough architecture or engineering now. It should have become a mandatory part of any archaeology curriculum. Willburton, therefore, welcomed Archie Baldwin's presence. And Archie, the grand man from the Smithsonian, had sweated like a pig and worked his ever-loving buns off for two months teaching the young graduate students how to take a roof off a three-thousand-year-old gem without shattering the whole business. There was a crew of Maya-speaking Mexicans, but they didn't know any more than the kids about taking off these kinds of roofs. The result was that all Willburton's knowledge about Petén and Yaxuná periods wasn't worth a hill of beans, especially if the hill collapsed and crushed all the beans, crushed all the beautiful stelae with the hieroglyphics. So Archie not only saved the day, so to speak, but gave Willburton something to write about that would possibly make the young man's reputation.

Archie came back tanned and as fit as he had ever been in his fifty-two years. He still had the grime under his nails from the dig. But he felt great. How often does a guy at this stage in his career really get to go out there and muck around anymore? Usually it was just pushing numbers, approving budgets, sitting on august boards with a bunch of old farts. Christ, for a year and a half he'd had to serve as acting department chairman at the Smithsonian until they'd found a new one. What a drag that had been. These last two months had been fun. Really fun. The kids had worked hard. They didn't exactly treat him like a contemporary. He wouldn't have liked or expected that. But they hadn't treated him like a father confessor or Father Time, either. There was no romance, no flirtations, but gee whiz, you couldn't have everything. A warm body, however, on a chilly Mexican night would have been nice.

He walked into his front hall. Everything seemed in order. There were several stacks of mail on the small hallway table. He could see that there was more on the dining room table and, he assumed, more at the office, but at least Ruth Goodfellow, his secretary, would have that taken care of. He took his bags upstairs and then came downstairs praying that there might be a beer in the fridge.

There was a six-pack in addition to eggs, bacon, juice, milk, bread, and even tomatoes for a proper English breakfast. Along with it all was a welcome-home note from Goodfellow. God! Did she ever fail? How British. None of this Wheaties, breakfast of champions, business. This was a breakfast fit for empire builders, or uncoverers, as the case might be. He suddenly was starved, even though he had had dinner on the plane. He took out some bacon and began frying it up. When the bacon was done he slid the tomatoes into the pan, chased them around with the spatula for the better part of a minute, removed them, and put in the eggs. When it was ready he took it to the kitchen table with his beer and flipped on the television set. The picture frizzled. There was a short blizzard of snow and then an unmistakable voice.

"Neddy!" Archie popped open the can of beer. The picture had resolved itself into a crisp image. Archie blinked and opened his eyes wider. "Neddy!" he exclaimed as he saw the tall lean figure of his cousin on a stage with Lorne Thurston, the television evangelist. "What the fu—"?

"I think we have to look at this whole issue of what we have been told is human evolution. I just don't think the final word is in on all this evolution stuff, and if . . ."

"Stuff!" Archie exclaimed. This was not Lorne Thurston talking. This was his own cousin. He was actually standing on a platform with the guy and mouthing this garbage. Neddy was no genius. Everyone in the family knew that, but there was a difference between being a dim-witted Republican and this! "This is, I think, a philosophy, this evolution stuff, more than a—"

"Oh, no!" groaned Archie. The film report ended two minutes later and the newscaster was talking about rumors that Lorne Thurston might be seeking national office and looking for endorsements from high-ranking conservative Republicans. "What are you doing, Neddy? You need this guy like a hole in the head!" Archie was fuming at the television set. "This has nothing to do with you. Didn't you give up running for office so you could serve better? You call this serving—getting this nut national exposure so he can run? What the fuck are you doing on the stand with these jerks?" He slammed down his can of beer, leaned forward, and flicked off the television. This was ridiculous, screaming at the television. He'd call up Neddy directly. He lived in Washington now, just a few blocks away. He had become used to the Washington area after serving for eight years as a cabinet officer and then as chief of protocol. So after his term as ambassador to the court of St. James had ended, he had returned to Washington. It was a good base to take off from for all of his board meetings and goodwill missions for chiefs of state. Of course, he still kept the old family place in Dover, Massachusetts, and another summer place in Maine. Where was he now? The home front would know. He dialed Ned Baldwin's D.C. number. It wasn't that late. Someone would be up. The phone rang twice.

"Lacey?"

"Big Lacey or Little Lacey?" a youthful female voice said.

"Oh, Lace, it's you. This is Archie."

"Oh, hi, Archie. What's up?"

"Trying to track down your dad."

"Oh, no problem. Hold on a second while I get the schedule." She was back within a minute. "Okay, let's see, tonight it's Thursday, so it must be Dallas, and it's the Hyatt Hotel." She then rattled off the hotel phone number and the area code.

"Hey, kiddo, you're fantastic. I think they ought to be putting you up for a cabinet post." There was a slight pause.

"Archie?" The voice had a plaintive note.

"Yes, dear?"

"Did you see Dad with that sleazeball preacher? Is that why you're calling?"

Archie sighed and spoke. "I did indeed."

"I was somehow hoping that this would escape most of our relatives—you of all people, too!" Lacey almost wailed.

"Don't worry about me."

"I know, worry about Dad."

"No, no. Don't worry about your dad. That's not your responsibility, Lacey."

"It's a little humiliating."

"It shouldn't be, sweetie. People, I really believe, are able to separate the children of public figures from those figures and treat them as individuals."

"Should be able to, but not necessarily *are* able to. It's still humiliating."

"That is exactly what it should not be—humiliating. Your dad has his humiliations, and you will I am sure in time have your own."

"Oh, goodie!" Lacey rejoined.

"No, it's the truth," Archie said firmly.

"You want to hear my most recent humiliating experience?"

"What's that?" Archie laughed.

"I'm thinking of not going to Harvard."

"Well, now that's not humiliating. I did the same thing. So are you thinking of following in my Dartmouth footsteps?"

"Nope."

"You got in, didn't you?"

"Yes. But that's the whole point. I am thinking of going where no other Baldwin feet have trod or left their mark."

"Yale?"

"No, Antioch."

"Antioch! Well, now that is an imaginative choice."

"Imaginative has sometimes been considered humiliating."

"Oh, come on now, Lacey. You're making us into caricatures. Do they have kayaking at Antioch?"

"I doubt it."

"Hmm." Archie hated to see a great pair of shoulders like Lacey's go for naught. She had Olympic potential, and he had been the one to introduce her to white-water kayaking. "What do your folks say?"

"What do you think?"

"Hmm."

"Yeah, you got the picture. Mom's not too upset. She's coming around."

"How is Big Lacey? She with your dad now?"

"No. She flew on to someplace else from Dallas, a step ahead of him, so to speak, in, let's see . . ." There was a pause. Archie could imagine her looking at a bulletin board with a map of the world and pins tracking the movements of public figure parents. "She is in Dayton, Ohio, receiving an award for her work with the Youth Literacy Program."

Big Lacey had always been a step or two ahead of Neddy. She was one of those large, slightly horsey looking patrician women who were immediately identified as being not only suitable but quite desirable because of their extraordinary common sense. This recommended them highly as effective wives and helpmates for men like Neddy, who were not very bright but were exceptionally good looking and possessed great geniality and charm. These men, due to their old money and genealogy, could rise effortlessly despite incompetency, but they really did require smart and skillful wives at their sides. Lacey had done just that for Neddy, beginning with his first run for the state legislature. Where was she now when he was making a fool of himself mouthing off about evolution on the same platform with that idiot Lorne Thurston? Being given an award for her work with a literacy project. How ironic! Archie said good-bye to Little Lacey, giving her his blessing for Antioch, hung up, and dialed the number in Dallas.

"Archie!" The warm rich voice on the other end exploded with genuine delight. Oh, God, he felt rotten about this. "Still got the last ten days in August slated in, fella?"

Well, he might as well come right out with it.

"Neddy!" He sighed deeply. "What the fuck were you doing up there with that asshole Lorne Thurston?"

"Now, now, calm yourself, Arch, just calm down. First of all—"

"First of all you don't know a goddamn thing about evolution or any science, and you know that as well as I do because you flunked that biology-for-poets course they used to give at Harvard *twice* and only made it through the third time because I tutored you solidly for two weeks while we were sailing."

"But you know this evolution stuff is not necessarily science."

Archie rolled his eyes and chewed on his pipe. "Oh, yeah, oh, great. This is the argument that the creationists are all using these days. Spare me, Neddy. I know their line. They are saying that we are saying that we cannot prove evolution, therefore evolution is a philosophy, a faith, conjecture. I heard you tonight on the news. But the fact is that evolution is a fact. There've been experiments with everything from corn to fruit flies, and remember the black moths in England . . ."

"Black moths in England?" Ned said in a bewildered tone.

"Yes. It's a clear-cut case of genetic change in a natural environment. The environment was getting to look like hell,

112

sooty, dark, awful because of the factories. The black moths prevailed in this sooty atmosphere. Why? Because they blended in with the scenery and could escape predation. The gene pool changed. The start-up of new species, new genera, is based on just this kind of thing. This is evolution. Proven in labs and in nature. It's no theory. What is theory is natural selection."

"But Archie, I'm going to tell you that these guys are coming up with evidence."

"Oh, no! Don't tell me they're doing the scientific creationist number on you."

"They're not doing any number on me, Archie, and look, believe me, I know that you know this stuff cold, but there is something to be said for some of the data that they're coming up with."

"Data!" Even hearing his cousin say the word in this context shocked Archie. "Neddy, this isn't polling results we're talking about here. Don't say that word *data* in conjunction with these people. May I remind you that the last data these people came up with—those nutty Paluxy footprints, trying to show that man and dinosaurs tiptoed through the tulips at the same time—was total bullshit, and I was one, along with Farlow, Glenn Kuban, and Steve Schafersman, to call their bluff. They were the most pathetic fakes I've ever seen."

"Okay! Okay!" There was not even a shadow of testiness in Neddy's voice. "I hear you, cousin. Now take it easy. It's not worth getting your blood pressure up. Don't worry, I am not a fundamentalist, and believe me, one can do a lot worse than stand on the same platform with Lorne Thurston and pretend to hate Darwin."

"This is bad," Archie said grimly. "You are dealing with a small, regional—"

But Neddy cut him off. "It is not that small or regional. Lorne Thurston has a broader appeal than you might believe from your—"

"Don't say it, Neddy."

"Ivory tower? I wasn't going to say that, Arch, I was just going to say that he is not as dumb or as redneck as you might think."

"I never had thought that he was, either. Anyone who can

113

rake in the money he does through that prayer network of his is not dumb."

"What I am trying to say, Archie, is that he is not only smart, but a lot less rough around the edges than he projects, and they are indeed coming up with some interesting evidence in the field of scientific creationism."

"They are coming up with a legal strategy for getting religion in the schools and hobbling free inquiry and that is all. Nothing more."

"You're really being awfully stuffy about all this, Arch. You should come down here and see some of the work going on at Lorne Thurston's college. They've got some very convincing evidence."

"For what, that crazy Flood theory of theirs, where four billion years of strata are squashed into the Genesis time frame?"

"No, no, it has more to do with some human skull analysis."

"Oh, terrific. Listen, just pray I don't come down there. I seem to have a nose for fraud these days—Paluxy Creek in Glen Rose, Texas, with the dinosaur prints. Then need I joggle your memory about the recent Harvard fiasco at Rosestone with the seeding of that site?"

"I'm going to be in Cambridge tomorrow, as a matter of fact."

"Giving a lecture on scientific creationism?"

"Very funny. No, it's a WGBH fund-raiser wingding. Remember, I'm on the board."

"I can't keep your boards straight. I wish you'd get off Thurston's board or whatever you're doing with him."

"I'm not doing anything with him, nor am I on any such board. I just went to a simple prayer breakfast, that's all." He sounded weary with Archie.

"Well, I think you're going to need a prayer or two yourself if you keep this association up."

"Okay, okay. But I really do not think that you would find Lorne Thurston all that loathsome."

"How does Lacey find him?" There was dead silence on the other end of the phone. Then a sigh.

"Okay. Be careful." Archie refrained from saying the obvious—that Lacey was smart, and it behooved Neddy to follow his wife on this. Neddy knew that Lacey was much smarter than he was, but he did not have to be reminded of it constantly.

"Don't worry about me, pal," Neddy said warmly. "I'll see you August twentieth for sure, if not before."

"Okay, good luck, Neddy, and do take care."

"Same to you, Arch."

17

Blood anomalies? Charley had wondered about that at the time. He wondered how he could find out more and had spent a very brief time considering whether he should hack into the police department's computer to see if anything had been added to the pathologist's report. It hadn't taken him long to decide, about five seconds. Nothing new had been added to the report. Charley knew very little about blood other than that type O was the most common, and from the report it looked as if Norman Petrakis had had type O blood. And yet there were these other letters listed, a sequence of K's and H's. Were these the anomalies? He hadn't even known what the word *anomalies* meant until he'd looked it up in his dictionary. Now he was going to have to find out more about blood. He wasn't going to go to a dictionary this time, or his *World Book Encyclopedia*. Who needed books when there were people? At the Martin Institute there had to be someone who could tell him all he needed to know about blood.

Charley got off the subway at the Kendall Square stop, crossed the street, Main Street, and angled to his left. Behind him to the south was Massachusetts Institute of Technology. To the east was the Charles River and a mess of construction. To the north was a hive of new office buildings housing bioengineering and computer firms with names like Biogen and Symbolics. These were for the most part started by MIT folks who didn't

115

want to move too far away. They were all of brick construction, which was the dominant material of the Cambridge-Boston area. The Martin Institute was just beyond these firms, enjoying a plaza of its own. Charley liked the fact that it was not a multistoried building like many of the new ones in the Kendall-Tech Square area. It had a low, chunky look somewhat similar to Boston City Hall. He headed for the main entrance. It was Saturday, and although Charley would not be expected to come in on a Saturday, he knew that the lab would hardly be empty. They worked around the clock at the Martin Institute. Saturday looked just about like any other day. Sure enough, Steven Gillespie, his "mentor" and the project coordinator for the Look Ahead program at Martin, was there at his bench. He was bent over, pipette in hand, sucking up something to put into the centrifuge machine. Lab workers were seldom without their pipettes, the daggerlike instruments similar to eyedroppers that sucked up solutions. They spent more time with pipettes in their hands than pencils.

"Charley Jacobs! What brings you here this morning?"

"Blood," Charley said simply, deciding not to beat around the bush.

"Blood . . . blood . . ." said Steve somewhat distractedly as he made his way to the centrifuge machine. He put something in and then switched it on. He turned toward Charley. "So what can I do for you?"

"I need to find out what these letters and numbers mean," Charley said, drawing out a piece of paper from his pants pocket.

Steve Gillespie looked at the paper and squinted. "I might be able to help you with that. Let me finish with this centrifuge stuff."

Half an hour later they were sitting in Mary Chung's, a Chinese restaurant just a few blocks away on Mass. Ave. in Central Square, eating spring rolls, dun dun noodles with shredded chicken, and moo shu pork and drinking Coke.

It's the antigens that are the anomalies. That's what those letters are. They represent antigenic markers, and they're getting a weird protein profile here."

116

"What's weird about it?" Charley asked.

Steve looked up from the little pancake he was neatly wrapping around a bundle of moo shu pork. "It's not human," he said quietly.

"Not human?"

"Yeah, I know. Weird. Where did you say this guy was killed?"

"The Sheraton Hotel here in Boston."

"Not a place where you'd tangle with animals—at least not the kind these antigens might indicate."

"What kind of animal would it be?"

"I don't know. I'd have to go look it up."

"Will you?"

"Sure, no problem."

"Good." Charley settled back in his seat.

Steven was a nice-looking fellow, but he dressed horribly. He wore pale plaid short-sleeved shirts in thin materials and very stiff jeans that always appeared too new and too dark. His clothes looked like something his mother might have bought for him. He dressed like a nerd, a classic MIT nerd. He even carried a package of plastic pens in his shirt pocket, and if he had worn glasses, they would have been broken over the nose bridge and taped. But he was nice, and Charley hoped that he had girlfriends despite the way he dressed. Charley also hoped that when he grew up, if he had muscles like Steve's, he wouldn't even consider wearing those wimpy shirts that made your arms look awful no matter what.

As Steve told Charley about the sophisticated blood analyses they were able to do now, Charley grew sorrier and sorrier for him. Somebody should tell Steve how to dress. It was sad to have your mother as your only clothing consultant. And he was now sure that this was the case with Steve. But it would hardly do for him to give advice. After all, in Project Look Ahead Steve was supposed to be his mentor, not the reverse. Steve was the one who had coined the term *mentee* for Charley and Matthew and Louise. He used the word as a kind of nickname or form of address on occasion. "Hey, mentee, want to see how we do these gels?"

117

"So you say this dude was a friend of your mom's?" Steve asked as he opened another can of Coke.

"Yeah. Not real close. They knew each other through their work."

"Well, I'll look into this blood thing for you."

"Gee, I really appreciate it."

"Hey, it's the least I can do. I mean, you, Matthew, and Louise have really worked your buns off around here. Leventhal's very pleased."

"He is?" Charley said excitedly.

"Yeah, I know he seems so busy you think he doesn't notice you, but he took those graphics of yours to that talk in England, and he thinks it's really neat all those models you got that software generating. It really helps us look at structure. And now next week you're going to start working with those brain proteins. That's the big debate going on now. It's hot."

"What's hot?"

"Well, not exactly what you're doing." He didn't want Charley to get the wrong idea. "But in the last couple of years there's been all this stuff coming out about intellamine and intellicone."

"What are they?"

"Well, this was going to be Monday afternoon's lecture from the mentor to the mentees, but I guess you'll get a preview."

He would need more than a preview, Charley thought. It was complicated.

"Can you run that by me again?" They had ordered a round of Peking ravioli and more Coke. "You mean that there are two different—what do you call them . . . these intellamine and intellicone things?"

"Neurotransmitters, proteins found in the brain."

"Okay, and how did they discover them?"

"A couple of years ago a lab, I think it was in California, did an experiment. The researchers out there wanted to figure out how neurotransmitters in general might affect higher-level thinking. So they exposed the subjects to a gas containing methadrill, which basically shuts down all creative and speculative thought. They gave the subjects spinal taps before and after the exposure to the gas. One specific protein was found to be missing from the second spinal tap, and not only was it missing, but on further analysis when it was finally pinpointed in the first tap, it was found to actually be a totally new neurotransmitter . . . Ta-da!" Steve held up his hands and snapped his fingers. "They discovered intellamine! It wasn't exactly earth-shaking news, but still it caused a few ripples in some of the scientific backwaters. The first article was published in *Endocrinology Abstracts*. Not a cutting-edge publication by any means. Basically they just talked about how this intellamine was a simple protein with four hundred bases. A primary structure was described, but they didn't have the vaguest idea about what the tertiary structure was. . . . See, get it?" Steve looked directly into Charley's eyes. "It's just like the modeling you're doing now on the protein folding problems: first you get just a long chain of amino acids, peptides in the primary structure, and then you try and find if and when it sheets, or curls into helices, the kind of stuff I was showing you the other day with those Styrofoam models. And that's the secondary structure, and then you take all that and jumble it around and see what kind of complicated molecules you get that could go into a tertiary structure. Anyway, on with the intellamine saga. They're trying to figure out all this, and in the course of it a second research group at University of Pennsylvania, I think, finds a different neurotransmitter—"

"That's intellicone?" Charley asked.

"Right. See, you're getting this. It only has five bases that are different from the other one, intellamine, but they come up with a tertiary structure for it. See, they figure out how these proteins fold into big fat smart-acting molecules."

"So that's pretty good that they figured that out."

"Yeah, very good. They published their report in the *Journal of Brain Chemistry*. Part of your assignment this week is to read that article, or at least the abstract of it. It just came out a few months ago. Now this got the folks at Duke and University of Minnesota excited, and they decided to jump on the bandwagon. This isn't a big bandwagon, by the way. It's not considered nearly as sexy and glamorous as AIDS research, but anyway, they wanted to find out exactly where intellamine and intellicone are used in the brain, if anywhere."

"How do they do that?"

"Complicated. They have to schedule time at the Brookhaven National Laboratory's positron emission tomography scanner. It's called PET for short."

"How does it work?"

"You synthesize the protein you wish to study using radioactive oxygen-eighteen. Then you inject it into the patient. The PET scanner lets you actually watch where the protein is in the brain. Ideally, it only gathers in the parts of the brain where it's being used."

"Jeez, sounds terrible. Who would allow themselves to be a victim for that?"

"Rats . . ." Steve paused. "And prisoners. They can make money, get sentences lessened."

"I don't know whether it's such a deal," Charley said. "So what do they find out? Where are these things used in the brain?"

"They find out that intellamine isn't used in the brain anywhere interesting—not anywhere connected with logical thought processes—but intellicone is used in the upper cerebral cortex near what they call the planning centers of the brain, and they're going to get a paper published in *Cell,* very distinguished scientific journal, and that's very hot stuff. So then there's a conference on it, a small one, and this thing starts looking kind of racial."

"Racial? How do you mean?"

"Well, the conference itself was kind of boring. I went to it. It was down in New York, and they mostly just showed graphs indicating the occurrence of intellamine and intellicone in various individuals, correlations with IQ and with different drugs, including recreational drugs. But at lunch I'm sitting around and listening to these guys talk, and it becomes apparent that all of the researchers who found intellamine were working with prison inmates, and those working with intellicone were using people from psychiatric wards. So first they figure intellicone is in crazy people, but by the second day of the conference they are saying it's racial. It just happens, of course, that all the prisoners are black and all the folks in the psych wards are white. This in itself is an obvious bias, and it does happen all the time, I am sorry to say. It's easy to get prisoners to be subjects for testing, and in a lot of prisons there are more black people than white people. The same is not true of psychiatric hospitals, where you usually have to pay to get in. This isn't the first time that researchers in their zealousness have overlooked the obvious.

"But in any case, they hypothesize that intellamine is in black people and intellicone is in whites. That was a year ago. Now these researchers are getting letters published in the *New England Journal of Medicine,* and they're finding slightly different variants in every race."

"They are?"

"That's what the literature says. But the clincher just came in last week. There was an experiment done where they injected a black male with intellicone and claim to have raised his IQ by twenty points."

"No shit!"

"So they say. They claim that intellicone is directly related to higher-order thinking."

"What's higher-order thinking?"

Steve Gillespie smiled at Charley's question. That's what he liked about this kid. He had a wonderful, raunchy sort of skepticism. He was always asking these knock-your-socks-off questions. He took a swallow of his Coke. "I'm not sure," he answered. "But supposedly we white honkies have it, and they don't." He didn't smile. "With this latest test they seem to be saying that if you have another form of it, the intellamine, your brain isn't doing as well. It's as if other races were trying to synthesize this brain chemical and just never got there."

"Do you believe that?"

"I got to look at the data. But this should be interesting to you mentees."

"I don't quite see the connection."

"Look—all that modeling stuff you've been doing is really a kind of mapping exercise. I've asked you just to look at the primary structures of a whole mess of proteins, find the similarities and correlations and see how they map into tertiary

121

structures. You guys, granted, don't know how it all happens because you haven't had the background biochemistry yet. But you sure as hell know what you are looking at. You are familiar with the patterns. Okay, admittedly it is not a high-priority project. It's one that no one else here really has the time for, but it is interesting and it still is important and it could apply to this intellamine and intellicone stuff."

"But what about this racial thing? You say that it's like they're trying to synthesize it, black people?"

"Well, no, not trying. That in itself is a very racist interpretation. Who knows? Their lack of it might be benefiting them in some hidden way. Remember, the gene that causes sickle-cell anemia also confers resistance to malaria. You know, it's like four million years ago or whenever it was that apes started evolving into hominids . . ." Steve took another swallow of Coke. "I want to say this very carefully because I don't want to draw any racist analogies here. I'm your basic skeptic in this whole thing. But look back then."

"Back when?" Charley asked.

"Back four million years ago. The forests were shrinking and the savanna was expanding. There was less room for chimps to be swinging from trees. Fewer branches available. So if survival, in the Darwinian sense, is survival of the fittest, who would be considered the fittest in the high-rent district of the jungle where available real estate is shrinking?"

"The guys who could keep the turf," Charley said.

"Exactly. The big strong apes who could cling and swing the best. It was the weak guys who didn't cling and swing so well who got pushed out onto the savanna and were forced to adapt and walk. You can look at the savanna as the evolutionary bottleneck that caused the walk genes to float to the top and helped to create hominids and eventually human beings."

"So you're saying this lack of intellicone might do the same thing?"

"Not exactly. You can't anticipate evolution. You can look back and say where species have come from, but you can't say with any certainty what they might evolve into. It's just that one group's loss might be another's gain. But it makes me real nervous when science starts looking at stuff like this."

It made Charley nervous, too, but for reasons less sophisticated than Steven Gillespie's. "You know that guy who got killed? Did I tell you about his book and the guy in the audience?"

"You mean the book on human evolution that he'd written?"

"Yeah, that's the one."

Steve nodded. "You told me about it. People get real upset about this evolution business."

"Yeah. Did I tell you what the words were that were scrawled on the wall in blood?" Charley asked.

"Nope."

"Monkey's Uncle."

"Phew!" Steve Gillespie leaned back and raised his arm to run his hand through his hair. There was a damp ring in the armpit of his shirt.

18

There was dinner for eight at Julia Child's house. There was a lost letter from Edgar Allan Poe's mother when the family had lived on Carver Street in Boston, now Charles Street. There was a poetry reading by Seamus Heany and Richard Wilbur to be performed in a private home in the greater Boston area. There was a chance to carry a spear, or whatever Sarah told you to carry, in a Sarah Caldwell opera, and there were also a pair of original works of art by Calista Jacobs from her Caldecott-winning book *Puss in Boots*. Fifteen hundred dollars was the floor at which all bidding opened, and the proceeds would go to WGBH, the Boston educational television channel that for over two decades had provided classics in public broadcasting. The event was billed as the annual WGBH Five Star auction in which five priceless items or experiences were put on the block. It was about as glitzy an event as Cambridge-Boston ever put on. If it had been in New York, it would have been held at the Metropolitan Museum in the Temple of Dendur, and one of the items would have been a cruise on Donald Trump's yacht or the like. But this was not New York. So it was held at the Charles Hotel, a kind of new wave Algonquin in Cambridge. It was forever hosting literary and artistic events.

Calista arrived just as the auction was about to commence. She had missed the cocktail party beforehand on purpose. Calista hated cocktail parties. She found it awkward to stand with a drink in your hand and try to carry on a conversation. But worse than that, she always had the feeling that whoever she was talking with was scanning the room to find someone more powerful or better-connected to talk to. She hated the formlessness of a cocktail party, the lack of structure. There could be no beginnings, middles, and ends to conversations or exchanges. No smooth transitions. It was very hard to know how to move on at a cocktail party. So she had avoided this one. She spotted her neighbors Herb and Ethel Goldman. They waved to her and indicated that there was an empty seat by them.

"Do you want to bid on the Julia Child dinner?" Ethel whispered. "We could go halvsies."

"What a great idea. Sure," Calista replied.

"You know"—Herb was leaning over—"if we had really gotten organized about this, we could have enlisted some other people."

"Oh, you're right, Herbie. Why didn't we think of it?" They dropped out of the bidding when it got to $2,400. The Poe letter brought in the most at $15,200. Calista's pair of drawings fetched $8,750.

"Not bad, Calista! Not bad!" Herb said as they got up to go out onto the terrace for the buffet supper.

"Oh, doesn't it look lovely!" Calista exclaimed as they came out the double doors onto the terrace. Ficus trees in box planters had been strung with tiny lights, and on the tables covered with pink cloths there were soft explosions of anemones in baskets made from dried vines woven through with moss. It was a black-tie event, and the women for the most part wore long, somewhat dated evening gowns. There was not one of those ridiculous confections called "poufs" that made women look like spun-sugar bonbons. None of that at the Charles. The women were dressed in gowns of chiffon and brocade or beaded sheaths. Some had been bought especially for the occasion, but very few were designer dresses. Most had been worn to other events—a wedding, a debut, an anniversary party, a Boston symphony event or a gala at the Wang Center. Shoulders showed, and there were discreet peeks of bosoms. The women looked nice.

They looked special, but they had not dressed for any photographers. They had dressed for themselves and their husbands. Calista recognized across the room old Mrs. Belmont. She and her husband, Montgomery, lived in a beautiful house on Brattle Street. She was a stalwart of the Cambridge Plant and Garden Club, had even written books on gardening. Monty had been a lawyer for Harvard since God knew when. They were in their seventies. Calista could imagine that when Sally Belmont had come down that lovely curving staircase of theirs this evening in her indigo blue chiffon, her ample bosom crushed into the jet beaded bodice, Monty had said something wonderful about how she looked. She had a little mink stole around her shoulders on this fair spring evening. Now where else would you see a mink stole except in Boston? Calista thought.

Calista herself had on the most expensive thing she had ever bought in Filene's basement. She was convinced that it got there by accident. It was a long gray cashmere dress by Armani. It had a wraparound bodice that was cut to the waist and was sprinkled with tiny chip rhinestones. It possessed that deceptively simple tailoring combined with the soft luxurious fabric that was Armani's hallmark. It was fluid. It was sensual, and it went with her hair. She looked rather a knockout in this outfit. She knew it even when she had tried it on over her jeans in the basement that day. The idea of the dress was to wear a minimum of underwear with it. She had no bra on and a string bikini.

She was standing now with Herb and Ethel. She hoped they didn't think she was clinging to them like some lost child. But she supposed she was. They were her neighbors, and they had been so kind to her and Charley since Tom had died. There wasn't a month that went by when they didn't have her and Charley over for a Sunday dinner. If there was any Harvard event that they thought she would be interested in but might feel awkward going to as a single woman, they always called and invited her to join them. When Herb had been on sabbatical at Stanford last year, they had still called every few weeks. As she stood there talking to them now telling them about Charley's experience at the Martin Institute, she caught sight of a familiar face across the room and stopped midsentence. That face! Hadn't she just seen it somewhere? Where?

"What are you looking at, Calista?" Ethel asked.

"Isn't that what's-his-name? Uh, Ned Baldwin?"

The Goldmans looked in the direction she was looking.

"Oh, yes, Governor Baldwin, or former Governor Baldwin," Herb said. "Of course, he'd be here. He's on the board of GBH. Has been for years."

"He has a roving eye. . . . Look at him," Ethel said. This was a typical Ethel remark. She specialized in certain kinds of information—gossip about public figures. She seemed to know things about these people that the rest of the world didn't, but she was usually right.

"Yes," said Ethel, now looking over at the tanned patrician figure of Ned Baldwin. "I've heard about his chasing about for years. No names. At least none that I recognized." She sniffed as if to suggest that if one were not sleeping with a major novelist, a critic for *The Times Literary Supplement,* or Margaret Thatcher, what was the use of even discussing it.

"Well, he might have a roving eye, but he's got something else, too," Calista said.

"What's that?" Herb said.

"A brain the size of a pea! Did you see that news clip of him on the *Today* show the day before yesterday?"

"No. What did he do?" Ethel asked.

"It showed him at some deal down in Texas with that guy Lorne Thurston."

"Lorne Thurston?" Herb said, somewhat bewildered.

"Yeah, that TV preacher."

"What in the world was he doing with him?" Herb asked.

"Discussing evolution, or rather the lack of it."

"What?" the Goldmans replied.

"I'm not kidding. It was the most preposterous thing I ever

126

saw. He's up there on this platform with the guy, and he's saying things like 'They haven't got any proof for this evolution stuff.'"

"What? I can't believe it!" Herb exclaimed. "I mean, the guy is no genius, but he can't be that dumb. Why would he say such a thing? I . . . I . . . I mean . . . how . . ." Herb began to sputter. "How can he be on the board of directors of WGBH and not believe in evolution?"

Calista and Ethel both burst out laughing at this. Herb ran his fingers through his curly gray hair and squinted through his thick glasses.

They went through the buffet line and sat down at one of the tables with two other couples they knew from Cambridge. As dessert was being served a band started playing and a few people began to dance. Ned Baldwin was standing with two other men near the table where they had been seated. One was another board member, and the other was a producer for GBH.

"Hal, I think we've lost Sid," Ned said to the board member.

"I'm sorry," Sid said. "But that woman dancing with that rather squat man . . ."

"Oh, my goodness," whispered Ned. "She is lovely."

"Isn't that the artist, the children's book illustrator whose pictures they auctioned off tonight?"

"Calista Jacobs, of course!" said Hal Marteau. "The one whose husband was killed, the famous astrophysicist, Tom Jacobs, and all that mess with the CIA, and oh . . ." He waved a hand as if to clear away the mess. It had been a mess. Hal Marteau knew too well. He was on the board of overseers of Harvard.

"My, she looks better than she photographs," Ned said. "You know, my cousin Arch Baldwin helped her out quite a bit in that situation."

"She's very stunning in an unusual way," Sid said.

The three men gazed at her appreciatively. She looked like a column of moonlight in her soft narrow gray dress as she moved across the dance floor. Her weather-front hair now looked like a silvery nimbus around her head. She had just finished dancing with Jensen Reed, whose head came up approximately to her

127

sternum, which in the case of this particular dress was partially exposed. Jensen chattered away animatedly about his grandchildren and how much they enjoyed her books. She thought he might have stolen an occasional glance across the moraine of her bony breastplate in search of a breast, but she had wrapped the bodice so that there was only a suggestion and no bosom visible.

A younger man suddenly appeared and tapped Jensen on the shoulder. "Cutting in, are you, Sid?"

"Indeed, sir."

My goodness, thought Calista. She didn't know when was the last time she had been cut in on.

"I'm Sid."

"I'm Calista."

"I know. I couldn't afford your drawings."

"That makes two of us." He laughed at her remark. "What do you do, Sid?" she asked.

"I'm a producer for *Earth Stories.*"

"Oh, that's a neat program. My son watches it all the time. Do you get to go to all those places—the Arctic and the Galápagos?"

"Not always. Sometimes. Mostly I sit at desks and in editing rooms."

Out of the corner of her eye she caught a glimpse of Baldwin dancing with none other than Julia Child, who was a good two inches taller than he was, and Baldwin was nearly six feet. It didn't last long, however. For she soon saw him guiding Julia toward her table, where he chatted briefly with the other people. Amazing, she thought, how fluidly he moved between these two worlds. He was so much a part of this one. It became all the more unbelievable those brief minutes—seconds, probably—that she had seen him on the television news screen.

She and Sid chatted on for a few more minutes, and then Calista felt it happening. She saw the figure threading through the dancing couples, and she knew, just knew, that he was coming toward her.

"Sorry, Sid, my turn."

"All right, Ned. I never argue with a board member, and remember my graciousness when I ask you for funding for *The Vanishing People* series."

"Good sport." Ned chuckled as he took Calista's right hand. She was appalled. She hadn't been prepared for this repartee when she had seen him coming toward her. All the light talk might be a joke, but still she was the butt of it. It was her femaleness that made it work. She had just been bartered for, plain and simple. It wasn't fair. Calista's rules about ethnic or minority jokes were that they were acceptable only if they were told by a person identified with that group. She hadn't told the joke. Nobody had asked her permission. It wasn't funny. It wasn't just small talk. It was rude. But she didn't know what to do. And now she felt his right hand on the small of her back, pressing her lightly into the rhythm of the music, and his left hand beginning to steer her on a course.

"I'm Neddy Baldwin." He smiled warmly, and the taut skin around his eyes crinkled.

"I know." Calista nodded stiffly.

He continued to smile. "I just took a whirl with Julia. I must say you're more my size."

Don't count on it! Calista thought. She was madly ransacking her brain for an idea of what to do, how to end this, but she felt her anger welling up dangerously. This stupid jerk had been on the same platform with Lorne Thurston, and now he was dancing with her!

"I always make a point of dancing with the female stars of the auction."

"Too bad the old lady's not here," Calista said.

"What?" he asked, slightly bewildered.

"Mrs. Poe—Edgar's mother."

"Oh, ho ho!" He threw back his elegant square chin and laughed while pulling her closer to him. "Oh, my! You're very clever. That's cute. I like that in a woman."

"You do." It wasn't a question, and there was something rather chilling, an unnerving light that emanated from the dark hooded eyes, that made Neddy Baldwin swallow and look at her again. Had he said something wrong? God, she was intriguing. The silver-shot hair swirled about her head like smoke. Archie, he had sensed, had been quite taken by her, but there was something funny going on here.

Just at that moment Calista, as if searching for what to say or do next, looked up at the sky. It was a clear night. The stars were brilliant in the spring night sky. *Follow the arc to Arcturus and speed on to Spica!* So went the exhortation of ancient navigators. She saw Arcturus burning bright in the constellation of Boötes and Spica below, lead star in the constellation of Virgo, but suddenly she realized the Charioteer was missing. Where was her starry Charioteer! Slipped out of the sky on its transit through the seasons? Why in heaven's name was she dancing with this idiot?

"Are you planning to do a program on *Nova* on scientific creationism?" she asked suddenly.

"Wh-what?" He cracked a grin. "Whatcha talking about?"

"You, Mr. Baldwin. I saw you on the news the other day with that Christian thug Lorne Thurston."

"Oh, thaaat!" He tossed the noble chin back again and laughed. "You know, you're in a position like me, you get around all over . . ."

"Precisely!" Calista had stopped dancing and dropped her hand out of his. This was a point that had never been covered in the proper dancing school that Neddy had attended some forty-five years before: what to do if the young lady simply stops cold in the middle of the foxtrot and drops her hands to her side. He had never seen anyone as still and as coldly angry as this stunning woman who stood before him like some blazing column of moonlight. He tried to reconcile those breasts, lovely mounds quivering under the soft cashmere of her dress, with those dark hooded eyes and the anger. She had seemed so delectable just minutes before, but those breasts were actually quivering in fury.

Calista's heart was pounding. Her chest seized in a tachycardia. She had never made a scene before, but she felt she might now. He seemed mesmerized by her, and he still had this silly grin on his face. God save this man if he said she was beautiful when she was angry. She'd kick him right in the nuts. She lowered her voice, but the words came out in a ratchety noise. "I think Lorne Thurston and all of those television evangelists are bullies, and I'm sick of their screaming from their bully pulpits. You should be ashamed, Mr. Baldwin. You and your storm troopers for God!"

With that she turned on her heel and left. Left Neddy Baldwin with his firm, aristocratic jaw dropped into a profile that made him look a hair's breadth away from being declared a certifiable moron. But worse than that, she had left this handsome scion of patrician New England without a dance partner for the first time in his life.

19

"Rabbit's blood!" Charley repeated. Steven Gillespie had just called him.

"Yep . . . and that other sequence you gave me, the trace sequence, indicates monkey's blood. But you said that was only in very small amounts."

"Yeah, at least according to the police report." Charley paused. "How does a human being get murdered and spurt rabbit blood?"

"In a Sheraton Hotel, no less. Sounds a little weird to me. Did he keep any pets? Travel with them?"

"He wasn't a circus. He was a science writer, a children's book writer, to be exact."

"Bunnies!"

"What?" Charley was shocked. There was something in the way that Steve had said that soft, plump little word that was absolutely horrifying. Some macabre connection was fighting to the surface of his mind.

"Oh, I was just thinking," Steve began. "You know, all the books for little kids. . . ."

But Charley wasn't even hearing him. The shadow of a monstrous notion began to slide across his brain. There were so many oddities in this situation, so many unlikely events and contradictions, that it was hard to know where to begin to look for a pattern, and if one could even exist within this batch of illogical elements—bunny blood, monkey blood, strangula-

131

tions, and the words *Monkey's Uncle,* scrawled in rabbit's blood by what? An irate creationist who thought someone was taking potshots at God? Charley could live with disorder, with chaos, with breaks in the pattern. He found them intriguing more than threatening. It was what made black holes, singularities, and the origins of the universe so exciting. It was what had compelled his father to devote his intellectual life to the study of such phenomena, and it compelled him to look at chaos and not see it as the absence of order, but rather as the presence of randomness and the unpredictable. Chaos in Charley's mind could be another kind of order, an order that followed different rules entirely. But right now a monster shadow spread its wings like a dark dragon. A dragon! He suddenly remembered those dragons at Margaret McGowan's house. Sweet velvet dragons with satin wings and some spitting tongues of satin flames. He had to see that book again. It was a wild hunch, but nonetheless . . . "You going to be at the lab late?"

"Sure. Why?"

"I might want to bring something in for you to look at. It's just a hunch, but . . ."

"No, fine, Charley. I'll be here."

It was just a hunch, but thank God the police department was so inefficient, Charley thought as he biked over to Foster Street and Margaret McGowan's house. When Calista had finally gotten a message through to the two detectives about the defaced books she and Margaret had received, the police were supposed to have sent over someone to collect the evidence. This had never happened. It had not surprised Calista or Charley. Calista had started to think of cops like appliance repairmen. They never returned calls. They never showed up, and if they did, who knows—they might charge you twenty-five bucks an hour for labor plus parts. So Charley was sure that the book would still be at Margaret's, although Margaret was in Scotland and not to return until the end of the month. Mammy, however, was house-sitting for her, and when Charley biked up she was out sweeping the walk in a bright rose-colored running suit and billed cap that said La Costa.

"Why, hello there, Charley. You playing hooky or what?"

"Naw. It's an early release day. Public schools get out quarter to one so teachers can have meetings."

"That's nice. What can I do for you?"

Charley was chaining his bike to the front-gate post. "You know that book that Margaret got, the one with the—"

Mammy scowled. "You don't have to tell me. I know the one. Disgusting. Depraved! Lord, what sewer minds some people have . . . and going on to do something like that to Margaret! I said to her I hope Leo never sees that."

"Leo?"

"Leo Krell, her illustrator on that book. Sweetest little man you ever met. But he's had two bypass operations, and I think he's got himself a pacemaker now, and seeing that horrible, horrible thing might just short-circuit him!"

"Well, Mammy, I have a favor to ask."

"What's that, son?" She stopped sweeping and looked up.

"Could I borrow that book just for a short time? I really need it."

"What you need a book like that for? Gives me the willies just having it around, but Margaret says we got to keep it for the police, but the police never come."

"Well, I got this kind of loony hunch, and I just want to borrow it for a short time. I'll bring it right back."

"What kind of a hunch you got on?" Margaret said, clasping her hands over the top of the broom handle and resting her chin.

"Well, if you don't mind, I'd rather not say right now. If my hunch turns out right, you'll be the first to know. I promise."

He broke that promise.

"Rabbit's blood!" Calista exclaimed. "That's rabbit's blood, not paint." Calista's finger trembled as she pointed at the picture of Rothgar on the Plain of Crystal Doom and the seven meticulously drawn slits spurting the teardrops of blood. "Oh, God." She touched her hand to her cheek. "I would have thought it was Aquatext seventy-two."

"No way, José," Charley said.

"You're sure about this?"

"Absolutely. They ran it through the blood analyzer in the hematology lab at the institute."

133

"How do they run a book through a machine?"

"Easy. All I did was lift some of the dried blood off using Scotch tape. Then this girl, Inga, dissolved it in some solution and ran it through the Ultra centrifuge machine. Then it was ready for the blood anaylzer. It can analyze for about eighteen jillion things at once—hemoglobin counts, platelets, antigens, you name it. It was the antigens that gave it away."

"Bugs Bunny, huh?" She bit her lower lip lightly as she contemplated this information.

"Yep." Charley sprawled on the winged chair in the study and looked at his mom, who had about three pencils sticking out of her hair and was clutching a paintbrush as if it were a weapon.

"This is really getting sick," she muttered, and thought how both Walt Disney and Beatrix Potter must be turning in their respective graves.

"Listen, I promised to get the book back to Mammy. As a matter of fact, I promised that I would tell her first if my hunch was right, and I came home and told you instead."

"How did you ever hunch this in the first place?"

"I told you that the blood on the wall was rabbit with a little bit of monkey's blood."

"Oh, yeah, yeah. And you got that from hacking into the police files. That really makes me nervous."

Charley wanted to say that that should be the least that made her nervous, but he didn't. "Look," he said, "people do it all the time. It's absolutely untraceable, and even if it were, I didn't do anything criminal."

"Hmm."

Charley couldn't tell if it was a sigh or a moan coming from his mother's clamped mouth. Whatever it was, it sounded slightly skeptical but not totally condemnatory. He suddenly noticed a VCR tape to the left of his mother's drawing board. "What's that?"

Calista slid her eyes to the left and this time did sigh. *"Eddie Murphy—Raw."*

"Mom!" Charley grinned. "Are you kidding?"

"You know I've always thought Eddie Murphy was funny."

"Yeah, but . . ." The words hung in the air, begging an

134

explanation. How could she explain that after dancing with Ned Baldwin the previous evening, the best antidote she could think of was Eddie Murphy? She had been so furious at that party that she had stormed out, barely saying good-bye to the Goldmans and claiming to have a headache. What she had was a monumental case of fury. She had almost felt a sense of contamination after dancing with him and staring into that genial but vacuous face. "The banality of evil," that fantastic phrase of Hannah Arendt's, was all she could think of. With Ned Baldwin, of course, it wasn't precisely evil. It was more like the banality of ignorance. But it was a case where ignorance could very easily slip beyond the border and into evil. And Eddie Murphy was about as far away from Ned Baldwin as she could get. He was bawdy, scatological, savvy, and even though he was for all intents and purposes antifeminist, he was so extreme and funny that in the end he merely became a caricature of what was considered macho. So who cared if he bragged about his big dick and used the word *fuck* like a comma? He came off as essentially smart, good-hearted, and hysterically funny. She had laughed until she'd cried, something that Ned Baldwin had not made her do. And now that she was staring at bunny blood, she needed all the laughs she could get. But she wasn't sure how she could explain the Ned Baldwin part to Charley.

"Did I tell you that I met Ned Baldwin?"

"Ned Baldwin? You mean that creep on television the other day?"

"The very one. And Archie's cousin, although he bears no resemblance whatsoever."

"You're kidding. Where?"

"At that GBH party last night."

"What was he like?"

"Well, I thought loathsome. Although I'm sure he passes." Her voice dwindled off as she thought of him chatting so amicably with all the A-list people and profiling so nobly.

"What do you mean, 'passes'?" Charley asked.

"People like Neddy Baldwin always slip through until they slip up," she replied, and then added somewhat cryptically, "It comes with the territory." She paused. "Anyhow, getting back to this blood thing. Somehow it doesn't make sense at all. But how in the heck, Charley, did you ever even hunch that those . . . those . . ." She hesitated, searching for a word. "Drops on Margaret's book, Rothgar's wounds, were really blood? That's just astounding to me."

"I don't know. I was just looking for patterns, not logical patterns, really, just something beyond surfaces, like beyond event horizons."

Something very deep ached within Calista. He was so much like his father. "And you found it. You found a new pattern."

"I don't know whether it's a new pattern or a new puzzle." He paused, his eyes becoming opaque. Calista tried to think, think like Charley, think like Tom. They so easily traveled beyond the surface order of things, across the lines to where the rules stopped and chaos began. They were not afraid to contemplate new complexities. She should try.

"Maybe it's not a pattern—the rabbit's blood."

"What do you mean?"

"Maybe we're asking the wrong questions."

"I wasn't exactly asking any questions," Charley said.

"Well, I was, sort of. I was trying to figure out that if we assume that a God-fearing Christian creationist was so outraged by Norman Petrakis's view that he would scrawl in blood the words *Monkey's Uncle,* how could he kill a rabbit to do it?"

"You mean how could Christian love kill a cute little furry bunny even though the guy was mad enough to kill another human being?"

"Yes, in a sense. I guess I think they would use lamb's blood or goat's blood. It's sort of the symbolic sacrificial media of the Bible. It's more religious."

"I don't know. Look at the Easter Bunny."

"Well, I never have been able to figure that one out. Not that I'm doing so well on this. But somehow rabbit's blood in this case just doesn't fit—at least not with these fundamentalists or scientific creationists."

"I don't know. You said that guy at the conference was pretty mad."

"Not exactly mad—obsessed."

"Obsessed enough to kill a rabbit—that would be kind of

small potatoes for someone getting ready to kill a man. A little hors d'oeuvres."

"Oh, Charley!"

20

Dear Sirs:

I am interested in applying for admission to the Lorne Thurston College of Christian Heritage. I have a feeling that it might be what I am seeking in furthering my education both spiritually and intellectually.

Charley held the paper and read in a small voice from the top bunk. Matthew in the bottom bunk was spending the night. It was a Saturday night, and Calista was still prowling around. He didn't want her to hear this.

"I think it's real weird—just the name of the college," Matthew whispered up. "To say that it's a college of Christian heritage and then use a guy's name right in the title, weird! I mean, if you were to start a college of Jewish heritage, would you call it the Charley Jacobs College of Jewish Heritage? It's like this guy Lorne Thurston owns it all, the philosophy, the religion, the works."

"I know. It's sort of like a franchise operation."

"McDonald's."

"Right. McDonald's."

"Well, there you go. It makes me think of hamburgers, not God," Matthew said.

"You got to understand that these people are into owning things and franchising religion. They got radio stations and TV networks and colleges."

"Okay, go ahead. This is the first letter, right?"

"Yeah, I got an answer."

"And your mother didn't see it?"

"No, luckily it came on a Saturday when I was home to intercept it, and the other one—"

"There's another one?"

"Yes, confirming the receipt of my application and my interview date."

"Interview date? You joking?"

"No. But I'll tell you about that later. Anyhow, I told Vicki, our cleaning lady, to try and intercept that one for me, if it came when I wasn't here."

"And she did?"

"Yeah."

"Okay. Read on."

I really want to learn more about God and the Bible, and for the next four years I would like to attend a Christian college for this purpose. I think this will help me grow in my walk with God.

"Whew-eeee!" Matthew exclaimed. "Walk with God! Charley, too much!"

"It's not too much for these people. Wait till I show you their brochure. Everybody's taking walks with God and talking about being in a closer relationship with Jesus and studying with Jesus by their side."

"Come on and dance with God, do the boog-a-loo," Matthew sang.

"No. They don't dance. It's against the rules of Christian Life Standards." He continued reading the letter aloud.

I would very much appreciate it if you would send an application form and a catalog describing more about your college and the courses you offer. Also my mother and I shall be visiting in Texas in June and would very much like to take the opportunity at this time to come out and visit the campus and arrange for an interview if that is possible.

I look forward to hearing from you in the near future.

Sincerely,
Charles Jacobs

"I was going to sign it 'Your Friend in Christ,' but I thought that might be overdoing it."

"I think going for an interview will be overdoing it, Charley."

"Look, Matthew, how am I going to find out about anything if I don't investigate this? I got a hunch about these guys, and I'm going to follow it."

"But you don't know that it's Lorne Thurston and his guys. There are hundreds of these televangelists. Why does it have to be him?"

"Because he's the richest and the most powerful, and it was people from his college, at least some of them, that were involved in the fake footprints of dinosaurs and men down in Texas at Paluxy Creek, and they are spearheading this whole scientific creationism thing and all the stuff with getting it into the schools."

"Yeah, but Charley, how the heck are you going to pass yourself off as a college applicant? I mean, you're only an eighth-grader."

"By June I will officially be a ninth-grader, and you know I can fudge a little."

"But you're too short. You don't shave. You don't have much in the way of secondary sex characteristics, as they call them in sex ed."

"I don't have to stand naked in front of these guys."

Matthew laughed, and Charley felt the frame of the bunk bed shake. He was laughing too at the idea of him being interviewed nude and taking a naked tour of the Lorne Thurston College of Christian Heritage. "And I have the height problem solved."

"How's that."

"I'm going to get elevator shoes."

"What?"

"Elevator shoes. They make you taller. Mammy, this lady who works for Margaret McGowan, is going to take me to get them. She knows where. It's someplace in Boston."

"Are you ever going to tell your mother?"

"Sure. I'll have to. She's got to go with me for the interview. I just don't want to tell her yet. She's not totally convinced about the creationists' part in Petrakis's murder. But I am."

"Okay, read the next letter."

"Okay. This is the one where they just sent me the application and brochure. It's short but here. . . ." He reached over the side of the bed and handed down a large envelope with some materials in it. "You got to look at the brochure and the course catalog to get the full flavor of this place."

Dear Charles:

Lorne Thurston College of Christian Heritage is a great place to live and learn. If you are a person who is wanting to grow in both mind and spirit and deepen your relationship with our Lord Jesus, this is the place for you.

Enclosed you will find the application for admission to Lorne Thurston College of Christian Heritage. When I myself filled out this application seven years ago I had no idea of the far-reaching effects it would have. I met teachers and students with whom I have come to have deep respect and close friendships. They have taught me many subjects and I have gained knowledge, but most important I have learned how all they have taught me is related directly to God's Word. I think that you, too, if you fill out the application form, could participate in a similar experience. I pray that if the Lord wants you at Lorne Thurston College of Christian Heritage, He will work out all the necessary details.

When you and your mother know the exact dates of your visit to Dallas, please inform us and we shall be happy to set up an appointment for an interview and a tour of our campus.

Sincerely,
Tommy Lee Clayton
Assistant Director of Admissions

Charley leaned over and looked down at Matthew, who was lolling his head over the side of the bunk and holding the course catalog. "Well, what do you think?" Charley asked.

"I never really thought of God as a detail man. I mean, from the Big Bang on he seems to have gotten it okay. So I guess that is a lot of details."

140

"My dad, by the way, said that the Big Bang theory doesn't exclude God at all. That's why they liked my dad at the Vatican so much. He gave a speech there when they had the conference on cosmology. Standing room only at the Vatican. That's what my mom said. Pretty good in a place like that where the pope is the only game in town."

"Something tells me the Vatican is way ahead of Lorne Thurston Christian Heritage College."

"Yeah, they sorted all this out hundreds of years ago, according to my mom. She says they must look at all this stuff here going on in this country with scientific creationism as really weird. Like, where you guys been for the last two hundred years?"

"Did you read this catalog?"

"Of course I read it."

"Did you see some of these weird courses? Christian Anthropology—Searching for the Ark. It's only given in the fall semester. Sounds like an Indiana Jones–type course. And this one, Flood Geology. It's offered both semesters. I can't believe this. Listen to the course description. 'A close examination of the Noachian Flood as a cataclysmic model in which the general order from simple to complex organisms is confirmed in the geologic column. A hydraulic refutation of Darwinian notions of evolution.'" Matthew paused. "What in the world is a hydraulic refutation?"

"I'm not sure. I think it means that this ordering of fossils was predicted or determined just by the mechanics of the Flood, all at once, right after the land drained, and that the order had nothing to do with things evolving over a long period of time. The Flood drowned them and then redeposited them in the fossil order that geologists find them."

"Gee whiz. They really go on with this Flood thing. Here's a course that's about the greenhouse effect and the Flood."

"Yeah. You see, they're always trying to be scientific about all this, at least up to a point. I don't think they like to have their theories tested like real scientists."

"Did you read the rules for Christian Life Standards?"

"Yeah. They're a breeze. I don't smoke, drink. I don't fornicate. I'm not a homosexual."

141

"You say 'shit' and 'fuck.'"

"Well, I could give that up. I just wish regular college was so easy to get into."

"Yeah. So what is this other letter you got back?"

"Okay . . . here goes. Now, Matthew, just hang on when I get to one part. I'll explain it. Don't worry."

"What do you mean—don't worry?" He leaned farther out of the lower bunk and looked up at Charley.

"Just hang on."

Dear Charles:

We have received your application form and we would be most happy to have you and your mother come to our campus on Wednesday June 20 for a visit. If you plan to arrive here by ten o'clock that morning, there will be ample time for us to give you a tour of our campus and have a talk. We have enclosed a map for your convenience. It is only a thirty-minute drive from Dallas, and at that hour you should have no trouble with traffic. We shall be sending to you character reference forms, one of which should be given to your pastor, the Reverend Matthew McPhail.

"What?" screeched Matthew.

"Look, you had to list your religious affiliation, the home church, and your pastor's name. It's no big deal."

"No big deal! Charley, what are you talking about? I am an eighth-grader in a Cambridge public school. I am not a pastor of any church, and I am not called Reverend McPhail. Somebody calls up my house and asks for Reverend McPhail, my mother's not going to know what the heck's going on. She might think it's the obscene caller we had from last fall and that he's just changed his line."

"What obscene caller?"

"Some weird guy used to call up and pretend he was taking a survey. Then he'd ask my mom about her breasts or something."

"Oh, gross!"

"Yeah, well, let these folks from this college call up and ask for Pastor McPhail and she'll think it's him again."

"They're not going to call up, Matthew. So just cool it. I don't even have to send these character references in at all now. They're willing to interview me without them. They just say that when these forms are completed that the application is considered complete. So I don't see why you're upset."

"You'd be upset, too, Jacobs, if I'd done this to you."

"No, I wouldn't."

"Yes, you would."

"Let's not get into a fight, okay? I'll make it up to you. I'll pay for three rounds of games at Elsie's."

"And an Elsie Burger?"

"Yes, an Elsie Burger."

"A knish?"

"A knish for Pastor McPhail. Yeah, you got it."

21

Charley did not buy his mother a knish or a round of games or an Elsie Burger for a bribe. Instead he stood watching her doing the Buffalo shuffle, shifting to a ball change for two measures, then a toe, heel drop and culminating in a Maxiford break to top off the last of the sixty-four measures. It was not a laughing matter any longer. He tried not to look pained. He wondered if the other people in his mom's class were quite as bad as she was.

"Well, what do you think?" she asked eagerly.

He thought she should stick to illustrating. That's what he really thought. "Well, I think your tap dancing has really improved, Mom."

"Really? You do? Of course, you haven't seen me do it, really. I mean, I can't believe you asked to see me practice this morning."

"Oh, well, you know, I just thought . . . but anyway, yeah, you're a lot better. You're not as good as . . . who's that black guy?"

"Gregory Hines."

143

"Yeah, him."

"Well, no way. I mean, that's really black tap dancing what he does. A whole other thing. I mean, not that I'm going to be Ruby Keeler. But my teacher says I've really improved."

"Listen, Mom. I want to ask you something."

"Uh-oh!" She paused. "Is that why you were being so nice about my tap dancing?"

"No, Mom! No. I was really interested. I mean, I hear you tapping away in the bathroom and here in the kitchen, and your feet clicking under your drawing board. I was just interested." She didn't believe him.

"Okay. What is it?"

"Well, you know how I'm going with you to Dallas."

"Yes, dear. My moral support while I get the award. I'm much appreciative. True loyalty." And she meant it. A thirteen-year-old boy's idea of heaven was not being at a convention with forty thousand librarians and eating practically every meal with small groups of these librarians while the publisher introduced them to their favorite and most beloved children's book illustrator. But she in turn had promised to take Charley and two friends to a Grateful Dead concert in the fall. It was all negotiation. That's what parenting boiled down to.

"Okay. Now do you realize that Green Acre, Texas, is only a thirty-minute drive from downtown Dallas?"

"No, but why would I want to go to Green Acre? Is that like God's Green Acre?"

Charley rolled his eyes. "Guess so."

"Well, why would I want to go to Green Acre, Texas? Is there a Grateful Dead concert there?"

"No," Charley said quietly. "But the Lorne Thurston College of Christian Heritage is there, and we have an appointment for an interview on June twentieth at ten o'clock in the morning."

"Charley!" She stared at her son, her feet dead in her patent-leather tap shoes.

22

Charley was holding up his end admirably. He had run relays taking glasses of wine to his mom, Janet Weiss, and Ethan Thayer, chairman of J. T. Thayer and Sons Publishing, as they stood accepting the congratulations for the Caldecott Award in an interminable receiving line of librarians. The librarians loved Charley. He was polite. He was cute. And he read. But most of all his face was traceable in the scores of children's books that his mother had illustrated that they bought in multiple copies for their school and public libraries. They could go back home and tell eager young readers that they had met *The Selkie Boy* or *The Night Glider* or Edward from *I'm the Boss* or Peter from *Monster Pie*. And did they know that one of the boys in the *Wild Swans* was Charley Jacobs, the illustrator's son, and the rest of the brothers were his friends? Often they asked Charley to pose for pictures holding a book in which his face had appeared. Then when they returned home to their local public libraries or school libraries, they would put up Charley's picture on their bulletin boards in Peoria or Dubuque or Great Bend or Tacoma or Bethesda or Omaha. Charley, of course, did not tell them that he no longer read children's books or even Y.A., young adult, books. He'd finished with all that a couple of years before. The Y.A. books bored him silly. They were all about teenagers with problems. Even Janet Weiss, who edited them, had learned not to send any more to Charley and was sometimes heard to refer to this genre as the teenage-problem-of-the-month syndrome. My mother's alcoholic, my dad's gay, and I'm on crack—this seemed to be typical fare of the genre. Problem-solving novels, they called them. It wasn't that Charley didn't think these were worthwhile subjects for contemplation. He just thought there was something terribly mechanical about it all—the plots, the characters, the style. It was all, in one sense, too solvable. If a kid did the right thing, summoned the right kind of strength and gritted his or her teeth, he or she would make it. He preferred Robert Cormier or S. E. Hinton, who wrote very realistic novels in which the problems could not always be

145

solved but offered characters who indeed probed a more monstrous world and explored the darker side of teenage life. These "problems" might not have anything to do with drugs, but rather hideous power struggles and bouts with megalomaniacal gang leaders and corrupt adults. Charley liked them the best of the Y.A. fiction. But in reality his favorite reading material of late was stuff that would never be recognized by these librarians or make its way onto the lists of Best Books for Young Adults. They were mass-market paperbacks often published by companies with names that did not have any familiar bookish ring but sounded more as if they had something to do with semiconductors or silicon chips or even toys. Companies like TSR, parent company of Steve Jackson Games, that produced books like *Green Circle Blues* and *Bimbos of the Death Sun*. These books sold millions of copies, but they weren't on the reading lists of many of the librarians at this convention.

"Charley Jacobs!" a deep voice rumbled. He swung around with the glass in his hand that he was en route with to Ethan Thayer. A large lady with frizzy hair and wearing a stiff emerald green dress loomed before him, not unlike the Emerald City in the *Wizard of Oz*. He read her name tag quickly: Elsa Dineen, Petaluma County Librarian, Petaluma, California. He remembered her vaguely, probably from when he had traveled with his mom last year to California on a book promotion tour.

"You've been working so hard," the woman continued, "I thought you might need something yourself. Looks like this line is going to go on for another twenty minutes." She held out toward him a plate of goodies—little petit fours and pastries.

"Oh, gosh, that looks great. Let me get this wine to Ethan." It wasn't really wine, but Charley and Ethan weren't telling anybody. Ethan had arranged for a waiter to serve him vodka on the rocks. There was no way he could get through being so unmitigatingly charming to this endless stream to whom he owed his fortune without something stronger than Chablis. He loved them all, every single librarian from Petaluma to St. Petersburg. And they loved him because he was one of the last independents in publishing. J. T. Thayer and Sons had not been swallowed up into some disgusting amalgam of fast-food chains and amusement parks. His late father and his two sons had, over the course of nearly seventy years, published the books that they wanted to publish. They were the best. They promoted and marketed them skillfully, and they felt no compulsion to have a blockbuster every other list because they had a backlist that any other publisher would kill for.

They were Quality with a capital Q. And as the old man, Ethan Thayer, Sr., had once said before he died, "Any outfit like ours that thinks they're going to be bought, kept, and pampered like a nineteenth-century courtesan to a king is mistaken. They aren't. They're going to be treated like a hot call girl for a limited period of time and then be thrown out on the streets. It's pure fantasy to think that you are going to become the jewel in the crown of one of these conglomerates that makes hamburgers and runs porpoise shows." The old man saw it all coming before it really arrived. He saw this salacious union between books and food and knew, anticipated, leveraged buyouts before they ever got into full frenzy as they did in the eighties.

Calista Jacobs had been one of the jewels in the Thayer crown for nearly twenty years. She had come into their offices in Gramercy Park fresh out of college or, more accurately, the spring before her commencement from Bryn Mawr, toting a portfolio. She had gotten an appointment with the art director because her father, a midwesterner with a restaurant supply business, was also an expert poker player and trout fisherman and had written a book on both entitled *Bluffing*. It had turned out to be a best-seller, and it was through his connection that Calista got the appointment. But art directors and editors had hundreds of such appointments with aspiring artists and writers with a "connection" every year, and very rarely did they turn into anything. However, the minute Michael Ronay looked at her portfolio he knew he had a gem. It wasn't that she was flashy, and it wasn't even her line, deceptively simple yet endlessly manipulable in service to subject and style. She had first of all this intensity of vision, an undivided attention that resulted in distilled images of great power. Then she possessed an uncanny intercourse with the classical world and a nearly magical ability to make it serve her without hesitation or pretension. It was all quietly there. Dürer, Altdorfer, Brueghel, da Vinci, the Limburg brothers, Grünewald. She integrated it subtly, gracefully, without ever missing a step, and yet it was all somehow her own. No one ever mistook a Calista Jacobs illustration for anyone else's. Michael had thought of her, in this almost mysterious relation with the classical world of painters and print makers, as some kind of idiot savant, similar to the autistic people who could do computerlike calculations in their heads and be able to tell you that Valentine's Day in the year 2093 would fall on a Tuesday. But she was no idiot. She was charming, sexy in a funny, offbeat way, yet perfectly normal. She was also very tough and soon became knowledgeable when it came to negotiating contracts—although she was quickly plucked up by an agent, which was all to the good since she would never have had time to draw and deal with all the subsidiary rights and ancillary deals that began to pour in. Tonight was her second Caldecott Medal, an award that guaranteed handsome profits for the publishing company and herself.

Calista looked around now for Charley. He really was a sport. She supposed it wouldn't hurt to follow this hunch of his and go out to this stupid college tomorrow. All of their official obligations would be over by then and they would be taking an evening flight back to Boston. Charley was very insistent about how she should look, and one of his ideas was that she had to do something about her hair. The gray had to go. It just wouldn't look right. He was probably right. Judging from the good Christian women she had seen on the television evangelism shows, which they had taken to watching in preparation, nobody let anything go natural. Helmet-style hairdos or cascades of rigor mortis curls, all dyed chromium colors, were in abundance. Makeup was basically applied with backhoes. But she was loath to dye her hair. Low maintenance in gardens and cosmetics was the name of the game. That's why she had granite in her Cambridge yard and gray hair on her head. You start dyeing your hair, she had told Charley, and there's no end to it. You got to keep fussing with the color, and it never turns out the same way twice. But leave it to Charley! He had found a temporary rinse at the pharmacy. Guaranteed to wash out with one shampoo. So she had agreed to become something called a Rosy Dawn redhead the next morning. She had wondered when she bought the bottle if the name was intentionally a classical allusion to Homer's rosy-fingered dawn that seemed to greet Odysseus every morning when he broached the wind in his sailing vessel. The things she did for this kid! Right now, however, he seemed to be bearing up quite well. A large green librarian was plying him with goodies.

"Umm, these are good," Charley was saying as he bit into something with whipped cream. "You know something?" he said, pointing to another pastry on the plate identical to the one he was eating.

"What's that?" Elsa Dineen asked.

"They got a thing in this city about squirting everything out of tubes and making it fancy. Every meal I've had since I've been here, if they serve you something like mashed potatoes or even creamed spinach, they squirt it into these little decorations. You know, it looks kind of like corduroy all the time. Doesn't hurt the taste. Just wonder why they do that."

"Wouldn't know," Elsa said. "Tell me, what have you been reading lately?"

"You want an honest answer or the other?"

"Why, Charley, you mean you haven't been reading all the Newbery winners?"

"No, I try to avoid them if I can."

"So what's it been?"

"Bimbos of the Death Sun."

"What?" Calista had just walked up. The receiving line had finished for all intents and purposes.

"I was just telling Mrs. Dineen what I was reading."

"Great title. What's it about? And by the way, I'm not a Mrs. but a Ms. But you can call me Elsa."

Librarians were really the most tolerant people in the world. One had to be if one read at all, Calista thought. It was categorically impossible to be a bigot if one read widely.

But Charley was worried. If this lady liked being called Ms., she might not like some of the story of *Bimbos.* He took the plunge. "Well, it takes place at this sci-fi conference. Everybody there's a sci-fi writer, and there's this murder."

"Where does the bimbo part come in?"

"Oh . . ." He paused. How should he put this? "Well, one of the writers has written this story, and the idea of it is how women who work on computers are being affected by sunspots. . . . It's kind of complicated, but it's impairing their uh . . . brain . . . uh . . ."

"Hmm." That was Elsa's comment. She paused and then asked thoughtfully, "Is it corrupting you, Charley?"

"Naw, it's just fun reading."

"Well, you know we're in censorship territory down here. Home of the Gablers and all those people who want to edit textbooks."

"Oh, God!" Calista sighed.

"Yes sireee." Elsa Dineen nodded. "Powerful group, and don't you believe for one minute that the publishers with large educational divisions don't cater to them. If a text gets adopted by the Texas Board of Education for use in the public school system, well, that is fat city for the publishers. We're talking tens of millions of dollars in profits! Oh, they're very sneaky about it. Norma Gabler, who has really spearheaded the movement, talks about 'balanced treatment.' She talks about how it is 'liberal' to give both sides of an issue, that it is incumbent upon us as parents and teachers to present both sides, and then she goes on and asks for both sides in the field of biology to be presented. Why can't we teach creation theory along with atheism? She calls that academic freedom. You know, go ahead and let in every crackpot idea. Slippery, isn't it?"

Calista and Charley both nodded. Neither one of them could believe that they were having this conversation on the eve of their visit to Lorne Thurston College of Christian Heritage.

"It's a hard argument to counter, isn't it?" Calista said after a long pause. She knew what Charley was thinking. Don't even try and counter it tomorrow, Mom!

"Indeed it is," replied Elsa. "But really it has nothing to do with academic freedom. Have you ever heard what John Dewey said about the meaning of real intellectual tolerance?"

"No, what was that?" Calista asked.

"He said that being open-minded was like placing a welcome mat outside your front door and being willing to be hospitable to those who come knocking, but that it was not the same as throwing the door wide open and putting up a sign that says 'Come on in. Nobody's home.'"

"What a great analogy. Reminds me of something that Ray Bradbury once said," Calista replied.

"Oh, what's that?" Elsa asked.

"There're more ways to burn a book than striking a match."

23

There were rosy fingers all right at the dawn. Calista's.

"Oh, God!" she muttered as she gazed down at her rust-colored hands. She'd worry about taking it off after she had fixed her hair in a style that she hoped Charley would consider suitable for this weird trip. How could she let a thirteen-year-old run her life like this? But he had actually, for the first time since he was an infant, been up before she was. He was dressed in his elevator shoes and was busy in his adjoining room slicking down his hair with some concoction that he felt would make him look like a "Pentecostal nerd." At this point Charley knew more about this peculiar phenomena in America's religious history than Calista. One thing she had begun to understand was that it was far from a purely religious phenomena. It was a social one as well. Charley had explained that the Lorne Thurston College of Christian Heritage was a Pentecostalist one. All the fundamentalists were evangelical, but a minority called themselves Pentecostalists, or charismatics, which meant that they believed that the Holy Spirit could work directly through them and thus let them prophesy and heal. Lorne Thurston was in this tradition, a tradition he shared with some others such as Oral Roberts, Jimmy Swaggart, Jim Bakker. According to Charley, Jerry Falwell, Pat Robertson, and Billy

Graham were just straight evangelicals. Billy Graham was looking better and better to Calista. Why couldn't they be going to the Billy Graham University of whatever?

"You ready, Mom? How does it look?"

"You mean the color?"

"Yeah."

"Well, not so bad on my hair, but my fingers, I don't know, they might give me away." She looked up. She didn't look bad as a redhead. It was a very deep auburn color. Nothing flaming. But she didn't really look any younger, either, she thought.

"Remember, you can't wear it in that hurricane style. That won't do," Charley called in.

"Yes, Kenneth."

"What?"

"Kenneth. He's a famous hairdresser in New York. Does Jackie Kennedy's hair. Or rather Jackie Onassis."

Calista started to go to work with a curling iron, a blow dryer, and a can of industrial-strength hairspray.

"Great!" Charley exclaimed when she walked out of the bathroom twenty minutes later.

"More Annette Funicello than Tammy Faye, I think."

"It looks so set. Can I touch it?"

"Sure. This is up to gale-force winds."

Calista had pinned up the back of her hair into a French twist. She had then teased the top into a mushroom-shaped dome that was as rigid as it was smooth. She had pulled down a little fringe of hair over her forehead and curled it under with the curling iron into what had once been known as Mamie Eisenhower bangs. "You look pretty weird yourself," she said.

Charley had actually let the barber cut off quite a bit of his hair before they came on the trip. He now had it slicked down and was wearing nonprescription glasses. He wore a print cotton shirt that he'd found at T. J. MAXX and a narrow tie. Calista at the same time had bought a striped shirtwaist dress. She had never in her entire life owned a shirtwaist dress. She was also carrying a flat white handbag, the kind one always saw Queen Elizabeth carrying when performing her royal chores, at

152

least those that did not require her to wear the crown and ermine robes.

"I think I'm too nervous to eat," Charley said.

"You're too nervous! You're the one who thought up this harebrained idea."

"I'm the one who's applying for admission, remember."

"God forbid."

"And it's not harebrained, Mom. This is the college, of all these Bible ones, that is the most antievolutionary and pro–scientific creationism. You heard Janet say that she found out from Norman Petrakis's editor that they had put all of Norman's books on their banned list and that Thurston himself had spoken out against Petrakis."

"You didn't say anything to Janet about this little jaunt of ours, did you, Charley?" She raised her finger ready to scold.

"Of course not."

"She'd absolutely have a fit, and she'd probably tell Ethan, and Ethan would . . . God, I don't know what."

Both Ethan Thayer and Janet were taking early morning planes back to New York. Calista had made some excuse about visiting some old colleagues of Tom's in the Dallas area, and for that reason she was taking a later evening flight back east. She looked at Charley. She had one nagging question that he had not answered satisfactorily. She sighed. "Now tell me again. What do you really think we can accomplish by going out there and going through this whole charade?"

"Mom, I told you. You don't know what you're going to find until you find it. But you got to start somewhere. This is the logical starting point. It's not just that these are the most fanatical. They have the most money, the most power, the most satellite linkups for their religious TV programs."

"But by the same token they have the most to lose by getting involved with murder."

"I'm not saying they did it, Mom. But we might find out something. They're the ones who are pouring money into that whole Louisiana thing for balanced treatment of creation science. They also run the Committee for the Study of Natural Sciences and the Institute of the Deluge."

"Institute of the Deluge?" Calista asked.

"Yeah, I read about it. They study delugology."

"What in the hell is delugology?"

"It figures out theories about the Flood, you know the one in the Bible, and how the Flood can account for all the fossils in the rocks. They even have this water vapor theory to go with it. A kind of greenhouse effect that worked with the forty days and forty nights of rain. You got to understand, Mom, that of all these Christian colleges this one goes the farthest in trying to making the Bible into a science. They teach a Christian anthropology course, Christian physics courses, Christian biochemistry. This is the center of it. Real weird."

"I'll say."

"But it's a science according to them, and they offer two courses in the deluge, Flood Geology one and two. Then after you take those you can go on an archaeology expedition and look for the Ark."

"Sounds like fun. Where do they think it is—Disney World?"

"Ha! Ha! Very funny. Now look, Mom. You got to get all your jokes out of you before we go. All right?"

24

All the jokes were gone as they drove due east out of Dallas on Route 20 in their rental car—an enormous boat of a thing that felt like an aircraft carrier to Calista. But then again, Charley said it was perfect. Charley might have a future as a caterer with his attention to detail for occasions, Calista thought. They were quiet, Calista rehearsing in her mind not so much what she would say, but what she would not say. She didn't think it would be hard holding her tongue, actually. She would share nothing with these people. She had agreed to say that she was churchgoing, but if anybody asked her about when she had received Christ or last spoken in tongues, she was not going to say anything—or at most say that it was such an intensely personal experience that she found it hard to articulate. She was going as a widow. Her late husband had been a doctor, and she herself worked as an artist. That was all that she would say. Charley apparently had his whole spiel worked out. He wanted to come to Lorne Thurston College because he was indeed interested in a Christian education and walking closer with God, but also because they offered the best and most extensive program in creation science, a subject that interested him and that he had not been able to pursue in his public school education to date. As they drove Charley went over all the rationality of the creationist science that he had read in the previous three weeks: nutty notions all designed to jam the earth's history into six thousand years; notions that debunked, without data or any evidence whatsoever, everything from radiocarbon dating to geological stratigraphy. They were, however, very big on the second law of thermodynamics, which said that closed systems tend to become more disordered. Adam and Eve's Fall, the Garden of Eden, and the fact that the queen bee murders her sisters were evidence of that, said one creationist theorist. In creationist theory, therefore, organized living systems, such as humans, could not have evolved from less organized matter without divine intervention. Hallelujah. Praise the Lord and the second law! It all fit. Yes, Charley was well prepared—so well prepared that he had completely neglected to do a last research paper for school and would have an incomplete or possibly a C if he didn't do something about it by the end of the month.

They had already seen several signs for the college and the town of Green Acre. Apparently the town came first.

"What in the heck is that?" Calista asked.

"What?" Charley asked.

"That." She pointed ahead toward one o'clock. On a nearly barren horizon a silvery sphere loomed out of the parched earth. A sign soon appeared: Lorne Thurston College of Christian Heritage, One Mile, Exit 22a.

"They even get their own exit," Charley whispered. None of the others had *a*'s or *b*'s. There wasn't a 21a.

"Hmph," Calista growled. "I'd like to give them their own exit all right."

They turned off at 22a. Where the exit road joined another road there was a second sign for the college, this one with a picture of Lorne Thurston on it.

"Imagine Derek Bok putting up his picture as you crossed the Larz Anderson Bridge into Cambridge."

"Mom, be quiet!" Charley said sharply.

The parched land suddenly turned green as they drove through an entry gate. At a guardhouse they were directed to the Dale Thurston Administration Offices. They parked in the lot in front of a bleached-yellow brick building. Calista took a deep breath and closed her eyes briefly.

"You okay, Mom?" There was a plaintive note in his voice as if suddenly he might have regretted this whole thing. If Charley lost courage, God, what would she do? It was so hard lying, not being yourself. She should have probably taken a Valium. She had considered it but decided not to since she was driving. She should have taken a drink, is what she should have taken!

"No, I'm fine." She said the words tightly. "Let's go."

The heat was oppressive as they stepped out of the car. It was only ten o'clock in the morning, but Texas had started to bake hours before and the temperature was nearly one hundred degrees. As soon as they stepped into the lobby of the building Calista felt better. There was a crucifix on one side and a cool tinkling waterfall that spilled into a pool on the other side. Calista noticed pennies glittering through the water on the aquamarine tile. By the pool was a small sign: "It is possible to give away and become richer." Proverbs 11:24. She wondered if this was really how they collected for their alumni fund. Almost immediately a young girl with silky blond hair and a band of freckles across her nose came bouncing into the lobby.

"You must be Charles Jacobs and Mrs. Jacobs!" she said, extending her hand.

"Yes." They nodded.

"I'm Beth Ann Hennessey. I'm going to be your guide for today. Why don't you first come into our lounge. After that you can meet Tommy Lee Clayton, our assistant director of admissions, and talk with him for a while, and then we'll go on the tour."

Five minutes later they were sitting in a lovely lounge while Beth Ann chatted on about how Lorne Thurston College of Christian Heritage had changed her life. She was a junior, and she had qualified for a scholarship.

"Now if you have any financial needs, we have a wonderful financial aid program here, and there's just so many ways you can supplement that. Like I'm working as a guide this summer. And I also work in the television studio."

"Television studio?" Calista asked.

"Sure thing. Right here. Didn't you know that *The Lorne Thurston Gospel Hour* is produced and broadcast from right here on campus? We got the satellite linkups. Didn't you see the big dishes when you came in—or did you come in from Route twenty?"

"Yes, we did."

"Oh, well, all that's over on the other side of campus in what we call the southeast quadrant. You'll see it on our tour. You saw the pictures in the brochure, didn't you, Charley, of our studios? And you know we have a wonderful communications program here. You can major in television ministry work. But even if you're not a major—like me, I'm majoring in youth ministry—you can get jobs in the station. Some pay, some don't. It's really fun. You learn a lot about TV production. I work there six hours a week in the summer and about four during the school term."

"Oh, that'll be neat to see."

"Is that the broadcasting studio—that large silver ball that we saw from the highway?" Calista asked.

"No. That is the Sphere of Faith." Calista must have looked a little blank, for Beth Ann quickly added, "Where we have our chapel services. And behind it is an outdoor amphitheater so that in good weather in the evenings we can have services outdoors under the Texas stars. It's just beautiful. Will you be here this evening?"

"No," they both answered quickly.

157

"Oh, that's too bad. There'll be an outdoor service. And Lorne Thurston's wife, Clarella—we all call her Mom—is preaching. She's wonderful." Then she lowered her voice to a conspiratorial whisper. "I think she's better than the reverend myself." She paused a moment and continued. "Sometimes they do broadcast from the Sphere of Faith. It has all the equipment, but that's only on special occasions. Are you interested in communication, Charles?" She paused briefly. "Do you like being called Charles or Charley?"

There was something very warm and engaging about this young girl, Calista thought. She seemed lively and intelligent. It was hard to believe that she could be as limited as one might suppose such an environment would suggest. And if she were, Calista thought, she wondered how flexible or inflexible those limitations, those boundary lines, were.

"Well, most people call me Charley. Yeah, I guess I might be. I'm really interested, though, in your science program here—the scientific creation courses."

"Oh, you are? Well, as you probably know, we really have a wonderful department in that area. I'm not so good in science myself. So I haven't taken that much. But it is one of our most exciting departments. So I'm glad you told me because I'll take you over to the Creation Center, that's where most of the courses are taught and where the labs are."

"Labs?" said Calista, her eyes widening. She shouldn't have said it. She knew it as soon as the word was out, and she could feel Charley tense beside her on the couch.

"Yes, you know, the laboratories where they do their experiments and all that stuff." Beth Ann spoke rather offhandedly, so maybe she hadn't noticed Calista's incredulity.

Tommy Lee Clayton was one of those persons who precluded wondering about. One would never entertain the slightest notion about his limitations other than that they were fixed and eternal. Beth Ann had ushered them into the assistant admissions director's office. Tommy Lee didn't look much older than Beth Ann. But he looked set from his plastic molded hair to his sharply cut powder blue suit.

"Well, I am so pleased to welcome you to the college. We

don't often get visitors from Massachusetts here." Did she imagine it, or was there a funny note in his voice, a slight sneer as he said the word *Massachusetts?* The same sneer that came into the voices of certain conservative politicians and presidential candidates when they spoke of that liberal state as if it were some arrogant and eternally erring child.

"And as I understand it, Mrs. Jacobs, you are a widow?"

"Yes. Yes," she said tersely. "My husband was a doctor."

"And do you work?"

She was taken aback by the question. There was something definitely wrong here. College interviews never started off with questions to the parents. It was the kids they were supposed to be focused on.

"Uh . . . yes . . . uh, I'm an artist . . . a comm—"
She had started to say "commercial." But something stuck, and she coughed slightly.

"Commercial." He filled in the word, and she nodded and regained her composure. When you sold as many books as Calista did, you could certainly call it being commercial even if it wasn't advertising. Finally he turned to Charley and began to ask him some questions.

"So you like to skateboard, and I see from your application that you have worked through your church on starting a youth skateboarding group."

Holy moley! Calista thought. What was this? Skateboarding for God! What in the hell had Charley gone and written on that thing?

"Well, yes," Charley was saying modestly. "At a church fair we put on an exhibition and had a safety clinic for kids just starting out. You know, just about wearing pads and helmets. We actually raised fifty dollars."

"Well, good for you, son! I got a nine-year-old nephew who loves to skateboard. And I don't think you can stress the safety thing too much. 'Thrashers,' isn't that the slang word for skateboarders?"

"Yes, sir." Charley's face suddenly brightened. God, had her child really found something in common with this guy? That Charley! "You know what we call ourselves, Mr. Clayton?"

"What's that, son?" he asked eagerly.

159

"Gospel Thrashers." He beamed.

"Well, I'll be." Tommy Lee Clayton slapped his thigh. "That really has a ring to it. You ever think of going into communications, Charles? You know, we got a great department here. Real on-the-spot opportunities. See, the main transponder for *The Lorne Thurston Gospel Hour* is right here."

"Yes." Calista nodded. "Beth Ann told us about it."

"Yeah. . . . Well, as I was telling Beth Ann," Charley continued, "I'm really interested in your creation science program here."

"Oh, now you're talking." Clayton pointed his finger directly at Charley. "We're really blowing some of these other so-called scientists off the map. We got some outstanding research going on down here and some real new breakthroughs which you'll be reading about in the not-too-distant future. You be sure to have Beth Ann give you a complete tour of our William Jennings Bryan Creation Science Center. We've got some excellent new young professors on board."

"Yes." Charley nodded. "I've been reading about this man Ferneld."

"Ah, yes, Gerry Ferneld. He'll be coming to teach here next fall."

"Yes, I've been reading about his theory of the vapor canopy that shielded the lower atmosphere from cosmic radiation and why that means that radiocarbon dating isn't really accurate."

"Well, my goodness, son, you are up on things."

"Yes, sir. And I'm trying to plan an experiment for the Westinghouse Science Fair that, well . . . you know." Charley squirmed and gave a very good impression of bashfulness. "I mean, it can't prove conclusively . . ."

"Yes, son, yes!" Tommy Lee was leaning forward, his elbows on his desk, eagerly awaiting Charley's words.

"Well, I think that there's a way that you can prove the water shield theory and the specific reduction of radioactive carbon if you start using amber samples."

"Amber? Well, I'll be."

"Yeah, you see, amber really keeps all those precipitates intact that come from the atmosphere . . ." Charley was off and running with his theory of amber precipitates as an index of an antediluvian vapor canopy. It was total gobbledygook. He was talking iridium and zinc indices and atmospheric scrubbing particles that could be evidence of a great deluge four thousand years ago. It was a bizarre mixture of chemistry and particle physics and Scripture. Light on the Scripture. He apparently had only read the creation part.

"And what happens if it doesn't turn out right?"

"Right?" Charley looked bewildered. Calista felt totally disoriented. Had such a question really ever been asked in such a way about scientific inquiry? "You mean if the experiment I do for the Westinghouse thing shows that there couldn't be a vapor canopy that would interfere with radiocarbon dating?"

"Yeah." Clayton's voice was flat. This was a trap. Shit! Calista thought, Why did Charley have to go mouthing off about this? Why couldn't he have come in here like any other admissions candidate? When was the last time they had one in this office who had aspirations for a Westinghouse Science Award?

"Well . . ." Charley paused. "It will be the wrong experiment."

Suddenly Calista saw what Charley was doing. "Right," she said. "No need to throw out the baby with the bathwater—or the Flood waters." She smiled weakly. At this a huge grin cracked Tommy Lee's simple face. What a pair of phrasemakers they must appear to be, Calista thought. "Gospel Thrashers"— "baby with the Flood waters!"

"Yes," said Charley, picking up on his mother's line. "You don't throw out the Scriptures. I must just be misunderstanding them in some way, and so I'll have to come up with a new experiment."

Tommy Lee smiled again. Calista breathed a sigh of relief. They had played the game right. Any model of a biblical deluge can be falsified, but the truth of the fact of the Flood cannot be. Models and experiments can be shoved and nudged, but not Genesis. Wasn't this in direct contradiction to the philosopher Karl Popper's dictum that a theory be in principle falsifiable? Tom had explained that Popper's dictum meant that a good theory not only explained fully, but also could predict what conditions or observations could prove the theory wrong or false. This meant simply that a theory could be proved conclusively false, or at least one of its statements false, if an observational consequence were false. Not here, however. If the observational consequence of the vapor canopy proved false, the scriptural statements stood truer than ever! Tom had explained falsifiability as being a cornerstone to scientific procedure and inquiry. But it didn't count for much in Green Acre, Texas, obviously.

Tommy Lee got up and leaned forward to shake hands with Charley. "I think you're going to do very well here. I think we might even be able to arrange for advanced placement."

Over my dead body! Calista thought.

25

They were now following Beth Ann along a baking concrete walkway that led from the Student Union Center to the BCN, Bible Cable Network, the real nerve center of Lorne Thurston's television empire.

"Over there." Beth Ann was pointing to a low building that looked like a ranch-style house. "That's our computer center."

"Oh, wow!" Charley said.

"Oh, Charley'll want to see that." Calista laughed.

"Well, it's not usually on the tour, but I can certainly take you there," Beth Ann said.

"It's not on the tour? Why not?"

"It's the computer center for BCN. It's where they process all the donations, and it houses our direct-mail operation for BCN's giving programs."

"Oh, you mean it's not for the college," Charley said.

"Well, it is and it isn't. You saw Morton Hall. That's where the students go to work on computers and learn about programming. Well, this is where you can go once you've learned. Another summer internship that you can have here is working

162

in the computer center. It is directly connected with the television studios. Come on, I'll show you."

They walked into the building, which was much larger than it appeared from the outside. In the spacious lobby there was an immense color photograph of Lorne Thurston that dominated the entire space. If Jim Bakker was said to look like Howdy Doody, Calista thought, Lorne Thurston was certainly a dead ringer for an aging Buster Brown, the one who had lived in a shoe with his freckles, pug nose, saucer eyes, and red hair. He beamed down on them, and above the picture was the scriptural verse "Give, And It Shall Be Given Unto You"—Luke 6:38. On either side of this portrait was a glass wall behind which were banks of computers and telephones. They walked up to the wall.

"They call that the pit," Beth Ann said. There were at least thirty people manning phones and at computer terminals. "It can be really hard work during broadcasting hours. Those phones never stop ringing. This is the headquarters, of course, but we have seven other regional branches throughout the country." It was fairly state-of-the-art as far as Charley could tell. There was an electronic ticker tape flashing up-to-the-minute calculations.

"What are those signs—Sphere of Faith, Partners in the Kingdom?" Calista asked.

"Oh, those indicate the varying amounts that donors can give. If you give over a certain amount, you can become a Partner in the Kingdom, that means you get to go to an annual prayer dinner with Lorne Thurston. If you are a member of the Sphere of Faith, it means that for a certain amount your name will be inscribed on one of the window plates in the Sphere of Faith Chapel here on campus."

Calista understood immediately. It was an old selling tactic. She believed it had been called, by Madison Avenue, the unique selling proposition. In more ancient times it had been called buying papal indulgences. You bought prayer dinners or breakfasts with Thurston, or perhaps you bought bricks or glass in his campus and broadcasting empire, as Beth Ann was now telling them.

"Every letter accompanying a donation is individually read and prayed over."

"I don't see how there'd be enough hours in the day to do that," Calista said as she stood almost mesmerized by the ticker tape flashing the current tallies that looked as if they were indeed rising.

"Well, they say they do it," Beth Ann said ingenuously. It was the word *say* that made Calista think that this was perhaps the first time Beth Ann had questioned anything since she had come to the college. The word functioned like a slight hesitation in the scriptural recording that had been implanted in her brain. A tiny glitch in the tape. But she resumed perkily. "Now, you see that green light over there by the huge clock?" she said, pointing to a large green globe. "When they are on the air, that green light is on and then you can see a lot of activity in this room. You really notice the difference. The ticker tape, for one thing, is flashing a lot more, numbers really going up. The various clubs work on a kind of mini–goal system so that when certain donor levels are reached in the course of a broadcast, other lights and bells go off. It's real exciting."

"Goodness," was all that Calista could say. She looked at the green globe. She thought of the green light at the end of the pier that Jay Gatsby used to stare across toward, and she thought of the elusive green color that she had tried to track down at Houghton Library in the books of hours. This was not it.

"We can go into the television studio now. There probably won't be much going on today because I don't think they're taping."

"Clarella will not wear that dress on the air. She calls that puke yellow, and it's something like Tammy Faye would wear. . . . Oh, dear!" The young woman clapped her hands over her mouth as she came round the corner and met up with Beth Ann leading her charges around.

"Don't worry, Sue. We didn't hear a thing." Beth Ann laughed. "And I don't blame her. Yellow does not televise well, especially with her coloring. Are you taping today?"

"No. Not till tomorrow."

"Oh, by the way, Sue. This is Charley Jacobs and his mother. I'm giving them a tour. Charley is going to apply here."

"Oh, do!" Sue's eyes became dreamy. "It's the most wonderful experience you'll ever have. Next year's my last year, and I don't know how I'll ever leave. . . ." She sighed. "But, of course, that's the whole idea . . . sense of mission, that's what it's all about."

"What are you going to do after graduation?" Calista asked.

"Well, I'm hoping to get a job with one of our affiliates in California. I'm real interested in Christian broadcasting. And if that doesn't come through, I might go down to the park for a while."

"What park?"

"Oh, you know, the Bible theme park that the reverend runs in Virginia. Bible Times, it's called. It's really fun. I did a work-study program there last spring and helped them set up a day-care center, and there's talk of some children's programming that would originate from the park. You know, kind of like Sesame Street, only Christian."

"Oh," Calista said softly. Somehow she had never imagined Big Bird as an evangelist. And presumably Oscar the Grouch would be turned into Satan the Slouch or some such thing.

From the BCN building they moved on to the William Jennings Bryan Creation Science Center.

In the beginning God created the heaven and the earth. And the earth was without form and void; and darkness was upon the face of the deep. And the spirit of God moved upon the face of the waters. And God said, Let there be light: and there was light. And God saw the light and saw that it was good. And God divided the light from the darkness. And God called the light Day and the darkness he called Night and the evening and the morning were the first day. . . . And God said, Let the earth bring forth grass, the herb yielding seed, and the fruit tree yielding fruit after his kind, whose seed is in itself, upon the earth: and it was so. And the earth brought forth grass, and herb yielding seed after his kind, and the tree yielding fruit, whose seed was in itself, after his kind. And God saw that it was good.

165

These first verses of Genesis were engraved in limestone over the front entrance to the William Jennings Bryan Creation Science Center. Upon entering the lobby Calista and Charley found other verses from Genesis carved into stone slabs that were set into the pale yellow brick walls. Within the walls of this building there was no doubt and there would be no inquiry. That was for certain. The lobby seemed to function as a sort of lounge. There were tables and comfortable chairs, and Calista paused as she passed by a magazine rack to look at what was offered for light lobby reading. There was a selection of pamphlets from an outfit called Creation Life Publishers. She casually picked one up entitled *God's Plan for Air*. Next to it was *God's Plan for Insects* and another called *Unhappy Gays* and finally *I'm a Woman By God's Design*. There was also literature from a group called FLAG, which stood for "Family, Life, America, under God."

The whole thing was starting to become a strain for Calista. She hoped that Charley was getting what he needed because she was feeling increasingly uncomfortable in this environment. But they were presumably at the heart of the matter here in the William Jennings Bryan Creation Science Center. Charley was standing at another rack of reading materials and motioned her over while Beth Ann had gone to a water fountain to get a drink. "Look at this!" he said, picking up some sort of newsletter.

"Oh!" Calista gasped. There was a picture of Norman Petrakis. And above the picture was the headline SATAN'S SCHOLAR VICTIM OF VIOLENT ATTACK. They both read the article silently. "Norman Petrakis, a longtime children's book author of nonfiction works, was found dead in a Boston hotel room. Mr. Petrakis had written extensively on the subject of human evolution. He was an outspoken anti-Creationist, and those of us in the Christian Community had long deplored this man's depravity and influence on young minds. Once a member of the Socialist party and rumored to be a practicing homosexual, Mr. Petrakis was indeed the perfect embodiment of the degenerate mind fostered by modernistic ideas. We who have long believed that evolutionary thinking leads to degeneracy, depravity, and the general dissolution of society feel that, although we regret any man's death, the manner in which Mr.

Petrakis died is again proof of evolutionistic thought as the root of atheism, amorality, libertinism, and all manner of anti-Christian systems of belief."

Both of their hands had begun to tremble as they held the paper. Just at that moment Beth Ann walked up. "Ready to begin?" she asked cheerfully. Calista was ready to throw up. But Charley rebounded gamely.

The tour began with the lecture halls and some classrooms. They then proceeded to pass by what looked like standard laboratories where chemistry or biology classes might be held. It was difficult to imagine what such classes would be like or how observational data might be regarded despite the rather conventional appearance of these labs. "Now this is the lab where I took a course last spring semester—Biblical Archaeology. It was really neat. And then, of course, the Flood studies. I only took the first semester of that. It was kind of hard. You really had to learn a lot about hydraulics, and I'm not very good in physics and that kind of science. Professor Stark is a hydraulic engineer, though, by training. A dear man. He gave me a B minus, and I really think I should have just gotten a C. I think he felt sorry for me." She smiled sweetly. "He even encouraged me to go on the field trip this summer to Mount Ararat in the Holy Land. He goes every year in search of Noah's Ark, and they've turned up some really promising artifacts. But I couldn't go. It's really expensive, the airfare, and I just couldn't swing it. I mean, I'm on scholarship already, and my grandma and grandpa send me spending money from their pensions. I really can't ask for anything else."

"Can we walk through here?" Charley asked, nodding his head toward the archaeology lab.

"Sure thing." They entered. "Now if we go through that door, we get into the anthro lab."

"Anthro?" Calista asked.

"Anthropology," Beth Ann said. "It's a cultural anthropology course, for the most part. It surveys the biblical foundations of Christian missions. It focuses on practical methods which relate to cultural or racial barriers in the field. It's a requirement for everyone in the missions program. I took it, however, even though I'm not in the program. Next semester I'll take arid lands biology, and I will have completed my science requirements. Praise the Lord!" she whispered. "I'm just awful in science, but the anthro course is really interesting. And now we got this new neat professor and he came from up north, but he's really discovered some wonderful things."

"What?" Charley asked.

"Well, do you know that last summer they combined the Mount Ararat expedition with an arid lands biology expedition? They're doing a lot of that now that Professor Tompkins has come here. He's the one who came from up north, Minnesota or someplace."

"A lot of what?" Calista asked.

"Combining the anthropology and the archaeology with biology. I guess he's a biologist by training, but he's doing a lot with anthropology down here. And so they had this joint expedition, people from both departments went, and somewhere along the way they discovered these fascinating skulls."

"What kind of skulls?" Calista asked.

"Human skulls—very ancient ones from probably long before the Flood."

Now how ancient could they get? Calista was thinking. Weren't these folks trying to crush it all into six thousand years? She supposed that in their geological scale anything over two thousand years was considered ancient. Thus these skulls, from before the time of Noah, perhaps just outside the garden gates of Eden, seemed to them ancient.

"And do you know what they are thinking that they're on the brink of proving?" Beth Ann continued.

"What?" Charley asked.

"That the races were formed separately." Beth Ann's eyes widened.

"What do you mean?" Calista and Charley both asked the same question at once.

"It means that the races—you know, blacks and whites— started off separately from the beginning. I mean, we always suspected it, but now we know."

"We do?" Calista asked vaguely.

"Yeah, Wayne Tompkins, he's the professor who found the proof, dug it up."

"You mean this skull?" Calista asked.

"Yep. He showed a cast of it in a seminar he gives. My roommate saw it."

Calista worded her next question carefully. "But isn't this like evolution?"

"We don't believe in that," Beth Ann said firmly. "This is just like the Bible says in Genesis, really. Just as it says God made the beasts of the earth according to their kinds, and every winged bird according to its kind. He created man in his own image and then created the kinds of man."

"But it never says that, does it, in the Bible? That he created kinds of men?"

"No. You're right. It doesn't get that detailed, but Wayne Tompkins says that this fossil will certainly prove that the Book of Genesis could have indeed gotten that detailed."

Calista was confused. Had a fundamentalist switched the rules on her, turned revisionist? Could there be such a thing as a revisionist fundamentalist?

"Could we see the skull?" Charley asked suddenly.

"Well, I suppose I can ask Wayne. He's around here someplace. I saw him when I was getting a drink at the fountain when we first came in. Let me go see. You wait here."

They waited until she was out of the room. Calista wheeled toward Charley. "This is getting too friggin' weird, Charley. I don't know whether I can keep pretenses up too much longer."

"Mom, it's getting interesting. Can you believe doing science like these guys do it? Come on, we got to look at this skull."

"Have you ever heard of Piltdown man, Charley?" Calista hissed.

"No. What's that?"

"It was about the biggest fake in science, and these guys aren't even that smart. Incidentally, Piltdown man was rumored to be pulled off by a man of the cloth—Teilhard de Chardin. What we're going to see here is a papier-mâché skull. You can bet on that! Everybody knows that racial differences have never even shown up in the fossil record of hominids because there friggin' weren't any until twenty thousand years ago!"

169

"Mom, don't even say friggin'! Remember where we are." He peered at her through his nonprescription glasses. She could smell the gunk he had put on his hair.

"How could I forget?"

Beth Ann returned in a few minutes. Her color was high, higher than it should have been for this air-conditioned building, and she was visibly agitated. "I'm afraid that the skulls are unavailable at the moment. They are undergoing some further testing in another laboratory, and I really should not have mentioned anything about them at this point."

"Oh, dear," Calista said. "I hope we didn't get you into any trouble."

"Oh, no! No! Don't worry about it. No trouble." But she looked as if she were on the brink of tears.

"No trouble at all," a voice suddenly said. "Hello, Mrs. Jacobs and Charles." It was a nice voice, a reasonable voice, full of intelligence. From the moment Calista heard Wayne Tompkins speak, she felt more at ease.

He was around thirty, with a friendly, open face that was very nice looking but not quite handsome. He was dressed in khaki pants and rolled-up shirtsleeves. He walked over and extended his hand. "I'm just afraid that Beth Ann was a little exuberant here. She's a very enthusiastic science student. But announcing the find is just a bit premature. See, after our next round of testing we are planning a formal colloquium, and that is when it shall be officially announced. I'm sure you can understand."

Calista could not reconcile him at all with these surroundings. She could not imagine him walking through that lobby with those slanderous, vile pamphlets. He was in marked contrast with Tommy Lee Clayton, that was for sure. And it wasn't just that he was from the north and did not have an accent. He just seemed eminently reasonable to her and logical with no axes, biblical or otherwise, to grind.

"Yes, yes, of course," Calista said quickly. She looked at her watch. "You know, we must be going, Charley. We do have a plane to catch."

"You're going out of Dallas-Fort Worth, right?"

"Yes."

"Well, you might want to take a shortcut back. You take Route twenty back, but you get off one exit early before Dallas. Here, let me draw you a little sketch." He got a piece of paper and drew on it, then handed it to Calista. This will save you going through downtown Dallas."

"Oh, thanks, thanks so much."

"Sorry about the skull."

"Oh, no problem. Don't worry, we won't spill the beans."

Wayne Tompkins smiled. "I'm sure you won't."

26

Neither Calista nor Charley spoke a word until they had driven out of the gates of the college. Then Calista sank back against the almost broiling vinyl of the car seat. "Oy vay!" she growled deeply. "Charley, the things I do for you!"

"Mom, that's not fair. You didn't do it just for me."

She sighed. "You're right," she said, and thought of Norman Petrakis. "Could you believe that thing, that filthy rag they had about his death? God, these people are totally screwball."

"You see, they had a motive."

Calista thought for a moment. Until this day she would never have really thought they had a motive. She would have thought of them as just a bunch of religious fanatics, but there was such vitriol in that piece, such real hatred and paranoia. It was the Nazis all over again. The whole operation was a bunch of shit even if Beth Ann and Wayne Tompkins seemed nice and relatively normal.

"Look, there's that damn prayer ball or whatever they call it," she said, nodding at it in her rearview mirror. "It's like something out of a Mel Brooks movie."

"Sphere of Faith," Charley said.

"It is written, 'My house shall be called the house of prayer; but you have made it a den of thieves,'" Calista said in a low voice.

"Who said that?" Charley asked.

"The Bible. New Testament."

"I didn't know you knew the Bible that well."

"I don't. The phrase just came to me. Once upon a time I took a religion and literature course as an undergraduate." She paused. "So did you get anything out of this, Charley?"

"Well, you yourself agree with me that they had a motive."

"But there's no evidence. There is still absolutely nothing to go on. I mean, these guys might screw around with scientific data all they want, but we haven't got one shred of evidence. Just because they might be hateful people doesn't mean they murder. Could you believe that Beth Ann could murder?"

"She was nice."

"She was. I . . . I feel sorry for her. I really do."

"You do?" Charley sounded surprised.

"Yeah, I do. I have the feeling that there's a story there with Beth Ann, or at least we don't have the full one."

"What do you mean?"

"I don't know—intuition. I don't think that coming to Lorne Thurston College of Christian Heritage was a real choice in the true sense."

They were silent for a while. "Can you hand me that little piece of paper with the map the guy sketched? I think we're coming up on our exit, and I have to know what to look for."

They had been off the main highway on a smaller road for a few minutes when Calista noticed a car coming up rather fast in her rearview mirror.

"God, what's that guy doing? Is he going to pass me or what?" She looked nervously into the side mirror. "Talk about tailgating!"

"Mom, he's not just tailgating!" The car had cut out abruptly and was pulling up even with them while trying to press into their side.

"Jesus Christ, what's he doing? He's trying to run me off the road!" Calista honked the horn. But she sensed the futility of this gesture as a kind of awful knowledge flooded through her being. This is what they did to Karen Silkwood, she thought.

"Gun it, Mom! Gun it." There was a terrible hot screech as

172

metal glanced off metal. The fucking boat had no power. The other car was riding them hard, edging them over, easily keeping pace with them. Tail wagging the dog. Tail wagging the dog! That was all Calista could think of. Time for the dog to stop wagging. She slammed on the brakes. The other car spun out in front of them. Calista swerved sharply into the other lane.

"Good God!" Charley was on his knees on the seat looking back. The car had rolled down an embankment but left a tire behind that wobbled crazily across the road. "They friggin' tried to kill us!" she screamed, and gunned the car. She could feel her heart pounding, the blood pulsing through her temples. "Are they gone? They're not coming after us, are they, Charley?"

"No, they're finished. No way. Skidded into that deep ditch, lost a wheel. Why would they do that?"

Calista eased up on the accelerator. She looked at Charley. "They must have had a motive."

"Do you think it's them? The college?"

"Whoever it was knew who we were. They weren't kidding around. They were out to get us."

"Why are you going so slow now?"

"I don't want to get arrested for speeding in the state of Texas, Charley. Something tells me that in these parts Lorne Thurston has things sewn up. We're going to get home as fast as we can, but we're going to be careful."

Careful meant not waiting for their four o'clock flight to Boston but taking the first flight they could heading east. Within twenty minutes of arriving at the airport they were settling into their seats on a Delta flight to Philadelphia. Calista would figure out how to get the rest of the way when they got to Philly. They were still trembling as the flight attendant directed their attention to the safety features of the plane. Calista pulled the pins out of her French twist and began vigorously brushing out her hair.

"Okay. We're going to figure this out. But I need a very stiff drink first."

She ordered a double vodka martini. She had splurged and bought first-class tickets. The wider seats were kind to the

173

disintegrating disk in her back. Whenever she was on a plane she spent the first couple of minutes doing some invisible back exercises that her orthopedic surgeon had advised her to do before a long flight and once or twice during the trip. She did them now with a fierce concentration. Charley dared not interrupt her. His mother's mood had changed from scared to angry. "Profound piss-dom," he called it. It was just like the time two years ago when it had all come out about the CIA and his dad's death. They had sent in that creepy guy to seduce her and then steal the Time Slicer. They had hoped to embarrass his mom. But she didn't embarrass or shut up. She got mad. Real mad and had turned around and sued the pants off the government. They'd settled out of court for a huge sum. The government had hoped that it would save them having to have their dirty linen washed in public. But it hadn't. Then she'd doubly humiliated them by giving away most of the money to their nemesis—the nuclear freeze movement! And to make matters worse, she'd won her most stunning endorsement from that old conservative warhorse of the American Right—Barry Goldwater. Called her a brave woman, a true American, and if anyone should be embarrassed, it should be the federal government, whom she'd caught with their pants down, said he!

Charley looked at his mother now out of the corner of his eye. She had finished the exercises and was sipping her drink. Could they have been recognized? She hadn't looked at all like her pictures with the red hair and the new hairdo. Her picture hadn't been in the paper that much. Only that morning for the first time was it in the Dallas papers for winning the Caldecott Award the previous night. That seemed so long ago now—his conversation with the big green librarian and running vodkas to Ethan. But maybe the same people who had disrupted the conference that she and Petrakis had been at in April had come to this one. Maybe they infiltrated all these book conferences. If they were that scared of books, as the green librarian had said they were, maybe they made a practice of sending in spies. They could have been looking at her and at him, studying their every move for the whole three days. Maybe they had been on to them from the time Charley had first sent in his application to Lorne Thurston College of Christian Heritage. How many people

174

from Cambridge applied there? Maybe it was the same people who had put the diapers on *Nick in the Night* and the rabbit's blood on the pictures of Rothgar and messed up Owl. Holy shit, maybe they were just taking a long glide down the Plain of Crystal Doom and they would soon crash and shatter! Charley looked out the window. They were above a layer of neatly fragmented clouds that floated below them like sky biscuits, round and fluffy.

"Okay, Charley. I'm ready. . . . I think there are at least two separate questions here: Did they know who we really were? That's one question."

Charley looked up, surprised at this conjecture of his mother's. "You think they might not have guessed our identity?"

"I'm not sure, and even if they hadn't, they still might have done the same thing."

"Huh?"

"Look, Charley, supposing they didn't really know who we were—just supposing. Then they wouldn't have thought that we were there in connection at all with Petrakis's death. Think back: when did they really get upset? When did the whole tenor of the visit change?"

"In the Creation Center."

"Precisely—when Beth Ann came back to tell us that the skulls were unavailable. She had made, unwittingly, a major gaffe. They have something planned for those skulls, and it really threatened their plans when Beth Ann spilled the beans."

"Jeez, I hope she's going to be all right. She almost looked as if she were about to cry."

"I know. I'm worried about her, too. Somehow I just resist instinctually throwing her in with those jerks.

"In any case, it was the mention of the skulls that made them antsy." She thought back on Wayne Tompkins, all smooth and engaging and very offhand. And he had seemed exceedingly intelligent, a kind of oasis of intelligence in a desert of abysmal ignorance. She had felt at ease with him. But had that just been all for show? Was that some sort of glaze over the hatred that springs from ignorance? Calista thought hard. She remembered faces, and even if she hadn't been quite aware of it at the time, she had, on some subliminal level, tucked away several hundred k, as Charley would call it, on this man. The bits and bytes came back to her now, the smallest, subtlest nuances and contours and gestures of the face came back with a full intensity to the eye of a consummate portrait artist. She could see him now so clearly explaining about the further testing and the future colloquium at which a formal announcement would be made. There was a slight quiver in the left corner of his mouth, and with that fragment of an image came the cold sure knowledge: It was the liar's quiver, the palsy under the mask as one tried to lie and look casual, speak falsehoods yet come across as a real person. The quiver was the giveaway. It said, "Are you buying this?" And she, of course, was trying desperately to appear as if indeed she were buying this. So she was probably quivering, too. And then it burst upon her. "God, how stupid!" She put down her glass a little too emphatically, and some of the vodka slopped over the edge. She's have to order another one. "He set us up!"

"Who?"

"Tompkins, that's who. He sketched that map for us. Got us onto that road. There was hardly another car on that road. How do we even know if it would have led us around Dallas and direct to the airport?" Indeed, they had been so frightened that they had gotten off it at the first opportunity and wound their way back onto the main highway as fast as they could. It was so obvious that Tompkins had set them up, and yet they had never really thought of it until that moment. In the sheer adrenaline of the moment, and the aftermath, they had totally forgotten about Tompkins's map and the route supposedly being a shortcut.

"Well, I guess that's evidence," Charley said.

"Sort of. I don't know whether it would stand up in court. Do you still have the map he drew?"

"Somewhere," he said, digging down into his pocket. "Do you think he was the one driving the car, Mom?"

"I doubt it," she said quickly.

Charley looked up. "How can you be so sure?"

"I just have this hunch that he's the kind to get others to do his dirty work for him. He probably has a string of stooges." For some reason she thought of the paint-splattered stuffed Owl

176

figure ghastly in the moonlight of that frozen Cambridge night of two months before.

Charley brought out the small crumpled piece of paper. "Why are we going to have to stand up in court with this evidence?" he asked.

"Well, I don't know, to tell you the truth."

"We weren't exactly murdered."

"You can bet that you don't stand up in court if you're murdered. Attempted murder, maybe."

"But you haven't reported it to anyone," Charley said.

"I know. Somehow I just don't have the faith in cops that perhaps I should."

"We got to do something, Mom. Who do you have faith in?"

"Archie Baldwin," she said quietly.

27

Beth Ann Hennessey felt absolutely rotten all afternoon. She hadn't meant to "blab." What an awful word. It was too close to gossip, which, of course, was a sin. And Wayne Tompkins had accused her of this. She didn't even know him that well, but she would never have expected such an outburst. What had she done to deserve it? She of all people. She squeezed her eyes shut in the glare of the setting sun as she walked across campus. She had to set things right. She had never been in any kind of trouble in her life. She couldn't endure any kind of blemish on her record. It wasn't that she herself had sacrificed so much to come here, but others had so she could be here—Reverend and Mrs. Bottis, not to mention her dear grammy and grandpa. Grammy and Grandpa hadn't any money to spare for things like this, but they had backed her up all the way and were so proud of her. This would be a terrible betrayal of everyone's expectations. She couldn't imagine that this one incident after all her hard work and good grades could really do her in, but she had to have a flawless record and be able to get the best recommendations possible.

She would be a senior the following year, and she was already starting to worry about a job. There was a lot of competition out there for the good jobs—the ones at the counseling centers or the mission support bases and the youth ministry programs. She had never ever done anything wrong or anything to draw attention to herself. For Beth Ann the distinction between the two was not that clear. Well, she was going to settle it up right now. She didn't want Dr. Tompkins going to Tommy Lee Clayton as he had muttered about doing. How was she to know that this stupid skull thing was top secret? No matter, she would go and tell Dr. Tompkins how truly sorry she was and that she would never ever say anything again.

She wasn't sure if she should specifically ask him not to say anything to Dean Clayton. Tommy Lee Clayton had always thought the world of her, and she was counting on him for a good recommendation in her job file. She just wasn't too sure how smart it was to let Dr. Tompkins know how much she was counting on the dean's recommendation. She had liked that mother and son so much, the Jacobses. They just seemed special somehow to her. The boy, Charley, was so friendly and real smart, and his mother . . . well, although she appeared kind of nervous, she also seemed very sweet and kind—real Christian kindness. You could just feel it in her. It must be so nice to have a young pretty mother like that. These were the thoughts that were swirling in her head as she entered the William Jennings Bryan Creation Science Center.

She turned down the long corridor and then through the door of the anthro lab. The place was deserted. She walked through the lab and out a back door that led into a corridor where Tompkins's office was. The door was slightly ajar. She could look in.

"Dr. Tompkins," she said softly.

There was a figure reclining on the couch. She soon realized from the sound of the breathing that whoever it was might be sleeping. She poked her head in a little farther. She certainly didn't want to wake him up if that was the case.

That was the case. But there was something strange. She

178

froze in a posture of dismay. There was blood on his shirt and a big bruise on his cheek. "Dr. Tompkins," she gasped out loud, "are you okay?" He stirred, rolled over on his side, and opened one eye. He didn't seem to recognize her.

"Yeah?" he said roughly.

"Are you okay, Dr. Tompkins?"

There was an ugly little smile, as if he were enjoying some private joke. "Yeah, sure thing. Now why don't you git out an' leave me 'lone."

Beth Ann backed away in a daze. That voice just didn't seem like Dr. Tompkins at all—flat and nasal. But it was he. Even with his bruised cheek and the gash over his eye, it was certainly Dr. Tompkins. He must have had some sort of accident. Suddenly behind her she heard footsteps. They stopped abruptly. Then she heard running. She turned just in time to see the back of a man disappearing where the corridor made a right-angle turn. What in the world was going on here? Beth Ann thought to herself.

Things were made no more clear that evening. Beth Ann had just hung up the phone in her dorm room. "Well, I declare," she murmured.

"What's that?" Her roommate, Sandy, looked up from her white Bible with the gold gilt letters of her name embossed on the cover.

"That was Dean Clayton. I'm getting to go to Bible Times. They got a job for me in the park—at the child-care center."

"Oh, you lucky duck!" shrieked Sandy, and plopped her Bible shut.

"Strange are the ways . . ." Beth Ann didn't finish the thought.

"What are you talking about, strange—this is terrific! It's what everybody would love to do and always has to wait until senior year, usually."

Beth Ann thought a minute. She had been about to blab again. There was no reason for Sandy to know just how strange this really was. This was a blessing, that was all. She must receive it that way. Tommy Lee Clayton hadn't been angry at all when he had called her. In fact, quite the opposite. He was calling up to apologize for what he gathered had been Tompkins's unseemly and rude outburst. It wasn't her fault at all, he had assured her, but, you know, Dr. Tompkins was just one of these weird scientists and had overreacted. He didn't want any more tours given of the science center because of the sensitive nature of the work going on there. These people had to be humored, you know. But Tommy Lee Clayton was not going to humor them at the expense of a fine, hardworking student like Beth Ann. As an apology to her, he felt that they owed her something. So why not take this plum of a job down at Bible Times? A girl in the day-care center had to leave suddenly and there was an opening.

Beth Ann hardly had time to pack her bags and no time to write her grandparents before leaving. The very next day she was on a plane to Lorne Thurston's religious theme park, Bible Times.

28

"There is only one thing wrong with Harvard." The man's florid face pushed across the table toward Archie Baldwin, filling the tight space between them. Just his luck to be seated across from this bozo benefactor.

"What's that?" Archie asked politely.

"They give too many goddamn honorary degrees to women, Jews, and blacks."

Archie was stunned. The words came on a wave of boozy breath. Whoever said vodka didn't smell was wrong. This guy smelled as if he had been marinating in it for days.

"You agree?" the man asked. His name was Hugh Eth-elredge. "You see what I mean?" he whispered as he leaned closer and nodded toward a tall black man at the end of the table.

"I think I see all too clearly what you mean," Archie said, regaining his composure. "For your information, I was the one

180

to suggest that Germain Beyers be appointed to the board of overseers for the Peabody Museum of Ethnography"—Baldwin emphasized the last word, then continued—"and Archaeology."

"You and your goddamn ethnics, Archie." Ethelredge chuckled. "Glad your cousin Neddy isn't that way. Wouldn't have gotten my vote when he was running for governor." And he wouldn't have gotten mine, either, Archie thought, but he refrained from saying anything. Of course, Hugh Ethelredge would never understand that Archie Baldwin and Neddy Baldwin would never vote for each other on anything, but that both cousins would always reserve the last ten days in August to go sailing down east together on the sleek old Hinckley yawl, *Rogue Moon,* as they had for the last thirty years.

Baldwin sighed. "It's not my goddamn ethics. It so happens that Germain Beyers is the best damn lawyer in nonprofits there is, and he's also raised more money for them than you ever dreamed of contributing."

Ethelredge's color rose. One eyebrow flicked and took on an antic life of its own. "I'll have you know, Archie," the man fumed, "that I've contributed over two million dollars to Harvard in the last—"

"I know. And how much did you contribute to *The Green Review,* Hugh?" Archie paused just briefly. "I was sent a copy of it this spring by the Anti-Defamation League as an example of the most vicious and ugly sort of journalism," Archie said, getting up just as the waitress slid a plate in front of him with a glazed petit four inscribed on the top with a crimson H. "Now, if you'll excuse me . . ." He walked away from the table, leaving Hugh Ethelredge fuming and turning as dark as the crimson H.

Archie Baldwin desperately needed some fresh air. He ducked out of the dining room and into the entrance hall of President's House. Every president of Harvard since Lowell until Bok had occupied the elegant Georgian structure at number 17 Quincy Street. Now it was used only for entertaining and special functions such as the one this evening, the semiannual dinner meeting of the board of overseers for the

181

Peabody Museum. Baldwin, of course, was shocked by Ethelredge's remark, yet he had been recruited for this board precisely because the director had hinted that they were in desperate need of fresh blood. The curmudgeon index was becoming intolerably high. The director of the museum had used an excruciating mix of metaphors at the time, actually—fresh blood and deadwood. The metaphor had proved apt, however.

Baldwin had been asked to join the board. They had literally begged him after the Peter Gardiner disaster of eighteen months before. He had been instrumental, along with Calista Jacobs, the eminent book illustrator, and her son, Charley, in uncovering the biggest scam in archaeology ever, which had been operating directly out of the Peabody Museum.

Hugh Ethelredge was obviously part of the deadwood that the director had been referring to. But Baldwin had brought in the fresh blood. Along with Germain Beyers, he had convinced Steve Herbert, a curator from the American Museum of Natural History, to join the board. The director had been jubilant. There had to be a better way of keeping the museum solvent and vital than relying on people like Ethelredge. Baldwin had just not anticipated the remark. Good Lord, why would people like that ever want to sit on the board of a museum dedicated to celebrating the diversity of human culture?

Archie glanced at his watch. He had time for a quick turn around the block before the after-dinner remarks and the slide show. He bemoaned his hard luck of being seated directly across from Ethelredge. His own social life wasn't so great that he needed to waste evenings having dinners with such people. Well, tomorrow night there would be a definite improvement in dining companions.

Calista Jacobs. She had called him, frightened to death. Someone had tried to run her and Charley off a road down in Texas. It had something to do with a strange story of skulls and the death of a colleague of hers. She had sputtered on about visiting this weird college run by that nut Lorne Thurston, whom she also had seen on television with Neddy. It was a complicated tale that she'd said she would rather explain in person—if that were possible. It turned out that he was coming

182

up the next day for the Harvard meeting. So they'd made plans for the following evening.

As he took a turn in the neighborhood, he realized that he was actually quite near her street. He had wanted to see her again. But it seemed as if they were always just missing each other. When he had come to Cambridge last year at the time of the annual meeting, she had been invited by the Rockefeller Institute in Bellagio to come there for a month, a month coveted by many scholars and artists, to pursue her work in the tranquil beauty of the Villa Sebolloni. Then she and her son had traveled extensively in Europe. She also seemed to spend a lot of time at her vacation home in Vermont. Last fall she had been invited to Japan, where her work was being honored. At Christmas, when Archie had come to visit his family in Boston, she had been in Indiana visiting hers.

But tomorrow night he would see her—see her for the first time since the awful time, that crystalline fall day when she had come very close to losing her only child after she had already lost her husband. He tried to picture her face now, but it kept slipping away from him as it had for the past eighteen months. It was, as he remembered, a lovely face, strikingly enigmatic. So at one point he had gone to a children's bookstore in Washington to find one of her books in hopes that there would be a picture of her on the back or inside the dust jacket. What caught his attention on a display table was not a photograph of the illustrator, but an illustration of an incredible swashbuckling cat from her new illustrated book *Puss in Boots*. The cat standing on its back feet in thigh-high boots, a cape flaring out behind, and a plumed hat looked for all the world, in terms of posture and bravado, to be a feline version of Errol Flynn, except for the eyes. The eyes were her eyes—slightly hooded, very dark, with fierce sparkles of light that seemed to suggest other universes, distant and unreachable ones. Had her husband, Tom Jacobs, the astrophysicist, found analogs within his own wife's eyes? When he'd died in the desert in Nevada, bleeding to death from the bite of the rattlesnake that had been placed in his sleeping bag, had he looked up into the black dome of the desert sky, pricked with the light of the stars, and thought of his wife's eyes?

Baldwin slipped into the living room of the President's House just as the first slide was coming on the screen. It was the photograph of an umiak, a skin boat, that would be included in a joint exhibition with Russia that was to highlight East and West's shared cultural heritage through the Arctic connection. Baldwin could feel Ethelredge squirming on his seat with this latest wrinkle in the *glasnost* lovefest.

An hour later Archie was sliding the key into his parents' town house on Louisburg Square. Will and Nan Baldwin had already gone to their summer home on the coast of Maine.

"Archie?" a thin, scratchy voice called out.

"Yeah, Heckie! I'm in, all safe and sound. No need to worry. Didn't wreck the car, no necking on the Common."

There was a sound of parched laughter and a door closing. Heckie, gardener, handyman, sometimes chauffeur when he was younger, and on occasion taskmaster and baby-sitter for various Baldwins in their youth, had stayed up out of habit, a habit of over fifty years. He was now nearing eighty. He had come with Will and Nan Baldwin when they were a young bridal couple and previous to that had been in the employ of Will Baldwin's father, Tut.

When Will Baldwin married, and life promised to become immediately more complicated, Heckie came along, not as a servant, but more as a co-manager with Will and Nan to help run a large house in the city and ride herd over the five children that started arriving almost immediately. Will Baldwin had always been considered slightly odd by the extensive Baldwin family, whose genealogical tendrils, through blood and marriage, had intertwined with Saltonstalls, Warrens, and Cabots over generations of Boston breeding and interbreeding. Will Baldwin not only acted like a Democrat, he actually voted the ticket fairly consistently and espoused a lot of "Bohemian" causes like nuclear disarmament, worker-managed firms, and environmental groups. He had also, in a distinct break with recent tradition, made several millions of dollars in his own ventures. These ventures had ranged from publishing a small chain of local newspapers to getting in at the start-up of some of the mushrooming computer companies out on Route 128 and beyond. "Wang!" Will's uncle had said to him three decades

184

before. This was obviously the first Chinese that any Baldwin had dealt with since the China trade merchants of one hundred and thirty years before.

Archie, Will and Nan's second eldest, was considered as curious as his father. Passionate about his archaeology, he had become the boy wonder of the field thirty years before with his extraordinary work in the desert West and the Paleo-Indian cultures of that region and the nearby Great Basin. He was now considered the dean of American archaeology. Just grazing fifty with close-clipped gray hair and intense blue eyes, he was startlingly attractive but lacked the gregariousness of his father and seemed to present a granitic exterior that women just loved to think they could crack. They seldom did. And when they failed they always went away telling themselves that Archie Baldwin was shy, or that maybe he was gay. He was neither. He just had not found too many women that he felt he could go the distance with. But he had sprinted with several. Of late he was finding these sprints less satisfying.

Now, as he went to his father's study, he could not for the life of him remember Calista Jacobs's face. He should have brought the *Puss in Boots* book with him. It had her picture on the flap, and of course there was that wild cat on the cover and through-out the book with her eyes. He remembered that even the cat's fur looked like her hair. He had brought a beer up with him to his father's study and sat down on an easy chair and began browsing through a *New Yorker*.

It was a curious collision of events, he thought as he looked at the cartoons, his seeing Neddy on television and Calista seeing him. Well, it had been on the national news. But then her going down to that dingbat's college in Texas, and how did her murdered colleague fit into all this? And why was she so scared? Had someone really tried to run her off the road? And these skulls, what was that all about? Come to think of it, hadn't Neddy mentioned something to him about some skull analysis? Well, he guessed he'd find out tomorrow.

Just at that moment the telephone rang.

"Archie . . ." It was his father's sonorous voice. His mother was on the extension. They chatted for a few minutes about some mundane matters such as timing for summer visits and could he please try to make it this summer for a good spell before he went sailing with Neddy, his nieces and nephews so adored him. "By the way," Will said, "I've been meaning to ask you since you got back. Did you by any chance catch Neddy a few weeks ago on the national news with that disgusting Bible thumper?"

"Lorne Thurston? I did indeed."

"It was absolutely mortifying." His mother's voice came through clear and soft. It was always soft, even when she was angry. And he could tell she was now.

"I mean," continued his father, "we always knew Neddy wasn't too smart."

Nan Baldwin spoke crisply. "I, I was so angry about his stand on abortion, but this is even more irksome in an odd way."

"I don't know what we can do about it," Will Baldwin said.

"I don't either. I called him up at the time, though, and bawled him out."

"Good for you, Archie!" his mother trumpeted. "You are a man of action. Well, I think I'll do the same. The more pressure brought to bear the better. Poor Lacey. God, she puts up with a lot."

"Yes, and Little Lacey isn't so keen on the notion of her dad up there with this Bible-pounding jerk, either."

"Is she still thinking about Antioch?" Nan Baldwin asked.

"Yes."

"Terribly refreshing choice, I think," Will added.

"Oh, before I forget, Archie dear, I have a great favor to ask you."

"Anything, Mother."

"Well, your father's underwear is in absolute shreds. Would you mind going to Filene's—the basement, of course—and picking up a dozen boxer shorts for him and some undershirts? Size thirty-six waist on the shorts. Extra large on the shirts. And it probably wouldn't do any harm to replenish your own wardrobe. If you go to the second floor of the basement over on the far left in the men's section, they usually have some good buys on sports coats. I got Will a wonderful Harris tweed on a second markdown for seventy-five dollars."

186

"Okay. I'll look."

"Good, dear. Thank you so much."

29

Calista had been stripping in Filene's basement for years. It was an acquired skill, which, when honed by veterans of the basement, could be raised to a minor art form. Basically one pulled the skirt on over the skirt or the trousers one was wearing and then dropped the nether garment. If you had planned ahead and worn an undershirt, you had it made, for it meant that you could actually strip off your sweater or shirt and try on a new top quite easily without baring too much. But if you had not planned ahead and found yourself just popping into the basement for a quick tour, and indeed discovered something worth trying on, it required a bit more dexterity to put on a blouse or a sweater with a modicum of modesty. Only a modicum was really necessary, as the basement shoppers were so involved in their tasks that eyes were rarely lifted from the merchandise. Next to the marathon it was the most competitive noncollegiate, nonprofessional sport in Boston, and the watchword in any race was never waste time by stealing a glance at the competition.

Today Calista found herself unprepared in the basement but nonetheless trying on a designer top that was on its second markdown. She had not worn a T-shirt under her sweater, and she had not worn a bra. So it was a bit tricky. However, she was very good at this business despite the fact that she did not possess the optimum specs that go into the design of a really great basement shopper. Shortness counted for a lot in the basement because it was really easier to see the merchandise between people crowding around a table than over them. Also, it was easier to strip without being seen if one barely reached the shoulder level of an average shopper. Shortness and a definite stoutness were the ideal attributes for ambushing merchandise and conducting table raids. Once one saw what one wanted on a table, it was often necessary to pry an opening in the crowd. There were certain basement shoppers who could do this with all the efficiency of a cold chisel. This was leverage buying at its most basic.

Being on the tall side and quite lean were attributes that normally would not work to the advantage of a basement raider. But Calista had become so skillful that it didn't matter anymore. She considered herself the Larry Bird of the basement. He looked clumsy. He couldn't jump. He was a white man in a black man's game. But he was so smart that he could look one way and pass the ball the other way. That was what she was doing just then. She had taken off the top and was still holding her sweater to her bare chest when she spotted the silk corner emblazoned with the gold chain links. Knotted gold chains and heraldic stamps meant just one thing—Hermès. Hermès scarves were as rare in the basement, especially in this area of the basement, as orchids in a field of soybeans. Her sensors warned her that there were most likely half a dozen women in the immediate vicinity who would pounce on the scarf in an instant if they spotted it. She looked the opposite way and reached for the scarf. What could be wrong with it?

"Calista!"

Shit! She clutched the scarf to her breast along with her sweater.

"Archie!" She was nonplussed. What was he doing here now? They were both speechless. She felt him look at her bare shoulders with confusion. He didn't understand any of this. He was not a denizen of the basement. It was egregiously obvious.

"You're early." That was all she could think to say.

"I guess so." He laughed, and his fierce blue eyes blazed. Jesus, she hadn't remembered he was so handsome. "I'm kind of lost, actually. I was looking for the men's department."

"Oh . . . oh, really . . . Well, you're in the wrong section. You've got to go upstairs to the second floor."

"But I thought this was the second floor," Archie said, obviously confused.

"No! How could you think that? This is the first floor."

"But first I went to the . . ." He began to point up. His

voice dwindled off. "I mean, wouldn't you consider this going to a second floor even if it's . . . Jesus Christ, this is complicated."

"Oh, I see what your problem is. Yeah, you thought . . . Oh, I get it. It's just a matter of perspective. It's actually quite easy if you think of it in terms of upper and lower level and not first and second floor." Calista's long fingers were jabbing up and down in the air as she explained the levels of the basement. Neither the scarf nor the sweater slipped an inch as she conducted what had to be the longest discourse ever held in Filene's basement. "You know, I'm really surprised at you, Archie, being an archaeologist and all. It's just the old classic stratigraphy. This floor we're on now is the lower level. See, the bottom stratum comes first, is the earliest; therefore, you call it the first floor. Then we move up through the layers of time, or merchandise, as the case is here, and you get to the second level. That's where the men's department is. Just apply your basic geological stratigraphy and you got it."

"Yes, I guess I just never thought of it that way," he said, looking around. "They sell wedding dresses here?"

"Yes, yes, everything. You name it. Listen, just wait a minute while I get dressed, and I'll show you where you need to go."

"Wait while you get dressed?" Again he looked slightly confused. "Should I turn my back?"

"Oh, you're not used to this at all, are you?" Calista laughed and shook her head. "Well, if it makes you more comfortable, sure. But I'm so good at this. I mean, it's like sleight of hand. There're naked ladies all over the place here. It's just that we dress and undress at light speed, so you never see us." And as she talked she pinned the Hermès scarf to her chest with one arm and slipped into her sweater. "Dressed!" she announced. "Oh, wait. I forgot to take off this skirt." Archie blinked as she stepped out of the skirt and stood in her well-tailored slacks. "Okay. Let me just quickly buy this scarf. It's on a third markdown, if you can believe it."

Archie looked baffled. "That's a scarf? It looks the size of a tablecloth."

"Yeah, I think I'm going to make something out of it."

189

Calista paid for the scarf and then led Archie to the upper stratum and the men's department. "Well, here you are," she said. "You think you can find your way out from here?"

"Yeah, I think so." He smiled. He wished she'd stay around a little bit. He would never forget running into her that way. It hadn't been her eyes that had caught his attention in the basement. It had been her shoulders. She had great shoulders, broad, with fabulously elegant bones. "So I'll see you tonight?"

"Yes, of course. What time will you be by?"

"What time's convenient?"

"Well, six-thirty, and we can have a drink first."

"Okay, see you then."

By her calculations Calista had exactly three and one-half hours after she got home to sew the scarf into something to wear for that evening. Queen Elizabeth might wear these scarves to batten down her tight little perms at the horse races, but, by God, Calista was going to turn this into something sensational. Originally the scarf had been at least three hundred dollars. By the time it hit the basement it had been one hundred and seventy-five dollars, and then by the time it was on a third markdown, when Calista got it, it was eighty bucks. Still too much for a head scarf, but quite reasonable for a skirt. She didn't want to do a miniskirt, as was now quite popular again. She loathed kneecaps, especially her own, out of context. But she wanted something mildly sexy.

Gads! She had not remembered Archie as being that attractive. Of course, at the time of their last meeting Charley had just been released from the hospital. No wonder she had not been in a state of mind to observe him more closely. But now she knew that he had a great face, a face that she would draw and that might eventually thread its way into her work. Robin Hood! She had yet to be pleased with the eyes. The face she had found on the subway that day a few months ago was fine for the contours and the structure, but the eyes had not measured up. Archie's eyes! They'd be perfect in that face. Because of the trip to Dallas and all the Caldecott hoopla, not to mention her and Charley's near demise on a Texas highway, her concentration had suffered and there had been scant time to really work on *Marian's Tale.* She planned to get back to it, if not today, tomorrow. A September deadline loomed.

That afternoon, however, found her not drawing faces, but sketching a design for the scarf skirt. Ordinarily a sarong-type look would have seemed appropriate considering the fabric and the fact that this was a scarf with beautifully hand-rolled hems, the hallmark of Hermès superb craftsmanship. The design should interfere as little as possible with the true quality of the scarf. The less cutting and darting the better. But the heraldic print of the chains and shields and ensigns did not look good on the bias. She wrapped the scarf around her and studied her image in the mirror.

"Yuck!" she muttered. At that moment she heard the door slam downstairs. "Charley?"

"Yeah."

"You home?"

"No, actually, Mom, I'm still out. This is my aura."

"Very funny. How was the Martin Institute today?"

"Fine, but I did not find the cure for cancer." She heard him bounding up the steps.

"Oh, shucks." Calista laughed.

"Why are you standing there half-naked wrapped in chains, Mom?"

Calista blinked at her image in the mirror and that of her son's. He had grown, but had he grown up that much? Good Lord, Charley could put things in an odd way. He was not ignorant about sex anymore, or of his mother as a sexual being. But this was a little much. Was this elegant scarf really kinky under its hand-rolled hems? A soupçon of bondage! Is that what Charley was saying? She had never thought of it that way. What did Charley know about such things, anyway? She looked at him, the aureola of red hair, thick and flaming around his still delicate face. The clear gray eyes.

"Well, I'm trying to make it into a skirt to wear tonight."

"Where you going?"

"Remember, Archie Baldwin is coming over and taking me out to dinner."

"Oh, God! Baldwin, I forgot."

191

"How could you forget? I'm hoping he's going to shed some light on this skull thing, not to mention the other events." She paused and looked at him. "I'd really like you to come, too, or at least be here to help me explain it. I still don't quite understand why you can't," Calista said. She did wish he would accompany her. She had never really thought of it quite this way until now. It wasn't just because she needed Charley there to help explain what had happened down in Texas. She could do that fine. She just wished Charley could be there. She knew why. She had found Baldwin uncompromisingly attractive. She had felt something stir within her during that nutty encounter in Filene's basement. She would feel safer, less accessible to her own feelings, if Charley were there. It wasn't fair thinking about her son like this. She could not use him this way. She was ashamed of herself.

"Now what was it you said you were doing?"

"I told you, Matthew and Andrew and I have to go and observe Scott."

"Observe Scott?"

"Yes, he's having a date with Anna Fredkin."

"A date?"

"Yes, a first date."

"How romantic having you three there to observe."

"But you don't understand. Matthew was supposed to have a date, his first date, with Anna."

"So, Scott beat him to the punch."

"Not exactly. Scott knew Matthew was going to ask her, but . . ." He paused. "It . . . you know . . . it just takes a while to build up your nerve to do these things. So Scott should have waited. It was very unfair."

"So do you think it's fair that you three little shy guys go and 'observe' Scott and Anna now? How do you think Anna's going to feel about that? She might never accept a date with Matthew if she sees him doing this kind of stuff."

"We're going to be very casual about it. They're going to the movies and then the Harvard House of Pizza. It's all going to appear very natural. Only Scott is going to squirm."

"Ooh, *les liaisons dangereuse!*" Calista said as she laid the scarf on the floor and began to mark it with her tailor's chalk.

"What's that?" asked Charley.

"Nothing. But why don't you come and observe me on my date with Baldwin?"

"That's not a date," Charley said.

"What do you mean it's not a date?" Calista said, looking up with pins sticking out of her mouth.

"I wish you wouldn't talk with pins in your mouth, Mom. It really makes me nervous. I'm scared you're going to swallow one and die. Then I'd really be an orphan."

Calista removed the pins and began putting them into the hedgehog pin cushion.

"Okay, now tell me why this isn't a date."

"Because you're just old friends."

"We're not such old friends. I've only met him once under very trying circumstances."

"Well, that's just it. It was just an accident."

"But now it's not an accident. When I called him he said he was coming up and that he would love to take me and you to dinner. Not just me."

"Well, see. It's not a boy-girl thing like a date."

"But it's a man-woman thing. I mean, what do you call going out to dinner?"

"Not a date," Charley said, getting up and tossing a little ball in the air.

God, kids could be dogmatic. Charley wandered into his room and dropped the ball into the miniature basketball net that he had on the back of his bedroom door. "Did I tell you I saw Bill Walton in Harvard Square, Mom?"

"No, you didn't. How did he look?"

"Old! Old! The guy had to be at least thirty-eight. I mean, he's almost your age. Matthew was going to go up and ask him when he was going to play again. But I said it wouldn't be nice. He's had so many operations. His knees must look like road maps."

"Charley, what about those incomplete assignments of yours, the geography thing and that other report that you neglected to tell me you hadn't done? If it's not in by the end of the week you get C's. Gee, and how will we ever send your transcript to Lorne Thurston College of Christian Heritage with two C's?"

193

"I've done the geography thing, and the history report is very easy. It's not even a full report, really just a very small, very, very, very minor report on Pliny the Elder. It's a breeze. He didn't do that much."

"I can hear him turning in his grave now. Charley, that's very insensitive of you. How about someday if you were famous, some kid a millennium from now was doing a report on you and referred to it as being a breeze, very small, very minor guy, that Charley Jacobs, didn't do that much. I mean, if you can be so sensitive about Bill Walton, why not Pliny the Elder?"

"Not the same. He's not a Celtic, for one thing."

"He's a Roman, my dear."

"Well, it wouldn't bother me if I spared some kid from having to write a long composition."

At six-twenty she stood before her bathroom mirror in the little navy blue grenadier's jacket she planned to wear with the skirt. It was an Yves St. Laurent jacket, another gem from the basement. She was applying some makeup, which mostly consisted of a variety of moisturizers and eye creams. Gone was her palette of iridescent eye shadows, bright lipsticks, rosy blushes, and even at one time false eyelashes. That had been the makeup of her twenties and early thirties, which she thought of as first-strike cosmetics. Now, over forty, she was into defensive stuff. These creams announced their intentions boldly with their lexicon of vaguely scientific-sounding words like "emulsion" and "hydration." There were references to "moisture traps" and even "antiaging systems," and there was one product with the rather homey but to-the-point subtitle of "dewrinkling, firming cream" for below the eyes. She had bought that last one simply because she was charmed by the sound of the word *dewrinkling,* which apart from its meaning seemed to have a music all of its own. None of it was first strike at all anymore. What it boiled down to was protective reinforcement reaction. She was on the defense, shoring up against the onslaught, the ravages, of time.

She slid into the skirt. It looked terrific. Straight, falling to her midcalf. There was a chic side slash to the knee with welt finishing. To soften the military effect of the jacket she wore nothing underneath except a fake diamond brooch slung on a strand of real pearls against the modest V of her chest. She eyed herself in the mirror. Was the effect too calculated? Of course it was. How could it be anything else? She had been calculating for the last four hours. She pinned up her mop of hair and pulled down a few of her brightest silver strands for bangs. She heard the doorbell ring.

"Charley, can you get that?"

"Okay."

She heard Baldwin downstairs greeting Charley warmly. She stood for the better part of a minute at the top of the staircase, where she could not be seen, and just listened. It sounded so good, their two voices in the front hall. She felt a storm of butterflies, bright monarchs, she imagined, beating their wings madly somewhere within her rib cage. She buttoned the next button up on the narrow little jacket, squared her shoulders, and proceeded down the stairs.

30

It was hard to find a restaurant to talk about murder in. Maybe the Michelin guide should adjust their symbols. Three stars, a fork, a knife, and a gun.

Calista had given a great deal of thought as to where they should go to dinner. She had an idea that Archie would not do well in one of those nouvelle cuisine outfits with plates of food that looked like Mondrian paintings delivered by waiters of dubious gender. The Harvest, which had the best food in Harvard Square, managed to serve it chicly without the nouvelle pretensions, but she felt the place was still too trendy for Archie. And then again the bar at the Harvest was very nearly a caricature of a singles bar with its own Cambridge twist on it. Muttonchops and pop tarts, that about summed up the denizens of the bar. There was always a mélange of aging Ph.D.'s with thick sideburns just out of stale marriages and concupiscent miniskirted young women in horn-rim glasses. It was okay now to show legs, to show boobs. That hard-line power dressing, well, let them do it downtown or in New York. There were also older women at the bar, the ones who knew they were beyond miniskirts but were still on the prowl. Eight, ten years ago they would have been wearing Marimekko dresses, a style Calista particularly loathed with its stiff fabrics and bold primary-color designs. Now, however, Marimekko was out, and these women would be wearing fiber-arts stuff. Sweaters and dresses with collages of knitted and netted appliqué work. Lots of yarn with weird stuff woven in—corks, feathers, you name it. They called it art. To Calista it all came off looking like a trawler's net. In any case, she didn't want to take Archie to the Harvest or her other standby, Legal Seafood—too crowded, too noisy. So they wound up in one of her old haunts from the years when she and Tom had first come to Cambridge, Chez André, halfway between Harvard Square and Porter Square, just off Mass. Ave. on Shepard Street.

The walls of Chez André were painted with some rather poor murals, and the wall-to-wall carpeting was an unfortunate shade of red, but the place was cozy and had an indefinable charm. The tables were covered with fresh white linens, and there was a bud vase with one or two bright flowers on each table. The menu was decidedly French, and the helpings were not at all nouvelle. With the entrées a heap of vegetables came in large covered dishes. No artfully arranged stringbeans on a plate. It was all presided over by a woman whom Calista instinctively thought of as La Maitresse. But she was not the owner. She was the headwaitress and had been for years. She had a beaked nose, a tiny pointed chin, and small dark eyes. She was tall and wore her dyed black hair in a style that had not been seen since the forties. Parted on the side and clamped with a barrette, it came to just below her ears and then frizzed into a little fringe. She always wore a black skirt with a white top and pinned a white cloth around her for an apron. She looked exactly like something out of a French Resistance movie. One could imagine her being quite pretty in her day, seducing Nazi commandants at the Ritz in Paris. After making love, she would slink out of bed to roll up her gartered stockings. Then wiggling her slim but delectable ass in the direction of Herr Goering, she would quickly fit the silencer onto the gun, turn around, and plug him right between the eyes.

"Ah, Madame Jacobs," she said softly, and handed Calista a menu.

Calista took the menu. She didn't even know the woman's name. She hadn't known it for all the years she had lived in Cambridge. And that apparently was the way it was supposed to be. One just knew that instinctively. None of this "Hi, my name is Mirielle, and I'm your server tonight." No, that was not how it was done at Chez André. They ordered drinks first—Archie a beer, Calista a Dubonnet on the rocks. It was a drink she rarely ordered, but it went well with certain restaurants, old-fashioned French ones, the kind with murals on the walls or old posters.

"You like meat, Archie?"

"Yeah, I like meat."

"They've got really good meat here. I don't eat that much meat, but it's so good here."

"Want to go for the Chateaubriand for two?"

That was precisely what she wanted to go for, but she had felt it might be a little forward to actually suggest the Chateaubriand. There were several other meat entrées that one did not have to share, but this one was the best. She nodded. "Yep." And then she paused. "I was kind of hoping you'd say that. It's the best one."

"Then why didn't you say so?" He looked over the top of his menu and smiled.

"I thought it would be forward . . . oh, Lord," she sputtered. "I didn't mean forward. That sounds so weird." Archie was grinning. "Forward about meat . . . oh, dear!" God, she needed a bullwhip for those butterflies that were now rampaging through her. Why couldn't she edit her speech a little bit more? Goddammit, Calista! she scolded herself. Just go ahead and utter any harebrained thing that trips across your alleged brain. She took a deep breath, swallowed, blushed furiously. "What I meant to say was I wanted to give you a choice and not

197

force you into this"—she laughed softly—"meat partnership because they only serve it for two, but you know, the veal is great, and so is the filet mignon."

Archie put down his menu and inclined his head toward her just a bit. "I've already made my choice. I'm glad it's yours."

Holy shit, he was appealing! "Uh . . . me too." She uttered those 2.5 words after some thought. Okay, Calista, get your head together. This is ridiculous. You cannot go through the entire evening putting your foot in your mouth and gasping. As a sobering thought, she reminded herself that she and Charley, a mere three days ago, had nearly been killed, run off the road by some religious fanatic, most likely, and that a dear colleague of hers had been killed two months before. She would just be quiet for a minute, sip her Dubonnet, and collect her thoughts. Archie was giving the order. "What do you want to start with, Calista?" he was asking.

"Oysters," she said crisply.

"Just one order, Madame Jacobs?" Oh, Jesus Christ, how mortifying! How could La Maitresse do this to her? Calista loved oysters more than anything in the world, and she always ordered two plates automatically. But that was two when she had been with her husband or by herself or with Janet Weiss or Ethan Thayer. But this was a date, and Archie was going to think she was Miss Piggy!

"Bring her two," Archie said without batting an eyelash.

"Oh, no, Archie, I couldn't."

"Oh, I bet you could. If you can't, I'll help you out, and I won't feel forced." He smiled and ordered something with artichokes for himself.

He looked at her after the waitress had left. She could be very quiet and still, as quiet and still as she was antic and lively and blushing. She didn't exactly blush when she said some of these nutty, charming things. She flared. You could see these spikes of red cutting across her cheeks and even down her neck. She was perhaps the most vivid person he had ever met. Her eyes, her mind, her language, her silvery hair. But now she was very still.

"You want to talk about this thing, this strange thing that happened down in Texas?"

She raised her eyes toward him slowly. They were hooded and

dark, and they looked a little bit frightened. God, he didn't want this woman to be frightened! Archie felt something deep within him turn, stir, something that had never stirred before in this way.

La Maitresse had just brought the dessert and poured the last of the bottle of wine into their glasses.

"So that brings us up to now," Calista was saying. "Do you think I should have done more in the way of notifying the police about getting run off the road in Texas?"

"The Boston police?"

"Yeah."

"You said you tried."

"I did. Kind of halfheartedly. One of the guys was on vacation, of the two detectives we had originally spoken to when Norman was killed, and the other was out. He never returned my call. They never do. It's unbelievable."

"Well, I think that's your answer. They really don't give a damn about this case."

"But I do. Look, I've been threatened, threatened three times, if you take what they did to my book and poor old Owl as a threat. First that, then the car. Luckily Margaret McGowan is in Scotland."

"Did she receive any more threats?"

"No, not that I know of. Mammy hasn't told me anything."

"Mammy?" Archie's eyes opened wide.

"Mammy's her housekeeper."

"That her name? Mammy?"

"Yeah, but that's a whole other story." Calista waved her hand. "No, as far as I know there's been nothing else sent to her, no threats of any kind."

"Now, can you repeat to me the stuff they said about the skull, or was it skulls?"

"Well, they referred to more than one, I'm pretty sure. And they said, or rather this lovely girl, Beth Ann, said—I know this sounds weird, my referring to her as 'this lovely girl,' but there was something so nice about her and rather vulnerable." She paused. "I really . . ." She stopped again. "I know it sounds nutty, but I really am concerned for her. Anyway, about

199

the skulls, Beth Ann said that they had these skulls that could prove that the races evolved separately."

"Did she say where they came from, where they had found them or dug them up?"

"Not really. Beth Ann talked about some fieldwork combined in a joint expedition for arid lands biology and the search for the ark at Mount Ararat."

"Holy moly!"

"Precisely."

"You mean they actually go out and hunt for Noah's Ark?"

"Apparently."

"So you think that's where they came across these skulls?"

"Well, she implied that it happened during this joint expedition, the one including the arid lands."

"That includes a lot! She didn't say which arid lands?"

"Nope." Calista shook her head.

Archie settled back in his seat and folded his arms across his chest. Calista waited. After a minute or more he began to speak. "I'm assuming," he began carefully, "that these skulls are fake, like the Paluxy footprints. Only this time they're moving more cautiously because they really got caught with their pants down on that one. They're not rushing to announce it for that reason, but there must be another reason, too. If these skulls were real, they would rush to announce it. It's hard for these finds to be kept under wraps for long—too much ego involvement. Paleoanthropology is a field that attracts massive egos. I'm not being critical here. It's just a natural consequence of the discipline— the study of human origins, what could be more fascinating to human beings than their own history? And yet, what could be more volatile in terms of interpretation? One of the best Ph.D. theses in paleoanthropology I ever read was one by a young woman at Yale. It was about the narrative aspects of the science of paleoanthropology. How anthropological accounts of human origins follow some of the basics of the storytelling tradition. Fascinating. She points out how we try to write our own story into these fossils and how the story has changed over the years with our own changing perception of ourselves."

"And this is the case here? These guys trying to write their own story, a racist story?"

"I think so—a racist story or a biblical one that puts it all in the Genesis time frame, or maybe one that combines both themes. Grind any ax they want to."

"But if you say everybody does this, then how do they differ?"

"The other guys use real data. They can't wait to tell the world about finding the oldest common ancestor. Look at the Leakey camps down in Olduvai and Koobi Fora in the Rift valley, or Don Johanson in Ethiopia. My God, every time you open the paper they've found a scrap of something older, a jaw fragment, fossil footprints, a skull. This is the sexiest, the most glamorous, of all the sciences. Louis Leakey made sure of that. Some of these people are better scientists than others, and the very best ones admit their biases and confess readily to the natural biases ingrained in the nature of their work. But all of them still rush to share their finds with the world, because the fossils they find are real, not fake. It is absolute torture for any real scientist to sit on a discovery. They want to get on top of the highest peak and scream the news to the world. They call press conferences in the most godforsaken places imaginable. They practically have hot lines to the *National Geographic*. They can't wait to name the goddamn things they find—often indirectly after themselves, or the region they have become associated with through their work, or perhaps after a benefactor.

"No, this is all wrong in terms of the nature of the field. If these folks have a skull that is real, there is no reason they'd be sitting on it. Even if it wouldn't turn out to be all they hoped, they would still bring it out. Eugene Dubois back in the last century, the guy who discovered the critter that is now known as *Homo erectus,* thought he had discovered our oldest ancestor, an upright-walking ape. The missing link. But the scientific establishment said no. He was so furious he went and reburied the bones underneath the floor in his own house. He didn't agree with them at all, never would. But as a scientist he had rushed back with these bones from Java so that they might be examined, scrutinized, and, he had hoped, welcomed with great applause. Why? Because the bones were real. They were still real even after the rest of the scientific world decided they could not be called the missing link. It was a question of semantics, and it pissed Dubois off royally. But he only hid them away after

201

he had subjected the bones to testing. This is science—formulating hypotheses, sometimes by intuition or analogy, then deducing conclusions that can be tested directly or indirectly by observation or experimentation."

"They do claim to be doing some further testing. That's why they said the skulls weren't available to look at."

"But why haven't we heard about the initial discovery? And if they're doing testing, I sure as hell haven't heard anything about it. I talk to the Berkeley folks almost weekly. The molecular guys out there work hand in glove with the paleoanthropologists now. They got all the hardware to run every kind of test. State-of-the-art stuff. I would have heard about this from them. Good Christ, Vincent Sarich figured out ten years ago how to biochemically determine when humans separated from apes. This would be small potatoes for him to figure out this racial thing. He would have been the first person they would have gone to. No, Calista. There have been plenty of bruised egos in this business when fossils haven't turned out to be as old as someone hoped, or a newly declared species turns out to be the same old thing. Mary Leakey and Don Johanson have been going at it hammer and tongs for over ten years as to whether Lucy, the little three-million-year-old gal from the Afars region, is a new species or not. Bones of contention, that's what this paleoanthropology business adds up to more often than not. But these skulls aren't bones of contention. They are bones of pretension." He paused. "And for some reason your presence down there made them very nervous."

"So what do we do?"

"Try to flush them out. They're looking for the right time to expose this skull, or skulls, as the case might be. We've got to throw off their timing."

31

There was no question of timing—or will she, or would he? It was prim, it was proper, and it was as tense as all get-out. They sat on their respective libidos in Calista's study and sipped brandy. There was no choice because there were three sprawling adolescents in the living room watching a Monty Python movie. They had finished observing Scott and Anna, and now Calista guessed it was her and Archie's turn. But as objects of observation they apparently were not as interesting as Scott and Anna or Monty Python. Charley had come in and talked with them for a while, and Calista had reviewed what Archie had said about the skulls, and then Archie had talked about some people he would call and a bit about how he hoped to flush these guys out. Then Charley went back to his friends, who were going to spend the night, and Calista and Archie were left alone in the study. So they sat there, taut and wary, wary not of each other, but of the situation, and there was nothing more they could say or talk about in reference to the skulls at this point. Archie asked about her work. She showed him some of the drawings from *Marian's Tale,* and there was this great gulf of unspoken things and unexpressed feelings that became almost unbearable. So he left, and when he left he gave her a kind of sideways embrace, wrapping his left arm around her shoulders, the way she had seen coaches embrace players, slightly injured players, in those crushing hugs of empathy. However, it didn't feel like empathy at all. It felt hungry and slightly desperate. But it looked like a coach's hug, so she resisted dropping her head against his shoulder and curling up against his chest forever and a day because after all there were these three boys sprawled in her living room—three skilled observers.

32

"Did you hear?" Louise said as Charley walked into the computer room at the Martin Institute.

"Hear what?"

"Steve is putting our names on that crystallography paper he's doing, and if it's accepted we'll all be famous."

"What? How can he do that?"

"They do it all the time," Matthew said, looking up from his terminal screen. "That's the way it's done."

"What's done?" Steve had just walked into the computer room.

Louise turned to him. "We just told Charley what you said about putting all our names on the crystallography paper that you're going to submit."

"But how can you do that? We didn't write a word of it."

"But your ideas and your work on the protein-folding problems helped me, furthered my thinking. Louise is right. That's the way it's done. The head of the Martin Institute will be named, too, at the very top above my name, and Leventhal, as head of our lab, will be on it, and Felicia and Nate. That is the protocol; everybody in the lab puts their name on the paper whether they've worked on it or not, and oftentimes they haven't even read it."

"Like us," Matthew said. "We haven't read it."

"You should at least read the parts that show the graphs based on the modeling you did. Nate has yet to read it. Felicia has. She helped me a lot with the editing. But don't be shocked, Charley. As I was explaining to Louise and Matthew, this is standard operating procedure in biology. Besides, the paper probably won't be accepted anyhow. I heard that this particular journal has published an awful lot on the topic recently." He walked over to the computer where Louise was working. "Meanwhile, back at the ranch here, what are my mentees coming up with? Have you solved the intellamine, intellicone problem?"

"Nope," Matthew said.

"Oh, by the way, Charley. How was Texas? What with the Fourth of July weekend and all, it feels like ages since I've seen you."

"Oh, it was fine. Interesting." But Charley's mind was suddenly skipping ahead—or actually back, he realized. When Steve had mentioned intellamine, something had clicked in his brain, and why hadn't it clicked down in Texas when they had stood in that lab with Beth Ann and heard that wacko tale of skulls and races? Why had he not thought of those elusive brain proteins, the neurotransmitters, then, and the experiments that seemed to be coming up with evidence that intellicone was apparently absent in black people?

"It was so hard reading those papers," Matthew complained. "They were beyond us."

"Look, I'm your mentor. What didn't you understand?"

"All of it," Louise moaned. "Or at least as far as I got."

Steve scratched his chin and looked at his charges. "Okay, you guys," he said thoughtfully, "I'll buy lunch today."

"Yeah!" they all cried.

"Hold it!" Steve said, lifting his finger. "It's not going to be at Mary Chung's."

"Oooh!" they all groaned.

"We'll order in if you want, but the deal is we get the west conference room and I lead you through these articles. But you got to try reading them first and write down your questions."

Five minutes later Steve had brought in the articles and tossed them on a table. "Well," said Charley, picking up one. "Let's see . . . one, two, three, four, five, six, seven, eight. Eight authors on this one. How many do you think actually read it or worked on the project?"

"Don't know," said Steve. "But they're from good places— Duke, University of Minnesota, University of Pennsylvania."

"What's this Coastal Research Institute?" Louise asked.

"It's an institute, kind of like Martin, not quite the same power or clout or money. But it's loosely connected with Stanford, the way the Martin is with MIT. The head of it is James Atwell, a biochemical engineer. He's done a lot of work in cryogenics. Okay, kids, start to work. See you in two hours."

"Wait a minute!" Louise said. "First things first. Who's going to order from Mary Chung's?"

"You can. But please don't spend the whole morning figuring out the order or I'll have to delete your names from the cyrstallography paper."

He started out the door.

"One more question!" Charley called after him. "Is Mary Chung's name on the paper?"

"Jacobs, what a wiseass you are." He waved and left.

"Not wiseass enough to figure this out," Matthew muttered.

"It's so boring," groaned Louise.

The three youngsters plugged away for the better part of an hour marking up the papers with highlighters and scribbling questions in the margin. "I don't understand a darn thing I'm reading," Matthew finally said. "I mean, I can kind of interpret these graphs, but there's nothing I know about in these papers."

Charley looked up suddenly. "You're right, Matthew. There's nothing we know about!" And he had been reading hard, trying to link up the hypotheses of these papers, all the stuff about neurotransmitters and the stuff he had heard about down in Texas. How could you link bones with molecules, fossils with proteins? he wanted to know. He knew a little bit about both, but one thing suddenly startled him. For over three months they had been working on models of protein structures, similarities in the primary structures of proteins and how they mapped to tertiary. It was sort of interesting work, but hardly earthshaking and definitely not a priority. Yet so far in these papers not one had addressed the subject of structure in regard to intellamine and intellicone.

"Have any of you guys come across the words *primary structure* or for that matter *tertiary structure* in these papers?"

"No, come to think of it," Louise said.

"Me neither." Matthew shook his head. "But I'm a slow reader, especially with this stuff."

Charley's face was lively. "Hey, guys, that's our question! That's the most interesting question around. How come there's nothing about structure in all these papers? Steve had said that in the very earliest papers there was something. But in these, nothing."

"But we're not sure," Louise said cautiously. She was a robust girl with a thick mass of curly black hair. "We'll have to read everything first. I mean, it still might crop up."

"Don't be ridiculous." Charley jumped up. "You want to die of boredom? We don't have to read all this stuff to find out."

"The scanner!" Matthew shouted.

"Right-o."

Along with its marvelous machines for splicing DNA and synthesizing peptides, the Martin Institute possessed another wonder that did neither of these but instead was a computer that could encode written text into binary symbols directly from paper into its memory and then scan it. For some peculiar reason the folks in the computer center had named it Susie Q. So while Susie Q did her work scanning for the key words of the question—*primary, tertiary, protein folding,* and *structure*—the children spent twenty minutes arguing over their order to call in to Mary Chung's. When they came back with the food, Charley, who had been left to monitor Susie Q, greeted Louise and Matthew with a single word: "Zilch."

If Steve was impressed with his mentees' question, he was even more impressed with their newfound zeal. First they had requested the earlier papers on intellamine and intellicone, where structure at least had been initially mentioned. Based on these, it looked to Steve as if they were going to try and do some mapping of their own. The kids were staying late and coming in early. They were doing boring stuff, or so it seemed to Steve, making long, laborious correlations of everything they had discovered to date. There was foot after foot of computer printout listing the regularities in all of the hundreds of proteins for which they had made structural models. When Steve saw how gung ho the kids were, he was not only pleased to let them run with it, but gave them all the help he could. More specifically, he requested that one of the hotshot programmers, Liam Phillips, come down and help them figure out a sorting and categorization program so they could organize and compare the regularities even more quickly. This sped up their work immensely.

Liam was an elfin-looking man of indeterminate age but

probably closer to thirty than forty. He had black electric hair that stood out around his head in a full-voltage nimbus of darkness. He took a swallow of his Coke and sat back. "So now that you've got all this data so neatly cubbyholed and observable, what are you going to do with it?"

Both Louise and Matthew looked at Charley. It was his project, ever since he had told them of the strange events at Lorne Thurston College. So it was for him to speak.

"There are these new brain proteins, and we just want to see how their structures compare with all the proteins we've already got structures on."

"You're just mapping the structures of these babies, right?" Liam asked.

"Yeah. Why?" Charley asked.

"You running any energy tests on these new brain proteins?"

"Energy tests?" all three kids asked.

"Yeah. How much free energy there is running round in the molecules of them. Another guy and I wrote a program for calculating free energy in molecules of structure proteins."

"No shit!" Charley gasped. "That's great. Gives us another thing to look at beyond the structure."

"Before the structure. They can only have so much free energy to exist."

"No kidding. So you know the energy range on all these proteins we've already been working with?"

"Sure. You don't even have to run the test on them. I'll just bring a disk down with all the data, and you can feed it into what you already got. Then you can run the program on these new brain proteins and see how it compares."

They would work for four days nearly around the clock, going in at seven in the morning and coming back after midnight. The Martin Institute fed them and gave them cab money, or rather Steve got it out of petty cash. He didn't inquire too closely as to what the kids were doing, but he knew they were going and going hot. He figured they'd come to him when they wanted to. They did at eleven o'clock on the fourth night.

The three youngsters stood in front of him, looking wan and somewhat exhausted but excited nonetheless. Charley jammed his hands into the pockets of his jeans and took a deep breath. "Guess what?"

Steve looked up and blinked. "What?" he said quietly, but there was a funny little pulse jumping around in his temple.

"They blow up."

"You ran the energy program of Liam's?" The three kids nodded. Steve coughed slightly. "Both of them—intellamine and intellicone?"

"Yep," said Charley.

Louise shook her head. "They can't exist. There's so much free energy they simply cannot exist."

"Not stable, huh?" Steve said.

"They'd just blow themselves apart," Charley said.

"Not only that, Steve." Matthew spoke. He was holding a sheaf of computer printout. "You should see the other stuff besides the energy thing. They have none of the regularities found in any of the other proteins we've mapped."

Steve smiled quietly to himself. This was where drudgery paid off. What the kids had done was to begin to sequence or, as Steve liked to think of it, walk a peptide chain of the amino acids that made up proteins that were in turn governed by DNA, the genetic coding molecule. A protein could be as many as four thousand bases of these amino acids. They had looked at a few thousand of these proteins to see how they folded into primary and tertiary structures and now added their own twist to calculate how much free energy each protein could maintain without literally falling apart, or blowing apart, as they called it. There was a critical mass beyond which a protein could not maintain its internal structure before disintegrating. There was nothing elegant that they had to do. All that, the designing and cloning of the probes, the splicing and recombinant work of the DNA, which governed the synthesis of these structural proteins, had been done by others. Even the rough sequencing and mapping had been done. All the kids had to do was to look at the tiny stuff and just search for patterns. It wasn't that these patterns didn't matter. It was just that searching for them was not top-, or even mid-, level priority in cancer research work. It was an all-guts-no-glory job.

In physics they might call these small patterns and correlations that the kids were looking for the butterfly effect—a syndrome that suggests that the fibrillations in the air caused by the wings of a butterfly stirring in Melbourne, Australia, could affect weather changes the following month in London. The technical name for the phenomenon was "sensitive dependence on initial conditions." Steve preferred the more lyrical name of butterfly effect, and he began to think of his young charges standing before him not as mentees, but as butterflies. They had stirred their wings, but now it was up to Steve to reveal that the elusive brain proteins of intellamine and intellicone were not simply elusive but illusive and positively mythical.

First, however, Charley had to tell him the rest of the story—why and how he had been willing to stay up for four nights in a row doing the dreariest task imaginable and drag his two friends along with him as they tiptoed through the proteins. And when he had finished late that night, Steve Gillespie was very nearly mesmerized by the possible cascading results of this particular butterfly effect. After he had put the kids into a cab that evening, he headed down Main Street toward the Charles River. As he crossed the Longfellow Bridge he stopped at the midway point and looked down at the dark, placid waters passing underneath the bridge—billions upon billions of molecules flowing down the river to the locks and into the harbor of Boston. Beneath the recognizable patterns were events, phenomena that could be called random because they were unseeable, incalculable—chaotic. But perhaps not. He thought of his three butterflies, three little butterflies flitting around within the structure of the Martin Institute amid the soaring of the eagles, the Nobel laureates who headed labs and brought in millions of dollars to support their research and wrote papers that these three butterflies could barely get through. He looked at the dark, still waters of the Charles and thought of the poem so often cited to illustrate the butterfly effect:

> *For want of a nail, the shoe was lost;*
> *For want of a shoe, the horse was lost;*
> *For want of a horse, the rider was lost;*
> *For want of a rider, the battle was lost;*
> *For want of a battle, the kingdom was lost!*

Now what precisely was the battle being fought here, and who were the riders? And the kingdom—what kind of a kingdom did these people who had faked the proteins envision? He shuddered, feeling a chill pass through him on this very hot July night, and continued walking quickly across the bridge toward Boston.

33

It had been the second night that Charley had worked late down at the Martin Institute. He had told his mother that he would be working well into the night along with Matthew and Louise for most of the week. Steven Gillespie had assured Calista, as well as Matthew's and Louise's parents, that he would see the youngsters home safely, either driving them himself or sending them in cabs. All the parents were pleased that their children were so zealous about their work, and although it was another three and a half years off, not one parent did not indulge himself or herself in projecting how nice this would all look on a college application.

Calista probably indulged herself less than the other parents, however, not because she was any more confident about her son's prospects, but because, goddammit, it was very hard to think when one's hormones were in such tumult. She had long ago passed beyond mere horniness. It was there all right, but in a somewhat fossilized form. She did not, however, think of Charley's long nights at the institute purely in terms of enhancing him as college material. No. These nights could be a window in the long night of celibacy. But Archie was gone. Gone to see his parents in Maine! That really bugged her. And gone to do some preliminary snooping before he began flushing out these latter-day Piltdowners. That was a name that she had come up with and that Archie had begun to use.

He had been gone now for three days. Calista never went to bed before Charley got home. She couldn't, because although

211

she could sleep, it was not a real slumber, thick and soft. It was more like a thin, scratchy blanket pulled over her on a chilly night. She would only half sleep in a kind of prickly somnolence, awaiting the turn of Charley's key in the lock. So she had decided to work. She didn't need daylight or north light. She mixed her colors, trying to duplicate the effects of the old formulas by beefing up the acrylics with an odd assortment of stuff that ranged from egg yolks to crushed stamens of tiger lilies in her search for the fabulous colors she had found in the books of hours. She had gone back to Houghton Library twice more to pore over some of her favorites. In the narrative of *Marian's Tale,* Marian had just escaped the convent that Friar Tuck had helped her get into because of the persistence of Prince John, soon to be King John. She had to escape because of a crooked prioress. Not exactly crooked, but she certainly knew which side her nonsacramental bread was buttered on, and when she found out that the pimply prince was on the prowl for Marian, she was all too ready to turn her over before she got locked in as a bride of Christ. Heaven's loss, another kingdom's gain. Of course, Calista hadn't exactly written it so coarsely in the book. It all was done with great delicacy and followed the old narrative traditions of maidens in distress being pursued by ugly guys. The twist here was that this particular maiden went from relative passivity to activity. Tuck was an all right fellow, but he had gotten her into this pickle, and thank you very much, she would get herself out of it now.

It was a month later in the story than when the book had opened, so the green had to be greener, and of course Robin Hood was going to show up. Calista had figured out the face for Robin—it was the guy on the subway with Archie's eyes. But the resemblance ended there. This Robin was dreamy, slightly disorganized, and unsure of himself, and he didn't shoot as well as Marian. Not great on people skills, either, and his band was not a merry band at all when Marian arrives. They were grumpy, fractious, and disorderly. The story, however, was not really about how she whipped them into shape, but of subtler things about her experiences alone in Sherwood Forest. Marian actually spent very little time with the band in Calista's version, and there was to be no love story. She took forays into Nottingham and surrounding villages, always disguised, rather like the Scarlet Pimpernel, and performed daring feats of service and espionage. The plot revolved around her rescue of a baby. Good old Marian! Calista thought as she painted the scene where she swam in the tumbling waters of a stream. "No pubic hair, please!" she whispered, and shuddered as she thought of the diapers painted on Nick. How obscene that had been. The rush of the foam, the curling of water, provided the natural camouflage necessary for a mature young woman appearing nude in a children's book. There was simply no way you could show tits and ass of any female over the age of ten in a picture book. This Calista knew and accepted.

The telephone rang.

"Charley?"

"Nope. Archie."

"Oh, goodness."

"You expecting Charley at this late hour?"

I certainly wasn't expecting you, she thought. "Well, he's been working really late over at the Martin Institute, and he usually calls around now to tell me what time he'll be heading home."

"Oh . . ." The word hung there in the air for just a fraction too long. Was she reading too much into it—that "oh" and then the little oval of silence that followed? "Well, I just happen to be in Harvard Square, and seeing as I'm not a street singer and don't find their songs particularly fetching tonight, I thought I might walk over."

"Oh!" Her "oh" this time, and another oval of silence. She swallowed. "Yes. Oh, do! I'd love to see you. Oh, goodie!" She rolled her eyes at herself. God, why did she always say these stupid things? She had to be the only person over forty who still said "goodie"! If there was one thing that Calista was not, it was cool. She had no way of sounding detached or even moderately disinterested if she was otherwise. She was, in short, your basic bag of exclamation points, asterisks, and other emotional punctuation marks.

Ten minutes later there was a knock on the door. She opened it. He stood there for just a second on the other side of the screen door, his face still but smiling, and even in the night she could see the fierce blue of his eyes. She felt as if he were drinking her in for that sliver of time. Then he came in. No more coach's hugs. He wrapped her up. She felt his chest against her and she felt his heart beating and his face crushed down upon hers in one long deep kiss and she opened her mouth slightly and when he had finished he said, the words hitting her someplace between her nose and eyelid, "When does Charley come home?"

"Late."

Everything strained and ached within her. Everything seemed to be open and ready. They stumbled into the study because there was no way they could make it upstairs in time. She was wearing yellow nylon running shorts, high-top sneakers, and a tank top with no bra. Archie's hand was plunged down into her shorts, and she could feel him hard against her. His voice was hoarse. "We don't have to have any awkward conversations about anything. I bought enough condoms to last into the next millennium."

"What a gent! Please get your pants off," she whispered as they crumpled onto the Oriental rug.

He didn't get them all the way off. He didn't even get his shoes off. But she peeled off everything except her high-tops. He probed her with his hand and then took his hand away and pressed his pelvis against her, not yet entering her, while he tore open the condom. She didn't know how she could wait a second longer. "I'll help you." She took the opened package and withdrew the condom. He lifted himself into a push-up. "You're beautiful," she whispered, looking straight down at his erect penis. "All over."

"You're not exactly ugly yourself," he said.

She laughed low, from the back of her throat, and slid the condom onto him. If he felt this great in her hands, Jesus, she couldn't wait. He drove into her—slow and hard. And they fitted together perfectly—like a billowing sea and a clipper ship. They rocked and swelled. He plowed and she rose again. They did it once. They did it twice. They did it again. They went through all sorts of weather together, and sometimes for

Calista, especially when he came, it felt as if it were raining silver inside her.

Charley called at two-thirty. He'd be home in thirty minutes. They hadn't exactly intended to do it again, but they had been standing nude at her drawing board and Archie sank onto the stool and looked down at his crotch. "I can't believe it," he muttered to his rising penis. He then gazed up at Calista, who looked so lean and tan and silvery. "Please!" And she climbed on him right there, laughing.

"I hope we don't mess up your painting."

"I paint in plastics."

He left minutes before the cab pulled up with Charley.

34

In that drowsy penumbra between night and dawn, she awoke. She watched the earliest, weakest pink from her bedroom window steal over the world, filling the sky with its early tint as if it were some enormous transparent rosy balloon. It hovered briefly, this dawn color, and then began to drift on to a new dawn in another world.

She had once seen a dorado fish caught by her father in the Florida keys go through spectacular transformations of color, colors that would shame a rainbow, and she was reminded of this as the pink of the dawn stole into her bedroom and turned the cool gray walls fuchsia for moments only.

But she was far from thoughts of dying. She basked in the memories of her splendid night of lovemaking with this most wonderful man. She looked over at two very small Georgia O'Keeffe charcoal drawings that she had bought with the great windfall of royalties from *Puss in Boots*. She remembered what O'Keeffe had once said about her work: that she arrested beauty to arrest people and stop them from the business of their busy lives. Calista had always liked that notion, and suddenly she realized that for the first time in a very long time she herself had been arrested—arrested by beauty and love and some deep, unnameable goodness that seemed to flow out of Archie. And it was not only deep, this kind of love she was feeling, but it was deepening. She felt it within her. She felt something melt and turn and flow; some kind of spiritual unlocking and tranquillity was upon her at last. As she stared at those austere, dreamlike images of O'Keeffe's, she thought of the painter's later works— the huge monumental flowers with their vivid, intense colors and complicated interiors revealed by unfoldings of soft petals. She had become one of those flowers last night under the touch and the press and the rhythms of Archie. She fell back to sleep. When she awoke again shards of bright sunlight crashed through the window and something shrill scratched the air. There was a flash of blue outside her window. Goddamn blue jays! They were always batting around the southeast corner of her house screeching and squawking—the yentas of the bird world!

The telephone rang. Jesus, what time was it? She fumbled for the phone and blinked at her clock. Nine o'clock! Charley must be gone already.

"Hello."

"Hi . . ."

"Archie!"

"Yeah. I love you."

"Oh, Archie!" And that was all she could say. She loved him, too. But the word couldn't even begin to encompass her feelings. She remembered Woody Allen struggling with the inadequacies, with the brevity, of the simple little word in *Annie Hall,* or was it *Manhattan*? "I am in lurve with you," he had said to Diane Keaton, trying to stretch out the word, making it an oozing proclamation of love—an avowal. But Archie did not use words promiscuously. So it had been hard enough for him to say the word *love,* but the *r* was implied—she knew it, and she knew that this was an avowal that even Racine wouldn't flinch at, and certainly not Calista. They talked some more. He planned to fly to Washington that day.

"I want to talk to my cousin Neddy about this face-to-face."

216

"Maybe you better not mention my name."

"Why not?"

"He might tell you about our face-to-face encounter."

"Yours?" he asked, bewildered. "Where did you and Neddy ever get together?"

"At a WGBH fund-raising benefit."

"Oh, that's right—he's on the board. He's on so many boards, I can't keep them all straight."

"Well, he asked me to dance."

"I can think of worse things he could have asked you to do." Archie chuckled. "Pardon me, I shouldn't say 'worse.' But what did he do? Step on your toes fox-trotting?"

"No, dear. I stepped on his in the redneck shuffle. It was just before I went to Texas. But I had caught his stellar performance with Lorne Thurston on the news."

"This might not be news to you, but my cousin Neddy is not that smart." Calista resisted saying, "Yeah, and the pope's Catholic."

"In any case, we're very close. There's a bond between us, and it really pains me to see him making a fool of himself. I want to go down there and talk to him directly about all of this. But, Calista, believe me, my main goal is not to salvage Neddy. I want to get to the bottom of this skull thing and see what the connection is with you and possibly the death of your friend. I told you that I had talked to Neddy after I had heard him on the news and he mentioned some kind of evidence that the people at Thurston's school had come up with, and it did involve skulls. I had thought at the time that it was some antievolutionary, pro-creationist stuff. From what you say, these skulls were supposed to prove separate evolutionary histories for the races. So that isn't precisely antievolutionary. But I suppose if they could come up with a racist-creationist scenario, that might let a few fossils into the game; a kind of revisionist version that excludes apes but allows for separate evolution of races. You know—have their cake and eat it, too, any port in a storm."

"Sounds kind of complicated to me," Calista said.

"Well, if it sounds complicated to you, I don't have to tell you how complicated it must sound to Neddy."

"Yeah." She laughed.

"Did you really step on his toes—or was that metaphorically speaking?"

"I did worse." She paused. "I stopped dancing with him."

The image was vivid in Archie's mind. He could almost hear the music and see the other dancers, and he could envision Calista still as death in her cold rage and Neddy stunned as he had never been stunned before. It was an image that would stick with Archie for a long time.

35

It was too hot to be outside in Washington. So instead they sat in the winter garden room. It was a perfectly appointed room with a cool green-and-ocher tiled floor, dark wicker furniture, and giant Chinese floor vases erupting with soft explosions of Boston ferns. At one end of the room a tall mirror with a curved top and set-in trelliswork reflected the garden behind the Georgetown house that had been lovingly cultivated over the years by Lacey Baldwin. Lacey was not there. She was at their summer home in Maine. The kids were all away, and so apparently was the maid. A thin layer of dust covered the surface of the English and French antiques. Sofas and chairs in the living room were draped in white covers.

There were no fresh flowers, and Neddy Baldwin, like many a summer's husband, found this his perfect season. There were no restrictions. Long weekends were the norm. The exodus began on Thursday, sometimes as early as Wednesday afternoon. Men of power commuted to summer residences on Martha's Vineyard, the Cape, Nantucket, Northeast Harbor, Maine—often in private jets. But there was really no end to the weekends for some of these men. It seemed to continue in spite of the fact that they returned on Sunday nights. They returned to empty houses with draped furniture such as Neddy's and often a lovely woman waiting upstairs, if she were the kind of woman you could trust to let herself in discreetly. It was the best of all possible worlds. Thursday through Sunday you ate lobster, sailed with children and grandchildren, uncorked bottles of champagne, and made clever toasts to your wife's prize rose that had been recognized by the American Rose Society and bloomed as it had never bloomed before. You even played croquet with your eighty-five-year-old mother and let her cheat, and there was always good bridge. Then you came home and fucked your brains out for the rest of the week. Nice.

Archie had never seen his cousin looking better. He would refrain from saying that, however, because it might lead to a reference to Neddy's current fling, and that was always uncomfortable. For although they were the closest of cousins despite their many differences, and they could discuss almost anything, there was a code. And part of the code was that they could not or would not talk about Neddy's infidelities because that would be a way of doubly hurting Lacey. It was not a question of Archie's approving or disapproving of Neddy's sex life. It was a question of another kind of disloyalty to Lacey, one that would involve not merely Neddy, but Archie, too, if he had begun to discuss these girls of Neddy's. Archie cared for Lacey. Lacey knew, of course, that Neddy had had his flings. Perhaps there were more than she was aware of, but Lacey and Neddy had come to some kind of an understanding. It was, however, an understanding between Lacey and Neddy and not Lacey and Neddy and Archie.

"So, cousin, what brings you here?" Neddy said, settling into a wicker chair and opening his can of beer. "Isn't this wonderful, by the way?" he said, lifting his can.

"What, the beer?"

"No, drinking it from the can. You know I can't do that when Lacey's around—always glasses."

God, Neddy was simple. Now Neddy knew that Archie knew what was probably going on here, and it was more than drinking beer from a can, and remarks like this one just underscored it. "You know, it's just so much easier in the summer. I don't have the maid except once a week or so. Half the time I eat those TV dinners. Life is simpler. Really pared down."

"Sounds like you're ready for Outward Bound," Archie said.

Neddy threw back his head and laughed. "Not quite, fella! Hey, those dates in August still okay with you?"

"Yeah," he said tersely. The image of Calista absolutely still amid the dancers was incredibly vivid in his mind. What had Neddy done at the time? Had he said anything?

"What's troubling you, Archie? You seem a little out of sorts."

Archie looked up. How was he to begin? "Uhh . . . Neddy . . ."

"Oh good Lord, Archie, are you still upset about me and the preacher Thurston?"

"Yes."

"Now look, Archie, you and I both know that although I no longer hold elective office, and"—he raised his hand to emphasize his next point—"I have no intention of running for anything in the foreseeable future, the work I do—this ambassador-at-large stuff, all these presidential commissions and panels—it's politics. And don't let anybody fool you about that." He narrowed his eyes.

"You trying to tell me you're not a statesman?"

"You can't be a good statesman unless you're a politician, and I for one don't think 'politician' is a dirty word."

"You saying your neighbor over there two blocks away, Averill Harriman, was a politician?"

"The best. He only indulged himself in all that statesman crap when he got too old. Loved the guy. Wife's a pain in the ass. And he loved politics."

"I don't know. I remember that 'joy of politics' speech Hubert Humphrey gave years ago. Somehow I don't think of being on the same platform with that kook Thurston as being a joyous experience in politics."

"It isn't. The guy's an asshole. Although not as bad as you might think."

"But why are you with him? What's the angle?"

"It's a constituency down there."

"Are you trying to tell me that the president is worried about them? He won a landslide victory."

A look of relief swept across Neddy's face. Archie noticed it immediately. Had Neddy been tense before that? He hadn't

220

realized it at the time, but now his face seemed more relaxed. Was that really it? The president worried about these fundamentalists as a constituency? But Archie had the strange sensation that he had led Neddy to this conclusion—when he had asked what was the angle. Was this the real angle?

Neddy was off and flying. He was quoting statistics. "Do you realize that two point four million American households tune in daily to Lorne Thurston? And Jimmy Swaggart, Jim Bakker, and Oral Roberts are just behind him. Now, would you rather have one of them for president or keep the one we got, even though I know he's not your first choice? We're talking power here, Archie, my boy. And they don't want to see one of those ham-fisted louts from the White House down there. They want to think they're talking to a cabinet officer or better."

"They want to see a statesman."

"Precisely."

Had the president actually sent Neddy? Well, it really didn't matter because what Archie wanted to find out about were those skulls and if they were part of the evidence that Neddy had mentioned to him over the phone. Maybe the president had sent him to assure those guys about the Louisiana ruling that would be coming up. Maybe it had something to do with a Supreme Court appointment. In a few very tight Washington circles there were rumors about one justice and his prostate. That was enough to send the world into a tizzy if it got out. But now he just wanted to find out about this so-called evidence.

"All right, Neddy. Look, here's what I really want to know. On the phone when I called you that night after I saw the broadcast, you mentioned some sort of new evidence that was going to prove something or other about evolution. I want to know what it was. Frankly, I don't give a shit what you do, with whom, or why."

But why had he said "why"? There was a little click in Archie's brain when he realized this. These guys had their hooks into Neddy, and it wasn't because any president had sent him down there to massage egos or make promises about Supreme Court appointments. This realization flooded his brain, and he barely heard what Neddy was talking about. The evidence that Neddy talked about was referring more or less to some loony-tune hypothesis about the Flood being the product of some greenhouse effect and blocking the lower atmosphere from cosmic radiation. He didn't mention the skulls. Archie had heard all this other stuff before. It was the standard line issued by some Center for Creation Studies out in California. Now Neddy was going on about some top scientists, "real Ph.D.'s coming down to Thurston's college."

"Real Ph.D.'s as opposed to fakes?"

"Archie!" Neddy sighed. "You know what I mean. They're getting guys down there that have more than a degree from a two-year Bible college. They're not just ordained ministers teaching biology courses."

"Well, there's nothing worse than an ordained biologist. I'll tell you that right now!" Archie said, looking Neddy straight in the eye.

36

"Does this bedroom remind you of Lady Jane Grey?" Calista asked, yawning. Archie had caught the seven o'clock shuttle back to Boston from D.C. He was in Cambridge by eight thirty. And Calista and he were in bed by eight thirty-five. They had, in fact, made it to the bed this time.

"What?" Archie propped himself on his side and traced with his finger the hollows around Calista's neck and collarbone and then ran his finger down between her breasts. "You mean that English girl in the Tower of London?"

"Yeah, the one beheaded by Queen Mary."

"Well, no, actually not. I wouldn't say the bedroom reminded me of her at all."

Me neither. But I did it over, painted it and all, a year or so ago, and my editor, when she saw it, she said that. She said it looked so austere and virginal. Although I guess Lady Jane wasn't really a virgin. They'd married her off to the duke of Suffolk or somebody like that."

"Well, it reminds me of you. And I don't think austere or

virginal are two adjectives that immediately come to mind when I think of you."

"You getting hungry for dinner?"

"Possibly."

She had had all day to plan dinner. She hoped it wouldn't look too elaborate. But there was no denying that she had been so excited that she had felt all that day like a teenager preparing for prom night with a favorite beau. She had run over to a fish store on Huron Avenue and bought soft-shell crabs. And then she had sawed off a few ounces from her precious stock of frozen gravlax. Once every other month or so Calista made gravlax by smothering filets of Norwegian salmon in a mixture of kosher salt, sugar, and Lap Souchong tea leaves. She then weighted them with a brick for five days in a dish in the refrigerator. The stuff froze beautifully. She served it on thinly sliced bread that had been spread with ginger butter and a dab of what Charley called her weird mustard sauce, which meant that it wasn't made with French's and that it had "foreign matter" in it in the form of chopped dill weed. She had made a cold vegetable salad of dilled peas and cucumbers and had been toying with the idea of steamed potatoes. But they had decided to do it one more time, and that meant there wasn't really time to fuss with the steamed potatoes. Sex was vastly superior to potatoes. The thought struck her just as they had finished doing it and Calista, who had been on top, was sitting astraddle Archie. She looked down into his intense blue eyes. "Love's not a potato. You can't throw it out the window," she said softly.

"What?" Archie laughed. He was still inside her, and she could feel him laugh way, way up.

"It's an old Russian proverb."

"Whatever made you think of that—do I remind you of a potato?"

This time Calista laughed, and he could feel her. "Great! Lady Jane Grey and the potato. What a pair! No, you don't remind me of a potato. It's just that I decided not to make the potatoes when we made love again 'cause there wouldn't be time."

"Oh! Any more proverbs?"

"Oh, dear, I just thought of one, not a proverb, exactly."

"What is it?"

"You know what my mother told me when I got married, her advice to the bride?"

"No? What was that?"

"Never get on top after thirty-five."

They both started to laugh now. "Why the hell not?" he asked.

"Because, you know, everything starts to droop—droop down."

If blushing could ever be called violent and aggressive, this was it, Archie thought as he gazed up at her. Once more the red spikes raked across her jaws and down her neck. No slow suffusion of capillary action gently tinting the skin here.

"You're not so droopy," he said.

"Jeez, Archie, you sly, silver-tongued old fox, old honey lips. Last night, what was it—'You're not so ugly yourself'—and now 'You're not droopy.' Blow me away with all this romantic talk! I hope nobody's taping this conversation." They both laughed. "I think I better dismount here."

They took a shower together, and Archie marveled at how wonderful she looked wet. "You look great wet," he said, embracing her. "Most people look like drowned rats."

"Oh, my God. What a wordsmith!"

They dressed and went downstairs to the kitchen.

She had put the butter and the oil in the skillet for the soft-shell crabs and was letting it melt. "Want a glass of champagne? I got some chilling."

"Champagne?" Archie lifted an eyebrow and pulled down the corners of his mouth.

"Yeah. I'm big on celebrations."

"What are you celebrating?"

"Us, you fool!"

"Oh!" He was embarrassed. Gee, this was going to be fun with her. She was so ready for everything. "Sure, sure. Bring it on."

Calista kept her wine "cellar" in a pantry separated from the kitchen by a rood screen that had been salvaged from a sixteenth-century English church. She also kept her good

crystal and bone china there. She went to get out two champagne glasses. The kitchen was rather spectacular with its
gleaming two-inch, cream-color ceramic tiles and handsomely
finished wood antiques. The ubiquitous blond butcher-block
counters found in so many renovated kitchens gave way here to
polished black granite. The general style could be considered
Jacobean, for there were several dark walnut English pieces from
that period in the seventeenth century. But there was also a
slightly ecclesiastical motif running through the kitchen design
exemplified not only by the rood screen wine cellar, but also by a
prie-dieu used for a kitchen drawing table, where she often
worked on the coldest days of winter, for it was warmer than her
study. And instead of sitting on a stool she sat on a bishop's
chair. All the pieces had come out of English and Scottish
churches and been bought for the most part through an antiques
dealer in Bath. Calista usually did entertain in the kitchen
rather than the dining room if it was for less than six. A dark
walnut gateleg table with four mid–eighteenth century arm-
chairs upholstered in red constituted the dining area of the
kitchen. The tile ceased there, and a parquet floor began. She
returned from the wine cellar with the two champagne glasses.
She eschewed flutes. Although she'd heard that they made
champagne taste better, she didn't like their test tube contours.
It wasn't as much fun looking at the bubbles. She went to the
refrigerator for the champagne and came back with the black
curvaceous bottle.

"Veuve Clicquot!" Archie raised his eyebrows. "You don't
mess around."

"I started drinking it before I was a widow, actually. Funny
nobody noticed then. Now they all assume it's some sort of
signature with me. This isn't just the widow, however." She set
down the black bottle. "It's the grande dame." Darkly fetching,
voluptuous, maybe the most beautiful bottle ever designed, and
certainly containing the most wonderful-tasting liquid. Archie
was about to ask if he could uncork the bottle for her, but she
had already started and seemed to be doing it with an ease and
elegance that he could not have equaled. The cork popped, the
champagne frothed over the lip of the bottle. He was ready with
both glasses. She poured. They looked into each other's eyes and

225

recognized in those reflections new lovers but very old friends. They raised their glasses in a wordless toast to both.

She took her champagne over to the stove and started cooking the soft-shell crabs. She dusted them with flour, and when the oil was hot she dropped them in. Their claws curled up.

"Don't worry. They aren't alive. They cleaned them for me at the store. Clean is a euphemism for kill here. Once they made a mistake, though, and forgot to clean them."

"What happened?" Archie asked.

"Kind of gross. I mean, they looked absolutely dead when I put them in the skillet, but they started hopping all around." She paused and looked up at Archie and wrinkled her nose. "You know what they reminded me of?"

"Lady Jane Grey?"

"No." She laughed. "Cab Calloway."

"Cab Calloway?"

"Yeah, I'm kind of into tap dancing."

"Do you tap-dance?"

"Only in private. I promised Charley."

"I'd love to see you tap-dance."

"No, you wouldn't."

"You're very well coordinated." He took a sip of his champagne and his eyes crinkled at the corners, the deep sun marks disappearing.

"I'm better at that than tap dancing." Calista chuckled.

They sat at the gateleg table, pulling their chairs close to each other until their shoulders touched while they ate the crabs and the cold dilled pea salad. He tried to help her clear the plates, but she told him not to. She got the dessert.

"This is my own invention," she said, bringing the ramekins to the table.

"What is it?'

"Frozen crème brûlé. Kind of an oxymoronic dessert. You burn it, and then you freeze it."

Archie took the bottle of champagne from the cooler and poured them a final glass. He looked into the glass at the bubbles and then into those dark eyes that sparkled like twin galaxies. For all her jokes, for all her absolute candor, she was an infinitely mysterious woman. He wanted to say something.

226

But, after all, he was no wordsmith. So he settled instead for just drinking the champagne and looking at her.

Calista shut her eyes tight as she savored the last swallows of the champagne. She was thinking of stars and remembering the old blind monk Dom Pérignon when, after years of experimentation, he had finally captured the sparkle of wine at just the right moment and had called to brother Pierre, "Come quickly, I am drinking the stars!" And for a brief sliver of a second Calista's perfect happiness was tinged with sadness as she remembered the starry Charioteer, and her own husband, Tom, who had died in the desert facing the limitless cosmos he had devoted his life to figuring out. They would get back to the Charioteer, but not now, not right now.

Charley came in at two that morning and Archie left at one fifty-three.

37

Calista dragged herself up the next morning early so she could catch Charley. It seemed as if she had hardly seen him for the past two days, and she was not at all sure if he was eating right, for he often was gone before breakfast. The entire Martin Institute seemed to subsist on Chinese food and Coca-Cola. But this morning she had gotten an egg down Charley, a bran muffin, cantaloupe, and milk. He was certainly not telling her much about what he was doing over there and what was commanding such gargantuan hunks of time. But she had a sense that it was in some way related to their trip to Texas and the skulls, although she couldn't imagine how the reputed skulls and cancer research could ever cross paths. She had just sat down with a second cup of coffee and was dreamily reliving every moment with Archie from the night before. She supposed that someday soon they would have to face the music and tell Charley something. She didn't know what or how. But Archie could not forever skulk out of her house in the dark shadow of moonless nights and hotfoot it back to his parents' house on Beacon Hill. Of course, one day he would have to go back to Washington and attend to business at the Smithsonian. But if this continued, he would come up presumably for visits. Would he still stay at his parents', and would they still arrange their lovemaking around Charley's schedule? The telephone rang. Calista answered it.

"Oh, Janet!"

"Yes, Janet! Haven't heard from you in ages. How goes it?"

"Oh, fine, fine."

"And how is the lovely Marian?" Janet asked delicately.

"Who?" There was a small gulf of silence.

"Calista, Maid Marian, as in Robin Hood!"

"Oh, that Marian!"

"Yes, that Marian! Remember, you are doing a book for us. And that you casually mentioned something about finishes just after Labor Day."

"Oh, yes, yes . . ." Calista laughed nervously. She had not planned to tell Janet about Archie. Oh, she had been dying to, all right, but she felt so bad about Janet's single state with no prospects in sight that she didn't feel it was particularly tactful to mention her own happiness at the time.

"What is it, Cal? Something's going on. I can tell. Is it Charley?" Her voice was gripped with tension. "Did something happen to Charley?"

"Oh, no! No! Don't you think I would have told you?"

"Oh, God, you didn't get another marked-up book, did you?"

"Oh, no, please, nothing of the sort." She had better tell Janet lest she jump to other dire conclusions. How to put it? She paused. "Janet, the person from Porlock came."

"What? What in the hell are you talking about?"

"Come on, you old English major. You remember the person from Porlock in Coleridge. He came just when old Coleridge was smack in the middle of an opium dream and composing the *Kubla Khan.* Interrupted him and that was the end of it all. Poor old Coleridge lost his train of thought, and great chunks of the

228

greatest lyric poem ever right out the window, down the tubes, gone forever."

"And that's what happened to you? The man from Porlock came?"

"About eight times in one night!"

"Holy shit, Cal!" Janet shrieked. "Why didn't you tell me?" Calista was laughing very hard now. "Cal, you are absolutely cackling!" Janet said, laughing herself.

"I know. I must improve my laugh. Whenever I laugh—" And she had begun again and could hardly stop to speak. "Whenever I laugh about sex I cackle. It has something to do with being Jewish and midwestern and repressed." She had dissolved into another cacophonous fit of cackles.

"Hardly a sexual enhancement. . . . You sound like Old Mother Thwackham!" Old Mother Thwackham was a hen that Calista had immortalized years before in a book called *Barnyard Fables*. Mrs. Thwackham had borne a distinct resemblance to Eleanor Roosevelt but had possessed a sky-shattering cackle.

Janet seemed pleased, however, despite her disapproval of the cackle. Calista should have known that Janet, her best friend and only editor, would have rejoiced for her.

"Well, I didn't lose my entire train of thought on Marian. But let's just say that she hasn't been uppermost in my mind in the last few days."

"Oh, forget *Marian's Tale*. This is real life!"

That evening Calista and Archie had just finished making love when the phone rang. Calista answered it. "Charley!" She pulled the sheet up in a gesture of instinctual modesty that Archie found charming. "Yeah? You'll be home in fifteen minutes." Archie now got out of bed immediately and reached for his shorts. "Tell Archie not to leave? . . ." She looked at Archie, and her eyes opened wide. "You've seen him the last three nights walking down Kirkland Street just as your cab turns the corner? You have something to tell us. . . . Oh, dear, is it serious? . . . Very? Okay, sweetie. We'll be here."

She hung up the phone. This time there were even streaks of red across her belly. "Oh, my God. He knows about us!"

"Now calm down, Calista. Did he say that?"

"Not exactly. He just said that he had to talk to us about something serious. But he does know that you've been here—late every night. I mean, I didn't try to hide the fact that you are in town and have been over for dinner. But he's seen you, Archie."

"Look, you're jumping to conclusions. The first conclusion is that just because he has to talk to us about something serious, it has to be us. There are other serious matters in the world and his life even aside from us."

"Pliny the Elder?"

"What?"

"Nothing—just a report that he was overdue with."

"Okay, now your second conclusion is that he'll be upset about us, and I don't really think that is the case. I think that Charley likes me."

"Oh, he does, Archie. I know he does."

"And that's not all. I don't just like Charley. I care for him very deeply, deeply in his own right, and also because he is part of you—of you and Tom. I see both of you in him. And I cherish that."

"Oh, Archie!" Calista's eyes filled with tears.

He held her close and rubbed his fingers through the thick silvery-chestnut hair. "Come on, Calista. He's not going to be upset about us sleeping together. I really don't think so. I mean, I don't think he was born yesterday. But we don't have to rub his nose in it. We'll take our cues from him."

She knew he was right.

When Charley came in they were both dressed and sitting at the dining table in the kitchen drinking a cup of tea and looking very nervous.

"You are not going to believe this!" he announced as he dropped a thick wad of photocopied papers on the table.

"What?" they both said. A flood of relief swept through Calista. She knew right then that she and Archie were definitely not the serious item on Charley's agenda, if indeed they were on it at all.

230

"Okay, you know the project I've been working on at Martin since April? Right? Protein folding, all that?"

"Yeah, but brief Archie on it."

He did. Then he briefed both of them on the intellamine-intellicone project. Archie was vaguely familiar with it. He had heard mention of it through one of his colleagues, but it had very little bearing on his interests.

"Okay," Charley said. "Now, if you'll recall when we were down in Texas at Lorne Thurston College of Christian Heritage, they let slip about some skulls which they felt indicated separate evolution of races."

"Recall—of course," Calista was saying. "That's why Archie's here." The color rose violently in her neck. Archie blinked.

"Yeah, well, anyhow . . ." Charley was brushing by that easily enough, Calista noticed. "You get the correlation here? Racial differences showing up in fossil materials, racial differences showing up in brain proteins?"

"Yes." Both Calista and Archie nodded. Archie was actually feeling a horrible queasiness in the pit of his stomach.

"And Archie, you suspect those skulls are going to be fake if you ever get to see them—like the Paluxy footprints."

Again Archie nodded very slowly but deliberately. "I think they're going to hold out to the last minute, hoping not to have to show them at all. Waiting for something else—and . . ." It suddenly dawned on Archie. "You got the something else?"

"Damn right I do. But they're not going to like it, and it's not going to be worth waiting for. The intellamine and intellicone proteins are pure fiction. They blow apart. We figured it out this week. We've been working on this dumb-shit project for months that nobody is really the least interested in, this modeling stuff."

"But I thought you said that Leventhal liked it. Took your models to some conference with him."

"He liked our three-D diagrams. He liked the fact that we had mapped so many of these proteins. Nobody else has the time to do that kind of work around there. Made it handy for him. We were just like glorified file clerks. We just worked on ways to collate data and make it more observable. But we didn't discover anything, Matthew, Louise, and me." He paused. "Until this week. Nobody had ever mapped intellamine and intellicone. And it looked weird. It just didn't have any of the regularities that any of the other proteins had, as least not from the data given in these papers." He tapped his index finger on the stack of photocopies. "And then this guy Liam, he's this real hotshot programmer. I mean, the guy can write code like you can't believe. He wrote this computer program that calculates the free energy in proteins. Well, he comes in and shows us how it works, and we run it on intellamine and intellicone, and the things just blow up on us. Like there is no way this stuff can hang together."

"So they faked it," Archie said.

"They sure did!"

"So you've got something being faked presumably on two levels, the fossil and the genetic level. Very high-tech. I guess they've learned something since the Paluxy footprints debacle."

"Right."

"But I don't understand. You said that there are papers from major universities and that they went to Brookhaven to use the PET scanner," Calista said, looking at the abstract on the title page of one article.

"They didn't have to go anyplace, really. They just had to have a plant in one or two labs—to write up data. Or they could have gone to Brookhaven and played tiddlywinks and pretended to run the scanner."

"But how did they get all these people to sign on to these papers?" Calista asked.

"That's the way it goes—especially in biology." Archie sighed. He'd taken out his pipe and was digging at his tobacco. "It doesn't mean that all the people who signed on the paper as coauthors had bad intentions. They did not set out to subvert the truth. They probably didn't know. There was a famous case just a few years ago. A guy up in Toronto, a molecular biologist, was faking the most elegant experiments imaginable. His data made sense. His work appeared flawless until he was caught. You know how they caught him?"

"How?" both Charley and Calista asked at the same time.

232

"Conceptually there didn't seem to be anything wrong with his experiments. But when one postdoc started to figure out how many culture dishes it would take to do those experiments, it was an incredible amount. More than a person might use in ten years. They went back and checked the lab supply sheets. There was no abnormal number of petri dishes being used. The experiments had been a complete fabrication. The director of the lab had signed on to the paper—after all, it made sense—and so had the other people in the lab. They had all signed on."

"I still don't get it. How could they not know?"

"It's protocol," Archie said quietly. "They all work in the lab together. Any work that comes out of that lab has to have on it the names of the head of the lab and the director of the department or institute. My name goes on all the papers that come out of the Smithsonian's Department of Anthropology. And I do read them all. But it gets more complicated in biology. For one thing, you trust your colleagues. You might not have been hanging over every petri dish. But you trust the people at the bench working with you, and if what they write up hangs together, sure, you put your name on it. It's important, especially for young postdocs, to get their names out there associated with important projects. God knows they aren't getting paid adequately for their time."

"That's exactly what Steve said. And guess what, Mom? Even my name is going to be on a crystallography paper he's writing. My name and Louise's and Matthew's. Just because of the work we did this spring. They'll be at the bottom of the list. But they'll be there all the same."

"So whose names are on these papers—not that it apparently matters?" Calista said.

"Well, there's only one that really matters." Charley took a paper off the top of the stack. The article, which had been published in *Endocrinology Abstracts,* was dated three years earlier and was entitled "Effects of Methadrill on Neurotransmitters As Related to Higher Order Thought Processes." A name was circled.

"E. W. Tompkins," Calista whispered. "Tompkins!"

"Yes, Mom. Remember the William Jennings Bryan Creation Science Center—that guy in the lab?" Charley said.

233

"Wayne Tompkins—this says E. W. How can we be sure? Tompkins is a fairly common name."

"Remember Beth Ann said that he came from up north? Look where this article is out of."

"University of Minnesota—guess that's north all right."

"Is this what made you suspicious, seeing his name on this?"

"No. Not at all. I didn't even notice his name until about an hour ago, when we went into Steve's office to tell him what we had found out. Then we just started making a list of every lab and university and person that ever had anything to do with intellamine and intellicone. And that's when his name kind of popped out at me."

"Do you have the list with you?" Archie asked.

"Yep. You want to see it?"

"Sure do."

Charley handed him the list. Archie took out his half-glasses from his pocket and began to read.

"Know anybody?" Charley asked.

"Lots."

"Oooh!" Calista groaned.

"Don't worry." Archie patted her hand. They had completely forgotten about being embarrassed in front of Charley. "It's like Charley said. This is the way they work. These top guys aren't the bad guys. I know a lot of the heads of the departments and the labs at these universities—Duke, Penn, Minnesota—James Atwell. . . . Now why does that name ring a bell? I don't know him, but the name Coastal Research Institute . . . James Atwell." Archie scratched his head.

"Oh, God!" Calista jumped up. "James Atwell, of course! That loathsome man. You know, Archie—the Nobel sperm bank."

"Oh, good Christ!" Archie removed his glasses and looked very nearly white. "You're right."

"Of course I'm right. I saw him on *Oprah Winfrey,* where else? But why does this say Coastal Research Institute?"

"It's all part of the same thing. The connection between the sperm bank and the Coastal Research Institute isn't all that public, but at one time the institute did have a loose connection

234

with Stanford. The sperm bank is into high-tech breeding—
and guess what they call themselves?"

"What?" Charley and Calista both looked at Archie.

"Genesis!"

"Oy!" Calista said.

Charley looked at Archie. He wondered if Archie understood
any Yiddish. It was definitely an "oy" kind of night.

"Well, I got some good ideas on pursuing this now. But I
better go home and sleep on it," Archie said, getting up.

"Why go home?" Charley said suddenly. And if anybody had
asked him why he had said it, he would not have been able to
explain. It just seemed that Archie belonged here, here with
him and his mom. Archie and Calista looked at each other.
"You might as well stay here. It's late. You can sleep in the
guest room." Archie and Calista exchanged another glance.
This time it was not lost on Charley. "Or, you know, in my
room or Mom's."

Then Calista said the boldest thing she had ever said to her
son. "I don't know if he'd do very well on the bottom bunk,
Charley." And she smiled softly at her son.

"Well, I guess it should be your room, then."

And it was. But they didn't make love again that night. They
crawled into bed, and Calista sank back against the pillows. "I
don't believe this—where will it all end—murder, phony brain
proteins, fake fossil skulls, sperm banks named Genesis, and—
oh God, Archie, I forgot those vandalized books that Margaret
and I both received, plus dear old Owl. Everything's at stake
here—science, the First Amendment . . . ."

"The whole way and manner and principle of scientific
thought is under fire with these guys because in their view
nothing is ever open to skeptical inquiry. The evolution debate
is only the opening wedge in a battle. You see, now they're
proceeding on to a racist scenario. And for them, education is
not a quest that ever involves uncertainty—only the right
answers."

"Archie, how did you know all that stuff about the sperm

235

bank?" His eyes crinkled into a smile. "No, Archie, don't tell me you gave! You're not a Nobel winner."

"They apparently let a few lesser folk in."

"No, you didn't!"

He put his arm around her. "No, darling lady, I didn't. I just remember when the letter came in. Goodfellow—you know, Ruth Goodfellow, my secretary—she and I had an awfully good laugh about it."

"Well, I hope you didn't laugh too hard with her—I mean, Archie . . . you didn't give at the office, did you?"

"With Goodfellow? No. She wouldn't have me, for one thing." He was laughing now. "No, dear, I only want to give at the house on James Place in Cambridge, Massachusetts."

Calista sighed. "Sperm and drang!" she muttered.

Archie laughed out loud.

As Charley drifted off to sleep that night, he could hear laughter coming from his mother's bedroom for the first time in nearly four years. It sounded good, like watery bubbles. And that made him think of dolphins. Dolphins with their built-in smiles. He had once heard that there was a place in Florida where you could swim with dolphins. And when he finally fell asleep he dreamed of swimming with these dolphins with Archie and his mom, and all around them were swirls of bubbles and laughter.

38

The next morning Archie called up Steve and asked him and Liam to come over to Calista's house for a meeting. Charley called up Louise and Matthew and asked them to come, too. Calista and Charley first explained the extraordinary possible ramifications of this fraud. Archie felt it was imperative that this fraud not be revealed prematurely, because if it was, it could become more dangerous than it already had been for Calista and Charley. He didn't want to scare anyone unduly,

236

especially the kids. But he wanted to make sure that when they got ready to move they had all the pieces in place. Steve and Liam were more than agreeable. It was apparent that this was more than the usual run-of-the-mill fudging of scientific data. These guys weren't just looking for more research money. They were playing for bigger stakes. As Steve sat in the Jacobses's kitchen he realized the intellamine-intellicone fraud was just one skirmish of many battles fought for one rather frightening kingdom—a kingdom of skinheads and scientific creationists—an unholy alliance if there ever was one.

The first step was for Charley and Archie to go with Liam and Steve over to SIPB, the Student Information Processing Board, in Building 11 at MIT, and sit down in front of "Binkly." All the computers in this center, as in many centers, had names. The names at SIPB were taken from the characters in Bloom County, the comic strip. They used a finger program, which is a program for "fingering," or finding out, information about people. The only other person in the center was playing Towers of Hanoi, a favorite game of hackers, which involved stacking towers in a graduated order. There were about seven or eight terminals. On the walls were a few signs that would seem somewhat cryptic for those outside the computer world— "Happiness Is a Working Laser Writer," read one sign. Another said simply "rm is forever."

They "fingered" every single name that had signed on as coauthor on every single article. Fingering did not come up with the equivalent of an FBI file. It could not yield as much or that kind of information. For the most part you could just put together where someone had worked, if they had had computer accounts at these places, what their interests and their expertise were, and a few vital statistics like their user name, telephone number, and where they worked out of. The finger program, coupled with the directory access program of the Unix system, could yield information about which computers they had used and to a limited extent what information they had gone after. Every university and institution, including Brookhaven, had a Unix operating system. They searched the directories diligently for any signs of the authors. They were able to finger several of them, including Wayne Tompkins. If a person had a user account, they were listed. It was not possible, however, to track how they had used a system or what specific information they had sought.

"Most places don't clutter up the works with that kind of data," Liam said. "They might keep the last time a user logged on, but that's about it."

How had this scam jumped from the fossil scale to the genetic one? And what exactly were the implications of this in the Petrakis murder? She thought about it as she waited for the take-out order from Mary Chung's that she had promised to bring to the fellows in Building 11 for lunch.

MIT was a veritable maze. She had to ask four people before she found Building 11. Calista had walked down more blind paths, gone through more tunnels, than she could count carrying her bundles of Chinese food. She had finally gotten to Building 11 through Building 5—or was it 9? None of the buildings had names. It was all confounding, and as she wended her way through the maze she began to think of it as a metaphor for the tangled tale of murder and fraud and "religion," if you could call it that. If she had been a Christian, she would have found it profoundly insulting. Of course, that was the problem, wasn't it, with all of the fundamentalists and the scientific creationists, whom she supposed were a subset of fundamentalists. None of them had any capacity for metaphor. There was no symbolic level to their thought at all. They would certainly have laughed at her if she had told them what she really thought of Genesis—that to her the Adam and Eve story, the whole story of creation, had a more powerful truth, more eloquence and beauty, than could ever be weighed or proven by scientific procedure; that she believed in that story in her own way, which was independent of science and did not hinge, in terms of its moral veracity or compelling beauty, on demonstrability. It was an epic, and epics did have their truth and their value. But they could not be measured by the same methods as scientific hypotheses, for they were symbolic truths.

But these people had no inclination or affinity toward symbolization or disposition toward metaphor. How thin and paltry their lives must be. No wonder they were moral cripples. If you could not imagine beyond the here and now, how could you ever empathize with another's pain, or joy, or freedom of mind and thought? And if you could not do that, then you could kill quite easily. So she was back to Norman again! But where was it all leading, and where the hell was this subbasement tunnel leading?

A wan-looking girl with a backpack and running shorts jogged by her. "Pardon me, I think I'm lost," Calista said. The girl looked up at her. She was wan indeed and had a rabbity-looking face. Her eyes were rimmed with pink from lack of sleep or from endless hours of staring into a computer terminal. Good Lord, was this like the white rabbit in *Alice's Adventures in Wonderland*? Calista fully expected her to spout out, "I'm late, I'm late for a very important date," and rush off. But she didn't.

"What do you want?"

"Building Eleven."

"You're in a subbasement of Building Nine. Continue to the end of the corridor, turn left, go up two floors and down the corridor, the same way you're heading now, and it will take you right into Building Eleven."

"Oh, thanks." But the girl had already scurried off.

She did what the girl told her. But she could not get certain images out of her mind—rabbits and mazes and bunny blood!

When she arrived at SIPB she found Archie and Liam and Steve and Charley huddled over terminals. They looked up as she entered. She had a strange look on her face. She was thinking that if you could just pull one thread, the whole thing could unravel. "Charley, I saw this girl in the basement coming over here from Building Nine. She looked just like a rabbit, and it reminded me . . ."

"Bunny blood!" Charley blurted the words out.

"Bunny blood?" Archie and Liam looked bewildered.

"Oh, yeah—bunny blood!" Steve said. There was a slow dawning tone in his voice. "Those antigens I tracked down for you."

Calista turned to Archie. "The words written on the wall of Norman Petrakis's hotel room were in blood. It was rabbit's blood, and so were the drops of blood on Margaret's book, the

239

ones that were supposed to be the wounds of Christ. See, these people have no capacity for metaphor. They have to use the real thing!"

But nobody seemed to follow the line of Calista's reasoning. They were with her for the most part, however, struggling with her as she tried to make this intuitive leap. It seemed to promise something. But it was not a leap. It was more like scaling up an immense peak. "Who uses rabbits?"

"Lots of places," Steve said.

"Not the Smithsonian," Archie said.

"No, you know, biological labs, biology departments at universities. . . ."

"Would places like the Martin Institute that do genetic research use animals?"

"Sure," Steve said. "We use mice, monkeys on occasion, rabbits, but we try not to advertise that too much. The animal rights advocates get very upset about rabbits."

Calista searched back in her memory to that conversation months before in the Japanese restaurant with Norman. She remembered him telling about all the different kinds of genetic research being done—the molecular time clock stuff, cancer research, the thing that he had called the human gene project, the twins research project in Minnesota.

"Would they have used it in that twins research project out at the University of Minnesota?" she asked.

"Possibly," Steve said.

"And what about the Coastal Research Institute—the place that showed up in one paper as one of the labs involved in the intellamine research? Remember, Charley, it was on that list that you brought home and showed to me and Archie, the place run by that guy Atwell."

"The sperm bank man?" Charley asked. "Oh, yuck!"

"Well, Archie said they were into high-tech breeding. Maybe they'd use animals for their research," Calista said.

"Yes, I suppose so," Archie replied with a kind of weary disgust at the whole notion.

"Let's call them up and the University of Minnesota, the twins research project."

"And say what?" Liam asked.

240

"Well," Calista began, "I tell them I'm from a biological supply house and I'm selling rabbits or rabbits' blood. I'll ask them what they're paying, and I'll promise that we can give them a better deal."

"And then what, Mom?"

She paused. "I'm not sure," she said honestly. "But maybe it's kind of like those petri dishes that Archie was telling us about. Only in this case if they don't use any, we can maybe absolve them from any connection with Norman's death. But if they do use some or inordinate amounts—like enough to write 'Monkey's Uncle' on a wall of a hotel room . . . well . . ." she didn't finish the thought.

It was not a bad idea. It was at least another starting point. The searching for authors in the computer networks had not yielded the kind of refined information they really needed. They could at least narrow down the labs that used rabbits' blood. It was decided that Steve should do the calling. Having worked in biology labs, he knew the ins and outs of biological supply businesses. He could talk fluently about the price of outbred rats, nude mice, inbred mice, miniswine, and, of course, rabbits, be they outbred, inbred, or whatever. He could talk about strain designations and user benefits such as VAFS (virus antibody free) animals and COBS (cesarean originated barrier sustained) animals. He offered a toll-free number, genetic monitoring reports, and the guarantee that all animals were free of *M. pulmonis.*

The lab where Wayne Tompkins had worked at the University of Minnesota didn't use any rabbits—too expensive. This was a blow. At Duke they used them occasionally and would consider using the Ballard Laboratories (that was what Steve was calling his outfit), but he should call back next week when Robert Pitkin, the manager for the bio labs, was back from vacation. The Coastal Research Institute also used some. Lorne Thurston College of Christian Heritage did not use any lab animals at all.

"Figures," Charley muttered as Steve hung up and reported this news.

"I think we're still stuck." Charley sighed.

241

"Well," said Steve, "mice really are the favorite animals of genetic research."

"No, we're not stuck. No, we're not," Calista persisted. "We just have to build a bridge between this rabbit's blood thing and . . . and . . ." Her mind was groping. "When you did those searches to see if the authors' names showed up—what do you call it when they use a computer?"

"User accounts," Liam said.

"Yes. Did you check to see if Norman Petrakis's name ever showed up?"

"No. Why?" Steve asked. "He wasn't an author. He was a victim."

Calista smiled. "But he was an author, of very fine children's books on subjects like human evolution, and he also wrote on DNA. I remember his telling me and Janet and Margaret about it in the restaurant the night he was murdered. That's why I thought it might be a good idea to call the University of Minnesota, not just that it had been mentioned in those papers on intellamine, but because of Norman's connection."

"Petrakis had a connection there?" Steve asked.

"Not a formal one, but he was in the process of doing some articles—'Designer Genes,' he was calling the series. He had mentioned the twins research project at University of Minnesota." She again tried to conjure up the memory of that conversation at dinner with Norman, hoping for some shred of information that could help them. Had he mentioned anything about sperm banks? She couldn't recall. It would seem like a natural place to go in terms of an article on genetics. But she felt like a blind person, lost in a forest on a moonless night. Bits of remembered conversation from that night swirled about her meaninglessly, giving no direction.

"Well, I would imagine that he would have gone out to Minnesota and checked into this twins stuff, and then there's the molecular time clock stuff. I think they've done a lot of that work out at Berkeley," Steve said.

"Yes, yes. He mentioned that." She paused. "Do you suppose that Norman Petrakis uncovered the intellamine fraud before you guys? Maybe he wasn't murdered for his book on human evolution at all. Maybe it was because what Norman

242

found out was the same thing that Charley and Louise and Matthew found out." She bit her lower lip lightly.

It was a stunning intuitive leap, but it made more sense than anything so far.

"But what about the Monkey's Uncle?" Charley asked.

"Trying to pass the buck to the creationists," Calista answered.

"You mean the creationists are the good guys?" Charley asked.

"Well, let's just say they might not be murderers," Calista said, and then added, "I'm sure, as with all of us, there is room for improvement, particularly in the form of some real functioning brain proteins. But we know for sure that they don't use any animals in their labs. I'm not saying that this exonerates them entirely. But I think in this case we have to follow the . . ." She paused. "Blood tracks, as it were. That seems to be the only thing to go on. The monkey's blood and the computer network for the authors of these papers. Those are the trails. And we know that Norman was seeking out this genetic stuff and it led him to a lot of the places where research was being done."

While they had been talking Liam logged on again. "Got your man, here. Norman Petrakis. He had accounts all over the place, or more precisely the same places that all these authors had them. None in Texas, though."

"So," said Archie, "he might not have found out anything about the skulls through the computer, if he knew anything about them at all then. For him this was strictly on the genetic level. Or we have to assume that."

"I guess for now we do," Calista said. "It doesn't seem that he went anywhere near Texas for his research."

Liam had just dialed a number on the telephone between Binkly and Oliver. The screen on the terminal changed. "Holy shit!" He ran his hands through his bushy, electric hair, which now really looked as if it had a few volts running through it. "This guy, Petrakis, he had an account at LBL."

"LBL?" Calista asked.

"Lawrence Berkeley Labs." Liam looked up. "This is great! We're not going to have to assume anything. You give me two days. Another guy who's a computer security expert is out

243

there. He's a good friend of mine. Between the two of us I think we can trace Petrakis's path. Petrakis's murderers, whoever they might be, did not go to any trouble to clean out his accounts."

"But I don't understand. How can you do this, trace him?" Calista asked.

"Think of it like that powder they put in the bag with the money when a bank is robbed. It explodes and leaves stains all over the place. Only in this case it's electronic footprints. All I need is a little time and to keep it quiet. We don't want to tip them off. Because then they might go in and cover the tracks."

"Maybe we should decoy them," Archie said.

"How do you mean?" Liam asked.

"Look, I think Calista's hunch is right. Someone might have been trying to pass the buck off on the creationists about this murder. And yet there is evidence that something was going on with fossils as well as on a genetic level in order to put one over about this separate origins of races. In a sense we might be dealing with two separate but related frauds. One has to do with fossils and is, I think, strictly out of the creationists' camp. And the second fraud is the intellamine thing."

"You don't see that as being part of the creationists' fraud?"

"Not originally. I don't think they would have gotten into the genetics thing intentionally at the start. They simply don't have the wherewithal to even begin to pull it off. Creationist science doesn't get that high-tech—at least not as high-tech as genetic research requires."

"But you think they did cross at some point—these two separate frauds."

"Possibly—"

"And you see that point being Norman?" Calista said.

"I don't think he knew about the skulls. I don't think that was his interest."

"But the creationists did know about him," Calista said. "They hated him. Charley and I saw these pamphlets attacking Norman for his book on human evolution."

"But that book came out a while ago."

"Yes, but there was someone at the conference who stood up on behalf of the Christian nation to take issue with Norman's views of evolution."

"But was he really a creationist?"

"Are you trying to say he could have been a disaffected geneticist in disguise?" Calista asked.

"Calista, you're the one who set out the idea in the first place of the genetics folks, the ones who faked the intellamine research, trying to pass the buck to the creationists."

There was silence as Charley, Liam, Steve, and Calista mulled this over in their minds. Archie waited, then spoke carefully, for he himself was not sure if this was truly the case, but there did seem to be the possibility of a connection between the two frauds. Perhaps it had not started out intentionally, but somehow two paths had overlapped, and Norman Petrakis had wound up as dead as he would have if he had been caught in the cross hairs of a rifle's sights.

"I think it might be to our advantage," Archie began slowly, "to try and play along with the original scenario. You know, like we're going after the creationists and flush them out of the woods on the skull thing. Maybe the timing's right for them to make their little announcement to the world. It might take the heat off you while you follow Petrakis's tracks through the other labs."

"Not a bad idea," Steve said.

"Okay, I'll start," Liam replied.

39

They were not grasping at straws now. They were pulling at threads. Calista had pulled at the first thread when she thought again of the rabbit's blood, which had then, through some tangled way, led her to think of searching for Petrakis's name. When his name showed up, things promised to unravel quite nicely. Archie sat in Calista's kitchen. He had just begun to pull at another thread. He had made a score of calls to his own network of colleagues and media people and was now on the phone with Colin Mercer, his close friend and editor over at the

National Geographic. Colin loved a challenge like this. "We'll get these guys by the balls!" Colin had chuckled.

"Oh, and by the way, Colin," Archie said, "for all intents and purposes, I have disappeared. Out of the country for the next few days. I don't want to just keep a low profile in this thing. In fact, I want no profile of me visible. After the Paluxy footprints they're immediately going to think of me. . . . Okay? . . . Yes, if you have to reach me, I'll be at this number in Vermont." He gave Mercer the number of Calista's vacation home in Vermont, where they planned to retreat for the next few days. He hung up the telephone and smiled at Calista.

"This is great. We're going to get two birds with one stone here. Hopefully find out who killed Petrakis and then put an end to this so-called science of the creationists." He got up and slapped the table. "And guess what, Cal? We're doing it by good, old-fashioned science!" He patted the telephone.

Calista laughed. She knew exactly what he meant. People liked to think that science always was "conducted" in laboratories by people wearing white coats holding up beakers of fluids or peering through microscopes. But it wasn't. The year before he had died, her husband Tom had delivered a lecture on the role of gossip, innuendo, and scuttlebutt in science. Good scientists were great gossips. As a physicist Tom had logged as much time on a telephone as he ever had in a lab, at an observatory, or at a reactor. And so had Archie Baldwin spent more time on telephones and flying about the country and the world to conferences than he had spent in the field with a trowel digging up artifacts. For that was largely how science proceeded. As a procedure, gossip and scuttlebutt were neither scientific nor logical. But then again the scientist did not seek to prove hypotheses through talking about them. A scientist hears about some ideas coming out of somewhere. It could be an experiment or a hypothesis, and he or she is in turn challenged to pick up on that thread of thought. They compare it, or contrast it, with what they are doing. Use it with a slightly different twist on it or toss it out completely. If it works, an initial idea has not been plagiarized or copied, but refined. There are not perhaps that many original ideas per se in science, but rather original ways of looking at old problems. But you had to be plugged in to the network. You had to hear the scuttlebutt that was going on. You had to know what to do with all that scuttlebutt—how to filter it, look at it, and see where it fit in with what you were doing. The creationists resisted every other standard procedure of science that required that they examine and weigh data against existing data. Their only textbook they claimed in the science of creation was God's written word— despite the fact that biblical scholarship and archaeology had proven that Genesis was developed by Hebrews from older Chaldean and Babylonian myths and that there were four authors. Now Archie wondered how they would do with this, the least heralded of scientific procedures—gossip. It was out there now, blowing in the wind—the biggest fossil news of the century—separate origins for the races. How would they fare under the glare of this publicity? Archie was ready to sit back and enjoy it all.

40

Charley had not wanted to go to Vermont. He had wanted to remain in Cambridge, more or less glued to Liam Phillips's side while Liam and his California counterpart, the security expert, a certain Corey Feinberg, wended their way through the electronic maze of a vast computer network, tracking for the late Norman Petrakis. But Calista would not hear of it. He could come with her and Archie to Vermont. He could bring Matthew and Louise with him if he wanted, or he could go with Matthew down to the Cape as the McPhails had invited him to do. He elected to do the latter, which Calista had to admit was preferable to him and Matthew and Louise all being in Vermont. She supposed that these two days could be considered a little honeymoon for her and Archie, which was not an unpleasant thought. She hadn't been to her Vermont house all summer, and although her good neighbors and caretakers, the Potts,

247

looked after the place, they would not have had time to tend the garden. By this point of the summer the garden might look like some Rousseau fantasy run amok.

So Calista and Charley headed off to their respective destinations that morning just after Archie had finished making the calls. Charley seemed more than reconciled to his trip to the Cape by this time, and Calista had given him a substantial advance on his allowance so he could purchase a surfboard that was comparable to Matthew's. She had even agreed to go halvsies on the price of it, which was a singularly indulgent act for Calista. Charley had always told her that allowancewise she was the cheapest mom in town. She had always assumed that this was a typical adolescent complaint—everyone gets more allowance than me. But then she'd found out it was true! She hated materially indulged children. She didn't care if Charley worked or not, but if he wanted money beyond the five bucks she gave him each week for doing practically nothing, he was going to have to work for it. She watched him go down the walk, skateboard under one arm, surfboard under the other. He wore acid green jams with hot pink stripes and a T-shirt with the most god-awful graphics and the words BAD TO THE BONE. She had made him take back the one that said BADASS MAMA. On his head he wore a Benjamin Moore painter's cap. This was a fad that Charley himself had started: painter's caps. All the kids in school were now collecting them and wearing them. His red hair stuck out around the edges. He did look cute walking down the path, and when he turned to wave good-bye to her and smiled that sweet crooked smile of his, she shook her head in amazement and thought, He starts fads and discovers fake proteins, but for all intents and purposes he looks like a surfer. All Cambridge kids had this hankering to come from southern California—Malibu!

Norman Petrakis had been a proficient hacker. It had cost big money to track him originally. Corey Feinberg knew because he had been paid to do it. He didn't know who precisely had paid him. A call had just come in from the University of Pennsylvania. There was a suspicion that there was an intruder in the system. They were not even that concerned about it because

248

there was no classified information, really. This was not a military or defense contractor. It was a university. University systems were notoriously lax. The joke was that the reason for this laxness was that the stakes were so low in academia. But people were becoming more security conscious now with the rumors of damaging viruses loose, and even though Penn didn't feel threatened directly, they were correct in reporting this suspected intrusion. Any hacker who got into a system could inadvertently or advertently do damage, and it was a gateway to other systems. Corey Feinberg was the best electronic sleuth in the business. He was thought of as an electronic Sherlock Holmes. And he was a good friend of Liam's. The Petrakis case was distinguished in Corey Feinberg's mind only by the time it had taken him to catch Petrakis. The guy hadn't done any damage. He hadn't stolen anything. Corey Feinberg was in fact shocked when he learned that Wiley—for that was Petrakis's user name—had been murdered. He had handled lots of sensitive cases before, where crackers were going after volatile information and could have gotten murdered, but this guy had just been snooping around. The pressure to catch him, though, had built. But the case was so uninteresting that he had all but forgotten about it. It was nothing like the West Germans, who had broken into Defense Department data base systems. When he found the message in his E-mail to quick contact Lip, which was Liam's user name, he could hardly remember the nitty-gritties of the case. He called him directly on the phone first.

"He basically got into the system through a public library in New Jersey," Corey was saying.

"New Jersey?"

"Yeah, he must have lived there. It was a home phone linkup. And through the public library linkup he got into Princeton's computer system and Dartmouth's."

"Dartmouth? God, I can understand Princeton if he lived in New Jersey, but Dartmouth hasn't shown up in any of this. No authors from Dartmouth or anything."

"He got into a lot of places—at least fifteen systems, as I recall. See, once he got into LBL, it was easy—Penn, Dartmouth, Minnesota, Brookhaven . . ."

"Aha, Brookhaven!"

"Yeah, that mean something to you?"

"I think so. Tell me, how did you finally catch him?"

"We let him keep tunneling for a while. I think I even tried to decoy him at one time with some false information, but he caught on. I mean, the guy was slippery. But the idea was if we let him walk around enough in the system, we could catch him. I started wearing a beeper and any access port, the minute he entered, my beeper would beep and we would record, at that port, every friggin' keystroke the guy made."

The access ports were the points at which any telephone linkup outside the main computer gained entry into the system. "Let me tell you, this guy wasn't just skillful, he was fucking brilliant."

"What kind of information was he going after?"

"All kinds. But if there was any theme, it was biological data—DNA, genetic stuff. I think he got into Martin Institute at one time. But I can't remember."

"What? He got into Martin, and I didn't know about it? Why the fuck didn't you tell me?"

"It was brief, believe me."

"Hell, Corey, this is like not reporting a hit-and-run."

"It wasn't a hit-and-run—no such thing. As I recall, it was probably my fault, part of the decoy strategy. But it didn't work. I had the feeling the guy was tracking on his own, meandering around looking for evidence of other hackers—at least when he went into the biology labs."

"Huh?" Liam scratched his head. "What other kinds of information did he go after, other than biological stuff?"

"Jeez, I can't even remember what he was doing when he got into Brookhaven. And then he got into the files of that jerk newspaper, *The Green Review*. He was looking for stuff over there."

"No kidding."

"You want to know the weirdest thing of all, the thing I was never able to figure out?"

"What's that?"

"He had no billing address, yet every hour of on-line time was paid for."

"By him?"

"I don't know if it was by him or not. But let's just say it was all neat and tidy. Nobody was ripped off in that sense." Corey paused. "I kind of grew to like the guy. Had a lot of admiration for him, really. So he was really murdered?"

"Yep."

"Gee, that makes me feel real bad."

"And you never found out who hired you to track him down?"

"Not really. For all intents and purposes it was the University of Pennsylvania. The initial request came from somebody there."

"Who wrote your paycheck?"

"Penn, for the first installment."

"Then after that?"

"Well, that was a little weird. They told me to send the bills to this P.O. Box at Penn, and they paid me with a postal money order."

"How much did it cost them?"

"It wasn't cheap, let me tell you. It took me over seven months. I think it all totaled up to about thirty thousand dollars."

Liam whistled low. "Somebody had big bucks."

"Yep."

41

All Archie had to do now was sit back and try to relax and watch the fun begin. Through his network of colleagues in archaeology and paleontology, including Colin Mercer at the *National Geographic,* word of the skulls had spread like wildfire. Lorne Thurston's college would have to make some announcement soon. And Archie was enjoying the thought of them being bombarded by calls. Colin Mercer was calling up the college and saying that the *National Geographic* wanted to fly photographers down to Green Acre, Texas, and also to the site where the skulls had been excavated. He assumed that the college must have a team still excavating over there, wherever it was. It would be out on the U.P. wire services by now. A *New York Times* science editor was toying with flying someone down there. The story would definitely be covered, in any case. Archie had even called Goodfellow and had her call the college on behalf of the Smithsonian. Within twelve hours the academic world was abuzz with this news.

Sitting back and relaxing was not too hard a thing to do in Vermont with Calista. In fact, he could do this forever, he thought, skulls or no skulls! He rolled over onto his back in the black water of the pond and looked up at the stars. Calista was floating on her back next to him, and he stretched out his hand for hers. This was Calista's own pond, a lovely one just down the grassy knoll from her house. Sedges and cattails grew in thick clumps around its banks. At one end, where an old bullfrog presided, there were some lily pads with pale pink blossoms. They had been swimming naked now for almost half an hour. There was never any need to wear clothes even during the daytime at this pond, and they had gone for a swim that afternoon just after arriving from the hot two-and-a-half-hour drive. But tonight it was magical. Chips of moonlight were scattered across the water, and above in the sky were garlands of stars.

Calista knew not only all the constellations but the mythology that went with them. She had just started to tell him one he had never heard, about Vega, the brightest star of the summer triangle. It was a strange tale of jealousy and music and the casting out of the purest sister, the one who could tell no lies but was doomed through the spell of an evil stepmother never to speak. She sought refuge in a cave on a magical island with an old mathematician.

"Where was the cave?" Archie asked.

"Samos."

"Isn't that where Pythagoras went?"

"Precisely," she answered. They had begun kicking on their backs toward shore. "She had fled there because there was this tyrant, Polycrates, who was the governor of the island and making life miserable for everyone. The stepmother was Polycrates' sister—out of the same mold."

"Okay, I follow you."

"Now, keep your eye on the star while I tell you the rest of the story."

Archie did. But for the life of him he couldn't remember a myth involving Pythagoras and a young girl. There had never, for that matter, been any mention of female companionship in the cave.

"So she lived in this cave with this little old guy on Samos. It was really a beautiful island swirled with salt air and forested with pines. But she couldn't speak. He didn't bug her about it. He taught her that there was harmony in nature and variety within sameness and unity. That all this had a language of its own, the language of numbers. See, he was on his way to discovering the Pythagorean theorem, or the proof. That was just down the pike. But before that he was finding something just as exciting—even more exciting. It was the basic relationship between mathematics and musical harmony. For Pythagoras taught Vega that she did not need words. And over the years she developed the purest and most beautiful language of all—music. It helped him refine his ideas about the mathematics of music. Vega was humming Bach fugues long before there ever was a Bach."

"What?" Archie slipped his arm around Calista's waist. They sat now in the silty mud, chest deep in the water.

"Anyhow, eventually she died."

"Before Pythagoras?"

"Yes. She just sort of faded away. It was as if she had lived steeped in this world of abstractions and symbols so thoroughly that she had somehow become that. There was no material substance to her. She didn't die, really. She just left her body behind and climbed this starry staircase into the sky, to become part of the harmony of the heavens. She became the brightest star, Vega, in heaven's harp—Lyra."

"I swear I never heard that myth." He drew her wet body closer to his.

"Well, of course you haven't heard it. I made it up."

"You made it up?"

"Yeah, for Charley, years ago."

"Did you ever make it into a picture book and illustrate it?"

253

"No. I can't give away all of our secrets. I hate those authors who use their families constantly. Believe me, plenty of the Jacobses get into my books. We have to save out something that's just for ourselves."

"So you're a secret mythmaker."

"Not so secret. Some I've thought up I've written for publication. But not this one. Not many of the starry ones."

"It's funny. Here Tom was an astrophysicist, and you make up astromyths."

"Not that funny." She paused. "So what if astronomers can measure the speed and temperatures of stars millions of miles away. Everything needs a story. There's the natural history story that explains the numbers, the physics. And then there needs to be the other kind of story—the one that deepens the mystery and makes more awesome the beauty." They lay back in each other's arms, their shoulders and heads resting against the thick soft grass of the bank, their torsos and legs extending into the silty mud. "I've even got one about quasars."

"Quasars?"

"You know."

"Yeah, I know. But I get them mixed up with pulsars. Pulsars give those radio waves in short bursts, right?"

"Yeah. They're basically fast-spinning neutron stars. But quasars are more mysterious. They're those faint little starlike objects. That's what the word stands for, quasi-stellar radio source. They were only detected, when? twenty, twenty-five years ago? They're ripe for mythmaking. Tom had written a lot about them. I mean, they're part of the black hole scenario."

"Why's that?"

"Well, they think they're related to the collapse of whole regions of a galaxy—see what a story that could be!"

Archie chuckled. He could see her eyes sparkling in her wet face. A scroll of hair inscribed her cheek. She looked sleek as a seal, and she swam like one, too.

"What are you laughing at? You think it's weird, don't you? My talking this way."

"I like it weird. I think it's amazing. I think your mind is amazing."

"You know, Archie, it's not that amazing. People have been

doing this for years. Michelangelo looks at a hunk of marble and sees the David embedded in it waiting to be released. A geologist looks at a hunk of marble and sees the silicate structure or whatever you call it. Both are right. Both see stories in the marble. One narrative is called natural science, the other is called mythology or art. But each has its own truths. So there!"

"So there!" Archie grabbed her and rolled her over in the mud.

"Oh, God, I always dreamed of mud wrestling!" She laughed as he began to slide inside her. "What will the bullfrog think?"

"He'll wish he were a prince!" Archie sighed deeply.

There was one thing that had been troubling Archie all along. Where in this tangled web of fudged science and religious extremism did his cousin Neddy fit? That afternoon in Neddy's house he had come away convinced that things were not exactly as Neddy had presented them. No way did he swallow that the president of the United States had sent Neddy to Texas as a kind of high-level emissary to pay court to those jerks. No, he had come away convinced that Thurston had his hooks into Neddy some way. But he could not imagine that his cousin would be on the take financially. No recent administration had earned particularly high marks in the ethics department. Kickback schemes were rampant, and conflict-of-interest situations, especially those related to defense contractors, had become almost epidemic. But there was some other reason why Neddy was down there, and it could not be money. He was just too rich. He wouldn't take such a risk for money. Could it be something with a woman? It didn't seem likely. And if Neddy was involved with the creationists, was he in on this intellamine crap, too? No, there was definitely something fishy. It smelled bad, real bad. Sooner or later Archie was going to have to confront Neddy. He just didn't have enough of the cards in his hands yet. But he was getting them. This morning he was reading *The New York Times* article on the reputed skulls. Calista had driven down into the village and bought every newspaper— all three. *The New York Times,* the *Boston Globe,* and something called the *Upper Valley News.* The *Times* and the *Globe* had front-page articles on the fossil treasures of Lorne Thurston College of

255

Christian Heritage. A spokesman for the college was playing it very tight-lipped, not denying or confirming anything but nodding soberly that yes, skulls had been found that raised new questions about different evolutionary tracks for the races. No, he had explained patiently, this was not a racist theory, and it in no way compromised their views on the creation story and the scientific veracity of Genesis.

"See," said Archie, snapping the paper and folding it over to read the bottom half, "this is what these guys always do. They say that species can undergo limited changes because the Creator endowed them each with somewhat of a repertoire of genetic variability. Just enough to make slight accommodations necessary to survive in nature. No, monkeys cannot evolve into people, mind you. Just a few changes in hair and coloring. Now listen to this, Cal." She looked up from the paper she was reading. "This guy quotes here Henry Morris. He's one of the head honchos of the creationist movement. Holds a Ph.D. in hydraulic engineering. What else can you say? Every good flood needs a hydraulic engineer." Calista laughed. "Listen to this. It's the college spokesman quoting Dr. Morris on this subject of genetic variability. Dr. Morris says, and I quote, 'Since the Creator has a purpose for each kind of organism created, He would institute a system which would not only assure its genetic integrity, but would also enable it to survive in nature. The genetic system would be such as to maintain its identity as a specific kind while, at the same time, allowing it to adjust its characteristics (within limits) to changes in environment.' End quote."

"So they think these skulls show that kind of small change that races might make?"

"Yeah. They think that, even though LeGros Clark, the great English anatomist and anthropologist, has said that there has never been a fossil that has shown any kind of racial traces. A few people have been hoping, trying for something like this for years. Carleton Coon, a racist anthropologist if there ever was one, wrote a whole book about it back in the early sixties in which he declared that Africa might have been the cradle of mankind, but it was only an 'indifferent kindergarten,' as he called it, and that Europe and Asia were the 'principle schools.'"

"Oh, no!" Calista wrinkled her nose. "How vile. Do they say yet where they found these skulls and what exactly they are or show?"

"Not yet. But the pressure's going to build. Mark my words. That'll come out tomorrow. And I'll tell you precisely where they're going to say they got them from and what they are."

"How can you know, Archie?" Calista looked up from her paper.

"Because if I were going to fake a skull for the reasons they are doing it, here's what I would have to do—not that these people are concerned with facts, but it is a fact that *Homo erectus* was the first hominid to travel outside of Africa."

"Oh, now wait a minute," Calista said. "Refresh me. Which one is *Homo erectus?*"

"You know, tall, dark, and handsome, invented fire. Kind of the matinee idol of the hominid world, the first one you might have been able to have a meaningful relationship with." Archie's eyes twinkled.

"Oh, come off it, Archie!" She wadded up a paper napkin and tossed it at him. "Okay, so he left Africa," she said.

"Not all of them. It's not as if the whole kit and caboodle packed up and left. Some stayed behind, but some left. Traces have been found in Asia and places in Europe. *Homo erectus* is generally regarded as the root stock of *Homo sapiens*. There were two waves of emigration from Africa. Now what these guys, I bet, are going to say is in that second wave these separate clumps of *Homo erectus* evolved into separate colors of *Homo sapiens*."

"But weren't there intermediary forms? I mean, are you saying they've got *Homo erectus* skulls?"

"Yes, there were intermediary forms, and no, they're not going to come up with *erectus* skulls. *Erectus* is just their ticket. They are going to say that modern African skulls more closely resemble, say, Neanderthal skulls—one of which could be thought of as an intermediary form. That these modern African skulls resemble Neanderthal more closely than Caucasians. One of these skulls that they claim to have found is going to be a very old *Homo sapiens* one, found in Europe. And it will look very Caucasian. Then they can say we whites have evolved much farther than blacks. At least if I were going to try and pull off something like this, this is how I would work it."

"Well, if you were going to do it, you wouldn't have to fit it all into the Genesis time frame, so that might make it a little easier."

"True, but watch—they'll manipulate that time frame to make it still hold up and work for them."

"Will they have a black skull, then?"

"No. They're just going to make this 'white' one very old but definitely found in Europe and within their favorite time frame. Listen, they don't even need to fake the skull to stir up a hornet's nest. People see too often what they want to see in fossils— glorified visions of themselves. Look how they convinced themselves on the science of Genesis. This wouldn't be too hard. They look at a skull, doctored or not, and they can read in a whole racist, white supremist doctrine. In the last century, which was a veritable heyday for craniology, folks did it all the time. Samuel George Moreton ranked cranial capacity according to race. He measured the volume with mustard seed. You can bet he really pushed down the mustard seeds to make room for more in the white skulls."

"Oh, God!"

"Oh, by the way, he didn't even bother measuring women's skulls."

"What a shame! So anyway you say that they'll just need this one very old *Homo sapiens* skull and they'll basically say that the *erectus* that were left behind didn't evolve or did so into a black variety of *Homo sapiens* and the ones that came to Europe became white."

"Yep." Archie nodded.

"But isn't that almost mathematically impossible?"

"Exactly! It's mathematically impossible for three of four separate clumps of one species to evolve simultaneously into as complex an organism as *Homo sapiens* with only racial differences. It's the equivalent of saying that a room full of chimps all at typewriters will come up with Hamlet's soliloquy and only punctuation differences."

. .

It happened almost precisely as Archie had described. The skulls had yet to be revealed, but in articles in the next day's *Times* and *Globe,* more information, "official information," had been given. There was just one skull, and it was definitely modern but very old. "Oh, my God!" Archie said. "All these years they're going on saying they don't believe in radiometric dating—now when it suits them, they use it! Listen to this: 'Although we do not believe in the validity of any of the radiometric dating techniques, even using those methods we see that this skull is significantly older than any thus found of modern human beings.'"

"How can they have it both ways? If they don't believe in the method, why use it?"

"They're scrambling, Calista. We caught them with their pants down. Any port in a storm. They're hedging their bets. See, they're invoking now a little Flood theory for deposition. They go on here to say that what they believe is that the geological column and all of the fossil-bearing strata were—and I quote—'arranged and worked out by the Creator long before anyone ever heard or thought about radioactive carbon dating.' Their fossil was found in very deep sediments."

"Yeah, like someone's basement," Calista said.

"'We can no longer be accused,'" Archie continued reading, "'of not submitting evidence for scientific testing. We have. And there now seems to be proof that this is a very old Caucasian skull, predating any of the other ones ever found.' Nobody has ever found a Caucasian fossil skull, buddy!" Archie growled at the paper.

"Where did they say they found it? Minneapolis?"

"Uh . . . let's see here . . . northern Turkey."

"Oh, of course, near Mount Ararat, where Noah's Ark was supposed to have finally fetched up. All the smart would-be white people got on the boat. There was probably, what—a speciation event on the Ark—and when they got off they were white. Better than *Love Boat!*"

Archie laughed. "They're running, Calista. They're running hard."

"But why? Why would they do such a thing?"

"Remember, the Creator is supposed to have a purpose for each kind of organism created, and presumably you can extend it to each race since He has a purpose for each kind of organism created."

"So what would they perceive as the Creator's purpose?"

"I couldn't even begin to imagine."

"It scares me."

"Me too," Archie said quietly.

And there was still this other thing nagging at him in the back of his mind. Why Neddy? Where did Neddy fit in? How did they get to him? These people had big plans. They controlled networks now. Often they controlled textbooks. No presidential candidate, except for Pat Robertson, had ever claimed to have God tell him to run. And there had now been rumors of Thurston feeling out the terrain, he too claiming divine inspiration—a heavenly PA system. They were rich. The old Gospel tent had given way to the satellite dish. Notions of parish had given way to those of constituencies, and notions of constituencies might be giving way to those of kingdoms and empires. When Pat Robertson had won an early Michigan primary, he had declared triumphantly, "The Christians have won. . . . What a breakthrough for the kingdom!" But as one astute journalist had pointed out in an article, when Jack Kennedy won the West Virginia primary he didn't declare, "The Catholics have won. . . . What a breakthrough for the Vatican!"

The telephone rang. Calista got up to answer it.

"Oh, hello, Colin. . . . Yes, Archie's here. Hiding out, as it were. Just a minute." Calista knew Colin Mercer from years before when the *National Geographic* had done an article on Tom and his work with the Time Slicer in magnetic dating using trace elements.

Archie picked up the phone. "Hello."

"I didn't realize, Archie, that you were keeping company with the widow Jacobs. I envy you. That mustn't be such a bad exile."

"I'm bearing up."

There was a low locker-room-type chuckle from Colin.

260

Archie knew that Colin was not one of Calista's favorites. He was a classic chauvinist pig. She would not have liked this laugh. On her behalf Archie gave a short cough of disapproval and did not join in the chuckle. "So what are you calling about?"

"What country are you supposed to be in?"

"I don't know. I never got that specific. Just away."

"Well, I think you should be in Israel."

"Why's that?"

"You know that team we're covering working in the Qafzeh cave in lower Galilee?"

"Yeah, yeah, sure. They come up with something?"

"They sure did, and the timing couldn't be better."

"What?" Archie said. Calista looked up from her drawing board. She could hear the excitement in his voice.

"Okay, now," Colin was saying, "the Texas boys claim they got an old skull proving that whites evolved separately long, long ago, but in Europe, while black guys sat down in Africa and didn't evolve much."

"Yeah, that's the scenario. Come on, Colin, don't drag this out."

But he was dragging it out. "Curious, this sudden interest of theirs in radiometric dating, isn't it?"

"Yes. Now what have you got?"

"A ninety-two-thousand-year-old skull from a 'modern,' not an archaic, human being from a cave in Israel, which ain't all that far from Africa. Only this one's real, and it's going to blow their little Johnny Walker White right out of the water. This one—it ain't white. It ain't black. It's just a good old-fashioned fabulous specimen of an anatomically modern human being."

"Good Lord! This is timing, but beyond that you realize that this pushes back the date for modern humans by at least fifty thousand years. They always thought the first ones evolved, what, thirty-two to thirty-five thousand years ago? And it also firmly supports the hypothesis that they evolved in Africa." Calista had stopped inking in the figure of Maid Marian and was trying to follow the conversation. "You're right, the timing couldn't be better."

261

"These guys are going to shrivel up and die, be blown away in the wind. We'll probably never find out why they went to such lengths."

"Don't count on it."

"Okay, well, keep in touch. And give the widow Jacobs a kiss for me."

Archie coughed again and said good-bye.

"So did you hear that, Cal?" he said, turning to her.

"Part of it."

Archie related briefly what Colin had just called about. Calista's eyes opened in amazement as he finished. "Can you believe it?" he said. "I mean the implications, not just in terms of this fake skull down in Texas."

42   "I don't like it!" Lorne Thurston said angrily into the receiver. A secretary poked her head into the room, and Clarella motioned her out with a wave of the long peach-colored nails that she was filing. "I don't care whether it's a new game now. I don't care if it's hardball. You don't play hardball with my students. . . . This'll blow over. . . ." His eyebrows raised as he listened to the voice on the other end. "I am not deluding myself," he barked. "This is nothing compared to Jim and Tammy Faye." Clarella looked up and winked knowingly at her husband, blew on her nails, and then picked up a buffer and began buffing them. "This publicity might be a minor set-back," Thurston continued, "but we can overcome it. We're getting the numbers right on the Supreme Court. The textbook folks are backing off. In Iowa, Oklahoma, and Illinois we're getting education officials to insist on inclusion of biblical creationist beliefs along with the Darwin stuff. We are getting ahead. Our guidelines are going through for textbooks. The National Association for Christian Educators and the good people over at CEE are doing a great job. No, there is absolutely no way I will permit this. She is not a threat, and even if she

were . . ." He listened silently for a few more seconds. "You guys are going too far, and I don't think I should have to remind you where your funding comes from. You're acting like a bunch of paranoids. No   this is the end of it. Not another word. Good-bye." He slammed down the telephone and glared out the window. "You know, Clarella"—he sighed deeply—"it's hard to pray for people like that. But by gum I'm going to try!"

He walked over to a corner area of his office where the carpeting stopped and some blue flagstones had been set into the floor. There were two potted lily plants and a crucifix. It was his own private office chapel. He sank to his knees with a groan. Clarella put down her nail buffer, walked over, and got down on her knees. She felt a run shoot up her left nylon. "Dear Lord . . ." Thurston began to pray.

Beth Ann had never thought again about that flat, nasal voice she'd heard come out of Dr. Tompkins. Not once since coming to Bible Times, which to her had been a dream come true. She adored her work in the Little Shepherd Day Care Center. And because they were also shorthanded in the hospitality office, she had been working there doing everything from helping people with travel arrangements to working on the printed materials that showed the new luxury suites. It was a real education.

But it was the beginning of Beth Ann's third week at Bible Times when the first leak sprung, and it was then that she recalled that strange nasal voice of Wayne Tompkins. She had just come into the hospitality office to stuff envelopes. Nobody was there. Everybody was in the office next door. She could see them all huddled around a table looking at something. She went in.

"I'll be . . . ," a voice said in slow wonderment.

"They're saying Lorne faked this stuff."

"Not Lorne . . . the scientists. . . ."

"This is a plot . . . this is a commie plot. . . ."

"Work of the devil. . . ."

"What's going on?" Beth Ann asked a young man she knew who was standing on the edge of the group.

Before the man could answer she heard another boy say, "Gee, my roommate went on that expedition when they discovered those skulls. It was right in the region where they're looking for the ark." Beth Ann's heart sank. She felt a funny prickly feeling all over. Her head seemed to swim. "Look what it says here in the *Post*. . . . Yeah, and this here *New York Times*, well, everyone knows what that rag is. . . . Yeah, but the Fredericksburg paper has . . ."

It seemed unbelievable. Her blabbing could not have come to this—could it have? She suddenly had an image of her mouth, her tongue, reflected in an infinity of mirrors.

"Beth Ann, is something wrong?" It was John, the young man she had first asked what was happening.

"No, no . . . I'll be all right," she said, touching the edge of a chair and then holding on to it more firmly.

"Beth Ann, you look terrible." He took her firmly by the arm. It was as if her feet weren't even on the floor, but she could feel his hand on her elbow. It was a welcome support.

They were sitting in the far corner of a juice bar in a replica of the old city of Jerusalem. "So," John was saying, "you think that maybe the college did have something to hide; that it might be true what the papers were saying, that they did do something funny."

"I don't know whether they did anything funny or not with the skulls, and I don't understand anything about this science, but I told you what happened when I took that nice lady through, how mad the professor got at me. I mean, wouldn't you say that that sounds like they had something to hide?"

"Well, yeah."

"And then I get instantly shipped off to here. I mean, John, kids are dying to get these jobs. How long have you been on a waiting list for your job here?"

"Five semesters, I think."

"Well, see? I'd just signed up, let's see . . . this past fall."

"That is quick. But Beth Ann, you yourself said that Dean Clayton said it was just sensitive material. That doesn't necessarily mean there's some kind of funny stuff going on."

"Oh, yes. I know. But still I shouldn't have said anything, and I did."

"I think you're being too hard on yourself, and besides, it

wasn't you who really spilled the beans. I mean, you didn't call up the newspapers and the press."

"No, certainly not."

"See, it must have been that nice lady and her kid who did it."

"Oh, dear!" Beth Ann whispered softly, and touched her cheek. But she was filled with feelings not of anger, but of anxiety. Suddenly she remembered the bruised face of Wayne Tompkins, the blood on his shirt. The ugly little laugh. No, she wasn't worried about Wayne Tompkins. She was worried about Charley Jacobs and his nice mother. She didn't care right now whether they had called up the press or not. She liked them. She just plain liked them.

It took a little doing to get the Jacobses' number. She had to call the admissions office back at the college, and there was no number, but she finally reached him through his pastor's home—the Reverend Matthew McPhail.

Calista's house in Vermont was an old eighteenth-century farmhouse. Her gardens were furious, untrammeled explosions of color. In Cambridge she had had no choice. Not enough sun could filter through the immense trees to coax any color out of anything. So she had been confined to shade plants for the most part with the occasional splash of spring colors from spring bulbs that could grow before the leaves had unfurled, spreading their embroidery of shade. It was in Vermont that she made up for the lack of color in Cambridge.

Off the back of the house was a terrace made from salvaged old bricks that had faded to almost pink. In the summertime and the early fall days, Calista spent most of her time on this terrace sunning, cooking in the brick barbecue, reading, and looking down at the meadow that swooped below for a thousand feet or more. The meadow ended in a bog that in June was filled with lady's slippers and strange, tiny orchids. But beyond the bog the low New England mountains rose in shadows of gray and purple, sometimes swathed in cloud and mist. Always gentle under the sky, so unlike the Rockies, which reared and clawed at the clouds above them, these mountains reminded Calista of sleeping women.

The coals were hot enough now. Calista took the trout she had caught that afternoon, which she had wrapped carefully in long grass, and buried them in the embers. She had found a couple of tomatoes ready in her garden and began slicing them. Archie watched her as she padded around barefoot. She wore these funny little outfits that were sexy, but not blatantly so. At the moment she was wearing men's light cotton drawers, boxer shorts, over some kind of a lace-trimmed body suit. She had stuck some pink roses in her hair. She looked quite frankly daffy, but undeniably sexy, springing around on her lean, well-muscled legs as she wrapped up fish in grass, discussed the merits of sedges versus cattails as a wrap for baking the fish, popped a sliver of the gravlax into Archie's mouth. She was most remarkable, this woman, this spinner of tales, maker of myths, with her observations on life, which ranged from contemplations of Dom Pérignon to insights into the fundamentalist mind. You never stopped thinking when you were around her or, for him, the other less cerebral activity—screwing. So this would either keep him very young or the reverse: he might go from fifty-two to eighty-two within a month.

While the trout were baking Calista settled on a cushion by Archie's feet with her drink and a bottle of calamine lotion and some cotton. This in Calista's mind was the perfect summer evening—to sip Mount Gay rum very slowly and count mosquito bites, dabbing on calamine lotion. "You have very nice legs, Archie."

"So do you."

"They're nice and straight with just the right amount of hairiness."

"Yours, too."

She laughed. "Why do men have more body hair than women?"

Archie chuckled. "There was once an evolutionary theory that tried to explain body hair."

"No kidding," she said, intent on a huge bite on Archie's knee. "Some people will do anything for a Ph.D. thesis."

"Yeah. It was hypothesized that the reason humans lost their apish hair was because when men had to go hunting and run

266

around on the savanna chasing saber-toothed tigers and all, they could not perspire efficiently."

"But what about the women? Why did they lose their hair? They weren't hunting, I presume."

"No, that's what was wrong with the theory. For one thing it presumed that only men hunted. So there was no explanation for women's hair loss. And then it was a theory hatched in the heyday of man-of-the-mighty-hunter concepts. Now they're starting to realize that man didn't hunt all that much."

"Huh?"

"Yeah. Didn't have the social organization back then. Food gathering was a lot more efficient and a lot less risky considering the net calorie gain. So it's more likely that the first food-related tool was not a spear or a hand ax, but a basket."

"Oooh, I like that! And then if this skull from the cave in Israel turns out to be a woman's, it will all make perfect evolutionary sense to me!" Calista took a sip of her rum and looked up at Archie. He ran his fingers through her hair, taking care not to disturb the roses.

43

"You see, there was this woman guest on *You Bet Your Life*." Calista was talking through the screen door as she swept the terrace early the next morning. She was still in her nightgown. Inside, Archie was minding the coffee. She had been up since five working on *Marian's Tale*. The door swung open, and Archie brought out a breakfast tray to put on the terrace table.

"Yeah?" he said.

"So this lady had had twenty-two children, and she was explaining somewhat sheepishly to Groucho that, well, she just loved her husband. And Groucho says to her, 'I love my cigar, too, but I take it out once in a while.'" Calista very nearly cackled, but she remembered just in time and suppressed the cackle that threatened to explode. The phone rang, and she went to get it.

"Oh, Liam. . . . Yes . . . well, we're here. You've found stuff out . . . oh, great. Wait, I'll get Archie, and I'll get on the other phone."

"What?" Archie said. "No shit . . . *The Green Review?* You mean that nutty reactionary publication? . . . Okay, yeah, let me get a pencil and paper."

By the end of the conversation, Calista had sketched a diagram of the hacking path of Norman Petrakis. Archie gnawed a pencil and stared at the map of institutes and labs where Petrakis had intruded. They were all biology labs working on genetic research of one sort or another—cancer, species separation, twins research. The one place that made absolutely no sense was *The Green Review.*

The Green Review—how could that fit into all of this? Funding! Hadn't Liam Phillips told them on the phone that his Berkeley contact had said big money had been put up to snag this intruder? Something to the tune of thirty thousand dollars. Big money was behind *The Green Review.* It was a very right-wing newspaper that was funded by very reactionary rich Ivy League graduates. It was not associated with any one particular school but had drawn from them all—Harvard, Dartmouth, Yale, Princeton. The staff was young and virulent.

Big money would have to be behind this protein-fudging scam. And who knew, the same kind of mind attracted to funding a rag like *The Green Review* might be attracted to this. He was beginning to see exactly where the fossils and the genetics separated and where they touched. The creationists had their own sources for money—coffers filled by those satellite collection plates, but the biology labs had to scramble, always an uphill battle for funding. You couldn't exactly get on the air and pass the plate as a biological laboratory, and if you were not very well connected with a big university, it would be tough. The labs that would be the most vulnerable were those not well connected—like the Coastal Research Institute and its little Nobel Sperm Bank—Genesis.

"You see," Archie said, looking at Calista, "Petrakis was on to this for a long time. He probably had all his facts down about the scam, but he wanted to know how it got funded. Penn,

Duke, and Minnesota were places with labs that all had plants—people willing to corroborate the information, pretend they were carrying out experiments and getting other people in the lab just to sign on, as protocol so often dictates in these situations. Probably only needed two or three to get the ball rolling. Where they ran short of cash was in trying to stop Petrakis. Universities would only allocate so much for something like that, but the perpetrators needed the guy caught and were willing to spend, well, at least thirty thousand dollars. Maybe they tried Lorne Thurston. Who knows. But it was money that first got these two schemes—the fossil one and the genetics one—together. And one connection could have been *The Green Review,* which is the greatest assemblage of fascists and crackpots under the sun and probably makes the Lorne Thurston College of Christian Heritage look mild by comparison. The backers of it are a bunch of mean old farts like . . ." Archie paused.

"Like who?"

"Like Hugh Ethelredge." Archie's face drained of color.

"Who's Hugh Ethelredge?" Calista asked.

"A very, very, very rich old man, for starters. He is on the advisory board of *The Green Review,* and—brace yourself—he is also, along with me, on the board of overseers at the Peabody Museum of Archaeology and Ethnography. He informed me recently that there was only one thing wrong with Harvard."

"What was that?" Calista asked weakly.

"They gave too many honorary degrees to women, blacks, and Jews."

"How lovely. Sounds like he might be able to get a design job at the sperm bank."

Archie blinked. "Let's check!"

Fifteen minutes later Ruth Goodfellow called Archie back.

"Archie, I couldn't find the old Genesis pamphlet. I can't believe I would have thrown away such a rare document," she said in her cool, clipped English accent. "But I did find the old letter where they asked for your contribution, my dear."

"Just as long as you don't have it framed."

"Yes, I thought I'd put it on the wall with all your family

pictures. Most fitting. You know, people can check out the whole Baldwin gene pool."

Archie laughed. "So what did you find?"

"Well, your little friend Hugh Ethelredge is a donor, although of money and not sperm, to Atwell's Project Genesis. That's the official name, by the way."

"No shit. He really is?"

"Yes, and this is confirmed."

"How in the hell did you do that?"

"Well, his name is on the stationery as being a member of the advisory board. And seeing as the letter was old, I just thought maybe I should check up to see if he was still on the board. And then they said—and I quote the lady I spoke to—'Oh, yes. Most certainly. He is one of our major supporters.' So I just said, 'I trust by supporter you mean of money, not sperm,' and she confirmed this. Although she added that she was not allowed to disclose who the actual sperm donors were over the phone, but that Mr. Ethelredge had given generously in terms of financial support. I suppose we should feel relieved that he did not give in the alternate method."

"Yes. I guess so. Well, thank you, Ruth. This is above and beyond."

"Nonsense, Archie. But I do think that Nobel or not, your contribution could not help but raise their standards."

"Please, Goodfellow! No more cracks!"

"Well, as we know, they never give Nobels in anthropology or archaeology anyhow. So don't feel bad."

"Goodfellow!"

"Cheerio, Archie."

It wasn't five minutes later that the phone rang again. This time it was Charley.

"Mom!" Charley blurted out. "You'll never guess what!"

"What?" Calista felt something clench in her stomach. She told herself to calm down. Nothing could be wrong. Here, after all, was Charley alive and well and blaring over the phone. "It's Beth Ann. She's real worried, and she even got into some kind of trouble herself."

"Beth Ann . . ." It took Calista a minute. "You mean Beth Ann from the college?"

"Yes, that Beth Ann!"

"Well, how do you know she's in trouble?"

"She called me."

"She called you at the McPhails' from Texas?"

"Not from Texas. From someplace in West Virginia or Virginia. It got confusing. Her grandparents live in West Virginia . . . someplace called Blue Holler, or something like that."

"But how did she ever find you at the McPhails'?"

"It's a long story."

"It must be. Do tell."

"Look, when I applied to that college you had to list your pastor, so I listed Reverend McPhail."

"Fred?"

"No. Matthew."

"Matthew?!" Calista nearly screamed. "Matthew is your pastor?"

"Motherrrr! Not really—what have you done, lost your marbles?"

"Well, I know not really, but—"

"Look, Mom, that's not the issue. She found me, that's all that counts, and she was scared to death. Really scared. They shipped her out of the college for spilling the beans about the skull thing, and now she's in that Bible Disney World of theirs. And she didn't know about us being run off the road, but she saw that Tompkins guy, and he was all bashed up like he'd been in some sort of accident. She's trying to get to West Virginia. I guess it's where her grandparents live."

"Oh, my God! Oh, that poor girl. We have to think of something to help her." Archie had come over, his face tense and grim as he pieced together the part of the conversation he was missing. "Yes . . . yes, Charley. Well, let me discuss this with Archie, then I'll call back. Is Joan around, or Fred? I'll want to talk to them. . . . Yes, dear. Don't worry. . . . No, I feel terribly sorry for her. . . . Yes. . . . Well, we'll try to figure out something. Good-bye. I'll talk to you soon,

271

within the hour. . . . Yes." She hung up the phone and sank down on the chair.

44

So that explained the blood and Wayne Tompkins's bruises. Beth Ann Hennessey felt entirely washed out, devoid of any strength and almost numb as she thought about what Charley Jacobs had just told her. Her hand still rested on the phone as if to confirm what she had just heard, to make this horrible reality palpable, less abstract. But it seemed so unbelievable—Charley and his mother nearly run off the road, then the other car had spun out and pitched into a deep ditch. My word, she thought. What were they so fearful of? What terrible power did these skulls possess that they had threatened the lives of the woman and her son? This sounded like the Devil's business if there ever was any.

She must go pray. She must go this minute to the small students' chapel and pray. It was late at night, and she would be alone. That would be good. She could cry if she wanted to and not bother anybody. She needed to pray for strength, and she needed to pray for guidance. Wrong had been done, and the wrong was not her blabbing. This much she knew. It went deeper, and it was far worse than blabbing.

She entered the chapel. It was hot and stuffy, as the air-conditioning had been turned off at this late hour, but it didn't bother her. She went to the very front and lifted a prayer pad off the seat of the pew and sank to her knees. There was only one light on, and the gleam of the beautifully designed modern cross seemed especially lustrous in the fragile darkness of the chapel. She saw a shadow slide briefly over the gleaming surface of the cross, but she never heard the movement behind her. She just felt something cold smash against the base of her skull, and the light on the cross went out.

45

When Calista had drawn the diagram of Norman Petrakis's hacking route through various computer systems, it had started to look like a spiderweb to her. She and Archie had begun to explore it and now were on a flight to Washington, D.C., where they would then pick up a car and drive to Morash, Virginia, where Bible Times was located.

They were searching for Beth Ann Hennessey. Liam Phillips had busted into the college's files in Green Acre and found out all the pertinent information necessary about Beth Ann. Beth Ann had no living parents. Her next of kin had been listed as her grandparents, Ola and Milford Arnette of Blue Hollow, West Virginia. It had been Calista's decision to go after Beth Ann. That was what she felt was the number-one priority.

The papers were full of the controversial skull and the new find in Israel. This seemed to be a last straw for the scientific world, which was already fed up with the shenanigans of the fundamentalists' forays into science. Headlines like PALUXY SKULL and RACIST FOSSILS abounded. The tabloids were having a field day with it. There were longer, more in-depth articles addressing the subject in *The New York Times* and the *Christian Science Monitor*. Paleontologists from around the world decried in no uncertain terms the outrageous abuse of science. They reiterated that the themes of bigotry and superstition, so rampant in the battle against the teaching of evolution, were rearing their ugly heads here with simply a new twist. However, the world had not even heard yet of the fabrications of the bogus brain proteins of intellamine and intellicone that had been going on in the genetic labs for the past three years. Once the link between these labs and the Lorne Thurston College of Christian Heritage could be made and the full dimensions of the abuse known, it would reveal not only fraud, but murder. Archie and Calista were still fairly certain that the creationists had been set up to be the fall guys in Petrakis's murder, that it was most likely someone trying to pass the buck off on the creationists about this murder. Still, there was the gathering evidence that some sort of bizarre plot was going on with the fossils that linked up with the fraud on a genetic level. It was designed to put one over about separate origins of races. It appeared that the words *Monkey's Uncle* had been written to throw everyone off the scent of the genetic perpetrators and somehow link Petrakis's death to his book for children on human evolution. That would explain the defacement of *Nick in the Night* as well as Margaret McGowan's book. Calista had been thinking about all of this just when Archie interrupted her. It was as if he were reading her thoughts.

"Those people from the Coastal Research Institute and the sperm bank and all the other folks they must have had planted in various university labs probably didn't give a rat's ass about the Genesis story and whether or not creationism got to be taught along with evolution or not. They had their own agenda that had to do with genetic stuff. The Bible thumpers probably just provided them with a kind of modus operandi and very possibly funds. From what you tell me after your visit to Thurston's college, and what we read about these television ministries, these guys are rolling in dough."

"But you already said they could get money from rich backers like this Ethelredge person."

"Hugh's rich, but he doesn't have it coming in at the rate of these satellite collection plates."

"Well, if the intellamine folks got money from Thurston, what did Thurston get from them?"

"A patina of scientific thought. This guy Tompkins has a master's in biology as well as a degree in engineering. Didn't you tell me there was some other guy down there that they mentioned that had a degree in hydraulic engineering?"

"Yes, Beth Ann mentioned someone."

"Well, hydraulic engineering would come in handy if you're trying to prove Noah's Flood did it all. And Atwell, he's some sort of engineer. There're always engineers in this business. Even if they believe in evolution, they can't accept ultimately the randomness of it all. They equate randomness with life devoid of meaning or purpose. They can't live with that. That is where guys like James Atwell and Hugh Ethelredge have a great deal in common with Lorne Thurston. If you're an engineer, then you assume you can fiddle with the system, adjust it to your purposes or what you perceive to be God's purposes. Why do you think Atwell has this damn Nobel sperm bank? He cannot live with the notion that there is no design to the universe. He wants to impose his own. Thurston and the creationists want to do the same thing through a literal reading of Genesis. Thurston needs the imprimatur of 'real' science, and Atwell needs money. Tit for tat, and who gives a rat's ass if it has anything to do with truth? Everybody gets what they want and comes away happy."

"Except for Norman Petrakis."

"Right." Archie paused. "There was an eighteenth-century theologian, William Paley, who compared life to a watch. He said just as a watch is too complicated to have sprung into existence spontaneously, so must it be with all living things. Because life is so complex, it, like a watch, had to have a design and a designer. The fundamentalists cannot countenance the notion of a blind watchmaker, for it means a world without purpose or reason."

Calista looked down at the map she had drawn of Petrakis's tunnelings into the various computers. She had scratchy lines running between the sites. It was looking very much like a spiderweb now. Norman had been caught in it all right. But it had not been spun by Norman or blind designers. The web, however, was spreading. She traced over the lines with her fine-nibbed pen. The drag lines were extending from the far upper left hand corner, California, where the Coastal Research Institute was located, to Green Acre, up again to Minneapolis, down to Philadelphia, and then to North Carolina and over to New Hampshire. Which were the major sites, however, where the spinnerets produced the silken threads of this design? Was it the lab in California with its fragile ties to Stanford? Or was it down in Green Acre? Or was it somewhere else that she and Archie had never imagined? Were these spinners too obvious, and was Norman to be the only victim? That sent a chill through Calista, and she thought of Beth Ann.

Calista knew a little bit about spiders. As a fourth-grader, Charley had had to write a report on them for school, and she had helped him with it. They had looked spiders up in the *Book of Knowledge,* and Charley had attempted to rewrite the information in his own words. The chunky, abrupt little sentences came back to her.

There are three main types of web weaver spiders. There are tangled-web weavers. There are sheet-web weavers, and there are orb weavers. The web of a tangled-web weaver is the simplest. It is shapeless and attaches to a support like the corner of a ceiling.

Calista looked at her drawing. This was not a tangled web of the classical order.

Orb weavers weave the most beautiful and complicated webs of all. The webs are round, and the silk threads run from the center of the web like spokes on a wheel. Some orb weavers lie in wait for their prey in the very center of the web. Some attach trap lines to the center of the web and the spider hides nearby in its nest. When an insect lands, the trap lines shake. That's the tip-off!

"What are you thinking about—spiderwebs?" Archie said, looking down at the paper.

"Yeah. I'm starting to think that this whole thing resembles a spiderweb—an orb weaver's, to be exact." She traced the bridge line that went from California to Hanover and then the perimeters.

"Hmm." Archie scratched his chin. "It's starting to look kind of like an old boy network to me."

"Where do you think Neddy fits in, or do you?"

"I don't know. I don't know. I can't believe that his involvement has anything to do with the murder. I just wish I knew what it was."

"It disturbs you a lot, doesn't it?"

"It sure does. And do you realize in three weeks I'm supposed to go sailing with Neddy? Our annual down east cruise."

"Well, I guess a cruise on a sailboat will shake any skeletons or skulls out of the closet."

Archie sighed, almost painfully. "I guess so."

When they got off the plane in Washington, D.C., Calista could not help but think of trap lines. Were they crawling up one now? Had the vibrations already begun?

46

Calista and Archie were walking under a fiberglass sky down a painted cobblestone street. On either side were shops hawking religious items—framed prayers, pop-up books with Bible stories for children, other religious books and records. And everywhere there were posters and pictures of Lorne Thurston and his wife, Clarella. They seemed to favor a somewhat regal stance in their pictures evocative of those formal portraits of the queen of England and Prince Philip. Lorne stood erect in a dark suit behind Clarella, who sat on a settee with a voluminous aquamarine gown flouncing up around her like a turbulent sea. Her hands were primly folded over a white Bible. Under his arm a larger black Bible was pressed. The message seemed to be: We are not just bringing the Word. We are the Word!

There were dolls of Clarella displayed in all the shop windows and selling for upward of two hundred dollars. If Lorne was the undisputed king of the airwaves, Clarella was certainly the queen of this kingdom here in Virginia. Her plastic face was everywhere, and for some reason it seemed to serve as a macabre twist on an old nightmare Calista had had as a child where she would desperately be looking for her mother and encountering instead plastic facsimiles. It had been a very unnerving dream of her childhood, and she had not thought of it in years. But she was not looking for her mother here. She was looking for a child—not her own, but nonetheless a child in need. And what had that child Beth Ann Hennessey been looking for? That was the real question, Calista thought.

There were ice-cream shops and theaters showing Animatronic presentations of the most dramatic of the Bible stories, ranging from "Daniel and the Lions" to "Noah's Ark." They were heading for the day-care center in hopes of finding Beth Ann. They walked through some brightly painted gates and found themselves at a desk tended by two scrubbed young girls.

"Can we help you?" one asked. The sign above read "Little Shepherd Day Care Center." In bright, air-conditioned, sky-lighted rooms beyond, Calista and Archie could see the little lambs.

"We're relatives of Beth Ann Hennessey, and we're just down for the day from Washington and wanted to stop by and say hello."

"Oh, Beth Ann," said the one girl, looking at the other. "Yes, she was working here. But then they switched her just temporarily." She paused. "Did they put her over in the water park, Mary?"

"Yeah, I think so—on the River Jordan ride, the kiddie part of it."

"The River Jordan?" Calista said softly.

"I think that's where they sent her," the girl named Mary said. "But come to think of it, I haven't seen her at supper for the last two nights."

"Beth Ann? Beth Ann Hennessey?" A young, athletic-looking man in a muscle shirt, bathing trunks, and a whistle around his neck was staring out as if trying to place her face. He was looking directly at a gigantic water slide. His face suddenly clenched, and he blew his whistle. "None of that, fellows! Too rough!" He was pointing at two teenaged boys who were horsing about at the top of the slide. "Now let's see. . . . Yeah. Beth Ann. I remember her. I think she had to go on home. Something about some ailing grandparent out in Califor-nia."

"Her grandparents—in California?" Calista said, slightly confused.

"Yeah, I'm sure they said that she was going to California, and it was something to do with her grandparents. You can check with the office. It's over at the broadcasting center. They'll know."

. .

The big question was, should they really check with the office? Would that tip off someone who could cause problems? Archie felt they should. None of the kids they had spoken to so far had been lying. He was sure of that. They genuinely did not know where Beth Ann had gone. She admittedly had not made much of an impression, but then again she presumably must not have spent much time there. It had barely been a month since Calista and Charley had left Beth Ann down in Green Acre in her job as campus guide.

Calista and Archie had cut through the replica village of Old Jerusalem to head for the administrative offices. Just as they exited the village they saw a long silver limousine pull up in front of the stucco offices.

"Look, it's him!" Archie said. A bright carrot-top head bobbed out of the car followed by a platinum one. Aides rushed out of the building, and some others got out of the car. Two young men ran around to the back of the limo and started unloading what looked to Calista like Vuitton luggage.

"No, honey, put that back in 'cause we're goin' to be goin' right over to the Manor," Clarella directed with a thin, jeweled hand.

"You really want to go in and ask for Beth Ann?" Calista said. "With the lion in his den?" She paused. "Archie, I think we better lay low. I got a hunch she's not here."

"But we know for a fact that her grandparents don't live in California. Liam found out they lived in West Virginia—Blue Hollow, West Virginia, which is definitely not California."

"There's only one thing in California as far as this mess is concerned." She looked at Archie levelly.

"The Coastal Research Institute," he replied.

She nodded.

"Do you think that there's any chance that she could be with her grandparents in Blue Hollow, or that they would know anything?" he asked.

"I don't know."

"And if she's not there, I guess we have to assume she's in California. Although why they would feel she constitutes so much of a threat that she would have to be removed to California, I don't know."

279

"Me neither. Unless they have other plans for her at that sperm bank. . . . Oh, God! It nauseates me just to think about it. I suppose it might be worth a try going to her grandparents' place in West Virginia. What did you say—that place they live in is only one hundred miles from here?"

"Less than that. It's just over the West Virginia border."

"I think we should get out of here before we're found out, or before anybody gets any ideas about running us off any roads."

"Okay. I'm with you."

47

"You see," Ola Arnette was saying. "I think we were just too old for her. She came to live with us when she was just four, and we were already almost seventy then." She spoke in a soft but husky voice that for some reason reminded Calista of morning mist or ground fog. It seemed to lie on the evening air like a gentle hush, muting things, blurring them just a bit. They were on the front porch of the Arnettes' log house deep in the hills of West Virginia. "This holler warn't no place for a young, growing thing. Oh, yeah, there were a few youngsters around, but they all had young parents and most of them moved down to Benton after a time." Ola paused as if to contemplate the migration of younger, stronger people. "We were old and poor when she came to us. We got our patch here and do fine by it. Mind you, we're not complaining."

"Not complaining," Milford echoed. He appeared to be totally absorbed in his whittling, but every now and then he would say something, usually repeating a phrase of his wife's. The low mountains turned blue in the dusky twilight.

"I think it was loneliness that drove her to the church," Ola said.

"That and the indoor plumbing," Milford said, running his thumb along the piece he was working.

"Milford!" Ola exclaimed. Archie and Calista looked at one

280

another. "She was always ashamed that we never had indoor plumbing. We have a johnny house out back. But as more and more of her friends started moving down to Benton and then when she started goin' to the junior high down there, well, she took to some ideas."

"Plumbing and sidewalks—the church had both," Milford said.

"Milford, these folks're going to think we're all heathens. It's not as if we don't go to church, and when we think of church, we just don't think of them conveniences you mentioned. It wasn't all that with Beth Ann."

Ola put down her work. She was braiding a rug, and she had long hands. They were gnarled and callused, but they were beautiful in their strength and now in their absolute repose as they settled very peacefully in her lap. "It wasn't just those conveniences." She paused as if to reflect. "It was the convenience of friendship, of being young with youngsters and being . . ." She paused and rested her elbow on the arm of the rocking chair and then rested her head heavily on her hand. "It's hard to explain to you folks, but, you know, Beth Ann's father, well, he warn't no good. He was a drunk, ran off from home before she was born. And her mother, well, Eulie, though she was my own daughter, she was not a kind child."

"She warn't really mean, Ola."

"No, she warn't mean. But you don't have to be mean to be unkind. She just didn't know how to be kind. She was too busy with herself and her own plans and dreams. So that's why she brought Beth Ann to us. And we was so old at the time. Two seventy-year-olds—ain't no place for a four-year-old to be. Oh, we loved her the best we could. But it's not the same. She knew she'd been passed off to us. At first her mama used to visit and sometimes write letters. But then she just stopped. And it was about that time that Beth Ann started going to church."

"And we don't just mean Sundays," Milford said, shaving off a curl from the wood with his knife.

"No, every day she could get down to Benton to church, she was going. I said to Milford when Beth Ann was just eleven years old, 'We're going to lose her. We love her as much as the church does, but there's no way we can compete.'"

281

"Ola was right."

"Yep." Ola rocked backed and forth now and tapped her foot briskly as if for emphasis. "She moved down there that spring. Stayed with the pastor's family all the way through junior high and high school and then got that scholarship to college."

"Does she ever come back?" Archie asked.

"Oh, sure. She's dear to us. Brings us presents and stays with us and all. She don't even complain now about the johnny house and the no sidewalks. She's a loving child. We just couldn't give her the kind of love she needed when she needed it."

Calista looked around and tried to imagine what it must have been like growing up in this shady mountain hollow of West Virginia with its blue smoky shadows and scent of pine, with no electricity and no plumbing, with these two gentle old people.

They were handsome people both with their snowy white hair and fair complexions. They looked almost as if they had been powdered. They must have taken great care to keep the sun off their faces. Calista could imagine them working their patch shaded by straw hats with deep brims. Their clothes were clean and neatly patched. They could neither read nor write, but Milford had built the house and made every stick of furniture in it. Several vegetable gardens surrounded the house all perfectly kept, and they had referred to a field. These people were warm and loving, but it might not have been enough, especially for a child who already knew she had been rejected. Wouldn't there always be this nagging doubt at the back of one's mind about being loved by "real" parents who were young and lived in houses with toilets on streets with sidewalks? Doubts like these might become compounded during those years of adolescent uncertainty and lead to a quest for a perfect and unconditional love. And could that not lead in turn to a confusion between plastic facsimiles, the kind of mechanical doll mothers that terrorized Calista's own dreams as a child, and the real thing? And the real thing in this case might seem at first to be old worn rag dolls made from flour sacks, worn threadbare from work but still loving the best way they knew how.

"So you think that our Beth Ann's in some sort of trouble?" Milford stopped whittling and looked directly at Archie.

"Well, we can't be sure, and we don't want to jump to conclusions. But Calista told you the long story about her and her son's visit to the college, and Calista's son, Charley, said that when she called she seemed . . . uh, quite upset."

"And you say that she said she was at that amusement park they run over there?" Ola asked. Archie nodded. "Seems funny that she wouldn't have written us 'bout it. That had been something that she'd talked about doing someday and it being so near to home . . . seems mighty funny. Dear me!"

"Now, don't get worried." Calista tried to soothe the old woman.

"Is this something we should talk to Buford about?" Ola seemed to be wondering aloud.

"Who's Buford?" Calista asked.

"He's the sheriff."

"Well, I don't think he could be of much help yet," Archie said.

Both Archie and Calista were trying desperately to sound concerned, but not overly so. They hadn't dared mention anything about Norman Petrakis's murder or that their next stop was the Coastal Research Institute. If the notion of indoor plumbing and sidewalks seemed exotic to the Arnettes, Archie and Calista could not even begin to imagine what they would think of a bank specializing in the harvesting of human sperm.

Before they left in the gathering shadows of the evening, Calista walked with Ola around the small farm. They kept one cow, some geese, chickens, and a sow. That was about it. The vegetable gardens were perfect, several with raised beds. It was unimaginable how they tended all of this, yet it was still very clearly a subsistence-level operation. They were now walking between two rows in one of the gardens. "There she is!" Ola exclaimed. "I declare, she's put on another pound overnight." A most immense pumpkin lolled on the rich dark soil.

"Goodness!" exclaimed Calista. "It's this big and the summer's just half-over!"

"Here's what does it!" Ola said, lifting the pitcher of milk she was carrying. "Now watch how I do this." She bent over. Her plump figure in the faded blue dress looked like a sack of laundry tied in the middle. A thin stream of milk slopped into the tin bowl set by the pumpkin's vine. "You see, I got it wicked."

"Wicked?"

"Yeah, I cut a notch in the vine and just lead a wick right up to it. The milk soaks in and climbs right up there to the vine. Pumpkins love milk. Makes them grow twice as big. And their meat tastes so good that way."

The first stars were just winking out of the dusty purple of the sky. A bobwhite whistled. A breeze came, and now along with the pine scent Calista smelled the sweet fragrance of Ola—of talcum powder and fresh milk. This was real. Calista had to help Beth Ann find her way back to reality even if it was not this one. She just had to help her.

48

"What are you doing bursting in here at this hour? For chrissake, Archie!" Neddy Baldwin came downstairs looking totally disheveled. There were lipstick smears on his cheeks. They had driven directly back from the Arnettes in West Virginia to Ned Baldwin in Georgetown. It had taken less than three hours to bridge these two disparate worlds.

"Just be happy I'm not your wife," Archie said. Neddy scowled at Archie. The scowl said, No fair! He'd gone off limits, limits that had been carefully preserved over the years.

"Hi." Calista came up the walk.

"What in the world?!" Neddy was absolutely speechless. This seemed to be his usual response to Calista, if two meetings could constitute usual. She wondered if she should ask him to dance. But she wasn't feeling cute.

"Come on, Neddy. You got some talking to do." He took his cousin firmly by the arm and hustled him inside. From upstairs a female voice called down, "Ned! Ned! You all right, honey?"

Archie rolled his eyes. "Neddy, you got to train them better than that! How the hell does she know it's not one of your kids or something? Tell her you're fine and to go back to sleep."

They went into the winter garden room. "Okay, now I'm not going to waste any time, Ned. You got to tell us everything."

"What are you talking about?"

Archie walked over to the cupboard that served as a bar and brought down a decanter of Scotch. He poured some into a glass with no ice and handed it to Ned.

"I'm talking about your association with Lorne Thurston. I'm not buying that crap about your going down as a special emissary for the president. How did they get their hooks into you?"

Neddy paled visibly. He swallowed. He was not groping for words, just a voice. The first sounds came out all croaky.

"Why does she have to be here?"

"Calista is not *she*." Archie nearly spat out the words. He suddenly found himself sick to death of Neddy, Neddy and his dumb good looks and his dumb attitudes toward women. He thought of lovely Ola Arnette's assessment of her own daughter: "Not mean. Just unkind." What were her precise words? "You don't have to be mean to be unkind." And maybe there was a certain point when plain old dumbness just slid over into unkindness. You simply weren't smart enough to be sensitive. "Calista is here"—Archie was choosing his words carefully— "because a friend of hers, a man who had been harassed by creationists, was murdered."

"They didn't do it!" But it was too late. There was a stricken look on his face.

Archie sighed deeply. "Let's sit down and talk about this. It seems you have a familiarity with the case. Would you care to share your views?"

Neddy lowered himself unsteadily into an armchair and then crumpled forward; a great sob shook him. Calista looked away. She didn't want to be here seeing this. She knew what would come out in the next few minutes would be even worse—some scummy, awful thing. Archie walked over to Neddy and put a hand lightly on his shoulder. "Just start at the beginning, Neddy."

285

It was not a long or particularly complicated story at all. Not the kind that involved laundered funds and elaborate cover-ups. It was short and sordid—a tale of betrayal of public trust and private indulgence. But it had snowballed into something more. "Snowballed" had been Neddy's favorite word in describing the accretion of bad effects from his initial action. And now this snowball in Neddy's mind had acquired a kind of demonic speed and weight, a life of its own. "It's getting out of control," he whispered.

"Do you have prints?"

"Yeah. They're in my wall safe."

"Can we see them?"

"Why not?" Neddy said with resignation. He rose and opened the safe, then handed the pictures to Archie.

These were not pictures that would make people gasp, at least not immediately. They were not lewd in the obvious sense. Nobody was fornicating. There were scantily clad girls all right, and one seemed to have her tits stuck in the face of a dark, very thin man. It was a party, and the picture was taken at a table. In the background there was a couple who appeared, for all intents and purposes, to be snorting cocaine. But was that so unusual these days? No. What was unusual was that this particular party was occurring in Panama. And the man at the center of the table was Neddy Baldwin, and he was flanked on one side by an infamous Central American political leader known for his connections with the drug world and on the other by an equally notorious billionaire arms dealer. Bad company for anybody, let alone a man on a diplomatic mission.

"Jesus Christ, Neddy!" Archie remembered when Neddy had been sent down years before to Panama on that diplomatic mission. "So what happened after this?"

"I wasn't very smart, Archie." He got up and began to walk over to the ferns in a gigantic vase. "The pictures in and of themselves weren't enough to kill me, just enough to scare me . . . scare me into turning my head on the drug dealings and money laundering. That guy . . ." He pointed to the face of the Panamanian. Feline eyes appeared behind a face that was thickened with cruelty. "He is absolutely evil, Archie, and the

286

country, Panama—good Christ, it was like a Disneyland for gangsters! Secret banking systems, corporation laws that allow principals to remain anonymous. Smack-dab in the middle of one of the greatest trade routes. It's got it all going for it. Narcotics, no problem, laundering money, no problem. A fucking Disneyland for the scumbags of the earth!"

"So, what? It was just all too tempting? I still don't get it," Archie said.

"Archie, you're so naive. I didn't do it for money. I haven't made a cent. I got no need for more money. And you know I'd never touch drugs." He sighed. "Archie, what's the one thing I have?" But Archie said nothing. He knew. "I got this." And Ned Baldwin almost magically drew himself up into a posture of incredible dignity and authority. Despite his disheveled state, he looked positively ambassadorial. For over thirty years he had played the role consummately. This was his stock-in-trade, his sustenance, his aphrodisiac. He was born to it—so tailored to it by some mysterious makeup of breeding and culture that his lack of real intelligence did not seem even to matter.

"So they used you?" Archie said. Neddy nodded. "But I still don't understand. How did this thing snowball, as you keep saying? How did it get from them to Lorne Thurston?"

"All too easily." Neddy sighed and stared into his glass of Scotch. "The Panamanian ran dope. Well, he didn't run it himself. He was at the heart of it. 'The facilitator,' they called him. And I became the facilitator's facilitator, especially after I began to serve on the president's commission on drugs. I didn't have to do anything except look the other way and try to steer the commission away. Nothing I did could have implicated me, at least I don't think so. These were sins of omission rather than commission."

"Just like the pictures."

"Yes. There is nothing precisely criminal, at least that I'm doing. It's just being there. But still it wouldn't have looked good. And that was the opening wedge. That was the leverage. I should have just said to hell with it and let them do what they wanted with the pictures. But I was scared."

"And it kept getting scarier."

Neddy nodded. "I kept getting drawn in deeper. I was always afraid of the CIA seeing this stuff. Imagine my shock when instead of the CIA, Lorne Thurston shows up. Not Lorne himself, one of his henchmen. They were down there trying to open a teleministry in Panama. They were, at the time, trying to start up several abroad. In any case, they were having some trouble, and they got hold of those pictures and put the screws to me. I pulled some strings for them there. No big deal."

"And?"

"And they botched the thing."

"Who botched what?"

"Thurston. They had people sending money for these damn ministries down there, but the money just wasn't going down there. So then the FCC gets on their tail and . . ."

This time it was Archie's turn to sigh. "So they leaned on you again, and you helped them get around the FCC."

"Yep. And from that point on it never stopped. They knew after that that they had me by the balls. Two years ago they came to me with all this creationist business. If they couldn't cut Darwin out of the textbooks, they at least wanted equal representation. And textbooks were their primary target. California and Texas dominate the textbook market. They account for more than twenty percent of total national sales. Books written for use in these states are often sold without any changes or modification to the rest of the country. I sit on the board of directors of the largest textbook publisher in this country."

Archie and Calista both groaned, and despite the heat of the summer night a dark chill feeling stole through the room.

There was something so essentially pathetic about all of it. Calista felt as if she had just listened to stories about experiences that one simply did not discuss in polite company. If there was any irony in this situation at all, it was not that a man of such patrician quality had sunk so low, it was the irony of his perceptions of himself. He had lived his life totally, completely, as an image, nothing more and nothing less. And it was a photographic image that had destroyed him—needlessly destroyed him. For although that picture was embarrassing and perhaps compromising, it was not enough to deliver a coup de grace, at least not to someone who had life beyond that of an image.

But where it had all led! It stunned Calista. She dealt in images. She made images. Images were her business. She abstracted from life and with her tools made representations that became distillations of life. But she knew the difference between what was real and what was not; what was image and what was actual. And now, in some odd inversion, sitting across from her was an image that had disguised itself as a pile of protoplasm. Throw water on him and he might dissolve like the Wicked Witch in the *Wizard of Oz*. Images should never come to life, and life should never come to images, she thought.

"But you say they didn't kill Norman Petrakis?" Calista asked.

"No. That's definitely not their style."

"Somehow I'm not relieved," Calista said coldly.

"Whose style is it—James Atwell's?" Archie asked.

"You mean that sperm bank guy out in California?"

"Yeah." Archie's voice was flat, his eyes steady as they observed Neddy.

"The guy's a loony," Neddy replied.

"What do you call the rest of you?" Calista shot back.

Neddy ignored her and continued to speak. "I don't know why they got in with Atwell and that Coastal Research Institute and his damn sperm bank. For some reason they felt they needed more real scientists around."

"I can understand why," Archie said dryly.

"They were getting ready for this Supreme Court showdown on the Louisiana law mandating equal time for the teaching of creation science in the public schools," Neddy continued.

"I suppose we should be thankful you weren't appointed a Supreme Court justice," Calista said. Neddy gave Archie a withering look as if to say, "Where'd this broad get that lip? You're going to have trouble with this one, Arch!"

But Archie did not respond. He merely continued to stare coldly at Neddy, and for the first time it occurred to Neddy that maybe Archie might not want to go sailing with him in August.

Neddy continued, "The guy's a Nazi."

289

"No wonder Hugh Ethelredge likes him," Archie said.

"Oh, yeah, Hugh. He always has been drawn to that sort of thing."

"So they gave Thurston some science, and what did he give them?"

"Money for their operations. Stanford cut them off. I mean, Atwell was a mechanical engineer out of Stanford and taught there for years, but they realized he was going off the deep end. I never did think it was a good move on the part of Thurston to get involved."

"Do you know about that research that Atwell was doing?"

"Naw, not really. He was getting into some of that genetic stuff."

"He was cooking it, was what he was doing," Archie said, not trying to disguise the disgust in his voice.

"What do you mean, cooking it?"

"Faking it. It's all going to come out. Same way this skull stuff is coming out."

"Yeah, I guess Thurston cooked his own goose on that one."

"They were trying to do the same thing on the genetic level that they were doing on the fossil level—this racist bit, separate evolution for the races."

"Oh, Jesus!" Neddy shook his head and sank back in the chair.

"Well," Archie said briskly, "no time for remorse now, fella." He strode quickly across the tile floor and put a firm hand under Neddy's elbow. Neddy looked up, slightly bewildered.

"What?" he asked.

"You're coming with us, Neddy."

"But where?"

"To the Coastal Research Institute. We've still got an unsolved murder, remember? And there's another even more pressing problem concerning a young lady who seems to be missing."

"I don't know what you're talking about, and I certainly don't know how I can help you."

"With the one thing you still have—your image. It's going to get us in there. Then I'll do the heavy work."

"Archie, what are you doing? Taking me hostage?"

"You can call it what you want, Neddy. But you're really going to start working now."

49

There was always a point, Calista remembered thinking on the flight to California, during long summers when one became fatigued by the monotony of the perfect days, hot weather, and the prevailing lassitude of it all. There was that time when one looked ahead longingly to schedules and the crisp weather of fall. Calista was at that point now, and Neddy reminded her of one of those long feckless summers. She wanted to be back, back with Charley, and it would be very nice if Archie were there, too. But the last place she wanted to be was on this plane with Neddy Baldwin.

Neddy was amazing. He had regained his equanimity and seemed to be as affable as ever. They flew first-class, and several people recognized Neddy and a few even addressed him as Mr. Ambassador, for that indeed had been his last foreign assignment—ambassador to the court of St. James. He enjoyed their attentions.

Archie had relaxed, but he seemed morose to Calista. He hardly spoke a word during the entire flight. Occasionally he would look across the aisle at Neddy and just stare at him with a kind of disbelief. It was as if Archie were giving himself exercises in realization—realization that his cousin, his lifelong friend, was indeed a bastard. At one point Calista saw Archie's eyes fill with tears. It was then she realized that he was actually going through a kind of grieving process.

Archie did have a plan of sorts in mind. The first priority was to find Beth Ann. They had called Charley before leaving to see if Beth Ann had called again. She had not. Archie intended to use Neddy as his front for busting in there and making demands. He did not want Calista to go with them to the

Coastal Research Institute. They were obviously on to her, and it would be best if she kept a low profile.

"Besides," Archie said after the flight attendant had set down their breakfast, "What's a woman going to do at a sperm bank?"

"Collect!"

Archie laughed, leaned over, and kissed her on the neck. It was the first time he had laughed during the flight. She supposed she should feel relieved. But she didn't. She didn't feel good at all. There was some uncontrollable element in all this. Just then Neddy leaned across the aisle.

"Calista," he said, "I never got to tell you how much our grandchildren love your books. Just crazy about them. What's that one you do with the two little animals?"

"Hedge and Owl," Calista said coldly. This guy was unbelievable!

"What are you working on now?"

"Something about Maid Marian."

"Maid Marian?"

"Yeah," said Archie. "You know, from Robin Hood. Kind of a feminist twist to it."

"Oh!" said Neddy. "That's very interesting."

"Yes," Calista said, leaning forward a bit. "I'm thinking of doing a whole series." She had never thought of doing a series at all. It was a lie.

"What on?" Neddy asked.

"Warrior women," she said quite distinctly. She heard Archie stifle a chuckle. "Yeah, you know, like Boadicea, the Celtic warrior queen with the blades in her chariot wheels," she continued. It wasn't a bad idea. Of course, how would one deal with the likes of a Tamara in a children's book? Tamara, the twelfth-century queen of the Caucasian empire of Georgia, had distinguished herself not just through her political clout, but through her sexual voraciousness as well. These appetites had been immortalized in Georgia folklore.

Thoughts of a horny medieval warrior queen from the Caucasus were only mildly distracting to Calista at this time. Were they flying into the dead center of the orb weaver's web, about to jiggle the trap line? And what about Archie? Was he too distracted over his own grief about Neddy to be totally alert? She felt deep in her gut that she should go with them to the institute. Relaxed and affable as Neddy was, as passive as he always seemed to be in his actions and morality, he was not her cousin, not her friend, and she didn't trust him for a minute. She knew that in Archie's mind Neddy was just weak-brained, cursed by moral lassitude and cowardice, not capable of sins of commission, just omission. But it didn't make her feel one bit better or more relaxed. People like that, through their abject passivity, were capable of great destruction. Their own laxness and ability to turn their heads the other way and not see had a kind of energy of its own that could spill out of control and leave in its wake victims. Their survival instincts were quite strong, and cowardice had its own kind of manic energy. She didn't trust this sucker for one minute.

50

But Archie had convinced her that she should not go with them. "Just don't tell me a sperm bank is no place for a woman," she said as he kissed her good-bye in their hotel room at the Mark Hopkins.

"No! I would never say that." He paused. "It's no place for a mother."

He got her there. She knew he was right. Charley was her first priority. "Don't you think you should notify the cops? Take someone with you?"

"I got Neddy. He's better than the cops. He's the feds!"

"You know what I mean."

"The cops aren't going to come with us now. It'll sound like a wild-goose chase to them. Look how great they did in Boston when this was supposed to be a priority."

"I guess you're right, but it just seems . . ." Her voice dwindled off.

"It's premature," he said. Calista's lips curled into a funny little smile. "What are you laughing about, Cal?"

"When you say premature and I think of you guys at a sperm bank—well . . ."

Archie laughed. "Yeah, I know. These places do lend themselves to a lot of puns. Listen, I better go." He gave her a kiss and squeezed her. "Don't worry."

"Okay. I could make a joke about getting caught in a crossfire of you know what. But I won't. Good luck."

Archie and Neddy had rented a car to drive out to the Coastal Research Institute and Project Genesis, which was just outside the town of Inverness. Archie promised to call her as soon as he knew anything. Calista, in the meantime, decided to walk through Chinatown. Chinatowns everywhere were her favorite stomping grounds for art supplies. An artist could buy paper and exotic brushes there that could not be found anywhere else. She spent the better part of three hours wandering through the streets. She had to buy a string bag to carry her purchases. And she especially liked the way the clerks wrapped things in wonderfully thin, crackly brown paper. She spent $150 on brushes and special pens that had bamboo shafts with beautiful sharp stainless-steel nibs. They were the most perfectly balanced pens one could buy. She had one store send thirty pounds of her favorite vellum paper back to Cambridge.

She dropped her bundles in her hotel room, taking a few minutes just to unwrap some of the brushes and pens to admire them. She laid them out on a table and gazed at them in anticipation. She couldn't wait to use them. She then grabbed her pocketbook and left the hotel, heading for Gumps on Union Square.

She loved Gumps and went straight to the second floor where the Chinese antiques were. There was a beautiful eighteenth-century Chinese painted screen with a waterfall and cranes hanging in flight above the fall's mist like benign specters from another world. It was lovely. It would look perfect in her living room, where she had tried for an effect somewhat reminiscent of the *japonaise* style in some French impressionist painting, notably Berthe Morisot, who combined a definitely French feel with an Oriental line. The screen, however, was $20,000. One quarter's royalties from *Puss in Boots* and *The Seal Woman* would cover it easily, but Calista was not that much of an impulse buyer. She would have to think. Oh, well.

She went to look at the antique kimonos. This was where she knew she was most vulnerable. She owned one already that hung on the bedroom wall in Vermont. Now she saw another one, even more beautiful. It was stencil-dyed in rich blues, pinks, and yellows. It was a woman's winter kimono, and it cost $2,500. This was tempting: $2,500 didn't seem as big an impulse as $20,000. She could wear it and hang it on a wall for decoration, too! On second glance she noticed the lovely orangy center of one of the flowers. The color reminded her so much of Ola's giant pumpkin. She was weakening.

As she walked up the hill to the hotel, there was a bounce in her step. It was the bounce of the inveterate shopper back in her element. She clutched the stunning Gump's shopping bag in her hand. If one couldn't wrap a purchase in that lovely brown paper, she supposed it was best to go the other direction with a lacquered black bag emblazoned with huge red poppies. What was the saying that her dad always kidded her mom and herself with? When the going gets tough, the tough go shopping!

That was what she was thinking when she slid the key in the door of her hotel room, hoping also to find a message from Archie. She shut the door behind her and was busy putting her packages down on the chair, so she did not look up immediately. But then she saw it and raised her hand to her mouth in a long, silent scream. The scream would not come. It was frozen as she stood transfixed before the bloody wobble of letters scrawled on the wall, the words coming together slowly in her brain—*Monkey Bitch.*

51

"Ninety-six percent of our semen is frozen in these liquid nitrogen tanks." James Atwell gestured to a phalanx of chrome canisters the size of water coolers. A woman in a white uniform was opening a hatch on one of the tanks. "Sally, can we come over and have a peek?"

"Sure thing, Dr. Atwell."

Inside the canister the space was divided into compartments. "What you're looking at are straws containing ampules of frozen sperm." Sally drew out one of the color-coded ampules. "Close the lid, Sal. We don't want to thaw out anything that's not supposed to be. You got somebody coming in?"

"Yeah. She'll be here in about forty-five minutes. So we're going to get this started."

Archie presumed that they did not put it in the microwave that he saw in a lounge area near Atwell's office.

"A tank like that can accommodate up to five thousand vials of sperm. You might have noticed that they are coded by number as well as color. With the improved methods of freezing and storing semen, we can now send frozen sperm through the mail. United Parcel, to be more precise. And we now have satellite banks. We don't call them branch banks—this is not money we're dealing with, after all. This is a much more valuable currency. In any case we can send semen back and forth. This capability is crucial to our program."

"Why?" Archie asked.

Atwell's eyes narrowed just for a sliver of a second. "Well, we can discuss that more completely in my office, but as you know, we here at Project Genesis want to make the genes of extremely able and intelligent men available to as many women as possible."

"But what about your recipients? Do you screen them as carefully as the men?"

"No, of course not. We screen them, but we don't have any hard and fast rules about who can and cannot receive semen. That, in our eyes, would be discriminatory. Look at it this way.

If a woman wants to have a baby and has the biomechanics to do it, well, she's darn well going to do it. So why not inseminate her with one of ours? Why go to K mart when you got Neiman-Marcus?"

"If you can afford it," Archie added dryly.

"We have donor insemination assistance programs. We call them motherships rather than scholarships." He smiled at the cleverness of it all, then continued, "We firmly believe that the more high-powered fathering we do, the higher the level of intelligence in our society will be."

"But still, don't you need high-powered moms? You're only focused on half the genetic material," Archie continued.

"Hey!" Atwell paused in a corridor. There was a glass window that looked across a separate corridor into another room. A young woman sat reading a magazine. "Look at that. There is one of our recipients—master's from Stanford in clinical psychology, cellist, scuba diver. Can't beat that, can you?"

"Sounds like the mom we all dream of," Archie said quietly.

Atwell furrowed his brow as if he were not sure Archie was being serious or joking. "Well, my point is this, Dr. Baldwin, and believe me, we would welcome your donation . . ." Archie smiled tightly. "But my point is this . . . ."

It was hard talking about points in a sperm bank. Calista was right; every word took on a double meaning.

"We, of course, like our recipients to be bright, but in truth, only a dozen or so truly superb, what the Napa Valley people might call 'grand cru,' specimens are required for our program to work." They had continued walking down the corridor. "This area off to the left here is our donor area. So I would like to emphasize right here that we do not limit ourselves to Nobel sperm. We want bright, successful men. Creative people who have demonstrated achievement. This means that there is an implicit lower age limit because after all it takes a while for a person to make their mark on the world. We have no medical students, who traditionally have been the heaviest contributors. You see, a single ejaculate from a young man can yield as many as sixty inseminations. But that's not what we're after—quantity. No. We're after quality. We therefore have no upper age limits because although quantity and motility of sperm often decreases in older men, the quality remains unaltered. You see, quality in this case means just one thing—genes!"

Archie still could not help but wonder if all those old Nobel codgers could withstand the rigors of being frozen in liquid nitrogen. But he put the question more delicately.

"What's the survival rate with frozen sperm?" It couldn't compare with the on-the-hoof rate, he was sure—Nobel or not.

"Yes, of course, fresh sperm has a higher viability than frozen. But as you probably know, cryogenics is my field, and just in the last year and a half we've improved our thawing procedures to such an extent that we now have a thirty percent higher motility rate than ever before in thawed sperm."

Archie felt as if his balls were receding on the spot—instantaneous testicular collapse. This guy really nauseated him. "In our catalog we list whether the donor's sperm is frozen or not. By the way, Dr. Baldwin, in our catalog, if you were to become a donor, we would list you only by number and a color code. Your area of expertise, hobbies, interests, and ethnic heritage would then be listed. The young lady we just passed is waiting for number twenty-six. See, this lovely young woman already has a two-year-old fathered by number twenty-six. In this way they shall be full siblings."

"Oh."

Archie and Neddy followed Atwell through an outer office where an attractive middle-aged woman was spraying a large potted plant.

"Hello, Anne. I'd like to introduce you to Ambassador Baldwin and his cousin Dr. Baldwin. Anne is in charge of our donor recruitment program."

"So pleased to meet you." She extended her hand toward Neddy first. She looked at both of them, her eyes burning brightly, as if she were scrutinizing prize bulls. Neddy, Archie noticed, shook hands very vigorously. Archie himself delivered the first dead-fish handshake of his life. The phone rang, and she went to her desk to pick it up.

"Really? No kidding?" she said. "What's his IQ?"

. .

Archie and Neddy followed Atwell into his office. It was well appointed. One wall was plastered with degrees and honors. James Atwell had made his mark as a biological engineer in the area of cryogenics. The Coastal Research Institute's abbreviation CRI served as a handy acronym as well for what had really been the foundation of the operation. He had figured out how to freeze all sorts of things—from human sperm and ova to French white asparagus and lingonberries. There were citations and plaques from medical societies as well as agricultural associations and culinary institutes. On another wall that was covered with corkboard were blueprints for some new machines and compressors in the works that would help with his quest to freeze the most delicate and precious of the earth's resources.

Atwell sat at his large desk and made a sweeping gesture toward the window behind him. "Across the courtyard out there, in that other wing, is our genetic-engineering and research center. We have a few bungalows on the other side there where some of our staff lives."

Archie wondered if that was where they had stashed Beth Ann. So far there had been no sign of her.

"So, Dr. Baldwin, you're interested in our overall program?"

Archie nodded. He wasn't sure how long he was going to let this bastard run on, but he might as well hear the whole grisly thing.

"Well, it is our feeling—and I'm sure you would corroborate this from your position as a distinguished archaeologist—that societies, civilizations, have been declining at an alarming rate. It's all deceleration and degeneration. You see, Project Genesis has been badly maligned in the past and misrepresented. We don't think we're going to get a Nobel Laureate out of this. That is not the realistic vision of this program. But what we do think we can do is improve the general gene pool. It's a question really of drawing a slipping species up by its bootstraps. Now as I have said, we want quality. IQ is the most reliable predictor. That is why we seek high-IQ, high-achievement scientists, even if they are not Nobel Prize winners." He nodded directly at Archie as he said this.

"So you really believe in the predictive value of IQ entirely."

"Entirely and absolutely. I don't call myself a raceologist like

299

some scientists, but we are starting to see that blacks have inherited certain biochemical deficits in regard to intelligence that indeed makes the races 'color-coded,' in the words of William Shockley."

"What do you mean by biochemical deficits?" Archie asked.

"There is some very exciting research going on in our labs"— he nodded toward the wing across the courtyard—"that I am not at liberty to disclose right now. But you might have read about some of it in a few academic journals. This research is not going on just here, but at other universities as well, and we are coming up with some very interesting data concerning neuro-transmitters."

The phone interrupted him. He picked it up. "Yeah. . . . no kidding. Can you beat that? What a loss. . . . Okay. . . . Well, sure. We don't have to freeze it. . . . Yeah, he's to be around here for a while. . . . Sure. Good idea. Put Topaz on the fresh list in the catalog. . . . Yeah, we're reprinting this week. So you got to move!" He hung up the phone and looked up. "That, gentlemen, was in reference to one of our younger donors—our first Olympic medalist."

"Didn't sound good, Jim," Neddy said.

God, thought Archie, how can Neddy already be calling this guy Jim? He had slipped into his old role again, so easily. Of course he shouldn't complain, that was what got them into the institute so quickly and even got Atwell out of a meeting.

"Not all bad. He flunked the freeze tolerance test. We do a freeze tolerance test on all of our donors. Can you imagine an Olympic medalist flunking it? In any case, we'll just offer his fresh. He's very interested in developing a real pool of Olympic talent in this country. You know, the Russians and East Europeans nurture these kids from the time they're infants. They spend much more money on it than we do. Not the sperm banking, but just the training. It's hard when an American athlete sees that kind of focus going on in another country and not his own. This is this boy's way of contributing."

Archie shifted on his seat. He had had enough of this. It sounded just like *Lebensborn* to him, the Nazi selective breeding program in which elite German troops were encouraged to impregnate Aryan women to produce racially pure children.

300

"The gifts of the führer," Himmler had called them. It was time to get to the business at hand. He tried to catch Neddy's eye to alert him, but Neddy seemed to be staring off into space. Oh, well. He had it fairly organized in his own mind and felt that the order of business should be first Beth Ann, then the cooked data on this neurotransmitter shit, and then the biggie—Norman Petrakis.

Archie leaned forward. "Dr. Atwell . . ."

There was a change in the entire atmosphere. The air suddenly seemed as charged as in an electrical storm. Archie saw Atwell's fingers coil under his desk and Neddy came back from wherever he was. There was no denying it—Archie Baldwin, although lacking any shred of the ambassadorial trappings of a Neddy or the gaudy charismatics of an evangelical preacher, could be incredibly formidable. There was no pomp and circumstance, nor was there the bright work of medals and gold braid; no visage bathed in the unearthly luminesence of divine knowledge. Just Archie. He leaned forward—a granite face slashed with bright blue eyes.

"I want to set the record straight: I am not here as a potential donor. I think your program is an affront to humanity." There was a stunned silence. Archie felt Neddy shift in his chair.

"Now, now, Arch."

What the fuck was Neddy doing? He didn't take time to look.

"I am here at the specific request of Ola and Milford Arnette."

"Ola and Milford Arnette. I don't believe I know them."

"They are concerned about their granddaughter, Beth Ann Hennessey." There was a slight twitch near Atwell's left eye.

"I don't know anyone by that name. Is she one of our recipients?"

"I hope not. We have reason to believe that she is here."

"Well, she is not so." He had begun to get up. "I don't know how I can further help you gentlemen."

Archie leaned forward and smashed his fist down on the desk. Neddy and Atwell jumped. "Sit down!"

"I beg your pardon? Dr. Baldwin, I'm going to have to call security if you don't leave this instant."

"I think you'd better call your lawyer."

Atwell sat down and tried to look casual. "Why would I need a lawyer, Dr. Baldwin? If I may be so bold."

"Two counts. First, that research you're doing on intellamine and intellicone." This time Atwell looked up. His gray eyes had turned to stone.

"How do you know about that?"

"Read some of those journals you mentioned."

"So what about it?"

"It's shit. You faked it."

"I faked it? I'll have you know there were four other labs that had projects going on concerning these brain proteins. There was just a seminar two months ago on it in New York, very well attended, I might add."

"Yeah, I know. I know all about it. So does the Martin Institute."

"What does the Martin Institute have to do with this?"

"They've got the evidence. They ran the energy tests. You can read all about it tomorrow in *The New York Times*."

"I don't know what you're talking about." He was visibly nervous now.

"The Martin Institute took up where Norman Petrakis left off. Do I make myself clear now, Dr. Atwell?"

"Perfectly." Atwell's hand went for the phone, but it came back with a gun.

52

"Howdy!" The voice, flat and nasal, sounded different.

"You!" Calista gasped as Wayne Tompkins stepped out from behind the window curtains in her hotel room. He held a length of narrow-gauge wire. Her hand was still at her mouth. She spoke through her fingers. "You . . . you killed Norman, you sent the books, you ran us off the road." He just smiled as if enjoying this litany of his deeds.

302

Calista's mind was racing. He was walking toward her slowly, carrying the wire casually in his hand. Was there anything she could use as a weapon? Why, why had she shut the door? She knew what he was going to do. He was going to garrote her as he had Norman. You can't talk when you're being strangled. She'd better start talking now. What would she say? . . . Anything . . . anything that would come into her mind that might throw him off.

"Where'd you get the nice red paint?" she said, glancing at the wall with the writing.

"It's not paint. It's blood." He smiled slowly. "Animal blood. Messes up the police to find it."

"Oh, how smart."

He seemed to brighten at this. "You think so?" he asked with genuine interest. There was something very odd going on here. This was Wayne Tompkins, and yet his voice sounded different and his whole bearing was different.

"Of course I think so. It not only confuses the blood issue, but they're probably trying to track down cult-type murderers. It's very smart. Very clever."

Calista wasn't so sure how long she could keep the compliments coming. He had stepped closer. She had no weapon. She had no strength. You didn't build muscle tap dancing. "You could, of course, have used something else, too."

"What's that?"

"Why, these." She gestured slightly to the table by the door where her newly bought art supplies lay and backed toward it. He came very close to her and looked down. In that instant she grabbed the hollow bamboo pen shaft with the double-pronged stainless-steel tip in a swift upward stroke that caught him in the eye. There was a terrible scream.

She raced out the door. A maid stood stunned in the hallway. "Get security!" she cried at the maid. "A man just tried to kill me."

53

"I don't believe this, Neddy.
How can you?"

"Sorry, Archie, but you and that dame basically took me
hostage, brought me here against my will."

In an extraordinary forty-five seconds Neddy Baldwin had
convinced James Atwell that indeed he was on his side. "As I
was telling you, Dr. Atwell, I have long believed in your
endeavors and felt that there has not been the political climate to
support them in this country until recently. But in my discussions with Lorne Thurston, and in detecting a change in that
climate, I do think that I can help you both; as you know, I am
in a position to do so. There is no need whatsoever that this
business with Petrakis has to come out. I spoke to Lorne. He was
admittedly ruffled about, uh . . ." Neddy hesitated and
coughed. "The fact that suspicions were raised in reference to
his group, but I think you got some bartering chips here. And I
definitely have some now—at last! But you can trust me. I think
together Coastal Research Institute and Lorne Thurston's ministry can forge a good bond. I think we can see some of your
dreams come true. This will be a new coalition."

"What in the fuck are you talking about, Neddy?" Archie
shouted.

"Shut up, Archie! You know, sometimes you're just too
honest for your own good."

They were both insane, and that was why this was working.
After years of deluding himself, Neddy had bought it all. There
was no There, there. He was like a vessel waiting to be filled up.
If Archie had been holding the gun, he would have been making
a coalition with him.

"Okay," Atwell said carefully. "You will just wait right
there, Dr. Baldwin. I'm calling my security people to help
escort you."

"Where?"

"You'll see soon enough."

At that moment the door opened and two rather burly-looking surfer types—donors themselves, no doubt, *cuvée* Malibu, Archie thought—came in.

"Did you boys clear the CRI lab?"

"Yes, sir," they both answered.

"Those big freezers on full blast?"

"Yes, sir."

Archie got a queasy feeling—big freezers were not necessary for freezing sperm. Big freezers were meat lockers. Terrific!

Another man entered the room. It was Wayne Tompkins. Atwell looked up.

"Any report yet on the Jacobs lady?"

"She should be taken care of by now," Tompkins replied.

"What?" Archie asked. "What did you do to Calista?"

"Sit down," Atwell barked. And Archie felt the heavy paw of one of the blond gorillas shove him down into the chair. He ignored Archie's question. "We are now going to walk to the CRI lab, Dr. Baldwin."

"I take it this is not for donor purposes. I doubt if I'd be able to perform under the circumstances," Archie said. Neddy started to giggle. Archie felt the hair stand out on the back of his neck. He felt himself fill with hate. He actually hated Neddy.

They had walked down the halls, which had all been cleared of personnel except for Anne, the donor recruitment director. "You the one who's going to jack me off?" Archie said, looking at her. Her eyes narrowed.

"You know," he continued as they entered the lab, "I hope this is an object lesson for all of you. You might just possibly get some first-class sperm here from me. I mean, look at Neddy and me, both of us descendents from the oldest of New England families. Our family tree's peppered with Cabots, Lowells, Adamses, and Saltonstalls."

"What's the object lesson?" Atwell gave a superior little smile.

"Well, these are genes that according to your standards are very desirable."

"One might say we're going to kill for them!"

The gorillas laughed.

"Well, you should be careful," Archie continued, "because

305

despite my impeccable breeding and my degrees from Dartmouth and Harvard—who knows, I might have had a Nobel even, but they never seem to give them in archaeology—one of the soft sciences, you know. In any case . . ."

"Yes, do get to the point. What's the object of this lesson?" Atwell said.

"Well, isn't it obvious? It can all go wrong. Imagine if my genes get out there. You'll not just have smart folks. You'll have all these people who see through shit like this and will rock your fucking little genetic dreamboat." Archie was shouting now. "They might have values that cannot be color-coded or predicted by IQ."

Just then there was a commotion in the hall, the sound of running footsteps.

"Okay, freeze!" Two cops burst in the door. Calista was behind them, looking distraught, disheveled, and wonderful to Archie.

"Boy, are we glad to see you," Neddy said loudly, and smiled. Archie's jaw dropped. But before he could say anything he heard Calista.

"Stand back, asshole!"

Atwell had dropped his gun, and Neddy had started to reach for it. But Calista slid across the floor and picked it up.

"I don't know what she's talking about, fellas." Neddy spoke with a slight quaver in his voice.

"Keep your hands up, Mr. Ambassador, until we can clear this up," one of the cops said.

As the hands slowly went up, Calista caught sight of Wayne Tompkins. Her mouth dropped open. He appeared completely normal. "That's the guy who . . . who was going to kill me!" She gasped, pointing at Wayne. Wh—what's he doing here? There's not a mark on him! I'm confused."

A smug grin slashed his face.

"I think I can clear this up." It was the voice of Anne. "Everybody freeze."

They turned. She stood in another doorway holding a chrome canister in her hands. The word *Danger* was printed in blue letters. "I throw this and everything explodes. So why don't you just put down your guns, Officers. Make it quick!" she snapped.

They dropped their guns. The gorillas scrambled for them. "Thanks, Annie," Atwell said, taking back his gun.

Calista was standing now by a tank of liquid nitrogen. She had been staring at the label when it finally dawned on her what it contained. Next to it were a pair of tongs and rubber gloves. A lever on the side of the tank read "Push to Open." She did. The lid popped open.

"Put that back down," Atwell barked, and Anne's face solidified into a mask of horror. Calista thought quickly. She jumped behind the tank, shielding herself with it. They'd dare not shoot her now. She peered into the tank. "Mr. Right, I presume?" She looked up merrily. Archie almost laughed.

"Mrs. Jacobs," Atwell said in very even tones, "I suggest you move away from that tank."

"I think that I'll just stay right here," she said, wrapping her arms around the tank almost lovingly. This was her ticket, their ticket, out of here. The rubber gloves were hanging on a hook attached to the tank. She managed deftly to put them on while embracing the tank. Everyone seemed mesmerized as they watched her. "Now put down those guns or else I'm going to start showing you my juggling act with Nobel sperm. You know, most people do use balls, but . . ." She found another lever that automatically raised the basket out of the nitrogen bath.

"You must lower that, Mrs. Jacobs," Anne said quietly. "If they are exposed . . ."

"Oh, dear. Well, I don't hear any guns dropping, and I was actually thinking of microwaving a few of these in that little oven we passed that you folks use for your soup." She had now used the tongs to take out a slender straw with a light turquoise band on it. She raised it in the air like a maestro about to begin conducting. "Drop the guns now," she ordered, and with her foot gave the tank a shove. It rolled wildly across the room. The cops lunged at Atwell. Archie decanistered Anne and sat on her. Three more cops had just arrived and clipped the two gorillas as they tried to dive out a window.

It was quick, like a squall. And suddenly it was over. Anne, the gorillas, Atwell, and Neddy were handcuffed.

Calista was still standing there stunned with her baton of

semen raised in the air waiting for the Philharmonic to stop tuning up and settle down. Archie came to her side and wrapped her in his arms.

"What the hell do I do with this?" she muttered in his ear.

"Drop it!" he whispered.

She did, and a thousand little splinters and icy crystals scattered across the floor.

54

"You don't think they did anything . . ."—Calista paused—"you know, weird to Beth Ann, do you?"

"Well, we know they abducted her and drugged her, but if by weird you mean try to artificially inseminate her, no, I don't think so. When we found her she was still so drugged up, and look, she'd only been hauled off from Bible Times, what—thirty-six hours before? They just wanted her out of the way, possibly for good. So I don't think they were looking upon her as a vessel for their prize bulls."

"Oh, yuck! The whole idea just turns my stomach."

They were sitting in the bar of the Clift Hotel. It was one of the most beautiful bars in the world with its soaring walls of redwood and immense reproductions of Klimt's paintings of Oriental women glitteringly robed in golden embroidery. They were dazzling, bejeweled, and gilded—benign she-dragons. Calista sighed and took a sip of her champagne.

"The poor child seemed so traumatized. I'm glad we could get her a room here next to ours." She paused. "What do you think she'll want to do after all this?"

"Not go back to Lorne Thurston College of Christian Heritage—that's for certain," Archie said, taking a sip of his beer.

"You know, she has only two more years to go. I wonder how many of those credits would be transferable."

"I would imagine several of them, except maybe the science

ones. She probably took a pretty standard undergraduate curriculum. Why?"

"Well, maybe she'd like to come to Boston. I feel so bad for her, Archie. She deserves a break of some sort."

"She deserves a chance to think without being frightened into dogma, is what she deserves."

"That's it, exactly." She took another sip of her champagne and smiled. "Charley was telling me that at MIT the brother of a friend of his who goes there said that in their dorm there's a de-nerdification zone."

"De-nerdification zone?"

"Yeah, isn't that a funny name?"

"What is it?"

"It's a lobby or corridor or something where there are no computers but, you know, chairs, and sofas and coffee tables—furniture set up into congenial configurations to encourage socializing. It strikes me that Beth Ann needs to go to a de-dogmafication zone."

"I think that actually her dogma is falling away from her in great chunks," Archie said. "Just from talking to her during dinner I could see it."

"It'll be interesting to see what kind of person she really is—I'm sure she's a good one. I just had that feeling about her from the start."

Calista went in to check on Beth Ann when they went back up to their room. She appeared to be sleeping, but then rolled over. "Calista? That you?"

"Yes. How are you doing?"

"Oh, okay . . . I guess. . . ." Her voice quavered.

"That doesn't sound too good," Calista said, walking over to the bed and sitting on the edge. Beth Ann's face was blotchy from crying. Calista picked up one of her hands. "This is going to take a while, Beth Ann. You've had a lot taken away from you all at once."

"I want to have my faith," she said almost fiercely.

"You can still have your faith. It's just not a faith in one man's vision. Have faith in yourself. You have every reason to. If you have faith in yourself, you'll discover your own visions."

Beth Ann's brow furrowed. "Are you a Christian, Calista?"

"Nope. I'm Jewish."

"You are of the Jewish faith?"

Now it was Calista who furrowed her brow. "I was born a Jew. I practice it in my own way. But I am one of these people who has never been very comfortable with anything organized, especially religion." She paused. "I have never felt close to God in a building."

"So when do you feel close and feel His spirit?"

"I cannot discuss it," Calista said quietly. "It is such a deeply personal thing with me that I simply can never discuss it."

"Do you ever question?"

"Of course—constantly."

"But how can you, with your deeply personal faith?" There was no sarcasm in the question, only a tone of deep wonderment.

"It is because of it that I can." She looked at Beth Ann carefully. "I shall not be betraying my private feelings if I tell you that it is my most profound belief that God loves skeptics." She paused. "And some of the most religious people I have known are the greatest skeptics—my husband, for one," she said, thinking of Tom with his wily blend of skepticism and reverence in the face of the universe that he probed.

When she went back into the bedroom, Archie was just hanging up the telephone. "They caught him."

"They did?"

"Guess Wayne and Dane aren't identical twins anymore. Dane's missing an eye." Archie paused. "They were never that identical. Apparently Wayne had the brains. That's how he got hooked up with the genetics lab at University of Minnesota. He came in via the twins study along with his brother, Dane. He had been studying engineering. Dane, on the other hand, had been a born-again Christian, but then he had some falling-out with the church. Dane was only too happy to set them up for murder. Or at least that's how it looks now. Dane did the dirty work."

"You mean the books, the stuffed animal in my garden, and all that."

"Yep. And Wayne was the mastermind behind it all. But he

was basically working for Atwell. Atwell needed money, and it was through Dane's connection with Thurston that they tapped into all that money."

So she had been right about Wayne getting stooges to do his dirty work. In this case it had been his own twin brother. This would be a new wrinkle in the classic Minnesota twins study.

Archie patted the bed where he was sitting. "Come on to bed. You've got a donor waiting here to do it the old-fashioned way."

55

"Oh, my God!" Charley said over and over. "Mom, I can't believe this! Jeez, Louise. You and Archie really killed a few birds with one stone here." Charley had newspapers spread out on the kitchen table. Calista was putting the finishing touches on Friar Tuck. In the mornings she always worked at her kitchen drawing table at this time of year. There was more available light, and what was available in late summer and early autumn had a special golden quality. "So it was Dane Tompkins who killed Petrakis and tried to do you in, too?"

"Yep. He was the connection. He was the one with the foot in both camps. He got his twin brother into Lorne Thurston's college as a professor. Wayne was not really a creationist per se. More or less a biological engineer with Nazi dreams along with Atwell. They needed the money for their dreams. Dane was only too happy to help them screw Thurston and the creationists out of money and lay the blame for murder on them. It wasn't supposed to come to murder, of course, until they figured out that Norman was on to them. Money had been the original intention. Norman must have got on to the intellamine thing, or at least to Wayne's role in it, when he was doing the research for those articles at University of Minnesota. He had mentioned genetic stuff up there in relation to the twins study."

"What about the skull stuff?" Charley asked.

"Well, it's like Archie said. The creationists down there were

311

dying to have a patina of science. That was what Tompkins was supposed to provide in exchange for the big bucks for Atwell's lab. So he came up with this skull idea—a bizarre and clumsy attempt that would not exactly disprove evolution but add a nice racist twist to things. The creationists weren't so interested in the racist thing as in getting a scientific scenario for Genesis. Their number-one priority was the textbook thing. They wanted to get scientific creationism equal time in textbooks. To do this they needed, quote, 'real scientists,' and Neddy Baldwin, who served on the board of a very powerful textbook publisher. But Atwell and his guys didn't give a hoot about Genesis, at least not the biblical one. They were just your basic Nazis with notions of a super race and insuring that those genes got out there."

"In other words, they could do their racist bit on two levels—the genetic and the fossil bone."

"Right," Calista said. "I can just imagine in Tompkins's and Atwell's twisted minds how elegant it all seemed—fossils and genes—you know, a double whammy!"

"A real double whammy if you consider that the creationists hated Petrakis for his views on evolution as much as Atwell and Tompkins hated him for finding out their fraud."

"Yes, truly a case of killing one bird with two stones!" Calista said. "But it was really Atwell's camp that was responsible for the murder."

"It sounds like this cousin of Archie's had a foot in a few camps, too."

"Indeed!"

"When's Archie coming back?"

"I hope soon. He had a lot to do. Deliver Beth Ann down to her grandparents."

"But she might be coming up here to live, right?"

"Yes, maybe. I wanted to ask you how you'd feel about that."

"You mean we could give her the room in the back?"

"Well, just for a start. I'm going to go over to Lesley College and find out if she might start there. I think most of her credits would transfer, and it might be the right place for her—small women's school, specializing in education—she has a lot of early childhood courses. And it's so convenient. Just two blocks

312

away. So near Harvard Law School. Maybe she could meet a nice lawyer." Calista laughed. "I don't think I could get her into a dorm at this late date."

"Naw, it's okay with me if she lives here."

"Well, we'll see."

"Who'd pay for it?"

"Archie and me." She bit the end of her brush. "We have faith in her," she said quietly. It had been Archie's idea, really, her going to Lesley and his paying for it. Archie, too, after all, had lost something. He needed to invest his faith in something else. Calista had insisted on paying half.

"So where's Archie now?"

"Dealing with Neddy's family."

"I wish he'd come back and deal with ours."

Calista looked up and smiled. "You like him?"

"Yeah."

"He'll be back."

56

He did come back. They sat on the faded brick terrace in Vermont. The long, low-angle golden light of autumn that Calista treasured bathed the terrace. They were caught in a blaze of autumnal refulgence as the last blast of the day's sun sprayed out over the mountains to the west, igniting the russet and bright yellows of the turning leaves. The scent of sweet potatoes baking in the coals of the grill mingled with the scent of the apples on a nearby tree. They were momentarily alone with their thoughts. But Archie scratched softly on Calista's back as she sat on a cushion by his chair sipping her bourbon on the rocks. The rum of summer had given way to bourbon, her fall and winter drink. "Here comes Charley up from the pond."

"Did he get any trout?"

"How could he miss in the pond? He's so lazy about certain

313

things like that. Won't go down to the stream where it's a fair fight."

"He's a fair fighter, Cal, if I ever saw one."

She dropped her head on his hand and kissed it. He ran his fingers through her thick hair. She knew what he was thinking about. Neddy. Everyone else's fate had been conveniently sealed except for Neddy's. Thurston's empire was crumbling around him. In the aftershocks of the fraud of the skulls and the revelation of his connection with Atwell, all sorts of other scams had been revealed. They were not guilty of the murder of Petrakis, but of influence peddling, FCC violations, and tax evasion. Atwell was behind bars without bail for being an accessory to murder, attempted murder, mail fraud, and a host of other charges relating to the intellamine-intellicone scheme. Dane and Wayne Tompkins were both in jail—Dane charged with Petrakis's murder, the attempted murder of Calista, and the kidnapping of Beth Ann; Wayne charged as an accessory to murder. It turned out that it had been an old classmate of Dane's from the Lorne Thurston College of Christian Heritage who had disrupted the children's literature conference in Boston that spring. He had needed little or no persuasion to do so, as these fundamentalist groups had been regularly sending out their troops to heckle at such conferences. Dane knew he could count on Petrakis being heckled, which meant a readily available scapegoat for murder. They needed Petrakis out of the way. He was on to their intellamine scam, and it would be the end of Coastal Research Institute and all of their dreams. The fundamentalists were a scapegoat made to order. They had also outlived their usefulness. Thurston was getting pressure on other financial fronts, and the well for Coastal Research was running dry.

It was Neddy whose fate seemed peculiarly unresolved. Neddy Baldwin was in McClean's Hospital in Waltham, Massachusetts, a mental hospital specializing in the breakdowns of the rich and distinguished, recovering from a botched suicide attempt. And the indefatigable Lacey, after years of being the perfect helpmate and wife, seemed to have broken as well. She was drinking and taking large doses of Valium. Little Lacey had just called Archie to tell him that she and her older brother were taking their mother out to the Betty Ford Clinic.

"Here they are!" Charley said, holding up the fish. "Cleaned and ready."

"Thank you, dear boy, just put them there beside the grill. You look wet."

"That's the way you get when you go swimming."

"You went swimming?"

"Yep. It's nice."

"Not too cold?"

"Mom, this is the warmest month of the year to go swimming. The water still has all the summer heat."

"It's certainly been a long hot one," Calista said, getting up to poke the coals into new life.

Archie had never seen Calista look as beautiful as she did that night. They had gone swimming, just the two of them, very late. It was chilly, but as Charley had said, the water was warm. To walk back up to the house, she had wrapped herself in her beautiful newly purchased antique kimono. Her dark hair was wet and molded to her fine head. Thick strands of gray ran like quicksilver back from her brow. He slid his arms under the kimono.

"I know this is an antique . . ."

"I take it you're referring to the kimono and not me."

"And I know it's very chilly."

"But Charley might still be up. . . . Look," said Calista. "This thing has survived one hundred years, but I think I'll just . . ." She let it slide off her right there on the small beach.

The moonlight blazed all around her. And across the grassy meadow surrounding the pond the night dew crept, spreading its veil of gray gauze. Her dark eyes shone like small galaxies with their faint glitters and mysteries. She looked as bejeweled and exotic as one of the Klimt ladies. But she was absolutely naked with the kimono crumpled about her ankles. She was unique. He had never met anybody like her. Where others might be *September Morn*, not Calista Jacobs. She glinted like some odalisque of the autumn night. She tilted her head up now to look at the sky. "Look," she said, "there it is." And she pointed up.

"What?" asked Archie.

She imagined it now so vividly, with the starry tracers, driving across the sky in its autumnal transit.

"It's coming back," she whispered. "Auriga—the Charioteer."

"Another myth?"

"If it only had been!" she said quietly, and pressed Archie's hand to her mouth.

ABOUT THE AUTHOR

KATHRYN LASKY KNIGHT is the author of many children's books.
Her adult mystery debut, *Trace Elements,* was a featured Mystery
Guild selection. She lives with her husband, Christopher Knight, and
their two children in Cambridge, Massachusetts, where she is at work
on her next Calista Jacobs mystery, *Mumbo Jumbo.*